THE ASSASSINS

Everybody considers dying important;
but as yet death is no festival.

—NIETZSCHE

The
Assassins

A BOOK OF HOURS

joyce carol oates

THE VANGUARD PRESS, INC.

NEW YORK

The characters, families, institutions, political
situations, and events in this novel are fictitious, and
no resemblance to real persons or events is
intended or should be inferred.

For Raymond

CONTENTS

Part One HUGH

1

I was born. It was born. So it began. It continues. It will outlive me. People whisper, stare, giggle. Their eternal privilege. My eternal curse. I am in a tiny place without walls. It is stifling here—but the walls are gone. No ceiling. A black hole of a ceiling. Floor? Invisible. I believe there is a floor. There must be a floor. It is invisible, like the ceiling. The walls are shoved up close, that is why the air is opaque tonight. Is it night? It has been night for some time. It is night again. Night sounds are with me always. Like the sea, the distant sea. Water in my ear—droplets— Can't shake them out. Can't shake my head. They have fixed my neck to a steel rod. The comedy continues. At a distance people are staring, giggling. Someone sighs. Coughs. Perhaps there is an audience. Folding chairs in the tiny cell, in the aisles between the beds, in the corridor outside. I don't know. The lights have been turned off. Fluorescent lights turned off by a master switch. Dim, soft explosions in the dark—the trickery of an optic nerve someone has been gnawing. But my brain survives. It will continue. It will outlive me.

I was born. I don't regret it. I still make jokes, I have always made jokes. People shuddered. Some turned pale, some blushed. Some sniggered. Now they can't hear me—they pretend not to. My mother, a beautiful woman, died just before my twenty-third birthday. Thereafter, the date of my birth was haunted. Poisoned. Bitter, was I? Not at all. Hateful? No. Hate got me nowhere. Ironic? My, yes. And subtle. *Hugh Petrie, the subtle one.* Subtle with my father, whom I feared. Subtle with all whom I fear. It did not save me. I was gentle, the rest were vicious. A family—descended from a deranged Puritan minister—famous for the transactions viciousness can make with civilization.

My mother died. I continued. The rest continued. A great pack of them. Of us. I am not bitter, I am really smiling. No one can see. The dark is stifling. Had I lungs, I could not use them. A stench here of disinfectant—cleanser—rust—oil smoke. The incinerator is nearby. Perhaps I am on a conveyor belt? No. I am not dead, I am fully alive. I cannot die. I can die, yes. Possibly. With effort. Bitter? No. Broken? No. In love? No, not now. Cured. I cannot die at the moment. It isn't a trick, it isn't that easy. My brother died: provoked someone into killing him. Selfish to the end. My older brother, "hero." Korean War. Silver Star. "Hero." Arrogant bastard. Ex-senator. "Radical pragmatist." "Radical conservative." A fascist, of the urbane variety; curiously American. He died at the culmination of a long chilly spring. He was made to die—provoked innocent people into killing him. Children? Young people? I don't know. I am not sure. They were innocent—perhaps. Unless someone else killed him. But he provoked them. Us.

Andrew in my mind's eye: not the stocky muscular perspiring aggressive flesh, not the slightly curved legs, the wide shoulders, the gray assertive gaze. Not that voice, rapid-fire and then drawling, mocking. Not the ugly grin. Instead, a thick-bodied creature made of stone. Trapped in stone. Petrified. A gigantic angel, enormous ungainly wings, brutal dark-stained muscles of stone. Stone-smooth eyes, blind. The face contorted with its usual rage. But silent. Silent! Thick-muscled chest, muscle-bound torso, shoulders, arms. Neck. So he crouches above the earth, that ridiculous wingspread useless to him, the cruelty of his wit useless, his money and his fame and his young wife useless. Useless.

The comedy continues. It will outlive us.

2

The telephone rang in the other room. One of them called me. I did not recognize Doris's voice at first. I listened, I murmured a few appropriate words. Yes. No. Of course. Certainly. Standing in an alcove, staring at the dismal blotched Atlantic sky. Heroic, I was. No sign of terror. My backbone seemed to lengthen; the muscles of my jaw tightened. No one was observing me. Still, I showed no alarm. Yes. No. Of course.

A noisy group in the other room, sitting at dinner. Dining room and playroom combined. I returned to my place at the table—a picnic table, inexpensive pine, benches instead of chairs. No carpet. Someone glanced my way. Someone beside me asked about the call. One of the children at the far end of the table cried *Uncle Hugh!* Yes? What? It was a crowded mismatched merry group. I loved them, the children especially. I was sitting at my place, groping for something. My wine glass. I lifted it, studied it. Charmingly ugly. Chunky. The wine was a very dry white wine, not my favorite. . . . Kathy, Simon's daughter from another marriage, was teasing me; she had answered the phone; she was eight years old; one of the adults had given her some wine to sip and she was giggling, flush-faced, bright-eyed, I could hardly bear to look at her. A woman had asked for me—was that my girl friend? Simon's wife Maggie tried to quiet her. Another of the children took up the question. A little boy— startling blue eyes—red-blond hair—someone's cousin's stepchild, I believe he was—parentless in this group and therefore disturbingly precocious. We had labored at sand castles and dams all day. Now he took his revenge.

I decided to tell the truth: the woman on the phone was a silly blowsy balloonish creature, an ostrich's head atop a rhinoceros's body, not my girl friend, not anyone's girl friend. My sister, Doris.

There was the usual laughter. Simon looked at me. Shrewd Simon, all black hair and fuzz, the sleeves of his nautical jersey shoved up to show beefy forearms. He believed himself my closest friend; he and Maggie my closest friends. Why they were anxious to please me, what they sought in me, or sought to gain through me, I never knew. A puzzle. Simon's amiable concern was irritating. I finished my glass of wine. I poured another. In a perfunctory voice I told Simon the news.

That silenced the table. Even the noisy children.

Even the bulgy-eyed woman in the peasant outfit, someone's un-married or divorced acquaintance of an acquaintance, dragged along on this outing for Hugh's benefit. She had been leering my way, her face prepared for a big hearty grin—her teeth reliably white and straight, her only good feature—on the assumption that whatever I said, in however morose a voice, was meant to be amusing. She was mistaken.

A fine moment. Exquisite. My well-bred refusal to be dramatic, to be emotional, had them all in my power.

What? someone cried.

Shouldn't joke about something like that, Maggie murmured. In front of the children.

Simon's features shifted. Clouded. My wit sometimes offended him.

Benjamin, another "friend" of the Mays, another charity case, shook his long cornsilk locks dramatically; he was trembling with ex-citement.

Joke? I said mildly. Who is joking?

Is it true? Maggie said. My hostess. Pretty in a plain, understated way. A few years younger than I, in her mid-thirties. Windblown hair, ordinary, brown, curled at the ends; maternal, in her cheerful knockabout manner. The girlish role no longer practical, she chose wisely to be everyone's motherly sister. I liked her. Always had. Loved her, perhaps. Did I say I loved everyone here? Not true. Exaggeration. Rush of sudden feeling—sickish, it came so strong. I didn't want to die.

Who is joking? I said. Raising my arched jester's eyebrows. I looked from one end of the table to the other. A respectful au-dience. Eight or ten silent, puzzled people. Never could I have an-ticipated the pulse of power in mere survival. *I survived you, Andrew. How simple it was!*

Who is joking? I? Do I joke? Would I joke about death? Murder? A man gunned down? A probable assassination? Would I joke even about that ludicrous hysterical clown, my brother Andrew?

Not in front of the children, Maggie begged.

It's true? He's dead? Andrew Petrie is dead? Simon asked.

They stared at me. The moment was mangled, lost.

Do you mean to say . . . ? Andrew Petrie has been . . . ?

Who did it? When? Where did it happen? Was it . . . a political killing?

The moment was lost. My power was lost. Dead! I wanted to scream at them. Dead, dead! And so what? Aren't there other topics we can now discuss? Why must it always be *him*? . . . And these people had seemed to like me for myself. My friends always seemed to like me for myself, until an issue arose that dispelled my illusions. Knowing how I detested Andrew—detesting him themselves, for everyone detested him, everyone with intelligence—except of course his unaccountable admirers, some of whom were perversely intelligent— knowing my position, knowing my sensitivity, misreading it perhaps —as people do—perversely—misreading it perhaps as envy, but honoring it nevertheless—people who drifted into my acquaintance never alluded to my older brother, not even to criticize him, to call him the necessary names. They honored my privacy, they honored me. And now, in two minutes, all ceremony is violated and they are questioning me directly; even the bug-eyed woman whose flirtations had so unnerved me last night, who had been coached (by Maggie no doubt) not even to allude to *my* profession and *my* modest fame, now reveals herself as interested only in Andrew Petrie.

They stared at me. I smiled bitterly at them.

My power was snatched from me. The artistry of the moment would be forgotten—misinterpreted. Ah, it went sour. Everything in my life goes sour. If not immediately, then eventually. If not in public, in private. Depend upon it. They had insisted upon this weekend at the very tip of Long Island—had insisted on dragging me along—absurd fears of my working too hard, driving myself too compulsively—the kind of issue friends create from time to time to reaffirm their friendship—knowing better than I what is best for me —Maggie warm and solicitous and sisterly—Simon more cunning, alluding to remarks made about me—a gathering I had not attended— remarks about my living too intensely in my work—excellent as that work is—formidable—brilliant—genius—that sort of thing—casual harmless lies—had insisted I spend the weekend with them—had been out to Montauk Point the summer before, to their cottage—I could relax, walk along the beach, enjoy the children, get the city out of my brain. They had insisted, they had overcome my natural objections. And things had gone surprisingly well. Very few people in early June. Excellent air. Chilly, damp, temperatures in the 40's and 50's at night, rising sluggishly to the low 60's during the day; awkward sleeping quarters; more people in the cottage than I had antici-

pated; sand—wind—drizzle—rain—surf—ocean spray—a shivering fit
though I was dressed as if for a blizzard; the goggle-eyed woman perfumy and overbearing; Benjamin stealing the show from time to
time, doing bird and animal noises that quite rivaled, with the children, my magician's and ventriloquist's tricks; toys underfoot, cigarette smoke drifting everywhere, an actual television set (portable)
blaring away; still, the weekend had been strangely pleasant. And
now it had soured: now it was ruined.

The children were taken away. The adults converged about me.
Serious? Are you serious?

I am always serious! I finally screamed.

3

You are alone. My shadow falls before you.
Waiting for the others to pack. The children running along the
beach. Crying of gulls. Screaming of children. *You are alone. You
are jumpy. As always. No, it is worse now: far worse. When you return to the city, to your squalid apartment, it will be even worse.
The visit to the funeral home in Albany: the funeral itself: the
journey to the cemetery: the formalities afterward.* Worse, far
worse. *Is it Andrew's revenge?* Striding along the beach. Gasping.
Lenses of glasses specked with water. Too thin. Too tall. Thirty-nine
years old. Too old for beginning anew, too young to shrug shoulders
and admit failure. Too old, too young. *You are alone: you turn as if
sensing someone with you: a few feet to the side. But the shadows
are gulls' shadows. The cries are gulls' cries.* Alone, alone. Sanctity.
The very end of the island: as far as the eye can see, nothing but
water. Beautiful, the others always say. Beautiful? No. Intimidating,
immense, unspeakable. *You are alone as always, brooding and joking
to yourself, moving your lips silently. The others, whose weekend
you have ruined, are back at the cottage putting things in order,
washing dishes, whispering to one another. About you. About
Andrew. About your family.* Striding out of the range of their lives,
oblivious, angry, frightened. Superior to them all. Perhaps. Who can
tell? My father—who loved Andrew best, of course—once took me
aside, whispered of my "potential" superiority; information based (I
suppose) on I.Q. tests the schools had administered. But perhaps he
lied. He often lied. Chief Justice of the State Court of Appeals at

that time. Art of lying, gracious and impenetrable. *You are alone.*
My shadow falls before you. You look up from your work, blinking.
You rise from the drawing board, not knowing where you are;
startled at being called back to yourself. What is it? Your next-door
neighbors quarreling again? Traffic out on Ninth Street? The un-
governable spasms of your own heart?

I jerked my arm in a careless motion—eradicating everything.
Let it collapse, let it sink back into itself. I deny it. I can rip it into
pieces. I have ripped it into pieces many times. I will again. *My*
shadow falls before you. It darkens your vision. It threatens to em-
brace you. A rectangular universe in my hands: my own art work.
The power to deny it is mine. The timid, tentative shadow is my
own. My own hand, my own arm. No one else is here. I am alone.

I staggered, panting. It was too much—the wind, the pace I had
set for myself. I wasn't well, even then. I hid my sickness from the
others. No sympathy, no pity—no thanks! Hugh has always been
scant of breath, overly sensitive, allergic to innumerable foods—odors
—people—situations. The murmur in Hugh's head is sometimes his
mother's, but with an eerie brassy undertone, a mockery of the love
his mother did feel for him—intolerable, such a parody! I am Hugh
pitying Hugh, pitying his helplessness, encouraging his defiance. *My*
shadow falls before you . . . blocks your way . . . gets between you
and the sunlight, you and the children squatting at the water's edge,
you and the rest of the world. . . .

A lie. I looked at the ocean, at the waves breaking a few yards
away. I was here, I was alive, I had outlived him. A triumph. Later,
possibly, I would repent my extraordinary elation: I always did. But
this was new, this sense of joy in mere, brute survival, in the survival
of my physical being—no matter about my imagination, my intellect,
my "personality"! The body lived now, trembling with cold, in a
world that no longer sustained that other body. A curious triumph. I
could not have guessed at such feelings, such simple, blunt, and yet
rather overwhelming observations. Such as: the sky is overhead, the
hard-crusted sand underfoot, the choppy waves a few yards before
me. Realities in space. Experienced in time. The children—Kathy,
Davy, Kevin, the little blond girl whose name I can't remember, and
the boy, the skinny boy with the glasses, Billy?—Bobby?—the children are shivering, tired, ready to be herded back.

Life. The ocean. The wide rough beach. Gulls: supremely and ar-
rogantly alive. A few yards away, a partly decomposed fish, taking the
light in tiny scattered jewel-like flashes—its single dark-glittering eye

also like a jewel—almost Byzantine, its queer beauty—hypnotic. I stood triumphant, breathing one breath after another, another and another and then another: indestructible.

A woman said to be my sister had telephoned—had told me hysterical news—the day's death—the day's murder—a man said to be my brother, whom I had not seen in years—with whom I had never been close—found dead, shot to death on a Sunday afternoon—a man said to be *my brother*. But all this was difficult to take seriously, out on the beach. What did it mean? Or, rather, why should it mean anything? Did not the ocean continue to break at my feet, didn't the children continue to yelp and play, didn't I continue as always? Life is unconquerable. Indestructible. I knew. I did not doubt. Life would continue.

And so, in a sense, it does.

4

Detached. Unemotional. Courteous as always. But distant, reserved, cautious. Of one of my masters, Goya, it has been brilliantly said that he discovered his genius the day he dared to give up pleasing others.

I have given up long ago—saw it as useless. I could not please others.

I tried. Failed. I tried again—failed—and a few times more—and that was it. My lifetime as a "member of the Petrie family." I gave up pleasing them and thereby discovered—I believe—my own soul. Genius? Contemptible hack? At least I am my own.

Hugh in Albany. Hugh at the old mansion on Van Schuyler Boulevard. Hugh at the funeral home. Hugh amid the floral displays, darkly courteous amid the murmuring throngs of "mourners"—as if more than two or three people mourned the death of Andrew Petrie! —Hugh solemn before the weeping tear-stained women of the family —Hugh shaking hands with the men—an adult like everyone else.

Isn't it a tragedy. Isn't it a catastrophe. So the hushed incredulous voices went. My sister Doris, a besotted girl of forty-six. Astonished. Round-eyed. But that had been her public manner, her social manner, for three decades. My aunt Louisa. Uncle Roderick. Cousins Harvey, Hannah, Pamela, George. Memories. Of Pamela especially. But no time for reminiscing. Who is Andrew's executor? . . . Standing over there. Yes. A second cousin, another George, married into the wealthy Hauptman family. Didn't you know? No invitation to the wedding? Pity. But to be expected. *Isn't it a tragedy, cut down in the prime of life. And the young wife left. And the sordid complications that surely lie ahead. Publicity! Always publicity.*

Hugh detached, unemotional. Clearly not intimidated by death. The others—yes. They are intimidated. They are grateful for the uniformed guards and the police escorts and the closed casket.

Death is death. The Angel of Death should not matter.

. . . My brother Stephen appeared. Making his way forward like a man in a dream. Someone spoke to him and he did not hear. Someone else spoke to him and touched his arm lightly and he did not respond. Making his way forward to the casket, to the floral displays, his manner abstracted, strange. A shock, seeing him. Had not seen Stephen for some time. Rumors of having been out of contact with the family—"sick"—disgraced. The baby of the family once. Now in his early thirties. Became a Catholic as a boy, entered the seminary, was asked to leave; now making his way past the aunts and uncles and cousins and grief-stricken friends of the family—past Cyril and Norman and Harvey (his snout reddened, not his eyes: Harvey Petrie the only member of the family in public office at this time) and Joan and Irene and Elizabeth and poor plain dowdy unmarried Hannah and the Bausches—Pamela with her face powdered an unearthly but rather attractive dead-white, and of course the paunchy silly Charles, whom I could never take seriously—Stephen unseeing, rude as usual—would have brushed past Doris herself had my sister not squashed herself forward into his embrace. Stephen! Oh Stephen! . . . I eased closer, wanting to overhear their conversation. Wanting to whisper *Death is merely death, why all this fuss?* The publicity one could understand, since the media are starved for fodder, for filler, but the private grief, the sense of catastrophe—*why all this fuss?* . . . Disappointing: Doris was telling Stephen what she had told me and what I had already known. Stephen did not seem to be listening. He stared past her. Stared. I drifted deliberately into his line of vision but he did not see me.

. . . The wife had found him, had found him dead. At the country place—the old farm in Natauga County. Why were they there? Why there? How could anyone have known they were there, how could anyone have gotten to him *there?* Everything repeated, repeated. Again and again the recitation of facts. Always facts, always tears. Incredulous anger, grief, befuddlement. He had been dead only a day or two!—already it seemed he had been dead forever. Enshrined, immortal. Why, why, why was the question—which nobody dared answer—there would be an eternity of it now. Was this survival? The triumph of Hugh's survival?

Doris was still telling Stephen what she had told me. I drifted nearer them, I was a surviving brother, I had the right to overhear anything I wished. Tall, elegantly dressed (a rented costume), pinch-faced, agreeably homely and harmless, my head slightly bowed as if in honor of death—

Where were you when you heard, Stephen? Doris said.

Stephen with his babyish curls and smooth complexion, madder than I recalled: Stephen looking at her for the first time and saying quietly that he had known—had already known.

You had already—?

Had already known, he said. It was God's will, he said. It can't be resisted.

5

Hugh at St. Aidan's Episcopal Church. Hugh at the funeral ceremony. Hugh gentlemanly, reserved. Solemn. But not emotional.

So many people!

Faces, faces. Dizzying. A kind of masquerade—costumes and masks of mourning. Only the police and the security guards looked real. Beefy faces. Gym coaches. A bit bored with Reverend Thayer's impassioned creaky voice.

So many people: so many of them familiar. A dream-like situation. Of course they knew me. Sitting in the reserved pew, in the old family pew, a sister on my right and the widow herself on my left. Must be Hugh Petrie. Isn't he the. . . ? The cartoonist. . . ? Odd, he had never seemed especially amusing.

I had begun to tremble.

The minister's voice. The altar. The rose window with its pale subdued well-bred colors. Christ in beige and white and black. The floral displays, the gleaming handsome costly black casket, the gleaming brass handles, the odor of animal panic. I had been here before: my mother's funeral. Had not been to church, any church, since.

My mother had died the summer I was in England. Had been

renting a tiny room in South Kensington. A non-graduation present from my parents, I assume—my father didn't want me in Albany. I was to enroll in art school in London. I was to "come to terms with myself." Had had to fly back, a dazed creature in his early twenties, little more control over his motor movements than an infant. Desperately sick. Terrified. Dark night of the soul? And of the body too. In the lavatory of the airliner bowels turned to fluid, tears streaking my cheeks, eyeglasses befogged. Mother. Mother's death. Unbelievable. Is it always? Must it be? Always? Bound for New York City, caught in the tail of a hurricane, landed instead in Washington, D.C. Panic. Edge of death. Begging for it—begging for the release of it. Insides slipping away. Turning to hot scalding fluid. Praying—yes, actually praying!—incredible—humiliating. *My God please let me get there, please let it be a mistake, please help her live, please let me get there in time. Is that too much to ask?* Yes. She was dead, of course. Had been dead. The causes of her death "complicated." Had been struggling, it was said, for many months. Had had an operation. Or two. Internal organs weakened—liver—heart—"put up a valiant struggle"—died at the age of fifty-three. Looked much older—shocking!—a pity. Hugh, don't behave like that. Not in public, Hugh. *Hugh.* You are not a child, Hugh. For God's sake, Hugh.

I returned. A telegram drew me back. I returned, sat in this very pew, alongside my father. I did not embarrass him in public; even in private, I did not accuse him of murder. It was known that the Petries—male and female—wore out their mates. A kind of family history, humorous, spicy, tragic, educational. Going back of course to the seventeenth century, when the men had to marry after their wives' deaths—had to remarry—and then again remarry—had to have children, especially sons. A family tradition. There were Petrie women in the nineteenth century, the tough ones, who wore out their men: Susan Petrie Montague, for instance, who married first a wealthy older man (one of the partners of the Irish immigrant William James, in fact) and then his son and then the son's closest friend. A heroine for those times or for any times. So I did not accuse my father of murder—of having slowly destroyed a sensitive and intelligent woman—nor to my knowledge did anyone else accuse him. Reverend Thayer had consoled me. Reverend Thayer, then as now officiating like a clerkish angel, greeting death as one of the events in the church's calendar, an occasion for ceremony.

Let us pray.

And afterward the idiotic solemn procession—the stately limousines—the hearse—the motorcycle escort—a dozen mounted police. Andrew's funeral, not my mother's. My mother's funeral had been fairly small compared to this. No excitement, no subdued hysteria and elation. Very well, she died; and I stopped blaming the old man. I no longer blame him. I don't blame him for anything. He could not fly East—was said to be in poor health—trouble with his blood pressure again—at a fashionable nursing home near Palm Springs, California. So he missed his dearest son's last rites. He missed the ride in the limousine, the photographers, the television cameramen, the wave-like murmuring that surrounded us. *Isn't it a. . . . And he was so brave, so. . . . His future lay all before him. . . . What a loss to America!* Had the old man attended the funeral, I would have leaned over to whisper in his ear: *Do you know who finally killed him?*

As if the specific Angel of Death mattered. . . .

Many were called, few chosen. Many made the leap, the attempt, the imaginative venture. Like plunging into an icy sea. Like sucking at the tip of a revolver's barrel, a finger playing at the trigger: no retreat, no self-respecting retreat. Of course everyone wanted to know who had done *it; this*; what group of people had actually carried out their plans and murdered Andrew? Assassination, was it? With reluctance I had to suppose so. An innocent unarmed man gunned down —"innocent" in a technical sense—five bullets in him—two in the face, at a distance of inches—instantaneous death—fortunately!—but so brutal. Everyone wondered who had done it.

But I did not wonder, not much.

There had been attempts on my brother's life in the past, some publicized, some kept secret. Some leaked to the press—of course. If the Petrie clan had reached its peak, in a sense, at the turn of the century—less money then but more power, more men in public office and in control of public office—it was nevertheless a fact that no one had been significant enough to shoot down. No doubt Andrew was well aware of this fact. A self-proclaimed historian of our family, conscious of the past, ridiculously proud of his name. . . . He knew everything. No doubt.

A close call some years ago, in Buffalo. I believe it was Buffalo. Andrew lecturing to a packed Masonic Auditorium—"The United Nations: From Farce to Tragedy"—at the peak of his career, though he didn't know it at the time—had certainly been feeding himself freely with dreams of the Presidency, the fool!—and an angry man had jumped from his seat and run down the aisle toward the stage, shouting at Andrew, a gun in his hand. How astonishing it must have been, how remarkable. . . . Andrew's confident impassioned well-rehearsed "spontaneous" speech interrupted suddenly by *life itself*. The man was mad, people said. Laughable. Perky and wiry and doomed, a minor character in a Hogarth mob, bald, rather short, silly. No one took him seriously—except for those few chaotic moments.

Three shots fired. Wild. Futile. He was disarmed—wrestled to the floor—arrested and taken to the police station—arraigned—no necessary involvement of Andrew at all, so far as I knew. By then he and his beautiful young wife were safely elsewhere. The would-be assassin was to have had a psychiatric examination the next day, but he hanged himself in his cell. It turned out he was no one special—no one "political" or important—certainly not an old acquaintance or enemy of Andrew's. Just an unhappy maniac, the commonplace kind. An autopsy showed unusually high levels of lead in his blood (he had been a demolition worker) but no gross damage to the nervous system. Police unearthed no significant information, no obscure and jarring connection with my brother. For the man it was perhaps time to kill, time to kill and be killed. Perhaps the posters announcing Andrew's lecture annoyed him—or articles in the papers—or remarks of Andrew's made on television. Or perhaps there was no reason at all.

And there must have been, over the years, other abortive attempts —desperate young Maoists—unbalanced blacks—perhaps even a personal enemy or two of his own class, after Andrew's term as state attorney general—individuals provoked by the man's arrogant statements and intolerably sanctimonious public manner—people teased into attempting murder by a human being who seemed to court it. Such things are kept secret. Of course. Even from me. But I was never so naïve and unobservant as Andrew thought me.

An egomaniac, he was. Megalomaniac. Thought himself unkillable —immortal—a blustery gray-eyed god. *Time to kill and be killed: that's all.*

6

And now I will try to describe her.

All this while I have been shying away from the task . . . from her

. . . from my emotions. Even at Montauk Point; even on the beach, my glasses misted over, my lungs aching. The bride. The wife. The widow.

First of all it must be stated clearly: I was not jealous of Andrew. Nor he of me—I think. It may be that he was jealous of me—he hid his feelings, always. He might have envied me my freedom. My life in New York City. My independence from the family. My talent. My devotion to my art. My singleness of purpose. I wanted nothing from anyone—I had moved away from Albany after Mother's death —I remained on the coolest possible terms with Father—refraining even from the vulgar melodrama of rebellion. (That play-acting I left to Andrew—who outraged the Judge and placated him and outraged him again and placated him again and again outraged him— politically, that is—and over the divorce from Willa Fergus—always the bright aggressive exhibitionistic favorite son, daring his father's Olympian fury because he is certain of being forgiven; and to Stephen as well, a slightly demented minor figure of our household, hot-eyed, dark-plum-eyed, with an extraordinary luminous olive-pale complexion, a moron's habitual, sensuous appreciation of anything and everything he encountered, so moved by "religious" promptings —which no one was cruel enough to assign a more clinical term to— that he repudiated the Episcopal faith to take up the Roman Catholic faith, even to enter a Jesuit seminary somewhere in Massachusetts —deliberately inviting, perhaps even requesting—so far as I know— the old man's censure: and disinheritance. Such shrill play-acting I left to others.) I was free, as Andrew certainly was not. I had discovered my soul on the day I gave up trying to please other people. . . . So it is possible he envied me.

It isn't impossible, at any rate.

And now I must deal with my sister-in-law; I must not shy away from her. In St. Aidan's—in the family pew—I sat beside her, on her right; and Stephen (I think) sat on her left, on the aisle. There was a beefy-faced amiable creature squatting in the aisle, protecting us. As if anyone would care to kill us—as if we, unlike the glorious Andrew, were worth killing—but such is police procedure—and I was a little elated by it, I suppose. Flattering, such attention.

Beside me sat, in utter silence, doped and leaden and smelling slightly of animal fear, Andrew's second wife.

An artless and joyfully confident bride, not long ago. Had shaken my hand—at Father's retirement party in the autumn of 1973—given me as little attention as if I'd been one of Andrew's innumerable sycophants—or a ward politician—or a tax lawyer. Blue-black hair worn straight, parted in the middle, horsey, coltish, not so beautiful as she imagined herself, dressed as if she and Andrew had just strolled in from an outing in the country—trousers and a turtle-neck sweater and a white coat-sweater, thigh-length, bulky-knit, innu-merable strands of amber and violet beads about her neck—casual, insultingly artless. Andrew had always played such tricks. Like him, the young woman had pretended not to take me seriously—had pre-tended not to know exactly who I was. (Yes? Which brother?) Only a few months earlier, my first collection of satirical drawings had won a small but prestigious award—*Eminent Contemporaries:* judged the outstanding book of its kind by the Pennebacher Founda-tion—a small medallion and a token $1000—certainly Andrew knew of it, and would have mentioned it to Yvonne—but she said nothing. He said nothing. She already had been corrupted by him, prejudiced against me. (As Willa refused to be prejudiced: but of course Willa had been sloughed off years before.) I flinched slightly before her, the glare of her slightly protruding eyes, her self-assurance, her youth, the recklessness of her vigor, the strong facial bones, the exaggerated lower lip—I found her offensive—exasperating. And stupid. A brainless young woman with striking looks, radiating the kind of confidence that is always a mistake. I could not look directly at her, I found myself stammering, blushing angrily. Rude, she was. Stupidly rude. Those sharp staring brightly-dark eyes—the eyebrows that were too thick and far too theatrically active—Yes? No? Is that true?—an aggressive and harshly virginal manner—already imitating Andrew's warrior-like stance. Quirky, questioning, flat-footed. Secure in who-ever she imagined herself to be: Mrs. Andrew Petrie. Long-limbed, long-waisted, her hips slim as a boy's, her voice throaty, low, in fact rather boyish—an epicene creature despite the constant (perhaps un-conscious?) seductive smile. The other women were pretty. At least feminine. Objects of attention, as if on display. I pitied them and was bored by them—by most of them, anyway—but at least I respected them—I knew them—and here was the new Mrs. Petrie looking quite frankly about her, watchful, bold, as if counting the guests, assessing them with part of her mind while with the other—the least significant—she carried on an ordinary banal conversation with a man said to be Andrew's brother. "The artist." She struck me gradually, over the course of the evening, as resembling a woman whose portrait had once hung in my parents' house—upstairs or in one of the guest rooms, or maybe I had come across it in the attic—a

Petrie woman of the late nineteenth century—unmarried, an heiress, who traveled alone in Europe, eventually settled down and died in Rome, gave much of her money to some questionable charities—a long, stern, arrogant, horsey face and a level dark stare—restless, brooding, an inappropriately full bosom, tightly laced, swelling as if she would burst—freakishly contemporary. No doubt she had offended people in her time, no doubt it had given her pleasure.

Rumors had been flying back and forth among the relatives for months, about Andrew and his probable second wife—the "fiancée" he had acquired so suddenly. I hated the tribal jealousies—I hated especially Doris's whinings—her occasional telephone calls—as though I had not extricated myself from that world of petty obsessions with money and social status and who might be marrying—or divorcing—a fortune; who might be a possibility for a high political appointment, or who might have ruined forever his chances for a career in government; who might be enormously lucky because of the passage of certain tax exemptions, or who might be close to disaster. My father saw to it that Doris—with her puffy face, her perplexed gaze, her hockey player's figure, her perpetual head colds—"sniffles"—was married off in her early twenties to a mild-mannered, unimaginative, rabbit-faced creature some years her senior—not so likely, therefore, to leave her someday for another, younger woman—an obsequious gray-faced trust officer in our family's investment house—Arnold Laubach: handpicked by Father, I had always believed, so that she would not make some idiotic blunder of her own—as more than one of our adventurous, liberated girl cousins had done—or would not marry at all. Doris Petrie Laubach, formidable in her own way, ludicrous of course to those who knew her as a girl, but capable of savage and shrewd decisions nonetheless—and vengeful, too, as she revealed in those conversations with me—calculating how best to make Andrew regret his decision to divorce Willa Fergus (all that money! —and those boy cousins, just the right age for Doris's Jessica and Stacey!)—as if anyone might ever get the better of Andrew. And of course divorce frightened her. The Petries "did not divorce." At first she had told me wild, outlandish things about the girl Andrew wanted to marry—that she was an opportunist, an ambitious young woman who wanted a career in politics for herself, that she was marrying Andrew only because of his fame—his notoriety, Doris must have meant—and his money—though nobody knew how much money Andrew actually had. What a fool Andrew was! But men did such things, men of early middle age, perhaps they could not help themselves. . . . And of course there were the rumors (really facts) about Willa's precarious mental health: and she had let Andrew down so dismally in Washington: who could forgive her for that? And on and on, Doris febrile and shrill, I limply at my drawing board—the receiver held against my ear by my shoulder—inspired in a way by her manic worries to sketch a few distraught faces—a few scrawny or obese bodies—some of them Petries, some of them strangers. And Yvonne Radek. One night I sketched the woman's face—unconsciously—and it turned out to bear a surprising resemblance to the woman herself, though less hawkish about the nose—a coincidence?—or the eerie flowering of my intuitive genius?

Rumors, rumors. Fears. Wishes. And then it turned out that the young woman, Yvonne, was evidently the daughter or granddaughter or niece of a very well-to-do Pittsburgh woman—part-owner of a downtown department store. Very good. And there were other holdings in the background—so Doris told me, reluctantly at first, as if doubting the turn things had taken—something to do with land in Colorado—a copper mine, was it? Yes. It turned out to be a copper mine. In fact, several copper mines. So the girl was not marrying Andrew for his money. Perhaps—and here I was tempted to join Doris in her ridiculous speculations—Andrew was marrying *her* for her money? From Andrew one learned nothing. Of course. That was his style. He demanded to know everything about others but revealed nothing about himself.

So he married Yvonne Radek and brought her home to Albany. And people liked her—as naturally they would, being fearful of Andrew. Father himself liked her—was enchanted by her—not yet senile, but with that donkeyish, placid, perpetually benign manner he developed in his later years—compensating his earlier savagery—and when I met her, at that party for Father, she still had the look of an exuberant newcomer—a bride. They said she was beautiful. She was not. Had she been beautiful—in the usual feminine way—had she made an effort to behave beautifully in my presence—I, who see beautiful women all the time, would hardly have noticed her. It was her arrogance that intrigued me.

And her triumph.

Now, transformed. Diminished. Smelling of panic. Sickness. Yes —I smelled it. Her. Sat close beside her, like an escort. Was I to be this woman's escort? Face burning with an emotion I could not understand—probably simple shame, self-consciousness. The rites of death—Anglican ceremony—so sad, futile. No word more accurate than "sad." Pomposity masking animal fear. The skin flames up, fiercely blushing, confronted with such futility. Beside me the man's wife, the widow. Bride—wife—widow. Did not want to think of her. There was Reverend Thayer, his voice, words. Comforting, were they? To others? Such sonorous somnambulistic mock-certainty. Beneath it, the litany, the words, what quivered and gasped and did not dare reveal itself? Pinched white lines on Thayer's forehead—yellowed hair—color too high in cheeks and nose—capillaries too close to the surface of the skin—my grandfather the same way, Father's father—secret alcoholics?—men of improbable wisdom—Father as well—Andrew as well—but no humanity to them, no human style. *Quisque suos patimur manes.* Then the translation. Then a passage from one of Andrew's speeches or essays, read to the mourners in a spirit of desperate bravery. Old man's histrionics. Should have retired —been forced into retirement—the Petrie funeral his last *fête*. Andrew's words thunderous, sad. The usual. The Widow sat quietly. Drugged, I believe. Someone had said. Doped-up. Sick. Flu symptoms. (I had overheard Doris chattering earlier.) Andrew, from out of the costly black casket: *Ages that endure the rebellion of the masses against the principle of order have always been characterized by an illusory belief in progress, a linear development under the control of man*— And on. More. The usual. Conservative rhetoric masking the same old piggish morals. The Widow moved suddenly, jerkily. One hand clasping the other.

Andrew? Dead?

Her left hand was bandaged. They said she had hurt herself somehow. Ring on her right hand, third finger: entwined rods or vines or snakes. Platinum or white gold. Gleaming. Snakes dancing on their tails, woven together. An antique ring. Andrew had given it to her, no doubt. It had not belonged to my mother—too exquisitely ugly—possibly to someone else in the family. Didn't recognize it. Hypnotic, the gleam. Church too dark. Always too dark. The gleaming ring—the woman's bluish-pale flesh—heavy, leaden, unattractive—veins enlarged—knuckles too big—fingers clasping fingers. Dead? Was someone dead? Were they gathered here to celebrate death?

It began to occur to me, as the service neared completion, that my brother had actually died. . . .

7

You're afraid, aren't you. Always afraid.

I'm not.

For Christ's sake, look at you—your face—your lips are blue—

Stop. Shut up. *Shut up!*

—lips are blue like a drowned person—a corpse—

Leave me alone!

Sunlight on the back of my head—so hot—my head pounding with heat—I started to cry—I heard myself crying—he had dared me, bullied me into this—I was trapped—I was going to fall—I was going to die—

Hugh, for Christ's sake! It isn't dangerous.

Leave me alone!

Shrieking. I was shrieking. Nearby there were grackles—starlings—ugly jeering creatures—the elm's branches rubbing against the roof, so close—not possible that they should be so close. . . . From the lawn the roof looked different, from a distance the slates were pretty—delicate hues—blue, blue-violet, violet-gray—the sunshine was pretty—the birds in the big elm—iridescent feathers—black and greenish-black and—

You didn't have to climb up here, didn't have to follow me.

Andrew jeered. Whispered. He had inched his way back to me. Slowly. Slowly or he would fall. He was afraid—afraid he would fall—he lied saying he wasn't afraid. I was crying. I hated him. I didn't care—I didn't care if I was killed. He would be blamed. They would blame him—punish him.

Why the hell did you follow me, you damn little coward. Goddam baby. Nobody asked you to follow me. Why are you always—

I could feel myself slipping. I was slipping down the roof. My fingers couldn't stop what was happening.

Hugh! Stop!

I was screaming, banging my face against the roof. I couldn't stop what was happening. I didn't care, but I didn't want to fall. It would be awful—sickening—the sensation in my stomach would swell—explode—I had been sick like that before. I didn't care if I died—he tried to kill me—he wanted me to die—I didn't care but I was afraid to fall. My fingers hurt. Everything was throbbing. I couldn't

remember where we were. It was flat and ugly and hard—but tilted—
I was lying on my stomach—my face pressed against the dirty ugly
thing—I was crying—Andrew tried to touch me and I pushed him
away—I slipped—I screamed and slipped—

Hugh, for Christ's sake—

I slipped but didn't fall. I slipped an inch or two inches. Andrew
was afraid—he tried to touch me—he was whimpering too—he was
afraid but wouldn't admit it. He tried to talk to me but I turned my
face away. My cheek hard against the roof. Eyes shut. There was
such heat pounding on me—on my face—but I didn't move.

Hugh? What's wrong?

I didn't move. I was on a mountainside: my fingers were bleeding.
It was dangerous to breathe. Andrew was talking fast—trying to talk
like Father—pretending he wasn't afraid. He had tricked me into
climbing on the roof. He had dared me. He hated me. He laughed at
me. He poked me—pinched me—called me names. Called me baby,
sissy, coward, bastard. He told lies. Got everybody to laugh at me. I
hated him—I wished he would die. I would tell Mother what he had
done—I would tell about him tricking me—wanting me to die.

I hate you, I hate you.

Hugh—?

Hugh, he said, pretending to talk like Father, Hugh—? It isn't
dangerous, Hugh. You can't slip if you're careful. It isn't steep. Hey.
Hugh? Are you listening? I said—

I hate you.

—It isn't dangerous, it isn't that steep along here. What's wrong,
can't you move? Are you paralyzed? Hugh, for God's sake—nothing's
going to happen to you—I've been up here before—you won't fall if
you're careful—just go back the way you came—can't you go back
the way you came? Back there? Hugh?

He was frightened now. I could hear it. I wanted to laugh—he was
frightened now—he was going to be sorry.

Maybe if you turned over on your back—Hugh—I could help you,
huh?—and you could use the bottoms of your shoes—the soles—
rubber soles—maybe that would be easier—it isn't dangerous—we can
both get down again—go back the way we came—hey, are you listening?—what's wrong?—just go slow enough—back over by the chimney—okay?—Hugh?

But I couldn't move.

Hugh—?

You go first, I whispered.

What? I can't go first.

You go first.

I can't—I can't crawl over you, for Christ's sake—

You go first.

My eyes were closed. It was like being asleep—but awake at the same time. I wasn't afraid now. I couldn't feel anything—the places where I might be afraid—I had had to go to the bathroom a minute before—it had been hurting me—now I forgot it, I was numb, it was like being asleep and I didn't care what he did to me, if he punched my arms and shoulders and squeezed my neck and pulled my ears and called me names and—

Hugh, I can't crawl over you! Are you crazy?

You go first, you go first. I was whispering. Smiling.

Stupid goddam coward! Baby! Stupid baby!

They're going to punish you. Both of them. Both of them are going to punish you. I'll tell them what you did. The names you called me. They're going to—

He touched me again, tried to put his arm around my shoulder. I screamed and pushed him away. No! no!

He was close beside me. Panting. I could hear him. He was afraid —afraid! I hated him, but he was afraid like me—he was trapped like me—couldn't get down—couldn't move—the two of us were trapped —he was starting to whimper—he was going to cry too—he thought he was so brave—the liar—he said he didn't cry any more but he was going to cry now—

It's going to be all right, Hugh, he said, trying to talk like Father, pretending, pretending he wasn't afraid, it's going to be all right— you won't fall—anyway it isn't far to the ground, is it?—what if we were on the big roof?—Hugh?—it's just grass down there—flowers— stuff like that—it isn't the flagstones—you wouldn't be killed if you fell—it isn't that far—but you won't fall, Hugh, look—look—all you have to do is crawl back over that way—you could be safe in a minute—it's only a few yards—as soon as you get by the chimney you'll be safe—I can help you—in a minute we could both be safe— we could be on the ground in a minute—just go back the way you came—Hugh, please—

I didn't answer. I didn't move.

Hugh—

Then he was going to crawl over me. Then I thought—

*I could kill him now. Could raise up on my elbows and—*I didn't move. I lay there, paralyzed.

8

Rattled, rocky. Shaky. I suppose I talked too much in the limousine. The more nervous, the more witty. Can't bear silence. The silence of people who detest me, are embarrassed by me, shrink away from me.

Unreal, the service. Unconvincing. Interior of St. Aidan's—costly—the white marble—stained glass—white-haired trembling old man in black—holy man, I suppose—reciting his holy words—magic—unconvincing. A once wealthy parish. Old mansions on the Boulevard. Old money. Endowment kept the church going—millions—pointless wealth—trusts, interest—endowed for centuries—no matter that the parish had shrunk, the sons and daughters of the old families moved away: saw and pounced upon an analogy with the evil modern practice of keeping bodies alive—hooked to tubes, machines, fed through the veins while the interior of the skull turns to mush: the futile stage-magician tricks of a dying society. Realized, a moment too late, that it might have been the wrong thing to say.

My impetuosity—my spontaneity—

My irrepressible wit—

Unnerved by the procession. The solemnity, gravity. The size of the casket!—enormous—wide enough for a small whale. Pallbearers. Mourners. Photographers. Television crew trucks. Police, State Troopers, security guards. Plainclothesmen. Important mourners—most of whom had hated Andrew—the Governor himself—old enemies—faces half-familiar—faces decayed, cheesy, grotesquely changed since I saw them last. And a crowd of spectators. Unnatural quiet. Hateful quiet.

And all for my brother!

How he would have loved this spectacle!

In the rear of the limousine, an eerie comfort. Cushioned seats—an elegant gray raddled with black—even the walls cushioned. Like the inside of a casket. But I did not utter that observation. *I did not utter that observation.*

Being impoverished for so many years had made me less of a Petrie; less oblivious to pomposity, wealth, the undeniably real and demonstrable comfort of elegance. I sat back, I sighed, I sank into the cushions. The Widow on the far side—an insignificant cousin—

Hannah—between us—and my silent dazed baby brother on my right —sniffing—brushing his hand unconsciously against his nose—hair in his eyes, dark ringlets and frizzy curls—fingernails edged with dirt. Air-conditioning. Relentless spurts of cold steely air. A glass partition between us and the uniformed driver. He wore dark gray flannel. Even a hat. Even gloves.

It's cold, it's ridiculously cold. It's been cold for the past six weeks. Why air-conditioning? Can't it be turned off?

I tapped on the partition. I suppose I chattered.

The mousy cousin stirred.

The brother rubbed at his face with both hands—no sign of having heard—

The Widow— But I could not see the Widow.

Helicopters! Impossible! And yet there were helicopters: airborne police. How Andrew would have gloried in the hideous exaggeration, expense. A farce, really. Roaring—chugging—throbbing—brutal beat of propellers. Grateful after all for the thick glass and the cushions and the air-conditioning. Yes, modern life is vile. Unlivable. Better to be deaf, blind, insensitive, a smiling drooling amiable old donkey like Father—like most people.

Something I said hung in the air. Stephen murmured a reply.

Sorry if I have offended you, I said. Meant it. If I stop joking, I stop existing. Superstitious. Can't help it. Sorry.

Please, Hugh—

Yes! Sorry! Sorry!

The Widow not listening.

If I've offended—

Yes, all right. Fine.

—I'm truly sorry. —But the situation is—it's been made—we are all forced to be—so public—on display—public mourners—stared at— even photographed—I believe in a way envied— Thayer put the fear of God in me for a moment or two—the old charlatan—have been assuming mortality for so long now—frightening to think—to doubt —sanity itself wobbles at such times—

Crossing a bridge. Slow stately procession. Traffic in the other lane —the startled faces of ordinary folk—must have pleased the Widow, crouched over there in her corner—silent and offended. Would never forgive me. Had never liked me anyway: Andrew's distortions, lies, contemptuous little jokes at my expense. Of course. I could imagine. Seventy-five dollars for a floral display. Waste. She would never even know—never bother to discover. Could not know how much seventy-five dollars is to me. I, whom certain individuals of intelligence and taste have called a genius: I, impoverished. Would never go to the old man for money—never again—after the humiliations of my youth.

—there just aren't words to—to—there aren't any adequate words to—

Yes, Hannah said.

—the words have been used—countless times—squeezed dry of their meaning—stereotyped and banal—one risks caricature by simply speaking—

Then don't speak, Stephen said suddenly.

Meager sunlight. A most disappointing spring.

Two weeks into June and still cold.

The vivid green of the cemetery—grass clipped short—oddly bright, fresh. Wet-looking. Rather like England—English churchyards—the chill to the air, the bright but damp sunshine—you expect the day to be far warmer than it usually is.

Gravel drive. The limousine following the hearse. And behind us the other limousines—like English taxicabs, in fact—formal, overbearing—everything rented and fraudulent. This cemetery was newer, of course, the "new" cemetery east of town; St. Aidan's churchyard was filled—filled to bursting—the quaint aged gravestones and markers beneath the oaks—some mossy and stained, surprised at being exposed where elms had been cut down—"historical" dead—slabs dating back to the 1700's—cracked by their own weight—high granite walls and iron spikes—gate locked at night—city noises, traffic noises—would disturb the sleep of those snobbish dead—still, Andrew would have wanted burial back there: it would have irritated him to see his final resting place.

A *nouveau-riche* knoll: spanking new gleaming-marble fronts, gravestones the size of telephone booths. Important people here. Take notice.

A few Petries already here. Mother, uncles, a young aunt. Handsome stones. Not ostentatious. The usual flowers—the usual spare, trim evergreens—an expensive but unimaginative place—I did no more than glance at Mother's grave—had been so long since—futile, anyway—always futile—the remembered shock of the actual name carved in the stone—Beatrice Anne, Beloved Wife of—and my father's name also—already carved—1907–1960 beneath her name—

1903–   beneath his. Awaiting him. Theodore Pratt Petrie. Out
in Southern California. Awaiting him, he awaiting it. Hateful to
think of. Ludicrous. Farcical, really.

My will—scribbled out one night, late, after a party, after a bout
of vomiting in my tiny bathroom—my will insists upon cremation.
Insists.

The hell with the Petrie domain.

The hell with—

Women's tears. Ghastly doughish reverence. Necessity for those
who have no reason to mourn—no earthly human reason—to pretend
—to fix their faces in attitudes of grief. Not for me. No thanks. Cremation for Hugh, rascal-Hugh, gangling huge-eared sharp-nosed
weak-eyed Hugh—unloved Hugh—not this ritual of—the surprise of
the grave's size, so wide—deep—actually it is a hole in the earth—actually it is in the earth—real—very real—the physical earth—the earth
itself and not merely an idea of or drawing of or premonition of—
My God, what is awaiting us?

Another ceremony concluded—and now the contraption working
creakily—the best money can buy and yet creaking—and—

And it flashed into my mind—

An instant's temptation, a sly sliver of an idea—

Hugh, you wouldn't dare! Hugh!

As the coffin began its slow descent into the grave—slightly comic
mechanical lowering—not quite a perfected gimmick—it occurred to
me that I might project a high squeaky voice—ventriloquism an art I
had halfway mastered—for parties, for the delight of children— I
alone among the mourners, I alone among the drawn-faced sag-
mouthed individuals surrounding the grave, I alone was capable of
transcending the situation—rising from farce to high comedy—I
could project a tiny voice into that pompous coffin—

Help! Let me out!

Sonsabitches!—let me out!

Did I faint? Or only fall to my knees?

Of course they grabbed me.

I had gone sick—weak—delirious with panic—had had to clap my
hands over my mouth—both hands—to keep from doing it—to keep
the squeaky little voice inside me—*Help! Let me out!*—had heard it
already in my imagination—*Help! help! let me out of here!*—stagger-

ing—falling to my knees in the damp grass—my hands flat against my mouth, my glasses knocked off—*Help! help! help! let me out of here!*

9

Poe, a rhapsodic maniac like myself, gave it a name—the imp of the perverse.

Yes, I am susceptible to it; to more than impishness; to more than perversity. Can one go beyond perversity? I think one can.

For instance. . . .

My friendship with the novelist T—— was destroyed a few years ago by a sudden impishness on my part. I a mere thirty-five years old, he a beautifully coiffed, beautifully tailored gentleman in his mid-fifties, secure in his fame, winner of innumerable awards, grants, citations—the envy of all who knew him—even those who knew him intimately—since he was, and still is, a fairly normal individual—divorced but not unhappily—married again, not unhappily. Distinguished, he was, no way to avoid such clichés in dealing with him, for his hair had begun to turn gray—no, silver—at the temples—and the wise philosophical lines of age became him—the creases about the mouth especially, from too much sweet-ironic smiling. You all know him. Of course. Witty, urbane, profound, and yet—and yet not overly profound—able at the slightest encouragement to turn into the grimacing Jewish jester he had been in his youth, when he had become famous "overnight," as they say. We were acquainted; we had mutual friends; we even became friendly in a way. At least I believe he liked me. (Surprising, the people who seemed to like me!—and I gave so little encouragement.)

This famous man consented to give a reading from a work-in-progress for a charity of some kind—drug rehabilitation—Manhattan Committee for Clean Air—the Ras Dashan Flood Relief—the usual thing; gave an excellent reading, moving his audience and himself nearly to tears, so impassioned was he, at the same time so well-groomed, so successful, the air quivered with sheer joy that he existed —as an example to the rest of us; he plunged bravely into a question-and-answer session—rather an aristocrat, yet robust and good-natured and very very sincere—one couldn't help being impressed; got a few excellent laughs from the audience; the tension eased; he was "one

of us"—almost; smiling warmly and rubbing his hands together, looking out into the audience, frank and open and not at all frightened;
and—And I jumped to my feet, far to the side, far over by the Exit—
jumped into the aisle and demanded in a thunderous voice—meant
to be funny, of course—how could it not have been funny?—
demanded of him *Why did you kill Our Savior?*

If ever a joke fell flat. . . .

Almost immediately I sensed that it had misfired: for one thing,
he was nearsighted without his glasses—and too vain to wear them
on stage—so he couldn't see who it was shouting at him, couldn't see
that it was only his friend Hugh Petrie—Hugh, who is always so—
Hugh, from whom one expects—and others in the audience of course
did not catch on—slow-witted and inclined to hysterics—perhaps a
little paranoid, too, from living so long in the city. It wasn't my style
to explain myself. Nor to back down. Apologize? Too late. Always
too late. The high-pitched question hung in the air—the famous man
stared—could not speak—a few titters from people near me should
have informed him that it was only a joke, a harmless joke—albeit a
devilishly clever joke—but he was too stunned, too overcome by the
surprise of it—and the challenge in my mock-furious voice. He could
not reply. He just stood there. Seconds passed—hideously; the audience was murmuring; the man who had introduced him came out of
the wings, anxious to see what was wrong; and the famous novelist
seemed to crumple—

I don't know how it ended exactly. My memory has always been
whimsical. But the friendship was over—he would not forgive—even
after it was explained to him countless times, by mutual friends,
after I wrote him a long letter explaining—not apologizing—he never
forgave me; he was embittered, vicious, small-minded. Some said he
even came to hate me. . . .

The perversity that overtook me at Andrew's graveside, however,
had intriguing consequences. Shameful, of course—the kind of thing
you remember suddenly in the street—your face shatters—teeth gripping themselves, eyes rolling—the kind of humiliation that pokes you
as you wake from sleep—returning to the irrefutable world of one's
personal destiny: shameful. But the consequences. . . .

A legend, a myth, I told Simon. Grief so overwhelming—love for
my brother so powerful—alone among the relatives I broke down—
had to be helped back to the car—staggering between Harvey and
someone else. Sobbing, evidently. I don't remember.

Then it turned out—for you—

Simon curious, inquisitive. A former editor at my former publisher's; had known each other earlier, distantly, at school; years passed
before I could overcome my initial dislike of the man. So self-assured, he was. So aggressively normal.

What do you mean, I asked irritably.

It turned out well—?

Death might as well turn out well, I said. What choice is there?

And now you're back to work, settled in? Now you don't think
about it at all—Maggie mentioned—

Of course I don't think about it, I said. Stared at him. Refused to
understand. *It*. *It?* The hell with *it*.

But your family—

They have nothing else but *it*.

Simon paused to stare after something. Someone. (We were on
Sixth Avenue, a few blocks from my apartment.) A little beggar-girl,
one of those playing at begging, I think. Pale chunky legs. Bare feet.
A jersey-like blouse pulled down over her large loose breasts and hips,
a man's shirt perhaps. Ugly. Repulsive. She drifted one way, we another. Simon turned back to me. Casually. No change in his expression, looking from that monstrous child-cow to me.

Maybe the grief was real, he said.

I did not reply.

—if the fainting was real.

Did not reply. My face burned.

If anything at all you tell me, anything you tell yourself, is real. If
that son of a bitch is really dead.

10

He died. He was dead. No mistake about it. I recovered, came to
my senses, left Albany. A few hours on the train—a few days of more
than usual work—at my enormous workbench from 6:30 A.M. till
dusk—a few weeks of sudden warmth—summer once again—temperature in the eighties—the usual complaints of humidity, heat,
stagnant city air—a chorus in which I could participate. Back to normal. As always.

As I told Simon, I didn't think about it at all.

Forgot.

Dürer's *Oswolt Krell:* the ever present frown, evasive gaze. Nose rather pronounced at its tip, as if fashioned for a much larger face. Small mouth. Firmly pursed. Inherited from my father's father. I think. Hair lighter than Oswolt's—but limp and fine and tending toward ringlets—like his—unfortunately I couldn't wear it to my shoulders as he did—couldn't hide my enormous ears. My face thin, long, hungering. Would never tan—only burn. The others tanned without effort. Hugh pinkened. As a boy. As an adult he remained pale. Aloof. Detached. And chaste.

Yes, Oswolt Krell. Except for the chilling confidence of his stare— the frantic but pleased—satisfied?—expectant?—glare of those black pupils. I had tried to get in line with them—to fix my gaze to his— one rainy inspiring day in Munich. Not possible. No. Also, I was not nearly so solid as he: my shoulders always sloping, my chest narrow, hollow, neck a scrawny stalk I could never keep clean—even as an adult—always a minor obsessive worry.

In such terms did I describe myself. In writing. Never on the telephone—the few times I dared let the call go through.

Hello, hello?
Yes?
Hello, who is this?
Who is calling?
Who is this?
—a private unlisted phone—please identify yourself—
Don't you recognize my voice?
No.
Is this Yvonne Petrie?
No, it is not.
Is this her number?
Who is calling, please?
I asked—is this her number? Is this Mrs. Petrie speaking?
Who is speaking, please? I must hang up unless—
But don't you recognize my voice?
Please. Sorry. Good-by.

It was July. I planned to leave the city for a week or two in August. No more: I detest vacations. It was July, mid-July. I worked from six-thirty (I was a morning insomniac that summer—at other times I had been a night insomniac—both are hellish—but I prefer morning) till dusk, went out often for lunch—sometimes skipped dinner—worked till bedtime more casually, grateful to be exhausted. Of course there were interruptions. Friends, appointments with my doctor, dentist, and analyst, unexpected calls from Doris with "news" of arrests and probable indictments—tiny bitter gulps of gossip—the will to be probated—the insurance not so very remarkable ($300,000)—the estate and taxes and court papers already being served against the widow's claim—banalities I dared not pursue—did not care to allow to flood my consciousness. Interruptions pleasant and unpleasant. The girl across the hall—special-delivery letter inviting me to give a lecture on the art and history of caricature—West Coast university so I couldn't accept—being fearful of air travel and too easily nauseated—a perfumed letter on violet stationery, anonymously sent—in a handwriting I halfway recognized. And more. And more. The texture of my ordinary life. My independent life, apart from *it*.

And from *her*.

So it was July. July 18, to be exact. A month and two days after the funeral, after the disgusting scene in the cemetery. I worked hard as usual, I was myself once again, I had forgotten entirely.

Yet, oddly, I hallucinated the following conversation:

> Hello, hello?
> Yes?
> Hello, who is this?
> Who is this?
> May I speak to her?
> Her?
> May I speak to—Yvonne?
> Who would like to speak to Yvonne?
> Don't you recognize my voice?
> Please—
> Are you pretending not to recognize my voice?

Then again, swaying over a stranger's telephone—no, it was in a bedroom—must have been a friend's—an acquaintance's—a noisy party in the other room and Hugh swaying drunken in the dark—dialing long-distance—surreptitious—trembling:

> All right. It's Hugh. It's Hugh Petrie.
> *Hugh. . . ?*
> Yes, Hugh. Your brother-in-law.
> (A pause. Must have wanted to hang up—but couldn't.)
> *Hugh.* Oh yes. I do recognize your voice. This is Hannah. . . .
> Hannah!
> Hannah, yes. I'm staying at the apartment. Yvonne is. . . .
> What do you mean! What! What the hell!

Yvonne is with the Greasons at Lake Placid. She. . . .
(My torso gripped with anger. Spasms. Could not breathe.)
Hugh. . . ? If you want Adrienne's number there. . . .
(Could not breathe.)
I'm helping her with some of Andrew's papers. . . .
Hannah?
Your cousin Hannah, yes. Is something wrong?
You're not Hannah. That isn't Hannah's voice.
What?
I said—you're not Hannah! You're lying!
(Now she was silent. Now the bitch was silent.)
Didn't know you and the widow were so close—such friends—
didn't know you and your wretched branch of the family
had wormed your way in—or isn't this Hannah
after all—how *could* this be Hannah—plain good-
hearted unimaginative Hannah—teaming up with
a woman who stole another woman's husband—eh?—
no, Hannah's harridan-mother wouldn't allow it—
wouldn't think of it—divorce forbidden—adultery
unthinkable—how could this be Hannah!—whose
infatuation for her glorious cousin Andrew was
so touching— Hello? What are you doing there?
Is anyone there? —Not Hannah: but Yvonne herself.
Is that it? Is it? Hello? Hello? *Hello?*
Why won't you speak to me, Yvonne? Why are you hiding?
Lying? Why this masquerade? Why this farce? I'm not
drunk: I'm beginning to see things with a frightful
clarity. You won't speak to me, eh?—you loathe me,
eh?—as he did? Is that it? Hello? *Hello?* What
were the lies he told you? I demand—

And more. I think. At least one more of these. Then on July 18 I
climbed onto the stool (a bar stool, and very convenient) at my
workbench and wrote a long hysterical formless letter—to her, to his
widow—filling page after page—my handwriting fairly recognizable
at the start and then increasingly slanted, crabbed, manic—writing in
black ink—sometimes jabbing the point of the pen so hard into the
paper that it tore—splashed the ink—writing and writing until my
hand ached, my breath was ragged, my heart threatened to jump
into palpitations—*What were the lies he told you? Why do you hate
me? I demand*—

Of course, I never sent it. Ripped it into shreds. I think.

11

Does a demon beckon?
Do you follow?
Do you turn aside, mashing your fists into your eyes?

You won't know until it beckons. To you. So long as it tempts others you can judge—can sneer—can express shock, disgust, outrage, and prim disdain—the usual emotions of punitive people. But you won't know. I didn't.

There is Hugh Petrie dream-haunted, fantasy-stung, not in the brownstone on Ninth Street—which he could not afford until his work began to sell to the larger magazines—but in his kitchenette apartment on the Upper West Side. One in a series of depressing, inadequate apartments. Hugh at the age of twenty-nine or thirty. Years ago. Nearly forgotten.

There is Hugh filling up on tea, chewing the chewable brands of vitamin pills, muttering to himself in the cramped loneliness of his room, trying to draw, trying to justify his existence—his continued existence, anyway—by creating art. Five feet eleven, weighing a feeble hundred and thirty pounds, already worried about his eyes—with justification: all his worries were legitimate or turned out to be so—sitting and then standing and then sitting again at his drawing board, a rectangular universe always before him, more teasing and cruel than the rumored exterior universe (where is it? who has seen it?)—at first dismayed by the light-headedness of hunger and then rather intrigued by it—the rapidity with which ideas, shapes, outlines leaped out of his mind—sometimes astonishing and exotic. He was trying to draw in the crude-seeming but highly sophisticated manner of Van Gogh: a reverence for his subject, always simple and ordinary. What effort! What strain! The results were clumsy. Sentimental. He dared not show them to anyone, not even his one or two friends.

At that time Andrew Petrie began his first term in the Senate. The brothers were not close—hardly kept in touch—Hugh valiantly resisting offers from his family—mysterious offers of jobs here in the city—an advertising firm on Third Avenue, a weekly newsmagazine—a position in an art school on Long Island. Andrew's secretary wrote to Hugh offering him an associate editorship on a monthly journal Andrew had begun, many years ago, when it looked as if Andrew would be a university professor all his life—a specialist in comparative constitutional law and the politics of Anglo-American states. Andrew's secretary wrote. Not Andrew himself. A letter sent from Washington, not a telephone call. Offering Hugh Petrie an associate editorship on *Discourses: Essays in Contemporary Culture.* At a salary Hugh could not believe. It was nearly double the salary of the teaching position. And, as Hugh knew very well, the journal made no money at all—paid none of its staff except the secretarial help—was at that time hardly more than an academic-political journal, right wing but not yet frenzied. (During the sixties *Discourses* was to go national—a glossy cover with pulpy hysterical insides—editorials by Andrew Petrie and political cartoons by his hack artists— vicious, unforgivable, bigoted in classic American Know-Nothing style—anti-black, anti-youth, anti-welfare, anti-federal spending—except that which "aided a sick economy"—anti-United Nations, anti-medical programs, educational programs, prison rehabilitation programs, anti-life itself. And very successful, of course.)

Hugh tried to call Andrew in Washington.

Sorry. Not in. Leave a message?

Hugh, already a few hundred dollars in debt, sitting for long motionless periods at his work—his "work"—unconscious of what he was doing, vague and lethargic, unshaven, unwashed, slowly going insane.

Does a demon beckon. . . ?

No, no.

When it became unbearable he ran out—four flights of stairs to the sidewalk—sometimes not knowing whether it was raining or cold until he had walked halfway down the street—coatless, hugging himself to keep warm, his gaze fixed on the dirty pavement a few yards before him. Had he a personal life at that time? Of course. Loves, hates. Confusions. Snarls that were undone to reveal—nothing. Other snarls that deepened. Torments, small joys, many expectations. But personal life did not concern him. Not really. Not then. He could not handle it—he had never been able to handle it—but it was his other life, the life of his art, that obsessed him.

Behind the offer from his brother was—?

Contempt.

Or possibly—?

A brotherly generosity, charity in the more acceptable sense of the word.

Then again—

Might Andrew be trying to ask for Hugh's forgiveness? (For Andrew had engineered one of the great wounds of Hugh's late adolescence—not to be acknowledged by Hugh until, at the age of thirty-six, he began seeing an analyst twice a week.) Forgiveness. . . ?

No, it was contempt. The gesture was typical of Andrew: an offer of a job made to a younger brother not suited for the job, in no way deserving of it or of the absurd salary attached to it, an offer made to underscore the brother's failure. And Andrew's success.

But then possibly—

It was possible their father was behind it. Judge Petrie, regretting his cruelty toward Hugh—the middle, neglected son—the one "potentially superior" to all the rest. The old man had far more money than he needed, and since he knew the exact amount Hugh received from his grandfather's trust— Since he might be capable of human, paternal concern—

No.

A generous offer? An insult? An attempt to thwart Hugh's plans for the future? An open, frank gesture—typical of the extraverted, aggressive personality—baffled by subtleties, genuinely puzzled by the resentment of others? (For Hugh realized even then, bitter as he was, that men like his brother occasionally meant well; it was their style of meaning well that provoked murder.)

Dream-haunted, even while awake. Moody. Sickly. For a while friendless—curtly rejecting invitations—and then despairingly lonely. Days passed. A week. Another week. Destroyed several months of labor in a few minutes—panting and gasping and muttering in a shrill voice—*No! No! I won't! I will not!* Too excitable to work for very long, even when inspired. Scrawls—scribbles—the pen point jabbing the paper—his beloved subjects turned into cartoonish Grosz creatures—splashes and blotches of ink—chaos. And his health was poor: dizzy spells that lasted for hours, tachycardia so violent he could hardly breathe, dark clamoring headaches that sometimes followed, and sometimes stimulated, his depressions.

His thirtieth birthday. No one knew. A card from Doris would come eventually—sent to the wrong address, as usual. He no longer had any interest in his work—the work itself made no sense—banal and sentimental and hopeless; he had no wife, no child, no job, no

future. A dead man. In a way. And so might he be absolved from
guilt if he did compromise himself? . . . if he did accept his
brother's offer. . . ?

Being talentless, how could he betray his talent?

Being soulless, how could he betray his soul?

He wrote to Andrew. He accepted.

His letter read in part: . . . *I hope you didn't offer me the job out
of pity . . . or in order to have the occasional pleasure of criticizing
me . . . or ridiculing me . . . or worse. But thank you.*

Sent the letter special delivery, on a Monday morning in October;
on Wednesday afternoon received the reply, also special delivery,
typed in evident haste—a telephone dictation, since Andrew was in
Los Angeles. Read and reread the letter—at first could not absorb it
—could not comprehend. The job at *Discourses* was "no longer available." Hugh had been "dilatory." Being "dilatory" and therefore
"self-defeating" was one of Hugh's worst traits, going back to boyhood. Egotistic, short-sighted, self-indulgent, unsuited for employment in any capacity that required responsibility and a sane
awareness of the external world "beyond the world of art and fantasy"—all this was Hugh Petrie—though it "grieved" Andrew to be
so explicit. The job was no longer available, that was all. Sorry.

A fairly lengthy letter, on official stationery. Impressive. And even
rather conversational at the end—as if Andrew had dictated it with
only part of his mind, had forgotten the trivial matter it dealt with,
but before signing off remembered it was his brother he was writing
to—so he complained cheerfully of the "hectic pace" in Washington
and the "very very considerable surprises" both he and Willa had
had in the past few weeks.

Hugh ripped the letter to bits.

But how much?

Yeh, you're just joking; son of a bitch joking.

Maybe yes, maybe no. How much?

How much d'you think?

I—I—have no idea.

He wore a dirty mashed hat. Grinning up at me. His companion,
slouched on the park bench, began to giggle. I could smell the
sickish-sweet wine. Another odor, sour. Vomit? Dried on their clothing, perhaps. The one in the hat got slowly to his feet. Not quite my
height, thank God. Even skinnier than I. In a filthy plaid sports coat,

only an undershirt beneath. Not so groggy as he had seemed a few minutes before. Eyes bright, malicious, netted in red. It was Sunday —Sunday morning. The bells of St. Aidan's sounded. Not, not St. Aidan's. I was in New York City. I was home. I had wandered a few blocks from home. I was not drunk, not now: but exhilarated. High. In white shoes, bought the day before. Stylish white shoes. Borrowed money. Why not? Why not, again? Now I was thirty-one years old and very wise. Experience had deepened me.

Do I wake. Or do I dream. Did I suddenly run away—hearing someone giggle behind me—or did I remain, unflinching at the stench, meeting the madman's gaze levelly, quoting prices in an uncharacteristically precise accent—an English accent of the upper-middle class, to be exact. Maybe yes, maybe no.

One thousand dollars?

Silence.

Two thousand—? He's a very evil man—has been evil to so many of us—

Interrupted by a sudden commotion: a tall emaciated boy with long bleached hair and a green headband, high on drugs, had seized one of the park's yellow wire trash cans and lifted it over his head, staggering in circles with his eyes shut, as if he were waiting for the right intuitive moment before he threw it. Black children were shouting at him.

I think I—yes—I am joking—

Huh? What?

Joking—only joking—

My life story.

And then a confused sequence: handing out money, a few bills, offering them eagerly, desperately, a few dollar bills, only a joke, only a joke.

My life story.

12

August 5. More questioning. I detached and civil, the interrogators respectful, sympathetic. They knew of the grief at the cemetery. I suppose. Perfunctory at the beginning—the identical questions they asked me back in June—a young man taking it down in shorthand— or seeming to—turning to another page when the questions touched upon something new. Evidently they had some new information. *And do you know of. . . ? And are you aware of. . . ? Is there anyone who. . . ?* Must have asked hundreds of people. Hundreds of questions. People, questions. Repetitions. Contradictions. Exasperation at finding no leads—did they use the expression "clues"?—muttering and complaining in private, in secret. Of course they were rivals with the other interrogators. Teams of them: federal, state, counties (Natauga County, where the murder had occurred; Albany County, Andrew's place of residence), the Police Department of the little town of Fremont (three men, I believe, one of them a professed "disciple" of the late messiah—and all the more fired to locate the "cell of murderers") and the Albany police, whose commissioner had been a personal friend of A's. And more. Insurance investigators, certainly. And at least one private investigator. Hired—I supposed—by Harvey. Expense account—his congressional office—or perhaps he could find a way to deduct it from his income tax: Harvey, among the cousins, famous for his stinginess. Really rather pathological. . . . Very likely there were other private investigators; the widow herself might have hired one (though Doris mentioned the woman's "unreasonable anxiety" over money); Doris might have goaded Laubach into it; and no doubt among A's conservative associates, those half-dozen he had not managed to offend this past year, there was at least one wealthy enough and mad enough to spend $50,000 or more . . . all to bring some fanatical little band to justice. I had no doubt that the assassination had been carried out by a dedicated group of radicals: whether of the left or of the right, who knows? That anyone should go to the trouble of killing another human being—should risk his own life—his own psychic balance—should in all probability condemn himself to a miserable existence afterward—what a puzzle! An impulsive killing might be something different. "Crime of passion"—"temporary loss of sanity"—whatever such terms mean. But a political assassination involving such planning—such evident planning—months of theorizing and preparing—learning of the man's movements, his frequent disappearances (a surprise to me: the Andrew I remembered had been boyishly and offensively gregarious, had liked very little about our place out in the mountains—where he was killed—except the possibility of shooting a few pheasant or rabbits or deer in season) and where he disappeared to—and how might be best to kill him—and *when*—and how, afterward, to *escape*— Amazing. One might envy such devotion to a principle.

That day, they asked me if the name "Joseph Rasch" or "Raschke" was familiar to me.

No—not at all.

No.

Never heard of the name.

They continued, but the crucial questions must have been blanketed in a dense cloud of words: I answered whenever I could, tried to figure out what they might be getting at, but grew bored finally and gave up. I yawned several times in quick succession. One of the detectives might have taken offense, his tone altered, he stared coldly at me—asked why I showed so little interest, so little human curiosity, in this investigation.

I feel interest, I said quickly. I feel curiosity. Even if I don't show it. . . . I want very much for the killers to be found. Very much. A terrifying thing . . . horrible, that they should still be free . . . that, with every day that passed, the likelihood of their arrest was lessened . . . and the police made to look ridiculous. A shameful thing. Tragic.

Smiled. Stood. Prepared to leave.

A moment's pause—some tension in the air?—but they were too stupid to sense my sarcasm—veiled by a bland hopeful earnest smile. And my extended hand, my eagerness to shake hands—like a gentleman—like a Petrie.

Any time I can be of help to you. . . . My diffident murmur, met with a gracious grunt; a routine farewell.

August 29. Back from a week at Montauk Point—Simon and Maggie again—too many house guests, too many children—impatient to return to my work. The ocean, the sky, the tedious bracing air: *déjà vu.* All had happened before. Left a week early. Returned in the late afternoon—pleasant garbagey smell in the foyer—climbing the flights of stairs a genuine treat—some unaccountable excitement as I unlocked my door. As if someone might be in there. Or the trace, the memory, of someone.

Nothing. Nothing.

The apartment was one long room, essentially. A "studio." People who dropped in were generally appalled and confused by it—by the mess—but I knew my way around, I felt at home in the clutter. An antique rocking horse; coconuts painted to resemble human heads, hanging from a curtain rod; a tarnished brass angel, child-sized; a bright green pillow; various old and presumably attractive things I had bought over the years as gifts for friends—and then, suddenly doubting my own instincts, or the wisdom of giving those particular gifts, or any gifts at all, decided to keep. And stacks of unframed canvases—piles of papers, books, magazines—towels, items of clothing, rags—at the kitchen end of the room a table weighted down with dishware—some of it cut glass and antique—acquired, for no particular reasons, at shops in the area—all but a few items thickly coated with dust. Never used. A space of about two feet square was kept clear, so that I could eat at the table if I chose; but most of the time I ate standing by the stove or the sink, or hunched over my drawing board. Beyond the kitchen alcove was a small closet-sized room, my bedroom; nothing in there but a bed without a headboard, a sagging mattress, rumpled sheets, a once handsome but now rather scruffed Victorian cabinet, a crook-necked lamp from Woolworth's, a single curtainless window that looked out upon a brick wall—a place to sleep, ideal for dreams. Blank.

I closed the door behind me. My heartbeat was still accelerated, expectant.

What—?

But nothing.

Like a sleepwalker I made my way into the room without a misstep. No real need to look at anything. So many things, odd amusing agreeable: *Hugh Petrie is such an odd personality*, people whispered: I could hear their whispers. Before me, around me, on all sides. Elegant taste, childishly joyful taste, idiosyncratic, rather reckless—careless—to be expected, with his genius. I noticed an urn that must have been an antique—Oriental—at least five feet high—with a plastic plant stuck in it, an obscene manufactured rubber plant, tilted forward, very dusty. Shoved to the very edge of my fifteen-foot workbench, amid the clutter, was a glittering Infant of Prague, lacy and pink-cheeked and lipsticked—someone had given it to me as a joke. There were several antique clocks, one of them a full-sized grandfather clock, beautifully carved, rather silly and expressionless, with no hour or minute hand and its brass pendulum permanently stilled. There were valuable works of art in here—several ink-and-wash drawings by Otto Dix—a transfer lithograph by George Grosz—work by Ben Shahn—several dozen reproductions of the caricatures of the eighteenth-century draughtsman James Gillray (on whom I had done three-quarters of a master's thesis some years before, when it looked as if I would have to live professorially and parasitically off others' art)—and copies of limited editions of my own work, said to

be modest collectors' items now. What else? A Leonard Baskin
woodcut—one of his deathly, anguished men—or had someone stolen
it? I had not seen it for some time. A woodcut of Felix Valloton's, a
violent swarm of starkly black human figures—hateful—exciting—
human beings reduced to ants—not by the artist but by their own activities—contemptible creatures! I knew them well. Framed, hanging
crooked above the kitchen table, a pencil-and-brown-wash drawing
by Lasansky, one of the Nazi drawings—about which a girl once said,
How can you like something so ugly?—the dear sweet contemptible
child. Most of the art work was my own, most of it drawings and caricatures already published, in which I had little interest—never got
around to framing anything but the marvelous beast-Prophet that
appeared in *Eminent Contemporaries*—and a leprous President in
the last stages of phosphorescent decay, overtly in the Grosz tradition—that had attracted some attention a few years before, when
there were still individuals unaware of the President's true nature—
naïve, scandalized. And the tricky little experimental piece to be
used for the cover of *Down & Out*, unless my publishers thought it
too obscene. My eye moved easily over these things. No snag, nothing out of place.

Had the telephone been ringing as I hurried up the stairs? Silent
now, pushed halfway under the kitchen table, on the floor. From another apartment came brief enigmatic noises—my neighbor Eva
quarreling with a lover?—or talking angrily to herself?—or just a
radio or television turned too high? But everything in my studio was
peaceful, undisturbed, still.

Went to the drawing board. A sheet of paper there—fragmentary
sketches, mere exercises—doodling. Nothing. Nothing unusual. I
studied the crude hurried figures—the exaggerated eyes, mouths, a
few of the people missing arms or legs, one of them gagged and
eyeless—mere doodling, done in haste or in vague frantic boredom.
There was a perplexed creature with a pear-shaped face melting into
grease-drops—a certain expression about the eyes—someone I knew?
—Andrew? no, impossible. . . . At the bottom right-hand corner
there was a faintly sketched face that drew my attention. A woman's
face, angular, rather long. Ugly and striking at the same time. The
eyebrows too dark and thick for the narrow forehead, almost meeting
above the nose. Haggard, bereaved, yet pouting: the lower lip was
thick, almost muscular. Her hair flowed upward from her forehead,
springing lustily away with a vitality of its own, and fell to her
shoulders—which had not been sketched in—and the deep-set eyes

seemed to be staring at me, forcing their angry sorrow upon me as I stood there, a stranger, suddenly frightened at what I had found.

She had been the one to find him—to find the body. She had gone back into the woods for him—back to the cabin by the river—the old cabin we had slept in a few times as boys—she had called his name, had run to the door that had been left partly open, had found his body inside— She, and no one else. I stared at the face, at her. At it. I swayed, stricken. Unaware of what I gripped so tightly in my hands —a few days' mail—I swayed above my own drawing board, about to pitch forward, suddenly faint, frightened, as if I were standing at the edge of an abyss—

13

I work my way through the paper, through the canvas. I take shape: I was always there. You labor over me, sweat running into your eyes like tears.

I went immediately to her. Up the Hudson River Valley. Offered myself to her. Selfless. No self. Art the oblivion of, annihilation of. Constant process of. Motions of the soul, which the body unquestioning obeys. I offered myself to her, to it. Generous with love. Cannot regret it—even now. Cannot imagine another Hugh—another self—another turn in the maze—another way out of the maze—

And she accepted me. In spite of what the evidence suggests.

14

—A shock, seeing her.

Nothing like my memory of her. Nothing like the woman I had expected to open the door. Yes? Hello? How do you do? How are you, Hugh? A haze of impressions—my eyes watering with absurd tears. Skin about my eyes tightened. Suspicious. Shook hands rather formally. Cool, moist, not very soft hand—rather thin. Must have spoken of something casual—desperate—the fine dry surprisingly cool weather—the scent of autumn already—the fact (which I mentioned) that I had never been in this apartment before.

No? Never?

Confused for a moment. Could not remember.

I laughed without embarrassment. Andrew and I—never very close —two entirely different careers—extremely busy lives—

Yes—

Offered me a drink. Rather early in the day for me—but perhaps some sherry? Invited me to look through the apartment—to look at the view—the woman like a hostess, a paid hostess—with that smooth throaty melodic voice. Alone for a moment, I took some wadded tissue out of my pocket—wiped my eyes—wondered why they were stinging. Not for him, certainly. Not for it. Maybe it was the sight of her—opening the door when I knocked—his widow standing there in the doorway, alone, an easy, welcoming expression on her face—and yet the vague bewilderment, the quizzical turn of the lips— Men approached her, men spoke to her. Men surrounded her. No doubt. But none of them were him.

Found myself standing before a window—a series of windows and French doors—an entire wall. A view of Jefferson Park, part of a golf course, a small lake or pond; in the distance the river, illuminated by sunshine, perfectly immobile. Impressive, yes. It would be. Beautiful in a cool, perfunctory way—a professional beauty—paid beauty—paid-for. The twenty-sixth floor of the building; quite silent up here, quite safe.

Staring out the window. Wondering.

She returned with the drinks. Small clatter of heels—parquet floor —the sound drum-like, stirring. Beautiful, isn't it. The river at dawn —in the early evening—at night, when there's a moon—restful, hypnotic.

I did not tell her about *my* studio. Did not mention *my* view.

So silent up here—surprising.

But why surprising, she asked, melodic and yet abrupt; the walls and the ceiling and the floor are backed by steel sheets—meant to be soundproof. Nearly. Sometimes from the corridor there is noise— neighbors' children running—and if the windows are open there is noise from the sky—but in general it's perfectly—

Noise from the sky!

A curious expression. Made me think of battalions of dark-winged angels—trumpets—the muscular turbulence of Michelangelo's *Last Judgment*—the apocalyptic crumbling of walls of cloud. Lovely.

We stood. Talked. Some nervous strain on my part. Like a cocktail party: the two of us standing a little to one side, in the dining area, by the plate-glass door. Chatter, harmless chatter. Hello, hello?

Yes? Continual murmuring, smiling; careful not to look too intensely into each other's face. I suppose I talked too fast. Kept fearing we would be interrupted at any moment—someone would appear at the far end of the living room—people would converge upon us from all sides. The curse of my youth and manhood: consciousness of self.

Not so young-looking, the glamorous Mrs. Petrie. Not now. But her glossy black hair was attractive—shorter than I remembered—had she had it cut?—swinging about her face as she moved her head, the pretense of animation a bit annoying. Bangs lying flat across the forehead; the eyebrows straight, dark, strong. Eyes abnormally bright. Deep-set, as in the sketch; darting from place to place, then back to me. The social manner. Mechanized, memorized. Routine. She led me from the window to a grouping of chairs—Victorian, high-backed, dark green velvet—speaking now of her work, how busy her days were. Husky-voiced. A certain confidence about her—not altogether convincing. She set her glass down, seemed to forget it. Gestured. Moved her hands in a way I believe I remembered—Andrew's —but not so aggressive, not so manic. The diamond rings on the left hand; the snake ring on the right. Slender, doughy-pale fingers. Colorless nails. Uneven: not manicured. My sister-in-law. Sister. Spoke of her "work"—a committee of some kind—an institute of some kind, government sponsored—the possibility of her teaching somewhere—and of course she was concentrating her energies on Andrew's manuscripts—sorting through them—hundreds of them, evidently—in preparation for—

Was it true he was writing a book, I asked innocently.

A book! —It would have had to be two or even three—

They were saying, yes—

—this past year, trying to get time to himself whenever possible— mainly weekends—wanted to take an entire month off later—later in the summer— Twenty-five years of work: various essays and outlines and ideas. Most of it published. Most in *Discourses*. But a good deal of it in crude preliminary form—first drafts—

Difficult for me to remain sitting. Wanted to jump to my feet. Wanted to laugh. Andrew and his hideous vanity! Vanity even as a boy. Fascinated by the pus-pointed bumps on his ugly face; would pause reflectively to study his handkerchief after he had blown his nose. Vanity. And now this deluded woman—

The topic?

She gestured helplessly. As if to indicate—

The fallacies of contemporary political and philosophical thought,

I suppose? Global errors? Suggestions of political strategy in the future? And wasn't he connected with—enthusiastic about—some kind of international "open conspiracy"—a network of superior men—or perhaps men and women both, I don't know—concerned with the survival of civilization?—the survival of what is valuable in Western civilization? I seem to remember a news item—New York Times—

The Times never treated him fairly—

Never.

Even the obituary—even the follow-up stories—prejudiced—distorted—

Silence.

A clock ticking somewhere behind me: solemn, righteous.

We began to speak at the same time—I remarking on the bloated extravagance of the capitol buildings—the new Mall here in Albany; she on the fact that the "case" was going very slowly.

Encouraged her to speak. Sat back, crossed legs, attempted to relax.

Emotionless, a woman speaking of the "case" of her husband's death. Unsolved. Innumerable leads—letters and telephone calls— even confessions (by "disturbed" individuals)—but no one arrested. Ill-coordinated teams of police. Even the townships involved. False witnesses stepping forth—claiming to have seen "suspicious" people in the area—informing on their neighbors—very strange people, up there in the mountains. Only eighty or ninety miles northwest of Albany; but the natives quite different. Was I familiar—?

Not very. Spent some summers there, on the old farm. Ten, twelve years old. Once when I was fifteen. Can't remember. Stayed on our property—didn't really meet anyone.

They seem—

I finished my glass of sherry. Tiny glass. Hardly more than a liqueur glass. Italian made: scarlet-stemmed. Lovely. Expensive. An antique—probably from Grandfather's estate.

—seemed unfriendly.

Yes, unfriendly. To outsiders.

The Petries had had a farm up there for—since— Someone in your family built that farm back in—it must have been the eighteenth century—

Smiled sympathetically. Watched her. Had the idea that she knew our family history perfectly—in greater detail than I knew it myself— was simply pretending not to know the man's name. I would not help her; I detested the Petrie "family," the absurd lineage. Rejected its values, its traditions, its morality, its property, its money, its people, living and dead.

—Governor of the state, wasn't he? And then he retired? To the country? To devote himself to philosophy—poetry—an autobiography of himself and his era?

Aaron Petrie. Married one of John Montgomery's daughters. Yes, he built the farm as a retreat; turned his back on politics—do you know why?

She smiled. Did not know, apparently.

A papermill factory on the river—a woman worker fired for disrupting the other workers—for singing, in fact—a boisterous, popular woman—rabble-rouser, she was called by the newspapers—several nights of rioting—nothing like it before or since in that little town. Soldiers sent in by the Governor: a small massacre. Even children. So afterward—a few months afterward—according to legend the Governor heard "the voice of God" instructing him to resign—to remove himself to a quiet place—to the mountains—to gentlemanly exile. And so he did. Built the farm on the river. Unfortunately he died after one winter. Could not bear it, I suppose—the snow, the freezing temperatures, the exile, the guilt.

She stood, offered me more sherry.

Fine. Thanks.

Watched her walk away: the guardedness of her body. Conscious of self. A curse. She too. Pretending to be at ease, girlish, "social." Would I ask the wrong question? Make the wrong remark? Would she blunder, would she break down, start to cry? What then? Unlikely. Steely calm, practiced. The Bride transformed into the Widow—rather beautifully—must admire the transformation.

Irritating, though, to have come so far: to be balked.

The person I wanted was keeping herself from me, denying me. Hiding there. A shell of a woman—pale, discreet. Returning with the sherry bottle—absolutely inscrutable look to her—could be a party hostess, a call girl in some new, sophisticated style—sexual beauty played down, innocently denied—a dress of raw black silk that fitted her tightly at the waist, emphasizing her gaunt figure—narrow hips, long thighs, long slender legs. Perfume? None. Nothing. I detected nothing, not even the exciting stink of panic.

And so you're in the city because of—?

I had mumbled something about legal, financial complications: something about property in my name that I wanted sold. Not quite true—not quite. The property had been sold years ago.

When I did not speak at any length she went on to say that she sympathized with me—with the difficulty of it—the heartbreaking burden of it—trying to straighten out financial matters. There were, of course, many complications concerning Andrew's estate— And—

I nodded. Hoped she would continue.

And—

People are filing suits? Making claims against it? What selfish bastards—

She blushed angrily.

—hard to believe, I murmured. The grossness of—

She changed the subject.

Art. Exhibits at the local musuem. In New York City: she and Andrew had seen the Giacometti show at the Guggenheim together —not long after the wedding. Had I seen it? But of course—of course I would have seen it; living in New York, I probably saw everything.

Hardly Andrew's taste, was it?

—and he bought something at an auction—an unsigned painting— it's there, on that wall—from colonial times I think—

Glanced at it. A coaching inn portrait. Obviously. His Majesty George III.

An antique—historically interesting—

Very interesting.

—the auctioneer said it dated back to—

Remarkable.

Not drinking her sherry. Long legs crossed at the ankle. Guarded. Aware of something detached in me—observant, ironic. Would have liked to ask me what I wanted; why I was really here. But shy. Shy of such directness. Reminded me of tough-talking soiled creatures I sometimes befriended—was amused by—detecting beneath the brassy high-pitched giggles and the strawlike bleached or dyed hair a certain childlike innocence—terror. Hid my own. Always. One learns to. One must.

She was calm, sociable, as she had been trained. No doubt her family had trained her: someone in Pittsburgh, an aunt or a guardian. Details vague. Though possibly Andrew himself had trained her. His first wife, Willa, very well-trained. Obedient. Effortless-seeming behavior at all times—perfectly normal a day before her attempted suicide, people said. But perhaps a rumor. Many rumors. Willa, whom I had liked so much, who had seemed to like me—Willa Fergus —fawnish-brown hair, delicate features, regal and vulnerable at the same time—a princess left in charge of a fortress. Had learned early to interpose for Andrew—a gracelessly brash young man just out of law school, lustful to enter politics, bullish, outrageously opportunistic, something of a joke except for the Petrie fortune. For years Willa made excuses for her husband's inexplicable actions, small rudenesses, mysterious absences—until the pretty façade shattered, the pathetic creature was hospitalized in Maryland—their small son Michael left without a mother for nearly a year. Now Willa and the boy lived in Manhattan and Palm Beach, as far as I knew. Manhattan: no more than a few miles from me, probably. But no contact. None. Divorce absolute—like death. Divorced from her husband, divorced from his entire family. Everything done through lawyers—very properly—ascetically.

Willa's replacement, Yvonne.

Yvonne.

Sister-in-law, sister. But no relative of mine. No kin. A stranger seated on Grandmother's velvet chair—or one resembling it—informing me of certain developments in which I had no interest—speaking impersonally, brightly, as if I were a fawning interviewer. A scholarship fund in Andrew's honor, sponsored by *Discourses*. Offers from publishing firms for Andrew's papers—anything at all—journals, memoirs, essays not yet collected in book form, correspondence, notes, scraps—anything at all. (She did not intend to accept—so she said.) A posthumous award. Lovely. Hundreds of letters. People so wonderful, supportive. Sympathy. Hundreds and thousands of cards. Donations. (Donations for what?—she did not elaborate.) Almost, a sense of community through his death—his dying for what he believed—certain moral principles—shared values—

Small prepared speech. Glanced at me, at the mere surface of me, to check my attentiveness. Why was I slouched so in that love seat? As if boneless, limpid. Why did I stare at her? Was I rude, or simply gauche? Her hands suddenly nervous. The snake ring slipped around, her finger must be thinner, jewelry loose.

Her voice thinned. Faltered. Some banal remark—a committee of state legislators formed to investigate any possible—

Are you very lonely? I asked suddenly.

Her gaze swung away. Heavy lidded.

A telephone began ringing.

Excuse me—

Of course. Of course.

Wandered through the front rooms. Alone. Jumpy in spite of the drink—plagued by the absurd sense of someone overhearing us—about to burst in upon us. Abnormally quiet here. Must be right about the steel sheets between the walls. Soundproofing. Unlike my brownstone, hardly more than a high-priced tenement, really; traffic noises, people on the stairs, children playing outside. A different life. Entirely different.

Furnishings handsome. Expensive, naturally. Interior decorator's taste—conventional mixture of harmless styles—greens, browns, pale yellows—a little velvet, a little leather—the ludicrous portrait of an insane king on one wall—painting of the Erie Barge Canal on another—a silver tea service—Mother's, no doubt—candelabra here and there, useless, not even quaint, just silly. The apartment of a wealthy bachelor. Someone rarely home. A place for occasional gatherings—painfully dull parties—intimate dinners at which certain decisions are made, deals completed. Parquet floor in the dining area; dark-stained hardwood floor elsewhere. Oriental rugs. Bought at auctions, probably. When the household with Willa was dissolved—they had lived in an immense Greek revival mansion in Riverdale, one of the older sections of town—everything had gone to her except a few of Mother's and Grandmother's things. At least I had been told so. The newer pieces of furniture here were formidable—an immense black leather sofa curving around a low-lying coffee table of smoked glass—various hard-edged mirrors—a highly polished little table that looked like a work of art.

Casually, I wondered how much money the man had actually had. I wondered also how much money Father was going to leave. Without Andrew's share—and of course Stephen had eliminated himself—with only Doris and me inheriting, of the immediate family—

But now I was thinking as *he* had always thought. . . .

Andrew's presence. Andrew's little kingdom.

A half-dozen handsomely framed paintings: nineteenth-century "realism." Pretty green hills rolling into hazy brainless skies. Small cattle grouped beneath picturesque oaks. Streams and meadows and exquisite fluffy clouds in exquisite blue skies. Hudson Valley School. A horse auction in colonial times—attempt at "action." "Vitality." Above the marble-topped mantel, exactly harmonizing with the proud gleaming brass fire irons, a Flemish-inspired landscape of offensively slick proportions—more comforting green hills, more cattle, a meandering stream, a sky heavy with dramatic storm clouds.

Andrew's little kingdom, Andrew's stubborn graceless taste. Such paintings—such flat, slick technical perfection—irritating to me—maddening—that flat-footed pragmatic vision of the world—a world to be parceled off into lots—manipulated, bought and sold, sold and bought, a world to be controlled by any means possible—*Republican majority in state senate*— You stood in the center of the late Andrew Petrie's living room, looked from wall to wall, from painting to painting, experienced the dizzying sensation of being transported to another era, another dimension, those six or seven paintings transformed into windows—ordinary windows—looking out upon rural scenes that assured the permanent stability, the absolute fixedness, of the cosmos.

Off the living room was a kind of sitting room, a small library. Its single window overlooked downtown Albany and the high-rise buildings of the Mall some distance away. The view was not so attractive on this side of the building. Another hardwood floor; several leather chairs; bookshelves crammed with books, some of them quite old—broken-backed—probably collectors' items—Washington Irving's *A History of New York From the Beginning of the World to the End of the Dutch Dynasty*—Crèvecoeur's *Journey into Northern Pennsylvania and the State of New York*—several shelves of the green-bound collections of the New York Historical Society, the most recent dated 1923—must have been Grandfather's books—and those twenty volumes of works by Theodore Roosevelt—certainly Grandfather's—Grandfather had known Roosevelt—according to family legend had been "crudely treated" by him. Throughout history, even back in England—back in the early 1600's, where one Michael Petrie, an Anglican minister, had been suspended for "nonconformity" to Anglican ceremonies—thereby encouraged to remove himself to New England; and certainly in recent history—one Petrie or another was "crudely treated" by his superiors or by the members of his parish or by his constituents or by his relatives or—in Andrew's case—by persons unknown. Unfair. Unjust. Stoicism outwardly—whining and puling and weeping in secret. Except for me: ill-treated, yes, and by no means rewarded with the income and prestige my genius might deserve. But I have never succumbed to self-pity.

Andrew's little kingdom!—and Andrew nowhere in sight.

A telephone on a writing desk, by the window.

Found myself before it. Fingers twitching. Trembling. Dread—joy—excitement. Dare I lift the receiver, dare I—? Eavesdrop—? Impossible.

Glasses sliding down nose. Must be perspiring. What if— But—
Unthinkable that—

The woman would hear me lifting it. A small unmistakable *click*.

Very excited now. Forced myself to look away—scan the titles of
books at eye level—saw nothing—blurs—leather-bound blurs—an ornate clock no longer ticking—hands stuck at 4:30. The telephone—
the receiver—

Gently.

But no. Impossible. Really out of the question.

Crammed shelves: floor to ceiling. Untouched, unread. Papers of
Thomas Jefferson—works of James Buchanan—Edmund Burke—
Disraeli—Churchill—translations of Juvenal—Marcus Aurelius—
hodgepodge of famous names—heroes—a half-dozen books on Alex-
ander the Great (did Andrew identify with him more than with the
others?)—sixteen volumes of Woodrow Wilson—my God! —Gently.
Heroically. As much courage needed for this as for leading a cavalry
charge—slaughtering barbarians—Indians—Irishmen— As much courage as—

Somehow the receiver was in my hand, had leaped to my ear. My
trembling but forceful forefinger remained on the apparatus that
kept the line dead. Marvelous inflow of adrenaline. Excited—very!
Something physical about the operation—keeping my finger there—
allowing it to rise gently, gently—hardly daring to breathe—physical,
sensual, every pore of my body sighing—my eyeballs throbbing—
vision nearly gone— At such times in my life (ah, there have been
many!) a phantom Hugh breaks away from me and stands staring—
wringing his skinny hands—moaning—unable to believe that this act
will really take place—unable to accept its meaning in terms of
Hugh's soul—in terms of the consequences Hugh may have to pay.
Shame, shame! Stop! How can you—what would Mother say? But so
laughably feeble is that dull phantom—so declassé the very conception of a conscience—and of course Freud's superego is sheer vapor—
that the trembling yearning sweating Hugh has only to allow nature
to course through him—a few shallow cautious breaths to transpire—
and the deed is done.

> . . . as soon as he leaves. No, didn't I explain?
> I can't. I can't. I don't have time. After the
> reception. . . .
> When can I see you, then? If Tuesday is. . . .
> . . . the Greasons will take me home; I think they
> will; Leon wants to talk to me about . . . some
> investments . . . a shopping plaza . . . it's very compli-

cated. But I don't think I will sue the paper.
I was never serious about that. I was hysterical,
please forgive me, now I must hang up . . . there is
a visitor here. . . .
Who did you say it was, Yvonne?
I didn't say.
It isn't someone—?
Someone—?
Someone dangerous?
I don't know, he might be dangerous—

Nearly fainting. Could bear it no longer.
Gently broke the connection—put the receiver back in its cradle.

Ah, what triumph.
Quiet now. Sated.
Sipping sherry—poured myself another glass—slouched in the charming love seat with one long skinny leg crossed over my knee, humming idly to myself. *Might be dangerous.* She had been talking to a man, voice unrecognizable, Yvonne rather hurried and distracted, the man eager—pushy—on the verge of being annoyed. A lover? *I don't know, he might be dangerous. I don't know, he might be dangerous. I don't know, he might be dangerous.* Before me a magnificent view of the Hudson River—a sky not so intensely blue but far more subtle and intriguing than those insipid skies in the late Andrew Petrie's landscapes—in another room a woman in a black silk dress whispering into a telephone—worried—wondering—*I don't know, he might be dangerous. I don't know—*

15

SETTING: a tower overlooking a featureless, insignificant landscape.

SCENE: the lover kneeling before his beloved, accepting without protest her sudden, irrational blow—the flat of her hand striking his cheek—

DIALOGUE:

Someone leaned over my shoulder. Someone's hair fell against my feverish cheek. I blew it away as if it were my own. No more curiosity, no more passion, than if it were my own.

Hugh Petrie? Is it you? Cruel, famous Hugh Petrie? Himself?

The Artist sits at his drawing board.

Mid-September heat. No rain for many days. But it is weatherless here. Climateless. The room—the walls—the long table more cluttered than ever—dizzying to consider, if one considered it. No time for it. No time here either: timeless. The external world falls away. Fades. Colorless, two-dimensional, finally one-dimensional and invisible.

Imagination struggles to free itself.

Bound for where—?

A great white bird—an albatross—struggling to free itself from something that holds it down. (Mother spoke of seeing these enormous lovely birds—a world cruise many years ago with her parents—watching them from the ship—indescribably lovely—wingspan of eight or ten feet!)

The Artist sits at his drawing board. Albatross; dove; snowy egret. Something of surpassing beauty struggling to free itself: as if from a tar pit. Ancient times, prehistoric unconscious times, all creatures sleepwalking. No one thinking, brooding, recording. No one responsible. Tar pits. Tigers. Saber-toothed tigers. Tusks—horns—claws and teeth. Ivory. Ivory—

Is that something you're supposed to do? For who? What does it represent?

The girl spoke querulously, familiarly.

Two assignments on hand. No, three. Backlog of promises. A national political figure had published a book—muckraking amidst the diplomatic corps—and his ex-wife was to publish a book—an "intimate memoir"—in a few weeks: some delightful sketch involving the two of them was needed. No problem. Should be no problem. Another, more ambitious drawing: innumerable political and cultural and moral "leaders" of the moment reduced in scale, clawing squirming biting wrestling disemboweling one another, like wolverines perhaps, all with fanatic godly eyes. Should be no problem—but might take some time. Wolverines? Or sharks? Possibly sharks. Gargoyles with fixed maniac grins—used in a drawing a few months earlier—can't use again for some time. Must stress the righteousness—the sanctimoniousness—the *certainty*—with which each trivial creature disembowels another.

But the haphazard sketches have nothing to do with the assignments.

A woman with savage hair rising lushly from her head. Medusa?

But sensual, sensuous. Innocent as well. Long straight Byzantine nose. Eyes very dark, staring. Long powerful arms and legs—such legs as might wrap themselves around a man—break his backbone. High, girlish breasts. Hard-looking. The breasts of a statue. Belly and pubic area shadowy, not quite sketched in; only suggested. Crucial to get the proportions right—the feel of the whole, its rhythmic motion— the way the head holds itself—the tension about the mouth.

Dialogue:

Nothing. A blank. What did we say to each other?—she to me? *I'm sorry, I must be leaving shortly, I can't ask you to stay.* And I rising slowly, lazily, perhaps insolently to my feet. *I was leaving anyway. Thanks immensely for allowing me up.* Walking with me to the door—silent, shyly angry, confused. No handshake. A farewell of murmurs, averted eyes. (For she knew very well I had eavesdropped: knew I had picked up that receiver.) Cowardly, she was. Would not accuse me. But perhaps she was being simply shrewd. . . . Andrew's technique. Strategy. Never allow your opponent to know the extent of your information concerning him; always appear to be friendly, open, innocent. At the door, some pretense of formality—allusion to our meeting again—clearly insincere—and I, bowing from the waist like a suitor in a stage comedy, though not quite so rakishly gauche as to seize her hand and kiss it, *Yes I think we will meet again: yes, fine.*

What did the woman with the dark, frantic stare and the hair that rose from her head like flames seem to be whispering?

Would you kill for me?

But no: nothing. A blank. Really nothing.

Neither asleep nor awake, the Artist sits at his drawing board. Neither hypnotized nor attentive. Dull sweet hummings in his head. Yes? No? What? No. He has no face; is faceless. No history. If someone leans over his shoulder to inspect his work—if someone's hair falls against his cheek—he returns to himself from a great distance, irritably, and asks her what she wants.

How did you get in here? Did I leave the door unlocked? I must be getting—

I'm more interesting than these ugly people, she said. You know I am.

I had thrown down my pencil; was now moving my fingers across the paper, trying to read the faces, the tiny mangled inconclusive faces, and *her* face, like Braille.

Faces!—the mysterious fleshly expression of the soul! All we have to work with in this life; and not nearly adequate.

Eva, I said vaguely, do you believe that a face expresses the soul— or do you believe, perhaps more reasonably, that a face is simply flesh like any other, symbolic of nothing? Nothing?

My face is beautiful, Eva said flatly. That man who—the other night—do you remember?—our discussion in the foyer and you ran down to investigate and—

That pimp with the sideburns?

He is not! He's—he has—he's with the United Nations—of a Latin temperament and therefore fiery and passionate— Carlos. Carlos said that my face was beautiful; that I was selfish and spoiled like all beautiful women. —Another time, after an audition, a man told me I had the grace of a gazelle. "The grace of a gazelle."

My fingers moved of their own accord. My eyes were closed.

Any secret? Any whispering?

Nothing.

When I was a child, Eva began, sitting now on the edge of my workbench—careless of how her wraparound gown fell open—we lived in a basement apartment in Newark—five of us and a tiny baby —the baby died of pneumonia and my mother almost went crazy— my father was a nice man but always drunk. There was a man in the building, a veteran of World War II, he lived all alone—have I told you this, Hugh?—no?—you're sure?—he had been supposedly wounded in action—I don't know—had a medal or a Purple Heart or something—anyway he stopped me in the hall after school one day and talked me into coming upstairs with him to his room—and—and he did things to me—I was only nine—he did things to me and warned me that if I told he would strangle me—said he'd strangled a girl once—in France—described how her eyes almost popped out and the same thing would happen to me if—

Eva, twenty-seven years old. Small, with smudge on her eyelids, a perpetual querulous edge to her voice; prettily depraved; at least fifteen pounds underweight. She lived across the hall. Came to visit occasionally, for mysterious reasons—not always evident at first— sometimes just lonely. Spoke of herself as a former photographer's model. Or a former "actress."

Eva, why are you telling me such things?

Why not? Why shouldn't I tell you?

You speak of outrages in that flat whiny adolescent voice—

How should I speak of them? Should I scream? Should it be poetry?—blank verse? Would you like that better?

Why are you here, do you want another loan?

She poked my shoulder, rather hard.

If that's all you think of—

You already owe me ninety dollars—and I owe other people money—even if I finish these assignments I'll still—

But she had no interest in my life. She sighed, tightened the sash of her festive green-and-scarlet "Oriental" gown, looked sadly at me. Well, your family has millions of dollars, she said; what the hell do you care about the rest of the world? Not that I blame you—I don't! —but—

I'm poor, I'm in debt. What do you want? I must work—maybe we could talk later—we could have coffee or something later—

I want to talk now, she said harshly. Nobody ever listens to me. They talk—*they* talk. Men. They talk about themselves. I don't know what they talk about—I don't listen. But they don't talk about me. If they do, it isn't about me; it's about them and me. It's their idea of me. I want to talk to you—you're an artist—you're different from the others—I want to talk to you and I want you to listen. If—

What you told me, Eva, I said suddenly, was all lies.

What? What do you mean?

Once it was an uncle who "did things" to you—once it was a Catholic priest—

No! It was not! It was never a priest—never! I'm not Catholic—

Once it was a high school principal—

That isn't true, she whispered. Breathing hard. Absurdly hurt: giving off an odor of heated, exasperated flesh. Around me, she rarely bothered with disguises—adornments—her platinum-and-brown sprayed hair needed shampooing—her small, slightly bowed legs were bare and stubbly—her stylish bright red lipstick, from last night, was badly flecked. Still charming. Perhaps even "beautiful."

That isn't true, she repeated. You're the one who lies. *You*. All these drawings—some of them are just nasty cartoons—what is that ugly thing on the wall there?—a bunch of bats and owls and crap flying down on a man's head—

That isn't mine, I said. That's Goya.

Anyway it's nasty and ugly and distorted—

So are we all.

I'm not! —Why don't you look at me? Why don't you do a study of me? A drawing—a pen-and-ink drawing—or even a painting?—the way painters do, of women? I would model for free; I would be honored.

My eye had been drawn back to Yvonne's face. What did she seem to be saying? What had she actually said? Our dialogue came to nothing. *Dialogue: nothing.* But perhaps she had been trying to tell me something—

I'm more interesting than those drawings, Eva said shrilly. Look at me—think about me—why don't you care about *me?*

I stared at her. Who was she? Who the hell? Babyish whining voice—hot-eyed, as if rehearsing a melodramatic scene—"anger"—"passion"—"despair." A bruise on her upper arm. A small pimple near her hairline. When life went well for my neighbor, I would not see her for weeks. Would hear a man's voice—the excited clatter of her fashionable stacked shoes—her high-pitched laughter—music from her apartment turned up high. Sometimes she disappeared from the building entirely—a vacation in Hawaii, or the Barbados, or Spain; sometimes she gave parties that lasted for a day and a night and part of another day. I had minded at first—had been depressed at first—ready to move out to yet another apartment—but had made the effort (as Dr. Wynand suggested) to "adapt" to unpleasant features in my environment. To some extent this worked. I "adapted" to her. I was even fond of her. But—

I suffer too, Eva was saying. I'm worthy of your attention. Just because your brother was killed—you people with your big-deal connections—politicians—other people get killed too, don't you know that? Huh? My best friend at school, her mother was shot to death in a hold up—in a dry-cleaning store in Newark—some black bastards that didn't give a damn about anything and the police just as bad—black bastards on the police force now—what do they care? What does anybody care? A girl I used to know, she had a place over on Bleecker Street, some drunk bastard ran her down—broke both her legs—does the *Times* give a damn? Such a big deal about somebody like your brother—and now it's that Governor out in—where is it?—Utah or something—that one of his children is missing—well, so what? Lots of people are missing! I'm missing! Nobody gives a damn about real people any more. One life is supposed to be as important as another, but—

I'm not concerned about my brother's death, I said quietly. People live—people die. "Thou owest God a death." As far as I'm—

Maybe it's my face that goes against me, actually, Eva said slowly.

People hesitate to believe that a pretty girl—a basically cheerful and healthy girl—can suffer. And if you're beautiful—well, forget it! Homely people—elderly people—blacks and chicanos and what d'ya call them—and of course crippled people—everybody feels sorry for them already, and guilty, and they have no feeling left over for the rest of us. You—*you* would notice me if I was deformed—or had a scar on my face—you'd probably beg me to model for you, huh? It isn't fair, it's unjust—

Eva, please—

But you don't *look* at me! Your mind is never here! No wonder you aren't married—or maybe you're divorced—is that it, are you divorced?

No.

Can I ask you, then—what the hell is that rocking horse for over there? I've been wanting to find out for—

It's nothing, nothing. Just nothing. It was a mistake.

—and the stuff hanging over it, that shirt or whatever it is, you know it's been hanging there since last winter? I mean it; since last winter. After I had the flu and you were so nice and I came over here, I remember it very well, I just peeked in one day and noticed it draped over the rocking horse and that was last February—and—

You let yourself go, you're worse than I am. Something awful is going to happen to you. You don't care about the real world—you don't even notice it—you're always sketching or doodling or seeing things in your mind—

I folded the sheet of paper. Folded it again.

Tossed it into the wastebasket.

My mother worries about me, that I let myself go—don't eat right —that kind of thing, Eva said. But you're worse. —You know what my mother said? Last time I was there? She said maybe I should move, maybe there was danger living here—in the same building with you—I sure as hell regret telling her that I knew Andrew Petrie's brother!—damn it!—she said—

Said what?

Maybe there was danger here, for instance if someone came to— well—someone was hired to—to go after you—and by mistake he broke into the wrong—

I began to laugh.

What? It's funny? Why is it so funny?

I waved her away.

Somebody with a gun—a machine gun, maybe? Is it so funny, is it so improbable?

I jumped down from the stool, walked away. Walked into the kitchen. Eva followed, protesting.

Look—there's a columnist for the *Newark News*—my mother sent me the clipping, in fact—his theory is that the assassination is actually solved—but the people that did it were—well, people on *his* side—I mean, some secret group—very right-wing group—you know?—with lots of money and high connections and power—people who can hire anyone to kill anyone, you know—so it could just happen all at once—somebody coming up the stairs here—knocking on your door—sometimes you don't even have the door locked when you're home, you're so trusting or absent-minded or stupid—aren't you?—and why is it so funny, that my mother should be worried? I'm not worried myself—I hardly even think of it—if I started getting paranoid, Jesus Christ!—where would it all end?—but it isn't exactly crazy of my mother, Hugh, and I resent it that you just dismiss—

Forgive me, honey. I can't help it.

—just laugh and ridicule everything people tell you—

I can't help it.

Can't help it. Can't help it.

16

September 19. In the pocket of my natty dark-blue-and-powder-blue-striped sports coat, a cocktail napkin of linen, claret-colored. Rolled into a loose cylinder. Monogram *P*.

Evidently I had stolen it while at my brother's apartment. Could not remember. Almost remembered—but could not.

The Widow in the other room—in one of the back rooms—a bedroom, probably. Talking to her lover on the phone. Excited, perhaps a little bitter, I might have rolled the napkin up and shoved it in my pocket. Might have done so. Don't really remember.

I was bullied as a boy. By him and by others. He knew, he did nothing to stop it. He knew. Everyone knew. The chaplain took pity on me, but no one else. Horribly abused, humiliated. I paid for my superiority—why shouldn't Andrew pay for his?

Had to run through the hall, down from the fourth floor, naked. They cheered and hooted. Whistled. Stamped their feet. Andrew was in the next house—Andrew knew what I suffered. Did not care. Professed to be ashamed of me. *Coward, coward!* Too cold to be vicious himself. —I know I'm drunk! So what? People are listening?—so what! Let them listen! Let everyone listen! I've paid for my sincerity many times—I don't mind paying—my character is my fate—*his* character was *his* fate, inescapable. We experience nothing but what we already are.

No roommates. They moved out—always moved out. No friends. They got me to cry, then laughed and jeered. Snatched my glasses away. Made me beg. I asked my brother for help—he refused. Laughed at me, said it wasn't serious, said I should ignore it. *Said I should ignore it.* —My refusal to accept their estimation of me: that caused the trouble. They thought I was negligible—stupid—weak. Frightened of Andrew, resentful of Andrew, so they took it out on me. Jealous of us all. *Petrie.* Jealous of the name. I fought them—fought against their tyranny. Always have. Tyranny!—must be destroyed. No tyrants. No tyrants. Must be free. —One day I jumped the noisiest bastard of them all—marching downstairs—fire drill—the one who had teased me about being so skinny—Saxton, his name—son of the state attorney general at that time—the ringing of the fire bells excited me, made me think of sudden catastrophic events—bombs, earthquakes, impersonal death—deaths— Realized death could be impersonal—no one to blame! Those bastards were vulnerable, despite their bravado and jeers, very vulnerable, actually very accessible—victims like myself. I spoke to him. He ignored me. I spoke to him again. He glanced at me, muttered something. Ignored me. Hurried away to be with his friends. I jumped him from behind. Grabbed him by the throat. How easy it was, how easy! We fell downstairs together. I was screaming—sobbing—the other boys pulled me away—such people must pay, must be punished— They respected me after that. Were afraid of me. No roommates—no friends. But they respected me. Father came to visit: took me to lunch. Angry at first. Then serious. "Impressed"—I think. Unaware of my maturity—a boy of thirteen speaking to him nearly as an equal—explaining how brutish behavior must be stopped, punished—*someone must do it.*

Why should I leave? Where are the people I came in with? Who are you?—why are you touching me like that? I'm not drunk. I have to speak like this or no one will hear. If you think you can paw me—if you think I'm helpless—

You must all pay—you can't escape. The cruelty of your childhood. The way you tortured others. Mocking, jeering, hurting— You must all pay, escape is impossible—I won't let you escape—I will remember —I condemn you all to—

Woke thrashing from side to side. Hands against face—thumbs pushing against eyeballs. Must punish. Must.

Woke damp with perspiration: the metallic taste in my mouth, the ache of my eyes. Began to remember. Strangers' faces—a boy with long snarled red hair—brittle, dyed—eyebrows and eyelashes dyed that false defiant orangish-red—the chemical reek about him— "perfume," was it?—a parody of perfume—parody of woman's scent —parody of woman. Had started out with Simon and Maggie and friends of theirs—and Deborah Tracey—the daughter of—sensitive, intelligent, as reserved as I—mid-thirties but still girl-like—charming —had known now for many years—many, many years—a quiet relationship—no fuss, no melodrama, no demands—no passion— Deborah the daughter of the man who published my first book— whom I admired—wanted to please—and yet could not quite please except at the cost of compromising my vision—but he understood, he was a gentleman as well as a businessman—a superb editor—must see him again soon: make that effort, seemingly so difficult, dial his number and arrange for luncheon sometime. But no. Wait. He died a few years ago. Died suddenly. Coronary thrombosis. Deborah upset, missing him so; Deborah unmarried, daughterly, my possible fiancée; what happened to her? Dinner at that French restaurant on 53rd Street, Simon's favorite—good lively conversation—martinis, wine—tart red wine—and someone disagreeing with me—what?— why?—and I witty and contemptuous—in French, I believe—and something about a taxi—a driver objecting to—what?—to me?—and confused exchanges—Maggie pretending to be hurt—pretending to cry—Simon and I shouting at each other in the street, while passers-by gaped—the contemptible fools!—the little sullen group resentful of me, perhaps, directing their resentment of all creative personalities against *me* personally—not able to forgive me for being what I am— annoyed that I insisted upon paying the bill for dinner—and what a bill!—my God!—so much money for a mere two-and-a-half hours' diversion! And—and— And I unable to bear the burden of their dim-witted fantasies of the Artist—unable to stand by meekly as imbecilic clichés are uttered in my presence—

A din. Voices. Din rising to thunder. Can't shut it out—can't beat it back. Dragged myself out of bed. My glasses? Had someone taken them? —Clothes on the floor. The straight-backed chair overturned, lying in the doorway. Odor of vomit—mine?

Never. Never again.

Never again.

Who's here? Is someone here with me? I called out shrilly. Naked —whimpering—staggering into the other room. Was he here? Had he stayed? What had he done? Where were my glasses?—had he taken them? Broken them? Remember getting out of a cab—handing my wallet over to—to that soft-spoken young man with the curious hair—plum-colored velvet collar, despite last night's warm temperature—shoes with six-inch heels—Spanish in design—pop-Spanish—the boy beating someone else back, saying *This is my friend—this is my newfound friend—you all stay away!—I know how to make you stay away!* I was dizzy, trying to stand up in a booth—bumping my hip— he helped me out, helped me up the steps—must have been a basement—up on the sidewalk a small crowd milling, mostly young people—stylish and flamboyant and merry—past three in the morning, and so merry!—and the stumbling walk back here to my apartment—four or five blocks—the boy with his arm around my waist, cooing to me—*Just fine! just fine! everything's gonna be just fine!*—must have taken my keys out of my hand—must have put me to bed—

My glasses lay on the floor. Evidently tossed there—but not broken. The wallet—tossed down also, a few feet away.

Never again.

17

Began to experience difficulty with my work. Assignments— commissions—somehow depressing, where once they were inspiring. Found it hard even to sit still for long. Climbed down from my stool; stood; climbed back up again; fidgeted, sighed, leaned forward until my hot dry parchment face touched the paper.

Across the street and a few doors down, Berger Bros. Funeral Parlor. Red brick. Brass trim. Always a funeral—always busy. Enormous black hearse and rented mourners' cars. Funeral: funereal. Ludicrous. Enough?—too much.

Out on Sixth Avenue, Roy's Famous Pizza. A medium-sized pizza with cheese, Italian sausage, mushrooms, and anchovies. Please. Will take it back to my apartment, thank you. Stringy cheese, grease droplets coagulating on the slightly too-scarlet sausage bits, the anchovies devilishly salty, the crust always too thick and underbaked on the very outside—but tasty, tasty. Can't deny. And cheap.

Afterward, stomach cramps.

So what?

The mouth can chew away lustily, the eyes can mist over with idiot pleasure, while knowing full well—with the intellect, that is— what will happen later. Mouth-pleasures, visceral-agonies. So? So what?

Where once my drawings excited me, now they depressed me. To have a drawing due next Tuesday—depressing indeed. My mind swerved away from work that had to be done. It fastened itself upon—upon other matters. A caricature illustrating the canny parochialism of a certain prominent New York literary "spokes-man"?—the detailed drawing of those "American leaders" in a snake's coil, tearing at one another with their teeth and claws, disem-boweling one another gleefully?—suddenly very hard to execute. Began and tore up innumerable sketches. Angry. Sad. Frightened. Yearning for a drink.

Supper at Blimpie's, on Sixth Avenue. A front of yellow tile, a huge pink neon sign. *Blimpie's.* Hamburger and bun and side order of six French fries. Pickle very green—*very* green. Lonely, tired. Hands trembling so that the cashier noticed.

A long walk—to Fourth Street maybe—and across—thereby avoid-ing Berger Bros.

Antique shops. Rare books. Florists. Taverns—pizzerias—news-stands—"Adult Books & Continuous Live Entertainment"—boutiques —delicatessens—butcher shops—life, life—all races, all ages—cos-tumes—wide busy avenue—buses, taxis, trucks, cars, bicyclists, mo-torcyclists, delivery boys. Marvelous—tiring. Dreaded seeing someone I knew. What if—? Out of a subway entrance—? But he was dead. What if it had been a hoax? A political trick? An insurance fraud? More antique shops—junk shops. Estate clearing houses. Old chairs, old bedsteads, pitchers and vases and coatracks. Multiplicity of forms. A & P dreary, warehouse-sized. Quite busy. Saw a young man who resembled Stephen—walking in a daze, black-bearded, frizzy-haired, obviously insane. Wore an oatmealish caftan. Sandals. Head bowed, fleshy lips moving in—what? A continuous prayer? A con-tinuous curse?

Considered telephoning Stephen. Did not know his place of residence. Somewhere in West Virginia? Brandywine? Might ask Doris. But—what point to it? Why telephone baby brother? *God's will.* Visions and hallucinations and soul stammerings as a boy—teary-eyed— so hideously embarrassing to the rest of us. Mother was "religious"— in her way. Conventionally religious. Did or did not "believe" in God—would certainly not have said—would not have embarrassed anyone. Stephen—no restraint! Gushing, sentimental, idiotic. A pity, since he had been intelligent at one time. Promising. Father wanted law school for the boys—naturally. Only Andrew complied. And then sailed beyond Father's dominion.

Now dead? Lowered into a fresh-dug grave, at least.

Dead?

Murdered?

God's will.

Did not telephone Stephen. Forgot about Stephen.

Clarity is my only sin.

Frankness—the refusal to lie—to sugarcoat the necessary pill.

Always be ready to speak your mind, and a base man will avoid you. The story of my life, exactly. Wrote to Yvonne: tried to explain. Sitting hunched over the table, so agitated I had to stand— shuffling from side to side—gnawing at my lip. Words so difficult for me—torture—hell. Could sketch in a few cartoons the story of my life, my relationship with the deceased; could do it elegantly, wittily, no self-pity at all. But words are hard. Very hard. Unless you are very careful they will reveal too much.

Yvonne? Are you very lonely? Did you sense how I. . . ?

Eyes aching. Ripped up the letter—threw the pieces away—scattered on the floor. Impasse.

Where was Eva? Would have welcomed her bright aimless chatter. Not around this weekend—left without saying good-by. Owed me a hundred and thirty-five dollars now. Needed "emergency funds"—her hair dry and brittle as straw, starting to fall out— required an eight-hour conditioning and oil-restoring treatment—so she said—desperate and chagrined—"emergency appointment" at Saks. Eva, Eva. The breath of life in her. Somehow enviable. Not my kind, not my species. How to cross over—? How?

Impasse.

Hello?

Yvonne?

Yes, who is this?

This is—

Nattily dressed, but not as before. A new outfit required. Autumn now—lovely lovely season of crisp decay—bright damp mornings and hazy sunsets—the beauty of maples and oaks along the Hudson River enough to blind one, to turn the soul inside out—a savagely flaming gold-orange-brown-scarlet-green sycamore not fifty yards away—my poor gaze fastened to it as I spoke to Yvonne, hoping—silently begging—that inasmuch as beauty of such heartbreaking authority does exist in the world—the maligned material world—inasmuch as we two are alive—living—I relatively young (forty now) and relatively vigorous (not quite true: but perhaps my state of health would improve) and relatively successful (a "known" artist if not commercially gargantuan, "known" in the New York City area at least)—inasmuch as I scrutinized my wardrobe and pronounced everything hopeless, dashed out wild and elated, took a cab uptown—hurried into a Fifth Avenue shop as if drawn by something extraordinary in its window—or guided by interior voices that gave me the courage my own voice might argue away—excited, euphoric, pirate-ish, with the liquid-dark gaze (I saw it myself in the three-way mirror!) of a virile young lover, a courtier, a Renaissance servant-of-love frantic to dash into his beloved's presence—inasmuch as I risked a prison sentence by writing—in a well-tempered hand—a check for $365.98 against an account fortified by no more than forty-five dollars and possibly less, since my system of bookkeeping had deteriorated of late—and emerged giddy with purpose into the street again, aggressively handsome and eye-engaging in an outfit of rust tweed edged with suede leather—no time, even, for alterations—no time!—wearing a silkish shirt of pale yellow and a gorgeous wide necktie that looked as if it were varnished—clutching a package containing yet more purchases: socks, underwear (blue!), an alternative tie designed by Christian Dior, scandalously provocative zebra stripes, and even a handkerchief—white, monogrammed P, expensive—"genuine Irish linen"—in case the Widow should, at one time or another, begin to cry in my presence—for could a lover, could anyone, offer that extraordinary woman a crumpled Kleenex?—inasmuch as I left my heaped-up work-table behind, left two editors' expectations cheerfully unfulfilled, left, in short, my self-respect and my pride and my sanity behind, to stride nervously back and forth through the corner of Jefferson Park facing my beloved's place of residence—darting across the street every ten or fifteen minutes to telephone her—again and again no answer!—fruitless maddening ringing, ringing!—until finally at two-twenty-five the telephone is actually answered—inasmuch as—

But I'm sorry. I can't. I can't see you. No, it isn't possible. Today? Now? I can't—no. I've been out all morning—I must go out again this evening—a reception for the new French consul—I have to work this afternoon—all afternoon—I have to work with Andrew's papers —I can't see you. I'm sorry. Tomorrow? No. I'm sorry. Tomorrow is filled—the entire day filled. Every day is filled this week. I'm sorry. And then Sunday—no, Sunday is out—on Sunday I'm due at—the Slossans are having people over—Andrew and John Slossan were always so close— I'm sorry, I can't see you. Very sorry. —Who did you say this was?

Bitch.

Hung up. Had muttered the word, teeth clenched. Did she hear? Bitch. Bitch. *Bitch.*

18

Your passion is a sickness. More specifically, it is just another symptom of your general sickness.

Thus spake Dr. Wynand.

But what—after four years of analysis—what should I presume to be the nature of my "general sickness"?

Silence.

Free association. A stream of words—phrases—bright and bubbling and insubstantial—airy—rather like music—without tedious referents to the real world. At first rather difficult: a tongue-tied phase, years back. Censor stern and immediate. Some rhymes, some riming-words, are surely offensive? Cannot lead to edification? Are merely alliterative, at best? But no—no—the censor defeated—prim rationalism defeated—the tongue loosed—flapping and salivating for fifty minutes at a time—hard to stop, actually—*hard to stop.* Outside and on the street, hurrying along, *hard to stop* that monologue. In a taxi; painfully hard. *Hard. To. Stop.*

Cost me my friendship with the Mays—dear Simon and Maggie!—

so long understanding and forgiving of me—of my "sardonic wit"—
ability to turn phrases—my artistic temperament, my testing of the
loyalty and affection of friends. They had not called for weeks—I
would not call—dare not—too ashamed, proud, bewildered. *Hard to
stop* once I begin. Psychoanalysis the liberating force—a mere faucet
turned on—a veritable Niagara unleashed.

The general nature of my sickness?

Not yet clear. A mystery. At the present. But gradually . . . gradually . . . a pattern is emerging—yes, a distinct, definite pattern—
emerging—must not hurry the process—the unconscious must *not* be
hurried—in fact, cannot be hurried—cannot be dictated to—the goal
of restoring one's miserable self to the "general unhappiness" of
mankind cannot be achieved by mere desire—petulant, childish
desire.

Rebuffed.

Yes, I know. Meek—"reasonable"—must now court Dr. Wynand
back—the danger of his suggesting that therapy be terminated always
present—a nightmare possibility—so much time and money and spiritual investment these past four years.

Yes, I know. I know. Cannot not know. In fact, that is what
depresses me: I am no better now than I was at the age of thirty-six.
New symptoms appear almost daily. Since the—it—the event of last
June—since that hideous highly publicized event—my family name
once again thrust in the headlines—since he was—it—

Silence.

Dr. Wynand surly, clever. Would not hint of any knowledge of
A's assassination. Would *not*.

Nor would I.

—since mid-June my entire system seems to have been altered—
really beyond my control or comprehension—two separate electrocar-
diograms showed nothing—a blood test showed nothing in July—and
nothing last week—I was dreading the possibility of—well—diabetes
—leukemia—anemia—and my stomach has been so quirkish lately—
refuses to digest the most unpredictable, bland things—arranged for
a test for ulcers—drank chalkish-milkish fluid that was supposed to
coat my stomach but had the effect only of inducing violent vomiting—returned again for the test—vomited again—back and forth the
vile white stuff went—vomiting like a baby—gagging even now when
I think of—

Hugh, please. Stop.

—I'm all right! All right! Just a little—a little spasm—I'm not
about to vomit, really, Dr. Wynand—it came and it went—nausea in

the imagination, not—not in the flesh— I assure you, this goatskin rug of yours is perfectly safe.

Paused. Recovered. Went on to describe to Dr. Wynand my frantic trip to Albany. Never in my entire life—never!—any behavior quite so ludicrous. Inexplicable, really. Destestable. *I didn't even like her.* Had explored—ah, many times—my ambivalent feelings toward all women—tendency to react to them as if they were Mother— aspects of Mother—a by no means uncommon complication of the Oedipal predicament—rivalry with Father—and older brother—possible confusion between Mother and sister (Doris being the eldest of the four children, now forty-six—my God!)—Dr. Wynand and I on familiar ground whenever "ambivalence" was an issue—and so—how to grasp what had happened—what had propelled me to risk so much —for a woman I did not particularly like but was evidently in love with—?

Dr. Wynand silent. Contemplative.

—or maybe I should arrange to have more tests? A neurological examination, maybe? To see if my nervousness—inability to concentrate—insomnia—possibly a brain tumor? But that hideous test, I've heard, is very nearly as dangerous as brain surgery itself! Dr. Wynand, what do you think? Should I? Or—? I've already made an appointment with someone just around the corner from me—feel the need for a urinalysis— Dr. Wynand? Oh—well—I suppose I'm just excessively sensitive. Hypochondriasis, you're thinking. Tendency that way since childhood—yes—Mother eager to baby me, prop me up with pillows in the sunporch—read to me from *Mary Poppins*— probable genesis of sexual confusion—male/female uncertainty. That ubiquitous umbrella of hers—! But one genuinely valuable thing emerged from the trip: I was able to get a loan to cover my present debts. Thank God! My brother-in-law Arnold Laubach— without Doris's knowledge—willing to give me a quite reasonable interest rate—seems very open, frank, friendly about these transactions —of course he knows I am due to inherit a great deal upon Father's death. Doris and I will share most of the estate. Nor should you worry either, Dr. Wynand—I'm prepared to pay not only for today's session, but for the last two. And I'm very grateful for your having carried me—

Not at all, Dr. Wynand said. Clearing his throat. Surprising—that he should react to this remark—not sensing the coy circumlocution of the past five minutes. Not at all—least I could do—knew you could be trusted.

You did, eh?

A recitation of my problems.

The neurotic is one who cannot function as his talent—even his genius—demands; the neurotic is continually frustrated, thinking about what he wants to do while doing something else, thinking about something else when he does what it appeared he "wanted" to do, half here, half there, grappling with and embracing phantoms, whispering to himself, pleading and cajoling with himself, -self, -self, to the exclusion of the world. A recitation of my problems: a series of portraits of -self.

Tuesday and Thursday. 9:00 A.M. Dr. Bruce Wynand, East Seventies, highly recommended by Deborah—who was one of Dr. Wynand's patients also—had been with him on a four-day schedule for a decade now. Of course she did not speak in any detail of her progress; nor did I; together for dinner once or twice a month, or meeting at others' apartments, we might allude to "the doctor"— "him"—our shared "father figure"—"authority figure"—always aware of the vulnerable nature of our commitment to him, and at the same time willing to testify in his behalf, willing to defend him against critics. His value was— His incontestable value was—

That he should listen so attentively. That he should not judge.

I had demanded the nine-o'clock slot from the very first. Wanted him fresh, clear-minded. Was jealous of the demands of his other patients. Obviously, he'd be drained even by noon; exhausted and incompetent by four. Even so, I sometimes sensed his mind wandering —sometimes feared I was boring him—if his chair did not creak for a certain space of time I grew anxious and began to chatter away. At my first session after Andrew's death, I was dreading his allusion to it —surely he would mention it!—out of curiosity if for no other reason ("Have the police or the FBI arrested anyone yet?"—asked by everyone else who knew me)—and so I chattered wildly—on and on and on—freely associating—Rimbaud, Baudelaire, Mallarmé hissing ever new and ever more fanciful images—dreams I could not actually remember springing up into consciousness, to be rattled off in the silence of Dr. Wynand's cave-like office. How I dreaded his mentioning that death—it! But he did not mention it, he remained courteous and sly.

It's life itself that is the problem, I said, isn't it? *This long disease* —that's it, eh?

Pessimism can be simply a defense against maturity, as we know.

Yes, yes!—I remember you telling me that, Dr. Wynand. Yes. —Anyway, I suppose my pessimism is no more than mental—intellectual?—my character is so blotched and scrambled that anything—any attempt at a judgment—a philosophical stand—is just an aspect of the neurosis? —Sometimes I'm convinced that is so. Only my work redeems me—carries me out of myself—my drawings and occasional paintings—my—my career—my *art*. The rest is—what is it?—a feeble charade of adulthood?

When Dr. Wynand did not respond I continued, hurriedly: And so—the crucial thing is—if my work is taken from me—if my ability to concentrate disappears—not only my livelihood will be endangered, but—but—my psychic equilibrium itself—such as it is, yes!—I know!—a paltry kind of equilibrium, but my own; my strategy of survival. If that is taken from me by the forces of— By fate— By my enemies— If my art is taken from me— If Andrew laughs and jeers at me from beyond the grave—dictating failure for me—ridiculing me—my life's-blood—my identity, destiny, *soul*— If— But that won't happen. Will it? Won't. Can't. For one thing, I am a real professional. Have been, now, for years. Other artists are capricious, but Hugh Petrie is reliable; will deliver on time, sometimes ahead of time. Quite a fine reputation in the city, actually. Second only to— Well, to a certain rival of mine. Won't mention his name—am *not* jealous of him—but think his talent outrageously over-estimated— and repetitious also—always the same noses and twinkling eyes and dwarfish bodies with big heads and ears—hesitates to commit himself to the truly daring—the possibly obscene—libelous—hesitates to slice into his subjects as I do—must—for nothing less than utter abandonment to the Muse will satisfy me—do you understand?—are you listening?—the founder of my art, one Annibale Carracci of Bologna, stated many centuries ago the aim, the ideal—*to grasp the perfect deformity, and thus reveal the very essence of a personality*—but my rival is comic and cute and altogether too human—too decent— But I am not jealous of him, of his fame and the reputed income he enjoys; why should I be jealous? My time will come.

Optimism also, Dr. Wynand said quietly, can be simply a defense —against the irrefutable facts of the objective world, as well as against a more fashionable pessimism.

Yes?

Appropriate anger must be expressed. Axiomatic for mental health. A textbook platitude, sold back to me for thousands of dollars—and yet unworkable. Where were the objects of my "appro-

72 THE ASSASSINS

priate" anger? Why did they seem so remarkably indifferent to me?—
indifferent to my anger? And what did "appropriate" mean, anyway?
Andrew had temper tantrums as a boy—his face beet-red—eyes
screwed up as if he were aping a paralytic stroke—fists clenched, dangerous. Either he got his way at once or was sent upstairs at once.
Mental health? Was he mentally sound, or had the "considerable
surprises" of Washington permanently unhinged him? A young
Senator—his career going well—suddenly his wife's collapse, his with-
drawal from politics—reappearance in staid old Upstate New York—
another aborted career in state politics—and into the madness of the
late sixties—a controversial magazine, a frantic personal life, a divorce and a second marriage—the *bête noir* of what passed for "liberal" Republicanism in that part of the world—and of course the
death, the sudden death. Someone expressed anger. Person or persons unknown. Marvelous mystery!—to be solved, no doubt, in some
tedious way. But until then—marvelous!—and who knows how appropriate the anger really was? Who can judge?

They spread rumors about me. Grotesque rumors.
Not true—as Doris informed me some of the relatives believed—
that I lost money by gambling or investing in speculative schemes—
land development in the Yukon, offshore oil in the Gulf of Mexico—
though I did lose nine hundred dollars back in 1972 in the Florida
Keys Realtors Association—simply bad luck—but never again, never
again. And yes: a paltry three hundred fifty through having co-
financed a young friend's "evening of plastic theater" in the Village.
A gift, really. I had not expected to get it back.
Better such rumors, however, than the truth.
Doctors: all sorts of specialists. Kept changing general practi-
tioners because they grew weary of my passionate search for what
was wrong, for the Key to my malaise. Insensitive men, for the most
part. Ignorant. Not aware, probably, of my drawings—associated the
name *Petrie* with my brother solely. *Are you related to—*? Certainly
not. Went to Dr. Wynand when my hands were trembling so that I
could hardly work—despite my desire to work—was immensely relieved when he accepted me as a part-time patient. Twice a week
all I could afford. In fact, more than I could afford. Vicious rumors
back in Albany that I threw money away—around—"bought" friends
—tried to wheedle editors and editors' assistants into commissioning
my work—what is money for, except to invest in oneself? Let them
lie. They can't be stopped anyway. Nor can I. Could I. Went to Dr.

Wynand to have the indigestible past tugged out of me—hand over
hand—an endless piece of spaghetti yanked out—sometimes roughly,
without mercy—went to him begging to be saved from myself—
*Who can defeat us except outselves?—who are our enemies, what
power have they to suffocate us, to strangle us, to beat us back to
zero?—what can I do—what can I surrender to—in order to be saved?*
Taller than I, but not much heavier; in his late forties or early fifties,
I would guess; tastefully dressed, soft-spoken, very fine brown hair
with a tendency to flutter up, a coin-sized pale pink bald spot on the
back of his head—rather like my own—except I keep my own better
hidden; glasses with tortoise-shell rims—of the kind I had as a boy,
but came to think were rather unfashionable since—though perhaps
they came back into fashion?—eloquent when necessary, strongly silent most of the time—attentive and yet not judging—not judging.
Not repulsed, not disgusted. At least giving no sign. He reminded me
of someone—could not recall who—whether a man or a woman, a
friend or an enemy, a peer or an inferior or someone who had been
unquestionably superior to me—could not recall who—
But now I no longer care about the past, Dr. Wynand. My voice
rose, begging. I turned to face him. It's the present I want—want to
possess—want to live in— I feel such yearning, suddenly—such passion—
Dr. Wynand looked away, at a corner of his desk. A paperweight,
thick costly free-form glass. But I did not look at it, I continued to
stare at his face.
I want—I want so badly— It's difficult to express in words—
difficult for me even to comprehend— Such yearning, suddenly, such
a sense of—a hope that—there is life still to be lived, for me—as for
others—as there has always been for those happy few, those *others*
who live in light— It has nothing to do with my brother's death, Dr.
Wynand. Nothing. I'm convinced of that. No—nothing. I really feel
nothing about that event—except normal sorrow, mourning—loss of
a brother—that sort of thing—hit me quite hard, of course—though
not so hard as my mother's death—as one might imagine—and while
I am as anxious as the next person that a horrible murder should be
solved—the people responsible should be apprehended, arrested,
taken out of society so they won't harm anyone else—political fanaticism has always bewildered and frightened me—don't you feel the
same way?—of course!—maniac feverish one-sidedness—neurosis
justified by a political slogan—any slogan will do—that sort of thing—
What was I saying? I— The point is— The point I came here to

make— Oh yes: the sudden trip to Albany, the unaccountable excitement and hope and—emotions of a kind I don't remember having
for some time—for a very long time—do you?—I mean, do you, Dr.
Wynand, remember my having had such emotions?—in the past four
years? Of course not— And so—now— I feel that— I feel there is a
possibility— In fact—

You imagine you're in love. With a woman you don't know.

Ah!—could not think for a moment—had Dr. Wynand actually uttered these words, or had I? Had he spoken at all? Or had I interrupted him, completing his sentence? Had I simply read his mind?

—in love. Love, yes. With a woman—

Whom you don't know?

But I know her! I know her very well! She and I—

At the conclusion of the hour, at that penultimate moment whose
approach both Dr. Wynand and I were keenly aware of—both of us,
I believe, regretting the session should come so abruptly to a
finish—as always—for my cleverness did manage, on most days, to
overcome and refine and make even entertaining the sordid degrading vaudeville of my soul—at that moment I rose, attempted a smile,
brushed tears from my cheeks, and shook hands. Man to man, one
adult to another. Professionals, both of us. Rather waggishly I said—
for now the "session" was over in the official, emotional sense—and I
could afford to be cavalier, knowing that my remarks were off the
record—that I had read a fascinating essay by a psychoanalyst not
long ago—in one of the popular intellectual weeklies for which I did
work occasionally—perhaps Dr. Wynand subscribed to it?—no?—but
familiar with it, surely?—a hypothesis that the life-force itself, most
keenly experienced when one is "in love," is simply a strategy of defense, a refusal to acknowledge the grim truths—the lofty tragic
vision—unflinching, noble—that Freud put forth?—that any attitude
contrary to this is necessarily sentimental—short-sighted—and of
course neurotic? That—

Possibly, Dr. Wynand said.

Yet I had faith in him.

Deborah had faith in him. And Stanley E_____, the painter. And
even the R_____'s, an attractive, formidable couple whom I knew
slightly. Once, after an especially turbulent session in my seventh
month of analysis—during which the ghastly details of my first sexual
"experience" were recalled—I could not break the spell, could hardly

be induced to leave Dr. Wynand's office. His receptionist called a taxi for me—helped me out into the street. But I refused to get in the taxi. Sent it away. Banging on the roof with my fists, demanding that the idiot drive away, leave me alone. He did. The receptionist retreated—I feared she might tell Dr. Wynand—feared also she might call the police—I ran up the street and into the park—weeping like a child, not caring who gaped at me. An hour or more of exquisite agony, wandering about, softly knocking my fists together—*Dr. Wynand! Please! There's more—much more! More! More! Help!*—finally doubled back onto his street—approached his building once again—unable to break the spell. Wisely, I stood on the sidewalk opposite. A lovesick stranger, an enchanted child, a hypnotized bird. Stared at the handsome slick-green door—the brass knocker—the bars on the basement and first-floor windows—wrought-iron bars belling out gracefully, as much ornamental as functional—the neat, clipped, four-feet-high evergreens in redwood tubs—and of course the windows—*the* window—with its partly closed Venetian blinds. I saw Stanley E_____ leave by the same door I had left by; Stanley not so aroused as I, but obviously much moved, his ordinarily satyrist manner subdued, abashed. Then Harold J_____ arrived—on foot—his stride alternately hurried and reluctant: Harold J_____, the fearsome critic, in oversized dark glasses and a trench coat and hat of the same material, as if in disguise—what a shock!—of all people!—and, later, in the afternoon, a chauffeur-driven limousine drew up to Dr. Wynand's curb and a man who resembled the president of the publishing house at which Deborah's father had been a senior editor got out—I think—that is, I think it might have been that man—but I could not be certain.

The adults of the world? All, all in disguise.

I felt better as the day progressed. Went home, finally, in fairly good spirits. A human being wants nothing so much as a communal secret—the delight of sharing—worshiping alone and yet knowing—knowing full well that others—and all adults!—powerful adults, even! —that others worship his god—or at least will not mock.

Ah, how I dread mockery! Is that too a symptom—?

19

Bitch.

Nevertheless I wired her flowers: a dozen red roses. Banal, I suppose. Predictable. Yes—all right—but very expensive as well. Incredibly expensive, in fact. What has happened? Why is the world so accelerated? I came of age so long ago—in the fifties—could never quite adjust myself to what passed for reality afterward—the sixties—and now the seventies—phantasmal, unlikely—but good material, thank God, for caricature.

Wired her flowers. Signed? *Your brother-in-law, Hugh.* Or maybe *Your devoted brother-in-law, Hugh.* Or, possibly, *H*—the initial *H*, and no more. Or *Yours, Hugh. Your fellow mourner, Hugh Petrie. Yours always, Hugh (Petrie). With continuing sympathy and regard, yours devotedly, Hugh (your brother-in-law).* Any or all of these. I forget which I used. Considered *Love, Hugh;* but rejected it. Wisely, I think. The woman was oddly shy, toughly virginal, would have to be courted with impeccable logic.

While in the florist's, seized with generosity. Elated. "Grand." Like a sneezing fit, it was. Sent a half-dozen red roses to the former wife, dear fragile mouse Willa; a potted mum plant (bright cheerful yellow) to Doris, to whom I had been carelessly rude the other day—hanging up as soon as she identified herself; a "variegated" bouquet of roses, carnations, asters, and miscellaneous to Deborah, up on Central Park South—an effortless gesture I should have made weeks ago; another mum plant (autumnal orange), but a more expensive one, to Maggie, whom I had obscurely insulted—didn't remember how and certainly not why; a half-dozen Miss All-American Beauty roses (bright red; by now the florist's assistant and I were quite friendly) to my beautiful but treacherous second cousin, Pamela, whom I had deliberately snubbed at that pompous funeral; and even a potted plant to my poor, ailing, declining father, out in Palm Springs. (Had not written to or telephoned or even thought of him for a very long time.) Something Southern Californian would do—I left the choice of plant up to the florist in Palm Springs—nineteen ninety-eight or under. *Your loving son, Hugh.*

Easily done—easily done. Once I began spending money it was easy to continue. Ah, the gratification of generosity! Like St. Francis licking his lepers—or whatever he did to them. Like the stanchless flow of blood from one's side, when that flow is in a good cause. And I had a ridiculous reputation for being cheap. . . .

Left the shop. Returned at once. Ordered a "grave blanket"—yes, that was the term—for A's grave. More costly than any of the other purchases—an incredible eighty-five dollars—but could not change my mind. *Love, Hugh.*

And so it was done.

Uncle Hugh! Uncle Hugh!

Wandering through Rockefeller Plaza one afternoon—unable to work—sick with anxiety that I would never be able to work again—pondering the recent and inexplicable rejection of the only drawing I'd been able to complete in weeks (an ingenious solution of the problem of the Senator and his wife: the wife triumphant, an Astarte cross-legged on his chest, holding his blood-dripping testicles aloft and greedily devouring them: ingenious, daring, quite perfectly executed, in my opinion, and yet rejected by *The New Republic* for the feeblest of reasons)—sifting again and again through my mind the dialogue I had had with Yvonne back in August—the two of us alone, intimate, sequestered there on the twenty-sixth floor of the tower—totally alone for the better part of an afternoon. She had said— And I had said— And she had replied— And then I— And she—and I—and—

Uncle Hugh—?

A gaggle of tourists passed. They carried tiny red flags on sticks. Yammering in a foreign language. Atrocious. In their wake stood a boy of about eleven or twelve, grinning at me. My nephew Michael —Andrew's son.

My first instinct—does everyone have such base instincts?—was to run.

But no. Why, for Christ's sake? I liked the boy—I had liked him— I didn't know him very well, but believed I had liked him. And he had seen me: was approaching me. Uncle Hugh?

We shook hands. Exchanged greetings.

A surprise to see you— Wonderful— Remarkable— Such a long time since—

He wanted to thank me, it seemed, for having sent the flowers to his mother. At first I could not remember—wondered what the hell he was referring to—then my splurge on Madison Avenue came back to me—I blushed and told him it was nothing, nothing—but was happy that Willa had been happy.

We walked along. Not watching where we went—headed into a cul-de-sac—our way partly blocked by a bold begging urchin in coveralls—thrusting a plastic orchid into my face— *Please sir, for the drug rehabilitation of thousands, sir! Wait a minute, sir! Not so fast, sir!*—and little Michael fended the boy off, precociously authoritative, his voice nearly an adult's. I thought: My God, he sounds like Andrew! And for a moment it seemed I was with my dead brother again, Andrew as he had been at that age, as he might have appeared to an adult: a charming smiling oddly confident boy with frank green-gray eyes and thick, wavy blond-brown hair, a dwarfed adult, really, and obviously very intelligent. I must have stammered replies —must have struck the child as peculiar—but the vision of Andrew, Andrew-returned, Andrew-again-incarnated-in-boyhood, was upsetting to me.

He and his mother had been in France, it turned out, at the time of the "assassination." He used the word gravely but easily; without quotation marks around it; without embarrassment.

Ah—France! You were in France—how interesting—

Not very interesting, really, Michael said. Mother was with friends of hers—those pathetic, tedious Denhams—do you remember them? Denham, Denham, and McKillop? *Him.* And *her.* So when the news came, Mrs. Denham asked me to inform Mother—imagining that Mother would be distraught or hysterical—and our tour of Versailles ruined. But of course Mother was neither distraught nor hysterical; nor was I. All of us—I'm sure this includes you too, Uncle Hugh?— knew that my father's days were numbered—he was as good as dead, in my opinion, years ago—taking the stand he did on desegregation. It was only a matter of time till they got him. And there was a rumor about a television show up in Albany—taped, but never released—a panel discussing the Glasberg prison riot and what happened there— the Governor ordering those prisoners shot—and rumor has it that Andrew said *very* inflammatory things and the show was never broadcast. So it was a foregone conclusion—wasn't it? Only a matter of time.

Strolling on Fifth Avenue now. I and my nephew, I towering over him in dread, trying to hide my bewilderment.

Yes—I suppose—a foregone conclusion, did you say?

Mother is sorry, of course. I'm sorry too. But—what can you do?— it's history, isn't it? He was a public man—lived a public life—had to expect a public death. It's history. It's objective—outside us—unsullied by personal intentions. Did you know—I'm going to be a historian? I intend to specialize in the politics of Anglo–American states—I'm already auditing a graduate seminar at Columbia—taught by a man whose scholarship is dubious, but he's well-intentioned and eager to hear my opinions—

Yes—is that so? And did you say—you're twelve now?

Twelve! he laughed gleefully. Uncle Hugh, you should know better—you should know I'm seventeen going on eighteen. Why—! It's been many years since we've met, but—really—

Seventeen going on eighteen—

Certainly. I may be somewhat underdeveloped—Mother attributes it to the psychic trauma of you-know-what—the curious cold-blooded way Andrew departed from my life—but it might be simply genetic. Mother is *not* exactly robust, you know. Though she's filled out in recent years—no longer quite so neurasthenic—her own woman, now—remarkable. She's in the phone book as W. B. Fergus—she'd be delighted to see you again, before she leaves for Palm Beach. She's going a little earlier this year—wants to look over a condominium village outside Miami—with the possibility of investing in it. Did you know?—I set up a kind of investment business of my own—nothing terribly speculative or daring—like Andrew, I know that the most conservative behavior is the wisest in the long run—not necessarily in the short run, of course—but it's the long run we should be aware of. Well, I had a bit of luck at the very first—I won't go into it—if you like, I'll send you a copy of *Forbes*—back in January they did quite a nice little piece on me—inflated, of course, as journalism always is. But nice. I can't complain. It's just a game, of course—making money—and the income I had for 1974-75 brought almost more trouble than it was worth—queries from the IRS—a ridiculously suspicious team to audit me—and Mother's poor tax lawyer, Mr. Berger, unable to cope. Really unable to cope—I've never seen a man so stymied. But—well—as you know, Uncle Hugh, it runs in the family—Andrew used to say that if he failed at doing what he most wanted to do, he could always fall back upon money-making—

Did he say that? Did he? Those words?

—yes, just around the house—not for publication, certainly. Investing is a game and it does take intelligence, but I intend to be a historian—a scholar of the present era—I intend to buy into a publishing firm maybe, to insure the publication of my books—well, not the publication, actually, since that's no problem—but the promotion, the distribution, the advertising. I'm nearly eighteen now: I'll probably have my Ph.D. by the age of twenty-three, from Harvard, and can start publishing around the age of twenty-five, if I'm careful to be respectful to the significant elders—don't come on too brash or too brilliant at first—till I get supporters—backing—sentiment in my favor. Being the only son of an assassinated man, you know, is equivalent to almost unlimited capital.

A remarkable boy!—I found myself listening for once—hardly daring to interrupt. And how uncanny it was, the sensation of being beside a version of my dead brother—hoping once more to learn from him—eager—nay, almost fawning—wondering if perhaps the secret of his personality—the key to his radiant being—wondering if—what might be revealed, offhand?—a throwaway tip? I had not remembered how, when things had gone well between us, as a boy I had followed him around, had been his most admiring audience—

You said—a moment ago— You said something very interesting a moment ago—

About Andrew's contempt for money-making? But everyone knew that.

Did everyone know that—? I'm not sure I did.

If he failed at accomplishing his great project—

Which was?

—totally reforming the Republic of the United States along the lines originally set up by the Founding Fathers—totally recasting the "democratic ideal" in the light of the fiscal and moral and political disasters of the post-war world. We corresponded occasionally. We weren't close—of course. That would have insulted Mother. She's quite easily insulted—not as robust as she appears. Yes, Andrew was always open with me—about his political intentions, I mean—and it was evident from his editorials in *Discourses* that he was set upon a heroic task—would not have feared martyrdom for the cause—in fact, he *didn't* fear martyrdom. His death was a foregone conclusion, as I said. The rabble would pull him down—as it always pulls down great men. But this isn't interesting to you, Uncle Hugh, is it? You were always—of the family—always so disinterested in public life, so introverted, a true artist's nature—I remember envying you, in a way, life seemed to come so easily to you—in contrast to Andrew's need to fight—always swimming upstream—and it was remarkable—for a Petrie—that you should be satisfied with so little: that's what Mother always said. To Father. *I admire Hugh*, she always said. *I admire him because he's satisfied with so little—and you require so much.*

Oh—did she say that? Always? You must mean when they were arguing—

Taxi! he called suddenly.

Must you leave?

Must be downtown in ten minutes—an appointment with
Denham—going to chew the old man out over Mother's investments
—conservatism is one thing, but my God! a broker in Queens could
do better—or in Boston—

But—perhaps—

We'll all have to get together one of these evenings, the child said,
shaking my hand firmly. He smiled, squinted against the sun,
climbed into the rear of the cab. A navy blue blazer—a white shirt
with French cuffs—immaculate blue-black trousers—Italian-styled
shoes—and that gleaming dazzling smile. *It was Andrew.* But no, no:
it was not Andrew. This one—this version—was somehow more formidable than the other. Wiser, older, shrewder. He grinned out the
window at me. —have to get together one of these evenings, Uncle
Hugh, before Mother leaves for—

But—wait—

Mother would be delighted, I know—

—what is your opinion of—do you know anything about—any information, any secrets—about the widow? *The Widow?*

The child's face hardened. He sat back; seemed to dismiss me;
snarled an address on Wall Street to the driver.

The widow, I repeated, do you know anything—?

The cab started off. I lunged after it—hesitated—stepped back.

A bitch, the child called out the window. Which *you* should know
—*you* most of all—

And the cab drove away.

I? I? Why I, most of all?

Have they been spying on me?

20

The Artist sits at his drawing board.

The dead man, resurrected, paws his widow—slobbers over her—
falls atop her in an ungainly heap—forces her long slender legs apart,
all the while moaning and slobbering and bleating—whimpering
with the self-pity of the prematurely dead. *Am I big enough for you?*

*Am I hard? Am I hurting you? Are you in pain? Are you? Are you?
Are you?* His head bobs frantically, his buttocks dip and lunge and
thrust, the woman beneath him arches her back as if to escape him—
as if to slide out from under him—but it is hopeless, he holds her
fast, holds her in a maniac's death grip, whimpering and slobbering,
Don't you ever forget this! Don't you ever forget me! The woman's
head strains backward—her arms are outstretched—backward, reaching backward, yearning to escape—her eyes roll in her head—her hair
hangs down, wild, futile—she is about to scream but the dead man
pounds himself against her, into her, his voice guttural, grunting:
*Am I big enough for you? Am I enough for you? Will you ever forget
this? Will you? Will you? —Bitch!*

Mother's ermine stole. Mother holding me against her, closing the
stole part way about me. The soft fur—the perfume of her body—the
tickling sensation in my nose and eyes. *Are you cold? Are you still
shivering?*
Long afterward, her death. The corpse of an attractive middle-
aged woman, rather fleshy about the jowls, but nicely colored: actually the healthiest she had looked for years. They did something to
her—not just the usual makeup and hair arrangement, but a device
of some kind stuck in her mouth to force the lips into an expression
of bemused serenity. *Isn't she pretty! Isn't she lifelike! —Actually, the
healthiest she has looked for years, poor thing!*

The closed coffin: not much face left, they said. No look of
bemused serenity. No look at all. Must have been a shock for her—
A series of shocks. *Will you ever forget this?* Yvonne staggering, sick.
Yvonne in terror. Very easy for the Artist to imagine—that shy stubborn social manner turned inside out. If a man can be reduced to
whimpering sniveling terror, why not a woman?

One otherwise eventless day in November, news came that the
murderer had been found.
And—executed.
I seemed not to be startled. Took the news placidly. Was eating
breakfast—at one o'clock in the afternoon—had been standing at the
drawing board awaiting inspiration—an insecty Castro in various
stages of composition—no good, obvious failure, wouldn't work—sipping cool tasteless tea and chewing peanuts absent-mindedly—merely
reached across the mess to get the telephone when it rang.

Yes? —Really? Is that so? A local man? A robbery? Not an assassination at all—really? Just—? Well—! Thank you for calling.

That was it: the mystery solved.

I had to fight a sudden yawn. So that was it—? *That*—? Oh well: at least it's over. The mystery solved.

At least—

The God of Perpetual Motion. Perpetual Circus. My appetite cannot be appeased—my mind craves the miraculous even as it rejects it as banal—I insist upon reducing all to silly rubble.

Kicking the rubble about. Listless circles.

I must have wanted the "mystery" solved—like everyone else—it must have been a need for me—a tremendous unrecognized need—a thirst so intense it had gripped my entire being. But now that it was "solved"—

Now that it was solved—

THE MYSTERY SOLVED—

I scrawled these words on a scrap of paper—big balloony comic-strip letters—THE MYSTERY SOLVED! ! !

Now—?

Sick with disgust. Humiliation. After all that—all our expectations— After the publicity, even—

Knocking my head gently against the wall. In my bathrobe, barefoot. Had telephoned Simon—could not bear to be alone—didn't want to get dressed and venture out into the street—might be recognized—remembered the flowers I had sent to Maggie and assumed—presumed—they would take me back.

They did. Marvelous friends.

Simon answered. Unfortunately. Would have preferred Maggie—easier to win over, easier to persuade to share my emotions.

But I liked Simon. His voice, his no-more-than-momentary hesitation—Oh?—yes?—it's you?—his natural strident masculinity a good example for me.

I told him what I knew of the—

Yes, heard it on the six o'clock news.

Already? On the news?

The details were vague. Are there more? A strange, sad—

Strange! Sad! —Disappointing, you mean! Humiliating!

Must have talked to Simon for nearly an hour. Had not known I was so upset. Some family pride after all—a minimum of Petrie

snobbishness—only human. A petty theft! Imagine! Not a conspiracy
—not an assassination—only a holdup and murder—committed by a
man in the area—a farmer's thirty-year-old son—"a little slow," people said of him. An idiot! Or at best a moron! My illustrious brother
—the last hope of our degenerate branch of the family—shot down
by a moron. And a few trivial things stolen from the cabin—a fountain pen, a lamp—Andrew's fancy watch slipped off his wrist— Unfair, wasn't it? Jesus Christ, wasn't it unfair?

I hadn't even known anything had been taken from the cabin.
Why hadn't I been told? Was there more I hadn't been told? Had
the bastards suspected *me*?

Simon cautioned me to calm down. Remember your asthma, your
high blood pressure—

High blood pressure? Do I have high blood pressure? My God, I
didn't even know—or didn't remember—

Hugh, Hugh! Please calm down!

Maggie's sweet voice.

Maggie? Everything is going wrong, Maggie—my life is going
wrong once again—I can't control it— I tried to console the widow
but she wouldn't have me—rejected me—even before she had good
cause, she rejected me, Maggie! Like everyone! Like you and Simon
—shutting me out of your lives at will, on whim—people with the
power to exclude others—lonely, single individuals always at the
mercy of— And my drawings aren't right any longer—I can't concentrate—my hand just doodles or draws pictures of people I don't know
—I'm far behind on my work—I'll never catch up—the only thing I
managed to finish, some puritanical bastard rejected!—*as if anything
Hugh Petrie did wasn't the work of a genius!—as if it could be
rejected by untalented queasy-stomached stunted individuals with no
—with no—*

But you must calm down, Hugh! Should we come over?

—not a conspiracy after all—imagine!—not a real assassination—
there was a murder in the family before—back in the twenties—a
jealous husband barged into—was shot down—a hotel detective
responsible—Plaza Hotel—scandal, publicity—I wasn't born yet—
didn't have to endure it—people jeering, snickering—there had been
deaths before too—naturally—but we'd never had an assassination—
never—his son Michael will be crushed by this news—do you know
Michael?—no?—no, of course not—how could you— My mind so
busy, so confused today— The child will be crushed, utterly: he was
so counting on a legitimate assassination! And I don't blame him! I

understand—sympathize—don't blame him in the slightest—though he is a contemptible little freak—an egoist like his father—an opportunist—but I understand, I sympathize! The incredible shame of it—that Andrew Petrie should have been killed for such ordinary reasons —armed robbery—a moron—a *white* moron— Why, Andrew might as well be alive, for all the good this will do him!

Afterward, collapsed on my bed.

Swallowed four of Eva's sleeping pills—barbiturates big enough to stun a horse—swallowed them down with straight Scotch—Eva's also. (She had heard me on the telephone—my voice must have carried across the way; had come over to see what was wrong. Dear, sweet, cutely depraved Eva! I forgave her the $135 debt before I passed out.)

Slept for fifteen hours.

Woke. Remembered. Arose.

Nevertheless, arose. And staggered to the bathroom. Switched on the light (a tiny window in the bathroom, no more than a few inches square, and very dirty; never enough light). In the toothpaste-splotched mirror the same face as always. Same old face. *There are those who dwell in darkness, and those who dwell in light.* The thin-cheeked stubble-cheeked ghoul glaring at me, out of a cave. Eyes slightly protuberant; neutral-colored. Bluish rings beneath. Mouth a wavering harmless scar. Why had I thought she might love me? —She had loved *him!* Why had I thought there might be some nobility, some transcendence awaiting me? —But he had had so much, he had been so very *happy* with his life! Now it was my turn! My turn!

But the same face confronted me. As always.

The Artist unable to sit at his drawing board. Unable to stand. The Artist prowling through his kingdom. Listless. Hung-over. The Artist at a time of great sorrow. The Artist feeling keenly the sufferings of humanity. Thus Bosch, thus Bruegel, thus Dürer, thus Goetz, thus Hogarth, thus Rowlandson, thus Gillray, thus Cruikshank, thus Goya, thus Géricault, thus Delacroix, thus Daumier— And the rest. And Hugh Petrie.

Felt now the sickening horror of the event. That it should be for so little!

Was death always so disappointing?

The Artist in a philosophical mood. The Artist as Ascetic—that look of gaunt, haunted maturity. —Telephone ringing: unanswered. Let them call me—let them plead for me—beg for my work, beg for interviews—

Who was the main inspiration in your life?—in your career as a caricaturist?

Well—frankly—to be utterly frank—

Your work has been compared to—

Never mind! —To be utterly, utterly frank—I must admit that my older brother inspired me—somewhat—indirectly, that is—inspired me to—to— The truth is— I had been attempting a kind of art for which I was unsuited—a kind of—it was a—a human, sentimental, *touching* art—unfashionable—passé—and very difficult— I had been working for years and getting nowhere—and—and something happened in my personal life, in my relations with him—something violent and disappointing—though hardly surprising—and I began to vent my rage on paper—began to give way to it, perhaps even to stimulate it— With very gratifying results. As the world knows.

The telephone continued ringing. I answered it. Wrong number. A black woman who sounded irritated with me. *Who's that? Who?*

We both hung up angrily.

Appropriate anger must be expressed.

Telephoned Yvonne. No answer.

Telephoned Doris. *Laubach residence, who is this*—? A black woman, a maid. Trained like a robot. Mrs. Laubach was not in—Mr. Laubach out of town—message, please?

I said I might be up for a weekend sometime. Sometime soon.

Had to repeat my name several times—finally had to spell it. Not *you. Hugh.* Hugh Petrie. —The voice sounded dubious, must have believed I was an impostor. Thanked me. Hung up.

Considered telephoning Harvey. His wife Irene simple-minded enough—might have wheedled some secrets out of her. Such as: now that the case was over, now that the murderer had been found, now —what? Was Harvey terribly disappointed? Was he—would he— might the two of us talk sometime? And— (But I could not construct the conversation. It faltered, faded. Impossible. I wanted only to ask what Harvey's private investigator had unearthed—particularly in regard to Yvonne. But it was impossible. I could not get beyond a few sentences.)

Brought in the paper. Finally.

Dreading it—the news—the headline.

A pathetic creature named Pickard—Ezra Pickard—"Ezzy"—thirty-one years old—residence a small farm several miles north of Fremont—about eleven miles west of the "site of the murder"—shot to death by state and county police officers—resisting arrest—barricaded in the hay loft of his father's barn—armed with two rifles and a shotgun. Fifty-four police officers involved. Helicopter police—three helicopters converging on the Pickard property. Tear gas. Conventional maneuvers: complicated only by the fact that the man had taken his seven-year-old son as hostage. Hours of suspense. Vast crowds—roads blocked with traffic—even the highway, miles away, clogged. Ah, what drama!—almost, one might wish he'd been there!

The child had been released after six hours—the desperate man had fired "wildly and deliberately," shouting that he would not be taken—and so they had had to kill him.

A most unfortunate thing, a State Trooper captain said.

Evidently Pickard had hidden his meager plunder in the barn—some neighbor's children had found it—had "informed" their parents. They had done this months ago—in August. But for "personal reasons" the parents had not wanted to tell the police—had been frightened—not even the prospect of the reward ($10,000 from one source, $12,000 from another) had encouraged them. Why did they change their minds, finally? Not known. But they had changed their minds—and police converged on the old Pickard place—and the rest would be local history.

A Carter's fountain pen; an aluminum snap-on writing lamp; a watch of "unusual make"—probably one of Andrew's silly gadgets, expensive trash. Police had found these items hidden in an old paper shopping bag from K-Mart, behind a pile of rancid hay.

Pickard's father would not speak to reporters. Was said to be "distraught." Taken to the Gloversville hospital. Pickard "a little slow in the head." But had a bad temper sometimes. Flared up, seemed to get panicked over nothing; still, someone was quoted, he "didn't seem like the type" and so forth, though he "had always been afraid of the police." At the same time, someone who would not be identified to reporters said it had been Pickard's "lifelong ambition" to be a motorcycle patrolman. And so forth, and so forth.

No real news. The rest of the article dealt with Andrew. I did no more than skim it—had had enough of reading about my brother's career—"controversial"—"dynamic"—"youngest Senator from"—that sort of thing.

Felt sorry for Pickard. And for his father. "Distraught." An old man, a widower, his elder son evidently retarded— "Distraught." All of us "distraught." A murder committed, a murderer found and summarily executed: is that all? Distraught, distraught. If Andrew only knew!—*but of course Andrew must have known.* All along, the poor bastard had known!

Felt sorry for Andrew.

The Artist at his drawing board. Sketching. The Castro assignment—to accompany a supposedly "remarkable" interview obtained by a fierce old work-cow—temporarily set aside. The Artist in a subdued mood. A sorrowing mood. Figures appeared—tentative, questioning—some heavy, some insubstantial as fairies—all strangers—as all human beings are strangers to one another—players, actors, ghosts. Not farce, this. Not caricature. Death dancers. Clumsy and appealing. One of them—must be Pickard? Pickard. Thick-bodied, squarish head, small dumb bewildered eyes. Rifles. Shotguns. A child hostage. An elderly father. A barn: ah, a barn! How quickly it leaped into my vision! I had seen such barns many times—old, decaying, oddly beautiful, I suppose—beautiful to *me*—not very beautiful to the people who owned them. And the frame house, two-story. Unpainted. In the winter these people had to drag bales of hay to the house to insulate it against the cold—the incredible cold of the mountains. —Impoverished farm, land no longer used, outbuildings allowed to sag and fall. Chickens—maybe geese—certainly a dog—a few cats. How familiar, how achingly familiar! Lightning rods on the old house. Of course. A front porch—perhaps an old sofa on it—possibly—sometimes—an old refrigerator. Going back and forth to our summer place, to what was called the farm, we had seen such houses many times. Dirt roads, gravel roads. Splendid quiet. Isolation. In the near distance, hills; in the far distance, the Adirondack Mountains. There was Mt. Invemere—the closest. From the window of the room I usually slept in—Mt. Invemere—the beauty of sunrise—the eastern side of the mountain illuminated—

But no. Pickard. The Pickard farm. The house, the cinder driveway, the narrow gravel road.

Perhaps a motorcycle parked in the drive—?

A motorcycle.

Boyish. Husky. Yet sickly in the face—slack-mouthed. Of course he was a stereotype—how could he not have been a stereotype?—or the father?—"distraught."

Ezra Pickard. Ezzy. "A little slow in the head." "Bad temper sometimes." "Afraid of the police." "Lifelong ambition. . . ." Younger brother, seven. Only seven? How possible? Probable? No. Might be—might be a nephew. Or a son.(?) Probably a nephew, the father's grandson. *Times* story no doubt inaccurate. *Natauga County Sheriff quoted as saying . . . no choice but to open fire*. But no: not the sheriff's men, not the police. The Artist not interested in them, not at the moment. The others—the bodies, the faces—wraiths— "Pickards"—had I ever seen them? In town? In Fremont? Had I as a boy ever seen the child who would grow into—? Might have noticed him—if the mental retardation had been evident, obvious—habit as a child of staring at the abnormal, the crippled, the odd—scared myself by looking and yet—could not look away—pity, was it?—or loathing?—simple curiosity or?—possibly empathy?

Pickard: murderer of my brother.

Not possible to feel anything toward him. Against him. Enmity? Anger? Frustration?

Remembered someone in the family mentioning—happening to mention, as if I knew about it—Father blocking the construction of an atomic energy plant out there—fifteen miles from our property— on one of the lakes—because the water's temperature would be raised by the plant and fish would be killed off—and the stir it was causing locally, because people out there wanted the plant: wanted it. Jokes about Father acting for once in the interests of the people, or of nature, at least—and being rewarded by picketing, even a few acts of vandalism—tar spread on the old farmhouse, around back. I had not seen it, never went out there. Hadn't gone out for many years. The farm was Andrew's, more or less. Not his property legally, but he was the only person who cared about it. Doris and Arnold—a Swiss chalet extravaganza on Lake Champlain: Stephen—no interest in the material world. Hugh the artist, Hugh the solitary one, blissfully content in New York City. . . . He didn't want it. He did *not* want it. Two thousand acres in the Adirondacks. . . . Didn't want it, not really. Though now Doris and I would inherit it when Father died. Would put it on the market immediately—sell it to a developer— resort hotels, hunting and fishing camps—

An angel.

Hardly more than doodling, but quite recognizable nevertheless.

The Angel of Death. Enormous waxy dark-feathered wings—spread wide, very wide—muscular—all encompassing—ah, what power!—hideous power!—while I was thinking of other things, my mind wandering—while I was not thinking of *it* at all—the Angel of Death appears before me.

A boyish face, in a sense?—in a sense, yes. Innocent. Cruel. The feathers on those wings not feathery in texture—rather like scales—dark, glinting. He hovers at the top of the page, over the entire landscape—the jumble of faces, bodies, houses, barns, trees, roads—hovers above this event of local history—sublime and yet brutish—graceful, graceless—beyond grace or the recognition of it—a physical presence—where everyone assumes a spirit—a physical presence all muscle and enormous flapping wings— Why, the descent of that creature would be thunderous: the air throbbing as if a helicopter were landing.

No wonder Andrew died.

No wonder the wife stank of panic—bowels loosened—fluids turned sour—complexion like curdled milk.

Was that it—? The Angel of Death so irrefutable?

It occurred to me, afterward, that Pickard was innocent.

Didn't explore the thought. Too flimsy, peripheral. But—

He was innocent. Possibly. The individual, Ezra Pickard, had been used as a means—an instrument—but the Angel of Death had guided everything—had always been in control. The Angel of Death. Something beautiful about him—about it—so very different from me—earthbound as I am—spiky with intelligence and talent and yearning as I am—while the Angel is sheer essence, sheer act, physicality at the point at which it is spirit— I knew this was nonsense of course. Angels—! Death—! Tricky words to give body to vaporous abstractions: no meaning. Empty categories. And yet—still—it seemed to me that the man, Pickard, was innocent—had been mistreated by fate—bad luck—defective genes. Someone else had killed my brother —something else—but "history" would attribute the crime to a moron.

"History"—! What a joke, what an assemblage of lies!

21

Feverish with activity. Accomplished nothing. Missed appointment with Dr. Wynand—telephoned at nine-fifteen to cancel—too late—would be billed—slammed down receiver—thought at once of *it*—a consolation.

Cardboard boxes beneath the worktable. In the closet. Back against the wall. Dustballs, filth. A stranger's accumulations—a stranger's past. One of those eccentrics, like pack-rats, found dead in a basement flat—garbage decaying—toilet backed up, overflowing—filth everywhere—mystery of filth—mystery of dust, dirt, our essence—If I were found dead here, how would I be interpreted? The bastards!—they would be eager to misunderstand, to distort—their "history" is always a lie.

Boxes stuffed with old letters, clippings, documents. No time to examine them. Those yellowed, ripped newspaper clippings—reviews of my first book—no time to even glance at them now. My passport—hadn't known it was in this mess—hadn't used it for years—now lapsed, outdated. Ah, what a young skinny-cheeked creature! So young, so big-eyed! *I* would have been a brother to him—*I* would have protected him—how innocent he was, how cringing! Poor Hugh. *Poor Hughie.* Sailed on a wretched Greek ship—memory of ocean, wind, terror of the ship's sinking, stalling—a delirium of terror, almost precious—the crossing haunted by memories of home—mother, father, the old house—memories of Andrew—my last semester at Yale—memories the Atlantic did not obliterate. The faces of our past selves—how vulnerable now!—pathetic, knowing so little—younger brothers and sisters craving warmth, guidance, knowledge—salvation—craving true parents who would love them as their earthly parents never do.

Found a few snapshots. Family life, mock-family life. One of Stephen as a baby—rather charming. One of Doris—plump, pretty—about fourteen years old. But the ones I wanted were missing. Someone must have torn them up.

Where were they, who tore up my precious snapshots of childhood?

I wanted to show them to her—wanted to impress her—casual can-

did snapshots of Andrew and me—brothers, friends, boyhood equals.
Such snapshots did exist somewhere. Or had existed.

My haunches ached. Hands were fifthy. Ah—a spider!—unhurried,
fat, creeping out from under a batch of letters—

Should I squash it, or allow it that fat mindless life?

My first book, *Eminent Contemporaries*. A copy face down beneath some curling charcoal drawings—my only copy, I think—the
others given away—happily, hopefully—scribbled my initials inside
and gave away to newfound friends, most of whom I never saw
again.

A shock, the publication date. Only a few years ago.

The book might have belonged to another artist, a stranger. The
photograph on the dust jacket: what the hell had I intended, so disguised? Tiny mustache—nostrils enlarged as if sucking in huge panicked breaths—dark glasses with metal rims—a detached "ironic" half-
smile—hair (not yet thinning) deliberately touseled, boyish. A
turtleneck sweater.

Clever!—they cried.

Vicious!—savage!—hilarious!—profound!

But—

But perhaps *too* clever?

Yes. Perhaps. Too clever, too arch. Overbright. Shrill at times.
Rather nasty—but of course! No artist of "caricatura" can forego nas-
tiness! Anyway he is funny, they said. Amusing. Insightful. Nasty—
but amusing. An *idiot-savant's* merciless eye, someone said. Clever—
promising. Wise. Relentless but wise. Stern, compassionate, and yet
nasty. Debut of a phenomenally perceptive critic of our grotesque era
. . . cruelty tempered with an odd quirky charm . . . venomous . . .
at times obscene . . . always amusing.

Amuse us! Shock us! Disgust us!

Glossy black cover, handsome. Silver lettering—the putrescent face
of the former President of the United States also in silver, but with a
greenish tinge—Death-in-Life—sly cunning yet helpless Death-in-Life
—infected, infectious—unconscious and yet shrewd, deliberate, remorseless with himself as with others. The essence of the creature
captured, in my opinion, perfectly.

And the others, all the others—

Politicians—statesmen—cultural "leaders"—artists—celebrities—famous and notorious—line drawings one and all, no more!—no
more. The most wicked, most delicious was Andrew himself: his

nose thickened and shortened to a snout, his small malicious eyes even smaller, piggishly slit, gleaming, glittering, quite mad. Giving speeches in the Senate at that time—enjoying a good press—on his way up—impossible to stop. He saw the drawing—how could he have missed it?—how could one of his associates have failed to show it to him?—reprinted in *Time*, even!—very funny, very beautifully funny! The triumph of Hugh Petrie over evil, over sheer brainless insensitivity!

The triumph of Hugh Petrie over the others as well—over everyone—

Politicians—statesmen—kings, queens, Prime Ministers—rebels—rock stars—film stars—writers, poets, fellow artists—fraudulent celebrities—evil disguised as idealism, as beauty, as wit, as charm, as innocence, as knowledge, even—at times!—as Evil, fashionable Evil. I saw through them. I *saw*. To reduce a man to one or two traits, to twist them into the features of animals—to flatten the complex deceiving contours of the face to two dimensions—icy and illuminated, the cartoonist's art—the moralist's art—puritanical, selfless, dedicated —even at times a little fanatical. A craft. A life's craft. Far more effective than actual murder. Mockery—ridicule—underscoring of hidden weaknesses—secrets— I made them appear to be less than human, and therefore ridiculous and killable. Killable because ridiculous—ridiculous because killable. (Three of the men immortalized in that book alone were afterward killed: "assassinated," in the inflated jargon of the press.)

Hugh, how cruel of you! How merciless of you!, the cry went.

Hugh, how daring!

How amusing!

Giggling, shivering. My excitement could not match theirs. We're tired of being civilized—it's so limiting, so restricting—dull— We're tired of being complex and intelligent— Tired of being in three dimensions—

The Great Men and Women of our Era: freaky line drawings.

So I conquered them, obliterated them.

I.

Paltry—skinny—homely—hypochondriac *I.*

Applauded for it. Rewarded. Two or three honors—prizes—distinctions. The satirist is really a moralist: *of course!* One murders in order to create. An era of destruction, decay. Amusements. Everything is an amusement, everyone is an amusement. All subjected to the same playful twistings of my pen, the wry whimsical savage bursts of humor, the Great Men and Women, living and dead, dead and living, all brothers and sisters of trashy pretensions, indistinguishable from clever beasts. I saw them, saw through them. The former President and his ghastly crew; other residents who preceded him; foreign heads of state, foreign deities and gnomes; precious idols; fashionable souls. I had satirized as well more local, commonplace banalities—poets of "alienation," prophets of "apocalypse," third-rate mentalities babbling of doom—liberals who were too liberal—conservatives who, like my brother, tried to disguise the beastly selfishness of their lives—the sublimation of cruelty into ideals—"politics."

Most effective of all, whether dealing with an enemy or a harmless fool: making the face darkly lined, cadaverous. My special touch. All caricaturists distort—exaggerate—make absurd—sometimes playfully, sometimes not. But I hinted at death, I transcribed the beginnings of decay, spiritual rot made visible, exposed. I, I! And no other! The best way of discrediting someone's ideas is to discredit *him*—the best way to discredit him is to discredit his life—so limited, so mortal after all. "Death"—so embarrassing! And if made amusing, if made clever—

I let the book fall.

That book, the others, the next book—each and all—what secrets did they reveal of me? Had *she* read them?

Mere death does not canonize us, she said.

Standing close together—the dimly lit foyer of the apartment—she subdued, softened—I hiding my agitation—regretting that I had listened in upon her conversation—no, regretting that she knew—and knew also of my consciousness of the situation: I leaning over her, my brother's wife, wanting only to protect her from him.

Yes? What?

—death does not canonize us, she repeated. Andrew himself said that, used that expression, in connection with—in another context. It was as if he knew— But of course he didn't know— I don't mean to suggest that—

Mere death does not canonize us, I repeated.

So I have resisted making a hero of him—resisted making a god of him. In fact—

Yes?

I want only to forget him.

You want only to forget him!

To forget him, to forget him!

Her fingers closing about my wrist, surprisingly strong for a
woman—

No, erase that.

Cross that out. She said nothing of the kind, and did not touch
me.

Abandoned the search for the snapshots. Futile, silly. And what
did I care? What did I care for any woman, let alone that one?

22

Took Pamela to luncheon at La Petite Place, on Fifty-third Street.

The quick-darting movements of my pen had kept Chaos at bay
for years: now Chaos began to seep forward, inward. Brute ferocity
of life—ungovernable vitality—etc., etc.—all it is rumored to be—
kept stilled beyond the margins of my paper and the sturdy rectangular propriety of my drawing board—held back, calmed, muzzled—
now beginning to jabber and squeal with delight.

Hugh, you sick, sad thing!—so squealed my cousin Pamela.

I squeezed her cold skinny hand, like a lover.

—poor Hugh, poor little Hughie—

Unable to work. Saw a French film on Third Avenue somewhere
—didn't bother to read the subtitles—sat slouched in the seat, eyes
half closed, letting the nonsense wash over me. *Eh, eh bien? Non?*
Gentleman with an abbreviated haircut and overcoat carefully
folded on the seat beside him—licking lips—nervous—glancing my
way. I ignored him. No time for him. Then—he must have caught a
better look at me—must have realized how old I was—then he rose,
picked up his coat, left.

A pointless episode.

When there is no meaning to events, we are surly, dissatisfied,
deathly.

When there is too much meaning, we are terrified.

An ancient family, spotty but formidable. The Petrie tribe. An inclination for sudden conversions—my younger brother the example
closest at hand—going back to the Anglican priest who had, one

Sunday, fallen to his knees as the Lord shouted at him, centuries ago, in Lancashire. During a funeral service, a solemn droning service I can well imagine. The Lord suddenly began shouting at Michael Petrie. *Thou shalt not profane My Church with pagan vestments and pagan orations in praise of My Dead: Who art My Dead and not Man's.* Fell to his knees, endured the shouting of the Lord, wept, surrendered, cracked, and rose from his knees a changed man, utterly changed, a zealous preacher of the Word, a nonconforming, stubborn, querulous hero who braved the Atlantic Ocean with other maniacs and therefore set into motion—

The difficulty with stories, even true ones, is that they begin nowhere and end nowhere. Ultimately they encompass the entire universe and all of history. Yet—one must begin somewhere, after all! Order must be imposed upon events! *History* must be presented as *story!*

Hugh, Pamela said irritably, why do you talk so much? Why not eat? I can't enjoy this disgusting wilted salad if you insist upon—

Isn't the salad any good? Isn't it? Would you like me to call the waiter and send it back?

For Christ's sake, no. I'm dieting. I prefer tasteless food.

Pamela, you're so thin—why are you dieting? You look—you certainly don't look—

But am I beautiful?

Yes, of course you're beautiful. But you're very, very—

She smiled. Hollow-cheeked, she was. Emaciated—stylish—probably weighed no more than one hundred pounds—a girl who had been, during our teens, almost as sturdy as my sister. She had played tennis and field hockey. Had had ordinary brown hair, a pretty face, not striking, not exotic as she was now—or *was* this my cousin?—this woman picking at her salad, peevish and charming and very much aware of my staring at her?

Smiled. The mouth surprisingly wide in that narrow face. The upper lip outlined in pencil, in pink-red, meant to give the illusion of being very thin; the lower lip, for some odd reason, outlined and colored so as to seem unnaturally thick, almost swollen. Passionate, aggressive, tough. The face heavily made up, encrusted with something pasty (I had noticed Pamela's face out on the street, in the daylight; in this cozy comfortable dim place I saw no details, had only a general impression of a beautiful, nervous woman, of whom it would be said: *She can't be that old!*), cheeks glowing beige-rose, eyes fantastically tricked out with lashes and paint, something defiant and hearty about her, the mask composed with such patient art. Sable coat, sable hat. Rings. Bracelets. A brusque manner—almost masculine in a way—habit of shrugging her thin shoulders—smiling at me with one corner of her mouth.

So you're in love with her?

Who told you that?

So you're bothering her—telephone calls, letters, flowers? A visit?

How do you know such things?

Reached across, her fork jabbing into what lay on my plate—fish of some kind—could hardly remember ordering—sole too squishy for my taste, in a sauce that was no more than tepid—garbage, at such prices!—and ate from both my plate and hers, as if we were still children together.

I suppose she's under surveillance?

Pamela laughed as if genuinely surprised.

But don't you know everyone is?

Everyone?

Andrew was. Certainly. That's what is so confusing—I mean people say it's confusing—my husband and others—and Harvey especially, who is so obsessed with what happened—

I didn't know Harvey was obsessed.

Yes. Almost frantic, they say. He's terrified of being killed—at the same time he's making more public appearances than ever—very much in demand—*very* popular, suddenly—and he's shifted farther to the right, did you notice? Sounds almost like Andrew now. Welfare mothers and abortion and that sort of thing.

Andrew was in favor of—?

Wasn't he? Either he wanted them to—

No, it was sterilization. Years ago. Afterward he changed his mind.

But one of them—wasn't it Andrew?—or was it always Harvey?—no, Harvey hasn't any principles—I think he was categorically against abortion under any circumstances—especially free abortion—taxpayers' subsidy—it was either Andrew or someone like him.

Maybe Harvey will be killed too, I said suddenly.

Pamela raised her eyes. Smiled.

Oh you silly romantic thing!—always dreaming!

Maybe we'll all be killed—

That's ridiculous, Pamela said. It's romantic and infantile to think along those lines. Your imagination— You cripple yourself—

Women are supposed to be fond of cripples—neurotics—blacks—children—

But not *her*: that great strapping husky girl. Do you really feel an attraction for her, Hugh? It was bad enough with Andrew—his taste in women was always atrocious—but you, with your imagination, your cerebral good taste— Wouldn't you rather—just look at some of the faces in here, at this moment—that darling curly-haired waiter over there?—must be no more than twenty-one, twenty-two—with your exquisite good taste, wouldn't you—?

Don't humiliate me, Pamela.

Humiliate you! That boy is an angel.

—and what did you mean, Andrew's taste in women was always—?

Don't misunderstand me, please. You look so upset—your hand is trembling, Hugh—for Christ's sake keep it flat on the table, will you? —Charles has no shame either—trembling and quivering in public— staring at me as if I were the source of evil in the world—*I!*—who am more a victim of the era and haphazard circumstances than any of you—staring at me as if I were a pinprick, a rent in the cosmic fabric through which all sorts of ugly things poured— I simply tell the truth. Like Andrew: he always told the truth. Don't interrupt, please, I knew Andrew better than you did—was able to appreciate him in ways you couldn't—poor little Hughie consumed by jealousy —and the laughable thing was— Don't interrupt, please—

Jealous? You think I was jealous?

—the laughable thing was—

I was never jealous of that fool.

Pamela's perfume was tangerine, tart. She kept glancing at me, smiling her queer tic-like smile, using her eyes on me in a deliberate vicious parody of the way women use their eyes on men.

He knew so much—kept things from you—protected you— Your mother's death—

Don't speak of her!

—her *death*. I am speaking of her *death*.

I really don't want to hear any more. Shut up.

But making a joke of it: I grinned, screwed up my eyes, played at projecting a tiny voice out of the corpse of the sole. *Shut up! Shut up!* And then, befitting the occasion, *tais-toi!*

Distracted, she was. At once. Like a girl—like a woman slightly drunk—giddy, charmed, metallic in her laughter.

Always, Hugh, you've been so—

What someone *is*, begins to be revealed when his talent abates,

when he stops showing what he can *do*. Talent, too, is a form of cosmetics; cosmetics, too, are a hiding device.

So spake Nietzsche. Cannot remember where. Sinister of him, unforgivable. Prophetic, too, in his case. Andrew's enthusiasm, really—
philosophy, political theory, psychological motivation of others—not
my concern, such depths. Put my faith in surfaces, in bits and fragments, chopped-up digestible hors-d'oeuvres of reality.

Fearful coincidence, meeting Pamela like that.

Meaning-in-the-world vs. Meaninglessness-in-the-world.

The finicky gentleman in the theater—his abrupt departure—no
disappointment on my part, certainly—but perhaps—I must be
honest—a slight sense of . . . of . . . loss, perhaps—loss of my own at-
tractiveness, my own youth—a slight sense of—melancholy, defeat.
For *she* would not love me either: did not in fact even like me. Gifts
and letters went unacknowledged. A playful valentine—line drawing
in red ink—innocent and dainty and certainly not to be misinterpreted as any sort of declaration—a collector's item, probably (for
my work was being collected by a few individuals convinced of my
genius)—sent weeks ago, in a kind of cold-feverish trance, also unanswered. Stared at the screen, the French actress half naked—or do
they call it nude?—aging temptress—a seductive smile—flicking her
hair out of her eyes as a girl—Pamela, in fact—had once flicked her
hair out of her eyes—and it washed over me, the memory of her, of
it, of *them*—of women—so that I forgot the man with the coat and
forgot the movie and sat for some time thinking only of—

Of—

Then, suddenly, on the street. Daylight. The surprise of it being
midday. Emerging from a theater into daylight—something perverse
and disappointing about it—disorienting. More confusion: a small
crowd gathered at the curb, a rarity in this city of so many specta-
cles: men and women openly admiring a car. A black Rolls Royce, it
was, but a convertible; a two-door; the top down (though it was November); the driver a woman in a fur outfit, indifferent to stares and
exclamations, seated like a Russian princess in an open sleigh, sable
hat and coat, leather gloves cut to show the backs of her hands—her
profile arrogant, complacent. And who was it? Who?—after my having brooded over her for the past half hour?

So I yelled after her, ran to where the car must pass, and insisted—
gallantly, theatrically—on taking her to lunch.

Hugh, she said, you strange sad delightful thing! Have not seen you

since the funeral—have not seen you to thank you for the flowers—or
to ask what they might mean?

To lunch, to La Petite Place. They knew me there, they would
respect me.

I should not tease, not about anything so serious as your emotional
state, Pamela said. If you're unable to work— Well—

I'm self-supporting. My work has been enough for me to live on
for quite a while now. If— But of course it's only—

These things are always temporary, Pamela said. Patted my hand.
Her rings were quite extraordinary—gifts from her first husband—
diamonds and sapphires. But the fingernails!—why so long, painted
such a silly glossy beige?

Just teasing, dear. Not serious, not serious at all.

The family has always been contemptuous and scornful of those
few individuals who have attempted to—

Yes. I was just teasing. We all admire you very much—I know
Andrew did too, in his way, of course he didn't quite understand or
approve of—so I gather—he never criticized you in my presence—we
weren't that close—but I gathered that he was sometimes annoyed
by your political attitude.

Political attitude? I have none! I am an artist—I am apolitical—I
am *metapolitical!*

But the people you're most savage with are always *his* kind, Hugh.
You seem especially vicious when caricaturing certain—well—I must
be discreet, I suppose—you look so murderous, like an enraged
puppy!—but you and your kind are, you know, especially vicious
when it comes to dealing with men who represent very basic, *very*
basic principles of civilization—private property and law and—that
sort of thing—culture, safety, comfort, pleasure—

Look, Pamela: you needn't repeat to me, like an ingenue, the
drivel you've learned from—

—the élitism of the artist, the subsidies and rewards and adulation
—hardly what you'd receive, you know, if a classless society came
into being. To be absolutely fair, I remember coming across a drawing you'd done of—I think—Marx himself—an angry little beetle
waving a lot of tiny fists, a freakish gaint head stuck on a silly little
body—so amusing, really—it probably sums him up, was probably
worth a thousand words. But I remember being quite surprised because everyone in the family thought—

Truth is my only subject. Truth. The exposure of hypocrisy—vaporous idealism—

Andrew used to say—

Must we talk about him? Must we contaminate this place with him?—with the smell of him?—the reek of the dead?

Pamela continued eating lazily. I could see a curious white glow above her eyes—paint of some sort, spread on the bone—like a photographic negative—the skull's hollowed-out black holes mysteriously white, glimmering with life. My cousin. A stranger. Daughter of a former director of the United States Government Agency—busy cheerful gregarious and oddly idealistic, like a Boy Scout—horrible man—beyond caricature, really—like so many of them. Career patriot. Sincere. Pamela's mother a featureless woman, an amiable blur —my father's cousin—one of the wealthier branches of the Petrie family—but blurred, featureless, like so many of the women attached to such men. Pamela had married for the first time while in college—eloped in her junior year from Briarcliff—married the son of a Marine Corps officer—in fact, a general—some scandal attached to him years later—tax evasions, bribes, real estate—the usual thing—but Pamela had been very fond of him, very attached—so she said—and resisted divorcing the son for years out of affection for the father. A second marriage lasted only a few months: according to Doris it was a trick or a joke, a whim, involving a glamorous party-loving Costa Rican in his late fifties. The third marriage, to Charles Bausch, a tax attorney with the firm who handled Father's tax problems, seemed to be more successful: it had lasted now for seven or eight years.

You look so troubled, Hugh, Pamela said softly. Finished her glass of wine. Licked lips. Smiled. Is it about—?

Must we always talk about *him?* Think about *him?*

But you lead the conversation that way yourself—I haven't seen you for months, for years—for many years, really, in any intimate sense—and as soon as we're seated here, even while the waiter is hovering over us, you ask about—

But it was a shock, wasn't it, to learn that Pickard wasn't the killer?

Hugh, my God! How naïve you are! We all knew—we were all certain—

How? Why?

—even the police knew, really; they must have known he wasn't the one, it was just bad luck and a failure of communication—misunderstanding—his being retarded, you know, such a pity—couldn't

communicate—found the things scattered along the road and—
Well, it was natural, I suppose, for him to resist arrest: they probably frightened him with the helicopters. But most of us knew, really
knew, that it couldn't have been him: it had to be someone more—

Did *she* know? What does *she* think?

Hugh, it's delightful you care so much for her! At your age—with
your background—after that dreary long friendship or engagement or
whatever it was with—who was it?—a platonic relationship, you
called it?—so sad!—I find it delightful that you can feel interest, passion, for Yvonne. If we were all younger—

Doesn't anyone feel sorry for Pickard? Or is he just another casu-
alty?

Was that his name? I'm sure some kind of compensation will be
given to the family—but it's so complicated and confused, Hugh—so
many suspects—people arrested and forgotten for weeks—one pathetic black man, in the Albany county jail, stuck away and forgotten for—how long?—it was in the *Times* recently—well, it's pathetic,
of course, and something should be done about it—but in the meantime we all must live—I often think of Andrew watching us,
watching the entire panorama—smiling that sad smile of his—

Sad smile!

I had to laugh. Had to laugh. *Sad smile*: that contemptuous
sneer!

—as he did once when he and Willa visited Rafael and me, do you
remember Rafael?—came to a cocktail party at our place in Georgetown—Andrew and poor Willa—and I'd just redecorated the living
room, had all the walls painted white, to display the Tazu Tikuta
canvas I had bought—ah, what genius!—overpowering!—have you
seen it, Hugh?—why, I don't think you have—you *must* visit with us
sometime—don't mind Charles, he can't help being what he is—awfully considerate in his way—sweet, patient— But the canvas, Hugh,
is stunning. Everyone who sees it is astonished. There are seventy-five
interlocking canvas panels, encompassing the entire room—all together they measure over one hundred feet by twelve feet—simply
breathtaking—images out of America in the forties—politicians,
cakes, hairdos, Christmas trees, infants in swaddling clothes, hatracks
with moose antlers, an old-fashioned lawn mower, a woman's head
with her hair in pin curls—the most extraordinary *fidelity* to tiny details—each pin curl *perfect*—exquisite—you really must see it, Hugh.
I hope you aren't one of those envious artists who disparage successful people—but of course you aren't, you're far too tolerant and

open-minded—and you're quite successful yourself, aren't you?—in your way?—but there was so much bitterness about Tikuta's career—his exhibition at the Guggenheim—and many of the rumors are false, I can assure you: Rafe did *not* pay a hundred thousand dollars for that painting. The price was rather high, yes, but not that high. Of course he would have paid that much if necessary—he was awfully generous when it came to gifts to me— He and Andrew got along, surprisingly. Andrew came in, looked at the canvas, just stood there and stared—dressed beautifully as always—but rather casually—and there was a tiny nick on the side of his nose—from shaving, evidently—I remember seeing it and wondering if his hand was beginning to shake—what with Willa drinking so much—so sad—some women are just not suited for Washington—should just stay home, should just forget it. Andrew squeezed my hand, the way he always did when we met, as if—it was like—we had a secret understanding between us—like brother and sister, almost—though we were much closer than—than—and he would kiss my cheek—would look at me, deeply at me—would ask— He would—

She fell silent.

More wine?

She nodded. Stared at my hands, at the bottle. Seemed to have forgotten the thread of her remarks. Was the woman actually . . . subdued?

Your relationship with Andrew was always quite different from mine, I said quietly. Did not want to sound malicious. Of course he probably confided in you—probably preferred you to either of his wives—

No. No.

Certainly he was closer to you in many ways than he was to Yvonne—?

I'll tell you a secret about their marriage, Pamela said. So many rumors—so many lies— But the truth is—no one believes it, but it happens to be true: *they were utterly devoted to each other.*

They *were*—?

She married him because he was famous, I suppose—she was so much younger—but his fame was part of Andrew's style, after all—even as a boy he had the tone, the feel, of someone extraordinary—he always had that manner—that marvelous self-assurance—that voice. Do you know what I mean? No? Yes? So she fell in love with him. It was obvious—the few times I saw them together—obvious she adored him. And he loved her: it hurts me to admit it, that

Andrew would finally love a woman so much, so very much, when—
in contrast to—I mean it jeopardizes other arrangements, ways of living we take for granted—marriages—that sort of thing. You wouldn't
know what I mean, dear: you've never been married. She appealed to
his paternal nature, to the tender side of it rather than the authori-
tarian side—she was so daughterly, so obedient, so awkward and
sweet. He needed a woman like that—though I wish he had chosen
someone less fervent—she's so eager to live up to everyone's expectations—to be worthy of—

Do you know Yvonne very well? Do you see her?

Of course I don't know her well, Pamela said. I don't like her. She
doesn't like me. The two of us talked once—I did most of the talking, she's so painfully shy when it suits her—at the Greasons, I think,
my God it was in May—only a month before. . . . We talked—we
happened to be alone together for a few minutes—talked about
something very strange, I remember it being very strange—playful
too—what was it? Only a month before he was killed. She looked
quite striking that day: a Sunday. What did we talk about? I've had
so many conversations in my life—so many, many conversations—the
words slip out of place and become entangled, confused— Is that
life, Hugh, is that what we'll remember at the very end?—the din of
words, of conversations?— Now I remember: we talked about death.

Death. You talked about death?

I did most of the talking. She listened. I had the impression she
was frightened of me—frightened of something—as if I might say the
wrong thing. But I always say the wrong thing! I delight in it.
Death: I talked about death. How I insisted Charles make out his
will—make certain there were no loopholes—no ways by which his
greedy relatives could make claims—since of course he will die before
me: men usually die before their wives. I believe she blushed—
seemed very shocked. A darling girl, but those eyebrows of hers!—I
would have liked to take a tweezers and pluck two-thirds of them out
—but she's quite beautiful in her way, something fierce and clean
and horsey about her—you expect her to snort and toss her head,
stomp around restlessly. Poor Hugh, am I disturbing you? Of course
I don't see her as you evidently do—how could I? That day she
stared and stared at me as if I were a freak of some kind. Rather rude
of her, really. I chattered about death—the death of my first husband
Robbie—after we were divorced, but it's almost the same thing:
you've lived with them, made love with them, "one flesh" and "one
mind," that sort of thing. Death is perfectly natural, I told her. Per-

fectly natural! Adrienne Greason, for instance, is terrified of growing old—always running to the hospital for checkups—and I mean real checkups—didn't you know, Hugh?—the poor thing is worse than you—always checking herself for cancer—little cysts and bumps and pimples—checking herself all over—she's so terrified of death, of dying, of growing old, but of course you'd never know it—she's one of the few perfect hostesses left in our culture: they're all dying out. But I'm quite different. I'm entirely different. If it's time to die— why, we simply die—that's that. No regrets, no nostalgia. As for mourning—do people still mourn? It seems so quirky, so unrealistic. Mourning—for what? Why? I certainly don't intend—I certainly *haven't*—I'm a mature woman now, no longer a child— Nothing disturbs me in the slightest; I can live with anything. Friends have told me I've attained an enviable state of mind. But poor Yvonne!—she did seem bewildered, as if I were speaking in a riddle or a parable or something instead of directly, with absolute sincerity, as I always speak—

Two-fifteen.

Pamela gone for several minutes, in the powder room—I fussed, quite lonely suddenly—complained to the waiter about my filet of sole Véronique—and the innocuous too-warm wine—and the inflated prices. Since I had been here with Deborah and Simon and Maggie —such good friends!—lost to me now—the prices had been raised: tiny gummed labels fitted over them. Crude. Ridiculous.

Had drunk two bottles of wine. Should have felt sleepier, happier. Drained, instead. Tired, depressed, unreasonably lonely.

The woman I had been talking so intimately with: said to be Pamela. My cousin. Much married now, much experienced, rather like a stranger; or had I become the stranger? A child of the old, old days—the lodge on Lake Champlain—swimming, picnics, Mt. Desert Island, someone's father's yacht—happy simple innocent times. No: that's a lie. But one must believe something.

Pamela? Are you ill?

Walking slowly, carrying herself as if she might break. Ill? So pale! Her streaked hair exotic about that thin, anxious face—elaborate hairdresser's curls—a forty-year-old poppet—sweetly cynical—brightening as she returned to our table, smiling as if my presence tripped a lever in her brain. *If someone were to love her, it wouldn't be too late for her.* A sudden, surprising thought. Where had it come from? But it was hopeless; obviously it was too late.

Vomiting in the powder room.

Ate too much—was ravenous and ate too much—then it dawned on me that I'd lost control, eaten as much food as I ordinarily allow myself for a week!—gain weight so easily, you know, it's frightening —disgusting. I induced vomiting, got rid of it; most of it; but do I look ghastly now? It's the price one must pay for—

Beautiful as always, I mumbled.

Andrew always said I was too thin—didn't approve of the turn my life had taken—was always, you know, rather puritanical—possessive —he simply didn't understand, did he? The complexities of adulthood—the revelations no one could have predicted—

Yes?

—toward the end he really didn't like me. I could tell, I could sense it—his outraged morality—but of course he was magnanimous enough to have forgiven me if—if the situation had ever— But do I look sick, Hugh? Should I risk leaving this gloomy place? —Poor Hugh! *You're* the one who looks sick—and I stand here prattling about myself—

Sick? Who's sick? You look fine, Pamela: beautiful as always.

—worrying and fussing about myself, when in front of my eyes— They said how badly you've been taking it, how terribly it's been affecting you—breaking down at the graveside like that—no one could have guessed how— Poor Hugh! *You've* forgiven me, haven't you?

Long ago, I said weakly, long long ago.

23

December.

A fine wet mist. Then rain. Then something sharper, more sinister —tiny near-invisible nails—splinters—bits of ice. Sleet that ran at me, aiming for my face, my eyes. The weakness of the eyes: vulnerability to all who happen to gaze upon you: hideous unpredictable chance.

Meaning to it. His death: someone's meaningful act. (No, Ezra Pickard had not "done it," had not been responsible.) Deliberate. By choice. By design—art—scruple.

No meaning to it. His death, like his life: merely things that happened, to him and others bound closely to him. Stray formless events —whispers that never rise to coherence—repugnant to me. (Though

as an artist I had hated the solution of Pickard—as a Petrie I had
dreaded his joining us in history.)

   Meaning?
   No meaning?
Hypochondriac. Amusing. Aches, complaints, fears realized and
unrealized. Went to Dr. _____ (I forget his name) in an absurdly
garrisoned brownstone on Twelfth Street. Urologist. Knew me.
Knew of me. Had bought copies of my books—flattering, but also
upsetting—knew my public image and now, prodding and poking
and assessing, knew me inside and out. I chattered, joked. Flinched
from his cold instruments and cold rubbered hands. Spoke of my
eyes—tormented by soot, the evil air of this city—propensity to shed
tears though without sorrow (speaking ironically to the doctor, who
seemed not to respond to my wit)—a coincidence that I should be
subject to unreasonable fears of blindness—did a detailed study of
the draftsman James Gillray—great satirist—not honored as Hogarth
was—unfair, that Hogarth (whose sentimentality often revealed itself!—embarrassing!) should enjoy lasting fame, and Gillray forgotten. The doctor listened. Appeared to listen. A stupid man, for all
his specialization and his "interest" in my work: he seemed not to
know what I was talking about.

Yvonne entered me through the eyes: the spirit aiming for the
most vulnerable surface. Knife-like, so keen. Razorish. Sharp—cruel—
but delicious, an ecstasy merely in submitting.

   The Angel of Death.
Doodles. Small armies on the worksheet. Aimless, busy, insect-
sized. If the telephone rang—who heard? Who was present? Might
be my sister—might be what are known as friends—"friends"—
curious links to humanity—ways by which the individual (supposedly) asserts his humanity. Might be a wrong number. Might be
someone who would say Hello? Hello? Is no one there? What have
you done with Hugh?
   Poor little Hughie.

Slept poorly. Difficulty with breathing. Found it best to sit up—
sleep in a sitting position—less strain—easier to wake if necessary.
The day after that luncheon with Pamela, drained and heavy-headed
but unable to lie down, no sooner on my back than something fright-

ened me, I had to sit up, had to listen closely to determine if—but this was madness, of course—laughable—if someone had entered the apartment, slipped inside without a sound. Magic! But ridiculous, of course. Lay awake thinking of how they had killed Andrew—must have slipped quietly into his presence—must have announced themselves only when it was too late.

Slept poorly. Wondered why I had taken so little interest in *it*, in the details surrounding *it*. Too late now: would have to make a special trip to the library. Last June's issues of the *Times*. Weekly newsmagazines. The Albany papers, especially *The Union-Inquirer*—the publisher a friend of Andrew's—must have investigated the assassination—must have run many stories—photographs—interviews—features. No doubt my name was mentioned. Perhaps a photograph. Identification: artist. *Andrew Petrie survived by his wife Yvonne, his son by a former marriage, Michael David, his sister—his brother—his father—*My name not mentioned: deliberately omitted. No. Yes. *His brother, the artist Hugh Petrie, a resident of New York City and recipient of numerous awards and honors. A controversial figure. Books include. . . .*

Dearest Yvonne:

I hesitate to write. I know you dislike me—were perhaps poisoned against me by your late husband. Not your fault. Not mine either. Must I remain silent? *Let the dead bury the dead.*

Propped up in bed. Unable to sleep. The insomniac enjoys his wakefulness—are you perhaps an insomniac too? I lie here—sit here—wander around here—enchanted with the memory of you, the idea of you. This tragedy in our lives should bring us closer together—*must* bring us closer together.

But in the meantime—

I think of you often. Constantly. I fear your life might be endangered—it would be so easy for someone to get into that apartment—bribe the doorman—possibly show him false identification papers (think of the numerous detectives, official and unofficial, assigned to Andrew's murder!)—force the lock to your apartment—lie in wait for you. If I could be of aid to you in any way— I am thinking only of— If it suited your needs— Might there be the possibility of— Someday perhaps you could move to New York—rent an apartment near me—or I could rent one near you—a contract

of some kind could be arranged—I would honor your chastity
—beauty—sanctity—widowhood—

Must have you. Why not? *Why not?*

That old platitude—*If there were no God, He would have to be
invented*—obviously no longer relevant. There is neither
God now nor the invention of Him. Nobody cares—nobody
gives a damn—only the artists toiling ceaselessly, ceaselessly
—without reward or the expectation of—

Yvonne? Erase all this.
Obliterate it.

December. Midweek. Across the street a funeral: four rented cars.
Small, dreary. Must have been someone without friends. Theater
people, a woman with reddened cheeks and hectic tearful eyes, a fur
stole that might have been imitation fur—glancing at me as I passed,
returning from the grocery store, innocent, hurried, intimidated—
staring at me as if I were someone she knew—one of the mourners—
the mourner.

They were preparing to get into the rented cars, to follow the
hearse wherever it led them. The woman stumbled. Someone supported her. Too-red lips, the glisten of teeth that were too white, the
odd way she stared at me as if recognizing me—but I was a stranger!
—forced me to return her gaze—but we were strangers!—her face
garish with makeup—pitiful—

Who had died? But I did not want to know.

What someone *is* begins to be revealed when his talent abates,
when he stops showing what he can *do.* . . .

Saw a man named Reidenbaugh, friend of Andrew's. Former
friend. Midtown, he getting into a taxi, I hurrying along the sidewalk. Exchange of blank innocent stares—he taking the lead, pretending not to know me—I strangely abashed, uncharacteristically
shy—did not reveal I knew him, did not force him to smile and say
hello. Friend of Andrew's, an attorney, Republican State Committee, first name Herman or Harold: possibly he did not know me.
And he was in a hurry to get into the cab, to escape.

Shamefaced, all of us. *It* surrounded us.

Disturbing news.
Spoke with Doris on the phone—first time in two or three weeks—

tried to get myself invited up to Albany—Christmas holidays—
"family celebration"—Doris cool, not very sisterly—making up excuses—a vacation in the Caribbean—business associates of Arnold's—
why didn't I fly out to Palm Springs to visit Father?—hadn't it been
a very long time since I had visited him?—bullying me as in the old
days. Bitch. I told her curtly of the backlog of work I had—mentioned my insomnia, my watering eyes—but no comment from her,
no sympathy.

Eased the subject onto—

Not reported in the papers, Doris said, what had happened to
Yvonne—thank God it hadn't been reported—no more publicity
needed—

What, what had happened?

—someone tried to attack her—or actually did attack her—she was
receiving a posthumous award for Andrew—a man ran up to the
stage and threw something at her—

She isn't hurt? Isn't dead? Isn't—?

She's perfectly all right Doris said irritably. Why are you so concerned? What is that woman to you?

Must love her: otherwise I would not have been so upset.

When I heard about Andrew—so many months ago—the news
had not affected me at all. It was "news"—impersonal, historical.
Andrew himself was "news." But when I heard of Yvonne—

No, the news of Andrew's death hadn't affected me at all. An interesting sidelight—diversion—more color and quirkiness to my
"character," perhaps—an aura of fashionable melodrama about me,
an advantage at parties—should have allowed me more license in my
art— But—

Telephoned Yvonne at once. No answer. Telephoned at forty-five-
minute intervals that day—no answer—why did she keep herself from
me for so long, when it was inevitable she should eventually surrender?

Completed, after weeks of anguished struggle, the drawing to accompany a long article for the *Sunday Times Magazine*—review of
the last two years' political infighting—obviously the best thing I'd
ever done—the creatures entwined, ensnarled, tendrils and tentacles
and guts and teeth claws hair genitals toes eyestalks arteries—
devouring and excreting one another—ferocious wavelike struggle—
my finest work, a drawing of genius—subtle, savage, frightening,

cerebral—enchanting, really—hypnotic—measured four feet by three —would have to be reduced for their paltry page-size—the most powerful thing I had ever done—*I knew*—almost ruined my eyes, the last six-hour stretch—working most of the night—inspired by—by what? —inspired—excited—the high pitch of my nerves transformed into these lines—incontestably my best work—would bring it with me to Albany to show her—and then she would see it in the *Times*—one Sunday morning she would see it, would marvel at it—would see my name there—*Hugh Petrie*—would murmur the name *Hugh Petrie*— would say *I know him: I know the artist: he and I are very close.*

Spoke with her finally.

Rather surprising, the confident sound of my voice. I was evidently at ease, in control—warmly concerned about her—as an older brother might be, quite naturally—without fuss or melodrama. Simply asked her how she was. Asked about the incident. Explained that Doris had told me—had sounded rather upset—and— But she was fine, not injured at all? Not even disturbed? Not even annoyed?

The voice informed me that such things did not disturb or annoy her; they must be accepted, as Andrew had accepted them; philosophically and with a sense of humor. There were, the voice told me softly, "unhappy individuals" in the world who were jealous of people like Andrew—these individuals could of course be "dangerous" but most of the time were only "pitiful." And—

What happened, Yvonne? What did he do?

—an inconsequential thing—had forgotten it already—had forgotten it in a few days. Very busy. Constantly busy. Not only working with Andrew's papers—which took up most mornings—but work connected with *Discourses* as well—editorial work—a few hours a week—and an attempt at writing on her own—unsuccessful so far— and had I heard, had Doris told me, the director of the New York State Commission on the Arts had offered her a position on the executive council, and—

But isn't your life in danger? Aren't you frightened?

—the day partitioned into units—blocks of time—each block of time filled with work—occasional blocks of time filled with social obligations—luncheons, cocktail parties, receptions, dinner parties— not many: she and Andrew had become so weary of dinner parties— Andrew had hated to waste so much valuable time—and there were hours taken up, of course, with chores—responsibilities concerning the upkeep of the apartment—responsibilities concerning the estate:

letters to write, replies to the innumerable kind people who wrote to
her—and replies, even, to those who were still writing to Andrew—
The voice continued. Not chatter: a litany.
I interrupted. Asked her what the hell she was trying to prove.
—correspondence of a kind no secretary could really handle—not
even Andrew's private secretary—and of course there were people
anxious to visit her, to talk with her—many who wanted interviews—
from as far away as Tokyo and Sydney—many who begged for simply
five minutes with her— She had to turn them all down, of course—
but it had to be done discreetly, courteously—so very important not
to antagonize or disappoint or even bewilder—
Interrupted. Must have said something extreme. The voice
stopped, in mid-sentence.
Yvonne?
Are you going mad, Yvonne?
Should I come to you now, Yvonne?
How else can I be of use in this world? I want only to be of use.
Don't deny me, Yvonne!

24

Extremely nervous. A suitor, a courtier. Unaccustomed to the gravity, the intimacy of such situations; an art to them I never bothered
to learn. The woman in that dense weighty reality—flesh, presence—
odor of skin and scalp—the constant surprise of her *otherness*—swift-
changing facial expressions—the movement of her eyes. Was she as
nervous as I? More nervous? More uncertain?
Encouraged by her air of timidity.
In control most of the time. Nervous—yes, extremely—and yet
able to disguise it. My light soothing witty stream of conversation
impressed her, held her in check. While she was gone—a telephone
call, I think—she did not explain—I slipped my vial of pills out—
meant only to take another—to wash another down quickly in order
to strengthen my position—fearful of the pills wearing out— Slipped
out the vial, spilled several onto my palm, at that moment the idea
occurred to me: why not put one in Yvonne's drink? Only one. Or
two. At the most, two. Helpful—soothing—not very strong, really—
one of the medium-mild tranquilizers— No one would notice. And it
would do both of us good.

The waiter nowhere near. Cocktail lounge of the old Andora—renovated a few years ago—not much character to it now—the old walnut paneling, still, and the handsome bar—everything else changed—but dark, nicely dark, wonderfully dark.

Slipped one pill in her drink. And another. Suitor—courtier—seducer. No new tricks along these lines—no need for newness.

Extraordinary courage! Where had I learned such cunning?

Finished my drink. Went to the bar to order another. Public manner easygoing tonight, even rather aristocratic. Imitating Father consciously. (Not as the old bastard was in his dotage, but as he had been in those smooth superficial charming middle years.) Andrew had tried to imitate him—unconsciously—and without success: Andrew always too strident, assertive, egotistic, without grace.

Saw her in the dusky mirror above the bar. Woman's figure in the doorway—hotel foyer behind her decorated for Christmas—galaxy of lights. A leap of something in me—lust, love, hope? But when I turned she was gone—I had lost her—what was wrong?

Yvonne?

Nervous, as you might expect. Yet in control of the situation, an artist directing what must happen. Inevitability to it—one event then the next then the next.

Comfortable booth. Dark leather cushions. Other couples in the lounge—heads together—murmuring, occasionally laughing—all very natural. Men and women, women and men. So natural. Nothing to it, really—the magic effortless—the miracle unnoticed.

Yvonne? Is anything wrong?

The pills must have dissolved by now—invisible, certainly—tasteless. She smiled. She lifted the glass. I watched—a hint of panic suddenly—oh why, why?—but she sipped at the drink, warm brown eyes fixed upon me, unsuspecting.

Yvonne, is it painful?—is it frightening?—is it embarrassing that I should want you so openly?—that I should be making jokes, chattering of inconsequential matters, leering and smiling and salivating like this?

She spoke of wanting to leave soon—to return to the apartment.

Went to bed early most nights. Always before midnight. Hoped I would understand. Usually in fine health—rarely ill—occasionally fatigued these past few months. Hoped I would understand.

Yes, yes.

Hugh in his russet tweed suit—suede trim—the zebra-stripe tie not quite right but at least daring, dramatic. Hugh murmuring Yes, yes.

People glanced our way. I saw them. A solitary man at the bar—a spy?—a detective?—a private investigator?—friend of Andrew's?—Yvonne's lover?—watching us surreptitiously through the mirror—outrageous simplicity to his style. The couple in the adjoining booth, heads together, whispering—of us—of her? Of *it*? A gentleman in a dark suit and vest passed by, looked at her and at me quite frankly but without recognition—unaccusing, curious. Some envy, perhaps. Imagining me—Hugh in his blue-patterned underwear, his fashionable eighty-five-dollar shoes—imagining me the woman's lover. And why not?

Why not?

Easy, intimate manner. Yvonne perplexed at first. As if unable to imagine what I wanted—why I had sought her out. Brotherly conversation, yet with a certain edge to it. Not flirtatious—by no means. Never crude. Incapable of being crude. Solicitous—gentle—"wise." Spoke of the disappointing lack of progress—the various police investigations that came to nothing—the pitiful death of Pickard—police recklessness, violence, stupidity—exactly the kind of cynical slovenly method—governmental, bureaucratic, military—that Andrew had detested, had so valiantly campaigned against. Taxpayers ultimately victimized. Huge machinery of government—colossal mechanism without check—limitless resources, supposedly, taxpayers always hurt. And people like Pickard, hurt also. It was inexcusable.

Inspired, I began to reminisce. Evoked memories of childhood. Andrew as a boy—strong-willed, intelligent, of a kindly and even sweet disposition—remarkably mature for his age—willing to accept responsibilities. A few examples of his prodigious talent: at home, at school, in public. There was Andrew Petrie at the age of thirteen, graciously accepting a trophy and a first prize of a hundred dollars and a complete set of the *Encyclopedia Americana* for a remarkably impassioned and persuasive and even rather scholarly speech he had given in a state-wide oratory contest: "Postwar America: the Collapse of the Republic?" At the age of fourteen, husky and good-natured, a little temperamental perhaps—due to his superior intellect—but athletic also, marvelously vital and competitive: sailing at Lake Champlain and Lake Placid and Bar Harbor, football and basketball and track in season, glamorously rough (had she seen his numerous scars? that severe pencil-thin one bisecting his right eyebrow? A boyhood accident, diving from the rocks at one of our summer places.) By fifteen he had his full growth—big for his age but carried it well—

weight-lifting an obsession for a while, one winter—and then he became very interested in boxing, against my father's wishes—and of
course against Mother's: took lessons at a gym in Albany, entirely on
his own, no connection with school sports or with boys he would
have ordinarily known. Really trained himself. Evidently wasn't
afraid to be knocked around in the ring, even: I never actually saw a
bout—by black boys and others of the kind—other boys of that kind
—whom he wouldn't ordinarily have known— A remarkable boy,
wasn't he? I had always admired him—of course. He was a semi-
finalist in the Golden Gloves tournament—lost his match—no one in
the family went to see it, for reasons I won't go into—got beaten
fairly badly, by amateur standards—but Father wouldn't go to
Syracuse, where the tournament was held—and Andrew never spoke
of it. Was stubborn and a trifle vain, even as a boy; but he had
reason to think well of himself. Everyone else thought well of him.
Destined for greatness. Strong ringing voice when he took part in
debates—or even at the dinner table, discussing with Father or our
guests certain complex issues—the constitutionality of the graduated
income tax—the secret meaning of the appointments of various persons to powerful state and federal positions—the need for fearless ax-
men in government on all levels. So prodigious, everyone said!—but
not in the usual inspired flighty way, as one might say of certain prodigious artists, but uncannily pragmatic, with a remarkable memory
for facts, dates, statistics, legal and historical precedents—and so personally charming, so winning—always a performer, our Andrew—obviously destined for politics. But, oddly, he wanted for a while to be
an architect—in his room he had model cities—city-states—and maps
on the walls—strange schemes whereby the East Coast was reorgan-
ized into sectors rather than states, and one immense area—most of
New Mexico, Arizona, and a few thousand square miles of Mexico—
was set aside for—for who I don't know—but set aside—I saw the
map myself. Ah, the cities he invented! He couldn't draw—one of his
very few handicaps—and occasionally asked me to draw for him—of
course it was generous of him to invite me to share his plans—
typically generous—but then temperamental differences marred our
partnership—too bad, too bad!—I might have learned a great deal
from him. Political geniuses, you know, *always* envision capitols and
palaces and boulevards and avenues and monuments and perpetually
flaming torches—*always* feel a compulsion to turn their dreams into
physical reality—

A genius, yes, but not tediously so. Not at all. No doubt people had told her—no doubt—how much Andrew's sense of humor saved him? That is, saved him from working himself to death? Even as a boy—especially as a boy—he possessed the most remarkable sense of humor. A little trickster at times. Practical jokes—roughhouse of various kinds—never sadistic, never intentionally cruel—just good animal spirits, the exuberance of youth—

During all this she stared at me. Attentive and greedy and slightly apprehensive (sensing my irony, yet not comprehending it). She stared—waited—her eyes filling with sentimental predictable tears—it became difficult for me to sit still, I was so excited.

Everyone loved him, I whispered.

She assented.

Everyone— But of course you know.

—was in awe of him, worshiped him.

Of course.

—of course.

And you—?

Yes, of course.

When you first—?

Yes, the first evening.

In Pittsburgh?

Yes. So long ago. I was introduced to him—I shook hands with him—I had wanted to argue with him about—about some minor point in a speech he had made that day—I had intended to—had wanted—

But you changed your mind? Forgot?

Forgot.

And did he love you immediately, as well? Was it—?

Yes. He said so. Afterward, he claimed that. And he never—

He never lied.

Never.

Incapable of lying, wasn't he?—a peculiarity of his even in childhood.

Was it? Even in childhood?

Peculiar—sometimes rather frightening—but of course noble, noble.

Incorruptible. People called him that and I thought they must be—

They weren't, were they?

No. They weren't. He never lied—he was incorruptible—he was a good man and he died—died horribly.

We all die horribly, Yvonne.

A panicked child clutching at a hot slate roof. Another child, stockier, with a blunt bullish chin and staring gray-green eyes, crawling over him. Careful, careful!—one quick sly shrug of the shoulders!—But no. Impossible. Dr. Wynand rejected it, as politely as possible. Dr. Wynand rejected. Knew better. A fantasy of the artist's—only a fantasy. Daydream. And the incident in the park— flirty zany conversation with the fake murderers-for-hire—all three too drunk to speak coherently—more fantasizing, the usual delusions of omnipotence.

What an imagination, Hugh! What a wry sense of humor!

Could get yourself an exotic wig—bobbing mass of red, red curls— could squeeze yourself into a girdle and other female attire—stockings, garter belt, high-heeled shoes—could dab plaster onto your blemished face and grind some scarlet lipstick onto your lips—could prepare a ten-minute comic routine and simply stun your classmates —win First Prize on Amateur Talent Night and even get into the local papers, with that sense of humor! The most daring, most iconoclastic, most *incredible* of all the Petries!

With that imagination—

And here is Yvonne laughing sleepily. Yvonne warm now, unwidowed. Eager to be diverted from thoughts of *it*—from dutiful memories of *it*. Finishing her drink. Childlike, trusting. Surprisingly sweet. I remembered her from years ago—that first meeting of ours— the woman cold, poised, careless of her appearance—a coarse beauty —something reptilian about the eyes. Rings on several fingers —long pale slender neck I had wanted to grab. Squeeze and squeeze and squeeze. That she should be indifferent to me, to *me!* That she should pretend not to know of my fame! But now, tonight, now she is softened—the drug has softened her—the drug and the alcohol and my discreet courting—the caressing of my words—my presence.

Now she says suddenly: I knew he would die.

You knew?

I knew, I knew.

But— Are you serious?

I knew.

God's will, someone had said.

Who?

Had always hated Him—God—it. Whatever. Had always hated not God—for there is none—but the idea. The hypothesis. The word arrangement itself. And those who babble of it—who are incapable of not babbling of it—GodGodGodGodGod. God's will. —Stephen at the funeral parlor, Stephen at the cemetery. Tall, abrupt, awkward, priestly. As I lost control of myself I looked wildly across the casket —sought him—sought help from him. Stephen? Is he dead? Is our brother dead? Am I next? Are you next? Staring across the lowered casket, across the wide grave. Perspiration on his forehead—horrible intensity to his dark eyes—Stephen staring wordlessly at me as I fell —hearing the zany little voice that cried for help. He alone heard it, of that crowd. He alone. Standing beside the Widow, not touching her—posted beside her in case she required him—the two of them startled as I collapsed—the two of them watchful—

But why were we speaking of Stephen?

Stephen?—no, Stephen was someone else.

Had always disliked him. Was contemptuous of. Could not take seriously—certainly could not. Andrew yammering and taunting— Andrew crawling over me that hot bright day—a physical creature, a miniature adult—the breath of life always evident in him, uncomplicated and soulless, as in most of us. But Stephen?—no, he was someone else.

Why did we begin to speak of—?

Yvonne sleepy now. Heavy-lidded. Asking of others in the family— childlike, inquisitive—a mere bride, really—a three years' bride to a man rarely home. Probably she had not dared to ask Andrew. Had not dared to seem curious. He did not approve of gossip—of personalities—of the personal life. In Andrew's arms she had lain voiceless. Smooth-limbed, of course, and meekly beautiful. For him. To him. In his presence. In my arms she spoke with the childish solemnity of one who is intoxicated— Why?—when?—who?—what? Why had so much happened to her already?—why, when her life had just begun?—had begun only a few years ago? When would it end, this siege? The pressure of other people, their insatiable curiosity?—their relentless hunting of Andrew?—and of her? Who was I, that I had pursued her? Had seemed to know her? Had spoken so sharply and so perceptively to her? What did I want? What would happen? What did it mean, that one of Andrew's brothers gave her counsel in her dreams?

Wanted to scream—Get away, you're not the one I want! Get away!

Innocent, brash, bewildered Eva. Eva in her kimono—fluffy pink bedroom slippers—a gift of a fruitcake left on my kitchen table.

Not the one, not the right one! —But there was some connection between us. Not brother and sister. Not cousins. Not lovers. I shouted—she retreated—must have seen something odd in my face. Stealthy bitch. Glanced at the clutter on my workbench—seeking evidence? clues?

Daydreams. Nightdreams.

You float—are drawn away from shore—the helplessness of your condition taxing, profound, humiliating. After the images of the vision fade, this condition of helplessness remains in the memory.

Numerous bells ringing—many churches—must have been Sunday morning. Albany, New Haven, New York City. And London also: the news came to me there, news of her death. When Yvonne lay in my arms she was as helpless as I. Blank faceless soulless people. Utter exhaustion of having split in two, a self broken in two. She clung to me—sleepy and desperate—I saw her once again in the waves, beyond the noisy surf—a shadowy uncertain shape desperate to live—desperate to get hold of me or of anyone—to wind her arms about my neck—to draw me down to her. Saw her. Did not recognize her at first. Did not recognize the water either, the afternoon of Andrew's death—had forgotten how, years before, I had teased and promised myself a death by water, the consolation of a death by any means, a death, my death, *the* death. Revenge, it would have been. Revenge on those who failed to love me—who surrounded me and observed, without affection—those perpetual spies and judges of my youth. An ecstasy of revenge—why not?

On a bridge. New Haven. Between sleep and waking—eerie clarity of the mind, late at night—calculating the distance the body must fall—calculating the possibility of shouts and screams from that body —the cowardly convulsions of a body that wants to live. Calculating coldly and wisely. One of the few lucid moments of my life. And then—

Then—

I sneezed. Sneezed twice.

And again. A sudden fit—a sneezing fit—caused by the damp wind.

Several minutes of sneezing—couldn't get the goddam tissue out—sneezed into my fingers the first three times. A mess. Hideous. Shameful. Thought the fit was over—blinking tears from my eyes—then it came upon me again—spasms not only in the head but in the chest, deep in the chest and stomach. Painful. Exhausting. When it was over—

Couldn't remember why I had come out. Why this bridge?—why here, so late at night? Suicide?—unthinkable! What a joke!

Everything about me is a joke, Yvonne! A joke! A joke! Why aren't you laughing, Yvonne? Why not, like the others? Why not, since I have been exposed to you?—to you more than anyone else? Don't you think it's amusing that I should have wanted you so badly, and then—and then *this*?

25

And did you—?
Yes. In a way.
You took her back to her apartment and—?
And helped her out of the cab—explained to the doorman that Mrs. Petrie wasn't feeling well—took her up in the elevator—got the keys from her purse and opened the door and— Of course it was a shock: stepping inside. She was leaning against me. Swaying. Head on my shoulder—my arm around her—like two people in a picture, a drawing?—an illustration? She must have been rather weak, to be so affected by the pills. I take a half dozen myself and hardly feel any-thing—must be getting immune—but I'm stronger than Yvonne, a stronger physique, morale. She was quite conscious, though. Kept asking what was wrong, why was it so late, what was going to hap-pen?—that sort of thing. Raving, but quietly. Could hardly hear her. What was going to happen—where was everyone—was she going to be late?
And—?
Simon, I swear—to my everlasting shame and delight!—I did these things, I did these things deliberately—rationally—bravely. I did not hesitate. Faltered only when I opened the door and helped her inside —for a moment—odd sense of someone already in there—one light burning in the living room and a book face-down on the coffee table. One moment only, at the most two. Felt a thrill of panic. But it passed, it translated itself into simple visceral and sexual excitement —entirely healthy—I regained control of myself and of the situation —and— Well— As I had planned, I did no more than assist her into the bedroom—*the* bedroom—fairly ordinary furnishings—Andrew's usual brutish taste—some quite attractive white draperies but in gen-

eral a dark sad place—not even very warm. The winds must be terrific up there on the twenty-sixth floor. Poor Yvonne! Poor deluded woman! —And, as I had planned, I did no more than help her lie down—took off her shoes, found a blanket in a closet, covered her with it. I lay her coat across a chair. Considered taking off her jewelry, then thought better of it—didn't want to distrub her or be misunderstood. As you can imagine, I was tremendously excited by now—my teeth chattering with it—with the daring, the desperation— With the possibility of—and yet the denial of—the deliberate chaste brotherly *denial* of it. I—I will admit that—there was something about the room, the feel of it, the presence of—and when I'd opened the closet door—well, it was one of the terrors of my life— can't explain why—had been set to see his things in there still—a man's clothes—and yet—when I—it was— There was— A slight shock, no more. My heart was pounding but because of her—because of me—the situation that was now irrevocable, a kind of marriage, don't you see, a kind of wedding?—honeymoon?—a ritual of a kind, far more remarkable than the ordinary version? And so— I— She fell asleep at once— Quite powerful, those pills! Wonderful invention! Had I had a love potion I could hardly have been more successful. This way, the delicacy of it would impress her. When she woke she'd remember—she'd realize—seeing herself fully clothed, the blanket over her—she'd realize what had happened, what an intimate bond there was between us now. There are so few bonds between people— I mean the real thing, the deep passionate gestures—connections—irrevocable unities. And—

And that's all?

Simon, what the hell do you think I am? What have you been anticipating? You misunderstand me entirely—it's an insult—a perversity on your part. I drew the blanket up to the lovely woman's chin. I bent over her, yes, one human being caring for another—very much struck by her sorrow, her loss, her—her features—her hair. Have you seen any photographs of her? Yes? But they don't do her justice! They don't! She isn't that—isn't that strong, that composed— Rather childlike, in fact— Trusting—helpless— A Botticelli. A Botticelli, I swear. At least when she was asleep—and I stood over her— and— And, yes: I will admit that I gave in. I kissed her two or three times, no more. On the forehead—which was clammy, surprisingly clammy—and on each eyelid. No more! No more. My heart nearly burst. But that's all—that's all. No more delicious an adventure has ever come my way—or sprung fully imagined out of my brain.

And— And then, afterward? The next morning?

Nothing comes next. Nothing can follow such ecstasy. There are moments in life, Simon—and though you're not as romantic and flamboyant as I, I'm sure you understand—Maggie would understand: but please don't tell her about this, she would only be angry with me again—you understand that nothing, *nothing* can follow such ecstasy. The mind refuses to function in that tedious cataloguing manner—the chronology of brutes. It comes to a stop. A full stop. And time itself is conquered.

When can I meet Yvonne? I would be interested in— Not out of morbid curiosity, of course, and not—not for other reasons— But—

You'll never meet her, I said curtly. She's mine.

26

At first a reverent hush. Then a murmuring—a wave-like swelling —pressure increasing—erupting into giggles and jeers and catcalls. Impotent, the audience cried.

IMPOTENT.

Slanderous lies. Charges brought against me by my enemies. A crowd of witnesses—a lifetime of witnesses—ringed together above the bed, cheek to cheek, grinning and giggling and gaping, like monkeys. Good-natured, of course—good-natured animal spirits. Always. Nothing sadistic intended.

The Artist exposed. Not only unmasked, but unclothed: kneeling in prayer above the idealized form of Love.

Is impotence real? Is it symbolic? Please—I must know!

Dr. Wynand sighed in his wisdom. As if—poor sick Hugh!—there could be any salvation through terminology!

The woman slipped from me—fell sideways across the bed—fell heavily, as if from a great height. Her head jerked backward at a painful angle. Asleep at once. Unconscious. Yvonne? I scrambled over her, clutched at her, my glasses riding down my nose. Yvonne? Yvonne?

Irrational fear that she would die.

Completely irrational, of course. The pills were not that strong. Had I wanted to stop her breathing—had I wanted to suffocate her with the pillow—or to strangle her— No, no. Not that strong. Anyway, I loved her: love reined me in.

Why did you abandon me? Why did you leave me alone in that terrible place? Like a tomb, it was. A high-rise building that swayed and creaked in the wind—bitter December wind sweeping down from the northeast, from the Atlantic Ocean and the Arctic. I could not tolerate it. Could not. And there was a smell of paint or plaster. A smell of something cold, dead.

Most humiliating, the scene that followed. Not at all the one I had presented—rather winningly, I think?—rather convincingly?—to my greedy friend Simon.

Yvonne? Yvonne?

I love you—isn't it enough?

But she fell from me. She forgot me. She moaned—her eyelids fluttered—I saw the dead-white white of her eye, blind, turned inward, awful. What was she staring at?—what fascinated her so, inside her head? Not me. Not Hugh. Not the witty cavalier Hugh. He remained behind, alone in the master bedroom—stooped over, partly unclothed, the touching blue of his underwear mocked—shivering, muttering aloud—brief mindless *oh God! Jesus Christ! God, no!*— the prayers of a futile boyhood. Hopeless, ludicrous. A caricature. She pushed away from me—stronger even in sleep than one would have expected—breathing hoarsely through her mouth. Slipped from me, escaped me, left me behind. Alone. In the presence of—

Why, the apartment stank with it!

Everywhere the smell.

Death. Death. Death.

I forced myself to proceed. I intended to go through with it. To complete the ritual. To make an end of it, of this phase of courtship. To satisfy myself—imagination as well as body—to prove that it might be possible to fulfill both love and simple lust—affection—admiration—revenge.

Yvonne? Yvonne, dear? Don't fight me—

She wore a long, loose dress of some soft fabric—jersey, perhaps— gray jersey—with neat plain schoolgirlish gray buttons—even the cuffs were buttoned, doubly. Silver earrings, several silver or white-gold bracelets—one of them a bracelet watch, the numerals too tiny for me to decipher—and the antique ring upon which the twin snakes coiled—and of course the diamond wedding rings. I wanted to strip her of the jewelry most of all—wanted to tear it off—force the rings off—throw them into the corners of his bedroom—yank the closet door open and throw them in triumph on the floor. There! There! What power have you now? But I trembled, I groaned aloud, I could not quite—could not quite—and I was a little drunk also—and exhausted by the hours of conversation—*my* conversation—my strained brilliant performance. What to do, how to proceed? I felt no desire—had only the angry memory of desire, the idea of desire—could not quite manage— A woman's body—yes?—and so?—the necessity to touch, to caress, to marvel at—to poke and pry—and squeeze—the necessity to unclothe that body—a feat, a ritual, a grim mad accomplishment—slowly, bravely! cautiously!—the necessity not to surrender to panic—the necessity to be guided by the will—the cold sane control of the will—though the instincts have dropped to zero and are, in fact, urging undignified flight. But slowly—bravely!—unflinchingly! The object being to gaze unimpeded upon the body of the beloved—to experience an intense secrecy—a delirious certainty of pleasure—a paroxysm of delight—of such violent apocalyptic magnitude that mere language could not serve to express it—

If only the apartment had not stunk with Andrew's presence—

—but no: nothing: an irrevocable nothing.

Nor did time stop, as I told Simon. It did not. Time continued—refused to give a leap—ticked away perfunctorily—yawningly—as always. My only moment of exhilaration or transcendence (if such a desperate act deserves such high-flown terms) was in opening the door to what was evidently Andrew's study—seeing by moonlight the enormous clutter of books and papers and magazines—not quite daring to switch on the overhead light (why? I tortured myself afterward with this question)—but snatching—so swiftly I hardly knew what I was doing—a sheet of paper from one of several piles on his old rolltop desk—snatching it, folding it, stuffing it in my pocket.

And then I fled. Adjusted my clothing as best I could being so agitated—stuffed the sheet of paper into my pocket—and fled.

Am fleeing still.

27

The Artist sits at his drawing board, omnipotent.
Omnipotent, at his drawing board.
Omnipotent: at his drawing board.
At his drawing board, omnipotent.
The Artist sits. Omnipotent, the Artist sits. At his drawing board.

The Artist sits omnipotent at his drawing board.

The Artist would multiply his loves—*his*—his "loves"—would multiply them endlessly. Toadstools popping up overnight. Anonymous —killable—endlessly replenished—forever at his disposal and his pleasure.

The reputation of being giddy, reckless, unpredictable. No one knew him, but he knew everyone. He eluded everyone.

Omnipotent.

The Artist would refuse to—would violently resist—would struggle to the death against falling in love with one of them. Unthinkable. Foolish. Obscene. For afterward—why, there would be no "afterward." He would never escape. Would no longer be unknown.

What childhood drama are you re-enacting?

Dr. Wynand's cursory question, meant to insult and deflate. The bastard! But I showed no emotion, was marvelously civil, articulate, "conscious" in the best sense of the word. (I had already betrayed him—had already engaged another analyst—and could foresee engaging still another—the deceptions overlapping—richly intricate—just as I had tried always to match one love with another—to keep always ahead of—detached from—quite self-contained, autonomous. What other technique, to assure my freedom?)

Omnipotent in the head. In the body, less so.

Alas, a devilish fine line between omnipotence and impotence. Very fine. At the drawing board I worked feverishly—experimenting —these were no longer idle doodles but grave magnificent experiments—the postures of her body and mine—the forms our connected bodies might take—*the* body we would comprise, no longer

split in two—no longer deprived of each other. United as we were
destined to be united, before his presence had frustrated us. Before—
long before!—he had even known her.

Yvonne a giantess at times—so tall and strong—immense arms and
legs—lovely smile, but cruel—giantess's smile, cannibal's smile. And
her teeth, ah—!

Her teeth.

Remembered that night in New Haven. The agitation—the certainty—the growing calm—the clear stoic intelligent will—and then
the sneezing fit, the insult of comedy at so sublime a moment. Impossible! Go home! You can't even die perfectly!

One of the oldest colleges at Yale. Not Father's choice—but he
had been pleased—evidently—pleased to some extent. Aged floors
creaking—creaking overhead—archaic plumbing—knocking of radiators all night long—the curse of insomnia—inescapable in such surroundings. Why was it "neurotic"? Why "pathological"? Normal,
entirely normal! The beasts who slumbered and snored and were not
awakened even by drunken singing in the courtyard or the hideous
banging of the front door or those radiators, those goddam radiators!
—those beasts were abnormal, not I. Sleepless. Nineteen years old.
Not only sleepless but acutely awake—acutely—intensely—horribly.
A lucidity to my thought processes unmatched before or since. Like
a lighthouse beacon glaring into an intimate sacred dark—like an X
ray—a laser beam—hideous unceasing activity of consciousness—carnival acceleration—Ferris wheel, merry-go-round, shrill hurdy-gurdy—
threat of madness—madness become a physical horror—a physical
possibility—a physical experience. Nineteen years old. Worn out.
Nerves jumping as if with electricity. And always the tensing—the
preparation for more drunken laughter outside—(the windows were
old, the sills warped, nothing fit tightly)—and the creaking of bed-
springs in the room upstairs—heavy footsteps—thuds—bursts of excited talk or laughter. My own roommates went elsewhere, to others'
sitting rooms—sullen,—resenting me, of course—since I had burst
upon them one pathetic night—weeping—screaming—begging for
quiet—rushing at the phonograph (where an overwrought version of
The Bolero was playing—overwrought even for that detestable piece
—had been playing and replaying for the past forty-five minutes)—
and afterward, after coffee and rum with the Master of the college—
after several more weeping spells—after a confession of "fear of insanity"—my shoulder gripped, my elbow held tightly—a treaty of

peace devised—an arrangement "less unsuitable for all concerned" sealed with handshakes all around. And yet!—still!—it was noisy, still!—unbearable!

I lay awake night after night. I thought of *her*, naturally: of Pamela. Of the two of us. Or was it the three of us? —Pamela at the age of sixteen, I a few months younger. Mt. Desert Island—end of summer—boating across Frenchman's Bay—her father's yacht— Andrew and an older man in charge—six or seven of us, approximately the same age. My mother had come to spend July and August with her mother, bringing the children; both our fathers were elsewhere. Cannot remember where. Andrew and Pamela and several others, strangers to me, even some local young people: aristocracy of the summer, secrets among them, dreaded and envied. I mocked them behind their backs. I loved them, detested them. I humbled myself before them. They ignored me most of the summer—then unaccountably took me along with them on their outings—then dropped me, forgot me—then remembered me. Then—

There was Pamela's strained face, her wet-glistening teeth, her eyes filling with moisture. And her breath: the surprisingly bitter smell of whiskey. Pamela digging her nails into me—grunting and clutching and—and then pushing at me angrily—kicking with her bare feet— Goddamn you! damn stupid bastard! In one of the cabins, in the lower bunk of one of the bunk-beds. The boat swayed and lurched. Everyone was drunk. I was drunk—had been drunk—was drunk no longer—would never be drunk again. She pushed at me, her eyes overbright, her lipstick smeared crazily about her mouth—drawling and mocking and beginning that nasal theatrical laugh of hers—of her girlhood—a humorless, rapidly ascending series of giggles— Poor little Hughie! Get the hell out of here!

Months. Years. Decades. Thinking of her, of it; remembering; hearing again her voice and that laughter; trying to comprehend the meaning—the possible or probable meaning—trying to figure out why?—why had she lured me down there?—why had—?—and why do such things continue to happen?

Lay awake thinking of her. Lay awake for years, for decades. Lay awake thinking, thinking. Hearing her giggle—the dismissive silly words—later that day a vague silly apology—superficial, cheerful—all forgotten—all forgotten, of course—insignificant, of course—grinning to show her childish white perfect teeth—grinning at me—grinning at Andrew—grinning and winking as she pinched my ear—in Andrew's presence—in the presence of the others—grinning and winking at Andrew—Andrew in white shorts and a white T-shirt, darkly tanned, coarsely handsome, his freshman year at Harvard already behind him and—and his marvelous future opening before him—

Andrew?

Pamela?

The wet, cold wind—the bridge's railing—my bare hands gripping hard—the familiar voices in my head chanting and jeering—Hugh, poor little Hughie, everyone knows about poor little Hughie— That laughing lipstick-smeared mouth: what had it meant? Why had it happened? Bells rang—the bells of many churches—I was back in the college, back in my bedroom—I was not going to die—I had not died —I would not die, just to please them. Would not. Would never. —Collapsed across the bed, must have slept.

Church bells. Sunday morning. Decision to leave Yale.

They almost killed me!—screaming at Dr. Wynand one morning, twenty years later. They—the two of them—not just the two of them but many, many—*many* people! Tried to kill me! Destroy me! Eat me alive—devour me—spit me out with a contemptuous laugh— Don't you believe me? Doesn't anyone believe me?

> Dearest:
>
> I hope you haven't misinterpreted the events of
> the other evening. What happened was only this:
> you became unaccountably tired, nearly fell asleep
> in the taxi, I helped you up to the apartment
> and to bed. I hope it wasn't offensive to you—
> I must confess I simply didn't know what to do
> under the circumstances. I hope you were warm
> enough with just that blanket. I hope that, the
> next morning, you felt better. I hope you
> will allow me to see you again. I hope you can
> recognize the seriousness of my feeling for you.
> I hope you weren't repulsed by anything. I hope
> you slept deeply and profoundly—forgetting every-
> thing—forgetting sorrow most of all. (Yvonne,
> it is my destiny to redeem you of your sorrow!)
> I hope you sense the depth of my commitment—the
> humility and sincerity of my love. I hope—

To Dr. Swann I recited hurriedly the important background facts —events—might have confused past and present—and future—spoke so quickly that saliva flew from my mouth. The main point—the only point I truly wanted to make—was that I loved her and pitied her and fully intended to save her—felt not only a lover's natural passion but a concern for her welfare that was brotherly—Christly— The two of us, after all, had been victimized by the same man.

Dearest:

Man has no Body distinct from his Soul; for that
call'd Body is a portion of Soul discern'd by the
five Senses, the chief inlets of Soul in this age.

(William Blake)

The Artist sits at his drawing board, once again omnipotent.

28

December, still. Mid-December.

The exterior world remained.

My drawing was returned—regretfully returned—an editor's embarrassed unintelligible scribbling—*Sorry cannot use not quite right not what we had intended Sorry sorry*—bastards who will not recognize what is before them—the quality, the ingenuity, the hours of anguished labor!—bastards uniting against me—persecuting me—trying to pressure me into conforming, into imitating the simpler shapes and brainless didactic art of my competitors! Ignorant! Envious! Vicious!

Revenge?

But how?

The exterior world remained. As always. It figured little in my life —in my essential life. And yet—there it was! Always! No matter when I woke—yawned and stretched at my front window—studied the windows and front stoops of the brownstones across the way— the funeral parlor a few doors to the left—the damp look of the street—the impassive featureless sky: no matter when I turned to it, no matter that I was vexed and tormented, or murderously excited, or simply bored and desirous of being filled, the world remained.

New York City. Said to be the center of the world. Center of civilization. Said to be immensely intricate—a maze of riches—infinitely mysterious: yet experienced by me as fairly small and negotiable. A backdrop for the continuing mystery of my life.

The week of the Birth of Our Savior, for instance. What had it to do with me?—with Yvonne and me? Nothing.

With Andrew, dead now six months and nearly forgotten? Nothing.

Midtown. Along the wide avenues Christmas carols—Christmas jingles—frisky organ tunes—hordes of shoppers—fir trees and aluminum trees and cardboard trees garishly trimmed—a prosperous Christmas for all—prosperous always and forever—no matter the "grim" Wall Street predictions—the hell with all "grim" predictions! This is America, this is New York City. This is the Nativity. Manger scenes—Muzak—snowmobiles and skis and heaped fur coats in the windows of Abercrombie & Fitch—a mannequin in one of Saks's windows with head and shoulders exactly like Yvonne's—stopped me dead, the sight of her—of it—slender columnar woman in a long, long silk dress—black, with small yellow flowers—like a slip—thin straps—the bosom nearly exposed, and so white!—the head regal, the tough mouth not even painted, the eyes heavy with lashes, slightly recessed—only the too-shiny black hair was unconvincing, and the freakish small waist. *Yvonne!* Dozens of Santas. Snow falling on their angel's-hair beards, their mittened hands ringing bells, begging. Along Fifth Avenue a stampede of shoppers. Smell of chestnuts stronger, more poignant than ever. A boy wearing a plaid cloth cap shook a tin can beneath the noses of passersby—begging, harassing—approached me and rattled the can—practically threatening me— Mister? Wouldyaliketo donate? Small contribution? Spastics of America, Inc.?—his voice jeering his ugly face set in contempt his free hand in a cautionary gesture to keep me from pushing past. I muttered no—tried to get away. He followed. Shaking the can, rattling the coins in the can, by my ear—still that jeer in his voice, almost an elation to it—until I turned on him and began shouting.

No! Get away! Go to hell! Leave me alone!

The external world: always.

May I try again, Yvonne?

Dr. Wynand bemused. Not exactly disbelieving, and yet not enthusiastic. Betrayed him with Dr. Swann. Each Wednesday at four, with Dr. Swann. Betrayed her, in fact, with a creature too trivial to figure in this narrative—homely, battered, and yet attractive face— eyes sometimes soulful, sometimes dopey—a pickup in a cafeteria on the West Side. Too trivial, too trivial. Spoke to various relatives on the phone—various friends—a warm pseudo-frank conversation with Deborah during which both of us explained several times how busy we were—I with new assignments, she with holiday partying and entertaining—and alluded to minor points meant to inspire sympathy—sympathy at a distance—I to a problem with an unhappy cousin of mine, grieved and alcoholic, Deborah to the possibility of her mother entering the hospital for tests. And we had as always our hints of Dr. Wynand, our hints of complex stormy sessions, uncovered memories, ravaging but cathartic "truths." I did not mention my new analyst, Dr. Swann: it would have been a confession of adultery.

Let us sin, the ancient heretics prayed, *that grace may abound.*

But what of us—what of the multitude of us who can experience neither sin nor grace, who are stuck forever tramping the city streets or opening a tin mailbox that will contain nothing of interest or sitting at the drawing board in despair—? What of us, the masses of humanity?

The external world. Intoxicating, tiring. Sometimes lovely. But always distracting: drawing me from my work, my life. Irresistible. Unfathomable. Buying five-dollars worth of groceries at the local A & P —repassing the tawdry hotel that had had a "kitchen fire" months ago and was a devastated, smoke-smelling ruin—watching an ecstatic child who held an immense pizza in both hands, his rosy cheeks belled out, eyes shut, a child-giant towering into the sky above a franchise "Italian food" restaurant—fantastic! monumental as art! On Seventh Avenue, a small store I passed often: windows plastered with advertisements and posters, most of them old election posters— X for Congress—a balding, sincerely-smiling man with a doomed look—unlike Andrew's triumphant look—Andrew for Senator—triumphant ubiquitous Andrew Petrie—"one of the youngest men ever": but the newest posters in the store window showed a pious gentle-eyed Indian—skin wrinkled like a leather glove—elderly, beautiful, mysterious. Temple of the Spirit. Guru Krishnarama.

I carried the letter from Andrew's desk around in my pocket. Sometimes, having coffee or a drink, I took it out, unfolded it, chuckled. She too had to endure the external world. She was going to need me—was going to need me desperately.

Dear Mrs Petrie,

Read of your heartbreaking tragedy and continue to follow it whenever possible. In regard to the fact that the murderers

are scot-free to this day, have been thinking of whether
to risk this but [words crossed out] for your own good and
the nations, am already in possession of some general
knowledge as to height and *coloring* of the leader of the
murderers pack. But must have more evidence and something to
hold in my hand before deeper truth is revealed. Could you
send me by special delivery a cherished gift of the late
Senator to you, would be even more powerful if something
of his given to you as a gift—like a ring he used to wear or
a sweater or lock of hair or cuff-links—the thing is, if he
carried it close about his body and then gave it to you, it would
help me a lot and then of course I would contact you at
once if the actual identification of the murderers came to me.
Would report to the police at your wish and be a witness
at the trial if necessary. I hope to hear from you Mrs Petrie
very soon and also want you to know how deeply struck
with sorrow I am, and everyone I know, with the loss of your
husband, who was the only one of them a person could
believe. That is why he died, of course. But his murderers can
still be found and brought to *EXECUTION.*

Possibly.
Spent Christmas Eve with—
One of the shocks of my life, the way she looked. And behaved.
Went home trembling—not even drunk—left her present to me on
the subway—left it behind deliberately.
A brocaded smoking jacket two sizes too large. Chintzy-looking
though expensive. Hilarious, the ironies of my life. A parrot-green
smoking jacket with a black silken sash—intimate Christmas present
from a woman I had once desired—had once been in love with—in a
manner of speaking—not with quite the passion and despair of my
love for Y., but in love just the same!—in love!
Have not the heart to recollect.
Ungentlemanly, for one thing. Disturbing. Rather sickening.

One of the ugliest visions of my life: in the limousine, being
driven from the funeral service to the cemetery, chattering away in
order to distract Yvonne from thoughts of sadness—how little I knew
the woman then, but how close I felt to her!—I had happened to
glance out at a pedestrian—a woman on the curb watching intently
as our funeral procession passed—happened to notice this woman—
and fell silent. In her forties, probably. Wearing tight red shorts and
a pullover blouse of some very thin, scandalously thin material, her

ravaged thighs bulging, her upper arms flabby, her hair platinum and perfect—obviously a wig—a woman not really fat, not freakish, not insane—just a conventional shopper—a woman of the middle class— with no intentions of shocking or dramatizing or even calling atten- tion to herself—no intention of being sexually alluring—just a woman, a shopper, quite normal for the era. She stood there, watching as the limousines passed. Expectant, curious, even sympa- thetic. It was the era watching us, the era itself—the normality of it —standing there on the curb, inexplicably disgusting to me, infinitely mysterious, as alien to me as if she belonged to another species alto- gether. I remember glancing across to Yvonne. Shocked at that dese- cration of female flesh, I looked to Yvonne. Mournful, leaden-pale, an El Greco-blue cast to her skin that day: she was pure, and the other woman was defiled.

Inexplicable purity. Some of them, a few of them, a very few of them. The rest: like that woman in the red shorts. Defiled, sunk in flesh, and somehow too brightly conscious—brightly alert—"sociable" perhaps the term I want. So difficult to explain—thirty seconds with a pencil or a bit of charcoal and I could sketch it—that intangible difference between one woman and another—frustrating, enigmatic, illusory perhaps but—but—so achingly irrevocably real—

The one sucks our love from us—love and awe and terror—slips into us through the eyes, through our vision—that most vulnerable and traitorous of the senses—that most delicious of the senses!—the one commands our imaginations—takes over our very souls: while the other merely summons forth a small thrill of disgust.

Willa, dear Willa— Willa Petrie née Fergus—

Christmas Eve. A total surprise. That body could betray soul— could betray the imagination as well— The surprise of Willa so al- tered, so physically conscious—conscious of her overripe blowsy body —prettily self-conscious, like an actress in a mediocre comedy—coy, eager, then checking herself and becoming cool—detached— My God, how unreal! How unreal both of us were!

Of course I wrote to her! Of course I sent flowers—a sympathy card—and quite a long letter! —So Willa informed me, patting my arm. So many many things to explain—so much to set right between his second wife and me—issues that had to be cleared up—not practi- cal, not economic—the lawyers took care of that, of course, and of course Andrew was forced to pay for his freedom—the poor thing, the poor man, we all know how dearly he paid. You see, Hugh, what men cannot help missing—yearning for—is—evidently—I've over-heard them talking this way personally—I am not, not exaggerating!—what they are absolutely helpless to resist—no matter how brilliant, how intellectual, how fastidious about money matters—no matter how messianic they may imagine themselves to be—out to transform the entire nation, no less, and rescue Western Civilization from a new age of barbarism—wasn't that it?—something like that?—I assure you I'm not mocking him, Hugh, *not!*—not mocking him in the slightest! But, but— What was I saying, Hugh?

Willa, I really can't stay. I didn't know it was for dinner—I've already eaten—I—I— I'm due at a friend's in a few minutes— A kind of family Christmas Eve—I have presents for their children— I—

A pity Mike can't join us, isn't it? Dear little Mike! And such a genius, they say. Of course—Andrew knew. Andrew *knew*. Wouldn't have been content with anything less than a genius—can hardly blame him—a pity he couldn't be with us tonight—he always speaks so admiringly of you, Hugh. If the subject of his Uncle Stephen ever comes up—why, the child just snickers—a born atheist, like his father —but *very* cheerful about it. As they all are, don't you know—true atheists—realistic pragmatic people—just so very content and produc-tive, unlike people like you and me, Hugh, far more sensitive—thought-riddled—is that the expression? From Shakespeare? But if the subject of his Uncle Hugh comes up, why Mike is positively *proud*. He has such plans!—he'd be embarrassed if I went into them in any detail, but he does hope—someday—someday very soon—to take control of certain presses and publications—I'm not able to say exactly *how*—I suppose through financial arrangements—or personal contact?—there's a kind of network, an invisible network of the élite —the molders of thought processes among the intelligent, so Mikie claims—as opposed to those who just manipulate the masses—the tel-evision viewers— Do you agree? Is it so? And Mikie has already put together some very detailed charts, connecting intellectuals with one another—editors, brothers-in-law, agents, former professors, that sort of thing—the charts are hidden away somewhere—he never speaks of them—the difficult thing about the charts, I gather, is the fact that they must be constantly revised—constantly. People are always dying or dropping out of the race or being betrayed by one another. That sort of thing. Well, Mikie has quite marvelous plans for *you*. He in-tends to give you a position where you'll have a real readership—where you'll become famous—and controversial—that sort of thing. Isn't it exciting, Hugh? He's just like his father! Much saner, of

course, and not nearly so interested in women as poor Andrew was—
and look where that took him!—poor deluded Andrew! So you see
how your nephew is counting on you and won't forget you and—it
might be a matter, he says, of adjusting your mind—shaping your political consciousness or whatever that sort of thing is— Artists,
Andrew once said, are simply not intelligent. Simply not intelligent.
Their talents must be taken in hand—guided—put to some use.
Otherwise—

Willa, please—

—why should the children of strangers mean more to you than
your own nephew? Who are these people? Of course you knew our
evening together included dinner—I'm sure I made that clear in my
note. Anyway, it's only eight-thirty. Eight-thirty on Christmas Eve.
The least you could do, especially in the light of—in the memory
of— Ah, I just remembered: the point I was making earlier. The terrible weakness of men, men of a certain age—what they simply cannot resist and will succumb to every time—no matter how devoted to
their families, how basically and fundamentally in love with their
wives— No matter how disastrous to their public image— You see,
Hugh, it's entirely unconscious. It's instinct. They can't help it—
can't help it—being seduced by young women—sometimes mere girls
—it's pitiful, pathetic, but explicable—in terms of nature—a phenomenon they simply can't help. No matter how unappealing the girl is,
for instance. Or how spotty her background. It's just her youth—her
tight flesh—I've heard men admit this myself, Hugh, don't blush and
look so shocked—you *are* a man, aren't you?—in a manner of speaking? And so—you should be sympathetic with— It's innocence, really. Innocence on the man's part. A kind of craziness overtakes him
—as in Andrew's case—a mania—an obsession—which is the reason I
never, never have spoken against him in public—Andrew, I mean—I
seem to be always talking about him, but—and it's Christmas Eve
also, and—but no matter, no matter—I have no vanity—I've left all
shame and hypocrisy behind—no longer darling victimized weepy
Willa the betrayed wife—the helpless ex-debutante— You see? No
longer, no longer that despicable creature! You should congratulate
me, I think.

Yes— I—

My flesh simply began to sag. Couldn't help it—nobody's fault—
not his and certainly not *mine.* An innocence, really, to the entire
catastrophe. I suppose I might have aged prematurely—it runs in the
Fergus family—and my pregnancy with Michael was a difficult one—

my labor protracted and very painful—and afterward I was stretched, I wasn't the same fresh young girl Andrew had married—and though he never mentioned it—how could he, since all this is entirely un-conscious—though he never—not once—though he was reasonably at-tentive to me in certain ways—at the same time— Hugh? You're about to spill that drink, don't you see?—why are you trembling so, dear? Would you like to telephone those people and beg off? Are you feeling guilty and nervous about them? —But you *knew*, you naughty boy, that you were having dinner with me! There was never the slightest ambiguity about my invitation—never the slightest am-biguity about our feeling for each other. Never! Going back to my wedding day, to that glorious reception on the lawn—your parents' marvelous home—and you looking so boyish and sweet and shy—shaking hands with Andrew and almost dreading—I saw it, I remem-ber to this day!—almost dreading having to kiss me on the cheek, because— Well— It was obvious, dear, so obvious. People chuckled over it, in fact. But I— I never thought it was amusing—I never alluded to it, even—your attachment to me—it was something—well—not exactly sacred, I don't want to romanticize it—and I don't be-lieve in such things anyway—you should see me swim those fifty laps every morning at the club!—and afterward my hour's workout in the gym—no, no, I'm far from romanticizing anything these days—but, at the same time, there's a kind of nostalgia about it— Very real, *very* dear to me. As it is to you, evidently, since you sent those flowers and spoke of me so warmly to Michael. How very, very thoughtful of you, Hugh!—you alone of all the Petries—a vastly over-rated family, I needn't tell you—married their money in each genera-tion—very little genuine contribution to government, in spite of their reputation—but I needn't tell *you*, you've been a most vociferous critic and a very, very intriguing personality of your own. I've often thought, Hugh, that—

The invitation had come a few days earlier. Willa's mono-grammed stationery—a warm, affectionate greeting—explanation of her being in the city at this time—as if I had expected her to be elsewhere: could not recall where—Florida?—Miami Beach?—apology for not having thanked me earlier for the lovely flowers. Would I come spend Christmas Eve with her?

Telephoned Maggie and Simon, explained that something had come up. A family emergency. Sorry, very sorry!

Bought a bracelet for Willa at Cartier's—silver—like the bracelets

Yvonne had been wearing. One of their least expensive items—only fifty-five dollars—but exquisite—just the sort of thing Willa had worn in the old days. Quite pleased, pleasantly apprehensive. She was not Yvonne, of course—and yet—I remembered her with such affection—an almost husbandly affection: Willa holding the infant Michael in her arms, a wide-brimmed straw hat perched gaily on her head, a white dress, white gloves. They said that Andrew had married her for her father's money and her father's connections: could be. But she was a remarkably pretty woman, very white skin, violet-blue eyes, a charming self-effacing manner.

Park Avenue apartment. A whispery black maid—from one of the Islands, judging by her accent—an impression of wealth, warmth—odor of pine from an eight-foot evergreen in the living room—handsome French provincial furniture—gilded mirrors—thick brown carpet—radio music playing rather loudly: those ubiquitous Christmas carols. And then— And then the shock of Willa herself.

My age, or at the most a few years older: but square-bodied now, with two rough rouged spots on her cheeks—unnecessary, silly—pajama-like tunic and trousers of some odd burlap-like fabric, earthen-colored. Her voice alternately coy and subdued; rising and falling. Flirtatious—then brusque and masculine—then rearing back to giggle, girlishly—then leaning far forward, her elbows on her knees, man-to-man. The first half hour careened by me—I accepted a drink—stared at her in alarm—tried to concentrate on her rattle and rush of words—found myself stricken, depressed. And on Christmas Eve! She kept taking my hands in hers—squeezing and rubbing them harshly, as if to warm them. She kept asking me why I didn't relax—why I sat on the edge of my chair—why I didn't take off my coat, if I was so warm. Was this Willa! Willa Petrie! A woman with haywire hair, quick-darting bright blue eyes, an ungainly sway to her torso. And reeking of alcohol.

I managed to relax. Had another drink. And another. Chewed curried peanuts—black olives through which tiny stale strips of Swiss cheese had been pushed—marinated raw shrimp. I heard myself laughing from time to time. Christmas Eve! Christmas Eve! My beloved in another city—my former beloved a few feet away—on the radio "Silent Night" playing in slow motion, as if under water.

A clumsily gay exchange of presents.

Dinner served by the black girl—Willa and I at opposite ends of a fairly long table—candlelight—evergreen boughs and red bows—Christmas red-and-green linen napkins. Dry white wine. A French dish—overdone, under-spiced. Could not decipher it. Too much oil in the salad dressing. A slippery little plum tomato fell into my lap—fell onto the floor. Willa continued talking. My mind disengaged itself. Stumbled around the table—out of the room—back through the foyer—to the corridor, the French-style cage-like elevator, the immense wrought-iron doors. Freedom! Even if it is nothing but emptiness and sorrow—freedom! Freedom!

In the taxi with Yvonne again. My arm around her—brotherly, husbandly. And then my other arm. My face brought up close against hers—lowered to hers—my lips touching lightly against her cheek, as if by accident—cautiously, delicately!—no sudden false moves! We drove along Delaware Avenue, past the Capitol buildings, the square darkly lit with new snow, the monstrous high-rises of the Mall illuminated even at night—office buildings perpetually burning—monuments, shrines—the megalomania of the former Governor shamelessly on exhibit—pride, wastefulness, stupidity—and yet there was an undeniable beauty to it, at least my pulsebeat quickened as we passed: my eager face beside Yvonne's, our two faces illuminated by the reflected glare. Andrew too had wanted to build monuments to himself—great cities—city-states—Andrew too had not shied away, at least in his less conscious youth, from fantasies of immortality. Unfortunate, the fact that he had evidently grown up—had been drawing these fantasies back inside himself—unfortunate, his being shot down like a dog—

Yvonne, I murmured, Yvonne dear?—Yvonne? What did you mean, Yvonne, by saying you knew ahead of time—? You knew he would die—?

She began to shake her head. Eyes shut, forehead tensed, tiny puckers about her mouth. Would not speak. I could not resist—closed my arms awkwardly about her—rubbed my face against the side of her head, her lovely silky black hair—kissed her ear, ran my tongue around her ear, breathing hotly and delightedly, calling her my dear, my darling, whispering to her that she too was a victim—she too was marked—the Angel of Death presided over us all—presided over the numerous agents of destruction—the Angel of Death was the Governor of what we called the external world, the Governor of all these messengers, puppets—like the person or persons who killed Andrew—like the man driving this taxicab at this very moment, perhaps! The external world: a maze of quests and theorems, far more mysterious than what we made of it, we artists. Did she know? Did she guess? I alone could save her from it—

redeem her—erase from her memory the awful sight of—what must have been the awful sight of—the bullet-smashed face, the bright raw splashes of blood—the shock of running to him, running to the cabin, calling for him—screaming for him—the shock of Death in the particular—Death in the flesh—*his* death, and no other's—

Willa was innocent. Had been innocent. In Europe at the time, with her son. With friends. I too was innocent: knew nothing. Questioned by the police—examined carefully—courteously—and seen to be innocent, quite innocent. A weekend at the eastern tip of Long Island, in fact. No connection. None possible. Others were innocent—a multitude. Was she? Yvonne? Was Yvonne innocent? Struggling to get her face free from mine—breathing stroke-like stubborn breaths—coltish, rather strong for a woman—could bring her arm around and bloody my nose if she liked— I released her, wisely. I respected her too much to continue.

Alone with her, later: I would get my revenge.

Irish coffee. Pastry of many wafer-thin layers—elegant in appearance but tasteless when eaten—or perhaps my mouth was numbed from the overrich food and all the wine. Willa still talking: gossip and rumors and actual facts (long ago reported in the public press, but she didn't seem to know that) about Washington people, New York people, some already dead and some still living. I pretended to be interested—pretended out of courtesy. That the Secretary of State had once been involved in . . . that the President himself had once, in New Hampshire, after a luncheon address to a devoted gaggle of Republican women voters—that an old enemy of Andrew's from his days on the State Industrial Relations Commission had once—in an elevator in the Mitter Club—and had I known of the many lawsuits filed against Andrew?—by former associates of his on *Discourses*, who claimed he had often rewritten their essays completely while publishing them under their names, and by various victims, and by—she hesitated to disillusion me, of course—by certain members of his own family? How innocent I was! How sweet, not to know such things; to seem to be surprised by them. Ah, she knew so much—so much! But it was difficult for her to order her thoughts, at least right now. Perhaps when her life calmed down a bit, she might consider writing her memoirs. Would I advise her to do so? Or might it be too daring, too vulgarly public?

Several gunshots: one of them in the face.

Yes? What?

Memoirs!

Yes. Memoirs. —More coffee? More pastry? Yes, it's hideously sticky—and it flakes in your fingers—would you like another napkin, dear? Where *is* your napkin, dear? Didn't Bernice give you one? Ah —there!

It must be Christmas. Christmas.

Merry Christmas, dear! We must keep living, you know.

A depthless evening that neither advanced nor retreated. Why insist upon chronological experience? Sipping B & B. Sinuses cleared— sibilant. On the enormous walls enormous paintings, over the radio— hidden in a carved walnut cabinet, a copy of Andrew's—the jingly and tinkly and cutely percussive Christmas carols, Willa's bosom heaving with laughter, a tiny scared pretty face inside the crepey sagging face, glass-blue eyes darting too often away from me to consult the others—the other guests—absent, mythical—and Hugh slouched, now rarely bothering to agree or nod but, lightly drunk, fascinated with a gargoyle-fetus staring at him from the highly polished surface of a silver fruit dish (stacked not with fruit but with golden ornaments)—fascinated, thinking it might work: might be just the thing: the image he needed for a rendering of a certain public figure, on the occasion of the idiot's daring to publish the first volume of his autobiography. The assignment, alas—when had it been due?— November?—but it was only December now—so little time had elapsed—it was Christmas Eve now—six months and more since the funeral—the "death" itself abstract and not within my experience, since I had not been present. Must calculate from the actual funeral, that dance at the graveside. Willa: Willa! Did you know the dead man spoke to me from the grave? As he was being lowered into the grave? Shrieked for help—so human, suddenly—so reduced—a childlike maniacal shriek—first time in both our lives he called for me, called upon me—Help, help! Willa, refill my glass. Willa, please turn that radio down!—turn it off! I am going mad, Willa. Willa: why? Is it symbolic, you in a filmy white dress, the infant in a white blanket, your eyes living—"sparkling," one might say—hesitates to say—it sounds so hopeless, so banal. Is it symbolic, or only real?

News of my impotence broadcast "far and wide." News of my impotence "spreading like wildfire."

Willa strode to the cabinet—turned the radio's volume up a bit— "Merry Reindeer Polka"—swayed—leered at me over her arched shoulder—Shall we dance? Dance? Merry Christmas and Happy

New Year and it is our duty—our responsibility—to keep living: to keep the world turning! As he would have wanted it—yes?

Yvonne's ring. Snakes in a minuet. Were there ever such creatures in the dismal thickets of reality? On her slender leaden-blue finger? I tried to work the ring free—the finger was limp, dead, puffy—had to snap it—had to snap the bone at the knuckle—Lie still, don't scream, don't fight me! Please don't fight me!

Willa sensing the arousal of my lust. Willa's face mask ending at the jawbones; throat too wrinkled, probably, to risk makeup. A Washington debutante, centuries ago. Do you know who killed him? —who arranged it? The mask of gaiety—the mask of grief—innocence floundering as my own—the arousal of animal spirits and animal lust—Christmas Eve—must be experienced as *a good*—necessary corrective to months of mourning—the body's soul too demands its satisfaction.

Hugh? Why are you crying? *Are* you crying?

Working too late at night, the Artist's eyes water. Working for hours—hours. No hope of being appreciated. No hope of being rewarded. Monstrous effort. Selfless. Martyr—victim—butt of many jokes. The girl sprang upon me, coiled as a snake—giggled and thrashed about and moaned—theatrically, horribly—I felt her warm tongue in my mouth—shrank away— Horrible, horrible!—and the squeaking on the steps—and Andrew in his summer's outfit—darkly tanned, hair cropped short as a Marine's, mouth slithering into its famous photographed shape. Yvonne too thrashed, begged me to release her—they thrash from side to side—heads on pillows—breasts, thighs, buttocks, the surprising length and power of their legs—their feet sometimes bare, sometimes not.

Can I cup your feet in my hands? Part the toes? Kiss between them? Can I kneel—lie flat on my stomach—can I crawl out of here? Where can I hide? Sleep? Turn off the lights in my head? Must be connected to a single switch, like fluorescent lights. Can I crawl to where you are lying? Can I sleep in your massive arms? Your loose flopping breasts, the promise of your soft stomach?—where?—here?— but not here, not with the radio so loud!—no, you are misunderstanding—no, no—no: I cannot dance.

Swaying and humming. Arms crossed, bracelets gleaming (she had slipped my present on at once: sweet girl!), trousered legs approaching me. I had no spine—was slouched nearly double. Knees therefore pointed. Elbows pointed. Humming to "Hark the Herald Angels Sing"—pausing now and then to grin at me—pert, the way

half her mouth moved and the other half remained frozen—a tic become a smile—interrupting herself to ask if I knew—if I knew who
knew—who had arranged it?—and then interrupting—in mid-inter-
ruption pausing—asking what I had heard—what Harvey Petrie had
discovered—what Michael had told me about her—he exaggerated so,
he didn't give her nearly enough credit for—! Asking if I had known
about Andrew's involvement in a global organization—headquarters
somewhere in Europe—built upon the assumption that nuclear war
was unavoidable, and that men of vision and power and money
would have to rebuild civilization?—asking if he had ever spoken of it
to me? Colonies of survivors—strategically sequestered—a kind of ark
to withstand the Apocalypse—what a pessimist the man had been,
eh?—and so like a Boy Scout, boasting of his incorruptibility—the
bastard—but pathetic, unable to adjust to middle age—bastard, bastard!—she had not minded for herself but for the child it had been
traumatic: and in the midst of his absurd secret weekend confer-
ences, those scholars and scientists and sinister statesmen from
Europe, babbling in broken English about the Post-Apocalyptic
World State and how mankind would not make certain mistakes a
second time around— Did I know? Had he confided in me? It was
true that Andrew had always spoken of me contemptuously, as one
might speak of a likable fool, but—and Andrew had so often played
this game—his public contempt might have been a screen for—
    No, no. Stop. Shut up.
    —might have been a screen for—
    No, I said. No. Stop: no. And again no. We detested each other—
he I and I he—everyone knows that!—everyone!—we had nothing in
common—we did not know each other—had we met on the street,
we would not have greeted each other—would not have acknowledged each other! There were no confidences between us—no plots—
no telephone calls—no secret messages— True, it was to me he called
—shrieked for help—it was to his most sensitive, most contemplative
survivor—
    Stop whimpering! Stand up like a man! Try on your present—try
it on right now!
    —sick, sickish: had better go home—
    Hark the Herald Angels Sing!
    Willa swaying before me—eyes shut—singing in a rich throaty
voice—swaying with the music—her left knee twitching with the
percussive beat—festive girlish uninhibited sheer holiday spirits cast-
ing-off of restraints—hypocritical crust of civilization—"veneer" of—

the proud sweaty perfumed Dance of the Body—rejoice, rejoice—
glory to the newborn King! Willa singing and singing. Willa singing
Singing. Hark the Herald Angels Sing—Glory to the Newborn King!
—Peace on Earth and Mercy Mild—*God and Sinner Reconciled*—
Singing and shouting. The left knee twitching. Eyes glazed with
gaiety—cheeks running with it—tears—hers and mine—from the
radio the lively tinkling noises without variation in depth or rhythm
—from Willa the words sliding to shrieks as I cringed before them:
Joyful all ye Nations Rise! Join the Tri-umph of the Ski-ies! Now
drumming on the little cigarette table before me—both hands, both
fists—drumming pounding chanting—hair disheveled, complexion
ruddy—rivulets of tears from her glittering eyes—tiny beads of perspiration or grease on the wings of her nose—Willa, dear Willa!—one
of her sleeves torn beneath the arm—noisy ecstatic rhythm—pounding so that the table wobbled—sheer joyful sound—sheer joyful ferocity of sound—

> *With An-gel-ic Host Proclaim*
> *Christ is born in Bethlehem*
>
> *Hark the herald an-gels sing!*
>
> *God and sinner re-con-ciled!*
>
> *Joyful all ye nations rise!*
> *Join the tri-umph of the ski-ies! !*
> *With an-gel-ic host proclaim—*

Afterward?
There must have been an afterward. Must have been several.
Images: Willa toppling into my lap, my lap inadequate, my poor
bony thighs crying aloud in agony. Willa scrambling to get up—one
patent leather slipper on, the other off—a wider tear beneath her arm
—something caught in my hair—my glasses skidding along the
parquet floor. Willa pushing my hands away—sobbing—protesting—
From the radio "O Little Town of." I crawling to get my glasses—
snatching them up in triumph—forcing them on my face. Willa's
sobbing fainter—the floor wobbling—a crystal chandelier with hundreds of lights suddenly fanning into one—
What—? What the hell you doin'?
—the black woman pushed aside, the other woman pursued—
Willa, Willa! Willa! Don't harm yourself! Come back! Willa, this
is—this is a friend— Willa, please! This is Hugh! Your friend Hugh!

A bedside lamp burning—the table topped with marble—the drawer yanked open—the tiny pistol seized—

No, for God's sake! *Willa!*

—kill myself— Put an end to—

Willa! No!

Image: a man hurrying, bent over. Coat unbuttoned. Tie flapping. Under his arm a large oblong box from Gian Martino's Men's Boutique. Crossing against a traffic light—wheeling about in mid-step—delighted guffaws from an invisible audience—rummies?—young lovers strolling hand in hand on the Eve of our Savior's birth? The external world in a good humor. The external world, as always. Bernice, succulent dimples that deepened cruelly into frown lines, Bernice in an immaculate stage-maid's white outfit, Bernice shoving my coat and my gloves and my Christmas present at me—fairly lifting me across the threshold—speeding me along my merry way—*Mrs. Petrie tired-out and high-strung, these holidays too excitable for her— G'night Mr. Petrie—G'night*—one of the many strong-willed performers the external world had sent my way in recent months: did she laugh as well? Or did I imagine it?

Image: the Artist at his drawing board.

A ragged dawn. Christmas Day, the caption informs us. The Artist examining tooth marks on his hands. Imagining them? The Artist with a vile hangover, a licorish indecipherable taste in his mouth, gaseous filaments of lobster and sherry. Imagining all this? Imagining the caption that gives focus to his pain, his honest befuddlement? Impossible. One simply could not imagine so much.

29

God appeared forty-five minutes ahead of time. God in a rumpled but stylish trench coat—dark iridescent green, many straps and buckles and buttons and pockets—with a belt and a matching hat— God in galoshes in the light-falling warm rain—God waiting with the others, confident that the *Sold Out* signs are mistaken—there will be tickets available— God in disguise. Always.

Upstate New York. Friday evening.

Ah, the line is moving!

Moving, moving!

What joy!

The small pistol with the mother-of-pearl and silver inlaid, God's arbitrary choice for the evening. Always arbitrary, God's choices. Always just.

What joy!

Posters show our Senator as a mortal man: as a minor god feigning mortality. Forehead furrowed with the brave pain of thought—thin lips stretched in an ironic smile. Balding, it seems. Aging: lines radiating out from the eyes, edging the posed smile. "The United Nations: from Farce to Tragedy." Bad news. Bad news, surely. The Senator's gaze locks into God's—an uncanny moment when the two of them seem one—a single force, a single pressure. And—

But the line moves, the line is moving!

There have been cancellations—tickets returned—tickets available for devoted followers! Somehow, God anticipated this.

Am not going to act this evening. Am not—repeat not—going to fulfill the prophecy this evening. God as one of thousands, God in 441 C, $3.50, God settling in the cramped seat, wiping his damp forehead with a tissue. Smooth-shaven, pale and eager. But contemplative this evening—am not going to act this evening—not this evening. Wise. Shrewd. The grace of genius.

Woman in a dress of angora wool—too tight for her plump body— Sorry! Excuse me! I believe that's my seat! Exchange of seats. Heated —hurried. God in His human form, susceptible to jokes. On one side the panting creature in the dress—on the other side a thin, nervous man of no apparent age—thirties, fifties?—nineteen?—with a retreating face, a head sunk upon his shoulders so that his meager chins bulged—neckless—a navy blue overcoat buttoned to his chin—nervous, very nervous—shaking his foot, tapping his fingers on the buttons of his coat. God in his agentry: ubiquitous.

The auditorium fills. The universe unfolds as it must.

Far away he appears. Is introduced—strides to the lectern—begins to speak.

What dazzlement! Even God's concentration is shattered.

The abrasive confidence of the voice—the percussive words— strings of words. What is he saying? What does it mean? Why must he be killed? The old Masonic Auditorium sold out. One evening only, Friday at 8 P.M., sold out. Sold out. And yet God trickled in— the seats are packed with fate—premature applause, to mislead the

Senator—delighted howls—chuckles of sinister cruelty. The Senator in a dark gray suit. The Senator rolling forward on the balls of his feet—a habit of his—unconscious—as his voice rises and falls—dramatic, cunning. Transparent. The feel of the pistol—the handle warm—warm and damp. Finger at the trigger: safely, safely. The catch is on. God in a near-swoon—God unable to breathe. This old auditorium! This unventilated trap!

The Senator presents himself as a victim. Attacked—crudely and viciously—ignorantly—attacked by small, envious men. Attacked by men in the East, by the power structure, by the secret coalitions our false Republic has allowed to breed, unchecked. Attacked by small envious vermin and also by giants—monstrous bloated international personalities—"names too well-known to be pronounced here tonight"—attacked unfairly, unjustly. The Senator presents himself as a martyr. The Senator is interrupted by applause—and again, applause.

International coalitions. Liaisons. "Adulterous affairs" in global politics. A network of connections—the world already mapped out for plunder—before the infamous treaties of the forties were even signed. Ah, everyone knew! Audiences knew! Americans knew, could sense!—had always known. Wisdom of the common man. Basic faith in America, Americans. Ability of the common man to see through grandiloquence—through mists of rhetoric—scenarios—cynical misrepresentations of the truth—distortions and scrambled statistics and outright lies—phantasmagoria of "liberalism"—bankrupt dead-end deathly suicidal—betrayal of—

For many shall come in my name, saying I am Christ. . . . There shall arise false Christs, and false prophets . . . showing great signs and wonders. . . . A gun without bullets. But perhaps it has bullets —but the safety catch is on—there is no danger tonight. Unless History intervenes— But God and History are one. God and History sit together, in seat 441 C. In the next seat a powdery perfumy bosomy woman thumps and claps—murmurs vehement assents—her elbow reckless, rude. In the next seat a gentleman wriggles his foot—taps his fingers—pauses to crack his knuckles. A gesture of unconscious violence. Is he—? Might—? Across the aisle a woman is knitting. Knitting and nodding and smiling. A row of high school students—pens and notebooks and surprisingly alert, intelligent faces—respectful expressions—no subtle cross-glances of irony, of hate. The atmosphere is stifling—the old building not adequately ventilated—what a mistake to come here! —But of course it is not a mistake, nothing is a mistake, nothing is accidental.

What if—? But the finger presses lightly against the trigger. The hand is oddly limp, weak. Little strength to it. No danger of drawing the gun out—drawing it from the warm shelter of the pocket. No danger, no danger.

So hot, so airless!

The Senator presents himself as a historian. Objective, even rather scientific. The Senator quotes Durkheim at great length; the Senator quotes certain speeches of his enemies. There is a brief but marvelously witty history of the United Nations. There are pauses for laughter, pauses for angry indignant sighs. The Senator is an Artist: a bully. Distance modifies his deformities—makes his voice rich and deep and compelling—*I stand here before you—I am willing to testify that—I speak for the vast majority of—I am not fearful of predicting—* The vast room fills with him. His words balloon, his gestures are immortal. The audience is enraptured. Empty—enraptured. People whisper together—their eyes snatch at him—they are biting their lips—they taste blood and cannot recognize it.

The inside of the mouth: suddenly a sharp salty taste, the surprise of blood. Chewing, gnawing.

Empty—enraptured.

The Senator is a passionate man. And then he is logical—precise—quoting statistics from memory. He leans over the podium, he leans on his elbows. He walks about the stage, springy on his feet, like a gym coach, actually rubbing his hands together in exhilaration. What is he saying? Why does he say it? Why does his stocky ugly body move so well, why does his abrasive voice sound so beautiful? Why are his deformities blurred, though he exhibits himself in a spotlight? Why—

There will come a time, and there will come a time. There will come a time when all I predict will be true: and then it will be too late.

And then we will all be enslaved.

Unless—

Unless—

Behind the Senator: a wine-colored velvet curtain with gold trim. Innumerable folds. Intricacies. Framing the stage a series of panels—grape blue gold scarlet—vaguely pastoral—styleless—gods and shepherds, goddesses and milkmaids—long white gowns, long bare arms and legs, bare milky-pale feet. What does all this mean? What can it mean? Chimeras. Mischievous cheats. The Senator's voice enchants us, his perfectly modulated gestures entrap us, only he and I remain —sharing the energies of this vast, terrible place—this tomb—this relic of a bygone day—only he and I are living—united—identical.

Suppose you wanted to assassinate the Senator?
Bodyguards. Secret Service men. Inconspicuous, of course—though the local police are in their uniforms, guarding the entrances. Trembling with anticipation, are they? This small army? But nothing will happen. Nothing. The gun with the mother-of-pearl and silver inlaid will not be used; the finger will not jerk spasmodically at the trigger. Will not. God appears, God observes. God moves in His own time. And yet squirming with a nearly sexual excitement. So airless in here, the atmosphere so oppressive! Hellish, the droning of that voice—its confidence, its tone of strength and wonder—now bemused, now harsh—now flippant, now grave—God eases into God—we are united —we cannot resist—though one of us is the Father of Lies, how can we resist? Applause. The woman in the tight angora dress weeps.
Suppose you wanted to assassinate the Senator?
The waves of applause. The wave-upon-wave of his voice, his deformed soul. Suppose— If there were— The marshaling of physical objects, the organization of events— If there might be— Signs and wonders, prophetic hints, *There will come a time and there will come a time*— Suppose the time were now, this evening? Suppose the martyr-assassin were present, in his human form?—and God in His primal form? And—

The distance narrows. Only he and I remain.
Will he recognize me at the last moment?
There is a painting of Klinger's—a nightmare—paralysis of sleep— immense hideous fingers starting out of the shadows—yearning— angry half-men shout at the dreamer—trapped, trapped—trapped in sleep—in the sleep of the personality—in the sleep of history, of time— Trapped—
Waves of applause. And then screams—the applause fading suddenly—a stark silence—suddenly this silence—what does it mean? Small screams—a man's shouts—a man shouting—somewhere near the front—in the aisle—running down the aisle shouting, shouting— And then there are gunshots. Gunshots! And I rise from my seat— jump to my feet like the others, like the thousands of others— Shocked, I am. Frightened. Hopeful that— Like the thousands of

others, like the small universe of others, I am straining to see, to know—my heart is a wild-flapping creature—I am in a near-swoon and the plump woman tramples on my feet—

God in his numerous forms. Ubiquitous. Agents everywhere—everywhere.

And yet—

ASSASSINATION ATTEMPT FAILS, the morning headlines inform us.

30

Awakened to action, reluctantly. The Artist abandons his drawing board for the wide pale terrifying sky—abandons Art for Duty—flying west, westward—outdistancing the sun. United Air Lines to Los Angeles, a shuttle to Palm Springs. Post-holiday crowd. Many children. Groggy, giggling, insipid. Several instances of vomiting.

The Artist, however, is nicely drugged for the occasion. A handful of pills—tranquilizers and motion sickness—a few martinis: terror kept at a distance and the Artist drifting, dreaming, reminiscing.

Had spoken curtly to Dr. Wynand a few days earlier. Rather more humbly to Dr. Swann. (Frightened me with his sweet fatherly smile —was it a caricature, was it real?) Presented to both men my recollection of that evening in Buffalo—Andrew's speech—Andrew of years ago, nearing the peak of his career—presented it first as a dream, then as reality. Dr. Wynand did not respond. A few murmurs, unintelligible. I became unbearably angry, but controlled myself. The man did not believe me! Did not believe me! Did not believe me capable of—of— I repeated that everything had happened just as I had told him. Yes, it had happened. In actual fact, in actual reality. *It had happened.*

Dr. Wynand guarded, polite. But he did not believe me. Asked a few questions—chose to pursue the totally irrelevant fact that a plump, matronly woman had been seated beside me—asked me about her, about my emotions or associations with her—*her!*—as if the entire experience had been nothing but a dream, to be broken into its component parts and analyzed.

That son of a bitch!

Denying me my reality! My soul!

With Dr. Swann I was less dramatic, my presentation of the experience more forceful, in my opinion, simply because I spoke in quiet, urbane tones. And with Dr. Swann one sits facing him—there is eye contact—awkward and embarrassing at times—at other times helpful, if one is anxious to show how he speaks the truth. Dr. Swann believed me, I think. Questioned me gently, intelligently. Ignored the defensiveness in my voice—which I could not help—still rankled by Dr. Wynand's obtuseness—and asked me precisely what the purpose of my trip to Buffalo had been. I tried to explain—stumbled over my own words—breathless, impatient—but he kept nodding sympathetically, kept his eyes fixed to my face—and somehow I managed to convince him. Yes, I had actually gone to Buffalo, New York —I, who travel so rarely, who detest the very idea of traveling—of sleeping overnight in a strange bed—I, impoverished as usual! Had been in Albany for family reasons, had heard the excited talk of Andrew this and Andrew that, Andrew one weekend in Houston and another in Seattle, Andrew to appear close to home in a few days— and then—and then— Then— It was so short a flight from Albany to Buffalo, so easy a thing to do— A kind of alibi, also. They would certainly believe I had flown back to New York. Would swear to it. An ingenious plot, wasn't it?—the work of an artist—and yet basically playful, not at all serious. Because I had never intended to shoot. Because I didn't even have a gun. That was the delicious, fascinating, mysterious thing about the entire event— *I hadn't a gun, I hadn't intended to hurt him at all.* (Or did I have a gun? To Dr. Wynand I might have said I had one—in order to convince the son of a bitch. To Dr. Swann, I didn't need that particular detail; and in mid-sentence it occurred to me that this gentle, wise, sympathetic creature might very well decide to turn me over to the police—or blackmail me—if I convinced him too well.) Ah, what did it matter?—a gun or not? A gun very much like poor Willa's, or not? The essence of the plot was its whimsicality—its sheer spontaneous action—overflow of imaginative energy: the Artist following the thread of a queer private dream, unafraid of the labyrinthian risks. And then—

The extraordinary coincidence, of course.

The coincidence that on that very evening—in that very audience —a would-be assassin would spring from his seat—run out into the aisle—would wave a gun and shoot several shots—wildly— Would make an attempt on my brother's life— A pathetic creature disarmed at once, wrestled to the floor, beaten and kicked—and hauled away (to his death: such was the price my brother and his henchmen ex-

acted from that man)— A coincidence, a remarkable coincidence—
  Had anything like it ever taken place in the annals of history?
  Dr. Swann did not answer that question. But he was respectful,
even curious. At the conclusion of the hour I stood to leave—briskly
—not a moment beyond the fifty minutes would I claim—and it was
obvious that he wanted me to continue—had many more questions
to ask.
  Such coincidences must happen often in your life, Hugh?
  I thought a moment. Then said: Yes. Yes, they do. In fact—yes.
How did you know?
  He smiled mysteriously.
  The world is so constructed, he said, that there is a network of relationships invisible—inaccessible to experience—if one has not an
awakened imagination. Certain artists, however—
  Artists—?
  The imagination, you see— It penetrates the surface of ordinary
reality, it sometimes waves aside the mists of what is known as "com-
mon sense"—and discovers certain patterns, certain non-causal
events— And so, since you are an artist, I assumed that you were
sensitive to such seeming coincidences—that you would note them, I
mean, while other people missed them entirely.
  Yes. Yes. But—
  Not a moment past my fifty-minute hour: I did not dare: I fled.

  Around the hero, it is said, everything turns to tragedy.
  And around Hugh Petrie?
  Comedy, cruel hissing laughter. The audience gaped—gasped—
clapped their hands to their mouths—witnessing the son's near-
collapse into the aged parent's embrace. Poolside, chemical-blue
water, mountains in the near-distance looking like travel posters—
shameless and insignificant, such mammoth beauty—and an eerie
too-white sun that made my eyes water. Father's poolside acquaintances gasped audibly, but had the grace not to burst into
laughter. Later, perhaps.
  It had been such a shock, you see—such a shock! Not the sight of
Father—who had of course aged—who was now a withered wearing-
down bodiless little gnome in green plaid bathing trunks and a
cherry-pink robe, wisps of white hair stirring on his skull, baby-blue
eyes sunk deep into his ravaged face—not the sight of him, not at all
—for in fact I had dreaded something far worse: but the impact of
my own feelings. Why? What was wrong? I saw him—recognized

him before he recognized me—began to stumble—to weep— *Father, what are they doing to us? What are they doing?* I tripped over something—a woman's big straw purse—and then Father was on his feet, wiry as always, and grasping my hand, my arm—helping to keep me upright while pretending only to greet me.

What was wrong, what was wrong? I did not break down. It was a shock, of course, but I did not break down. Sudden emotion—uncharacteristic of me—distressing, embarrassing. That bitch Doris had led me to believe the old man was doddering—might not have long to live—hadn't she told me he was using a walker last time she'd visited?—but he seemed lively and chirrupy enough, far friendlier than in the old days. Grasped my forearm so hard it hurt. Pumped at me, greeting me loudly enough so that the entire terrace would know he had a visitor: a son: one of the surviving Petrie sons.

Hugh, my boy! Hugh! I thought it was *next* Saturday you were coming!

A magnified sun, like a spotlight. You can't turn it off. Father glaring with Fatherliness: the terrifying insult of his enamel teeth. Has he become a salesman?—a self-made millionaire?—a Democrat? Yet —my God!—I happened to see, shoved partway beneath a towel on the chair beside him, a book the cover of which was familiar—bright red splotches, like blood—what was it?—had glimpsed it in a bookstore not long ago—picked it up, leafed through it—chuckling—my superior chuckle is thought to be my least offensive trait—crafty, sensitive, childlike, coy—ah yes: *The Plot to Take Over America, a privately subsidized investigation into the Assassinations of the Sixties and Seventies.* By one "Lawrence R. Bayley-Shuster." Published by "Gettysburg Press," somewhere in Maryland. Who had planned it, who was planning it still, who would gain the most from it, every aspect of *it?*— I had skimmed the book quickly, indifferently. Returned it to the shelf. A step backward, and the shelf bulged—the shelves bulged—with similar books: thirty, forty, seventy-five, possibly a hundred titles jammed in together. Each claimed to have solved the mystery of—

Hugh? Wasn't it *next* Saturday—?

Was it? No—no, I don't think—

Otherwise I would certainly have— You must think me rude or senile—

Rude or senile—? But I—

Led me away. An obstacle course of gaily striped canvas chairs of all sizes, all styles, in various stages of reclining—women's legs in various stages of blue-veiny deterioration—and men's legs as well—some puffy and dough-white, others scorched pink, some like sticks and some like—well—I did not stare long, I looked away at once as if having seen something forbidden: what tubs of flesh! what sorrow! Yet Father noticed nothing, Father still gripped my arm, asking about the flight—asking about the family—how well were they adjusting to the tragedy?—and the poor widow, the poor dear broken creature—and the boy Michael—that delicate child—

Father somewhat dwindled, shorter than I remembered. But not very ill: dismayingly healthy, in fact. Not nearly so pompous, judicial, so archetypally vain and censorious—was this really Theodore Petrie, retired from the State Court of Appeals, where he had served for decades?—chattery creature with a caved-in chest, an odd little bloated belly, the slight whiny edge of an accent—how perverse, Father's acquisition of a slight New York accent, out here in Southern California!—where of course he had come merely to die. He was deeply tan, especially on the arms; from a certain angle he had a sinister pygmyish look.

I was still trembling with emotion: did I love him after all?

Not possible.

Aged egg-pale man/woman, wearing a cap with a green plastic visor pulled onto its head, low over the forehead. Must be nearly one hundred years old. In attendance, a middle-aged nurse, puffy pumpkin-colored curls, open-toed sandals. There, Father whispered, there by the shuffleboard court—but don't look, don't be obvious about it!—there is—

My God, is it—?

You thought he was dead, eh? Father giggled. Oh yes: people think all sorts of things. But he isn't dead—he'll outlive us all. Remarkable, isn't it? Remarkable! Like gazing upon a chapter of history itself—like flipping through an entire book—an entire epoch. Everybody thinks he's dead and what a surprise it is, to be led up to him and introduced!—we don't stand on ceremony here at Joshua Tree, once you've been admitted to the colony. A very very surprising and livening place. —Hugh, for God's sake don't stand and gape! No Petrie was ever overwhelmed with awe for another person—not even royalty—not even historic personages. You're old enough to know that, aren't you?

But isn't he protected? Aren't there— There must be Secret Service men everywhere—

Not at all, Father said, we do things differently here: electronic surveillance, closed-circuit television, no one allowed in this part of the Manor unless he's been thoroughly screened, or a guest like yourself. If only poor Andrew—! If only he had listened to warnings—! But, you see, he was stubborn: and he had to fulfill his own tragic destiny, which no one could have prevented. Ah, history!—the demands it makes upon us, upon even ordinary mortals like myself!

Muttering, smiling, smacking his lips. The pink terrycloth robe had fallen open; his dry, dark skin was gathering itself into goose pimples. Impulsively, he hugged me. Or rather tried to: I stepped hastily aside, startled. He laughed in dismay—stared at me—baby-blue eyes like none I had ever glimpsed before—and ended by hugging himself in great excitement.

History—! You see—? It isn't—can't be—there is no way to— Fate —destiny—greatness—the synthesis of circumstance and personality— That gentleman in the wheelchair—and other great generals—heads of state—monarchs—prime ministers—presidents—and our Andrew, our Andrew among them—you see? It isn't—cannot possibly be— History— Cannot possibly and humanly be—be *understood!*

Yvonne beside me, Yvonne stroking my offended flesh. Yvonne ignoring the savage beauty of the sky, the mountains, the palm trees, the ornamental cacti—inclining her head toward mine, her lustrous dark eyes fixed upon mine, upon me exclusively: upon *me*. While the old man babbled about Andrew, making us elaborate drinks— chattering and sighing and wiping his nose slyly on the terrycloth robe—prancing—delicately calling my attention to the shrine in the living room—the old fool!—while he spoke of his survival of the shock of the assassination and his (and here he quoted the Manor's resident psychotherapist) re-emergence into the land of the living— his spiritual rebirth—rebirth! the old bastard!—his defeat of unnatural grief—his sloughing-off of personal mourning and his acceptance of impersonal and national and simply *human* mourning for a great man—only incidentally his son: that must be stressed—while he jabbered incoherently I summoned Yvonne to my side to see how I suffered, what distances I had traveled merely to suffer this final insult.

Why, the apartment was a museum—the living room especially— the walls hung with gravely mounted photographs of *him*, some

starkly black and white, rather exquisitely powerful—artistic, even—
one might be forced to say; some in impossible colors, shading toward
the violet, an ethereal cast to Andrew's square-jawed face. No, no.
And again: no. I refused to look after that first astonished minute.

Grief, you see. Grief—personal and impersonal—selfish and
supraselfish—do you see, Hugh? I've come to terms with it. With
all of it. Life—death—being a father, a son, a widower—seeing that
person as an infant—as a child—as a young man—as a mature adult:
seeing him, experiencing him, not simply as a father (for he might
have been born of any father, Hugh!—of any mortal parents!) but as
a man, a human being. I've come to terms with it. A very difficult
task—very! Almost killed me, the assassination, the terrible way in
which—the abruptness of—all the more horrible in that he and I had
not, as you know, been in close agreement on certain matters—or
didn't you know?—that unfortunate business about Marshall Frank
—the land-investment business—the conflict of interest—that sort of
thing—a very commonplace sort of thing, as everyone knows—
everyone but Andrew, of course. Too scrupulous at times. Rather
wooden—puritanical—priggish, I believe I called him once—in jest,
really—but of course we all wished Andrew might have been more—
if not more forgiving—at least more *unaware* of the private lives of
his friends and associates and admirers. Too bad, too bad! And yet it
was his fate, you see?—the glory—ecstasy—tragic horror—catastrophe
for the entire nation— Hugh? Is something wrong? Is the drink too
strong, or not strong enough? Are you shaky from the flight? Or is it
—is it Andrew's presence?

Yvonne beside me, stroking my arm. My soft fine silky hair. Whispering to me that all is well: I at least am not insane. *I* am not insane. The old man sits rather abruptly. Ice cubes clinking. Still in his
swimming trunks and that ghastly robe, wearing toe-strap sandals
that appear to be made of foam rubber. He is seventy-seven years
old, I believe. My old enemy: now a stranger.

Yvonne, the desert surrounds this place on all sides. Yvonne, who
was it said the desert is God without man? So beautiful! But I can't
get to it. Am confined with a lunatic—sipping a scarlet fruit drink
laced with vodka—sniffing, shuddering, hoping not to break down—
stared at from all sides by *him*, by the dead man, his face on every
wall—glaring self-righteous piggish eyes—him—he—it—that we imagined we had buried back in June. The desert air is uncanny, frightful.
So clear—stark—dry. It is January, and yet summer—it is summery,

and yet a terrible chill underlies everything—as soon as the sun sets, it will be cold. Yvonne—

Your grandfather was a martyr too, Father said suddenly. No one knows—he didn't want it known—and of course I respected his wishes—but— It wasn't ill health alone that forced him to step down, Hugh. His heart was weak, yes, but that wasn't the entire story. And it wasn't just betrayal either—though of course Theodore Roosevelt did betray him—cut him, most horribly—no manners, no sense of humanity—a brute, really—as everyone knows. Your grandfather had given so much—of himself—and financial aid as well—so generous in setting up the Academy for Eugenics Research—and of course the other great families of the nation pitched in—some openly, some anonymously—ah, those were the days, Hugh!—the new century barely begun, and the future so marvelous—so open to the imagination—*who* could have predicted the outcome? Relaxation of immigration laws—union agitation—amateurish handling of war —and it was a hop, skip, and a jump to the income tax and the New Deal and—and garbage-strewn streets—and Andrew dead in the prime of life. Fate—martyrdom—the price that must be paid for— for—

For being a Petrie?

He stared at me. Grinned. Repeated: *For being a Petrie.*

Yvonne:

This postcard cannot quite convey the sharp, acrid
beauty of this part of the world. Why do I think
of you, constantly? Wish only to love you? Again?
Love you once again? I loved you then, that night.
And it must happen again—it must! Again and again.
Don't be frightened of me, of it. Don't be frightened.
I would not hurt you, I love you. I think of you
constantly, for some reason when I am enduring my
father—his madman's babble!—then more than ever
I think of you, dream of you, lunge into you and—
and am kept from despair. My dear: please don't
deny me.

I had not said that, really. Those words: "for being a Petrie." Father mumbled and faltered and could not remember what he was saying—and I avoided his eye, I stared morosely at the red Spanish tile at my feet—sipped the drink in my hand. Silence. Let him complete his own thoughts.

—price that must be paid for—for—

A long pause. He sighed, drank. In his seventy-eighth year now—a miracle he had been allowed to live so long—my old enemy, my old disappointment, my mother's killer. But he had lived: most of them do. Now an elderly gentleman and *naturally* to be respected, admired, pitied, loved.

—price that must be paid for—for— Being a Petrie, I suppose.

I laughed suddenly. Giggled. How quaintly he had put it!—how unchanged everything was!

31

Unchanged, unchanged. . . .

Except for small puzzling things—tricks and quirks of the imagination—probably due to the ear infection I had had since Christmas Eve—or, more precisely, Christmas morning. Woke with it, my head pounding. Slight indigestion—the usual hangover following a night of such merriment—my eyes bleary, watery—and the beginning of a violent earache. Had she socked me on the side of the head, struggling to get the little revolver back? No, I think it was just the wind afterward. Ferocious city wind—a galaxy of winds—rushing along the streets, tunneling between the buildings, hungry to devour us all. How precarious our hold on—

But now I was in Southern California: and it was summer.

And in the background, beyond Father's frightening monologue, I heard stray inexplicable noises—the kind of noises I had been hearing for some time—had heard, in fact, the night I brought Yvonne home—almost inaudible, certainly indecipherable—the sounds of someone else in the room—invisible people bumping into things—passing quite near me. In my own apartment, even. At my drawing board. In bed. If I glanced around peevishly or boldly or angrily—if I allowed these creatures to know I was aware of them—it did no good at all. Sometimes the noises quieted for a few seconds; then they began again, as always. Of course it was all imagination. . . . Or, better yet, it had an organic basis: the ear infection. And it had not been my experience that, as my eyesight deteriorated, my hearing improved. Perhaps that is an old wives' tale . . . ? That the blind necessarily develop excellent hearing . . . ? It certainly wasn't my experience.

Joshua Tree Manor is the best thing that's ever happened to me, Father was saying. Now more subdued; now seated on a striking piece of furniture—a love seat with a fierce red cushion—heavy carved wood—Spanish design—massive-footed, sleepily sadistic, the kind of thing I would have loved for my own apartment. Brutal, corny, "beautiful"—a work of art in itself. Father sat there, legs crossed, puny and sweet and elfin rather than paternal. Ah, I had feared him for so many decades!—was it possible I had been mistaken? Or was I mistaken now? The pills, the martinis, the flight across the continent had somewhat unsettled me—my natural powers of observation were diminished. Father seemed to sense this, to speak clearly and loudly, as one might speak to a child. Yes, he said, sighing, yes, Joshua Tree Manor is the *best* thing that's ever happened to me.

The very best thing? I asked.

The *very* best thing.

Inconsequential images floated by: Father in his judge's robes, Father dining with the Governor, Father (this image out of a photograph) standing proudly beside his lovely bride. And Father holding an infant in his arms—any infant at all. He had had four. But such images struck me as only sentimental, what had they to do with Palm Springs?—with the marvelous clear dry sunny air, with the elegant palm trees and the blue pools and the high-rise apartment buildings? A nursing home disguised as a luxury hotel? What had they to do with me, sick with love, uncertain even of the exact arrangement of my beloved's features? Forty years old, was this it?—adulthood?—*this*? A seventy-seven-year-old gentleman faced me, in a pink robe, swinging his foot, informing me of the fact that nothing in his past was quite as meaningful as his present: moving his hand to take in the walls of this room, upon which my late brother Andrew had been affixed, in various stages of his life. I did not look —refused to look—but was aware of the curious, uncanny fact that Andrew's face—or faces—was always *unconscious*: that is, unconscious of the reality we now possessed, Father and I, having lived beyond the day of Andrew's death, knowing far more than he knew—poor boy. The advantages we, the living, have over the dead, *those others*, struck me as disturbing—somehow embarrassing. And shameful. Unfair, really, that anyone should survive anyone else even for a few minutes—

I've found God, Father was saying softly.

Found—?

God. Here. In this place.

Yvonne:

It is to be gradually revealed that the Hero of my Narrative
does not exist: is experienced by others in terms of random
paragraphs (of the approximate size newspaper editors demand)
that do not necessarily connect; or as random smears on
a wall—the slightly phosphorescent gleam of bygone cock-
roaches, dealt with frankly and directly by previous tenants.
Timid, like all angry artists, I came West not simply to fulfill
a kind of Christmas duty—not simply to obey my sister's
demands—or even to protect my right as an heir (the bulk
of it is in iron ore deposits near Lake Champlain, as you
must know—*from my mother's family* and not from the
Petries)—and not even out of filial love (which I suppose I feel,
being human as well as a monster): but for a revelation.

Do you believe me? Can you understand me? Are you even
reading this, or have you tossed it aside in disgust?
Does the memory of me as your lover upset you?—intimidate
you?—excite you? And—?

But it is true nevertheless. Or was true. I came to this
place for a revelation—I came to my aged, dying father for a
revelation. (In thinking back upon the events of the last six
months, I am forced to see that I've gone to many people—or
they have come to me—for revelations. And with what results?)

My father has found God: and thereby erased history.
Erased me. Andrew is reduced to photographs and newspaper
clippings—formidable in their own way, but hardly the
Andrew of old—hardly the crusading prince—hardly my brutal,
indefatigable brother—hardly your vigorous lover. *I've found
God*, Father told me, *and why shouldn't you? It may be
your time.*

Nothing changed, nothing. Nothing. Nothing ever changes.
Except—
Stayed in Palm Springs for three days. Guest room of Father's
well-appointed, costly, rather cubicule-like apartment—noted the oxy-
gen tank in the master bedroom—the hospital bed disguised as an ordinary bed, with a detachable crank at its foot—an immense closet of
supplies—linens—a bedpan or two—apparatus for IV fluids and
transfusions—a telephone in the headboard of the bed, direct line to
the emergency ward—evidently one of the Manor buildings, one-
story like a handsome resort motel, with red-orange Spanish tiles—all
very handsome, comforting. The Manor has its own golf course—

which appeared to my amateurish eye as rather abbreviated—though perhaps for the aged and infirm it was real enough—several chapels— a small theater where previews of new Hollywood movies are shown —an outdoor pool, an indoor pool—a small gymnasium where exercise bicycles face color television sets—the walls beautifully decorated with murals of Mexican landscapes and Mexican villages and "peasants"—swarthy husky male and female beauties. Attendants everywhere, in white. Doctors and nurses and physiotherapists disguised as resort managers, tennis professionals, masseurs. In the distance mountains like stage props: beyond beauty. Too grand, too compelling. Like everyone else I soon forgot them—no longer saw them. Homesick for the dreary view from my window—from my drawing board, center of the universe—displaced, here, at the center of the desert—my ear aching relentlessly, my eyes watering, my face set in a mask of incredulous unsatirical *interest* as Father babbled. Three days: quite enough.

Courteous. Detached. Respectful as always. Introduced as the "eldest living son." Seated in the Manor's elegant dining room, in charge of the wine menu (Father claimed to defer to my taste: liked to hear me prattle in French), reasonably sober. Rising, shaking hands, murmuring agreeable words. Yes, it was certainly a tragedy. Certainly was. But the FBI will certainly. And the various investigative agencies. Certainly. A crime of such magnitude: certainly cannot be allowed to repeat itself. The widow? Do I know her well? Has she recovered from the shock and the grief? Which widow? Ah yes: she is certainly mending as well as can be expected.

God, Father whispered, God came to me here.

Here?

One night—not long after *it* happened—God appeared to me—in white—I was dying, suffocating, clawing at my chest to get free—to be able to breathe— Oh Hugh: what terrors await us! Unless God intervenes—

Here, Father? Surely you jest: we're in the dining room.

Here, Hugh. The attack came upon me *here*. *Here*. At this very table. This very table! —A long marvelous dinner with delightful friends—new friends—one of them no longer with us, sad to say—a liver case—the kind that really can't be treated, you know—medical science has yet to—hasn't yet—penetrated all the mysteries of nature. But you know this, you're a New Yorker and so well-read! Another of my friends—a wonderful, wonderful young woman—physiotherapist specializing in water treatments—massage of a very special sort involving gentle caressing multistreams of water—various temperatures—*very* complex, just in the stages of being developed as a technique—another dear friend, a companion of that fateful night, no longer with us either: I would have liked you to meet her, Hugh. But frankly— Frankly, after my experience—nearly dying like that—at this very table—at the conclusion of a marvelous rich two-hour dinner—black cherries jubilee the last thing I clearly remember— Frankly, Hugh, I changed my way of living: renounced certain habits. Nearly dying—not knowing how deeply distressed I was—by my poor son's death and my wife's needless, needless death years ago —needless!—and very selfish—but we won't go into that, I've forgiven her—I've forgiven everyone who has wronged me. Nearly dying and being rescued—resuscitated—raised from the dead by Our Lord—in the form of a machine—His presence revealed to me as a white, glowing, throbbing, palpitating, throbbing, *living* machine— surrounded by agents, mere men, mortals, men and women in white —agents of God—angels of God—wired to do His bidding (as we all are, Hugh: never doubt)—frankly, that experience changed me—altered my thinking completely—forced me to see that certain habits of mine—certain practices—had to be abandoned. And so— And so, you see— You see before you a different man—humbler, wiser, happier. The woman—the women— That particular woman, a very wonderful person, I want to stress how wonderful she was—is—from a most pathetic background, like so many of them—so many of the ones I've met—that particular woman, whom I would have liked you to meet, Hugh, there's nothing secretive or underhanded about your poor old father *now*—she left Joshua Tree not long afterward, anyway—eloped with one of our most distinguished old gentlemen—and what a commotion, when his children showed up!—and their lawyers!—and private investigators! For they were very angry, you know: very. Not at all like you and Doris might have been under similar circumstances—you would want your poor old father to marry again and be happy, of course—I assume—and matters of money, of inheritance, that sort of thing—quite beside the point—embarrassing even to mention—I won't pursue the unpleasant subject any further, except to say that other children are not nearly so magnanimous! But she and I had already gone our separate ways, you see, at the moment God appeared to me—forced me to realize the error of my ways—of my past life. Now all, all is changed—*all*. I will be leaving most of my estate to— Ah, Hugh, you're so young: so young! If only— You can't have the slightest idea of what I mean, can you? So young—a mere boy—boyish—your face so perpetually innocent, as if you've never actually lived—as if you've been in preparation for it, observing, taking notes—that sort of thing—all in preparation for, for—

Father, I said quietly, Father, I said softly, Father: wait. You were saying a moment ago—

Our olive-toned springy poppet-waiter glided by—leaned over my shoulder—inquired if all was well at this table? Eh? Gave off a scent of salty warmth that would ordinarily have upset me—but his timing was bad, disastrous.

Father, I said hoarsely, you were—

Even before the tragedy of Andrew's death, Hugh, I hadn't been well. The years seemed to be dismantling me, part by part. Dismaying to be old—to discover oneself suddenly *old*—the body, so long a friend—friendly—now a stranger—indifferent and hostile. You're so young, in such fine health, you can't know what I mean! But when your mother died—in that horrible, horrible way— Of course it was hushed up, it had to be—not only for reasons of the insurance—and what a hard time those bastards gave us!—*us!*—not only for those reasons but because of—well—her family's reputation—her reputation—ours as well—not to mention poor Andrew, just getting started with his career, poor boy, uphill all the way—and with what results! But—you see—my point is—after your mother's death—after her cruel and quite public revenge on me—much of my life lost its meaning: the honors that gradually came to me, well-deserved though they were, and the good fortune in the stock market—and investments of various kinds—just ashes in my mouth, Hugh: mere ashes! My pride in Andrew kept me going to some extent. I loved Doris, as one must—a dear, dear girl; and Stephen—well, we will not speak of Stephen here—poor deluded boy!—but I wash my hands of his delusions—let *his God* pamper him. And you—always loved you, always—always—have great faith in you yet—so promising, people say —if only—but—this is no place for—no place for admonitions or advice or—and perhaps your life does actually please you, in ways difficult for the rest of us to appreciate—but I have always loved you, Hugh, as a father loves his son, no matter the son's position in life. I hope you know that! And so I did discharge my obligations as a parent to the fullest extent of my abilities—and I worked very, very hard on the bench, as everyone except my enemies will admit—but—but still—in spite of all this— The worldliness of the world had quite captivated me, you see, and I didn't know—how could I have known, until tragedy overcame me?—that it was mere ashes, ashes in the mouth—*ashes*. Until God appeared.

God, I repeated. God?

Yes—you see—at this very table—

God, at this very table?

Yes!

And has He returned?

He never leaves me, Hugh. A constant presence—assurance—

You are leaving your money to Him?

—His mere agents, Hugh. Agents—angels. Call them what you will: they performed His bidding, snatched me back from death. In my death trance God spoke to me: actually spoke to me: suggested that, when I awakened, I sign over my estate to Him. And of course—

God spoke to you? And suggested—?

But I am also, I have already invested a greal deal of—a number of us here, after Andrew's—after that most recent atrocity—a number of us, shocked and angry about the way Western civilization is going, have formed a kind of organization—no charter, of course—no lawyers—nothing official—hoping to finance a long-range investigation of—of the entire situation—a number of us got together on the shuffleboard court one day, and we've already invested a fair amount —a kind of communal citizen's venture—vigilante action—that sort of thing. But, yes, the bulk of the estate, what remains, must necessarily be willed elsewhere. The situation is a grave one, Hugh, involving the salvation of souls both in history and in eternity—do you see? You look so incredulous, so pale! But it's quite simple, really. From a certain angle. From God's angle, you see, *it's always simple*. Only in time, only in history, does man make a fearful mess of things. Mankind!—what sorrowful jokers! But God, you see, God knows all and forgives all and accounts for all—God is a perpetual presence—a throbbing palpitating humming living *presence*—without which, one single moment—one single moment, Hugh—we collapse: we are in hell.

Yes? Hell? Yes.

32

Even so, seeing me off, the old bastard could not resist clutching at my arm: asking me one final question.

Hugh, do you know—? Do—?

Know what?

—who was responsible?

Responsible for what?

Courteous as always, I was: but not overly helpful.

Do you know who—who might have— Assuming for the moment that— Excluding for the moment— Of course it isn't possible, and yet—history so often surprises—baffles— It's crossed my mind from time to time that—

Father, really. What the hell are you talking about?

—that— Well: that someone might know. Might have an idea. I have prayed and prayed for—hoping for— We have all, I suppose, been hoping for—the proper sort of enemy, let's say: and not just Harvey, by any means, though of course Harvey has the most to gain. And so—it crossed my mind—dining with you the other evening, noticing how you reacted to—to certain disclosures—how peculiarly you reacted to any mention of Andrew's poor widow—poor dear Willa!—and of course there's the new one—of whom I somehow don't think—just don't think: must be old age. But it crossed my mind that—in some way—

That I might know who killed my brother?

—arranged for, had a stake in— No. But yes: yes. Do you—?

Why, I said, sneering, couldn't resist sneering, looking with contempt upon a tanned wizened dandyish creature in sunglasses, lips trembling with the audacity of what he asked—asked *me*, of all people: couldn't resist sneering as I said, why, Father, it was God. God's will. How could you doubt? God—God's angels—agents, angels—ask Him if you want to know—ask *Him*, and leave me out of it! From now on!

33

Yvonne, dearest, I'm telephoning from another dimension—from hell—in fact, yes: hell—this is your brother-in-law, Hugh—Hugh Petrie—your knight, your slave, your lover—don't you recognize my voice at least? Yvonne? Dear? I'm telephoning from nowhere—the snowy wastes of Nebraska—can you hear me?—is my voice, my desperation, coming through?—Yvonne? *Yvonne?*—I'm telephoning from Okanogun, Nebraska—from the airport here—our plane has been forced down—blizzard—ice on wings—near-death, near-disaster

—in the morning you might have languidly opened the *Times* to read of—might have skimmed the list of names—yawning, unprepared for— Yvonne? What has happened to our connection? Operator? Yvonne? Isn't anyone listening?

Yvonne entered me through the eyes.

If thine eye delight thee—? But how to stop the deterioration? Weak eyes as a boy—the only child in the family, for many years the only one with glasses—among the innumerable cousins, those healthy beasts! James Gillray feared blindness, eye disease. Biographers thought him neurotic. Worse. Raving mad, at the end. But perhaps—it wasn't impossible—perhaps real disease, organic dysfunction? Does the soul direct such feats, or only know of them? Only suffer them helplessly?

Pushed Father out of my mind. His bright-white smile, his blood-thready eyes, whiff of cologne and after-shave lotion to disguise the greeny medicinal odor. Decaying from the inside out. Rotting from the top down, like Jonathan Swift, another of my masters. His babble—distressing to hear—must resist. What had he said of Mother?— the senile old bastard!

He killed her: he and no one else.

Will never forgive him. Never.

Will never think of him.

Small crisis—weeping uncontrollably—lavatory in airport outside Fort Preston, Kentucky (plane again forced down: the same blizzard following us east)—on an impulse extending New Year's greetings—a bit late, of course—but cheerfully and no-strings-attached—extending greetings to sweet-scholarly young man whom I had noticed on the plane a few seats ahead—reminded me of myself at that age: innocent, abashed, sensitive, doomed. Was repulsed. Viciously. Alone, weeping suddenly—out of control—thinking of Father, of Mother, of my failure as an artist, as a son, as a man, as a lover—thinking of Yvonne, hardly able to recall her face—and her body!—so elusive, so fantastically remote even while I was clambering upon it!—trying in desperation to console myself, to caress my*self*—and limp, hopeless, teat-sized, doomed. The end. Nothing to follow.

But—

A succession of dreams.

Unruly, vivid. Horrible. Yet fascinating in a way—caught myself

wanting to take several sleeping pills, just to get back—back into *it*.
Secrets to be revealed—mysteries to be explained—salvation—bliss?—
who can tell?

A far more clever artist resides in me!—diabolical at times. But
bliss awaits—I am sure—if I can interpret him correctly.

Undifferentiated midwinter days. January still? Yes. The longest
month of creation. Opened the *Times* one morning, hoping for a
few pinpricks of shock—luscious thrills of dismay—heart-sinking sensation that allows one to know (even in my tranquilized state) that
one is *alive*: despite the routine disasters abroad and near at hand,
to which we have become anesthetized. Hopeful, expectant. And not
disappointed: for there was a Petrie headline. *Petrie!* My eye leaped
to it, my heart lurched in that direction—

New Arrests in Petrie Case

Eleven people—seven men, four women—between the ages of
nineteen and thirty-four—arrested in a pre-dawn raid—surprised in a
farmhouse north of Milford, Pennsylvania, by FBI and state police:
members of a ring allegedly involved in recent bombings in the Philadelphia and New York City areas. No one was killed in the raid—
two people were wounded. FBI and police releasing few details—
secrecy surrounds—but a reporter for the *Times* was told that—

After the first spurt of excitement I calmed: went cold.

Tall tales, of course. Hoked-up arrests—fabricated news releases—
fantasies concocted by—by who?

The Government?

But—*which* "Government"?

Doris believes it: Doris rabid, hysterical, incoherent.

Maoists! She knew all along! Everyone knew! Andrew knew!—
would have known!—could have predicted!—probably *had* predicted!

How sweet for Harvey, I breathed into the phone.

Hung up.

Hideous dreams. A gigantic woman: body lithe, voluptuous, muscular. And her long dark hair!—could be smothered in it, groaning
and thrashing. Help me! Hold me! Tight!—tighter! But don't hurt
me—don't suffocate—

Left a message with Yvonne's answering service.

Please telephone me at once. At once! No more delay! No more of
your coyness, your female tricks! *I know you.*

Telephoned Pamela. Learned to my astonishment that something had evidently happened to her—New Year's Eve—an accident of some sort—the maid who answered the phone evasive, curt. But—! What was wrong? No details: Pamela away on vacation, a friend's villa in the Barbados, or in the Bermudas, or somewhere. Expected back when? No information, no details. But could I speak to her husband? Out of town. Madrid. And then Barcelona, and then Milan. And Rome. Business trip—would be gone a month—might even have to fly to Sydney, Australia. But where was Pamela, what had happened to her? What sort of accident? An automobile, or—?

Mz. Bausch not available at the present time. Sorry.

But is she— It isn't serious—?

Sorry.

Telephoned Willa. Michael answered: eager, as if hoping for another call. Subdued when I identified myself. Willa was in Palm Beach now—"not a moment too soon"—he was sorry he had been unable to join us on Christmas Eve—very very sorry, indeed—but Willa was recovering now, sounded as if she were in high spirits, Michael called her every evening, he'd give her my fondest best wishes. But could not divulge her number. Sorry. Hoped I would understand.

But I—

Changed the subject eagerly, and spoke of the arrests: the mystery solved at last! And so beautifully! Radicals—unfortunately all white —but radicals indeed, declared Maoists—of a peculiarly North American type—indicted not just for the murder of Andrew but for a number of violent acts—attempted extortion—and one of the cell members, a female, had a record going back to childhood—for *lewd and lascivious behavior*—could anything be more poetically and politically perfect? If Andrew could only have—

How dare you call him *Andrew*, I shouted. He was your father! He's dead! You don't have the right! We're all dead—nobody has the right to talk about us! You little—

January—still.

Relentless.

Several funerals in the street—yawning, I turned away from the window—scratched myself heartily—the most pleasure I've had in *months*. Sex, what was it? The idea of it evidently: a kind of Platonic essence, or cartoon-bubble, filled in with the (much exaggerated) elasticity of flesh. Pleasures mainly abstract—the ugly surprise of doodling at the table—still in my pajamas, unshaven, mouth rancid from the night (pills, nightcaps, dreams)—not even distracted by the ringing of the phone—the ugly marvelous surprise of—of what might emerge.

My "real" work abandoned, evidently abandoned back in December. Didn't quite guess at the time. The rejections from editorial assistants—mere brutes—clods—giddy gum-chewing creatures from the Bronx or Vassar able at last to spit upon the Petrie name—rejections as such really beside the point: I had already quit. The hell with *their* commissions, *their* assignments. Caricatures—no matter how arty and ingenious—and wicked—are nothing but illustrations to accompany either some moronic verbal twaddle or some frothy-ephemeral "idea" floating in the culture. What do I care! Why do I care! Why does my intuition always terrify me!

Studying the *Times* in a bistro on Third Avenue, someone else's paper, studied as if—as if it might be more authentic, less faked, than the one delivered to me. But they wouldn't be so clumsy, so brazen. . . . I skimmed, studied, yawned and scratched and sighed, by no means drunk at this hideous time of day (2:30 P.M.), impatient with the staged photographs, the headlines scattered in those columns and columns of trim deadpan type—as if the very tedium of it, the boringness of a recitation of catastrophes—the *predictability* of it, as in a joke heard many times—might convince a few readers that something was actually happening. The usual perking-up at the sighting of my own name—must be a biological reflex, untamed by intelligence (!)—feeble rush of adrenaline—rush and peak and subside in about eight seconds. Oh yes? Further developments? Handwriting experts, fingerprints that match? Tongue-in-cheek releases, possibly in Harvey's employ; though possibly not. Whoever is managing this is *possibly* not a friend of Harvey's, possibly not even a Republican.

Tongue-in-cheek releases. Action. "Drama." Saudi Arabia, Brazil, Waco, Texas. A Nobel Peace Prize winner photographed in the act of—of being photographed, judging from his/her odd expression. Murders in Central Park: nothing new: a spicy element in that murderer and murderee (alleged) were six and nine years old respectively. Color not given. The advertisements rather more artistic, because subdued—imagination toned down—restrained. Woman with a lofty forehead and long, long body wrapped in ermine—and barefoot!—a nice touch—peering at me idly, provocatively—considering me and rejecting me in about the same instant—as Yvonne did. News of upstate politics—Albany—tax surcharge—lobbyists—internecine squabbles—reform bill at impasse—reform of what?—no matter—such facts only mislead, are meant to mislead. Reality is elsewhere. We know. Want ads, amusements, obituaries. The deaths possibly not faked—possibly "factual" and "historical"—but certainly misrepresented. Recall Andrew's several columns of pious deadpan type!—distortions, outright lies, idiotic inflation of his worth. No mention of other prominent Petries *except* of course a few ancient embarrassments—scandals—libels. The hell with it.

Ah, a surprise: small pinprick of alarm. Julian W_____, the pianist, found dead in his apartment in the East Fifties—two years my junior—old pal—warm and then too-heated quarrel with him—someone's party after an opening—ballet?—silly American opera-attempt?—years, years ago—not so many years ago—fear flattens one's sense of time—demands distance: anyway the man is dead. Found dead. Two years my junior, and dead. But how? Natural causes? Or—? The notice is coy, offers few details. But I must know—I am shaking now—muttering aloud so that I am in danger of being— How old, how old was he?—and I?—when we quarreled, did I smirkingly obliterate him from my soul?—wish him dead?—is it too late? Too late—? For what? The crucial thing is— Must know how and why he died, otherwise— Are such things really happening? To ex-pals, ex-enemies, as well as to those who deserve them, like Andrew? And if so, then— But it must be interpreted, it must be filtered through—the restraint of the imagination—the soothing, calming processes of—

How the hell did he die! I am shouting. How the hell! And why! What a fraud this is, this newspaper! I want my money back—

Asked to leave. Will remember the place: smelly, crouched on a corner near a subway entrance, gypsy-ish girls (boys?) heckling me. Long Russian-style overcoats, fake sealskin collars, astrakhan hats. Heckling, were they?—or applauding me for what I shouted back into the bistro? The street rather lively for midafternoon, in spite of the cold. The usual beggars—no more than glancing my way—eager to approach the well-dressed well-booted tourists (always in couples or in family groups), not being so brain-damaged as they appear.

Met Eva in the street. Boisterous escort—escorts—three men and

my friend—swinging along arm-in-arm—waited to see if she would
greet me—when she refused to, when her absurd garish piggish eyes
flicked away, I called out to her: but no reaction. The foursome
strode past. From behind, called to her piteously at first—then irritably—then with a brave sort of indifference. As if her snubbing me
mattered in the slightest! As if anyone's snubbing of Hugh Petrie
mattered!

The bitches are all alike, however. As Father no doubt knew.

Later that night, having feasted on what remained in the refrigerator—having steadied my biological equilibrium by a massive forced
devouring of *vegetables*—carrots, rubbery celery, iceberg lettuce—and
what passed for tomatoes—and a bottle of sour wine—later, medita-
tively, I decided to go to Eva's door: exactly why I didn't know. To
apologize, to wheedle forgiveness, to accuse her of being a bitch, to
demand my money back? Don't know. Knocked on the door but
heard ominous sounds inside—bickering, giggling—wondered if I
should interrupt whatever was going on—or was it only a late movie?
—masculine voices raised in anger—feminine voice (voices?) raised in
ferocity— Drew back, did not care to knock again. Unimportant, really. Who was Eva? Who was Eva, that her betrayal in the street
should hurt me? *She* was not the one: that particular bitch did not
matter. As I well knew, as my dreams and doodles and various
agonies of the spirit informed me: *she* was not the one.

Paralysis upon waking. The ear infection still with me—spasms of
pain in the neck—urination burning, irritating—but the real problem
is the dreams to which I am subjected: crucifixions.

Emergency appointment with Dr. Wynand. Why doesn't he believe me, why does he translate everything into formulae! A
dream must have its origin in some repressed incestuous wish—and
also in some repressed memory—of something that actually, actually
occurred!—but such horrors *do not occur*—how can I convince him?
Banged my fist on his desk, but he refused to understand. Why, why
must that female monster be my poor mother? My poor helpless gin-
stinking mother? Why must I be dragged always into the past, into
the infantile past, when it is the present that is destroying me?
Showed him the scrappy amateurish drawing that awaited me
when I returned from California—in the mess of my apartment—ran-

sacked, possibly—I would hardly know or care at this stage!—shook beneath his fastidious nose the clumsy art work left by my tormenter —a mock-voluptuous female, stark naked, with innumerable breasts —dugs—a swollen belly—and eyes so heavily drawn that the pen had jabbed into the paper and ripped it—eyes overlapping—two eyes merged into a single eye—the pupil at the center a tiny pinprick, a hole in the paper— Horrible! Unfathomable!

All this is real, I cried. Real! Real! Nothing else! I am real!—she is real!—*it* is real! Please help me—

Reality unartistic to Dr. Wynand.

Cannot be reduced to his insipid formulae, so must be rejected.

But I am going mad, am being squeezed out of shape! And Yvonne will not return my calls. In desperation telephoned Deborah —forced myself to listen to her recitation of inane events—gallery openings, first nights, receptions for, dinner parties for—forced myself to keep from shrieking at her (for she was not the one: not she), pretending interest in the much anticipated fiasco of Edward M——'s new play, the story behind Gertrude E——'s collapse in a Fifth Avenue beauty salon. And Julian W——: had I heard? So sad! So very sad! Suspected of suicide but *evidently* not—evidently quite natural causes—simple heart failure, evidently—and how old was he? And Deborah understood, was sympathetic with, my decision to retreat from social life this winter—was sympathetic even with what might be called my rudeness (failure to R.S.V.P. invitations, alleged hanging-up on the telephone, general unsociability), for I was undoubtedly "undergoing personality upheavals"—"emerging at last into maturity"—"not responsible." Interrupted her to ask if people believed the latest story: the latest "arrest"? What were they saying? Were they saying anything? No, she didn't think so; the "tragedy of Andrew" had been to some extent replaced—wasn't I aware?—by the unpredictable kidnapings in the Boston area—kidnaping-killings— prominent families—both Democrats and Republicans so far— though all wealthy: such horrors, and so daily now! Indeed, people rarely spoke of Andrew—though people sometimes did ask about me —Hugh—asking if the rumors were true that—?

I am not dead. Not yet. Nor am I insane.

Stopped payment on my most recent check to that bastard Wynand—will never pay him another cent. Let him sue! Liar—fraud

—idiot! As if I could have drawn so ugly—so clumsy—so pointless a
picture—as if my nightly torments are trivia symbol-sessions—always
to be referred back to something else. Denying my reality, my life!
My soul! Telephoned him—the receptionist must have recognized
my voice—still, I could not stop—threatened the sonofabitch's life—
hadn't I a gun, eh?—hadn't I recently acquired a gun, eh?—and knew
very well how to use it? And was fearful enough and desperate
enough and—

Only a joke! Happy Valentine's Day! Happy April Fool's!— Still, I
stopped payment on that check: let the sonofabitch beg for it.

Began to contemplate certain possibilities, not previously entertained.

Such as—what if nothing is ultimately revealed? That is—what if
the mystery of Andrew's assassination is not "solved"? Months ago—
a small lifetime ago—I did not care in the slightest: did not give a
damn. How carefree I was, how blissful! Obviously, someone had
killed him—or had hired an agent to kill him—for personal reasons,
for political reasons, for insane reasons, for any reason—any at all—
obviously, obviously: and so why should it matter? It had not mattered. Had not seemed to matter. But now— Now it mattered very
much. It mattered constantly.

As it must matter to *her*. Constantly.

Unless—

But of course she was innocent: as innocent as I.

Dr. Swann, I said, what if nothing will be revealed? What if nothing will progress?—merely different facets exposed, different aspects
of—various fragments of— What if, what then? How can such things
be, Dr. Swann? How can they be allowed, Dr. Swann? Already the
defense for those suspects—suspect-victims—dupes—agents, angels—
fools—saints—martyrs—already the defense has charged outrageous
violations of civil rights—already defense funds are swelling—already,
do you see?—and the trial months away! And of course they are innocent: as innocent as the rest of us. And when they are acquitted or
the charges are dropped, Dr. Swann, what then? What will we do
then? Do you think *she* is as tormented as I, and merely more
stoical?

Dr. Swann?

34

A sidewalk, a street. Recognizable. Not recognizable. I am suddenly there. Identical with Hugh Petrie: trapped in his body. In the old raincoat, the trench coat with all the buttons. Alone. No pen, no pencil, no bit of charcoal in hand. Alone. Waiting. Suddenly hurrying forward. Uphill, sharply uphill. Sidewalk broken. Buildings fall away, cliffs arise. Maroon red, clayey. Unlike the only mountains I know well.

Ahead, somewhere ahead. Cannot see. Sidewalk broken, pebbly, vague. I am climbing, panting, my body vaguely realized. Unfocused. The place is familiar. I am familiar. Always Hugh. Hugh and no one else. Ahead, she is somewhere ahead, waiting. I am waiting. Waiting and hurrying. God removed Himself from history, someone has said. I knew it, I seem to have known it already. No God, never was. But the absence—!

The smell of her, suddenly.

The mountain air is dry, dusty. My nostrils ache with it. But the odor of the woman is wet: stale milkish stench. I feel faint, sick. I want to stop, to turn back, but I cannot. When I raise my eyes— something must happen between us. But the wenchy smell is so— The fact of her is— Seven feet tall, perhaps taller— A giantess— Breasts, belly, pubic hair, great muscular thighs— Arms that want only to clasp me— And the face, the eyes—

Waking, I lay in a paralysis of shame.

Shame, nausea, faintness. But also sorrow.

What is sorrow? I have never known. Cannot guess.

Dr. Swann begins to chuckle. Sudden ascending chuckle, such a surprise— So unexpected— When I open my eyes, however, the old man is gazing my way, somber, innocent, expressionless. He has aged since the start of my analysis.

HUGH PETRIE, PRIZE-WINNING CARICATURIST, DEAD BY HIS OWN HAND, IN MANHATTAN INTIMATES BLAME UNREQUITED LOVE

Had two copies made, one for Yvonne and one for myself. Sleazy shop off Times Square. One for Yvonne, one for myself. Chuckling as I waited. In the unmistakable type of the *Times*, under a mock-*Times* banner. The inspiration had come to me earlier, at the drawing board. "Breakfast." Quarter to one, no appetite, sipping at weak tea and trying to eat a container of yogurt. Serious work out of the question—"serious" meaning commissioned, paid for—out of the question—in fact hilarious at this point. No money for February rent. Would have to borrow. Beg. In the meantime unholy spurts of joy. Inspired: watching my hand in astonishment. A page of messed-up faces—hacked bodies—mutilated unrecognizable shapes—giants, dwarfs, mannequins, angels—and then the headline, concise and lyric and complete as a poem, a poem in three powerful lines, a poem for her, a *poem*, a *POEM*. For her.

Restless. Fearing insomnia. Out walking—must have been two in the morning—Sixth Avenue pleasantly busy. Insomnia feared, sleep feared. Drugs promise dreamlessness—blank dead weighted sleep—the temptation to take a handful, a fistful—but no: I refuse. Boy with wool shirt partly unbuttoned, black-frizzy chest and even a glimpse of belly hair. In this weather! Ugly. Despicable. Shrilly childish, arguing with me, wouldn't listen even when I explained who I was. Art demands structures, I said. He sneered. The very conception of a work of art necessitates a frame, I said, a pedestal, the exclusion of the rest of the world. He sneered, hiccupped, complained of being hungry. Friends appeared, all were hungry except me, all ate ravenously except me. Black-frizzy curls, a boy with a pudgy appealing look; an artist himself, he said. Printmaking his specialty. From Highland Meadows, Indiana. Boys in their early twenties but older in spirit and flesh than I. Pitted grayish skin—unwashed bodies —mock-fur collars and hats—teeth all ajumble in their busy hot mouths—the boy from Indiana with his head lowered, tearing at a sandwich, thick crusty bread gripped in his dirty hands. Loud music, amplified guitars, amplified shrieks. Not at my best, though they applauded me. One of them slipped away, weaselly bastard, but the others remained. Not at my best: had to struggle to draw breath, let alone shout.

Art demands structures, I said. Chaos may be entertained—often is —may be entertained and courted and even taken home—and bedded too (as the case may be)—and chaos may be entertain*ing*—but it is not art and cannot be art—it is an idea—chaos is an idea—an idea —nothing more!—an idea and nothing more!—therefore invisible, unprovable, outside experience. It doesn't exist! Art makes necessary demands, I said, though the boys giggled, the pudgy lad from Indiana impulsively wiped his mouth on my sleeve, hiccupped close to my face (salami, garlic, beer), the artist is doomed but optimistic, hauling stage scenery back and forth—arranging the audience into rows—hoping that by his continuous contortions and their expectations some revelation will be at hand: some fantastic unguessed-at truth. I was in disguise as a mere caricaturist—had become famous by the wrong means—sidetracked—my brother's influence, the extraordinary malevolence he inspired in me—in everyone he knew—but shortly my true nature would reveal itself, my true art would spring upon the undeserving mocking world—and—

Leaving a telephone booth, pushing someone out of the way. Later, was it? That same night? Much later. The boy from Pomona, California, ruddy cheeks and snarled red-brown beard and long black overcoat—a boy?—why a boy?—he could have been no younger than thirty-five!—struggling with me over the matter of an unpaid bill. We were in a drafty corridor. I began shouting—pushing at him—striking him about the head and shoulders. A sharp pain in my ear—but no one had touched me. We were in a corridor, unheated—the restrooms across the way—the amplified guitars lyric and torturous—omnipresent—inescapable. What the hell are you doing! What are you doing! Why am I always tormented! I had tried to telephone Yvonne, but could not remember her number; tried to telephone Dr. Swann, an emergency, request for ambulance, for forceful restraint and sedation and two weeks in retreat—began to dial Dr. Wynand's number, but lost interest—turned to Dial-a-Prayer and let the receiver hang loose—forgot to listen—

> In all that you do or say or think, recollect
> that at any time the power of withdrawal from
> life is in your hands.
>   —Marcus Aurelius

But they didn't tell us, in high school Latin! And the *Aeneid* was just a romp!

Dr. Swann: leathery-skinned, smelling of fresh tobacco, eyeglasses with thick lenses. Must be sixty-five or seventy years old. Ground-floor office on East Seventy-ninth Street, two blocks from the park, a minute's walk from Dr. Wynand's office. Books to the ceiling. Rug from North Africa—scratchy wool explosive black and yellow designs. In my normal state I would have been envious: Father's love seat, Andrew's Hudson River art, Willa's tricky costly silver trash, and this handsome rug—what a combination! Rolling over and over upon the rug, lost in the brawny sweaty arms of—gagging at the chest hair, the belly hair—rising again refreshed and ordinarily hung-over—ready for a morning's workout at the drawing board—what a prospect!—but unlikely. The self of other years and other accommodations waves good-by, sends me mock kisses as the train pulls out—I stand behind—underground—the subway stinking and vibrating—the very ground beneath my feet vibrating. Help, help!—wait! But Dr. Swann is going to help, otherwise would he accept these huge checks?

Wine-red rocks. Sandstone, shale?—dry, very dry—dusty—unpleasantly warm. The path broken, pebbly. The woman before me blocking my way—standing there with legs apart—waiting—grinning at me. What must I do? But why? I know very well what I must do —but why, why? Why? —Sometimes she is alone, sometimes there are other presences. Invisible, near-invisible. Shapes in the air that don't quite spring into focus, if you know what I mean—the way an ordinary scene appears when one isn't wearing glasses—and anything at all could materialize. —Sometimes they are visible: child-shapes, or dwarfs, comic little broken-off creatures perched on the rocks behind her or peering between her legs, gazing at me, blank and hideous. I imagine them smirking—but really there is this awful idiotic blankness, neuterness.

I can't approach her. I begin to cry. But it isn't crying (such as I will admit I sometimes do when awake): it's wailing. Long drawn-out piteous wails—shall I demonstrate?—and something terrible will happen—can't be avoided—not even a plunge over the side, not even death will allow me to escape—there is no way except past her—there is no way except—but the size of her!—and the moist, stale stench!— In one of the first nightmares she tried to touch me, tried to stick something in my mouth—but I struggled like mad, I fought her, fought it—was so terrified I was able to wake up—tangled in the bedclothes, the pillow partly over my face. Heart pounding so furiously I thought I would—

But I won't, will I? How can I? So stubborn, so sane, so much in love with life!—I won't, will I? It won't happen, will it?

Explained and explained to Dr. Wynand: Mother was a gracious, long-suffering woman, far too sensitive to survive. Of course I loved her—loved her very much—as a son normally loves his mother. Love mixed with pity and dread and perhaps some embarrassment. *But*—! No sexual feelings, really. Not really. It's true of course that I must not protest, or that will be held against me; I must not seem to resist. But—please—Dr. Wynand, please—if you could free yourself for a few minutes from your obsession with mothers—wombs—holes —nipples—if you could see that I am utterly sincere when I say— when I beg you to—please, please!

Explained. Pleaded. Dr. Wynand skeptical, courteous.

Of course it is the phallic mother once again: again. Threatening castration. Anxiety set off by recent visit to Father—near-uncontrollable wishes for his death—Hugh the child, the perpetual child, the daring rebellious child attempting to assert his manhood: the first act of which must be an incestuous one. Of course! Therefore an impasse. Your mother, disguised, has come to punish you and tease you and torment you with your own incestuous desires—with your infantile desire to be suckled once again—so offensive you have rejected all awareness of it!—and strenuously deny it. Your mother knows about the forbidden desires you have, and she has no intention of satisfying them—or of allowing you to forget them. Infantile and aggressive impulses are always with us, the unconscious knows no progression, no history, no time. The phallic mother knows no progression, no history, no time, no mercy.

Dr. Wynand, I must insist— The woman is not my mother but my sister-in-law— I know it's Yvonne, I can smell her—it!— *I know who it is!*

—a child of no more than eight or nine—fixated on his mother— severe infantile-aggressive impulses—no possibility of experiencing the female as anything except a symbolic expression of the mother, the only forbidden female. Ah, it will be a long, long journey before —before you will begin to experience any woman in her own being. Do you see? Certainly you see! A long, long journey—

Dr. Wynand, for God's sake—

But does this woman even exist?

What? *What?*

This sister-in-law you mention: does she exist? I had thought they were both killed, last summer—up in the Adirondacks, wasn't it?— your brother and his wife shot down by revolutionaries?—or was it—

My God, no! Not her!—not *her*. Only *him*.

—or am I confusing them with another couple? That Senator and his wife in—

Dr. Wynand, please!

It must have happened then, my screaming. Screaming screaming screaming.

Exists!—of course she exists!—she wasn't killed, not *her!*—wasn't my mother!—my mother was killed, is dead, buried!—no one can resurrect her!—*I* can't resurrect her!—I don't want to resurrect her!—must live now, must live my life now, now!—*now!*—NOW!

I MUST LIVE MY LIFE NOW
AND ALL OF YOU ARE PREVENTING ME!

Advertisement in the *Village Voice*. Hypnotist on Eighth Street, a mere block away. Classified ads, personal, help wanted, strayed lost & found. Categories. For sale, for rent, services desired, miscellaneous. HYPNOSIS: THE TURNING POINT IN YOUR LIFE? No. The newspaper was cruder than the *Times*, meant to give the illusion that its lies were therefore closer to rude natural living, the folk, good-hearted primitives in disguise as urban intellectuals. Lies, truth. Truth, lies. What difference? Read of the "fact" that the State of New York was directing its entire crime-fighting budget—a considerable sum, enough perhaps to wage a small war against a small country—into the prosecution of the Glasberg prisoners—whose exact crimes I didn't know, had no real interest in—what had Andrew to do with them?—or they with him?—was there a *clue* here?—but who could tell, who could judge, what difference did it make? Eighteen men, twelve of them black, charged with first-degree murder. Capital punishment voted in by the legislature—voted back in—for use against the murderers of law enforcement and courtroom officers—and—but —what about my brother?—is it too late for him?—for me?—for the rest of us?

Doctor Greenley, the hypnotist. "Doctor." Do you see how desperate I am, "Doctor" Greenley, willing to part with fifty dollars in cash for your services?—*you*, an obvious fraud? Must be calm, calmed down. *Must* be. Cannot fail with Dr. Swann. Cannot fail with him as I failed with Dr. Wynand. A hypnotist to calm me down—steady the erratic pulse—muffle the interior pain-shrieks—the noise in the inner ear as the antibiotics fight bravely and recklessly for my soul— *must* not fail with Dr. Swann, *must* not. "Doctor" Greenley asked who "Dr." Swann was but I refused to say.

One must be awfully, awfully careful of charlatans in the field of medical science, he said slowly, awfully careful especially in New York City.

I am calm. I am very calm. I am calm, calm, calm. One hundred, ninety-nine, ninety-eight, ninety-seven, ninety-six, ninety . . . ninety-seven?—ninety-eight, ninety-nine . . . ninety-eight, ninety-seven, ninety-six, ninety-five, ninety-four, ninety-five, ninety-six, ninety-six, ninety-seven?—ninety-five, I am calm, very calm, very very . . . when I reach zero I will be utterly calm, ninety-nine, ninety-eight, ninety-seven . . . when I reach zero I will be utterly, completely calm . . . never again nervous . . . no more anxiety. . . . Must count down from one hundred: one hundred, ninety-nine, ninety-eight, ninety-six, ninety-seven, ninety-eight, ninety— ninety-seven, ninety-six, ninety-five—

"Doctor" Greenley resembled one of the family's attorneys—corny, earnest, hair cut short and sticking up like a brush—a gushing breath—gaze fixed upon mine with the benign intensity of the quietly, unobtrusively mad—ninety-four, ninety-three, ninety-two, ninety-one — ninety — eighty-nine, eighty-eight — eighty — eighty? — eighty-one, eighty-two, eighty-three—pulses slowing, metabolism slowing—Dr. Swann, you must help me—must save me—Dr. Swann, do you exist?—is it already too late?—why am I hedged about with doctors, physicians of the soul?—why, when there is no soul? Eighty-nine, ninety—ninety! *Ninety!*

NINETY! *NINETY!* I MUST LIVE MY LIFE NOW AND ALL OF YOU ARE PREVENTING—

Leathery-skinned, sweet elfin features, a set of teeth like Father's, and those glasses—or should I say those eyes, magnified by the lenses —peering curiously at me. Ah, an artist! A genius! One of the prominent P—— family! An honor to treat him, always the possibility of writing the case up. Cave-like, the office. Shadowy and cozy. Outside the threat of the wind—winds—temperature in the 20's—February now—or is it still January?—still?—the grave long frozen, the tiny idiotic voice long silenced—*Help!*—Help yourself, you selfish bastard!—*Help help help!* Early on, I demonstrated that voice to Dr. S, who was genuinely interested—admiring, I think—like a playful delighted grandfather—as I projected the shriek for help into a tiny bronze figure on the desk before me—armless lad—charmingly naked—girlish, shy—Macedonia, fifth century B.C.—*Help help help*—and I witty enough to reply Help yourself, am I your keeper?—your elder brother? Dr. S memorized every word, every gesture, every facial subtlety. Mythical people on his walls, where the bookshelves gave way, Greek and Oriental creatures, some with innumerable arms and eyes. Gods, demons, angels. Fierce Islamic warriors. Dr. Swann, I said, I'm well aware that the dreams mean nothing—are probably associated with the antibiotics I've been taking—I'm well aware of the basic lunacy of pursuing such phantoms—after all I am a citizen of the United States—a citizen of the State of New York—a taxpayer, a newspaper reader, a mature male only incidentally and peripherally an artist—and by no means temperamental!—by no means!—though hardly a mediocre bourgeois like the rest of my clan. If I seem to have fallen in love— If I seem to be unnaturally concerned about my late brother— About the identity of his assassins— If I strike you as— Dr. Swann, where are we? Is this New York City? Is this the same world I was born into? Someone tried to strangle me last night —it was not so exquisite as I remember—am I growing old, jaded?— am I losing my sense of humor? Always my most redeeming trait!— as the Master of my college kept saying. Dr. Swann, I began to weep, it isn't serious—it never was—can't we call it a day, an era?—a lifetime? If only I could resolve everything into a joke—

I wept, he spoke, a siren sang in the distance, other sirens began, not even the promise of a fire—a catastrophe—cheered me. He spoke in a gentle gravelly voice. Far more perceptive than Father. But of course—he was not burdened by the nuisance of love—of having fathered the writhing mass of nerves before him. Spoke of the sacred nature of dreams: the great importance of what was being revealed to me. Spoke of—

No, for God's sake! Please!

—while behind him in a golden frame an eight-armed creature with a simpering smile quivered as if at the start of a dance—and I smelled yogurt—the strong sour natural kind, unsweetened—horrible —wondered if Dr. Swann ate it from the container, at his desk, ate hurriedly between sessions—ingesting stamina—nerve—energy. I wanted to know—needed desperately to know—but dreaded it, began to laugh at how much I dreaded it—preferred suddenly the simple-minded reductivist game of Dr. Wynand—where all mysteries are biological, are solved in terms of biology, genitals belonging to one "individual" merely yearning for genitals belonging to "another." Could not resist the impulse to jump up, peer into his wastebasket—to see if— Crumpled papers, a teabag, yes, but no evidence of— Dr. Swann startled at my curiosity, drawing away. Yes? Yes? Violence?

No.

There was a Petrie in the 1880's, I told Dr. Swann humbly, who was evidently "mystical"—began with an interest in Christian Science, soon drifted into occultism, séances, that sort of thing. (I did not tell him about Stephen—thought it best not to mention Stephen.) And so—perhaps—genetic precedence—heredity— If an inclination toward strange behavior is programmed in the chromosomes, surely it can be dealt with?—surely knowing about it, laughing heartily at it, must help? This deluded man, the younger brother of my father's grandfather, left the United States—lived in London— was tricked out of a great deal of money—yet never lost his faith— his faith in whatever it was: spirits, visions, occult practices. He married. His daughter, when about four or five, became seriously ill. No doctor—no hospital. No medical care of any kind. She died, manslaughter charges were brought against the parents, my great-grandfather had to go to England—it's part of our family history— I'm only recounting it in order to— Hoping to—

Dr. Swann, the human ego cannot hold its own against—

I've changed my mind, I think I prefer—

Dr. Wynand has warned me that if I attempt to enter his sanctuary, if I even ascend his steps— But I think I prefer—

The dream, Dr. Swann told me, is sacred. The dream, the dreamer. Your soul speaks—reveals itself—

That—!

—reveals itself if you are humble, if you maintain the proper attitude—not always joking, mocking, chattering away like a monkey—

—monkey?

It is possible that the female who appears to you—who causes you such distress—

Dr. Swann, I said, gripping the arms of the chair, the woman is clearly recognizable: my sister-in-law. I know her. I can smell her. Her. I realize I'm neurotic—isn't everyone?—and love itself is perhaps neurotic—a dependency, a defense—a complex—whatever —At the same time, my situation is a fairly ordinary one: I am in love. I am a lover. I need not a cure but a love potion—

Mr. Petrie, really—!

He permitted himself a dry chuckle.

Yes, I said, yes yes! *Yes!* I am a lover in search of a beloved! Is that so amusing? —I will take my leave of you: I will say good day.

You—a lover? *You?*

Yes!

In love with—?

—with, with—

The female who appears in your dream, Mr. Petrie, the giantess who threatens and disgusts you—you dare to imagine that *that* creature is a mere mortal woman, a woman of your acquaintance? Never, never! You see—? Never! Your pitiful ignorance will destroy you unless—

I'm a man, a lover! A deluded lover, yes! I want her—I intend to get her—I must take my time, must use my wits— You are not going to snatch her away from me—talk me out of her— Dr. Wynand insisted it was only Mother once again, but Mother is dead—Dr. Wynand is dead—I don't have to listen to this—I don't have to sit quietly while the woman I love is dissected—dismissed— And I intend to find the murderer! The two of us, united, will find him! Will find them! I will marry my brother's widow—it's a Biblical imperative, isn't it?—I will make amends for my past life—start afresh—I will buy a new wardrobe—take a lease on a new apartment—a studio with a skylight—she and I—what she did for *him* she must do for me —why not?—why do you sneer?—monkey, eh?—I'll monkey *you!*— the most beautiful woman, the most uncannily beautiful woman— mine—the two of us—no need of you—paltry little dried-up thing— face all dry and leathery like one of those bog people—peat-moss corpses—and jealous, aren't you? Jealous! *Jealous!* Jealous of my family's name—fortune—the role played in history— But you can't stop me—nobody can stop me—

Mr. Petrie, not so loud! Please!

But you—you— You want to snatch her from me, want to take my life from me— Like Andrew— Like all of them— Jeering and mocking and—

Mr. Petrie, please.

Dr. Swann smiled but I was not deceived. Frightened, the old bat. Not so much in control as he wished.

Mr. Petrie? You see—? The living woman—the sister-in-law whom you mention—she is not involved at all, not at all! Please. Calm yourself. You see, Mr. Petrie, it is very important that you realize—

You know her? You've seen photographs of her? In the newspaper, in the magazines? Have you? Of course! Everyone has! His wife, his widow— There is a woman behind those pictures—I've touched her, I've loved her—I intend to—

Mr. Petrie, the woman is not involved. Not involved. Your feeling for her is a—

Don't!

You have worked yourself into a frenzy, a passion—this is very bad for you—your health, your physical and emotional health—

But I love her! *Her!* I'll go to her tonight—I'll prove it to you—

The woman is innocent, the woman is—don't you see?—peripheral to your illness. She exists, but you have never met. You have—

She was responding to me, Dr. Swann. We got along well together —an evening a few months ago—cocktails—a quiet place, nothing strained or unpleasant— The day of the funeral, I admit I was rather shrill—and perhaps made a bad impression upon her. But— Love grows slowly—

Mr. Petrie, not another word of this! Not another word! You are pale, you are exhausted—this session has gone too far. In fact our work together has gone too far: I cannot advise that we continue. I fear that—under the circumstances—any further probing into your psyche, any stimulation of the deepest reservoirs of your unconscious, and tragedy may result. In other words—

Tragedy? What?

—the possibility of a breakdown, of psychosis. I am speaking frankly, but you are an intelligent man, and—

But I'm already crazy! I've been crazy for years! Everyone I know is crazy—all my friends, my ex-friends! You can't hold that against me!

How is it possible? How can an intelligent man like yourself say such things? There is nothing amusing about psychosis—nothing fashionable or communal—don't you understand? Life is serious, life is real—

But it isn't tragic!

—The hell of which the old religions speak is always near—always ready to flood into us—only the thin barrier of the personality pro-tects us from it. Yet you insist upon tempting it, tempting hell itself! But it is forbidden. No, don't interrupt—no, please—you must listen. Your dream is a warning—it is frightening even to me, even to me— as if such dangers might be contagious. The woman seems gigantic to you, a monster?—and perhaps she is—perhaps she cannot help herself. But the fact you must accept is your own smallness, your es-sential triviality—a blight of the spirit—one that your relative success in the world, and a certain blindness in yourself, have masked until now— Mr. Petrie, please—

I'm not paying you to insult me, Dr. Swann, I said, wondering at the authority of my voice, I'm not going to remain in this cave of yours—this hole—and allow you to insult—sit here helplessly while— I'm capable of extraordinary things! Do you comprehend! *You*, a wizened half-blind old—

—Your dream does not lie, does not flatter. It horrifies you, but it tells the truth. You are small—very small! An infant! the giantess is your own being, your own essence, slipped from your grasp—drawn back into the unconsciousness and now swollen, hideous, ready to devour you—ready to devour your sanity. The art of which you speak so constantly and so coyly—the "art" you claim as a value—of course you have realized all along that it is an infant's revenge upon the adults who surround him—an infant's art work—smearing of excrement upon a world others have created— It does no good to pretend anger! To pretend outrage! You *know* you are not a complete human being, you *know* because your dream has told us both! Your "art"— your caricatures—what value have they?—what hold have they given you in the world? Vanity—foppery—cruelty—a tragic delusion you share with your era— Your intelligence is everything, your emotional grasp is nothing, you are missing half your body—*she* has taken your strength from you—taken it back, since you did not know how to value it—and you cannot win it from her, Hugh, not in your present state—you cannot—it would be death for you, it would be madness for you to attempt it—for you to approach her. She is teasing you, she would like to get you in an embrace—but you must resist, do you see? You are too small for her, she would destroy you. Your conscious being would be flooded with her, you would lose all sense of yourself, your orientation to the world, you must not tempt it, not even in this way: not even by talking about it, as we are doing. Do you see? Can't you see? There is no woman—there is no sister-in-law —the widow is an illusion, an image your mind has seized upon—a crystallization of emotion—of raw passion—the particular form your madness would take. *She*—whom you have managed to elude all your life—she has too much strength now, she would break you like a matchstick. And so—we must end this session—we are both exhausted—we must end, we must leave each other—it would do you no good to tempt madness, your personality is not strong enough— perhaps it will never be strong enough. Certain visions are forbidden us; we must be very strong to experience them. Let it go, let your "love" go. Vanity—delusion. If your distinguished brother was murdered—what is that to you, to the burden of your own life? You must let him go. You must let the murderer go. Do you see—? You must let these things go: you must live with your impotence.

   You! What are you but a wizened dying old thing! Dwarf! Monkey! Walking corpse! Do you hear!—*you!*—jealous of my fame—my genius—the fact of my family's reputation—fortune— Jealous of my life, my love— My future— My—

35

February 1. All's well.

February 2. Worked at the drawing board for several intense hours —not satisfied with results—who is? what artist ever is? Worked for hours more. Worked. Hours. February now and all's well.

February 3. Examined mail, much of it postmarked many weeks ago. Mailbox stuffed. Postman evidently angry—the most recent letters and advertising circulars jammed in the slot—bent, ripped, mutilated. One for Eva, postmarked New Jersey. In the drafty foyer, mail in both hands, gazing out at the slick damp street—bemused, at peace—sense of purpose—a creature appeared out front—studying the addresses—dressed fairly well, hatless, gloveless, a shrewd hog's face—an investigator, perhaps—private detective—plainclothes policeman—someone in Harvey's employ—or perhaps one of *them*, the killers. Did I blink? Hardly. Tremble? Hardly. I stood my ground —watched him—he pretended not to see me—though my face, stern and ghostly behind the stained-glass window beside the door, must have given him something to meditate upon.

The Artist: not so easily destroyed.

February 4. Rapped on Eva's door. No answer. Several hours of work—annoying attacks of faintness—both ears aching now intermittently—drugs don't seem to help. Worked nevertheless. Worked hard. —Lifted my head as if from a moment's sleep, loss of consciousness that could have lasted only a split second—startled, blinking—discovered my serious sketches covered with ugly jagged doodlings—figures half human, half beast. Ripped the paper into many pieces without hesitation.

February 5. Party following the opening of a new opera— "American," so-called—managed to keep a straight face throughout —good behavior, semi-sober—first attempt at social life since *it* began. Folk-rock-requiem—"parable of American gypsy ethic"—noise so persistent I had trouble hearing anything—mind wandered, shot off in all directions—wanted desperately to leave at intermission— forced myself to stick it through—to subject myself to social life *as others did*. For us all, is this penance? But for what? Are we all guilty of—? What am I guilty of—? Impossible.

Party as noisy as the opera. Guests of honor not present. Extraordinary buffet—no appetite—mind wandering, wandering—not offended so much as startled when someone approached, tried to "start a conversation" by reference to Andrew—"the pity of," "the continuing mystery of," etc.—staring across Central Park—nighttime skyline routinely beautiful—drawn to a quick retort only when asked about myself: the rumor was out that I had had a breakdown of some kind, did I know?—about the rumor, that was.

Never in better health, I said.

The cruelty of rumors—!

The cruelty of swine like yourself.

February 6. A stranger answered Eva's door—girl in a maternity smock—beaming apple cheeks and a ponytail—looked seventeen years old, eagerly neighborly, puzzled by my questions. No, she didn't know about the apartment's previous tenant—her husband might know—though probably not, since he hadn't said. There'd been trouble about some of the furnishings and the fact that the place was so dirty—but— What trouble, I asked, what furnishings? What has happened? Didn't she move out? Wouldn't she have taken her things? What—? But the girl didn't know, her cheery neighborly grin abated, I thought it best to retreat. Something must have— But it was possible, simply, that— I would try again, would make other inquiries.

February 7. Nothing.

February 8. Asked her to marry me. Interior of St. Aidan's cold, dark—the two of us sitting close together—her frightened fingers closing about my wrist—Stop, please, no—no, I can't—no, no I'm afraid—I'm afraid of what he would do—what revenge he would take. I love you, but I'm afraid. I would marry you. But. I'm afraid, afraid. Christ in his cold splendor before us—rearing above the altar —Yvonne bare-handed, ringless, close beside me. How unnecessarily melancholy! I turned cavalier—witty—gracious—warm—teasing her with improbable hopes, plans for the future, honeymoons: Shall we fly to Acapulco, to Caracas, to the Barbados, to Hawaii? Stretch our souls on the outsides of our bodies for once, and grease them so that they shine?—gleam bronze? And what love might pass between us! And through us!

February 9. Worked. No results: nothing.

February 10. Nothing.

February 11. Telephoned Eva's mother—asked for Eva—the woman began a hysterical unintelligible monologue—angry, fright-

ened—too messy for me—I hung up. No: don't ask. No. Not a word!
—no. Returned to my work, returned to what I know. Worked. No
results, nothing. But worked, worked. Tore it to bits—returned to
zero—began again. What? No. What was—? No. Nothing. He clam-
bered upon her—burrowed, guzzled, grunted—thrust himself into her
—again again and again—the wet slap of their bodies—his slack
stomach—like this!—like this!—like this! He seized her by her delicate shoulders—would have strangled her, perhaps, had she resisted.
The first occasion of their love-making, years ago: their "honeymoon." I would be so much more gentle, I whispered to her, I would
respect you—be a friend to you—a brother— Marry me! Only marry
me!—we need not even consummate our union.

Love: a ritual. Love-making: the performance of a ritual.

February 12. Slept till one o'clock. Woke hung over, though could
not remember having drunk the night before. (When *was* the night
before?) Dragged myself from bed—light-headed—weak and euphoric at the same time—ringing of telephone a false alarm—the line
quite silent when I picked up the receiver—not even a dial tone.
Went to drawing board—saw there a different series of figures—not
just the woman but, superimposed upon her, a slim dark angel—Angel of Death—arms and shoulders and torso quite well-developed,
thighs slender as a girl's—enormous intense mad eyes—*God's love
sustains all human actions*—madness of course. Dark hair, curly hair,
thick hair falling upon his forehead. Angel of Death. Sexless, like a
child. Neuter. Innocent. And yet so brutal—one saw it first in the
eyes, then in the set of the mouth, then in the outspread warning
fingers.

Who has drawn these beasts, who is responsible?

Thank God I freed myself from Dr. S, a raving fool. Charlatan.
And dangerous, dangerous. Thank God I had the courage.

Fate guides my hand, deals me these ugly visions: I must only bow
down to them. So the fool said. Dangerous! Should be arrested. No
one draws these beasts—no one is responsible—no one need study
them, take them seriously, let alone submit himself. I reject them all!
—Still, they intrigue me. One may as well be an anthropologist of his
own life.

February 13. Gun in my pocket, gloved hands thrust in pockets.
Lean but strong—formidable—fearless. A rare sunshiny afternoon.
Went for walk—therapeutic stroll—gaze averted from the small fu-
neral procession taking off across the street—grateful for chill brisk

air. Health! Life! Brownstone next to mine in poor condition—
landlord allowing it to run down—fire escapes on front of building
rusty—garbage cans at the curb, one of them overturned—disgusting.
Avenue of the Americas gaudy-shabby in the winter sun: too much
activity. Jangling nerves.

Side street. Spanish-Portuguese Jewish cemetery, early nineteenth
century. Shaded, squeezed-in. Behind iron railing. The tombstones
looked so frail!—ah, so insubstantial. Sparrows picked in the spotty
snow—flew up at my approach—returned when they saw I was harmless. I gripped the rails, I felt my man's strength pour through me,
wanting to weep, to shriek defiance. Must have been there several
minutes—how long?—a split second—must have lost consciousness
without falling—awoke to West Eleventh Street and that tiny cemetery I've passed for years—could not remember why I was there, gripping the rails, breathing so rapidly.

Footsteps behind me—

Hugh?

I turned but saw no one. There was no one.

Hugh? Hugh?

No one.

February 13. Evening. My brother Stephen following beside me—
unshaven stranger—dark curly hair matted, disheveled—his steamy
breath an irritant to me. What do you want? Why are you spying on
me? Has *she* informed you—? What is your business with me?

Sorrow between us. Brotherly dislike. Not dislike, perhaps, but the
realization that there is no connection—nothing to say—no bond.
Stephen must be over thirty years old now, yet looks babyish as always; something obscene about that innocence. I am tempted to say
Father still loathes you! But it is more fitting that I pity him.

I felt I must talk with you, Stephen says softly.

Oh hell! To save my soul, I suppose?

Your life, Stephen says softly, your life. I don't fear for your soul:
your soul can take care of itself.

Tempted to pull the gun out, wave it at him. Thrust the barrel
into his priggish baby face. But there are people close by—packs of
strangers—it is a city street, a city scene—absurdly real—far more be-
lievable than my phantom brother, this hallucination of a brother—
with his mop of dark curls and his pouty ascetic look. How did he
find me, for one thing? Had he really followed me from home? Shy,

sinister, secretive. Inscrutable as always—though, as always, I rather suspect him of being simply naïve.

I suppose she's been reporting me to you, I said coolly, I suppose that business about the fake *Times* obituary—

But he pretended not to know. What obituary, he asked.

I suppose she's been complaining of me to the family, I said, hands thrust in pockets, grinning my sad sour grin, I suppose the Petries are transcending their jealousy of her—uniting to protect her against me, eh? The scapegoat Hugh, that queer one, Hugh—that perennial failure Hugh—

Pretended not to know. Sanctimonious little liar.

But you're not a failure, Stephen said, are you?

I merely laughed.

Only Andrew failed, Stephen said, only Andrew attempted anything—and therefore failed. But I don't believe in failure, Stephen said, pronouncing each word separately, with equal emphasis, as if he were translating from another language. Not deep, not inscrutable!—simple-minded.

I had always been bored by my younger brother. Could not comprehend others' adoration of him—my mother's especially. Aside from his olive-glowing skin and those magnificent dark eyes, aside from that puppyish manner, what charm had he? His religiosity was an insult, his pose of piety ridiculous. In my own way I was far more religious—devout—ascetic—disciplined.

What's my life to you, I asked him, and anyway my symptoms have disappeared, as always. At the present I am seeing *no doctors*: it's remarkable how my neurotic symptoms have vanished. I may have written a few joking letters to Yvonne—and of course she rushed to the family to complain!—like every other little bitch, eh?—she *is* like every other little bitch, isn't she? I assume you know her quite well, Stephen?

Basketball court, midwinter. Boys running loose. Like dogs, like colts, like deer. Black boys—of high school age mainly—a single white boy, no more than thirteen—shouting and darting from side to side—the basketball bouncing at odd unpredictable angles from the uneven surface of cracked asphalt—yells, screams, shouts of joy—disappointment—sudden rage—and then joy again, and again the pounding of feet. Stephen was watching them. My voice faltered, sounded shrill and womanish and—and what had I been saying? *You are Yvonne's lover, aren't you?* But that particular bit of madness I would not articulate; I was, after all, not mad.

You are Yvonne's lover—? Are you?

A handsome black boy rushed with the ball down to our end of the court—leaped magnificently—sank the ball through the crooked hoop—the others closing about him, their breaths steamy—their shouts ragged, raw. *Van Dyke Y.S.A.*: the boy's red sweatshirt. Incomprehensible message. For a moment the boy glared out at me—wiping his face, panting—and I felt a pang of—of what?—not of envy, not of desire, not even of simple admiration—for he was beyond that, he was another species entirely—but of awe. No: not awe. Not quite. A feeling of— A sensation of—
    The game continued, the boys charged to the other end.
    Of course he had not glared at me. He had not even seen me.
    I stood there alone, shivering, on what must be called the "outside" of that wire fence. Stood there alone, hands in both pockets, my right hand numbly caressing. . . .

A young man with brittle platinum hair invited me in—told me I was quite welcome to come in—but what could he tell me about Eva? He didn't know Eva. A rugless floor—cartons of books—canvases smeared with thick multicolored coils of paint. Can't tell you any more than the landlord told me, the young man said, pretending to be concerned while I stared at the amateurish canvases—noticed, in a pile of books on the floor, a copy of *Eminent Contemporaries* without its dust jacket. *Hey, I created that! Hey, that's me!* "Hugh Petrie" *is none other than me, me, me!*
    Can't tell you any more than the landlord told me, he said, and I shrugged and backed away and fled.

Though we live in jest, we die in earnest.

Stephen appeared beside me, my lost brother Stephen—touched my shoulder (as one should not do, in New York City)—explained that he had been following me for several minutes, had been calling my name. I was more angry than frightened. That someone should touch me, should creep up on me like that! That someone, even my brother, should interrupt my reverie—
    Hugh? Don't you recognize me? Are you—?
    Accompanied me to the Food Basket—taller than I by several inches—my baby brother. But why pretend? He didn't look babyish, didn't look like any brother of mine. Haggard, drawn, peculiar.

Watching without comment as I selected items from the produce counter—ostensibly health-producing vegetables—and from the dairy counter—several containers of plain sour yogurt—could not recall whose advice I was following—one of the doctors?—one of my fellow alcoholics? In order to drink well, they say, one must be reasonably alive; therefore one *must* eat.

And what shall I buy for you, Stephen? Of course you'll dine with me tonight. Such an unexpected pleasure, I find myself at a loss merely to comprehend it. . . . You'll be having dinner with me?

Stephen said he had no appetite, really. Wasn't hungry. Had already eaten, wouldn't be hungry now for many hours. Unfortunately he had to leave shortly—couldn't stay for very long—

This amused me. Where must you return to, Stephen? A monastery? A churchyard? Or have you broken with that world, have you completed that idiotic phase of your life? Father always said—and said again when I visited him recently—

You visited him recently?

—said that he thought of you with pity rather than anger: why should he be angry? You declared bravely at the age of twenty-one, wasn't it?—that you weren't really one of us, you rejected Grandfather's trust in your name, and what Mother left you, and made quite an impression on everyone—which had been your intention, no doubt. He isn't magnanimous enough a man to "forgive" you, I'm afraid, but you don't want—?

My father doesn't know me at all, Stephen said abruptly. He doesn't know any of us.

Ah, but he actually wept—embraced me—prattled of his love for me—admiration, even—as if he'd ever been capable of appreciating my art!—still, it was touching—I believe I wept also—a father-son scene of the kind I never anticipated. —Why, he collects my drawings! Remarkable, isn't it? Has a clipping service—keeps them framed—under glass—several drawings I had more or less forgotten myself, there they were on his living-room wall— And of course he had photographs of Andrew also: and even of Doris. Elderly, senile, but quite outspoken when the subject of his will came up—unhappy that Andrew was dead, of course, but grateful at least that Doris and I were still—could still take over the responsibilities of the estate after his death. Father and I have had our differences, of course, but I must admit—

He doesn't know any of us, Stephen said, interrupting.

In the apartment, putting things away, humming to myself while Stephen waited in absolute silence. He had never visited me before. He stood in the midst of my kingdom, staring from object to object —from place to place—his lips pursed in disapproval or shock. Or envy. I snatched some sheets of paper off the workbench—made a show of putting them away—as if he would be offended by the sight of such things.

You have never cared for my work, I said lightly.

He was looking at a messed-up line drawing, a kind of crucifixion —a copulation-crucifixion—that I barely remembered having done. It was a work of genius!—except for the fact that someone had blotted ink on it and smeared the inkblots. A copulation-crucifixion, my personal revenge upon the Angel of Death and the Woman—the Angel crucified on a ludicrous fleshy cross—a woman's body upside down—could barely remember having drawn this delicious thing— though I must have done it in the last few days.

You have never been sympathetic with my work, I said, taking the sheet from him.

I don't understand it, he said.

Ha, ha! Art isn't to be understood, it's to be experienced, I said, chuckling warmly. Stephen avoided my jolly brimming gaze. Art, like life, is only to be experienced, I said.

I have never understood that either, he said softly.

You can't fool me with your innocence! But never mind, never mind. The love of brothers should not be challenged by any difference of taste, however fraudulent. Sit down. Take off your coat. Relax, stay a while, it's been years. Don't look so intimidated. You'll make me nervous, and I'm so newly freed of nervousness—so newly healthy and happy. Would you like a drink? No? Nothing? But of course you don't mind if—? Of course, of course not. Why should you mind, how dare you mind. Nobody minds. Nobody cares. Nobody sees me, nobody visits. You're the first one in— Look, Stephen, I would prefer you to sit down. Clear off that chair. Sit down. From this angle you look at least seven feet tall—in this lighting you look ghastly, your face all blue shadows. You must humor me. You must entertain me. Of course *she* has told you all sorts of lies, eh? About certain offenses committed against her ostensible purity?

Stephen sat. His big clumsy fingers unbuttoned his coat—absent-minded, numb—but he did not take the coat off. Why unshaven, my baby brother? He was not so pretty now. Had the battered dazed ap-

pearance of one of those louts I occasionally mingled with in one bar
or another. I could not resist lurching across the room to him and
rumpling his hair—as one might rumple a sullen child's hair—half
affectionately, half cruelly.

Don't!

Sorry—

He sat. I sat. Scotch in a tumbler, no ice. Yogurt—my hands trembling as I spooned it—making a joke of my curious shaky hunger. I
might have been alone, I felt so uneasy. Alone and yet not really
alone, not at peace—alone in one room while someone is in another
—alone in a locked apartment while someone makes his way up the
fire escape, along the creaking corridor—while invisible presences
hover and whisper and brush against one's face. Silence. Awkward.
Stephen had always been shy, ungainly. *Don't!* he had cried. As if
frightened. As if truly frightened.

But what could I do to you? I—to *you?*

Began to laugh at the absurdity of it. He was strong—strong in the
shoulders and arms. I was thin, my upper arms flabby, hopeless. The
spoon clattered on the floor.

What is my life to you, I said coolly, since when did anyone in the
family ever give a damn about me? Or about anyone? Selfish bastards. Father cut you off without a penny, he wishes you were dead,
hadn't been born—told me so himself—drooling in his senility—
revealing certain long-suppressed truths. He's found God out there.
Brags about it. His God isn't your God, however. What *is* your God?
—You haven't come to save my soul, you said. Why can my soul
take care of itself? Why do you have such faith in my soul? Last
time I looked there was nothing there—a few roach or bedbug
smears—that's all.

Stephen shifted uneasily, trying to meet my gaze. He began to
speak—muttered something about having heard I was ill—hadn't
been able to work—

What is my life to you!

Hugh, please—

Hugh please! Hugh please! Hugh *please!* Should I blow my head
off simply to satisfy that woman's blood lust? Because I insulted her,
toyed with her, did a little poking and prying? Not everyone,
Stephen, is a eunuch like you. Some of us are reasonably normal
men— There was Andrew, for instance—with all his women— And
of course Father.

I offered the bottle. He refused.

Prig.

What is your motive for coming here, I asked. Not a concern for my well-being—hardly!

Muttered again something about "having heard I was ill."

There is no illness! Only varying degrees of perception! I see—I know—I'm therefore dangerous, eh? Like any lover, I gambled—I wanted to win, wanted desperately—but I will accept my fate—I'm an adult. Noble, aren't I? I'll surprise you all yet. My life is surfacing at last, Stephen, its contours are revealing themselves—a terrain I had inhabited for decades without guessing at its dimensions—so large, large—a continent—large enough to lose myself—I love her, Stephen, and out of spite I refuse to give her up to you. No doubt you have plans— But you don't really know, do you, any more than I do? Or *do* you? Do you know—?

Know what, Stephen said sullenly.

Who arranged for—?

Stephen shook his head.

It might be, he said after a moment's pause, it might be, yes, that I have some idea.

You—?

Have some idea, some dim idea, Stephen said.

But we're talking about Andrew's murder!

Of course, Stephen said, what did you think we were talking about?

And then—

And—

It was impossible to keep him: impossible to keep the creature in focus.

My head pounded—amplified pain from both ears, pressing inward —I snatched my glasses off to rub my eyes—not wanting to weep before him—and somehow I lost him, lost the focus of him, of what he was saying.

Stephen, don't leave yet—don't leave me—

Stephen, don't belittle me to her—mock me, ridicule me—don't humiliate me as Andrew did—

Don't expose me to everyone—

Mr. Petrie, how do you account for your genius?

I don't account for my genius: I am not accountable. I am unique.

Is uniqueness quite a "cross" to bear?

It's exquisite. But one does feel at times like rushing along—to find a suitable spot to dump it. (Of course that's meant to be witty.)

Mr. Petrie, what is that mask of wrinkles you are wearing? And that milkish stain on your chin?

In eighteenth-century Venice, my boy, a man who wanted to disguise himself would not be forced to wear an actual mask—whether of crow's-feet or not—he had only to wear a symbolic miniature mask attached to a coat button. V*oilà!*—he was disguised. He could go anywhere, do anything, he possessed a kind of omnipotence, he could not be held accountable, even to himself he need not be held accountable. —The milkish stain is from her. From nibbling greedily at her. My hands trembled, something fell to the floor, I was dizzy with hunger—must have lost consciousness for a split second—and they were both gone. Only you remain: please don't leave me! Your questions are fascinating— What did you ask me? Could you repeat—?

Why do so many people despise you, Mr. Petrie?

Because I speak the truths none dare utter! Because I smear excrement everywhere! Everywhere! Because I did not shy away—slipped into the bathroom—into the marvelous eight-foot bathtub with her—with her—where she was bathing herself luxuriously—lazily—an infinity of tiny white bubbles rising about her breasts and shoulders —her marvelous skin—high proud head, hair damp at the ends—her mouth parting in a reluctant smile. An infinity of bubbles—a galaxy of tiny worlds—popping against that body—popping, exploding, dying—tiny heartbeats exploding with rapture against her—against it— the weight, density, pull of her body— An infinity of tiny love spasms—unwitnessed, unsung— What was your question? Don't stop! Your question— You were asking— I need your questions, please don't stop—

Who the hell's this?

Some famous man, a congressman or something, or a guy from television. Always giving interviews. It's almost ten: that will shut him up.

Could work off energy if we unstrapped that thing.

Is he gonna jump from the window? Jump uphill?

He's quieter now, he's looking at me.

He can't see you or nobody.

Looking right at *me*.

Think you're a pretty boy, eh? —Jesus, he'd be a powerful source of energy, could be hooked to a floor-polisher—or what's-his-name's kidney machine—

A famous man, huh? Which one?

I don't know. They're all alike, always giving interviews. Fall asleep in the middle of a sentence, wake up in the middle of another sentence. I don't know who the hell he is—I don't keep up with the news.

36

February 14. All's well.

Rose from a mild hangover, already smiling and eager for the drawing board. The Artist thrives on work. Cannot be kept from it. Crawls to his work—clutches at the tabletop—pulls himself up by his straining splintering fingernails—a wide wide-screen enamel smile—for the biographers to note.

Hangover, but unusually mild.

No weather today worth mentioning. Sooty skies—or perhaps only a sooty window—overcast, undercast—comforting drone of the city in winter. Would I wish it spring? And Yvonne not yet won? Hardly. Weeks and months of work lay ahead.

My antique clock has wound down, the pendulum stilled. When the resumption of time is celebrated I will wind the clock; will give that tarnished old pendulum a helpful poke of my forefinger.

The night before, less memory than nagging hangover. Must have fallen asleep at the drawing board. Empty bottle of Scotch . . . empty container of yogurt and spoon at my feet . . . my lips encrusted with something hideous. It tasted black but was white, dried foam or spittle, a saltlike appearance but no taste of salt.

Memory of Stephen.

Fond drunken hallucination, nothing to worry about. No horror to it—not the D.T.'s, I assume—really quite acceptable, in a context of otherwise unremarkable events. . . . A boy I picked up somewhere, in a Greenwich Village dive or maybe at one of the baths? . . . or maybe, taking pity suddenly, not giving in to my impulse to shove him violently away, out on the avenue, peddling crepe-paper carnations or "real" orchids for a worthy cause? Or was it really Stephen? My only surviving brother?

Remember tousling the boy's hair. Would probably not have done so if— And his reaction? Irritable, flinching away. *Don't!* Unmistakable edge to his voice. Warning. Little-boy maniac, perhaps. Stephen? A dream? A soiled black-jacketed angel, sent to comfort me but not very comforting? (As, alas, is often the case.) Since this is February, and not a spring day of some time ago, the boy cannot have been exotic Bulgarian-born Dimitri of the Royal Ballet—no, he hadn't a bruise on his forehead—nor had he kept himself stiffly away, refusing to drink with me. No. Not at all. Either it was Stephen in person, or a bad dream. In either case I felt nothing for him—am incapable of feeling anything for him—the least attractive vice in my opinion (contrary to Dr. W's theology) being incest of any kind.

This morning: the apartment as usual.

This afternoon: all's well.

In the Museum of Modern Art, a work by Paul Klee, *The Mocker Mocked*: a man's head and the merest suggestion of shoulders . . . a man whose jagged, impatient being is a single line . . . jaw protruding, mouth and nose run together . . . mute with fury, intelligent fury, in an eternal spasm of discontent. The eyes are squibbles. Blind. No ears. The creature himself is contained within a block of darkness like a square of—linoleum tile. An ever-vigilant consciousness! Isolated, yes. Of course. Separated from his "fellow men," as the saying goes. What is his sin? Clarity! An unsentimental clarity!

Will no one pity him?

Will no one honor him?

Spent the day sketching, ripping up what I'd done, trying again. No point in despairing. Feasted on a concoction brimming with health: sliced carrots and celery in bouillon made from three tiny cubes. Practical, economical, nutritious.

Afterward, yogurt sprinkled with wheat germ.

Nutritious, brimming with health . . . somewhat sickening. Still, one must make the attempt.

Stephen, I said coyly, your pretty face isn't very pretty at the moment. You seem rather morose, eh? You've lost a few pounds, eh? And those shadows around your eyes are alarming; can't you sleep any longer, like the rest of the adult population?

At this his face actually began to turn rosy. Blushing, he was. My gentle, pious, innocent brother!

You look almost as if . . . as if you are in mourning, I said delicately.

He muttered something in embarrassment. He did not want to talk about himself. It made him uncomfortable to be spoken of in this way; it makes everyone uncomfortable; which is one of my strategies. . . . Yes, your face is thinning and the old bright puppyish gleam of your eyes is gone and—unless I am mistaken—there's a certain dull purple crepe-like tone to the skin just beneath your eyes. And—

All right, Stephen said.

. . . Do they work you too hard at your present place of employment?

All right, Stephen said.

What do you mean—all right what? . . . I asked you about your present place of employment, didn't I? What is it? Where is it? What do you do, what sort of life are you leading now?

I came to talk about other things, Stephen said slowly. Not myself but—

Then go away! Now! At once! Out, out, out!

Looked extremely startled, our Stephen. Christly prig. Stammering. What do you mean—what—why? Go away—why? I want to—

You offer nothing of yourself, it's a form of—

—want to—

Don't interrupt! —It's a form of egoism worse than—

But there's nothing in my life, Stephen said. There is nothing. Where I am, there is nothing— There is nothing—nothing—nothing significant.

Then get out.

He was silent for a moment then said rather briskly, I have a job at a children's shelter in Ogdensburg—it's only temporary—in fact I might not return—I'm not certain. Do you know where Ogdensburg is?—on the St. Lawrence, yes—a little south of Massena—this winter has been especially bad there, the temperature has stayed below zero for weeks at a time—I—I—I might return, I don't know—don't know. I left Brandywine last fall, for a number of reasons. —But don't you know this?—I would have thought Doris—

Doris tells me everything, I said, but her voice obliterates the content, makes it all trivial and embarrassing and not worth my effort to record—that must be it, eh? Possibly I did know some of this. But I forgot and I need to be reminded. —So you left the good folks in Brandywine and sought out some good folks up north and now you're leaving them and don't know what's next: marvelous. The family points to *me* as the failure—and it has always seemed that *you* are outside the context of failure and success, doing as you will, merrily and moronically. Since you're on the border now, why not slip over into Canada?—slide all the way to the Arctic, to the North Pole —preach to the sea birds and the bears and the walruses—and have done with *us*.

They won't let me into Canada, Stephen said evenly. Always, he deflated my tone; ruined my good humor. They don't want me—at least right now—

Because—

Of what?

Because—

Surely not because of—? The fact that Andrew was—?

Blushing again, an overgrown child. I did dislike him. Yet I liked my dislike of him—there was something familiar about it—fond, brotherly—childlike—childish: whom can we dislike, if not our siblings? Are not siblings the only human beings we are not seriously required to love?

Because of my police record, Stephen muttered.

Record! You!

A moment of astonishment: sheer exquisite astonishment.

But was it genuine, had I heard correctly? And why, now, spooning a sour coagulating mixture into my mouth, why did I remember it so skewedly, so *artificially*? In fact I knew of my brother's "record" —in the madcap sixties he had been involved in protests—demonstrations—draft-card burnings—a march or two on a courthouse or perhaps on the Pentagon itself—who knows?—who bothered to keep track of his late and protracted adolescence?—not even Andrew had probably cared enough, finally.

Stephen, I whispered, do you—? Are you—? Could you tell me—? If you could tell me assuredly— Not *his* death, particularly. I am desperate to know, yes. Desperate. Dying. But: If you could tell me assuredly of death in a more general sense—if you could whisper a few secrets about it—*it*— Stephen? If you could—? I would be so eternally grateful. Stephen!

Silence. An empty room, an empty apartment.

Stephen—?

Dearest Yvonne:

I must know. What is Death? Did you experience it with
him? Stumbling upon him like that, did you accidentally
comprehend . . . ? Was he dead when you found him, or was he
in the throes of death, of actual dying? If so. . . . If so, dear,
did he speak to you? Did he explain . . . ? It's true I love
you, I want you, but I would be willing to concede that perhaps . . . in a manner of speaking . . . it is your wisdom I crave,
your closeness to . . . intimacy with. . . . Do you see? I love
you but would be content with. . . .

Can we live without knowing?

How can we live? How? Without knowing? How can we bear
it, not knowing? How and why and in what context he
died. . . . It isn't a question of justice, dear Yvonne, but of
the survival of sanity; mankind cannot live with mystery. . . .

At least I can't.

Love—Love—Love

Hugh

Dissatisfied with the phrasing of that letter, nevertheless folded it,
put it in an envelope, printed her name and address in arty block letters. Stamp? No stamp? Pawing through debris, looking through pencil stubs and paper clips and letters, no luck, no stamps handy. . . .
Not long afterward, the buzzer sounded.

The buzzer sounded. Woke me from a deep, apparently dreamless
sleep. Very late—two or three in the morning—quite a surprise. I was
not, however, alarmed.
Went to the intercom. Who's there? Who is it? And the voice
that answered—unintelligible murmur—my dear friend Eva.
Eva? What's wrong? Where have you been for the past two
months? Eva? Will you come up? Eva? Are you alone?
Buzzed to unlock the door downstairs.
Slicked my hair down eagerly. In pajamas—not my most attractive
pair, either—baggy damask-patterned cotton. Put my bathrobe on, a
slight improvement. Where was the belt? Without the belt it would
swing open.
No time to search for the belt.
Went to the door, stood with the chain-lock on, peering out—
waiting—absurdly excited, pleased—as if this were an adventure—the

sort of thing people imagine happens often in Greenwich Village.
Eva appeared, hurrying. Rushed toward me.

Taller, was she? Different?

I unlocked the door.

Not Eva: but Yvonne.

Yvonne!

Already past me, brushed past me. She hurried into the room as if
afraid I would shut the door.

Yvonne, is it really—? But why—?

She wore a long dark coat, rather plain, not very attractive. It fell
below her knees: may have been fashionable, may have been out of
fashion. Her hair was hidden beneath an odd hat or cap, scooped up
and hidden inside it so that her face looked exposed, bare, raw.

Yvonne, I don't know what to—

She made no effort to smile. Her manner was brusque, barely
polite, irritable. Dark trousers, calfskin boots. No gloves. No rings either: I noticed that at once.

I'm sorry to disturb you, she said in a low, flat voice, only now
bothering to look directly at me, I'm sorry to come to you like this,
but—but— We must talk, isn't that so? You've been wanting to talk
with me, haven't you? And now—here we are— Now— Before I leave
we will have settled certain things.

Yvonne, I'm at a loss for— As you can see, I—

She would not take off her coat, would not sit down. She paced to
the kitchen archway, turned back, came headlong at me as if unaware
of me, sighing, harassed, continually touching her head, her hair, patting the dove-gray wool cap. My eyes began to water, I could not
help myself.

A drink? No? A cup of coffee? No? But at least let me take your—

Looked at me, unsmiling. Skin hard-glowing, mean, the opacity of
lard. Eyebrows too dark, eyes shrewd, suspicious, narrowed. My dear
My beloved? There was a shadowy cleft to her chin I had not n
ticed before.

The woman was panting, lips pursed shut. Her chest and should
actually moved with the effort—rose and fell.

If only I had known— You've come to me at such a— Yvon
you're so beautiful!—and I'm so ugly— And— And if you're c
cerned about that obituary, that fake *Times* story, why—why—it
just a joke—I didn't actually—

Yvonne laughed.

Obituary! Would I care about your obituary!

But I—

I want to know, Yvonne said, approaching me from the far side of the workbench, stepping with a kind of angry fastidiousness through the clutter, I want to know what you did to me that night—do you remember?—you remember! That night—that night in Albany—at the Hotel Washington—wasn't it?—you begged me to meet you, you begged me for an hour of my time, and—

The Andora, I whispered, it was the old Andora—the Red Fox Lounge—

The Andora, then! What difference does it make! —I want to know what you did to me afterward. In the apartment. On my bed. I want to know exactly what happened—what you did.

Did?

To me. To my body.

Why, Yvonne— Why, don't you know, I did—I— I did nothing— nothing at all—

What did you do! I want to know exactly!

I—

Poor eyes watering violently now. Could hardly see the woman.

—nothing, nothing— Nothing at all— I assure you that—I—I was never capable of—in my entire lifetime— Yvonne, please don't be angry! It was only—only— It wasn't meant to— I knew all along I'm not the man Andrew was—hardly!—he was always so fine a physical specimen, and so psychologically stable as well—so hideously *normal*: who can compete with normal men? You see— There's no reason for, no need to—

You're contemptible, Yvonne interrupted. You disgust me. You disgust everyone. *You!*—how dare *you* even speak of him! Of all people, *you*—! And the bragging afterward—the obscene remarks and hints— The rumors that came back to me—

Yvonne, that isn't possible! Cannot be! That anyone repeated— that anyone would have taken me seriously—

Look at you, look at how you live!—how contemptible! Her voice was low, rapid, flat. She made a sudden gesture—knocked something off a table—a small pile of papers that scattered across the floor.

That's quite all right, quite all right, I said weakly, don't bother to pick them up—I'll do it— If only you would stay in one place, Yvonne dear, if only you would have mercy, would listen to my side of the story— You see, for one thing you woke me from a sound sleep and I'm not at my best—haven't been at my best for some time—for many weeks—months— To tell the truth, I haven't been at my best

for years— Being waked like this, so suddenly, I'm at a disadvantage
intellectually and emotionally—

Aren't you going to answer my question?

Question . . . ?

Aren't you going to answer it?

You seem so hard, Yvonne, so stern—remorseless— Not at all the
woman everyone knows and admires— I fear there has been some
terrible, terrible—

You forget, she said, half-shutting her eyes, I'm not a Petrie: I'm
not one of *you*: who among you has ever known me?

But— But— That doesn't mean you must hate us, does it?

She was still panting. The fingers of one hand checked her cap
nervously, tucked in a few strands of hair. A coltish impatience to
her, nothing pretty about her, cheeks somewhat gaunt, hollow. She
did not glare at me: her eyes were narrowed, mean, as if she looked
upon me with the greatest reluctance.

I don't owe you any answers, she said. I've asked you a question
and I'm waiting for—

Yvonne, what a—

I tried to laugh. I managed to laugh.

—a joke!

The old brown flannel robe hung open—I unsnapped my pajamas
—groped for my penis—feeble, limp, tiny creature like nothing else
on earth—a joke, yes—it was a joke—must have been a— I shook it at
her, toward her, trying to laugh again, again with some minimal success: couldn't she see? wasn't this proof? A joke, a joke—I was never
anything but a joke—how harmless I was, how soft, limp, hopeless,
helpless—couldn't she see? Have mercy!

Yvonne, why so angry! Why so humorless! Anyone in his right
mind could—in her right mind— You're being irrational—short-
sighted—unfair— Do you think, Yvonne, that I—that *this*?—this tiny
useless thing? Please—it's beyond being a joke—it's wildly hilarious
now— It's— Don't you see? Don't you understand?

Stared at me. Stared at it.

Yvonne—? You don't really think that—?

For a long moment she stared, for a long moment she remained
perfectly still. Her lips still pursed, her brows still lowered; her eyes
fixed remorselessly upon me. She saw. Seemed to see. The tension in
her jaw relaxed, she very nearly smiled—but did not smile—did not
smile.

All right? Yvonne? Mercy? *Mercy?*

37

Alone. And my shadow falls before you.

Brooding and muttering aloud, as always, alone, pretending to joke but always serious; pretending to be serious but always joking, muttering so that no one will hear in this public place, now that the symptoms are finally banished and all's well.

Innumerable shadows now. Cast by innumerable lights. Not just the sun: there are innumerable reflected suns. In smoked-glass windows, in the enormous floor-to-ceiling dark green window, solid plate glass, of a bank on Fourth Avenue—or is it Third Avenue—and over at Radio City Music Hall an astonishing sight: a block-long procession of very young children, five or six years old, babbling, giggling, in couples, holding hands. A shadowy figure here, a shadowy figure there as you hurry across the busy street—no time to waste—no time even to glare angrily at the horns that sound so rudely—innumerable shadows blocking your path, so you must charge through them. Yet there is a trick to the light, I am still before you, crouched slightly, interfering with your conversation—ruining it, as always—standing before you—yet not quite visible—not ever visible. I am here, now. I am here, always. You are speaking earnestly to the woman—pleading with her, one would judge from your voice—and I ruin the opportunity, as always, and you are helpless to change anything. An elementary school teacher, sandpaper-skinned, wearing glasses, in a herringbone tweed pants suit—smiling at first, and then smiling with more effort—trying to determine if you are serious or joking or insane.

Would you like the services of another adult?—another adult to supervise the children, to sit with them for the matinee? I'm available, I'm absolutely free—just noticed you and the others a moment ago—and was impressed with—moved by— I'm free, really—have a luncheon engagement at La Petite Place at twelve-thirty, but I could easily break it if necessary—

The woman is smiling no thank you, no thanks, go to hell, crawl away somewhere to die, who needs you? Smiling and shaking her head. Thank you very much but there are four of us—we can manage quite well—

I'm an uncle, myself, I'm quite fond of children, it was evidently not my fate to be a father—to father my *own* children— But—on the other hand— I could help you with the tickets, you know: I'd be delighted to help. Somehow Christmas came and went, I was too busy, too absorbed in my own worries to— And before we know it Easter will be here—

Thank you. But sorry.

Procession of children, seemingly endless. Surging forward. Two by two, girls holding hands, boys holding hands, girls and boys, boys and girls, the adults among them suspicious of you, staring frankly at you, at your watery eyes and hands shoved in pockets. Can they see? Can they guess? . . . How small the children! Extraordinarily small. Children and not adults.

The procession is seemingly endless, filing into the theater. You stand to the side, you manage a smile, gape and stare and exchange a few awkward greetings, no harm, how harm?—a skinny child with glasses shies away from your grin—like you yourself at that age!—and there is a little blond girl in a scarlet coat who reminds you of—a scarlet coat with darling fake-ermine collar and cuffs—a child who reminds you of another child—someone you played with—someone you were close to—and yet another child who reminds you of— My shadow falls before you, not quite visible. But when it lifts, the procession is gone, the last of the children has entered the theater, you are alone.

Harm? How?

Never.

Panhandlers. One of them familiar—a boy in a soiled khaki parka —rubbing his nose even as he appeals to passers-by—rattling a cup in their faces. Ah! There! Let him approach *you!*

Sir? Madame? A worthy cause—cystic fibrosis— Worthy worthy cause—what's the rush?— Madame, sir? Just a minute, you—

Tourists, well-dressed and cautious. A veritable parade of tourists this morning. Fifth Avenue and Forty-ninth Street. The lively boy in the parka bounces along—follows one embarrassed couple for half a block—shakes the cup in their faces—grins wonderfully. The gentleman finally gives him something: a coin. The boy grins, grins. Shakes the cup even harder in the man's face.

You follow, gun in pocket.

The boy lets them go at the curb—bows mockingly—a final shake of the cup—turns away and for a moment his face is normal, his expression subdued and even a little tired—he strides back to his post and again appeals to pedestrians—some hurry by, some hesitate—a

few give coins—one or two mutter something at him and rush past—
he ignores *you*—does not seem to notice *you*—has glanced at you
indifferently and does not seem to be impressed. Sir? Madame? Any
change you can spare for a worthy worthy cause—

You walk slowly past. He ignores you.

You turn, look back. He ignores you. Is appealing to a nattily
dressed little man with black mustache and sideburns—hovering over
him—bullying and grinning. Sir? Please? Spare change for a—

You hesitate. Someone collides with you—mutters *Excuse me*
without looking—but still the boy ignores you, now attaching himself to a woman in a fake leopard-skin coat. You hesitate, wondering
if you should remain here—or walk purposefully away—or perhaps go
around the block and try again.

You are excited, in spite of the ugly bustle of the street. This is
not the place you would have chosen for your gesture of futility—
not exactly the stage you would have selected—but it will do well
enough. If only that bastard would approach you! If only he would
stick that cup in your face! And then—

Yvonne, opening the closet door—finding nothing, exclaiming in
irritation—as if you had hidden something from her, as a child hides
something that must be found. Yvonne, pulling the drawers out one
by one—then striding to the bed, your untidy rumpled bed, lifting
the pillow to reveal the gun—Willa's revolver—in that secret place
you had kept it—how did she know?—who had told her?

Yvonne, tossing the pillow to the floor, exposing the gun. There it
is! There! Take it—you know what to do with it! Take it! *Take it!*

Yvonne, watching with that pale, heated look of utter contempt—
of exquisite contempt. You know what to do with it! *Take it now!*

But the boy is trotting alongside the woman in the leopard-skin
coat—begging, whining, grinning like a clown—he even leaves his ter-
ritory and follows her across the street.

A pity. It would have been an enigmatic act—playful, Dadaist—a
filthy bastard deserving of death shot down at high noon—his murderer then turning the gun nobly upon himself—heard to proclaim
to horrified witnesses: I hereby protest the vulgarity of modern life!

Nothing sentimental about it. Reckless, cavalier, highly imaginative—in no way traced back to—in no way linked with—

Eyeglasses slipping down nose. Crowds at intersections—edging
out before the lights change—and the usual taxicabs bullying their
way through. Hurry. Must hurry. Six blocks to go—five and a half—

must hurry—reservation for twelve-thirty—nearly forgot—no time to
telephone Pamela—dear Pamela!—lately deceased, they said—though
perhaps they lied—perhaps it was necessary to lie. The latest arrests
in the Petrie case, the latest headlines: necessary lies. No point in
protesting. The corpse was not shown—hidden from view inside that
magnificent casket—no way for the average mourner to know that
Andrew was even dead—the only hint Hugh caught was the squealing for help—as the casket was lowered into the grave—squealing,
shrieking—horror—something comic about it, of course—but—
    Three blocks. Ah, no: two.
    Handsome façades of shops. Travel agencies. Plate-glass windows
—mannequins dressed for spring—red polka dots definitely *in*—silky
lounging pajamas—in Doubleday's a marvelous spread of bright
glossy books—none of them familiar, no dust jacket familiar—but no
time anyway, no time to waste. Midtown Manhattan, high noon,
rare splurge of wintry sunshine, frosty healthy breaths, a few faces
familiar—as always—strangers hauntingly familiar—but no time to
waste, no time. *Take it! Take it now!* And one minute before twelve-
thirty the maitre d' checks his clipboard in the gloom—Hugh Petrie?
—table for one?—escorts you halfway across the floor—seats you at a
tiny table not far from the kitchen's swinging doors—but why
protest?—you simply shut your eyes—swinging doors opening upon a
glaring kitchen—hellish—swinging doors like hell's gate—open, shut,
open, shut—waiters scurrying past—a boy in a tight-fitting waiter's
outfit seems to wink at you—recognizes you?—remembers you from
last time? Fortunately you have worn a necktie and a reasonably decent sports coat. Not very smoothly shaven, but acceptable. Hair
slicked in place. But that kitchen door—that constant swinging—
Hell's gate—hell—bright jarring radiance of—
    Monsieur? Yes?
    Brook trout meunière, please hurry!
    Playful, playful. Nothing melodramatic about it—nothing senti-
mental or coarse. A drink? No? Cannot take the risk of being
thought drunk, not today.
    Service slow. Interior smoky. Tables jammed together—a narrow
runway for the waiters—and that everlasting kitchen door—hadn't
noticed previously. Two semi-stale rolls in a basket—a few pats of
butter on ice—thank you, thank you—no wine today, I think—thank
you—cavalier smile—the impish serenity of genius—no need to
worry, all's well at last. Luncheon at La Petite Place. A pity none of
his—none of your—women could join you. And so it is a quite ordi-

nary occasion: these customer-spectators quite ordinary, ordinary.

A very poor table for so famous a customer: when would these ignorant peasants learn? Bastards with their labored fake-French!

Brook trout meunière. Slow in coming—very slow. Overpriced, as always. Prices raised since last time, in fact. . . . Should have ordered terrapin Baltimore style, intestines and all, a rare treat, rarely seen on a menu hereabouts. Too late you remember that price is really no concern of yours, not today. Habit of being economical—pointless now—spending little, trying desperately to save a few pennies, made to beg and cringe and crawl to the Petries simply in order to pay your rent—to exist minimally—a lifetime habit, no longer practical. Brook trout meunière at last: hideous, that eye staring at you!

Forgot about the scaly head and tail, the jewel of an eye! But here it is. And a side dish of asparagus, tiny and limp, not very warm. Perfunctory salad, two slices of pale tomatoes, hothouse tomatoes, inedible. Why did you come here? What was the point of it? A fish lying before you, tail and head intact, eye intact, ready to wink—sprinkled with lemon and parsley—overpriced and probably chock full of tiny bones— The anxiety of the first forkful—your nerve endings at the bursting point—

Monsieur? The boy-waiter is hovering at your elbow.

Go away! Leave me alone! I can't eat with people staring at me!

Fork slips, clatters against the plate. Napkin in lap, safely. Now what? What? Ah yes: must eat carefully, must avoid the dangerous bones. *Monsieur!* the fish pipes up, *Monsieur! Take care!* You poke it with the fork nonetheless. You laugh, astounded; but no one else has heard. *You would eat me, monsieur? How crude!*

The fish is protesting. Alive. Sprinkled with butter and lemon and parsley, but still alive, impudent. Somehow this isn't surprising: the service here is execrable, the food shockingly overpriced. And the waiters move about so fussily, brushing near you, without regard for you, unaware of your identity. Impossible situation. You signal the waiter—the waiter pretends not to see. What! What is this! And the kitchen doors are swinging, swinging—

Monsieur, I protest my position here on this plate—

Shut up! Who's master here!

People at a nearby table are mildly curious. A girl in a flaming orange dress—balloonish white-blond hair—must be a model—staring your way with a provocative smile—assuming you are someone important—impressed with your hauteur. Does she know you? Have you met? Too late, too late. Too late. Suddenly the revolver is in your hand.

Too late. The revolver is out. Sweaty palm, icy fingers that clutch. Everyone sees. Too late to turn back.

Courage is all that is needed.

Monsieur—

Shut up! You have no rights! I can't stomach you!

The revolver is exposed: now there are gasps and murmurs.

Partly premeditated, partly improvised. You knew that something would happen here—which was why you made the reservation and spelled out your name with care—and yet, until the moment the fish began to speak, until the luscious moment when you poked it into speaking, the exact scenario was not known. Genius. The first suicide of genius. A suicide/murder, first of its kind in Manhattan or anywhere. Who can stop you? Who is more deliciously imaginative? The fish lies helpless and tepid, scaly, lightly sautéed, a single beady eye fixed upon yours. An insult, such food. Such prices. Such inadequate service.

I protest the execrable downward slide of the conditions of life— You clear your throat and begin again, speaking shrilly. I protest— I will not tolerate— The conditions of life in our large urban areas— The rapid disintegration of values in our— I am a martyr—the first martyr—

Everyone is staring. It is suddenly very quiet.

I protest— By this act I offer my—

Nothing sentimental about *you*. Nothing that could be mocked afterward in the papers, in the gossip columns, by friends or enemies. Sangfroid, they will say. Impeccable to the last, they will say. Heroic, reckless, the most original gesture of our era—not a bit sentimental or murky, like other famous suicides!—in no way attributable to a personal failure of any kind—not to professional disappointments— not to love, certainly—unrequited love—or befuddlement over—helplessness in the face of—no, not at all: no. And again: no. Not the slightest connection with the assassination.

First in history, murder/suicide at La Petite Place, busy ordinary self-absorbed lunchtime crowd on Fifty-third Street—what a surprise for them!—the noted prize-winning caricaturist Hugh Petrie shoots his impudent brook trout and then, without flinching—without so much as a blink of the eye—

A woman's voice rises. What? What is—?

Someone is approaching.

No! Stay back! This is between me and *it!*

No flinching now. No hesitation. You aim the gun—pull the trigger—ah!—the first shot is perfect!—right into the fish's head—terrific noise, confusion, plates fly, the bread basket tumbles end over end, the water glass jumps into the air, you are somehow on your feet, the tablecloth caught between your legs for one harried instant —but you refuse to be intimidated, you refuse to give way to panic—

No flinching now. Only your brave shrill unfaltering voice: I hereby protest and offer myself as the first martyr—the first rebel— Deadpan mocking ingenious—what an imagination, they will cry— how we will miss him—who will take his place?—no one, no one!— they will cry in the streets—

I offer myself—

Without flinching, the barrel of the revolver in your mouth, gripped between your teeth. Wildly your eye careens across the tables—through the smoky fashionable gloom—your audience is staring, amazed—incredulous—the girl in the orange dress is crouching, both hands pressed against her cheeks—long painted fingernails digging into her cheeks—even the waiters have paused in midstep, their heavy trays held aloft—

Not the mouth, not the mouth! Suddenly it occurs to you that someone will misunderstand—Dr. W, for instance—or that maniac Dr. S—will interpret your act as symbolic and not real—deathly real —will place a degrading and perhaps even obscene "meaning" upon it— And so you press the end of the barrel against your forehead and pull at the heavy heavy trigger and—

Though we live in jest, we die in—

Part Two **YVONNE**

1

On the afternoon of May 4, more than a month before her husband's death, Yvonne Petrie realized he would die. She did not know, however, what the circumstances of his death would be.

2

Not yet a widow, that day.

She is, instead, highly spirited and enthusiastic. At the same time she is courteous, attentive, and reserved—always rather reserved, as a matter of principle, when she is in public. These people, even her husband's cousin Hannah, are a kind of audience: they stare, as if memorizing her.

She is smiling at her audience, a small gathering, no more than five or six people. She is trying to concentrate—someone is asking a question about the probable allotment of funds if a certain bill is passed by the legislature; she is trying to concentrate, to be polite, though why should he ask *her?*—what have she and Andrew to do with the squalor of state politics at the present time?—trying to concentrate while suddenly aware of a sensation in her left hand, numbness, tingling on the verge of pain. It is entirely new to her, this invisible trembling. She is distracted, annoyed rather than frightened.

She is visiting the Van Ruysdael School for Handicapped Children, on Seventh and Glengarry Streets, Albany, New York. It is an old three-story brick building in a neighborhood of warehouses and trainyards, not far from the river. She is sitting in the shabby, windowless teachers' lounge, at the conclusion of her two-hour visit, having coffee; she is ready to leave, but the others continue talking, asking questions, staring at her. . . . Her left hand, her left forearm: suddenly that tingling, that sensation of numbness. It is distracting, puzzling. As if there were an exterior trembling or vibration that has somehow brushed against her: now lodged in her hand and arm. She is in excellent health, as always—has been in excellent health all her life—has never worried, has never had time to worry. Her body has always taken care of itself.

The feeling in her arm now is one of panic: but subdued, small and treacherous, secret. Something is going to happen—something is already happening.

She shows no discomfort, no alarm. Someone speaks to her; she replies. Her voice is quick and assured. Perhaps a little too quick. She must guard against that, must watch herself: it is a temptation, to speak to certain people rather brusquely. But they are so routinely insolent, so complacently uninformed! She knows statistics, she knows the most recent reports, not-yet-official reports, she knows what is rumor and what is truth, and what is merely ridiculous propaganda—and since everyone has access to such information, why should it seem so surprising? . . . Again, that sensation of panic, an uncontrollable trembling in her left hand. She gropes for an arm of the chair to steady herself. But the chair has no arms. It is made of cheap lightweight plastic, scooped and hollowed to fit the standard contours of the human body. Too big, at the same time too low—too close to the floor for her long legs.

"What did you say? I didn't quite hear—"

The widow is self-conscious this afternoon among these hard-working decent people, the underpaid teachers of Van Ruysdael School; all the more awkward, that one of them is a second cousin of her husband's. But she gives no sign of being self-conscious. She is watchful—watchful of herself—as if something extraordinarily important is happening—is actually being recorded. These people are recording it, are even eager to record it, though their hostility—disguised by a clumsy, ill-orchestrated sociability—is obvious. She is handsome in her soft wool flannel suit—a blend of heather and gray —her hair brushed hard and flat, parted in the center of her head and drawn back, flat, fastened at the nape of her neck by a large gold barrette, only the tips of her ears showing. Her appearance is both stylish and trim, striking and understated, no superfluous details. The brandy-colored shoes gleam, highly polished as they are, but do not give the impression of being expensive: they look rather casual, almost sporty. Her manner is casual, not at all self-conscious. She is still smiling. She is not visibly distracted, not visibly alarmed.

"—your life with him, your work together— So close to him, knowing him in a way other people can't— The influence you must have— And then something happens like that panel, the televised hearings —which even I could see was biased, weighted against him— How do you deal with it, how do the two of you deal with it?"

"But there's no mystery!" Yvonne said. She was speaking to Hannah, smiling brightly at Hannah's serious, perplexed expression. It was Hannah who had invited her here, Hannah who was her hostess. "You know him as well as I do," Yvonne said. "You're his cousin, after all."

"Yes, but I don't know him," Hannah said slowly.

Was her left hand actually trembling? Yvonne risked a look—could see nothing. But the sensation was there, was spreading. She gripped the seat of the chair, propping herself up in a girlish, enthusiastic way. Why were they staring at her, what did they want from her? Even the black principal of the school—a woman in her fifties, with processed hair in the old style and a full, matronly bosom—was unnaturally attentive, watching Yvonne with a small fixed smile. A mock-gold clover-leaf pin on the collar of her dress—matching earrings—her fingernails nicely manicured but unpolished—courteous to the point of insolence. Having been introduced to Yvonne earlier, she had said she found Andrew's ideas quite stimulating and important—very important—in that they crystallized certain half-formed feelings—sentiments—prejudices—that, without Andrew's presence, without his intelligence, could never be comprehended; could never be dealt with, politically or morally. She had even asked whether Andrew intended to run for public office again—had expressed disappointment when told he certainly did not.

"I really don't know him," Hannah was saying in a slow, painstaking manner, "we weren't the right ages to become acquainted

. . . he was so much older than I, almost another generation. . . . I mean he *is* . . . he still is, of course."

Yvonne glanced at her, for a moment genuinely surprised. This plain, indifferently dressed woman had deliberately insulted her!—for they were the same age, nearly. Hannah must have been in her early thirties, only a few years older than Yvonne. She had meant, of course, that in childhood a decade is a very long period of time—she had probably not meant to be insulting. Still, Yvonne had the feeling that one or two of the others were aware of the insult, enjoying the moment.

"None of this is important, is it?" she said, smiling. "Personalities are not so important, are they? Your work with the children here, for instance, and your hope to get more money for the school—that shouldn't be interpreted in terms of your personal lives, should it?— your private lives? You would resent that, wouldn't you? It would be quite natural to resent it—?"

"But we're not famous," one of the men said cheerfully. "None of us are famous."

A young man in his mid-twenties; one of several teachers who worked with retarded children. Wunsch, his name was. Yvonne could not remember his first name. He had a small head, curly brown hair, eyes that looked weak but were thickly lashed—brown, staring, moist, slightly bulging eyes. He wore a jersey pullover sweater, dark green, tucked into slim trousers, and imitation-suede shoes.

"We are anonymous people," he said softly.

Yvonne laughed, thinking he meant to be amusing.

The others laughed, watching her. . . . Her left arm was tingling now, trembling. But she could not examine it, not in public. In her right hand she held a paper cup. Instant coffee out of a vending machine. She didn't want it, she didn't want any of this. Not now. The principal, that mock-friendly woman, was telling Yvonne about a talent show the school was going to present—would she like to attend, was she free a week from Friday evening?—might she and her husband both be free? Yvonne didn't want to sit here any longer, she didn't want any of this; unfortunately—she spoke with a quick sharp smile—Andrew was going to receive an honorary degree at McGill, would be in Montreal that weekend, unfortunately—but thank you all the same. And now—if she could—

"There's power in anonymity," the young man said. He cracked the knuckles of one hand contemplatively. Yvonne noticed a large ring with a black stone, too large to be genuine. "But there's more power in fame. There's more power," he said, "in power."

"A few years ago we had a talent show, some of the children were photographed and written up in the papers, you know, and the rumor was that they were being given contracts—recording companies, movies—you know? But it wasn't true. It was very disappointing then," someone said.

"Yes, wasn't it."

"Still, it was better than nothing. Wasn't it?"

"The newspapers shouldn't have done that."

"But who started the rumors? —The children themselves."

"More coffee, Mrs. Petrie? You don't have to leave so soon—?"

They were talking animatedly, perhaps for her benefit. She was quite nervous now. Both her hands were trembling. At one time in her life, long ago, she had considered being a teacher—had considered, even, working with handicapped children. Her life had gone in another direction, of course. Judging from what she had seen today . . . judging from the atmosphere of this place, even of the recreational area here, and the teachers' tired, grimly loud laughter. . . . No windows in the room, walls of solid concrete, several cheaply framed prints—one of those leprous Utrillo streets, and a skewed, flattened landscape that might have been Cezanne's but looked machine made, and a particularly ugly "abstract expressionist" clown who looked like a parody of one of the handicapped children—an atmosphere of tension, exhaustion, pointless flippancy—a cork-topped table, littered now at the end of the day, ashtrays overflowing with cigarette butts and ashes and several squashed coffee cups—even a broken black comb— And the floor of scuffed tile, worn into grooves, stained and sorrowful—

Yvonne set the cup down and prepared to leave.

"More coffee? No?"

The essence of life is ambiguity, complexity. So Yvonne knew. The essence of paranoia is the inability to tolerate ambiguity—even for brief periods of time. So Yvonne knew. Knows. She knows a great deal, but cannot act upon it. Knowledge: but no power. The teachers and the principal and Hannah Petrie—harmless, decent, hard working—of no importance whatsoever, really—no threat to her —her own bad habit of smiling when she is angry or perplexed—so that the dimple in her cheek sharpens, a sudden pit, a tiny scar: she knows, sees, but cannot act. She is paralyzed.

The young man in the jersey is questioning her, still with that air of good-hearted curiosity. He is fascinated. He is too admiring, too attentive. He catches Yvonne's eye as if to force an alliance between them, he and she against the others, *You and I are different, aren't we?—just a little different?*—at the same time needling her, returning to the subject of the televised hearings—the citizens' committee to investigate the riot at the Glasberg State Prison, some months before —and several remarks Andrew made that subsequently were taken out of context and distorted and used against him— Were there immediate consequences? Were there telegrams, telephone calls, letters? Threats? And how do they deal with such things, how do they live their lives, in the glare of such publicity?

"There are always letters," Yvonne says. Her cheeks burn. But she will not give this bastard the satisfaction of knowing he has annoyed her. "Of course there are always letters from disturbed people. Andrew has lived with it for a long time now. Threats—requests for favors—for money—for information—for secret information— But also very nice letters, letters of gratitude, letters enclosing good-luck charms—religious medals—recipes—prayers—even love letters— He receives every conceivable kind of letter, it really isn't very important. Sometimes there are telegrams, especially after he's given a speech or been on television. Sometimes there are gifts—sometimes there are things meant to frighten him—but nothing frightens him. It isn't important, really. He lives his life—we live our life—without being disturbed by any of this."

"Even the threats?"

"But all public figures receive threats!—don't you know that?" Yvonne says quickly. She is afraid her voice is trembling now. She is afraid everyone will see her panic. They are eying her closely, pretending to be friendly, pretending to be sympathetic. Hannah is even frowning at the young man in the green jersey, pretending to be displeased by his aggressive, naïve manner. Questioning Andrew Petrie's wife like this!—interrogating her, practically! But Yvonne continues to speak without hesitation: "Andrew and I read everything that comes in, we don't even trust his secretaries—since very clever people, very clever disturbed people, sometimes write in code—a kind of poetry, it is—strange—ugly—exasperating—but most of the time really innocent: not serious. People say things they don't mean. They write things they don't mean and they think anonymity will save them—I mean, they think the FBI can't trace the letter back—and in most cases, I mean in most of the problem cases, there isn't any genuine feeling, no real intent to harm—they just write to Andrew Petrie because they're angry about the state of the world in general, or about their own miserable lives— But he doesn't take this sort of thing very seriously: he has a talent for knowing what is serious and what isn't, when a threat is genuine and when it's just rhetoric. And the things I receive occasionally—those letters—they're laughable, really—they have nothing to do with me at all—no one knows *me* at all," she says, now breathing very quickly, almost panting. There is a pause, there is silence. She knows she is trembling visibly. "The exasperating thing about his—our— The tragic thing— I mean, the secret— You see, Andrew isn't a politician at all: he despises politics. He thinks of himself as a political theorist. A philosopher. An analyst—a historian—perhaps even a prophet, in a way. In a modest way. He works so hard!—spends months and months on a single essay—does so much research— He's a stylist, he's very concerned with style, with presentation—subtlety— He came to hate politics because everything is simplified, by the papers especially, everything is beaten down into headlines, reduced to a few formulas— Of course he's political because in a sense we are all political—all of life is political, isn't it? Nearly every aspect of life? The tragedy is—the theme of his writing is—the difference between what people *know* to be true and the way they actually behave—that terrible, inexplicable difference— It's the real concern of his life, not political power; he isn't even a conservative, in the usual sense of the word; but he demands that—he believes that—the only test of a person's belief is his action—his public action—the rest is rhetoric, the rest is illusion and deliberate mystification—"

The black woman is staring at Yvonne, smiling her formal, slightly cynical smile; Hannah is still frowning, pressing her glasses to her face with a forefinger, a stranger to Yvonne, not friendly, not even pretending to be friendly; Wunsch is leaning far forward, elbows on knees, chin on knuckles, regarding her with the look of a man watching television: his gaze wandering from her face to her body, down to her slim ankles and boldly colored shoes, back up again to her face. At the sink, rinsing a china mug, is a tall, thin black man who is nodding in Yvonne's direction. Yes? Yes? More—?

"He's not a politician, then," someone says.

"He doesn't think of himself as a politician," Hannah says. "Is he aware of that?—I mean, that distinction? Is he aware of it himself?"

"I don't understand," Yvonne says blankly.

"People do get the wrong idea about him," Hannah says. "It isn't his fault, it's the fault of people who try to simplify his ideas—

don't you think?—and in politics everything is so blunt—people become polarized so easily. People with certain murderous prejudices are so eager to—"

"I must leave," Yvonne says.

She gets to her feet. Picks up her purse. Trembling, still, but more confident now that she is moving, once again in control of the situation. She thanks them for having shown her through the school. She speaks of being impressed, of having learned a great deal.

Several of them walk with her. Wunsch even walks a little ahead, half-turned to her, slender, graceful, with a small man's agility. What is he saying? Why is he smirking? Asking her to visit the school another time—to visit his class—maybe to have lunch sometime at a restaurant not far away, on Washington Boulevard, a Greek restaurant she might like—?

Hannah is asking her about Andrew, whom she hasn't seen for some time. Is he well? Certainly. In excellent health. Is he still meeting with that committee, or has it disbanded? He resigned from the committee—couldn't bear the lies, the stupidity, the incompetence. And is he in the city, or traveling? He is— He is in the city. At home.

In fact Yvonne is not certain: Is he in the city, or traveling? Or in another city? Or in the mountains, at the old farm, alone, without even a telephone . . . ? She is not certain.

"He's at home," she says.

They asked her to peek into their auditorium. By far the most attractive part of the school, they said; a royal blue carpet had recently been installed, a donor's gift. Did she have time—? Rehearsals for the talent show were going on and it might be—

Yes. She had time. She could not protest.

Leather-padded doors with porthole windows. Swinging doors. The trembling almost uncontrollable now—her arms, her neck and head— They led her into the auditorium, Hannah on her right, Wunsch on her left. And there— There it was—

The noise! It was a drummer, a child drummer. The vibrations, the trembling—a boy playing drums—a drummer, drums!

Yvonne laughed, almost with delight.

"A drummer—" she whispered. "That noise—"

"What?" Hannah asked.

"The way the building is vibrating—"

"Shhh," Wunsch said, winking. "You'll throw him off."

Center stage, a black boy with a set of drums. He must have been eleven or twelve years old. What was wrong with him? Was something wrong? Not blind, was he? Yvonne couldn't tell—he *seemed* to be looking at the drums—*seemed* to be aware of them. One of the teachers, a black man, was standing in the aisle, hands on hips, a few yards away.

Only drumming!—only a child, playing drums! But how loud it was, how it made the old building shudder—still rather upsetting to Yvonne, who hated loud noises—and why didn't he stop, why did he keep pounding away? Was he one of the retarded children? But there was a queer flashing vitality to his eyes—a liveliness—cunning— He did not seem slow-witted and she could not see anything deformed about him, any physical hint of—

"Why doesn't he stop?" she whispered.

She took a few steps forward. Her heart was going wildly. What skill, what anger, what superb noise! The child had given himself up to the noise—tap-tap-tapping—a rattle—a clamor—a thunderous tolling that sounded both distant and immediate—drumming like a solid, fluid roar—a pressure on the eardrums and the eyes and the surface of the face—a pressure on every part of the body—on the brain itself—a pressure hardly to be borne. She wanted to scream. She wanted to get to him, to stop him. The noise echoed everywhere in the small auditorium, bounced off the walls and ceiling. She went forward, but stopped. The noise was overwhelming. A child with skinny arms—yet his arms and hands flashed, the drumsticks flashed and melted and were blurred, like light. The cymbals sounded: then again the drums. There were three of them, each with its own distinct noise. No music to it, no discernible rhythm—only noise. Sheer noise.

The black boy was gleaming with sweat and pleasure. Tireless. His body moved, ducked, jerked; both legs fairly danced. His head, which seemed large, slightly out of proportion to his thin body, bobbed and ducked happily. What joy in his grin!—and in the glaze of his sweat! And he was tireless, tireless. His movements were even accelerating, as if he were approaching the peak of a sequence of music—a sequence of noises—too complex for Yvonne to comprehend, except with her body—now trembling, trembling helplessly—caught in the drumbeat and the rolling clamorous echoing sound that grew louder, steadily louder, always louder.

The noise was in her eyeballs, even; pulsing in her eyes, in her vision. She was blinded. She was deafened. The boy ignored her, ignored his audience. What did he care! He did not care. He was superb, that utter absorption in the drums, that slack-mouthed grinning, the healthy gleam of perspiration—superb, unstoppable. Louder and louder and louder the drum-roll—and then the surprise of the cymbals—the fearful clash of the cymbals—then again the drums. A child's face, yet fixed in an attitude of exquisite pain; the grin sliding, retreating, growing slack again. The forehead a mass of furrows. Hair dark, frizzy, gleaming with sweat or oil. Was he brain-damaged, like some of the others? Blind? Partly crippled, partly paralyzed? Couldn't he speak properly? Breathe properly? He was so much in control of himself, of what he did—and yet wasn't something wrong with him, wasn't it necessary that something be wrong with him? And why wouldn't he stop? And why did he ignore her and the others?

Yvonne's lips parted. She must have been smiling, grinning. The lower half of her face went slack, limp. She wanted to laugh but could not. The child's grin tightened: a double row of teeth, the jaws taut, cords in the neck prominent, straining. No, please. No, no. Don't. Please. Too loud—too loud— And louder still, always louder— She could not bear it that the child's eyes were half closed now, in a kind of ecstasy—she could not bear it, his arms whirling, his hands flashing—the drumsticks trailing light behind them—delicate filmy strands of light—thread-like, luminous— And the noise! Always, always the noise. It was still increasing. She stared, had been staring so intensely that the boy's face lost all color suddenly—became a negative of itself, a photograph negative—now pale, ghostly—grinning at her—eyes still half closed. Something is going to happen, something is already happening, can you feel it happening?—now? She must have been standing there, paralyzed. She could not remember what had brought her here—who had escorted her—who had tricked her into this. The child on stage, the black child whose head sank and bounced and rolled—she did not know him—could not remember—his soul was pushing through his body—animating the entire body —the arms, the jerking legs, the drumsticks held so lightly by the fingers—even the drumsticks were part of his body, and the drums themselves—and the sharp frightening clash of the cymbals—the vibrations everywhere, now beating against her—clamoring—pushing—

She fainted.

3

She faints.

The widow, not yet a widow. She shrieks in dismay, her hands leaping to her face, to her eyes. Must she cover her eyes? But they are blind—blinded.

She recovers, drags herself away. Like an animal she drags herself away. And then considers: What does this mean? What can this possibly mean?

Must resist; must not give in. That day at the school—that ugly, smelly, depressing place—forgot the name—Dutch name?—no matter: forgot—that day she fainted, staggered and fainted, must have fallen to the floor while everyone gaped. But why? What did it mean? Her mind must fight free of the squalor that surrounds her— must gain distance, time, cunning. Must resist, must not give in. Must *know*.

A reason for everything. Nothing without its reason.

Causality: sanity. Chaos: insanity.

The noise was both outside and inside, a terrific pressure. Beating against her eardrums, her eyes, every inch of her face, every inch of her body. Hideous! She tried to resist, tried to break away, but could not. Paralyzed. The noise—it must mean something—it must mean something and she would grasp its meaning—would not be defeated by it. Music? Was it music? Was there a rhythmic pattern to it? Violent pounding—sheer pounding—hideous—maddening. Was that the only meaning of the noise, that it existed? That it would never end? Building and building in a crescendo, building to a climax, yet never ending? She was sick, sickened—she had gone blind—had been deafened by the noise for some time without knowing it—and still the noise reached upward, accelerating all the while—an infinity ahead, behind—on all sides—

An infinity—

She would run to where he was in hiding, to the secret place he hid himself. She would beg him to abandon the work he was now doing—would beg him to return to her—to the world—before it was too late and everything was changed— She would beg as she never did, she would plead and weep and scream at him as she never did—

She fainted. They must have helped her, must have helped her to her feet, must have pitied her, fussed over her, gaped at her. Must have touched her, handled her. She fainted, she fell heavily to the floor. They didn't have time to catch her—were taken by surprise. So she fell to the floor, in a faint. And they must have helped her afterward. But she could not remember any details.

4

Funeral services were held at St. Aidan's Episcopal Church on Otway Boulevard, at eleven o'clock, June 18, a weekday morning. The church was crowded, as the funeral parlor had been crowded; police formed a line to keep curious spectators back. A few individuals, men and women both, stood in the street and wept and waved at cameras and members of the family when they entered the church, and again when they left to get into the limousines. There were a few picket signs: *How Many Must Die Before the Traitors Are Exposed, Free Captive Nations of the World, Restore Death Penalty for Commie Killers.*

Everything went well. There were no unpleasant surprises.

One of the state police helicopters developed engine trouble while following the procession to the cemetery and had to land suddenly in the parking lot of a shopping mall—but no one was hurt, nothing serious happened.

A large, solemn, and essentially uneventful funeral, in sharp contrast to Andrew Petrie's turbulent life and most particularly his violent death, one of the innumerable commentators noted. Skillfully handled, the security measures especially, and a very shocked and grim occasion, of course—the widow closely guarded, as was the entire Petrie family—essentially uneventful—in spite of the publicity—but a genuinely happy note in the fact of the weather, which was not exactly tropical or even sunny but more what we should be getting at this time of year, temperatures in the high 60's and no rain as was predicted. . . .

5

One of them stood before her in a charcoal gray suit with a vest of lighter gray, a necktie broad and knotted like a fist, and his mouth knotted too, glowering and dense with humiliation. The white shirt was too white. It suggested another era. The black shoes were too black, too polished, like a dancer's shoes. What are the proper costumes for mourning? She was dressed in something that would not offend anyone, she could not remember exactly what it was—they had helped her with it, had helped her with the sleeves, the zipper—steadying her as she shook her hair free. The difficulty with her left hand, the thick clotted bandages. She had not wanted them changed. She had not wanted the hand treated. A small wound, nothing serious, very little danger of infection—the stabbing had been done with a fairly clean instrument, a pair of scissors she'd found in the farmhouse kitchen while awaiting the ambulance and the police. No, she didn't want the bandages changed, she could take care of herself—she wanted no attention for herself—she *wanted* them only to leave her alone.

"—What you should do, Yvonne, is send the bill directly to Fritz; don't pay a penny until he advises you."

One of them in his tight-fitting mourner's costume, like a bridegroom, trying to light a cigarette. His hands trembled badly. Was he next, was he going to die next? Speaking softly to the widow, sorrow gathered in pockets beneath his eyes, like rain pockets, bluish-violet, bruised. How terrible, terrible. Hadn't slept since then —since the news of it. Had been going to meet with Andrew on Thursday—day after tomorrow—not simply business but many other matters to catch up on—had known him so long, so many years. It was a terrible thing, terrible.

A kind of party: held in a chilly vaulted place, the size of a ballroom. Pilasters reaching to the high, high ceiling, absurdly ornamental at their bases. Chandeliers. Banks of flowers. Low-pitched voices and gestures that were subdued, held close to the body. Yvonne moved away from people who touched her, shrank away from a chattery middle-aged woman—her sister-in-law—and might have insulted her unwittingly. She wanted only to be left alone.

"What a terrible, terrible thing," someone whispered.

Her hands were seized. She winced, drew her left hand away.

"A terrible thing. . . ." The breath a fierce brandyish emission,
the eyes red-veined and shifting. She knew the man, did not know
the man, could not recall the name. She forced herself to be courteous, to listen to his grief. "You *know* who did this . . . ? You
know . . . ?" Whispering in a hoarse stagy voice, wanting perhaps to
embrace her—but she stepped back, was ready to shove him away—
and then Harvey or Leon or Charles or one of the others rescued her.

"Terrible, terrible thing! . . . But our enemies will pay for it!"

Yvonne smiled angrily. *Our enemies will pay.*

Though she was drugged, though the doctor had insisted upon
drugging her, only her body was numb and ungainly. Her mind
worked as always. Worked beautifully as always.

Their enemies would pay. His enemies. The ones who had killed
him—who had arranged for him to be killed. They would pay for it,
for this humiliation. They would be discovered and would pay.

This terrible, terrible thing, people murmured; wondering at her,
dreading to look into her face. She was a stranger, really. She was the
man's wife, he had married her—secretly, but officially—it was a legitimate union—but they did not know her, did not care about her. Except the fact of her widowhood, her grief. They dreaded to look into
her face, they preferred to shrink away, and if they spoke openly and
angrily it was out of her hearing, at the periphery of the crowd.

But she was not staggering with grief, she was not broken,
demolished. She was angry. Her mind worked as usual, her level
shrewd gaze moved from person to person, from face to face, working its way through the crowd—while whoever stood beside her
offered condolences and sighed and spoke of the weather, or the
beautiful floral arrangements, or the fact that the Governor of the
state seemed so genuinely moved—how ironic, what a surprise, had
he and Andrew become reconciled without anyone knowing—?

Yes, they would pay. His enemies. Their enemies. Whoever: whoever had killed him. They would pay, they would be discovered and
would be exposed and would pay for it, possibly even with their lives
—that would depend upon the circumstances—upon who they were,
how they were apprehended.

"The bastards. The cowards," Yvonne whispered.

"Yes? What?" her companion said, cupping an ear.

Her body was ill-coordinated. Her arms were too slack, too heavy to tremble. Even her eyelids drooped—what effort it took to stay awake! But her mind worked swiftly and beautifully as always, as if shock-protected, like one of Andrew's expensive watches.

And then in church, in that dark, quaint old church: her brain alert, wondrously aware. She knew people were watching her, she knew they were recording her—but how contemptible it was, their pity! She did not care for it, did not need it. The mumblings of strangers. That someone should grip her familiarly by the arm, help her with her coat—these insufferable, maddening rituals! One of Andrew's brothers on her left, another on her right. Protected by them, by two men. She had no use for them at all.

She had met the minister, the old man, only the day before. She had liked him well enough. The unctuous gravity of his voice, his other-worldly manner: annoying and even embarrassing in ordinary surroundings, but in this church surprisingly effective. Of course it was all ritual—theatrical—the Biblical incantations—the way certain words rang and echoed and drew tears.

She glanced at the casket and away again.

That did not matter. Not *that*.

They had killed him—had tried to stop him by killing him. But it would not be so easy. It was never that easy. They would see.

Flickering candlelight. White marble smooth as glass. Carved words and dates—the figure of Christ in quiet, chaste colors, one hand upraised as if in caution—the interior of the church shadowy, rather chill. He had disliked churches or had been indifferent to them and so was she, but it was necessary to endure this masquerade, as he had endured similar masquerades in his lifetime, without complaint. He had been stoical, brave. His enemies did not know how brave. They did not know her either, they had surely underestimated her.

Let us pray: but she did no more than bow her head. Dry-eyed, open-eyed. Watching the altar, the minister, the way the dark casket gleamed, as if highly charged with energy. Beside her, the younger brother hid his face—bending suddenly forward as if stricken with pain or grief—hiding his face in his hands—and she dreaded his sobbing, his breaking down. He was a stranger to her, she did not know him and had no connection with him; Andrew had disliked him intensely. They had argued once, in her hearing. And afterward Andrew had been upset, had kept to himself the rest of the day. . . . The other brother, Hugh, seemed embarrassed in her presence. Would not meet her eye. His remarks were difficult to comprehend, allusive and ironic and not very clearly articulated, so that she felt he wanted only to escape: to get through this ritual, as she did, and to escape. Restrained, distant, civil. Obviously quite intelligent. Andrew had spoken of him rarely, always with a kind of bemused exasperation—and then there was the matter of the money he had borrowed—six thousand dollars over a period of years—that Andrew assumed would never be repaid. But Hugh did not know that Yvonne knew, and she did not intend to embarrass him. That cold, uneasy, rather reptilian look of his!—the gaze never quite meeting hers, but sliding away, shifting away, his aversion for her disguised as courtesy.

Still she was dry-eyed. Let the others pray. She was enumerating his enemies: in her mind's eye making a list. She would type it up later. She would make a primary list and a secondary list. She would hand over to the investigators only the material that seemed to her really significant; otherwise, they might dissipate their energies, might follow too many leads. They would have to be directed. She knew the imaginations of bureaucrats, how limited their powers of speculation, how disappointing, always, their intelligence.

Once, not long after their marriage, Andrew had told her—in order to explain the mediocre performance of a friend of his, then presumably running for the Presidency, registered in the Florida primary—*The average person, and even the above-average person, isn't guided by a desire to be excellent, or even to be triumphant: he simply doesn't want to fail. He doesn't want to fail in public. He doesn't want to be exposed. He doesn't want to be laughed at.* She knew he was right. The fear of ridicule was stronger than any desire to excel. It was an American secret, the underside of the mythological American dream of success.

"The cowards, killing him like that," she whispered. ". . . bastards."

Waiting for the ambulance and the police, she had felt the numbness in her hand again—the very tips of the fingers tingling, as if she had brushed them lightly against a heated burner. It would drive her insane, that feeling! . . . so she found herself stabbing with the scissors, trying to stab some feeling into her hand, some sensation. Ah, that was better! That, and that! To feel pain, to feel it darting up her arm!—the sight of her own blood, so much better than that paralysis!

Afterward, of course, she had been stricken with shame.

There was no explanation. She could not explain. The doctor treated her for shock and cleansed the wounds and bandaged them, saying very little. She was ashamed, so ashamed. Her madness could not be explained and people would be talking about it, wondering at her, worrying . . . would she hurt herself further? . . . could she be trusted? She assured them she was all right now. She was in no danger.

At the cemetery: the rawness of daylight, the surprise of the actual grave. Pallbearers gloved and proper and rather absurd, trying not to pant with the weight of their archaic burden; the minister, unsheltered by his stained glass and his altar railing and his incantations, rather absurd as well. Voice faltering, aged. Yvonne stood dry-eyed, watching. She was stiff, and felt herself poreless and perfect as glass. How long, how very long this ritual lasted! . . . but she was not going to break.

Suppose he had been calling for her as he died . . . ?

No: impossible.

He had died at once. They said he had died at once. The bullets at such close range. . . . His murderer had surprised him and fired into his face at a distance of less than twelve inches. He died, died at once. Instantaneously. *At once.* He had not called her name . . . had not had time even to think of her.

A helicopter?—hovering at the edge of the cemetery, propellers pulsing, throbbing.

Yvonne wanted to turn away. She wanted to scream at them to leave Andrew alone.

Still the minister was talking. Still the service continued. He would not have wanted this: would have been humiliated by it. Let death be simple, direct, blunt, final. . . . He had wanted to be cremated, had not wanted a conventional funeral at all. But the family had protested. Had protested rather forcefully; so Yvonne gave in. It was true that Andrew had not been very adamant about cremation, and nothing in his will stipulated it; he had never given much thought to such matters . . . always too absorbed in the present, in his work, in life. It would have been embarrassing for him to leave detailed instructions concerning his death and funeral arrangements; that wasn't Andrew's nature. So Yvonne had yielded to the family, had not wanted to fight them at this time. Perhaps that was a point in her favor, something they would remember.

Then something extraordinary happened: Hugh began to whimper.

He was pressing both hands against his mouth, making a high, whimpering, whinnying noise. His glasses were crooked. His knees were visibly trembling.

He staggered forward and one of the men caught him. For a moment it looked as if he would collapse. Yvonne felt the horror of it, the childlike despair of his sobbing—the loss of control—the breakdown— For a moment she too was stricken. She turned aside dizzily. But no. No. She was stronger than Hugh. She was not going to collapse in public. The muffled sounds of the man's anguish repulsed her; she turned away. She was not going to collapse. She was strong, stronger than anyone knew.

"Are you—?"

She had groped for someone, had unconsciously laid her hand on someone's arm. It was Stephen; he believed mistakenly that she needed help. *Yvonne? Are you all right?* He gripped her arm. His voice was a murmur, his manner awkward, shy. As always he was clumsy. She drew away from him, shaking her head slightly, irritably. She did not want his help. She did not require anyone's help. On the other side of the grave Hugh was sobbing wildly; his relatives clustered about him, helpless. But grateful, perhaps, for the distraction.

Yvonne's face burned. She did no more than glance at Stephen.

"Yvonne—?"

But she was herself again, in control.

The ceremony came to an end. The funeral was over.

6

Fritz Sanderson, her attorney, studied the list of names. He did not speak for some time. At the funeral the other day he had looked pale and startled and fragile, especially about the eyes; now he looked merely ravaged, and older than his fifty years. On his left wrist was a complicated watch, like one of Andrew's—a chronograph —in what was probably a platinum bracelet, thick and chunky.

Finally he passed his hand over his eyes, and Yvonne knew what he would say. She said, before he could speak, that she had photostated copies of certain documents and letters—she had them with her, right here—would he like to examine them?

"There are thousands of documents," he said. "There are thousands of letters. —Thousands of enemies."

"Do you advise me not to give this list to the Attorney General?"

"One of them is the Attorney General's brother-in-law."

"I know that," Yvonne said. "What's wrong? —I know that."

"Do what you will," Sanderson said.

He lay the typed sheet on the desk between them. Yvonne hesitated, then picked it up. "Andrew always said he was hated more by his friends than by—than by the others. He always said—"

"But there were so many things he always said. . . ." Sanderson said weakly.

7

Tiny white dots. Suddenly they appear. They are alive, seething with life. Like snowflakes, so tiny—but living, near-microscopic pinpoints of motion, of life.

The widow begins to scream.

Tramping in the woods. Mountains—early spring—the world not yet awakened—everything neutral, somber, except the pines and the bright hard red berries and a few tentative leaves. It is early spring, it is a mute, subdued, colorless day. The Adirondacks. Or possibly the Rocky Mountains. No, the Adirondacks; Mt. Invemere prominent to the north; this is her husband's property, thousands of acres, the old farm and the boarded-up lodge and the cabin by the river. To the left, obscured by mist or low-lying clouds, is Royal Mountain. She knows where she is, knows what she is doing.

Her mind racing as always. Charging now this way, now that.

No, it is not Colorado: it is not a girl but a woman, not a child but a widow. A wife. She is a wife still. She has driven out from Albany to be with him, has been worried about him, will spend the weekend here. But he is harassed. He has little time for her. Polite, yes—expressing gratitude for her company—surprise that she should bother, driving to this ill-heated place she dislikes so much, especially when he will be back home by Monday afternoon. Perhaps he is baffled also by something urgent in her manner. A plea for some emotional response, a kind of blackmail uncharacteristic of her. But

he is harassed with his own work, he really has no time for her, and
of course she understands.

He didn't even bother with meals, he told her. Not when he was
working. Just ate where he was—camped out by the river—ate at his
desk, mostly sandwiches. No need for her to cook, to fuss over him.

She understood.

His mind was crammed with so many ideas, so many hypotheses—
almost, at times, he felt he was going mad—or on the verge of an extraordinary insight. Did she understand? He had so little time these
days—the hours raced when he was alone like this—he couldn't write
his ideas down fast enough, they came in such a rush sometimes—
and how would he synthesize these new ideas with the material he
already had—those hundreds of pages of—those thousands of pages
of—twenty years of— Did she understand?

She understood.

The widow in jeans and boots and a coarse-knit sweater, tramping through the old pastureland, through the old orchards. She understands, yet does not understand. Her hair is loose; it blows into
her eyes. She stares at the ground before her, brooding, talking to
herself, unaware of her surroundings. Where is she? In the mountains? But why? And why is her breath steamy, if it is May now and
no longer winter? She hears her own voice, questioning, she wonders
for a moment if it is Andrew she hears—he too talks to himself occasionally, rehearsing things he will say in public. Structure—rhythm—
style: of the utmost importance. *It is not enough to be correct, one
must also appear to be correct.*

Unconsciously she begins to walk faster. Her mind races, yet she is
not really thinking about anything. Something is going to happen—
or has it already happened? She does not intend to tell him about
the incident at the handicapped children's school, the way she lost
all strength in her legs suddenly, and evidently lost consciousness as
well for a few seconds and had to be helped. She does not intend to
tell him any of this. In fact, what is there to tell? There is nothing,
nothing to tell. Nothing to explain. He judges his own failings
harshly and he would judge hers harshly, if he could know.

She is staring at something—something that lies at the edge of a
field. As she approaches it, she sees that it is—what is it, that shape?
—too small, too flattened—a piece of cardboard, perhaps—a piece of
tar paper—yet she cannot come any closer, she stops, drawing her
hands out of her pockets, raising her shoulders, slightly hunched,
staring: no, it is not a dead thing, not the corpse of a small animal, it

is nothing to shrink from, nothing to make her gag. A piece of tar paper. It is too small, too flattened; not an animal, not an animal's corpse, not a dead rabbit teeming with maggots—no: it is not the wilderness of her childhood, it is not Colorado, not White Springs, but another world completely, another lifetime. She is his wife, not yet his widow. She is an adult. At the edge of the field something lies partly rotted, crumpled; but it is not a dead creature, it is nothing that will sicken and terrify her. Still, she circles it. She stares, she will not come any closer. There is a broken wall, an old stone wall, crumbled at her feet . . . several steps and she is on the other side, panting, triumphant. She will return by way of the dirt road, she will avoid the thing that lies at the edge of the field, having dragged itself there to die. A dead rabbit, was it? A dead raccoon? She doesn't know, she had to look away at once, gagging. No. No. Please. No! She hears herself screaming, but the scream is silent.

Those tiny grubby dots, appearing so suddenly: why, they are alive, seething with life! They cannot see her, they have no awareness of her, they are nothing of *hers*. They cannot even be named. What does it mean, to call them maggots? What does it mean, to turn aside, gagging, one's face contorted? Near-microscopic dots, mere pinpoints of motion, tough and living, alive. . . . What does it mean, even, to realize they are *alive?*

8

Not long after the body was discovered, not many hours after the widow came upon it, the first arrests were made. —But after the first sporadic arrests, after the hours of interrogation, suspects were released and the dead man was still dead. Suddenly it was the day of the funeral. Then it was the afternoon and the evening of the day of the funeral. Then it was the following weekend, and already the next Sunday—already the next Sunday!—and the dead man was still dead, and the murderer not yet apprehended.

"Is there anything we can do for you?" people asked.

"I'm not ill," she said. She smiled, to soften her manner.

"But is there anything we can *do* . . . ?"

She stared at them. Theoretically she was under sedation; her body seemed to be grieving, in a nagging, embarrassing manner—as if she had a mild case of intestinal flu; but in fact she was very much herself, in full consciousness, alert and wary.

"How do I know? How can I answer that question? How do I know what you can do, how much you can help me if you wanted to?" she said in her rapid, light voice.

"That was when it sank home . . . how awful, awful it would be . . . alone in the apartment without anyone to talk to . . . day after day after day. . . . I realized he was gone on Tuesday. Looked everywhere for him and couldn't find him. My sister, you know, who died last winter . . . well, she was seventy-six . . . she died last winter, we had been living together for about fifteen years, she came to live with me after her husband died . . . the thing is, he belonged to *her* originally and I didn't like him that much that I was aware of but now he's gone I don't have the heart to get another one, it's just too sad and such a drain on the spirit when something goes wrong. I had to go to the hospital for a checkup, you know, the last week of May. It was supposed to be a week but was actually twelve days. He was at the kennel all that time, I hated to put him in that noisy impersonal place, and there's no guarantee they really give the pets exercise—there's a runway, but how do you know they use it?—how could you actually *know?*—and the cost was so high, over a hundred dollars—I hated to take him there but I had no choice. . . . As soon as we were both home again, I knew something was strange. He seemed like a different animal, that's all. A big gray tom, he was, not a pedigree or anything special, but he could be quite affectionate when the spirit moved him, and he and I had always gotten along; but after the kennel, after those twelve days at the kennel, he just wasn't the same animal. He wasn't. It was all changed, all different, he refused to sit on my lap and he wouldn't eat his favorite foods, not even liver or seafood biscuits, and when I tried to pet him he just slinked away, sort of crouched down and scurried away as if he hated to be touched. It was so sad! It was the strangest thing! He went for the door though he had never been allowed outside in his life. He always went for the door, trying to get out. I scolded him, I tried to spank him—you know, patting him on the nose, not hard, just to discipline him—and he hissed and spat at me and even swiped at me with his paw—it was so exasperating and sad—it was just such a mystery. He had no claws, you know; Margaret had him declawed as a kitten. But he tried to get out anyway, one day I discovered him at the bedroom window, and he had the screen almost loose, and that should have warned me but I fed him and petted him and it seemed maybe he would settle down somewhat, but then it was the next day—or the day after that —when I came home from my hair appointment he wasn't around, didn't rush for the door when I unlocked it, and I thought maybe he was asleep under the bed—that was one of his places, all his life— sometimes he would sleep there all day long, practically—and it's hard for me to bend over, you know, to bend over far enough to look under the bed—so it was Tuesday night by the time I realized he wasn't in the apartment and so much time had been lost, so much precious time. . . . It turned out to be the bathroom window, the screen was loose just a bit and he had forced it, had squeezed out the bottom and then the screen clapped back, so you couldn't see how he had gotten out exactly unless you examined it very closely and then you could see the gray fur at the bottom, that bad cat! He must have forced his way out, must have pushed and pushed, and what strength he must have had, it's a wonder he didn't hurt himself. . . . If only I had checked that particular window, that particular screen, but it always seemed safe to me and Tommy ordinarily never went into the bathroom because I keep the door shut but evidently he had forced that door open too, just by pushing and clawing, isn't it awful, and I placed an advertisement in the morning paper and alerted the superintendent and both of us put notices on the bulletin board and on the bulletin board in the grocery store but it didn't do any good, he just disappeared, and I know he won't be back, I just *know* I will never see him again. . . ."

Yvonne listened without appearing to listen. She was at the Special Delivery window of the post office at Lake Placid, waiting in line. She had three letters to mail and had insisted upon taking them to the post office herself, though one of Adrienne Greason's children could have brought them over. She listened to the voice just behind her, but did not allow herself to turn, to see who the speaker was.

There were other voices, other conversations delivered with that subdued passion, that sense of weighty certainty Yvonne had begun to notice in overheard conversations. She listened carefully, her expression impassive. She wore sunglasses with very dark lenses; her hair was skimmed back from her face. Her poppy-colored sun dress, which wrapped around her and was fastened with a white sash, had the pert, pleasing look of a costume—she was costumed today, a day in July, as an attractive young woman. At other times she dressed like an attractive young widow, in dark colors. On the whole she preferred the dark colors, the sobriety of mourning; but she was able to eavesdrop more easily in an outfit like the poppy-colored dress.

Earlier, she had overheard on a telephone call Adrienne was making to a friend ". . . terribly hot back in Albany Leon says, he just called a minute ago, temperature in the nineties and very muggy . . . what? . . . oh yes! . . . the Fourth of July festival is very nice very nice as usual, the children always love it fireworks of course and a sailboat regatta and why don't you come over for drinks then dinner, yes she *is*, she *is*, though it's possible she won't come down for cocktails because she's very . . . not at all! no! not at all! . . . Leon was his closest friend, you know. . . . Yes, isn't it! Wasn't it! And what if. . . ."

Before leaving the post office she overheard two postmen talking. They were a few yards away, separated from her by an opaque green plastic partition. ". . . that son of a bitch, would you believe it? . . . saw it from the basement window, I mean I *saw* it . . . a good three feet on one side, maybe more, and he backs the truck in practically sideways and of course there was a long scratch. . . . That son of a bitch!"

On the steps of the post office, in the sudden sunshine, the widow feels dizzy for a moment: sees something dark and shapeless before her, then suddenly pinpricked by white, a seething clamorous white. She remembers a remark of Andrew's, made to someone else in her presence. A philosophical discussion. What was equality? What did it mean? Had anyone ever analyzed the concept? It was hideous! Loathsome! *Like William James I consider myself a radical empiricist; but like a friend of James's, whom he quoted in a spirit of objectivity, I find this empiricism a nightmare . . . too atomistic to be tolerated. It's hideous! "Like a sea of maggots on a carrion" . . . or whatever that expression is. . . . My public beliefs, then, are a matter of choice: I assert my faith in a hierarchy of. . . . I defeat my own metaphysics by an act of sheer. . . .*

Of what? Of—?

She was stricken suddenly by the memory of his voice: the manner, the tone, the courteous precision of the words: *I defeat my own metaphysics by an act of sheer. . . .* Standing in the brilliant sunshine, suddenly dizzy, saddened, weighed down by the slight sickness of her body, which lingered and would not be defeated, she realized it was some time now since his death: no longer hours or days but weeks, solid blocks of time that were weeks, countable in weeks. He was dead. Permanently dead. If she heard his voice again it would be only in her imagination, and she could not direct her imagination, could not will it to re-create him—she could not force it—was helpless—

I defeat my own metaphysics by an act of sheer—

Of will.

She told Adrienne she must leave, could not stay any longer at their lakeside house; she *must* leave, she had work to do, she had to return to Albany in order to do it.

"Don't argue! Please! You've been very kind," she said. ". . . very kind, Andrew would be . . . would be so grateful. . . . Your friendship meant . . . means. . . . But don't argue, please! I must go home."

9

They did not speak to her directly. They watched her, they addressed her by name—occasionally *Mrs. Petrie*, occasionally *Yvonne*—they spoke in her presence, spoke at her. But not directly. Not to her. Not to anyone she recognized as herself. The Petries who clustered around her and the friends, Andrew's friends, and the innumerable acquaintances she came into contact with did not speak to *her*, not directly. There was another woman, another ghostly image, whom they addressed by her name.

Of course she had always been something of an eavesdropper, a spy, an impostor: but in the past she had controlled the degree and the duration of her imposture.

The Police Commissioner was one of them. He spoke in her presence for many minutes, late one afternoon. *Mrs. Petrie*, he called her; and *Yvonne*. His manner was superficially apologetic. Beneath, always close beneath, was the belligerence she had formerly admired, knowing him as a friend of her husband's. He spoke for some time, not giving her a chance to interrupt, presenting her with a small, richly detailed speech . . . as if he were offering her information that had nothing to do with either of them, or with Andrew, but was the sort of information one might offer to the public.

The gun had been found: tossed into a few feet of water, in a ditch several miles from the shooting. A .38 Police Special, absolutely clean, untraceable. There were many suspects, and they were waiting for informers and other contacts to come forward . . . which might not be for a while, for various reasons . . . and though at the moment they had nothing strong to go on, nothing very convincing to work with, he was confident the people responsible would soon be located.

In the meantime it might be a good idea for her to leave town, to take a vacation somewhere, to visit with her family. Why had she left the Greasons? Mrs. Greason had telephoned his office, had been worried about her; why had she left Lake Placid so suddenly? He had had the idea she would be staying there most of the summer.

"I wanted to leave," Yvonne said. "I was bored there."

"It might have been a better idea to—"

"I wanted to come back to Albany."

"Yes, but—"

"I wanted to be home."

"Do you have any family, anyone you could—?"

"No."

"—your home?"

"My home is here."

He reddened slightly. She knew she had offended him with her tone of voice. Yet she went on, speaking as Andrew would have spoken: "Why don't you want me here? You don't think I'm in danger, do you? Why? Why would I be in danger? . . . I'm not in danger. I'm not important. I don't mind you telling lies to the newspapers or to one another, but please don't lie to *me*. It's like lying to Andrew himself."

"I'm not lying."

"You're not telling me everything, are you? You're not telling me everything. So in effect you're lying. I have a right to know, I'm his wife, he would want me to know everything. . . . When you talk to me like that, you're insulting me, it's like insulting *him* . . . it's like lying to Andrew himself."

"I never lied to Andrew," he said slowly.

Both were silent, thinking he had lied to Andrew—had lied several times in the past year. He and a number of other police officials, as well as the Governor's office and the prison authority at Glasberg, had lied.

"I never lie," he said.

He was addressing another person—someone who sat where Yvonne sat.

"You never lie," Yvonne repeated. It was surprising, how weak her voice sounded. She had the flu now—or a very bad, lingering cold—she supposed it was an actual disease, a minor illness that really had no connection with the death. Her voice sounded faint, remote, a little nasal. "But so many details, so many facts, such a listing of names—of 'suspects'—and that nonsense about the things stolen, as if anyone for a moment could take that theory seriously!—that it was robbery, that he was killed for a few trivial things—taking so long to tell me about *that*, as if I didn't already know—do you think I'm a newspaper reporter, that you must smother me with these misleading little facts, these lying *truths*? And you don't even seem to be talking to me. What's wrong? Why are you like this? Talk to *me*, look at *me*."

He rose from behind his desk.

"Mrs. Petrie, are you ill?"

"What? Why? Why do you say that?"

"You sound a little hysterical."

He stared at her as if seeing her for the first time. She saw the alarm in his face—the sudden fright.

"I'm not sick," Yvonne said irritably. "Don't touch me, please."

He went past her, went to the door. Called to his secretary in the same scared, vexed voice. ". . . isn't feeling well, if you could bring her some water. . . . Could you come in here a minute, Mildred, and. . . ."

Yvonne stood. "I'm not sick!" she said. "You won't listen to me, you want to—want to discredit me— Why am I hysterical? You weren't even talking to me, not to me! You were lying to me! It's a game, a pretense, you're taping this conversation and— Trying to trap me, are you trying to trap me? *Me*? It's like lying to Andrew himself, insulting Andrew himself—"

"Yvonne, please—"

"What do you mean? Don't touch me! I know you don't want me around—you're afraid they will get to me too and you'll be embarrassed in public—my safety isn't important to you otherwise, is it?—is it? You and your friends betrayed Andrew—he would never have taken such an extreme stand about the Glasberg riot—"

"*I* was betrayed," he said, "I was told lies—you can ask—"

"Don't interrupt me, please," Yvonne said quickly, "I can't stand that—it makes me nervous, I—I can't stand it— You would never have dared interrupt Andrew— You betrayed him, you lied to him—if you didn't lie to him you withheld information, your office withheld information, I know why you kept it from the newspapers but—

but— Your responsibility to Andrew was— You were friends, you had been friends— He was one of you— Now I can't believe anything you say and—"

"Yvonne—"

"You would probably be relieved if something did happen to me— it would make everything easier—except it would—there would be— you and your office would be embarrassed—"

"That's ridiculous," he said sharply. "You know that's ridiculous. I warned Andrew after that Glasberg publicity—I warned him there were threats reported against his life—informers called in—I warned him years ago, many times, and he always defied me and he always said afterward that I had been an alarmist, taking these maniacs seriously, and it never mattered whether one of them actually did show up—as they did, you know, fairly often—and once, in Buffalo, Andrew was nearly killed—it never mattered to Andrew because the mere fact that he was still alive was a sufficient argument in his mind that I'd been an alarmist. So he brushed it all aside, he took it lightly, he thought there was a kind of bullet-proof aura around him—"

"That isn't true," Yvonne said. "You're distorting everything. You sit in this office and refashion what happened and tell the newspapers grotesque things and lie to me, to my face—as if you could lie to me about my own husband—"

"I knew Andrew for more than seventeen years—"

"This bullet-proof image, this bullet-proof lie—*bullet-proof*—that grotesque expression was in one of the news articles—I suppose you were the—"

"I was not," he said hotly. "The comment was made by an unidentified person—I don't happen to know who it was—but it was common knowledge that—"

"*Bullet-proof!*" Yvonne said. "You deliberately gave the reporters that grotesque insane expression—you deliberately leaked it—to make your own position seem less responsible—to make people think he was insane and brought what happened on himself. I know what you're like, I know what the police are like, but you were a friend of his and— You betrayed him and you're betraying him even now— You— You deliberately—"

"*Stand next to me; I'm bullet-proof*," he said. "I swear to you that Andrew was known to have—"

"He was quoting someone else! He was mocking whoever it was! I know very well—I remember it very clearly—that was misreported too—whenever he gave a public address the newspapers distorted it, they singled out phrases for headlines and they missed his jokes and his ironies and his subtleties and—and—they missed *him*—they always missed *him*— People who listened closely to him were never mistaken, they always knew what he meant, and anyone who has read his essays knows—anyone who takes the time to examine— He— It was one of his jokes— He was mocking the man who had said that—I don't remember who—you are deliberately confusing me —but—but I remember that talk, I was in the audience, it was in Washington—Georgetown University—he was citing that remark as an example of—of— I think he was alluding in a way to John Kennedy, who didn't allow himself to be protected well enough—but I don't think Kennedy was the man who—"

"Yvonne, it doesn't matter, the fact is the remark was attributed to Andrew and even if it didn't originate with him it did express his feeling—in a way it expressed his feeling, his unconscious—"

"It certainly did not," Yvonne said angrily. "That remark was the very antithesis of Andrew—of Andrew's sanity—and the reason he made it, the reason he cited it, was to point out that certain men in high positions—like Presidents—especially Presidents—he wasn't referring just to Kennedy but to all of them, to any of them— These men, they become megalomaniacs—they forget they are human—the point of Andrew's talk was just that, I remember it, I was there, you weren't there and you're distorting everything and you lie to the papers and to one another and if he only knew—if he could only know— And you're fundamentally *stupid*: that's the problem. He never recognized how very *stupid* you people are. He knew he was surrounded by inferiors and he knew they weren't just the rednecks and the Imperial Grand Wizards and the—what do they call themselves—the White Guard—the Minutemen—he knew it wasn't just those men but men close to him, he knew his vision was being misinterpreted and simplified and reduced to—to idiotic racist nonsense—but he didn't know how great the difference was—he really didn't know—he was so *loyal* to the old families, to the past, to his friends —he wouldn't criticize except to me—he was so *loyal*— And now you are all betraying him by suggesting that—"

"Nobody is betraying Andrew Petrie," he said. "You have no idea how shocked and angry and—and how hard I've been working— You have no idea, Yvonne, you have no right to use that term—"

"I'm not Yvonne to you," she said.

He was silent. When she went to leave he said quietly: "Then you're not Yvonne. All right. Fine. But Mrs. Petrie, *my* Mrs. Petrie, the *Mrs. Petrie* I assume when I hear that term—*Mrs. Petrie* to some of us—is not you but another woman. If you don't want to be called Yvonne—"

"Go to hell," Yvonne said.

Someone telephoned. A stranger telephoned though she had a private number.

"Hello hello hello. . . ?" the voice begged.

She said nothing. She listened to the breathy panicked voice.

Gradually she realized it was her brother-in-law, Hugh. He was telephoning from New York but he seemed close, as if a block away or in the next room, jarringly intimate. She listened to him chatter and felt a surge of pity for him and spoke to him, reluctantly, at first noncommittal about who she was: was she Yvonne herself, or someone merely attending the telephone? She could have been one of Andrew's former secretaries or one of the Petrie family or a maid or a typist or an acquaintance of Yvonne's answering the phone because Yvonne was out of the room or out of the city. "Hello, hello," the voice begged, "Yvonne . . . ?" She was tempted to hang up. But she did not. She replied to a few of his questions, she was languid, resigned, thinking still of what the Police Commissioner had said, of how she might take revenge upon Hugh, knowing it was hopeless and she would never be capable of revenge or even of hurting or disturbing or insulting him . . . his cruel clever voice gave way to his chirrupy breathless pathetic voice and she felt pity for him, almost a sense of relief, of affection. He was not cruel; he seemed to be pleading with her. He was not cold and hateful and in control, like the others; he was meek as a child.

Still, she was puzzled. She did not know why he was talking to her so earnestly. Could he take a train up, could he visit? Could they meet for lunch or at least for drinks? Somewhere? Anywhere? At her convenience? . . . Gradually she realized that he too was not speaking to her. Not to *her*.

She told him it wasn't possible. It wasn't possible for them to meet.

Still he continued. He seemed not to have heard.

. . . None of them spoke to her, not to *her*. They did not see her. She was invisible. She did not exist. Had never existed. There was a phantom in her place, a near-transparent being or creature. She watched this creature and she watched and listened to the others in the creature's presence and felt only a dim, sullen contempt for the masquerade. They forced this imposture upon her. She had not chosen it. She was spying upon her own life and upon them. Where was her life, her self? . . . they had torn her out of it, had ripped her inside out. They had begun their work years ago, in fact. The bride herself had been effaced, defaced. Her face lost. It had begun then. It continued still. Someday they would kill her as they had killed Andrew: her face and body brutally assaulted. Torn inside out. Mangled. Mutilated. And then they would pretend grief and shock and sorrow and they would shake their heads and say she had brought it upon herself, she had willed it, she had *unconsciously.* . . .

"What do you want?" she interrupted. Suddenly she could not bear it, this masquerade. "Why are you calling?"

He could not speak. "I—I— As I said, I—"

She wondered if it was about the six thousand dollars he owed Andrew. She wondered if he wanted to bring the conversation around to that topic but didn't dare and was waiting for her to suggest it.

". . . is it about . . . ? Something personal, financial . . . ?" she said.

But how awkward! . . . she regretted she had said anything. Andrew had lent his brother a little more than six thousand dollars over a period of years, in uneven installments, at no interest rate; he had told Yvonne that, to save Hugh's pride, he had allowed Hugh to consider the sum a loan, but in reality, it was a gift—Hugh would never be able to repay it. And he was evidently in debt to others, to people who would not so easily forgive him. So it was a gift, it would have to be a gift. Certainly the man must know that by now—though perhaps his pride did not allow him to acknowledge it.

He talked, he talked. Chattered. Yvonne listened and then stopped listening. There was something edgy about him, something she did not like—did not trust—but he was harmless, Andrew had always spoken of him as eccentric but "harmless"—so her mind detached itself from the conversation and she made plans of her own, worked at calculations of her own, envisioning in her imagination the list of primary suspects that was now quite lengthy, thirty-two names of people or organizations that—

Hugh was asking again if he might come to Albany to see her.

She paused, as if seriously thinking.

Finally she said, "No. That's impossible."

10

I love you.

I love *you*.

So they said, so they said. They said those words. I love you, you know that don't you? . . . Know that don't you?

Eavesdropping, she had overheard.

Sometimes she overheard intentionally, sometimes unintentionally. She was innocent at times. At other times guilty. *I love you. Don't hurt me. . . . I love you, doesn't it make any difference?*

Her mother: the blond, feathery-blond hair, the slightly flattened but attractive features, that habit of smiling too quickly and then allowing her smile to slowly retreat, fade. The strength in her arms and hands that always surprised Yvonne. A short, delicately boned woman, but always quick—marvelously quick. *I love you. Doesn't it make any difference?* Sometimes whimpering, self-pitying. Sometimes angry.

Did it make any difference?

Her father: tall, abrupt, good-natured when sober and irritable when not. A mineworker in Wyoming and Colorado before Yvonne's birth. Then he became a deputy sheriff in White Springs, in northern Colorado; he died when Yvonne was eight years old.

They had loved each other very much, the parents. Yvonne remembered the flashes of rage, the quarrels, the thumps and thuds and tears—she remembered the quick, close, tense atmosphere of the house—even when he left, when he walked out, the house was filled with him, with her mother's thoughts of *him*. They had loved each other very much. So they said: and so others said of them. Yvonne had not thought about it, being too young. She had been too young to doubt.

And what difference had it made?

It was true, probably, that the Radeks were very much in love. They were both young, youthful in manner—almost childlike, at times—hot-headed, impulsive, eager to hurt and to be hurt. Yvonne had thought all mothers and fathers were like hers, so noisily passionate, so quick to take offense and to forgive. Her father in his soiled uniform, pulling off his boots—her mother scolding him—the exchange of lazy insults, the mocking questions—sudden laughter, but sometimes raised voices. Often her mother's wrists were bruised. He liked to catch her by the wrist, turn her small, fragile hand in his own, he liked to force her to cry out, to submit. Once, during the winter, she bloodied his nose—Yvonne remembered the dribbling bloodspots on the kitchen floor and on the fresh snow out in the drive—remembered the uproar that followed, though evidently it had been an accident, her slapping him. And of course he had forgiven her.

They were playful, her parents. Not quite adults.

Her father had died long ago, when still a young man. Not quite an adult, not quite a man. He had been brave—noisy and good-natured and brave—everyone had been fond of him—and his wife had gone a little mad when they came to tell her what happened—how he had died. Twenty-nine years old, and dead. Yvonne, now the age of her dead father. Yvonne now a wife, now a widow, thinks of her father with detachment, unable to remember him. It had happened so long ago, so many years ago. It had happened to strangers, really. What connection was there?

She had told Andrew very little about her parents. She stressed the fact that they had loved each other very much—but what difference had it made, that love? He had died anyway. Had been killed anyway. Had not valued that love, not his wife's or his own, really—had not allowed it to make much difference to him, to the care he had taken with his life.

Afterward, because he had died while off duty—on a volunteer rescue mission on the Colorado River, one flooding April—the county had refused to pay the widow a full pension. Yvonne remembered her mother reading the letter aloud, to Yvonne's grandmother, to neighbors, to Yvonne herself. She remembered being cornered and forced to hear that letter. She remembered her mother stressing certain words, certain sentences, as if unable to comprehend them. *Regret to inform you that . . . according to our records . . . no provision made at the present time . . . no coverage. . . .* Her mother had not been drunk at that time, but she behaved drunkenly. Repeating the key words, the key sentences again and again. What did these words mean? What was happening? It could not be controlled, could it?—what was happening to them?

Her father leaving the house on a Sunday . . . missing that day, missing that night . . . found dead, horribly mutilated, two days later. . . . One side of his face had been smashed. One arm nearly

severed, both legs crushed to the knee. And a few weeks later the letter arrived, a message with an official stamp and official signature.
Regret . . . according to . . . no provision . . . no coverage. . . .
Typed words in a letter. It could not be controlled, what was happening. It could not even be understood.

If he had loved her and her mother, Yvonne told Andrew, he
would not have died like that. He would not have risked his life. It
wasn't even an accident, really—he had been trying to rescue people
past rescuing—a rancher and his family already dead, drowned—lost.
He had tried to rescue people he could not have rescued. He had not
listened to the others. The house had been demolished, the family already dead. A waste, an act of recklessness, of stupidity. People had
called it heroic and the White Springs paper had called him a hero,
along with two other volunteer workers who were killed in the same
flood; there was a plaque in the courthouse square. But what did it
mean, what difference did it make? . . . The body broken, mangled,
horrible. The body designated *heroic.*

Her husband had been very moved by the story. He had wanted to
hear more. What had happened to her mother?

But she did not care to discuss it.

Was her mother still living?

No. She wasn't still living.

The pension—?

Everyone in town had liked her father so much that the pension
had come through after all. The sheriff had liked him, had often
gone drinking with him—so the county settled out of court, their attorney talked Yvonne's mother into signing a release for a certain
sum of money—not much, Yvonne guessed—and the money lasted a
while, maybe a year.

And then—?

She had not wanted to discuss her life. It was irrelevant, no more
than an encumbrance, an embarrassment. Sometimes she lied, sometimes she said nothing when questioned too closely; sometimes she
made up facts, dates, probable events—her father killed in Korea, or
in an explosion in a Montana mine. What difference did such things
make, she asked wearily, sullenly, why must one be burdened with
the past . . . ? She had been struck by Andrew's public statements
concerning the essential shallowness of the merely subjective, personal life; she knew, she knew he was correct, she *knew* . . . and she
did not care to talk about it.

"I'm inclined to think the personal life is over," Yvonne had said.

11

Sometimes she slept in the bedroom, sometimes on the couch in Andrew's study, once or twice she slept in the living room, partly clothed, beneath a thin blanket. The apartment was very quiet. It was usually very quiet. Because it was summer and the legislature was not meeting, the city itself was quiet, insignificant. It was not a "city," really; it did not exist as a city. Yvonne thought of it as a place she happened to be at the present. Had Andrew lived elsewhere, had he been born elsewhere, she would be somewhere else and that place also would not be significant in itself: but one must live locally, one must come to earth somewhere. So she kept the apartment, though everyone assumed she would give it up. She kept to the schedule she had had as his wife, with certain obvious exceptions.

There was an answering service. But sometimes the telephone rang in the apartment. Most of the time she did not answer it—not out of timidity, but out of indifference. Who would be calling? Who had anything to tell her? When Andrew's assassin was found, the news would not come over the telephone; she was certain of that. They would send a policeman over, or perhaps a plainclothesman, they would break the news to her in person. . . . The Police Commissioner himself would probably come over. He would tell her: We've found them. We have them. It's over.

But days passed. Weeks. She went to the cemetery—stared at the grave—tried to think what connection this had with her, or with Andrew—what it could possibly mean. One lived in the present. One lived half in the future, in fact. Of course there was a partnership between those who lived now, those who would live in the future, and those who had lived in the past—it was Burke, she believed, who had written so passionately on this subject—the dead, the living, and the unborn were a single essence, a unity: yet one lived in the present and the future, mainly. Andrew was always thinking ahead, planning ahead: next fall, next year, the next several issues of the magazine, and always the next elections, and the elections after that. Always the future, the future. He stared into it, yearned for it, as if there, *there*, the world he desired was at last complete. And he himself vindicated, justified. Triumphant.

It was the future, Yvonne thought suddenly, that would prove him correct: for the present could not endure as it was, it must collapse, fall in upon itself. It was bankrupt, a ruin. Yet it kept going on its own heavy, blind course—no energy, only momentum—every year more exposures of corruption—stupid, childish greed—piggishness, inexplicable in adult men except as a symptom of disease, the regression of a culture toward the primitive, toward death. A machine comprised of many machines, each rattling and clattering in its own way, at the point of breakdown, and yet not quite breaking down—for there was still enough wealth to keep these things going—a gigantic machine, self-justified, an end in itself, a government with no connection any longer to those it governed. Let the future come: it would prove Andrew right. Chaos would come again and, perhaps, out of that chaos something that was new and at the same time old, timeless, would arise.

And his assassins would be discovered. She felt a sudden sensation of gloating, to know that they *would* be found. It was wrong to despair, it was far too soon, not even August yet. They would be found. She had been assured innumerable times that the authorities wanted nothing so much as to bring Andrew's killers to justice—and even if one agency tried to hinder the investigation (the state, for instance), another agency, a higher agency, would pursue it. But it might take time, it might take time . . . she must be patient.

As time passed she slept more often on the leather couch in the study. It had been Andrew's bed at times; he would work late, would sleep on the couch, not wanting to disturb her. Sometimes she found him there, before dawn, fully clothed, even his shoes on, a book or some papers on his chest, the floor lamp behind the couch still burning. *Andrew . . . ? Andrew . . . ?* She would whisper, not really wanting to wake him. He slept so heavily, his chest labored to suck in air and expel it, as if a great weight were pressing against him.

The study was a large cool room, facing the northeast. From one window Yvonne could see the Hudson River; from a smaller window she could see only a few hundred yards, since the view was blocked by another high-rise apartment building, a newer building on the park. Yvonne sometimes stood at the big window, leaning her forehead against it. She had a great deal of work to do, but she was rarely impatient now. The river fascinated her. It meant nothing, it was the same every day, there was a pointlessness to it—the inevitable tedium of nature, of natural processes—yet she was fascinated. *He* had liked to work by the river in the mountains, the Natauga, hardly more than creek-size, cutting through the Petries' property. The old farm, the old buildings. Decaying orchards—pear, apple, cherry. Birds, small animals, occasionally deer. She had not felt comfortable there—it was a place of childhood memories for Andrew—a place that excluded her—and of course it was rundown now, they had not bothered to keep up the old stone house and the old barns. They had summer places, beautiful summer places, elsewhere in the mountains: on Lake Champlain, Lake Placid, and on the coast of Maine. She had not liked the old farm, had resented him driving out there. Why had he felt the need to drag his things a hundred miles into the mountains, why had he felt the need to work at that small desk in the cabin, by a window with a coarse, dirt-pocked screen, so that he needed a light burning constantly . . . ?

When the river was obscured by mists, early in the morning, Yvonne stared down into the park—across Jefferson Avenue to the war memorial—the lovely grouping of oaks and sycamores and spruces. At that time the park benches and the graveled paths were usually empty. She felt an unaccountable satisfaction, hiding here on the twenty-sixth floor, in a kind of tower, quite safe.

The study was nearly as large as the master bedroom. But it looked cramped because of the things jammed into it.

There was the leather couch, and a leather chair, and several cane-backed chairs upon which things were piled; but the main item of furniture was the old desk, an antique rolltop desk made of mahogany. It had a center drawer and on either side three deep drawers with brass knobs. It had innumerable pigeonholes, all stuffed with papers. Above the desk were portable shelves; from floor to ceiling, against two of the walls, were older shelves, of walnut. There were innumerable books, magazines, pamphlets, papers. There were encyclopedias, dictionaries in several languages, shelves of law books, law journals, bound volumes of *Discourses* in wine-colored leather with gold lettering, there were books on economics, history, political theory, philosophy; biographies of great men; collected letters; yearbooks; technical dictionaries; the works of Aristotle, Kant, Diderot, Hegel, Nietzsche, Burke, De Tocqueville, Beard, Marx, Spinoza, Durkheim, and others. On the walls there was space only for a portrait of David Hume, whom Andrew had much admired, and one of those Hudson River watercolors he had liked so much, and several

framed and glass-covered explorers' maps of the eighteenth century—
of the world, of North America, and of New York State and the
Hudson Bay area. The Turkish rug was well worn by now, an olive-
green-brown shade; the drapes were russet, made of a thick, substantial cotton; the ceiling was painted brown and seemed rather uncom-
fortably low.

Between the desk and the wall was a large filing cabinet, which
looked out of place; it was made of aluminum, smart and new and
gleaming. On the desk, pushed to one side, was an old Remington
typewriter and a large, costly office electric typewriter in its plastic
protective covering. Everywhere there were papers—some in Manila
folders with red or green edges, some in piles, some loose. There were
a half-dozen aluminum trays with card indexes and several shoeboxes
filled with clippings, notes, articles torn out of magazines, photostated copies of manuscripts, and miscellaneous items like paper clips
and rubber bands and stamps. At the time of his death Andrew Petrie had retired temporarily from public life—had even given up the
editorship of his magazine—in order to write a book, which he had
been writing, in a sense, all his life. There were at least a thousand
pages in the manuscript. Some were neatly typed, some were
handwritten, some only outlines. One chapter, which he had been
working on at the time of his death, lay on the desk where Yvonne
had placed it. *The United States of America: The Experiment That
Failed.* These pages, some forty or fifty, were badly wrinkled,
a few of them ripped, several splattered with blood and now dried
stiff, like parchment.

12

Why did she feel feverish when she was not ill, why was each involuntary breath a stab, a risk, as if she were high in the mountains
and surrounded by snow, killing piercing winter air one must breathe
despite the pain of each breath? Why, she did not inquire aloud, did
these creatures come to her and drag her spirit down to their level,
why did she tolerate it, why, dressed in green linen so dark as to
seem black, did she do no more than murmur assent or denial, her
eyes fixed upon her sister-in-law's distraught face without allowing
herself even to glance at the husband—when it was so often to hus-
bands she did glance at such moments, exchanging a secret ironic

dismissing look, *What a contemptible idiot you married!* But perhaps she would turn to the husband after all. Perhaps she would give him that look if things became really intolerable.

She had no time to visit Doris. She made excuses, she faltered as if deliberately embarrassed at the paucity of her excuses, but there was no time for this sort of thing, no time. So the sister-in-law came to visit her. It was inevitable, there must be a visit, a meeting of some kind, the dead husband's older sister must make her messy claim and return to tell the others about the life her deceased brother's widow was living. The husband, Arnold Laubach, came with her. He was genial and self-effacing. Yvonne detested such men. She could not bear it, the social subservience of such men, the public display they made of their ineptness. And he would not interrupt his wife though the wife was stumbling onto things that were not meant for Yvonne to hear, so that each breath she drew was sharp, really stabbing, and yet she could not shut out the voice and she could not refuse to breathe—she could not refuse to sit here and listen.

The Laubachs visited Yvonne one day from about five in the afternoon to nearly seven-thirty. They sat in the living room of the apartment, on Andrew's furniture, as if they had been invited and were welcome. They drank the drinks Yvonne prepared for them and did not notice, or did not appear to notice, that she merely sipped at hers and then set it aside and forgot it. She made them two more drinks, and then two more. She was quick to play hostess, rising in the middle of a tedious complicated proposition the sister-in-law was making—would Yvonne like to live with them? would she like Doris to help her with Andrew's work?—as if it were no more than a stream of words that might be interrupted at any time. She was feverish, she felt almost dangerously feverish, though she was not really excited and was not ill, and had had no more than a taste of her drink. But she spoke to them, as always, coolly and politely, her dark intelligent gaze fixed upon the sister-in-law's face as if she were someone to be taken seriously.

Doris was sometimes distraught. Then she was obstinately pragmatic. She used, even, one of Andrew's pet words—empirical. She seemed to believe it had something to do with common sense. *The empirical thing to do, Arnold and I think, would be . . . if the family could aid you more . . . if there could be more communication between us and more support . . . for you . . . this first year will be so hard, Yvonne, it's hard for all of us but of course it will be harder for you . . . for you in your. . . . We have so much room in our*

house, don't we, Arnold? . . . and you would be so much safer. . . .
And there would be a chance for us to become closer, at last. . . .

Yvonne interrupted to ask about being safer: what did it mean, *safer?* She was safe now, would moving to the Laubachs assure her of even greater safety?

Doris, however, did not respond to the question as it was phrased; she spoke vaguely of threats and rumors and strange coincidences and—and just the problems of living alone, a woman living alone in a city like Albany. It seemed to her and to the family that Andrew would wish nothing else for Yvonne than that the family come forward to help her—to support her—to protect her. There had been that outrageous Sunday feature story on her, after all—old discredited rumors dragged out again and quotations attributed to unidentified "former intimates" of Andrew's—and cheap sensational attacks like that might be prevented if—

Yvonne told Doris the *Journal* had wanted to interview her and she had refused and that was their revenge on—

Doris assured her she understood: she understood. The entire family understood. . . . *the way in which certain requests are turned down, however . . . there's a certain art to . . . you must be so very careful with. . . .*

When Yvonne did not reply, did not even assent, but continued to stare stonily at her, Doris went on to allude to certain problems that were arising because of the immensely complicated nature of Andrew's estate and his wishes for the family . . . *and there is Mr. Petrie to consider, in California, if he should ever be spry enough to take the trip he would want to feel absolutely welcome . . . in his surroundings. And there's the child, Andrew's poor son Michael, who. . . .* Yvonne felt the stabbing sensation, again and again; she tried to show nothing of the discomfort she felt, though her forehead was damp and very likely there was a film of perspiration on it that the Laubachs might note. *We want only what is good for you, what will help you adjust. . . .*

And the rumors! Already there were rumors. Of course many rumors had circulated about Andrew from the very first, from the first stage of his career in state politics, and that was no surprise—everyone was jealous of him. As they should have been. But now the rumors were also about Yvonne. She knew some of them—no doubt? Cruel and nasty and unjust. And yet made to seem plausible. In certain details. At the Golf Club a friend of one of Arnold's business partners had overheard. . . . And the daughter of one of Harvey's aides, in Washington, had been told quite seriously by her roommate in New York. . . . And there was speculation about. . . . And a story had been traced back to one of the girls in the District Attorney's office that dealt with . . . really quite private matters, details no one could know . . . details it would seem no one could know. Or had it been the Police Commissioner's office? . . . And, though this was another problem, maybe just the beginning of another problem, Hugh had telephoned from New York just the other night to report a rumor he had heard: an ex-photographer's model hawking her "memoirs" about town to various newspapers and magazines, a piece of nasty business that dealt with A and an alleged love affair. No grounds to it, none at all. The whole thing was preposterous. An attempt at blackmail, extortion, nothing more. . . . Yvonne need not worry about such things because . . . because the family knew how to handle them if they really became threatening.

They asked her to join them for dinner, at the club. Yvonne thanked them but declined. Her voice was quite steady. It was over now: evidently over. A few more vague fluttery words about the family, about "poor Stephen" who might also like to "feel welcome," and then Doris excused herself and left the room for a few minutes. Yvonne and Laubach remained. He had finished his drink but now raised it again to his mouth. When he set the glass down, he looked guiltily at Yvonne. Neither spoke.

She had no clear impression of him. A middle-aged man with quizzical harmless features. He was well dressed, like all the Petries, but undistinguished, unmanly. Though Doris was out of the room and Yvonne should have felt better, she did in fact feel suddenly weak; as if she were about to faint. Laubach rose from his seat and crossed to her, not very steadily. He asked if there were anything he could do?—anything?

Yvonne tried to smile at him. She failed.

Anything? Anything?

Keep that bitch away from me, she heard herself say.

He was surprised. Somehow she had not expected his genuine surprise.

Yet he touched her shoulder, lightly. He touched it as if to comfort her before he turned away.

There's Harvey too— he mumbled.

Yvonne said nothing. They were waiting for Doris to return.

Arnold said quickly that Doris had been under a terrible strain . . . wasn't really herself . . . had dreams and nightmares . . . had the idea, which she couldn't get rid of, that *it* might have been done for personal reasons . . . that *it* had nothing to do with politics at all or political enemies or. . . . That the murder had been committed by someone close to Andrew . . . someone he knew and trusted.

That's ridiculous, Yvonne said.

Then Doris returned, walking rather heavily. She stopped at one of the paintings and murmured a few words, something about having always loved that painting of the river, having had such a sentimental attachment to. . . .

But the visit was over. What had been intended to take place had not taken place; or perhaps it had. At any rate the visit was over.

13

Dear Bereaved One:

Read about your sad time & just wanted to write to ask who the hell you people think you are, your so special are you? My man is dying right here in the house, is only 51 yrs old & you cant tell me hes dying from any natural causes. Just has no energy left & during the night coughs & coughs & has no control of his body functions, then to hear about your husband, and you, ass-kissing all the way up to the President, worse will happen to people like you & *you will deserve it.* Last night on tv there was nothing but bitches like you & him & boys twitching and winking, I am talking about the party held for some nigger consul & televised for the rest of us to puke when we saw it. . . .

Dear Yvonne:

Do you notice the bloodstains on this stationery, that is to argue how serious I am. I AM SERIOUS AND NOBODY CAN RAISE HIS VOICE IN DIRISION AGAINST ME. NOBODY IS GOING TO HOUND ME OR PUT ME IN JAIL. IN THIS BUILDING THERE ARE PEOPLE OUT FOR THAT *REWARD MONEY* AND WHAT THEY SAY ABOUT ME IS LIES AND IF YOU BE-LIEVE THEM YOU ARE *CRAZY* BECAUSE I DID *NOT* KILL YOUR HUSBAND ANDREW PETRIE OR *ANYBODY ELSE* AND WILL NOT STAND FOR LIES BEING SPREAD ABOUT ME OR. . . .

Dear Yvonne:

Been meaning to write since June, I don't know what to say
actually, its so sad, but these things happen to people, to
all of us. I recognized you in a photo two or three years
ago but supposed you would want to break ties with the past,
who can blame you? People say your husband was killed by
a ring of killers, but I don't know if they want to kill women
too, but anyway I will not sign my name to this, in case
someone finds it with your things. If I say we were good
friends at Mrs. Danas in Colorado Springs, can you take the
hint??? Mrs. Dana is still going strong, my husband and I
drove down with the kids last summer, but Mr. Dana is dead
(did you know that?) and she can't take in any foster children
now so she is sort of lonely and loves people to come
visit. She showed me a magazine with your picture in it
and asked if it was *you*, but I just couldn't get her hopes up,
because she takes things so excitedly now and has high blood
pressure (she is at least 220 pounds now!) and Bob says
how those magazines just print shit anyway, and you can't believe them. Anyway I said to Mrs. Dana she wouldn't give you
the time of day if it was Yvonne, would she? After how
you walked out of here and said those things against her
and Mr. Dana, such things die hard. You just had to get
your own way and didn't care who you hurt. I am writing this
to say CONGRATULATIONS since now you are going to be
rich, aren't you, and inherit a million dollars, which was
always your scheme, wasn't it, so you can look down on
people like us like we are niggers, and laugh at. . . .

Dear Mrs. Petrie:

I am not one to write letters like this and frankly I do not
concern myself with the lives of politicians and their ladies.
However, it struck my funny bone as marvelously appropriate that. . . .

Dear Mrs. Petie:

My husband says that people like your husband deserve to
die, they are murderers themselves, all tied in with those crooks
in the labor unions & I do *not* mean the dues-paying members
but the men who run the unions who are taking bribes
from the companies and millionaire contrivers like the late
ANDREW PETIE, all down the line, & if some plan backfires the
innocent victims life is not worth a penny. Why do you

think you are different? I could give you six examples straight
off where. . . .

Dear Mrs. Petrie,

Hi! We have never met but. . . .

14

August. Outside the air-conditioned tower the days shimmer and
glow in a cloudless, rainless progression; the skies are wide, blue-eyed,
something maddening about them, heightened, remorseless.

He is impatient, she can feel him crowding against her, breathing
onto her. He peers over her shoulder at the papers spread so helplessly before her—why does she do everything so slowly, why is
nothing being put in order and why has nothing changed? Now it is
August. Two months have passed. Enormous blocks of time have
passed—boulder-sized, crushing blocks of time.

Not a tall man, but he gave the impression of being tall. Compact,
with thick, strong shoulders. Hair thinning, brown turning to a kind
of silver-blond—light, feathery, like a baby's fine hair. She saw that at
once, was struck by it at once. How curiously vulnerable he was . . .
looking at her so directly, staring at her, as if to intimidate her into
not really seeing him.

Arrogant manners. Eyes pouchy and sad when no one was admiring him. *Wanted to be loved:* so she had jeered at him that very
first night. His secret, his secret like everyone else's! Desperate to be
loved. Pretending to be so confident, so utterly sure of himself . . .
insulting those who gathered about him meekly, acknowledging him
as a kind of prince. That constant guardedness of his, what was it
but terror? She recognized it. *She* knew it very well.

She had lied in order to meet him. Had pretended to be the
daughter of a man Andrew had once helped—a political favor of
some kind, years back—a kind word with an employer, perhaps—
Yvonne with her bright dark glittering stare, inventing a father, a
background, a life, as she stood face to face with Andrew Petrie at a
reception in Pittsburgh. He had participated in a panel earlier that
evening at the Mellon Institute, discussing the phenomenon in recent years of violent, inexplicable swings in public mood—backlash

voting, reflexes in opposition to personalities rather than to legitimate issues, occasional outbursts of political hysteria that flared up
and did great damage and then disappeared again inexplicably—and
Yvonne had sat in the audience, alone, staring at him, hardly hearing
what he said. At first she had rejected his words disdainfully, they
could not be taken seriously—such right-wing fanaticism!—such
lies!—and then she noticed how the other three members of the
panel, two of them historians and one of them a Democratic congressman from Pittsburgh, disdained him but deferred to him, oddly,
involuntarily—always addressing Mr. Petrie or alluding to him,
defensively, irritably, with a certain air of self-conscious bitterness
and irony. *As if he spoke the truths they must not speak. As if he
spoke the forbidden, outlawed, unspeakable truths in order that they
might please the crowd by refuting him.* Occasionally the audience
interrupted Andrew—occasionally he was forced to smile, to acknowledge their right to drown him out with their hisses and boos
and sporadic shouts. The audience clearly favored the other speakers,
the audience sided with *them.* But Andrew had really triumphed.
Beaming, ironic, deft, theatrical, a born competitor, a springy resilient athletic manner about him even while he was seated, he gave the
impression of always knowing what would happen, of directing and
guiding and forcing not only his opponents but his audience as well
—forcing them into emotion, into the agony of hatred, the unmistakable quickening of the heart's beat that preceded and accompanied the desire to kill.

He taunted them, goaded them into hatred of him; *he* forced
them to succumb, never quite involved, himself, always courtly and
gracious and even boyish, outrageously innocent.

"Your secret is that you want control over people," Yvonne said.
"You want them to love you but that's too difficult—so you force
them into hating you. But it's the same thing. It's the same thing.
You aren't free of them, you're trapped by them—aren't you? De-
pendent on them, always dependent on them! You delude yourself!
You lie to yourself!"

In the taxi he laughed, seizing her hand. He twisted it slightly—
not meaning to hurt her—and she thought at once of her father
twisting her mother's wrist. It did not please her, it was a thought
she had not had for many years. She was repelled, angry. She disliked
him for having forced her into emotion—having inspired her into a
performance, an imposture, when she had vowed she would not lie
again. Her life, since the day she had walked out of a foster home in

Colorado and hitchhiked east, had been a series of lies, one performance after another. She was in her mid-twenties now, but still very
girlish, childish, susceptible to intensities of emotion that left her
drained, bewildered afterward. She told Petrie that it was impossible
to talk to him, impossible to discuss anything with him; he was not
an intellectual, he could not be approached rationally, sanely, though
he gave the impression of being so eminently logical, and therefore
nothing he said counted—it was unprincipled, like a jab in the ribs.
But even as she spoke she was overcome with emotion, her voice
went faint, she began to pant. She hated him for the excitement she
was feeling in his presence, seated beside him.

"You don't know me. You can't judge," he said simply.

"The things you said tonight—"

"I say lots of things," he said.

Yvonne had not much interest in men. As a part-time student at
the university she had been involved with a man, she had been "in
love" with him as far as she knew, and after a year or so the pointlessness of their relationship had crushed her, overwhelmed her—the
tedium of their raw, jangling nerves, the obliteration of their
differences in passion, in physical passion—and she had reacted
violently against him, against men, against the idea of "love." It was
so dull, really. It was not distasteful, only stupid and boring and dull.
She was capable of feeling a genuine interest in the *personality* of her
lover—a Marxist, a self-proclaimed revolutionary—but incapable of
loving him, of continuing to perform in the role of lover, beloved, a
creature whose primary connection with another had to be through
the body: that repulsed her. With Petrie that evening she heard herself as a voice, sharp, edgy, impertinent—she felt their connection
through the mind, through the antagonism of their minds. And then
it did not matter, suddenly, whether she felt affection for him or dislike; it did not matter, exactly what he said or seemed to say, only
that he existed, that he roused her to such an intensity of cerebral,
verbal excitement.

Later, after they were married, she was to recognize in him a certain pattern of behavior—the near-ecstatic pitch of his public personality, that bright, impersonal, aggressively happy manner, a god's
sense of omnipotence, almost, that led him to do quirky, unexpected,
foolish things (like leaving that reception with a young woman he
did not know, and inviting her to his hotel room, not even certain of
her name), giving way suddenly and abruptly and horribly to depression, sometimes as many as five or six days of depression, during

which time he was nearly inert, an old man suddenly, querulous and
fretful. But this Andrew Petrie no one saw, no one knew. He kept to
himself then. Like a sick animal he hid himself, ashamed, weary.
There was almost a defiance in him, in the way he sank into himself, withdrawing from others, not honoring commitments or appointments, forcing Yvonne—as, she supposed, he had forced his first
wife—to make excuses for him. First the ecstatic heights, the public
performance: a lecture, a speech, a television interview or panel, a
large party at which he was a guest of honor. For two or three hours
afterward, then, the euphoria continued—perhaps even grew slightly
—as he allowed people to get him drunk, to make him one of them;
it was the only time Andrew drank very much. Afterward, as soon as
he was alone—as soon as the crowd withdrew—the horrible downward plunge, the pitch into a kind of psychic oblivion. Then he was
weary, infinitely weary, so fatigued he could hardly undress himself.
Then his charming busy theatrical self was extinct—his handsome,
squarish face went ashen—and he had to keep to himself, resting,
sometimes lying in a darkened room with a damp cloth over his eyes
until the spell passed.

That first evening he had been extraordinarily talkative—interrupting her, joking with her, teasing her—begging her not to leave him,
not so soon!—though careful not to offend her, for he sensed her
nervous dislike of being touched, even by him. They had had a drink
together in the hotel lounge, and another drink in his room. It was
not late—only midnight—but Yvonne had felt exhausted, drained by
his attention, the relentlessness of his interest in her and the pace of
his conversation. She did not really intend to stay with him; it did
not appeal to her at all, not even the glamor of it, of having seduced
him. She did not want him—that smiling public man, so pleased to
be disliked, so eager to acknowledge his enemies. As a man he was
very attractive: his gray eyes, his soft silvery-blond hair, the sweet-
cynical curve of his smile. She knew little about fashions, cared very
little about them, but she could see that he dressed well, with casual,
indifferent good taste. He had had too much to drink, his speech was
slurred, more and more he interrupted himself, began again, forgot
what he was going to say. Still he was attractive to her. But she did
not care, she did not trust her own feelings, and she would have left
him had he not undergone so extraordinary a transformation—suddenly quiet, his face crumpling, an almost infantile exhaustion and
formlessness about him. The glass slipped from his hand, he groped
for it and was not able to find it, as if his vision had failed.

"Don't leave me," he whispered. "Wait. —Where are you? Wait."

"Are you ill? What's wrong?"

"Don't leave me. . . ."

"What's wrong?" Yvonne cried.

He stared toward her as if blind. He blinked. His mouth went slack, his face seemed to age.

"Don't leave," he whispered.

And so she had not left: she stayed with him not only that night, but for most of the following day as well.

After the fatigue, after the near-inert, sick depression, he would gradually return to normal; he always returned to himself in a week or ten days. During this time he needed from Yvonne an almost absolute attention or awareness; though she did not have to be with him, in the room with him, she had to be thinking of him, concentrating upon him, always *aware* of him, the center of her consciousness in him, not elsewhere. If they were in Albany she canceled all her engagements. She stayed in the apartment, read or worked silently, did not use the telephone, knocked on the door of his study only when she felt—when she sensed—that he needed her with him. He might be asleep, or in a kind of stupor; he might be lying on the sofa, a book unread on his chest; he might be at the window, staring down into Jefferson Park, or across to the river, his back to her, slightly hunched in his bathrobe. At times he did not even acknowledge her presence. But he knew, he was grateful. Afterward he would thank her. Afterward, when he came alive again, he would thank her for having saved his life.

And so, gradually, he would return to normal. His personality regained its stability—his moods leveled out—he returned to his desk, to his books, to the telephone; he was extraordinarily sweet, boyish, playful, even rather loving at such times—though loving in a boyish way, making no physical demands upon her. He seemed to want forgiveness, and of course she forgave him.

"Don't you love me?" he would ask at times, wistfully, doubtfully. "Don't you. . . ? But it doesn't matter, does it. It doesn't really matter."

"It doesn't matter," Yvonne said.

She did not love him. And no matter what he said, no matter how convincing or bullying he was, he did not love her; she was certain of that.

"No, it doesn't matter," he would agree.

Most of the time she held him in awe, was astonished by him—by the quick, darting movements of his intellect, by the way he leaped from one idea to another, by the range and depth of his knowledge and his capacity for remembering facts; she believed him to be a genius, the only really brilliant man she had ever met. At other times she was impatient with him—his vanity was so transparent!—and he did want to be loved, or hated, or talked about, he wanted it so hungrily, so painfully. When he was depressed or ill—for he was not in good health, he suffered from excruciating headaches and mysterious, ghostly chest and stomach pains that could not be diagnosed—she was moved to an anguished, almost self-lacerating compassion for him, as she might have been moved by the spectacle of a suffering animal. So this was Andrew Petrie! Her husband now! —She pitied him, was absorbed in him, took care of him. In a sense they were married long before he brought her to Albany, to a small, private, unannounced civil wedding at City Hall; in another sense, they were never "married" at all.

15

"And so—what conclusions have you drawn about the infamous Petrie family? Do you regret having become involved with us? Or has it been a profound experience of some kind? A *fiercely rewarding profound experience*, perhaps?"

He tried to speak casually, playfully. But his voice was shrill, his manner agitated and histrionic, as if he were on the verge of screaming. He stared at her face, at her forehead; he smiled, staring, licking his thin, dry lips, showing his rather poor, grayish teeth. He would not meet her gaze—not yet. He was staring at her forehead, or at her mouth, or at the bridge of her nose. He did not look at her body, either—except when she had opened the door to admit him and his gaze dipped helplessly to her feet and swung back up again as he stammered hello.

"I don't know what you mean," Yvonne murmured. "I think you must be joking."

"I—! Joking—! Never."

"I don't know what you mean," she said.

He had already finished his glass of sherry. He had swallowed it down without tasting it, nervously, automatically. His laughter was sudden, surprising, corrosive. It seemed to surprise him as much as Yvonne.

"The past two months have been very difficult, but everyone in the family has been helpful," Yvonne said quickly, hardly knowing what she said. ". . . everyone has been helpful, very helpful."

"Eh, they all hate you! They always have," Hugh said, grinning. "They're jealous of you. You see—it isn't just the money, *his* money —though in fact he doesn't have much, does he? I mean, by *our* standards?—since the old man hasn't yet died—and Andrew was counting on that inheritance, I assume, counting on it to back him for his next political adventure. But that's done now! All done! And I'm sorry too, genuinely sorry, I think the electorate always benefits when there are a number of candidates—a spectrum of choices—not just the middle-of-the-road boys but the fringe boys as well—the radical right and the radical left should definitely be represented—kept in plain sight—invited up on the platform with the rest. That's the beauty of our open society!—democracy, that sort of thing. Range of choices. . . . But Andrew's contribution to the show is over, a hideous loss—hideous. You must feel it doubly, Yvonne, having been his wife and I assume one of his most feverish—fervent—admirers? I wish there were something within my power I could actually, actually *do*—"

Yvonne could not believe what she heard: she sat facing him, listening to the dangerous rattling charge and slide of his voice, and could not believe what she heard. He broke off in midsentence, coughed several times in rapid, staccato succession, and poured another glass of sherry for himself. He was obviously very excited; she could smell the odor of his armpits, of his unwashed body. At first she thought he must be drunk. Then she thought he might be on drugs—that queer lilt to his voice, the glittering of his eyes, the way he kept interrupting himself to clear his throat and laugh. He must have lost several pounds since the funeral, for he looked far thinner, almost emaciated. His cheeks were hollow, the sockets of his eyes darkly shadowed, and his neck appeared to have shrunk inside the collar of his shirt—a lavender and pale yellow striped shirt with a button-down collar, years out of fashion. As he spoke he kept in constant motion, as if it were unbearable for him to be here—unbearable for him to have to sit still in one place: he crossed and uncrossed his long, lanky legs, showing an inch or more of exposed skin—stark white, with brown curly hairs—above his pale green socks, which seemed to have ridden down into his shoes beneath his heels; he kept setting his sherry glass down and snatching it back up again, clicking the rim softly against his teeth: he gestured with his left hand, the fingers spread wide, as if appealing to her. Yvonne could not make sense of his words. She tried to concentrate but was distracted by his manner, his tense straining grin, the way he seemed to be appealing to her in some secret, silent way, confidentially, conspiratorially. He was chattering about the investigation—the teams of detectives—the many false arrests, false confessions—the overlapping, jealous, rivalrous authorities—the spies everywhere, so that none of the Petries could ever again lead a private life—did she imagine *she* was any different? And what about the flowers he had sent to the funeral home, $85 or was it $95 worth of flowers, a "grave blanket" was the term, he believed—had she taken note of them, had she even had time to appreciate such gestures in the flurry and excitement of those days—? Yvonne was frightened. She could not follow him, he spoke so rapidly. What had Andrew said about him?—harmless—*The poor bastard is harmless*—but perhaps she should not have opened the door to him, she was frightened, sick with a sensation of blank helpless despair, the despair of being in error, of having made a mistake. That she could have been so stupid!—she, Yvonne Petrie! Now she was unable to think clearly, unable to think—what must she do?— what was possible?—for she must not offend or upset him, she must not allow him to know how he terrified her. It was sickening, that she had made this mistake: had not quite understood him when he telephoned those several odd times, had refused to interpret the rush of words, the breathy intimate pressure of his voice. And he had sent her a copy of a book of his, hadn't he—satirical drawings—inscribed *To My Dear Sister-in-Law With Highest Regards Yrs. Hugh Petrie*— and she had done no more than glance through it, in a hurry that day, mildly repelled by the squashed distorted figures, the gleeful madness—she had had no time to reply, to thank him—had put the book on a shelf somewhere, in the sitting room probably, where she rarely went—had forgotten about it completely. But perhaps he had forgotten as well? He was speaking so animatedly, so urgently of his family, as if testing her—or as if, in some peculiar way, he wanted to check with her, to see where their realities coincided.

"Then you don't regret it? Not even now? Joining our family? There's a clause in my grandfather's will, you know, 'in default of issue,' that sort of thing, so if I married and my wife were barren she would *not* inherit the Petrie money—I assume all the cousins have it, I assume Andrew had it, but perhaps this doesn't affect you?—

perhaps there are substantial funds elsewhere? Rewards of an emotional or spiritual nature? It is said of you, Yvonne, that you are so *intellectual!*—and they don't approve of that. You should hear Doris rave! To you, naturally, she shows one face—one side of that pasted-up clownish face—and I gather you are friendly with mousy little Hannah?—don't trust her either, she's eaten up with jealousy and rage and spite, *her* father married unwisely, and too late—was very shabbily treated by the old man, really vicious even for him—poor Hannah, the plainest and poorest of the cousins! As for Harvey: I hardly need tell you not to trust *him*. He and Andrew despised each other, as you know. And—did you catch it?—an item in the paper, Harvey giving a speech somewhere upstate, the dedication of a new hospital or a new prison or something like that, Harvey Petrie with tears running down his cheeks, picked up by the AP and sent across America with the rest of the daily garbage—Harvey eulogizing his dead cousin!—quoting the Bible, quoting Latin!—that someone must have trained him to pronounce. Avoid him, avoid that bastard. Just look at his wife—Irene's glazed droopy look—she used to be quite *beautiful*. As did Andrew's first wife. And you— You still— They say you are older than your official age, Yvonne, is that so? Did you lie? I heard it from a most reliable source—someone's private investigation agency poking around—courthouse records, I believe—or is *that* a lie? No need to look so startled, dear! I won't tell. —Then you don't regret it, marrying him? Not even now? Most people who marry into our family, especially women, wake one morning screaming—and find themselves unable to stop . . . but you don't look like the kind of woman who would scream, Yvonne, you look so strong, so stoic! Have you ever screamed? Lost control? Did you—that day?—then? *Did you scream when you saw him?* —My little brother Stephen used to be infatuated with martyrs—had a kiddies' book of the martyrs of North America—French Jesuits, I believe—I got hold of the book one day and read of the tortures—too ugly to describe, I'm afraid, under the circumstances—but the martyrs didn't scream, refused to scream—refused to surrender to their torturers' wishes—what will power, what egomania! And you, you strike me as— But I admire you, of course—as everyone does— I admire you very much. —What was I saying, what was my topic? Ah yes: the fate of certain women who have married into our family. Most of them were quite wealthy —I mean very, *very* wealthy—my grandmother was a Paxton, of Charleston, her father owned most of the West Indies at one time— I mean my mother's mother—and then my grandfather—my other grandfather—ah, it's so confusing, what am I saying?—and you look so very very stern with me! I fear I am wearing out my welcome. —Old George Petrie, Teddy Roosevelt's drinking buddy—did Andrew tell you about *him?*—incredible old bastard!—even Roosevelt got disgusted with him—most of the money channeled into eugenics research and foundations and 'institutes'—wanted to keep in with the Carnegies and the Harrimans but just hadn't enough cash, not really: the old booby, so fearful of having his ancestry sullied! He literally trembled, his spotty old jowls actually quivered if someone happened to mention a name that sounded Jewish—let alone Italian or Irish. Thought himself a ladies' man, too, until the very end, his gums all shrunken away from his dentures and a most amazing, persistent stink emanating from his long woollen underwear. Still—though one may mock—there were women not only willing to sleep with the old boy, but eager—nay, anxious— for the privilege; he was said to be very, very generous at such times. You might have liked him, I think—women did like him—at first. —Yvonne, may I trouble you for something else besides sherry? I don't like sherry. It doesn't agree with me. Some sort of English affectation, isn't it?—sherry?—Andrew brought the habit back with him from England, I believe, very impressed by one of the noble lords—an 'historic' house, that sort of thing—invited him and the other wife, what's-her-name, for a month of fox hunting and carousing and talk of politics—somewhere in Sussex, was it? Or don't you know? It's quite possible he didn't tell you about the glories of his past—when he was a Senator from the Empire State—the good old days of his prime. —But have you anything else, dear? Some Scotch? Bourbon?"

There were odd splotches on his cheeks—pale, bloodless spots, like frostbite. And the tip of his nose was waxen pale. Yvonne thought: *He's the one.*

"Do you mind if I get it myself? I assume the liquor cabinet is here?—over here?"

He got to his feet, rather slowly. Standing, there was a cautious, almost graceful manner about him, as if he were deliberately holding himself in restraint, not surrendering to the impulse to jump up.

For the first time since Andrew's death, since she had realized he was dead—had known of his death somehow—had sensed it, felt it— for the first time since that moment, Yvonne knew fear: the nullity of fear, the cold, helpless stupidity of panic. Nothing to be done, nothing to be done. She stared at Hugh's gawky, mock-graceful figure and could not reply.

"How quiet you are, Yvonne! How subdued this afternoon! I don't remember you being so quiet, dear—when did we first meet, we two?—that reception for my father?—my father's retirement? Ah, you weren't subdued then!—you were wonderfully, wonderfully alive —rather outrageously alive—as everyone noted at the time. You are taking your widowhood quite seriously—? And is it an interesting experience? A rewarding experience?"

"I— I'm— I don't understand you," Yvonne said faintly.

"I'm not to be understood," he called over to her. "I'm only to be experienced."

She heard herself talking. She heard her unfamiliar childhood voice, a girl's brave hollow voice, she heard it from a distance, hoping it would not falter, would not break, revealing her utter terror. The child at the Emergency Welfare Center in White Springs—taken from her mother and her mother's lover very early one Sunday morning—taken away in a State Trooper's squad car—wrapped in someone's jacket—nose bleeding, mad with fear—saying she wasn't hurt, they hadn't hurt her, no one had hurt her, where were they taking her?—and the same voice in the dining hall, in the recreation room, in the interviewing room—Yvonne always the tallest of the girls in her age group, always the most articulate, the most intelligent— Yvonne Radek always the most cunning—pretending at times to be shy, to be meek—but always alert, intense, with that glacial, uncanny calm: no one could intimidate her. Not her. In the first of the foster homes, and in Juvenile Detention—as a runaway—as an "incorrigible"—and in the last foster home—Yvonne always the most observant, the most clever, alert to the point of insolence. She talked, she knew how to talk, from the very first she had imitated one of the young brash matrons—the most popular one, the one whose cruelty was forgiven her: for wasn't she fearless, confident, without remorse? Yvonne imitated her. Yvonne imitated the voice, the quick empty smile, the rather ticlike grin. It had not failed her, that performance. It had never failed her so far.

"Ah, what a remarkable woman you are!" Hugh sighed. He wiped his face with a tissue; he took off his glasses and dabbed at his eyes. Strange, he was almost attractive—almost, except for his mottled cheeks, a handsome man. His light brown hair was frizzy, damp-looking, like a boy's hair; without his glasses he looked boyish. Then he put them back on and looked at her.

She shivered.

"Extraordinary," he said, "how brave you are—active—carrying on without him—that sort of thing. Everyone assumed you would simply take the money and run—if there *is* much of an estate—is there? Or hasn't it been cleared yet? I suppose not; these things take ages; and there are evidently libel suits still pending against him?—poor Andrew! Even in his grave he can't possibly be at peace. He must be enjoying himself! I like to think so! —And so you are carrying on as usual—I think it's to your credit—will hush the rumormongers—what a very good idea, a scholarship fund in his honor—he was such a fine scholar, you know, in prep school and as an undergraduate—mainly A's—a really outstanding record—made poor Stephen and me look awfully silly, needless to say. And you're going to edit his manuscripts? What a contribution to American letters! I wish I could help but I'm no good with words—arranging words on paper—my talent is for the visual, for the eye—sensual rather than cerebral, that's me—*sensual* to my fingertips—not very cerebral, never very intellectual, I'm afraid—unlike *him*. Yes, my dear, you've done beautifully so far. I want to congratulate you. And was there a cover story on you in one of the Albany papers?—a Sunday supplement? Doris mentioned it—said it was awfully cruel of them to do it against your wishes—without your cooperation—but that's your fate, Yvonne, as *his* widow. Eh, I'm sorry! Will this leave a ring? It's been so long since—used to be so conscious of—my mother had such exquisite furniture, you know, we had to be careful where we set things and I felt safe only in my room—or in the bathroom, where I could hide for hours —that sort of thing. Maybe you can buff it up? Is that the correct term? No doubt you have a maid—certainly you have a maid—*she* can buff it up. And now— You look awfully tired, Yvonne, am I exhausting you? I sometimes have that effect on people—and I swear I don't know why."

Yvonne laughed suddenly.

Hugh glanced at her—his eyeglasses sliding down his nose, his lips pricking up in a sudden, genuine smile.

"Eh? What? You think I'm amusing?"

She drew in her breath sharply. No: she must not laugh. She was in danger. There was danger here—danger surrounding her—she had made a mistake, allowing this stranger into the apartment—had blundered, had acted stupidly—all along thinking the assassin was not an individual, not a fleshly creature, but an abstraction—an idea —a theory: not a man at all. She had not understood, she hadn't believed, hadn't known. Theory: abstraction. Not men. Not a man.

Running out to the highway through the woods—escaping to a car on the highway—phantasmal laughing gliding shapes—hadn't she known they must be real, human like herself?—like this man? But of course this man was not the assassin. That was impossible. She had misjudged him, had been frightened for no reason, panicked to the point of nausea. No reason, no reason. He grinned at her, one leg crossed and bobbing, a patch of pale skin exposed—how innocent, her brother-in-law Hugh Petrie! She held her breath, watching him. No, she must not laugh. He wanted her to laugh—he was waiting, deliciously, waiting for her to surrender, submit, break into helpless laughter. His eyebrows were arched, a jester's eyebrows. He was inno-cent, innocent. The odor of his excited, lustful body reached her, but she would not laugh.

"Your husband hardly soggy in the grave, and already you are merry?—giggling?—flirting with a blood relative?"

Yvonne suddenly snorted with laughter. She could not help herself.

16

"What's wrong?" she cried.

There was a man staring toward her, as if he were blind. His fair brown hair disheveled—his lips moving silently. Something had slipped from his fingers, had fallen to the floor. The sound was muffled; the floor was carpeted. That floor was carpeted.

"What's wrong?" she cried. "What do you want from me?"

She went out during the day. She began to accept invitations. She went to libraries; arranged for a carrell in the State Historical Mu-seum. Daylight made her drowsy, dark made her awake, alert, tense, cautious. But she triumphed. She lay awake and thought: Insomnia. Others have suffered insomnia. During the day her drowsiness was a kind of comfort. And there were so many people now—when she left the apartment, when she went into the city—emerging from the ele-vator into the foyer, even—there were so many people, so much to take into account, she rarely had any need to think of herself, to con-sole herself. She thought: Sorrow. Others have suffered sorrow.

Emerging from the library, standing for a moment at the top of the steps. Here is the widow, here is *his* widow. She experiences the pleasant sensation of being involved—in all these people—the public square, the line of taxis—the limousine from the airport just pulling out—involved, absorbed in, obliterated in. It is an infinitely wide, infinitely fine web of nerves cast out everywhere, throughout the city and beyond, men and women caught up in work, in separate but ultimately connected activities: office workers, men and women, well dressed, some with briefcases, girls with shoulder bags and fashionable shoes—men with airline bags—valises—splendidly well groomed, most of them—people like herself and Andrew. Civilized, they are. Alive. Cheerful in the sunlight of early autumn—why should they not be cheerful today?—why should they not give the appearance of being cheerful?—secretaries, legislators, lawyers, tourists—the living and the dead both—hurrying across the square, along the paths, along the sidewalks—inching out into the street, eager for the traffic lights to change. She is exhilarated by the sight of them, of the commotion, the stream of life. She is reassured, the external world continues, *it* has not begun to slow down, *it* is supreme.

Between the enormous Schumacher Building and the fountain with the sprightly cast-iron sculpture at its center she is approached: someone speaks to her shyly. Spray from the fountain touches them. Neither can move, it is one of those clumsy social moments; she would—if she were less aware of his uneasiness—move back, away from the spray. What a shock to see her! He had been thinking of— at that very moment thinking of—of— *Of Andrew?* Of Andrew. Had been thinking of the magazine, the next issue—the first since—the first— The first issue with his name on the masthead as editor-in-chief. "Acting Editor," he had been. The past year and a half. He had been thinking of that and of Andrew and of her: yes, he had been thinking of her.

"Could I see you sometime? For lunch? For lunch, here, around here, where it's convenient for you?—so that we could talk—could talk of—"

She writes in a small notebook she keeps in her purse. She enters his name, *Eliot Stacey.*

Not long afterward Harvey himself dropped by. Shook her hand, held it hard. Warm dry hand, reassuring. Harvey himself splendidly blue-eyed, in a light wool suit, tweed, something sporty about the lapels and the buttons—the sort of thing Andrew might have chosen for himself. Asked her about the papers?—letters?—work on the "book"? Was she feeling better? Was she going to see people again? Not too many people, of course; and not the wrong people.

"Who are the wrong people," Yvonne asked ironically.

Harvey enumerated them.

Yvonne interrupted: "—That one is harmless, isn't he?"

"Everyone is harmless in theory," Harvey said.

"I don't see why I should listen to you," Yvonne said. "I don't see why I should take your instructions seriously."

"You wouldn't see, no," Harvey said slowly. He rubbed his hands together and smiled. "It's part of your . . . it's part of your condition, let's say, not to see; not to want to accept instructions. Andrew was like that too. He was like that even as a boy. If he had taken advice from certain members of his family, who wished him only well, who were *not* jealous of him and working against him . . . if he had taken their advice. . . ."

Yvonne looked away. He was silent, as if waiting for her to look back. He faced her across the massive smoked-glass coffee table, big dry hands clasped together, patient, sympathetic, sly.

"If he had taken that advice . . ." Harvey said gently.

". . . he would have been a mediocrity," Yvonne said, still not looking at him, smiling. She spoke rather softly but he did not ask her to repeat what she had said. "He would have been indistinguishable from the rest of you. . . ."

"He would be *alive*," Harvey said.

When Yvonne did not reply he went on, in a forced, conversational tone: "Have they called you in to ask questions about—? The latest development—? Maniac stopped at the Canadian border with guns and ammunition—an old acquaintance of our Stephen's, they say—name of Raschke?"

"They call me in often," Yvonne said.

"They don't call me in often," Harvey said. "They must think I'm innocent . . . must think I'm completely out of it. I resent that, in a way. . . . But you, Yvonne, you don't seem to think I'm innocent?"

"I don't know what you're talking about," Yvonne said sharply.

"You don't seem to trust me, don't care to confide in me. . . . Is there anyone else? There's no one else. I'm reasonably sure there's no one else. At the present time."

Her knifelike smile came and went. She experienced it as a sensation, something apart from her. ". . . don't have the right to talk to me like that . . . taunting me, bantering with me . . ." she said in a low, hoarse voice. "You don't . . . you haven't . . . there is nothing between us, no claim between us. You're stupid and vulgar and transparent, a transparent opportunist, *those are Andrew's words* and not mine. He would be disgusted to see you here, in his home, smiling that unctuous intolerable smile of yours . . . only fools could be taken in . . . seduced. . . . We know about your political deals and your women, your girls, your secretaries and stenographers and college girl Young Republicans and volunteer campaign workers. . . ."

Harvey laughed. He seemed genuinely amused. She could not look at him, however; she did not want to meet that fixed, mocking stare of his.

"*We* know about lots of things," Harvey said zestfully. "*We* are omnipotent. Aren't we miraculous, aren't *we* immortal! . . . And so virtuous!"

". . . You have no right to come here, to persecute me," Yvonne said. "I know you hated Andrew and Andrew made no secret of his feelings toward you. I know you despise me. I don't *want* you not to despise me. It doesn't matter that you're so powerful and influential and that the Petries are all clustering around you; they won't listen to you if you go against Andrew and me, they've changed their . . . some of them have changed their minds about me . . . they have told me personally . . . have expressed their feelings personally to me, after his . . . after the. . . . They accept me, most of them. They accept me as much as they can, under the circumstances, and I don't expect . . . I don't want . . . I'm not going to campaign for myself . . . I'm Andrew's wife and my time is completely filled with him, with his work, I am never lonely . . . social life doesn't interest me . . . I . . . I resent you coming here . . . I didn't invite you . . . you have no right. . . ."

"Circumstances make their own laws," Harvey said. His exuberant tone of only a moment before had vanished, or had been retracted. He spoke bluntly, with no desire to charm. "Persons . . . personalities . . . your elegant icy hysteria and my erratic compulsions . . . your being so fatally close to him, a twin of his . . . and my childhood fascination with . . . with *him*: these things don't matter. It's the circumstances that must be taken seriously, not the performers. Not the persons. Who are *you*, after all? Yvonne Radek. . . ? Who is Yvonne Radek?" He got to his feet. He spoke ponderously, without feeling. She looked at him now, slitting her eyes, fearful of him, but she saw that he was neutral, colorless; his gaze seemed flattened. "We'll be friends. I'm sure of that, Yvonne. Friends. Friendly. I don't take seriously your pretense of being superior to me . . . any more than I took seriously Andrew's pretensions. I am only stupid and vulgar and transparent when it suits my purpose. After all—I am not merely a politician, I'm an intelligent civilized man, and my family is older than the nation itself—I'm as good as your late husband in every way, Yvonne, and maybe better in some ways. But we have time, we have a future. Certain details can wait. . . . The one thing you must know, however, is that I am innocent . . . I mean that in every way—literally, metaphorically—directly or indirectly—you must know that, you should know that unless you've become unbalanced, seriously unbalanced. Really, it's beyond all sane speculation. . . ."

"Yes," Yvonne said.

"I wasn't Andrew's enemy. I was his cousin. We supported each other in public most of the time. I wasn't his enemy, I was his friend. And I am your friend. You'll need friends—living people. A living man. A man who is alive, eh? —You'll see."

"Yes," Yvonne said. "People are free to think that."

As the months passed she received a number of gifts from Hugh Petrie.

They included a dozen long-stemmed red roses, a white silk scarf from Bergdorf Goodman's with the price tag still attached ($65), another copy of *Eminent Contemporaries*, missing the dust jacket, with a simple "Love, yr. brother-in-law H." inscribed; a hammered gold falcon, ten inches high, from Cartier; three poinsettias in a large earthenware pot; a number of costly art books mailed directly from Manhattan bookstores—the photographs of Ansel Adams, the political satires of Goya, a history of the animated cartoon in the United States, with most emphasis on Walt Disney, *The Erotic Art of India, Scotland Yard's Most Sensational Cases: With 101 Unsparing Photographs*; a yellowed lace mantilla or shawl that, a note explained, Hugh's great-great-great-grandmother had worn to an inaugural ball at the White House, a framed lithograph by an artist of whom Yvonne had heard, but about whom she knew nothing—it portrayed a hideous creature with a crow's head and the body of a man, and Yvonne did no more than glance at it before she closed the carton in which it had come, thinking she would give it away— donate it to one of the local museums, perhaps. And he sent her a carelessly wrapped fake-fur pillow in the shape of a human tongue, feverishly pink; it arrived soiled and partly shredded. And a very simple pen-and-ink drawing of a man and a woman making love, locked in an anguished, complicated embrace, the woman streaming long black hair and the man rather like Hugh, with glasses slipping comically down his nose . . . it was not at all obscene and Yvonne studied it placidly before ripping it up. He sent her, also, a pen-and-ink map of Natauga County. It showed the north and south forks of the river, the lakes, the town of Fremont, and the acreage owned by the Petries; an X marked the spot, on the river, where Andrew had died. Outside the county were indicated the Adirondack Mountains, the foothills, Mt. Invemere, Royal Mountain, the Sacandaga Reservoir, the Mohawk and Hudson Rivers, and the cities of Gloversville, Schenectady, and Albany. The Hudson River was noted in an abbreviated, stylized way; as were New York City and Long Island. At the very tip of Long Island there was another X. Yvonne studied the map, could read nothing in it. It seemed to be a fairly accurate map. The land owned by the Petries in that county was considerable—but of course most of it was wild, acres and acres of woods. She studied the map, she was not angry, not bewildered. She had an impulse to make another X on it—the X that would mark her own position at the time of the assassination—but she resisted. She threw the map out, she forgot about it and about Hugh.

Twenty-eight years old.
Twenty-nine.
No one knew if she lied or spoke the truth. She herself did not know always. And it was inconsequential. Sometimes she lied, sometimes she told the truth. Andrew had always cautioned her: Tell no more than you are required to tell.
But she had not needed him for that wisdom. She had always known.
Do you recognize this person? What do you know about this person? What was your relationship with this person? What was your husband's relationship with this person? Are you still in contact with—? Have you any reason to suspect or have grounds for—? Did your husband ever indicate—? Ever mention—?
Thirty years old. Sixteen years old. A runaway. Had walked away, actually—in full view of them all—shamefaced, defiant. Who was going to stop her! Who would dare touch her! Nagged and slapped and, on the cellar steps, in the cold wet stink of the cellar with its dirt floor, mauled, punched, humiliated. But it's only tickling, they said. Teasing. He doesn't mean any harm, he's fond of you, you more than the others. She was fifteen years old. Seventeen. On the road, dressed like a boy, the checked flannel shirt loose over the

sleeveless black sweater, she was eighteen years old and hitchhiking usually to a town not many miles to the east; to an army officers' base where her father—separated from the family—was stationed. The long rides she declined, unless a woman was in the car. She was never going far, never risking much distance. Eighteen years old, she claimed, if anyone asked. Often they did ask. She was hitchhiking to visit her father, who expected her. She was saving bus fare. She had done it several times in the past.

In White Springs her mother had often shown her a certain snapshot: a stern but attractive girl, her hair prim and neat in a page-boy, standing before a DeSoto, arms folded, posture confident, fearless. A cousin of Yvonne's mother's, an older cousin, not seen for many years but rumored to be "well-to-do." In Pittsburgh, the girl was a thick-waisted woman in her forties, more vexed than surprised when she opened the door to Yvonne. What had happened? What was the meaning of this? She claimed not to have heard of the name *Radek*, claimed never to have known who her cousin had married or where she had ended up—Colorado or California or Alaska. Yvonne in the soiled jeans, the flannel shirt, the black sweater reeking of stale perspiration, eyes pink, nose running. "You're no real relation of mine," the woman said. "There's no blood connection. Anyway I don't believe in that sort of thing nowadays. . . . I just don't believe in it."

Nevertheless Yvonne was allowed to stay. She kept house, worked, went to high school at night. Her mother's cousin insisted that the name *Radek* was a total mystery to her, but she didn't want to hear about it—about what had happened—about any of it. Her own life was burdensome enough. Her own life was puzzling enough. Did Yvonne understand?

Yvonne understood.

"Do you love me?"

One of the widow's lovers asked her this question. She was teased, tormented. She wanted to tell the truth—wanted to discover the truth and then utter it, publish it, as the world required. She was nervous. Ferret-faced, ferret-clawed. Nineteen years old. And then twenty. Twenty-one. Sometimes nineteen again, sometimes twenty-two. She lost the drift of what was happening—could not believe that anyone would hold her responsible. After all, everyone was dead back home. Certainly no one remained living. She avoided the word *orphan*, which embarrassed. She was five feet nine inches tall, long waisted, with rather long feet and hands, a glacial chill to her brown eyes, bluish-black hair she wore parted in the center of her head; certainly the word *orphan* was inappropriate. Similarly, the word *chambermaid* seemed wrong; and *salesgirl*. *Student* was neutral. *Student* was fine. *Abortion*, at that time, was a word rarely uttered. It was never, never to be found on public billboards or in public advertisements. It was not often thought, even in the privacy of one's most secret life. Must she arrange for one?—must a friend arrange for one? Her lover, who worked at a Ford assembling plant, the graveyard shift, and at a bowling alley on the weekends, who was editing a smudged, rather crude and embarrassing pulp magazine—*Worker & Poet*—remained innocent, not knowing. This allowed her to forget him soon after. She forgot a great deal, so there was little difficulty in forgetting him. And it turned out there had been no need for an abortion. So she forgot about that too.

"Do you love me?" they asked. She could not take them seriously, could not concentrate. Unless concentration is possible, love cannot exist; cannot get started. The tiny quivering flame began. She blew it out. She yawned and blew it out. She was nineteen years old. She wore skirts and sweaters and boots, and a navy blue coat with a collar that could be turned up to protect her face from the wind. She narrowed her eyes: her eyelashes went white with snowflakes, frost, suspicion. She could not take them seriously—did not care to be pawed, teased, caressed, mauled, loved—*loved*, as people called it; *loved*. Fifteen years old or nineteen or twenty-six, she was not deceived. *Love* was the word they assigned to their need, their ephemeral, egoistic need; she was the accidental object of that need and might easily be replaced by another object. There was no connection, no necessary connection. She did not believe in that sort of thing.

Lover too was a word that embarrassed, that was inappropriate. But she could not think of another word.

Husband?

One must concentrate. Hands and mouth and body: there must be concentration, a studious intensification of the mind, the racing of the intellect stilled, excluded. There was a lover, the lover had a name, a personality, a history. One must concentrate, one must suspend judgment, one must not be critical and sharp edged and impatient. One must have faith.

Afterward, she forgot him. She had not been pregnant—had never been pregnant. Did not intend to be pregnant.

"I don't regret the one child I do have," Andrew told her. "A son.
A rather precocious boy, though terribly spoiled by his mother—
ruined by her and her relatives, in fact. I don't regret Michael, I love
him very much. But as for more children—"

After a moment Yvonne said she understood.

"In my generation there are thirty cousins," Andrew said. "Approximately. I don't think the world really requires more of us."

"And then the estates are divided in so many ways," Yvonne said.
"Everything is weakened, isn't it? —Which must be very disappointing."

Andrew glanced at her, as if in surprise. "Yes," he said. "Yes, precisely. *Disappointing.*"

Not *lover* but *husband.*

He was like her mother's cousin in some ways: liking or disliking
such people was inappropriate, a confused reaction. It did not matter
that one *liked*, it did not matter that one *disliked.* The personality
was supreme, untouched, indifferent.

When Yvonne moved out of the cousin's house, having rented a
room not far from the university, the woman, hearing her on the
stairs with the two suitcases and the grocery bag of books, preferred
to remain in the kitchen with the door closed, heating a teakettle,
humming loudly to herself.

"Good-by!" Yvonne called. "I'm leaving now—good-by!"

She must have been nineteen then. She worked part-time in the
university library, and on Saturdays at one of the bookstores in the
area. She had a lover then; there was a young man who was her
lover; but she was not moving out to live with him.

"Thank you! Thank you for everything!" Yvonne shouted from
the front door.

The house was silent, the woman's humming subsided. Yvonne
did not dare rush into the kitchen. She did not dare start to weep.
What point was there in that, what difference would it make?

"Thank you for everything!" she shouted from the front door.

The woman was a sales clerk in the Ladies' Lingerie & Sleepwear
department of Stern's, a large downtown store. Once Yvonne went
there not to buy anything but simply to confront her—to face her.
Radek? Had there been no *Radek?* She would see about that.

At first she could not locate the woman. Then she saw her—

behind the corset counter. Yvonne approached slowly, hesitantly. She would see about that! She would— But the change in the woman was enormous. Yvonne had not seen her for several years and now she was really an old woman, heavier, shoulders rounded, tired. She wore bifocal glasses. Her hair was a perky synthetic silver, pressed down upon her head like a helmet. She did not seem to notice Yvonne approaching.

Hello! I only wanted to say—

I must tell you about my good fortune—

I thought you'd be pleased to—

But no: she could not. She hesitated, stopped. What was she doing, what did she want? What connection was there between her and that woman with the wrinkled, peevish face?—now speaking irritably to a younger woman, another sales clerk?

I want my own mother, Yvonne thought.

Later she thought: Not really.

Much later, years later, she thought: Not really. No. None of them. Not even *him*. She was going to survive his death.

17

Always he brushed near her. His demands were not a lover's demands—he was not jealous—but he was acutely aware, always near, listening.

He was not jealous. She believed he took pride in her—smiling that infrequent wide smile of his, as if taken by surprise.

"So you live here. You live here," he said. He spoke as if amused, trying to disguise his nervousness. ". . . so high."

Yvonne said nothing. She stood watching him, studying him. He avoided her serene, level gaze, went to the balcony, said something about the view—a spire in the distance was his church—that is, a Catholic church in his neighborhood—miles away.

He went into the sitting room. He saw the piles of letters—the unopened envelopes—the cards in stacks. "Jesus! You don't have to answer all this, do you? —*GOD BE WITH YOU IN YOUR HOUR OF DEEPEST NEED. SOMEDAY THE CLOUDS*

WILL PART. HEARTFELT SYMPATHY FROM OUR
HEARTH TO YOURS." He picked up a magazine. Yvonne judged
from its pale yellow cover that it was the September issue of *Discourses*.
He leafed through it, said nothing, put it carefully back
down. "So you're alone now?" he said.

Yvonne did not reply. She remained standing in the doorway.

"The only thing I ever read of his," Wunsch said with an odd
defiant twist of a smile, "was an exquisitely mad essay in an anthology,
a collection of essays on the Rosenberg case. I was an undergraduate
at the time. I didn't quite understand your husband's position.
Whether they were *guilty* or not wasn't an issue?—*guilty* in the
sense of having done anything, or having conspired to?—but guilty in
terms of the evidence presented in the courtroom, during the trial, in
the physical confines of the courtroom—wasn't that it? Something
like that?"

"You're oversimplifying his argument," Yvonne said. "But basically
you're correct."

". . . and then his style, his style was unreadable. . . . His was the
only essay in the book that had a voice, a tone, it was really perverse,
and in a perverse way I enjoyed reading it," he said. So long as he
was talking like this, moving about the room, he had conquered his
excitement; he glanced toward her and then away. "However, I never
read anything of his again. I want to be utterly frank with you."

"But why?" Yvonne said. The nervousness was his; he seemed to
have relieved her of it. "Why should you be utterly frank?"

"I wouldn't want us to misunderstand each other—"

"But why should it matter to you whether we misunderstand each
other?" Yvonne said, puzzled. "Do you think—"

"I only meant—"

"—it matters?"

"In Pittsburgh I was a volunteer worker for a man who was running
for Congress, a very fine man, a black man named Dwyer. He
was a Democrat. He was an attorney but not an extremist of any
kind. He was very intelligent, patient, a little slow . . . slow in his
speech. He didn't expect miracles, he was always telling his people to
work through the structures that existed rather than tearing them
down; but the other blacks, the extremists, got most of the publicity.
. . . Andrew came to Pittsburgh, he introduced Dwyer at one of
Dwyer's rallies and gave a history of black politics, showed how certain
developments were part of a necessary pattern and how other

developments were not; how the moderate and the conservative survived while the extremist passed away, how the only hope for minority people was to work through the existing structures of government. He was really an optimist: he had faith in the future. But he connected it with the past, he said we must read the future out of the past. The freedom the blacks wanted at that time—the extremists—was like the freedom they were given after the Civil War—the euphoria of freedom, simple self-determination, the brutality of such freedom—the meaninglessness of it—without education, training—discipline—"

"But you're serious!" he said. "You really mean it. —Or am I misinterpreting you?"

"You asked how we had met," Yvonne said. Her voice was rapid, light, effortless. She might have been reciting a prepared speech, the words came so easily. But she had never said them before; she had never told this particular story to anyone. Most of the facts were authentic—there had been a Dwyer, in Scranton—but she had already been Andrew Petrie's companion at the time.

"Yes," he said. "But it's much more serious than I had thought."

"Everything is serious," Yvonne said. "Why are you so upset?"

They had met by accident, on the street. At first she had not recognized him—he looked so anonymous, nameless—insignificant. But there was something about his small boyish head, his curly brown hair, his rather impudent manner, that attracted her.

He had had several drinks. He was not so energetic now.

"I wouldn't want us to misunderstand each other," he said softly.

Yvonne laughed.

"In what way could we misunderstand each other?" she said.

He looked at her, miserable. He got to his feet, approached her, his fingers twitching.

"If you— Would you—"

"Yes?"

She had had her hair cut a few days earlier. Bangs scissored across her forehead, neat, severe, level with her eyebrows. A few gray hairs, they told her. But nothing to worry about: just pull them out as they appear, one by one. Until, of course, there are too many to pull out.

She had had her hair cut, but her old attitude, her old manner of intense, expectant cynicism was gone. In the past, in her girlhood and young womanhood, she had experienced a certain keen, gloating delight, a detached and even rather sinister delight, in her appearance: a jaunty cynicism of a kind. Her appearance had nothing to do with her, had no connection with *her*. It was superficial entirely. The long, thick hair, which could be brushed until it gleamed—the good, strong cheekbones—the eyes, the mouth—the strikingly pale skin: all, all were superficial. They did not represent her, in a way they masked her, allowed her to hide quite comfortably inside, somewhere deep inside, cunning and patient. She heard her voice performing when it cared to perform. She witnessed her own behavior from a distance, from a distance inside her, really oblivious to other people. There was a world of strangers, irrelevant and apart from her, not related at all. Of course *he* crossed over, *he* had touched her. But no one else. And even he had been deceived in a way; had been attracted by what was least significant about her, her appearance. That others should look at her and see only the appearance of her, the superficial husk of her, had been bewildering at first and then, as the years passed, a kind of consolation. She could retreat there whenever she wished. She could seem to *be* what she appeared to be; it was a sanctuary of a kind. That other people might be hiding, cleverly hiding, wearing their own faces like masks, would occur to her from time to time— but only when she was in the presence of someone who, like herself, was extraordinarily sharp witted, alert, suspicious. Most people dreamed, staggered through life in a dream, not knowing that they staggered, drifted, fell slowly forward and downward, imagining they controlled their destinies; there were so few of the others, the keenly awakened ones, so few Yvonne had met, and even with these uncommon people—even with Andrew—she could usually retreat, observe, perform as she thought it best to perform, all the while intensely awake, passing judgment. She was in control then, always in control. It was not that she wanted to manipulate people—though sometimes, of course, it was necessary that she manipulate them—nor did she want them to like her, to be attracted to her; certainly she did not want them to fall in love with her. That storm of misunderstandings, misinterpretations—that hallucinatory chaos—did not appeal to her at all. It was dangerous, ungovernable. She did not want to be loved—did not *want* what people called love—at all. But she did want to control their idea of her, their interpretation of her, the image they carried away in their imaginations. It gave her pleasure of a kind, a strong cerebral pleasure. It confirmed her cynicism, her detachment, her own pure and undefiled identity. Imposture forced upon her—as in the old days, in the foster homes and in the juvenile detention home, and even in Pittsburgh for a while—was repulsive, horrible; she felt a violent hatred for those who forced her to deceive them, to court them or elude them or deceive them outright. That was hideous, certainly. But imposture for its own sake, freely chosen: she delighted in it, like a child. It was play, purely playful, yet there was something sacred about it, an almost mystical seriousness about it, and she could be very much moved by herself at such times. Her appearance in a full-length mirror, that uncanny specter of herself as a *beautiful woman* . . . how marvelous it seemed to her, how she gloated in it! For it was the perfect disguise, *the* perfection of a disguise, drawing strangers' eyes to it while simultaneously blinding them, dazzling them, distracting them. And should she one day no longer appear to be beautiful, should she feel that kind of power fading, why would she care? There were other kinds of power.

But now her old, innocent delight was lost to her, now she stared indifferently at what was presented—the black hair cut so severely across the forehead, enlarging the eyes, making the neck seem longer. They said to her, flattering her, How this becomes you, Mrs. Petrie! how lovely! She was unmoved, indifferent. Even the small pleasure of having Andrew affect surprise at seeing her—approving of the change—complimenting her as he often did, easily and courteously, in that social manner she had noticed in a number of the Petries— honey-smooth and yet cool, effortless—that small pleasure would be denied her; he was absent, gone, dead.

The thick-lashed brown eyes, lighter than her own. Hazel with flecks of green. The curly hair, not cut in a very flattering style; or perhaps it had grown out unevenly. Filling with moisture, his eyes. Tears of dismay or anger?—chagrin?—rage?

". . . sorry," he murmured.

She said nothing. Her mind had been detached for some time: she was thinking of the fact that the apartment should be repainted, except for Andrew's study; he had wanted it repainted, had been talking about it for some time, and now she would make the arrangements. Except for his study: not that room. She would not change that room.

On the surface of her body she was sweaty, slick with sweat, and yet cold—shivering. She was not well, perhaps. She could not remember what it was—to be healthy, to be able to sleep, to feel well—what did that mean, *well?*—how had she lost it?—though possibly she had lost nothing at all, was remembering the past incorrectly. She detested illness, her own or anyone else's. She would not think of it, being ill, going to a doctor. And she did not believe she was ill; her symptoms were mild, some days there were none at all, only a sense of malaise, as if she were coming down with the flu. Sometimes she was feverish, sometimes she was unaccountably cold. But Wunsch too was shivering. He too was coated with sweat, and shivering, miserable.

He prepared to leave. Yvonne did not follow him to the door. She said in a quick, concerned voice, as if she had just thought of it: "Don't be upset—don't be disgusted with yourself. You don't like me, that's all."

He said nothing. She watched him from the doorway, half-pitying him. ". . . you don't like me, perhaps you don't like women. It doesn't matter."

"All right," he said. "Good-by."

Afterward she dressed and went into the other room to see if he had taken anything. But of course not, he would not have taken anything, he was not that type. She went into Andrew's study. It was dark; she switched on the desk lamp. The couch was empty—no one lay on it. The room was empty. It was filled with things, yet empty. The drapes looked heavy, oppressive. She did not bother to draw them. So high in the air, so high above the park, no one could see.

Andrew—?

But he was gone, it was absurd to think of him here, waiting for her.

Still. . . . The assassins would be apprehended, and he would triumph over them—she too would triumph—but they must have patience, he must be willing to wait as she waited. Already she had forgotten Wunsch, she had not even spoken his name—Larry, was it?—Larry—already he had receded, disappeared. Not the assassin, not him. Not that one. He was an enemy, but not the killer. She was certain of that, she knew he would be incapable of murder—was incapable, even, of ordinary passion.

She sat at the desk. She lifted papers, read them, recognized the words—which she had read many times—and in the same instant lost awareness of them, put the papers back down. The manuscript—so many sheets of paper!—but she would put it together, she would edit it, would fulfill her obligation to him. After all she was *his* wife; it would not have been said, ordinarily, that he was *her* husband.

18

There were patches of snow on the ground and on evergreen boughs, weighing the boughs down, flecked with dirt, melting slowly. There were bunches of bright red berries drooping from skeletal bushes. Birds flew overhead. Andrew pointed out a small flock of Canada geese. They walked together, he leaned a little against her, explaining something. He talked quietly and at great length, never pausing, not giving her time to interrupt or make any comment or ask any question, as if knowing her remarks would be inconsequential.

He had been betrayed by his political associates. He had been betrayed by his friends. Someone had assured him that someone else had assured *him* that a certain very guilty party—in this instance the warden of the Glasberg State Penitentiary—had been innocent of the charges made against him, the hysterical accusations in the left-wing press and elsewhere. Was it the first time, Yvonne wanted to know. Was it the first time anyone had betrayed him? She knew it was not, but he was behaving as if it were, going over and over the facts of the matter, the deaths of a number of prisoners and the deaths of a number of prison guards and the statistics released by the prison authorities and the evidence of Andrew's own senses—hadn't he, along with the other members of the citizens' investigating committee, spent the better part of a day being led through that disgusting place?—being assured, being assured—flattered that one of the prison authority's attorneys could quote verbatim Andrew Petrie in the *Harvard Law Review* of several years past—and then suddenly to open the paper and read in the headlines—

He spoke with a quiet, astonished outrage, as if it were the first time he had been outraged, either by his friends or his many enemies; he spoke at great length, at great length, leaning a little against Yvonne, favoring his right leg as he sometimes did in damp weather. When he was especially tired he walked with a considerable limp. As a child he had climbed on the roof of his parents' house and had slipped off, had fallen to a flagstone terrace and broken his leg quite badly—brutally—the thigh bone snapped and the kneecap very nearly crushed—served him right, really, for having been so foolhardy, showing off as he had so often in childhood. Fortunately his younger brother, who had followed him, had not fallen with him; the fall might have been fatal, for Hugh had been so delicate a child. And then, years later, as a parachutist, Andrew had broken the leg again, rebroken the thigh bone. . . . In bad weather the leg ached violently, both legs ached mysteriously, and he found walking difficult. But he needed to walk, needed to exercise himself, could not surrender to the temptation to spend every hour at his desk; he knew that would be disastrous.

When he's old— Yvonne thought. *When he's old he will need me even more.* And it gave her pleasure to think he would lean more heavily against her, and that she would be equal to it; she would be equal to him. Always, in the past, she had disliked weakness—had avoided people who might want to be dependent upon her. For some reason she did not feel that way about her husband. He was so strong-willed that any evidence of weakness was endearing; made him seem very human. *When he's old*— But of course he was not old. Would not be old for many years. He was in the prime of life now, forty-five years old. Though he seemed at times wearier than he had been, more inclined to repetition, to thinking aloud, he was still an extraordinarily vigorous, quick-witted man, exactly the Andrew Petrie others admired. —But he was so hurt, so baffled by this "betrayal," as he called it!—so hurt, he had forgotten even to be angry. It was unlike him. He had made a fool of himself in public—but that did not matter, did it; he had made exaggerated, rather inflammatory statements to the press before, had he not?—and still he was admired by his admirers, still he was the same man, proud and independent and contemptuous of others' opinions—and in any case, as Yvonne assured him, these matters would soon be forgotten. A public scandal remained in the public eye for only a certain number of days and then would be replaced by another public scandal. There was a pattern to it, almost a kind of rhythm. Didn't he know? He knew. And the case of the State of New York against the inmates accused of murder in the first degree would not be held for many, many months; and it would be held in Rochester, far enough away not to matter. Neither the prosecution nor the defense would want to subpoena him, surely—? He was out of it, safely out of it. What did it matter, what did such trivial things matter, everyone knew the state was middling-corrupt, not so bad as some states, of course, but bad enough; and everyone who knew Andrew personally would know he had acted in good faith, had simply been misinformed, and they would understand his resigning from the committee and even the rather extreme accusations he had made— They would understand, they would understand. And if they did not, why should it matter? But she did not argue with him. Not that day.

Naturally she worshiped him. It had not occurred to her at the time, in such simple terms. One fine bright autumn day she went again to the cemetery, stood at the graveside, waiting, listening, as if for instructions. Had he not taught her so much, so very much?—she must see the individual always in its larger category, always dwarfed and quieted by history, by the universal. Subjectivism was repellent to him. He was correct, certainly. She understood, she believed. What was the expression, quoted from which historian, "the pathology of subjectivism," and so she stood at her husband's graveside awaiting deliverance in the cool sunny autumn air. It was very quiet. Quiet. Birds chattered, automobiles passed in the distance, a child was crying somewhere in another part of the cemetery. "Andrew—?" He was going to be proved right.

19

Her husband's young brother Stephen stood at another graveside, some distance away. He was accompanying an old woman who wore a black cloth coat. Yvonne stared. She did not want to stop on the graveled path, did not want to call attention to herself. Stephen stood beside the old woman, he wore coveralls, he held in one hand a pair of gardening shears and in the other a branch of blossoms—no, they could not be blossoms at this time of year—small white roses, wild climbing roses, those roses that grew like weeds on the stone walls of the cemetery.

He turned, glanced toward her. It was not Stephen; it was a stranger.

Yet he had the same—

The dark hair, the quizzical expression—

And the shears in one hand, the spray of flowers in the other. A stranger, standing at a stranger's grave, one of the cemetery's workmen, no one Yvonne knew.

Perhaps he knew her? He smiled shyly and said something she could not hear. The old woman, intent upon the grave, noticed nothing.

20

An unemployed foundry worker in his fifties, separated from his wife, confessed to the killing in a downtown precinct late one Saturday night. He was not drunk. They knew he was lying but had difficulty persuading him. He wanted newspaper reporters, he wanted television coverage, he wanted them to telephone his wife and spring the news upon her. They had difficulty persuading him that he lied. A psychiatrist examined the man, questioned him for ten minutes, declared he was a paranoid schizophrenic, possibly quite dangerous. The man was lucid, convincing, sober, had even shaved for the occasion. "Give me a lie detector test!" he begged. The ambulance arrived the next morning at seven. When he was strapped into a restraining jacket by two tall black orderlies from the state hospital he began to shout: "I'm innocent! Hey! I didn't kill anyone! I read about it in an old magazine I found in—" One of the black boys seized him by the scruff of the neck and gave him a good hard shake. The ambulance doors were slammed shut. The ambulance drove off.

21

He asked her about the ring and she lifted it to the meager light—a hooded stained-glass miniature lantern on their table—and told him she had found it many years ago, had discovered it in a restroom in a bus station somewhere in Nebraska, lying on the filthy floor, a lovely little ring, a gift, a gift to *her*—she had been very sick that day, sick to her stomach—had been going into public restrooms not knowing what to do—and—and there, on the floor of this smelly place, there the ring lay, and she had snatched it up, had put it on her finger at once. She spoke quickly, warmly, not really knowing what she said. Eliot was listening without comment. She said it had not even occurred to her that the ring might belong to someone—to another girl, for instance—or that it might mean a great deal to someone else; not until months afterward did that simple thought cross her mind. By then it was too late, she was far from Nebraska. It was too late. And if she had taken the ring to the ticket counter, if

she had surrendered it there—probably it would not have been returned to its owner anyway. It was *hers*, a gift to *her*. It had been
dropped there, had been lying amid crumpled paper towels and loose
hairs, awaiting *her*.

Eliot said nothing, as if intimidated by her feeling; or perhaps by
the information she had given him.

He stared at the ring but did not take her hand. He was about to
take it, to touch it—but then he did not, he hesitated. Instead, he
stared at the ring. It was made of inexpensive silver, two half-moons
facing each other, one lowered slightly so that it fitted into the open
space of the other, like a hook.

She realized she had told him too much. She felt a pang of revulsion, of dismay. But he was harmless, not one of the enemy; perhaps
it would not matter.

22

Days pass, weeks pass. The mail begins to subside.

If she does not open it every day it accumulates in the sitting
room. Most of it is forwarded from the New York office of *Discourses*, some of it comes addressed to her c/o the Police Department, Albany, New York. There are hundreds of clippings: some
torn out of newspapers, some sealed in transparent plastic, the size
and shape of a bookmark or holy card. Several are mounted on stiff
white paper. One came on a sheet of cardboard painted white with
an elaborate black border around it done in India ink, painstaking
work that must have taken someone hours; it was mailed from
Phoenix, Arizona. FORMER SENATOR PETRIE SLAIN. . . . The headlines vary, take surprising shapes. Yvonne no longer reads them. She
no longer reads the letters, which come from as far away as Alaska,
Japan, "Free China." *Dear Mrs. Petrie, I thought you would like to
see this if you are keeping a scrapbook. My prayers are with you in
your time of great sorrow . . .*

From someone in Santa Cruz, California: a news report of a four-
teen-year-old high school girl found in the mountains there, raped,
murdered, partly dismembered. The clipping had been torn out of
the newspaper crudely; its final line was: *Police believe that the wire
used to strangle the girl* (cont'd 7A, Col. 2). No return address on
the envelope.

11 September

Dear Yvonne,

Do you think I don't know what you want? You want
XXXXXXXXXX & I am the man for you. . . .

August 29

Dear Mrs. Petrie:

Enclosed is a photostated copy of a letter I and my family
have sent to Tho vi Phy, Prisoner ID No. E. 4672, held
at Puolo Condor, Con Son Island, South Vietnam. We would
appreciate your taking an interest in this prisoner and
also in the estimated 300,000 political prisoners still being
held and tortured by the South Vietnam regime contrary to
Article II of the Agreements which directs the two South
Vietnamese parties to "prohibit all acts of reprisal and dis-
crimination against individuals or organizations that have
collaborated with one side or the other. . . ." Your husband in
his lifetime, along with others of his kind, have helped to
curtail freedoms here and abroad, and now that he is dead
perhaps you could use your influence to *counteract* the vicious
anti-life fascism of. . . .

Sweetheart:

Am writing this with yr. picture propped up before me.
Arent you something!—the photo from the Sunday paper,
such big brown eyes and luscious lips. You are just the right
age & size for my tastes. Let me describe myself: am considered
very attractive (*Tall, Dark & Handsome*), a nice sense of
humor, good spender, with a slight beer-belly from the love
of good times and company. If. . . .

Dear Mrs. Petrie:

Living in not-so-distance New York I wonder if you are ever in
the city, and lonely for male companionship outside the
narrow range of your society. Let me describe myself: 6'2,
red curls, green eyes, perfect posture, Ph.D. in experimental
psychology at Columbia, with many outside interests (music,
ballet, theater, gourmet food, etc.). Since I am an academic
I have access to many women, Yvonne, but they bore me
largely as I know you would *not*. You are someone special—as I
believe I am. With your looks and intelligence and social connections and *Cash* not to mention the hidden smouldering

depths there would be no limits to our relationship. This is a
serious letter. You will *not* be disappointed if. . . .

Dear Mrs. Petrie,

My garbage is set by the curb in garbage bags always perfectly
neat and tied, why do the garbage men knock the bags over
and step on my shrubs then? This is a problem not only at
our house but in the neighborhood as a whole. You can
drive down the street and see trash blowing across the lawns.
Last Tuesday when there was the hurricane warning and
those strong winds, youd think the garbage men would have
taken extra care to press the plastic lids down on the
garbage cans that have plastic lids but *think again,* there
they were blowing all over, across the lawns and into the street
and down as far as McKenzie where a lid was blown up
into the windshield of a passing car and caused a 4-car
accident, all the garbage men's fault. When they began their
union it was the beginning of the end, I thought so at the
time and am now proved right. Though your fine husband is no
longer with us this is the kind of issue he worked so hard to
combat, and it would be *very much* APPRECIATED if
you could use your influence with the Mayor to have some
action taken against the garbage men of the city who are so
bad. What a pity it is that your husband is no longer with us,
the common citizen desperately needs men of *anger and
honesty* such as he possessed in great quantity if we are to
survive in this troubled era. . . .

Dear Mrs. Petrie:

I have some information that would be of great interest to
you. It involves who killed your husband and also the plans
for taking your life as well. You must meet me *in person* without
any police in the vicinity or any other escort. Otherwise your
days are numbered and it is useless to. . . .

Dear Mrs. Petrie:

I am not one to rub salt into old wounds but I came across
a story about your husband and read it and just had to
laugh, this was the man who said on TV once that a certain
political opponent of his had the brains of a ditch-digger—
thinking he was so superior, why should he talk like that over
television, getting people to laugh and be scornful of pro-
fessions where men use their hands. In my family. . . .

Dear Mrs. Petrie:

Shortly before the terrible death of your husband I was watching
a broadcast on TV of him and some other people and
had such a strong premonition, like a vision, but it was
mixed up with a dream I also had that someone would die
within a 100-yard radius of our house here in Seneca Falls.
So I didn't know whether to warn him or not and let precious
time pass and am just sick with guilt to think that. . . .

Dearest Yvonne:

Do you remember? me? Hugh? Yr. brother?-in-law? Hugh?
May? I? see? YOU? & WHEN? ? ?

23

Sometimes she slept on the leather couch, sometimes in the bed.
Sometimes she did not sleep at all. Her mind raced, she was out in
the country again, at the farm . . . tramping through a back pasture
. . . thinking she would go to him, interrupt his work, risk antagonizing him . . . beg him to leave earlier than they had planned.
She was walking, walking. And then she was running. One night she
found herself standing at the far end of the bedroom, where there
was a closet door with a mirror. She was pressing herself against the
mirror, against her own invisible mirrored self, her fingers closed
tight about the glass doorknob, rattling it, grabbing at it. One night
she was hunched over his papers, at his desk, with only the desk
lamp burning, she was reading and rereading a sentence *It is the
"common good" that binds men together irreparably together in a
political community from which no one can dissociate himself no
one can be allowed to dissociate himself under penalty of* and there
was something about her eyes, her eyesight, it was going from her,
lost to her, she was helpless, blinking, frightened, and then from a
distance came the sound of sirens—then gradually nearer, nearer,
until it was in the room with her and she woke, terrified, had fallen
asleep at the desk and now the telephone was ringing a few feet
behind her, a shrill maddening noise, jeering, hideous, not to be
borne.

"Can't you leave me alone!" she cried. "What do you want from
me! —There must be some mistake."

24

Mere death does not canonize us. . . .

He spoke with a passionate, heated authority, with absolute certainty. He did not allow the others to interrupt. He spoke into the small microphone attached to a wire apparatus around his neck, he gripped the microphone and held it up to his mouth, speaking without hesitation, raising his voice only slightly to be heard over the sudden din.

The glorification of the dead, the apotheosis of ordinary people as martyrs . . . is based upon a misconception of . . . a sentimental and illogical. . . .

But the noise from the audience was too great, the hisses and boos and isolated shouts, the stamping of feet: a swelling wave, a chaos of waves, washing and breaking upon him.

I am merely saying— In the words of Immanuel Kant—

When Yvonne telephoned the studio to ask for a private showing of that television program, they told her the tape had been erased. The show itself had gone out live, but only on their local station; it had never been shown elsewhere in the country; the tape had been erased almost immediately. Yvonne said she happened to know that the tape had not been erased. She wanted to see it. Later, the manager of the station telephoned, to apologize and explain, but Yvonne had interrupted him—what did she care for his apologies and explanations? She wanted to see the tape, the next day if possible.

She and Eliot went one morning at ten o'clock to the fifteenth floor of the Schumacher Building, where the educational television network had its local studios. They watched the tape in a windowless room, seated at the head of a long conference table; the television set was attached to the opposite wall.

His face in that rectangular frame—his features and his voice so distorted, flattened, trivialized—

The shock of seeing him, again alive—

The surprise of, the panic of—

"I can't stand this," Eliot said.

"Leave me alone, go away," Yvonne said. "—I want to see it all."

"It might be a better idea if—"

"No. Please."

"Should I wait for you out—"

"Go away, please. Leave me alone," Yvonne whispered.

She was staring at the television screen, her hands pressed against her ears, not to drown out Andrew's voice—which was raspy, abrasive, too loud—but Eliot's.

"I'll wait for you outside—"

"Yes. Yes. Whatever you want," Yvonne said, not aware of him.

There was a former state legislator on the committee, a Democrat, a practicing veterinarian from the countryside near Catskill; he was Andrew's only supporter. There was a civil liberties attorney from New York City, as articulate and impassioned as Andrew himself, very contemptuous of him. There was a shrill black woman, another woman from the area who directed a New Opportunities program, and a professor of political science from the State University. There was a businessman, there was even a clergyman whose denomination Yvonne did not know. None of these people were very real to her. They were not real at all. The moderator's voice competed with Andrew's—but it was unreal, ghostly, unconvincing.

She stared, she tried to concentrate. But his presence, his voice got in the way of his words, his living essence drowned out everything else. Was he dead? Was that death! —It was not.

But the moderator continued to speak and finally the camera focused upon him. He was smiling nervously, stupidly. He was begging the studio audience to quiet down. There were still boos, isolated shouts—a sense of disorder—abandon. The moderator seemed both shocked and enticed by what was happening. He was a youthfully dressed man of middle age whom Yvonne believed she knew—had met once in a great crowd of people—but she could not remember his name. Stammering with excitement, perspiring!—she despised him.

—to the suggestion made by Mrs. Peters that a conspiracy existed between certain business interests and a certain faction of the Republican Party—that the Governor deliberately allowed subordinate officials to take charge— Mr. Petrie was originally making the point that—hypothetically, I believe?—that the Governor would not have been acting in any manner out of line with precedent—

The Governor is a Presidential candidate, Andrew interrupted, *he's been campaigning since the age of twelve—*

—that it would have been a frame-up—

—hypothetically!

—Professor Rowen has made the point that—from a legal point of —there could be no possible precedent for—

Men were killed! someone shouted. *Men were tortured and killed! Everybody knows— It's a matter of public record—*

But Mrs. Peters was saying—

The original point was—

Quiet, please! Quiet! We must have—

Men were tortured—killed—there were black prisoners in holes beneath the floor— There was murder committed by the—

The laws were broken! The laws of the prison! They rioted for three days and they were warned and the National Guard did only—

If we could have it quiet— If we could—

Are you saying those men deserved to die? They deserved to be shot down?

—anarchy and martial law and the need for—

At the conclusion of the forty-five-minute program each speaker summed up his position. First there was one small speech, then there was another. Yvonne's face was burning. She too could deliver a speech—as who could not? Everyone had an opinion! Everyone's opinion was being honored! It was as Andrew had said—as she had halfway known before meeting him—the world would end with everyone leveled to the status of everyone else—whoever could shout loudest would triumph—whoever was shrewd enough to manipulate public opinion would triumph. The issue did not matter. What did the Glasberg riot matter, what did the dead and wounded prisoners matter, or the prison guards who had died, or the mother of one of the dead prisoners—a black woman from Syracuse—interviewed so poignantly by the press? They imagined they were important. They imagined their cause was important. But they were not important, their cause did not matter, except as it might be snatched up and used by others—by their "friends"—by Andrew's enemies. They were all his enemies. They were shameless, they were hypocritical, they would snatch up any issue whatsoever—anything that would advance their own interests and work against those of their enemies—

What a clamor! And how humiliating that Andrew should be involved! It almost seemed to her that his image on the screen—on that dwarfish, vulgar screen and his voice competing with the others —it almost seemed to her deathly, a kind of death—the mere fact that he had acquiesced to appear with those others. Of course he was superior to the rest of the committee. That was obvious, there was no doubt about that. His manner—his intelligence—his refusal to qualify his position or back down when challenged—his refusal to become emotional like the others: it was obvious, his superiority. She did not really mind that so few people honored it. They were only dissembling, pretending not to recognize what was obvious; they were liars, hypocrites. They were deluded. And the way they blocked out the facts that weakened their position and emphasized and re-emphasized with quivering voices the facts that strengthened their position—the way they pretended this particular event had any meaning for them—any genuine meaning in their own lives— How it maddened her! She hated them. She had always hated them. The superficial optimism of government people—the "well-intentioned" welfare workers and social workers and experts on child psychology and directors of public programs—the "well-intentioned" who were not well-intentioned but merely stupid—sometimes not even stupid but demented, insane—always knowing what is best for the "people" —the downtrodden—always interfering, always drawing up new rules and procedures—always a tear rolling down a cheek, so idiotic, so insultingly pointless! She was trembling, she was so upset. She could hardly bear to listen to the self-righteous speech of the political-science professor—pretending to be "moved"—"shaken" as he called it—by the "reactionary" and "inhuman" views of certain members of the committee—how she hated him, the bastard! He was the enemy, he was one of the enemy. Not the assassin, for his kind had no physical courage, but one who encouraged the assassin and afterward, reading of Andrew's murder, reading as much as he could to get the full flavor of it, wanting to know every detail, *every* humiliating detail, afterward he would be gloating—digesting the news as if it were a dinner that pleased him. And his life was words, nothing but words! He erected an abstract tower of words about an event that, for him, in his life, was simply another abstraction—what did he care about anything except the erection of his abstract tower, the triumph of his words? Because he was safe from the prisoners—because they had been "put away" or "brutally murdered"—because he would never know them, never experience the sickening realization that— the knowledge that— Because he would never be challenged except by others' words—

Yvonne tried to calm herself. She knew this, she knew all this. As a young girl she had known it, though she had not been able to express it—not until meeting Andrew had she been able to express it—

to see how her instinctive knowledge was not that of a solitary individual's, but belonged to tradition, to custom. She was not alone. She was not even an individual. People must be protected from one another—there must be governmental force—not only the threat of violence but its performance, its regular, even routine performance— there *must* be control—organization—no exceptions, no room for emotion—no meddling by the well-intentioned—those educated people who were infatuated with the sound of their own words, but who knew nothing of life. They knew nothing, they were deluded, mad. They did not know what Yvonne knew. Murderers and criminals of all sorts were everywhere—everywhere—awaiting only the opportunity to act—awaiting the kind words and apologies of people like the professor from Cornell—now drowned out by a wave of cheers and applause. Of course!—of course he was magnanimous!—generous!— "democratic." He could afford to be so, resting secure in the knowledge that men like Andrew would continue to support and protect him; men like Andrew would make certain he would never live in a democracy.

I was not—must I repeat myself so emphatically?—I was not for a moment suggesting that anyone "deserved" to die—there is, I believe, still a tradition of law—a constitution that guarantees— No one has the power of execution—there can be no capital punishment without due process of— Only the State has— I was not suggesting that anyone deserved to die, though I believe Mr. Ackley said quite overtly that the black guard held prisoner did "deserve" to die?—that his allegiance to the authorities was a political choice, and he had to suffer the consequences?—I was suggesting only that the actions of other people, in this case the National Guard, do not confer any moral status upon us independent of our own actions— Prisoners found guilty after due process of law—found guilty and sentenced to prison—disobeying orders, rioting, attempting to take over the prison and by extension the prison system itself and the State of New York itself and the United States itself—these men are not suddenly saints because they have been shot down! We must concern ourselves with the context—the history—if we want to pass judgment on the event, we must detach ourselves from it— What has Christianity degenerated into, this slovenly pious hysteria over the "oppressed"—why, the majority of people aren't sufficiently "oppressed"! —And if one can become a martyr so easily, simply by provoking someone else to kill him— This is a mockery of our tradition, our very sanity— Mere

*death does not canonize us, has never canonized us! In the words of
Immanuel Kant—let me finish, please—I am well within the three-
minute limit of— In the words of— As Immanuel Kant expressed it,
a human truth other great men have known as well: "It is indeed a
great gift of God to possess right or (as they now call it) common
sense. But this common sense must be shown in action by"—please!
—let me conclude, please!—"must be shown in action by well-con-
sidered and reasonable thoughts and words, not by appealing to it as
an oracle when no rational justification for one's position can be advanced— Seen clearly, it is but an appeal to the multitude, of whose
applause the philosopher is ashamed, while the popular charlatan
glories and boasts in it—"*

But he was drowned out. They did not listen. She watched, hands
pressed against her ears, hunched forward against the table, in a
misery of rage and frustration. How his enemies had triumphed that
day!—and continued to triumph. Perhaps, at this very moment, at
the moment at which Andrew Petrie was being so rudely dismissed,
the assassin knew what he would do; perhaps at this very instant, the
fleeting instant this particular part of the program was recorded—

Whoever had killed him was present, had listened, had been
moved by the gross animal passions of the crowd—

There, it came to him suddenly, *there is the man, the very man!
That man must die, and no other.*

25

*He bathed and bandaged a cut on her foot. On the tender, inner
part of her left foot, it had been. Barefoot, she had crossed a patch
of sand and weeds, had been looking out at the ocean, had stepped
on a piece of glass from a soft drink bottle. The pain was such a
surprise, so incredible a sensation—she had been turning over and
over in her mind a conversation she and Andrew had had, walking
along the beach after breakfast—his passionate admission that, for
him, ideas were the only reality—the only permanent reality—the rational side of mankind the only sacred side—never really explored except by a few individuals, isolated, uncertain of their connection
with one another: the future of mankind was only through reason,
logic, awakened capacities in the brain that were now dormant in*

nearly everyone. They had talked of Aristotle, whose works he had given her to read—his boyhood books, they were, the margins filled with comments—the lines heavily underscored—they had talked of Plato's Republic, which Yvonne had once studied—but without the necessary guidance and insight. And then— And now— She had been thinking of—had been rehearsing in her mind the several objections and questions she wanted to make— What did Kant mean by, why was he so obscure in, could it be interpreted that—

The pain, suddenly. Her left foot. How quickly it had happened, and how the blood spurted out onto the sand!

Maine. Rails Bay. A lodge they had rented for a week. It was a honeymoon of a sort. They had been married seven months earlier, had had no time to get away, Andrew had been committed to so much work—so many public appearances, public responsibilities. Then, in September, they had gone away. The weather was poor: rain at least once a day, always rather murky, misty, cold. Sometimes the sun penetrated the clouds with a beautiful, harsh splendor— sometimes the entire day was overcast. But she loved it there. She loved it passionately. And Andrew, in old clothes, unshaven, at times playful and childlike—Andrew had seemed so happy—for the first four days, at least, he had seemed so untroubled—had been able to detach himself from his immediate work and was taking the time to reread certain books he had loved as a young man—

Then she had stepped on the glass, then the blood spurted out, so suddenly, foolishly. For a moment she was stunned—even the pain did not really register. Then she saw what had happened: for some reason she stooped to pick up the piece of glass, green glass, she stared at it for an instant and then threw it hard, hard, out into the ocean—tears of anger starting into her eyes. That so foolish an accident should happen to her, to *her!*

She had not wanted to tell him, but the pain was too great, the bleeding profuse. She limped back to the lodge, dizzy, hoping she would not faint; she sat on the top step, crouched over, hunched over, like an animal; unable to stop the bleeding by pressing against it with her fingers, unable to control what was happening; unable to quite comprehend how an instant's innocent distraction had led to. . . .

She called for him. She surrendered, called for him, there was fear in her voice she could not disguise: *Andrew!* she called. *Andrew, Andrew!*

So he hurried to her, he exclaimed when he saw the wound, he helped her up—walked her into the house, into the old-fashioned bathroom—exclaiming, murmuring—comforting—almost scolding her, as one might scold a child to distract it from panic. How had it happened! But she must not step on it, must try not to step on it! Look at the dirt, the sand! How had it happened, such a terrible accident? He sat her on the edge of the tub, a high, white enamel tub, he turned on the faucets, adjusted the hot and cold water, murmuring to her all the while as he cleansed the wound—squatting on his haunches—breathing heavily—a slight stammer as he comforted her, instructed her to close her eyes, not to watch the blood. He washed the wound with soap and water. He dabbed disinfectant on it. He rubbed white ointment on it, like cold cream, but the blood continued to flow and he had to keep the water running, all the while steadying her with one arm, talking to her, comforting her. It was not dangerous, really! It was only about two inches long! Not very deep! Only a freak accident, it would not happen again, he'd rake every inch of the beach again, he would be more thorough than he'd been, if only she would close her eyes and relax, the blood would stop in a moment, now he was pressing a cloth against it, now it was nearly stopped, she should lean against him, shift her weight against him rather than back against the wall. . . .

"A freak accident," he said. "It won't happen again. I can bandage it and we'll drive you into Rails Bay and have a doctor look at it—"

"Is the bleeding stopped?" Yvonne said.

"It's slowed, it's nearly stopped."

"—I don't need a doctor then," she said. "I don't want a doctor."

"—a freak accident, really. It won't happen again. What was it, a piece of glass? Was it a piece of glass?"

"—piece of glass—"

"I thought I'd raked this area so thoroughly—you and I had both raked it—"

"I threw the glass away," Yvonne said. "I threw it into the ocean."

"It was a freak accident, wasn't it," Andrew muttered. He seemed shaky, now that she was herself again; he smiled up at her, his eyes more gray than green, the irises pinpoints now, his gaze pale, innocent, as if washed clean. He wore old shapeless trousers and a pullover sweater worn at the elbows and tennis shoes without socks;

he was dressed like any other man. He was dressed like an ordinary man.

"Imagine if a child had stepped on the glass," one of them said.
"—it won't happen again, it was a freak accident."
"The glass is gone? —It won't happen again."

Afterward Yvonne made an effort to walk naturally. She wore sandals, there was plenty of room for the bandage, the wound was not cramped and did not hurt very much. Whenever he asked her about it, she said it did not hurt. It was healing, she said. Andrew decided to cut their vacation short, to drive back to Albany a day early—and Yvonne acquiesced, not liking Maine so much now—and when he suggested she see a doctor, their doctor Allan Jamison—she said there was no need, the wound was healing, it did not really hurt and gave her no trouble.

Eventually that was so.

26

The telephone rang. Very late at night—past two in the morning—but she had not been asleep, had been sitting up against the headboard of the bed, a pillow bunched up behind her. She answered the phone on the first ring because the noise was so ugly.

She answered the phone but did not speak, not at once. She listened.

"Yvonne? Yvonne? Is this Yvonne Petrie?"

The voice was familiar. But so many voices were familiar.

"Yvonne? Is this Yvonne? —This is Hugh calling. This is Hugh. Are you all right? *Yvonne?*"

"Yes," she said finally.

"Ah, Yvonne! I knew it was you—I *knew* by the very quality of—the texture of the silence— It was so *intense* a silence, so stubborn and cruel!—but how are you, my dear, are you well?"

"Why are you calling so late?" Yvonne said neutrally.

"But—is it late? I've lost track of time," the voice went on cheerfully, with a minimal, joking attempt at self-censure. "Surely there is no need to respect ordinary chronology in our lives?—in *our* lives? Your late husband often worked round the clock, didn't he, wasn't that one of his character traits, the ability to work with great concentration for long periods of time?—and then catnap, like Edison and other men of genius? Like Winston Churchill too, they say. And Lyndon Johnson. So you must be accustomed to having day turned into night and night into day and—and—that sort of thing."

Yvonne said nothing. She saw by the luminous, pale green hands of the clock on the night table that it was 2:25. Her own watch, a bracelet watch studded with small diamonds, lay nearby; it showed only 12:05; it must have stopped. Eliot's watch, an electronic watch with a black leather band and an extremely complicated, unreadable face—blue with innumerable black and white dots and clock hands that were mere slivers of light—lay at the very edge of the table where one of them had put it.

"I'm calling, frankly, because I have been worrying about you," Hugh was saying. The line was surprisingly clear for a long-distance call; the man's bright, lurching, insinuating voice sounded as if it were in the room with her. When Yvonne did not reply, the voice drawled something about being frankly worried about the other members of the family—the close relatives, that is—since there was so much madness loose in the world today, so much inspired envy and cruelty—had she seen the *Times* this morning?—that is, yesterday morning?—and it was obvious to him that whoever had killed Andrew was a madman and might very well have a plan—but of course she knew all this, she was intelligent enough to know this— certainly her late husband had educated her into an awareness and appreciation of the innumerable conspiracies that surrounded them—?

"Yes," Yvonne said. "Why are you telephoning me?"

"But I wanted to hear your voice! —I've been calling off and on all day, Yvonne, hoping to find you at home—of course it was always possible that you weren't in Albany—but somehow I sensed—and kept calling every hour or hour and a half—I think—and now it's very late at night, isn't it?—somehow it seems to be very late at night. —I hope I'm not disturbing you? Are you alone? —But naturally you would be alone—it's very late—but I'm puzzled about why you refused to answer the phone for so many hours—"

Eliot was awake now. His expression showed alarm, apprehension rather than curiosity; he sat up at once, blinking. Yvonne looked at him. She smiled her quick, effortless, rather critical smile, that he should know there was no danger. Still he stared at her, he stared appealingly at her, as if trying to read her thoughts.

Yvonne lay her hand carelessly over the receiver, not bothering to

muffle her voice. "You should be leaving, shouldn't you? Shouldn't
you leave? It's so late—"

Eliot stood, still apprehensive, shy, not turning his back to her—
easing out of the bedclothes with a peculiar subdued grace, as if he
were afraid to make any sudden movement. He stared at her, smiling
with one corner of his mouth, trying to read her thoughts, still
stuporous with sleep, groggy. Yvonne believed he did not know, really, where he was. She sensed his mind working, thoughts and half-
thoughts flooding his brain—and yet he did not know, could not remember. His genial, prematurely lined boy's face seemed to her now
almost pitiable.

But then too he was probably a little sick; he had had so much to
drink.

He turned away, still very silent, and intimidated, in his underwear, in his socks, he went stealthily to the far end of the bedroom
and, while listening to her brother-in-law's chatter, Yvonne watched
him mistake the closet door for the bathroom door, open it, start in
and then stop, as if befuddled; then he went to the right door.

"—someone's there? Is someone there?" Hugh was saying. "I heard
you speak to someone—didn't I?"

"There's no one here," Yvonne said. "I'm alone. I'm in bed. Who
would be here? There's no one."

"I thought I heard— Unless I'm imagining—"

"Who would be here?" Yvonne said dryly. "—You people flatter
yourselves."

"What? Who? What people?" Hugh said. When Yvonne did not
reply he said in a more normal voice that he had heard—it might be
just rumor—since it had been Doris who told him—confidentially—
he had heard that arrests were imminent. "Arrests are imminent," he
repeated. "But of course you would know—?"

Involuntarily, Yvonne brought her head back against the carved
headboard. Her heartbeat responded at once, quickening. But she
showed no emotion, no curiosity; she only murmured a vague assent.

"Arrests are imminent," Hugh said softly. "And it's supposed to be
a surprise . . . I gather. I mean I *gather* that. Have they been questioning you again?"

"No."

". . . of course Doris could be misinformed. It depends upon her
source of information: sometimes she hears of things through Arnold, who has some good connections up there since one of his partners handles the District Attorney's father-in-law's investments;

sometimes it's through Harvey; but sometimes it's just the girl who does her hair. . . . Are you sure you're alone? We don't *feel* alone. We feel as if someone is overhearing this conversation—I mean *I* feel as if—"

"It could be possible that the phone is tapped," Yvonne said.

"—as if— But— What did you say? —Don't you *mind?*"

"Why should I mind?" Yvonne said.

"But— One's privacy— I would have thought— Andrew was such a classic libertarian, wasn't he?—constitutional rights, states' rights, the integrity of the individual—didn't he come out against wiretapping very strongly? Such an invasion of privacy—something obscene about it. Don't you mind?"

"Why are you calling me, Hugh?" Yvonne asked.

But that was an error: she had called him by his name.

"I— I've been— I only— I've been so— The thought of you has been— You see, at our very first meeting—at that reception for my father—our very first meeting, Yvonne—I somehow knew—sensed— of course we didn't have much to say to each other—I don't believe we even *liked* each other—a sentimental allegiance on my part to Andrew's first wife, you know, poor Willa—a sad, sad case!—you should have pity on her, I think. If you have time for that sort of thing. —Do you think the phone *is* tapped? What should we do in that case?"

"We could hang up," Yvonne said.

"But—but— But we're not saying anything wicked, are we?—and of course we—we are— We're both quite— It's reasonable that I should telephone my sister-in-law occasionally and inquire after her health and—and— Someone saw you the other day and said you looked very *tired*, Yvonne. One of the cousins who promptly told—who was it?—Pamela, I think—oh that girl is very *very* jealous of you—I sensed it three years ago and I sensed it just the other day, it seems, in June—that day seems so recent—the funeral, I mean— that pack of ghouls crowded into Whittbacher's and you so elegant among them, aloof and—so very different from them, from all of *them*. I don't know if I detest the Petries, Yvonne, but I certainly feel an almost physical revulsion for them—my skin crawls—does yours? —Anyway it came by way of Pamela to Doris: you look rather tired. Are you sleeping well? Are you eating well? You don't brood over the past, do you? —I mean excessively? I've made every effort in my own life to mourn the dead as an act of piety—but I have no superstitious awe of death—I'm quite fearless, actually. I've been called reckless, even. Yvonne? Do you think the phone is really tapped?"

"I don't know," Yvonne said. "But why should it matter? We have nothing to say to each other, do we?"

"—and what else was it, apart from your health—looking tired, they said—'haggard' was Doris's unkind word, I believe, but that's just wishful thinking on that creature's part. Sorrow becomes you. It becomes most women. —Your health, yes, and—and your financial condition?—it's quite reasonable that I should inquire about—"

"My finances are too complicated," Yvonne said, "for me to know what condition they're in. —But now I think we should—"

"The main reason for my call— The reason I am calling at this particular moment— Yes, I understand about the financial complications!—my checking account is a chaos—my savings account is in rather better condition—money comes into it automatically, you know—so I needn't fuss. Money has never been important to me, but I'm grateful—I have to admit—I'm grateful I have quite enough to live on comfortably—so long as I resist the temptation to dip into my capital. But such matters are—aren't very—aren't very interesting, are they, and the real reason I am telephoning, Yvonne, at what turns out to be surprisingly late at night— The real reason—"

"Yes?"

"—is that I—I— Did you get a letter I sent recently?"

"I don't remember."

"Ah, you get so much mail! Yes, I understand. —And so—well—the fact is—I believe I would like to see you," he said excitedly. "I would like to see you. Just to talk. There's so much between us, so much unsaid—if it could be possible for—"

"I must hang up," Yvonne said uneasily. She had begun to shiver. She lay atop the silk cover; she was wearing a floor-length robe of light wool. But the room was rather chilly. "Yes, it might be possible —sometime—after New Year's, maybe— So much is happening now and I'm so busy and—"

"Yvonne, please," he said, barking with laughter, "that's preposterous. *Preposterous*. In the light of the fact that I am, at this moment, no more than a minute away from you—two minutes at the most—can't you have pity, can't you be reasonable—"

"Two minutes?" Yvonne said. She shivered again. She gripped the receiver against her ear more closely.

"Yes. I'm just two minutes away, I'm telephoning from a booth in the Highlands Motor Inn—just across the street from—I can practically see your building, dear, if I crouch down a little and—"

"What?" Yvonne said. She swung her legs around quickly. "I don't— What—"

"Did you think I was in New York, Yvonne? No, no. I should have explained. But it's so devilishly tricky talking to you, dear, you seem to lead me through a—a veritable maze—a rat's maze— But I suppose it's—I'm not that accustomed, frankly, to dealing with— with young women like yourself—but I don't at all mind, not at all! —your devices. The fact is, dear, I am in Albany; I'm a mere two-minute stroll from you; now may I see you, perhaps for a nightcap? There are innumerable—"

"What do you mean," Yvonne said, frightened, "what do you— Why are you— You have no right to do this," she said, now angry, "spying on me—it's degrading, I won't tolerate it!—how can you have come to Albany to see *me* without calling first? I don't even know you—I don't know you—"

"But I am calling first," Hugh protested. "What is this but a telephone call? And it's all so unnecessary, since I'm so close—and most of the subtleties in a relationship are lost in a—over the— Couldn't I come for a nightcap? There are certain things I want to tell you in person—things you really should know. I think you'll find my counsel very, very valuable—and— Yvonne?"

She began to speak rapidly and coldly. She told him she was sorry, very sorry. But she could not see him. And she must hang up—

"Tomorrow? Tomorrow for breakfast? I'll be right here—I'll be right in the vicin—"

But she told him she was sorry: she could not see him. She would be working all morning. There was a luncheon at noon—the executive committee of the Council of the Humanities, Arts, and Communications—and in the afternoon she had an appointment with someone—and she hoped to get in an hour or two more, working on the manuscript—and then there was a reception for the French consul—and the next day was filled also—and then she was going out of town—and then, on Sunday, she believed there was a dinner party at the Slossans—she couldn't refuse them—

He said something further, but she was not listening. She was excited, frightened. It occurred to her that she had made an error, long ago—something to do with this man—a thought she had had about him but hadn't taken seriously—she had lost her instinctive powers— something was going from her, fading, draining away—suspicion lay very lightly on the surface of her being now, skittering across her skin —and she stood back from it, did not heed it—the numbness was ris-

ing in her again as it had risen on *that* day—detached and cynical
and fatalistic—and she could not seize it, could not get hold of it as
in the past. Then she had known what to do, had always known. Her
mind worked beautifully, brilliantly. It came alive by solving problems. Now the problems arose but were strangely fragmented—now
she could not synthesize them—it had something to do with that
black boy's drumming and the hideous loss of her control—the realization, suddenly, that—the deathly certain knowledge that— He
would die, and it was not in her power to prevent—

"Leave me alone!" she cried, interrupting him. "There must be
some mistake! —What do you want from me?"

Her last words were pleading, almost musical.

"What do you want from me—all of you?"

Afterward, at the door, Eliot asked who had telephoned.

Yvonne was still upset. She held the robe closed, the embroidered
collar up close to her chin. She said reluctantly that it was her
brother-in-law—one of them—Hugh—the cartoonist, was he acquainted with—?

Eliot shook his head. He was still groggy, blinking slowly. He said
he had never met Hugh—but Andrew had mentioned him once at
the office—was irritated by a caricature the man had done, of someone in Congress—a friend of Andrew's. No, he had never met Hugh
Petrie.

"Andrew said one of his brothers pretended to be insane," Eliot
said, smiling, "so that he would be absolved from—from ordinary
life, I think it was. Hugh, was it? I don't remember."

"Pretending? Is he pretending?" Yvonne said.

She laughed.

He tried to join her, but failed. He smiled. He reached for her
hand and she gave it to him, knowing it was very cold, the fingers almost numb, lifeless.

"Good night," he said.

"Good night," said Yvonne.

27

After the private showing of the program, Yvonne had gone out to
find Eliot waiting for her, and their eyes snatched at each other—she

saw he was still upset, ashen. By now she was calmer; she had gone to the television set to turn it off when Andrew concluded his summation; she had had no interest in the last five minutes. In the room, walking slowly about the long table, she had forced herself to be calm—she knew it was absurd, such emotion—a waste of her life's energy, her vitality, a draining of her will. She knew, she *knew*. Anger that went the way of ordinary, unproductive emotion, anger that dissolved helplessly into sorrow—she knew very well it was idiotic, a waste—

That she might break down, might weep openly—that she might become hysterical, as others did—what a victory that would be for their enemies!

Eliot asked her to have lunch with him. He was a slender, rather boyishly good-looking man in his early thirties, of moderate height, with prematurely graying hair; at times his appeal was strongly, and again rather boyishly, intellectual—for he had been, at Dartmouth, Andrew's outstanding student, many years ago—had written a Master's thesis on the dizzyingly numerous influences and pressures that went into one of the more recent Amendments to the Constitution, a small book that had subsequently been published; at other times his appeal was childlike, his gaze liquid, questioning, as if deferring wistfully and yet eagerly to the other person—breaking off in midsentence, shy, yet rather clever—knowing *he* was inadequate and the other, whoever it might be, had all the power. He had been working with Andrew on *Discourses* for over a decade, had been acting editor for over a year, and was now editor-in-chief. Yvonne had met him several times but had been rather amused and irritated by his manner—still a student, still so obsequious to his elders—and clever, too, wonderfully clever—for by minimizing his own existence he inflated others, certain others—like Andrew, whom everyone courted in some way, but without Eliot's finesse. She had known at once what he was doing, had known from the very first—seated across from him at a lengthy dinner party—and again, more recently —back in February or March—at the Greasons—drawing him out, almost interrogating him, sly herself, teasing, feeling a kind of pleasure that so clever and probably so brilliant a man should be that faithful to Andrew, for so little pay—though he had a full-time teaching job at a small college along the Hudson, which Andrew had arranged for him—so little reward in editing *Discourses*—worrying about subscriptions, bills unpaid, threatening letters and telephone calls and even libel suits: still he seemed to love it, craved Andrew's praise,

never questioned Andrew's authority. So Yvonne had sensed something in him kin to her, to herself, and it had pleased her to draw
him out—as if she were a kind of princess, a noble lady—condescending to ask him about his life and receiving an account of him—of his
achievements—with intense, methodical interest, noting how reluctantly he spoke of himself, how he depended upon her to question
him, to draw him out. He gave the impression of being respectful, of
being deferential. Perhaps he really was.

She had neither liked nor disliked him. At the Greasons' dinner
party she could not really remember him—or herself—and she did
not care to remember Andrew—did not want to succumb to that sort
of nostalgic re-creation of the past, which might be dangerous. At
the Greasons', for one thing, Andrew had been extraordinarily charming—witty and provocative and energetic—giving, at least, the appearance of being energetic—for he had been quite troubled all that
winter, with the citizens' committee and with other matters, public
and private; it was to be his last dinner party, his last party among
friends, and Yvonne did not care to recall it—not at this time. Eliot
Stacey had been there, handsomely dressed, gap-toothed when he
smiled, shy, sweet, with a young, reticent wife, her pale blond hair
worn artlessly short, a small, pursed mouth, eyes that darted from
face to face—a former student of Eliot's, evidently—too young for
this company, out of place, uneasy. Yvonne had felt sorry for her,
had been irritated with Eliot for being so oblivious of her, but when
she spoke to the girl—meaning only to be friendly, warm—the girl
seemed to freeze, like a frightened animal, a wild creature confronted
with an enemy: Yvonne's presence, Yvonne's genuine interest in her,
evidently made her very uneasy. So Yvonne had let her go, had not
pursued any conversation, had been dully and unaccountably annoyed with the husband, with Eliot, who spoke at times in a way
that echoed Andrew so obviously, it was embarrassing—even using
his hands in certain gestures, a timid mimicry of Andrew. But he was
exceptionally intelligent; he was quick-witted, he knew a great deal
about political theory and even more about politics, could argue well,
would not back down, never said anything extravagant or risky. She
respected his intelligence, she liked him for that. The marriage was
possibly a disappointment to Eliot—so Yvonne sensed, without
curiosity—and perhaps he was not to blame for preferring the company of others to that of his young wife. She passed no personal
judgment on him, neither liking nor disliking him. When Andrew
spoke well of him, as he often did, Yvonne always assented; but she

did not offer any judgment of her own. Andrew's people had, in her imagination, a certain indefinable privilege. They were superior to her somehow. They were always superior to her. They were never really to be challenged, never subjected to any sort of emotional assessment; they possessed a mysterious authority she herself did not have.

"My father was a police captain in a precinct in Boston," Eliot was saying slowly. "You wouldn't know, probably—wouldn't be familiar with—names like Brewer, Follett—Hanrahan in the Treasury Department— No, I wouldn't think so, and it was kind of Andrew never to tell you. He never, *never* brought my background up to me. I was an undergraduate at the time everything broke, the various scandals—exposés—a one-man grand jury was handing down indictments of everyone, friend and enemy alike—nothing could stop him once he got going. And of course things were very bad, very clotted, sickening, disgusting," Eliot said, looking at her. He seemed unaware of his surroundings. Though he had had only one drink, he spoke with a certain belabored care, as if he were drunk. Yvonne tried not to notice the way his mouth twisted as he spoke. She did not want to imitate him, she did not want suddenly to start crying. ". . . My father was one of those men who accepted everything," Eliot said, "he had a certain good-natured, crafty acceptance of—of everything. Nothing could surprise him, he liked to say how immune he was, how much he knew about human nature. He wasn't a bad man, just coarse. I don't hate him. I never did hate him. It was just that he was part of—people like him are part of—the corruption, the bribery —the sickening deals and— Nothing surprises them, they make a show of being tolerant—so wise to the world— And of course they play along with it—they *want* to play along with it—it means more to them than anything else, playing along with others, going along with whatever is being done— I was an undergraduate at Dartmouth, a junior. Andrew taught a course in political science that was very popular—and there was an honors seminar that grew out of it that only seniors were supposed to take—but he allowed me to register for it. And—and— It was at the time of— Everything broke," he said, his mouth twisting, "everything was exposed back home. I got a telephone call from one of my brothers. I knew what my father was like but I didn't know how deeply he was into it—I thought a lot of his remarks were just jokes, boasts—I suppose I didn't really think about it, I didn't want to think about it. He was so good-natured, he had so many friends— He drank quite a bit but was never— Everybody thought, I mean people like him thought, that public offices, especially those that are politically appointed, were supposed to be supported by graft—as if it were a law of nature—because their salaries weren't much and they didn't have expense accounts. They tried to distinguish between 'clean' and 'dirty' money. That was the talk, that was the way they talked. But always joking, hinting, alluding to things, to complicated relationships—liaisons—that sort of thing—as if it were all, all—" he said, his voice going hollow, for a moment unable to think what he meant; then going on, with that childlike grimness, "—all illicit games, sexual games—adulterous affairs carried on by men, betraying one another and vowing faithfulness to one another and spying on one another and—in the long run—forgiving one another because it was all exciting, you know?— and the way the city was run—the way all cities are run. My father was one of the least important people, of course. He was only a precinct captain. There were judges, a whole string of corrupt judges, really cynical bastards—and so arrogant—all of them Democrats, though probably—I mean—they would have been anything, probably —they had no political commitments or ideals or awareness of ideals. My father thought he was privileged, being taken up by these people. He thought it was like being voted into a club—into one of the downtown clubs—and then I don't think he had very much—he wasn't very—he wasn't very *intelligent*," Eliot said. "So he went along with it, let himself be used, they said at the hearings that he had been involved for eleven years—eleven years!—and it all came out, it broke wide open, that was when a man named Follett was killed—he had turned state's witness and was killed— But the name means nothing to you, does it," he said slowly, now taking Yvonne's hand, seizing it, staring at her. "No. You don't know and you don't care. Andrew knew—he called me into his office for a conference, he knew very well what was happening, he knew *everything*—read a half-dozen papers, read constantly!—he knew what was happening but he didn't even offer me any saccharine advice—he just let me cry —he wasn't embarrassed, just let me sit there crying in his office— when the telephone rang he didn't answer it, when someone knocked on the door he didn't answer it—just let me stay in there with him until—until finally I was all right and we could talk and we could even talk about graft and corruption and how the climate can change, almost overnight sometimes, how certain people are left suddenly powerless—how their enemies rush to get them. He made me see what had happened. But in theory, in theory. It was something

that happened so often—it was part of a pattern—nothing
specifically individual, you know?—but the trap unintelligent people
fall into—manipulated by others—no idea of what is really going on.
They are used, exploited, because there is nothing in them of their
own. They don't believe in anything. They have no principles, no
ideals. They don't even *know* about the existence of such things!
They have no conception of history, of the tradition of their own
offices, they don't know how their governments were formed and
they don't give a damn and it's like a merry-go-round to them, a ride,
a game—they can't be blamed, in a way—they don't know what they
are doing. Andrew told me there are always people like that, especially in city and county politics. It wasn't just my father, it was a
type, a personality—a certain kind of jovial good-natured shrewd
man, you know?—he's all-forgiving, he's very tolerant—really he
doesn't give a damn. He just doesn't care. He doesn't care. He can be
made to be sorry after he's caught—he can be destroyed, in fact—like
my father—but he never grasps what he's done, he never knows how
he has violated a communal code—a principle of— He never knows,
he's not intelligent enough to know. The typical politician is this
man, this man I am talking about, he's shrewder than my father but
there's the same emptiness in him. —But the Petries are so
different," Eliot said, leaning forward against the table, now grasping
Yvonne's forearm. "Andrew of course most of all—but his father,
too, a very high-ranking judge—might have been named to the
Supreme Court except for politics—and other Petries in public office
—but you know all this yourself, how could you not know!—you
must think I'm crazy or drunk or—but I can't help it—I don't have
anyone left now, anyone to talk with—I used to talk with *him,* you
know, for hours—for hours—he'd have me outline the argument of
one of the articles the magazine had received and then we'd discuss
it—he was always so kind, so courteous—he allowed me to speak even
when I was going in the wrong direction, and he was never sarcastic
when he pointed out my mistakes—he was *never* sarcastic with me.
Of course he could be devastating with other people, he could be
murderous. But never with *me,* he was so gentle with me, he liked
me very much, Yvonne, didn't he?—it meant so much when he invited me to join the magazine's staff—and then appointing me acting
editor—though he knew it would antagonize certain other editors
who imagined *they* were next in line. He liked me, Yvonne, didn't
he? Did he talk about me with you? —And now, now," he said, suddenly exhausted, "now I have no one to talk with. And half the staff

is quitting—walking off. He kept them in line, you know, the John Birchers and the others—he could handle them but I—I—I don't think I—I don't think I will be equal to—"

He loved Andrew, Yvonne thought.

"I don't think I will be equal to it," Eliot said.

The hum of conversations, the eating and drinking, eating and drinking, gusto of men maneuvering forks and knives: what do we want from this, Yvonne wondered, what will come of it? Eliot was silent now. He stared at his plate. "Did he live and die for this, do you think?" Yvonne asked.

"This? What?"

He bent forward, not hearing.

Yvonne indicated the restaurant—the other customers.

"Is the smoke bothering you?" Eliot asked.

He loved Andrew, Yvonne thought in a kind of triumph, *he loves him. . . .* Someone close to her as a brother, an intimate friend; a stranger who turned out to be a friend. They said good-by. They parted. A few hours later he telephoned and wanted to see her. "Yes," Yvonne said. He brought a bottle of Scotch with him—he'd been drinking, he said, since noon.

Yet she liked him now. She liked him very much. He sat beside her and talked and his entire face twisted, took on a brutal, infantile expression, tiny near-invisible lines like a mask fitted over his guileless boy's face. *You love him,* Yvonne thought, *more than I do.*

Later they lay in each other's arms. They lay atop the bedspread, not undressed. He relived that Sunday evening: where he had been when his wife came to tell him the news of the assassination, what he had felt, what his first reaction had been. He relived the night, the following day, the following days. He relived the funeral. And the hours that followed—when it seemed certain that, at any time, the killers would be apprehended. Every hour the possibility of the arrest, *the* arrest! And then the long dull agony of days, weeks, weeks. Weeks and now months, now it was autumn and a new group of legislators convening and Andrew dead, still dead, and nothing changed—the enemy still free—free and jeering at them. He could not bear it! He despised them all!

He sobbed. Yvonne held him. She did not like the sickish whiskey odor of his breath, or the heat of his body, or the spasmodic twitchings of his muscles; but she held him, she comforted him. She too wept, but not from grief; from exhaustion. She hoped he would sleep but he continued to squirm in her arms, he buried his damp face against her throat, he moaned of the injustice . . . the film he had seen not long ago of the Glasberg riot, the ostensible liberation of the prisoner-held prison by the Governor's guardsmen, rows of soldiers equipped with gas masks and rifles, rows of black prisoners stepping forward in the rain, hands on heads, weaponless, coming hesitantly forward to surrender . . . and the sudden staccato noise of the bullets, the unarmed men shot down in the yard, in the mud . . . the sound of their screams barely recorded, so thin, delicate, piercing . . . distant. Then the guardsmen rushed upon the rest of them with clubs. Then the film went blank, the camera must have been smashed. No more popping of bullets, no more faint surprised screams, just silence. Silence. *Andrew had not known. Andrew had been betrayed.* Everyone lied afterward: the Commander of the National Guard and the warden and the warden's men and the Commissioner of Police and the Deputy Commissioner and the Prison Authority and their attorneys and the Governor and the Lieutenant-Governor and— Everyone, everyone had lied. Now he was dead and could never redeem himself.

Yvonne comforted him. Of course Andrew had redeemed himself! Long before he died he had— She pressed her cheek against Eliot's head, against the top of his head; she tried to hold him still. He was sobbing. Hot, babyish, his arms and legs jerking with grief. His clothing damp. She hoped he would not be sick to his stomach—she did not think he was accustomed to drinking so much.

The sobbing abated.

He fell into a deep sleep.

He left the apartment at about a quarter to three. When he was gone, Yvonne remembered his wife. Then she remembered the way he had looked at her, saying good-by.

Perhaps he imagined they were lovers . . . ?

"He will never know," she thought.

28

She sits at the desk reading an essay on Durkheim that is cross-referenced to Nietzsche and Thomas Jefferson and Carlyle and Marx and the Tao Te Ching and Lewis Carroll. The typing is poor, the margins very narrow, she has no room to make pencil marks, she finds it difficult to follow the line of thought from one phrase to another; the sentences are complex, convoluted, run-on as if for dramatic effect—something hypnotic about them, unsettling. She is thinking of a prefabricated building, an annex, she seems to see it, she remembers that it is the place terminal patients are put—the ones who never get any visitors. They are moved there, relegated there, the roof is made of corrugated tin and in the summer sun the air heats to one hundred degrees, the stench is unbearable. Grandma? Grandma? She is in the skirt and blouse the Beattie girl gave her because they were too worn; she is back in French Creek, back for the first visit in a long time, she is talking now to one of the student nurses, the girl is not much older than Yvonne but has a job, a uniform, a smart clipped manner explaining that the doctors are busy in the regular hospital and so are the nurses and what does she expect?—what does she expect? Only when she is alone again, safe and alone, does she begin to cry. Coarse ugly sobs. No inflection to them. Ugly, angry. Very angry. The woman blinked at her and recognized her and was perfectly clear-minded and remembered everything and did not seem to feel the heat and Yvonne is not weeping out of grief but out of anger. She has never wept out of grief, only out of anger.

She does not mourn *him.* She is mourning his absence, the loss of his power. His name, his prestige. His essence. She does not mourn *him* because, in a sense, he is only temporarily gone. He is out of the room, out of the apartment for a few days, perhaps there is a speaking engagement somewhere, an honorary degree to be conferred on him, there is something happening to him, with him, about him, no need to mourn *him.* She weeps with anger sometimes when she discovers how they are telling lies about him—pretending to eulogize him, using the opportunity to tell vicious lies. She is not weeping out of grief but out of anger. It is cleansing, it is good for her. For weeks now she has not been well—not quite herself. Lethargic during the day, wakeful at night; occasional dizziness, loss of balance, loss of appetite; sweating and shivering; waves of nausea, though never any vomiting. She weeps with anger, but it is a tearless weeping. It is cleansing, it is healthy and good for her, like retching—but it is dry, spasmodic, painful. Their lies! Their innuendos! Their jealousies!

She does not mourn him, she is not in mourning. She goes out, to

luncheons, to meetings. She flies to New York City to meet with
Andrew's tax attorneys; she spends the weekend with friends in a
hunting lodge near Lake George. The apartment is painted and she
makes arrangements for the sofas, chairs, and carpets to be cleaned.
She speaks with the Police Commissioner and with the District Attorney. She attends a reception at the Governor's mansion, she sits at
Andrew's desk eight hours a day, she makes an appointment with
Dr. Jamison and is then forced to cancel it, having been invited to
participate in a three-day conference held in San Francisco by the
World Relations Forum in early November. She is not a featured
speaker—they are an elderly Belgian nobleman and a chancellor of
one of the California state colleges and a lively, witty black woman
in her sixties, evidently a controversial figure on the West Coast,
president of the Oakland Board of Education; and a senator from
the south, one of the Republican Party's leading candidates for the
Presidential nomination; and a lean, trim, tanned young man, surprisingly like Andrew in his mannerisms, though not in his political
beliefs, who has worked for the past ten years as a doctor in a world
health clinic in India. She is not in mourning—escorted to receptions, to dinners, to a luncheon held high in the mountains, even to
a lavish memorial service held one misty evening for a former ambassador to Greece who had died of a heart attack quite suddenly before
the conference had even begun. She is not in mourning but chooses
to wear the colors of mourning, or subtle and tasteful variations of
those colors: a long black skirt with a pale yellow silk blouse, a velvet
suit, winy-dark, almost black, and a plain blue dress, long-sleeved,
high-necked, that shows off her gaunt, earnest frame to advantage.
The president of French, Wilton, & Brinton is very attentive to her,
and claims to have known Andrew during Andrew's senatorial days;
the chairman of the board of the Hanley Aircraft Corporation is attentive to her, as is the industrial relations consultant-arbitrator of
Proxmire & Aaron. She participates in several round-table discussions,
apprehensive at first and then, gradually, as other people speak, increasingly confident, knowing that the voluminous notes she has
brought with her contain insights and facts and even clever ironies
far superior to what is being offered—and Andrew's ideas are received
intelligently and respectfully, with only minimal questioning. The
French Revolution and the "romance" of continual revolution and
its close ties with decadence—the need for an empirical realism that
incorporates man's idealism—his indentification with the past, with
tradition—the danger of subjectivism, the disease of individualism,

the necessity for— Who is going to question such a statement, who can get his mind around her? As the discussion is breaking up, the tanned, pipe-smoking doctor asks Yvonne what the practical consequences of such a vision are, does she know, can they be predicted from such generalities or is it in the nature of such generalities that they are not to be burdened with the proof of history?—what might such ideas lead to? But no one is listening, the session is breaking up, Yvonne leans across the table to tell the man, her mouth shaped as if for a kiss, her voice low, level, in perfect control: "Assassination, of course." He is shocked, shaken, visibly offended, he stares at her, sucking his pipe, says that wasn't what he meant—she had misunderstood—but Yvonne pretends not to hear, being escorted to the door by a handsome gentleman with a faint British accent, who compliments her on the deep and thoughtful and provocative things she has said and asks her if she would like to join him for cocktails at the Fairmont, since there is at least an hour and a half before the banquet in honor of. . . . She hears the news of the Pickard affair: the police and the State Troopers and the helicopter patrol and the tear gas and the hostage and the death of Pickard, riddled with bullets, and the outcry and public apologies by officials, all in a few hours' time, and she is back in Albany, having returned earlier than she had planned, as if she had somehow made a mistake—imagining Andrew was accompanying her, when in fact he was somehow, in some way, still back in the East. Sick to her stomach on the plane, she feels she is being punished; she has been mourning her husband's death after all, and that is the one thing she must not allow herself to do.

29

After the Pickard incident there is a flurry of mail again. More mounted clippings, more holy cards, more editorials and columns torn out of newspapers and sent to her; the entire twenty-four-page issue of a rather attractive magazine called *Outrage, Inc.*, published in Atlanta, Georgia, devoted to an article with the title: "The Murderers of the Honorable Andrew Petrie Continue to Move Among Us" by one Leander Rawlings; astrological charts on both pulp and slick paper, with Andrew's sign circled in red; elaborate dream diagrams; numbered steps leading to the moon whereby prophetic visions can be "interpreted by the layman"; hexes for the widow's employment, as well as anti-hex formulae; mandalas, anagrams, riddles, quotations in Latin and Sanskrit, pages detached carefully from copies of *I Ching* with certain warnings underscored; drawings of witches, wizards, Christ, Indian holy men in full lotus position, the Infant of Prague in His splendor; invitations to join various churches and church communities and communes, like the Disciples of Our Living Christ; several copies of the same issue of *The Meta-Realist*, where November's lead essay is "How the Fascists Are Using the Petrie Case to Smash the People"; as well as miscellaneous items like a stainless steel crucifix, a thimbleful of white grainy powder—heroin? —arsenic?—in a pink envelope with scalloped edges, a copy of *The Consolation of Philosophy*, published in 1870 in London and sent to her by an unknown admirer, mimeographed newsletters from youth organizations, health food clubs, Hedonists Inc., a variety of paperback books: 1001 *Spells: How To Cast Them, Remove Them, Counteract Them*; *Conspirators Among Us*; *A Handbook of Organic Gardening*; *The True Astonishing Story of the J. F. Kennedy Assassination*; *The Occult Powers: If They Are Not For You, They Are Against You*; *Gods Among Us?*; *The Decline of the White Race and How to Combat It*. In a special-delivery package there is another publication from *Outrage, Inc.*, published in 1969, a book that deals in extraordinary detail with the Sino-Jewish conspiracy, which dates back to the year 200 B.C. and involves for some reason both Egyptian and German royalty; several American Presidents are related by blood to the original conspirators, and their positions on the elaborate family tree are marked by actual photographs, much reduced in size. *For Mrs. Andrew Petrie, with the compliments of the author, Dabney Reynolds III.* There are innumerable letters, some typewritten, some hand-printed, some scrawled in ballpoint ink; one, arriving in an envelope without a stamp, is apparently from someone in the apartment building. It asks the widow *Are you satisfied now that you have stolen a decent woman's husband and brought shame to an illustrious family?*

"Don't these things upset you?" Charles Bausch asked one day. He had come to talk with Yvonne about certain joint capital ventures he and Andrew had been seriously considering before the murder; he wandered into the sitting room and was struck by the piles of mail.

"Why should they upset me," Yvonne said coldly. "They mean nothing to me. They have nothing to do with me."

"But all these people—! Just the fact that they exist, that they are evidently thinking of you!" Charles said.

He whistled and patted his thighs nervously. He was a plump, well-dressed man in his early fifties, with very light, sweet blue eyes. His face was flushed, his manner more troubled than usual.

"They're not thinking of me," Yvonne said. "Not of *me*. They don't know me at all."

"All the same, if I received things like these, or if Pamela did. . . . It would be very disturbing, I think."

"It doesn't disturb me," Yvonne said. She was not lying. "I feel nothing at all when I open them. I just open them . . . I see what they are . . . I don't even laugh any longer, as Andrew and I once did, and I certainly don't feel any alarm. I don't *feel* anything at all," she said.

"Then you're very fortunate," Charles said neutrally.

He picked up one of the copies of *The Meta-Realist* and leafed through it. It was tabloid size, with cartoons and caricatures at the top of each page accompanying the smudged columns of print.

"They hate us," Charles whispered. "It's as Andrew knew, as he always warned . . . they hate us, they want to destroy us. The conspiracy is coming out into the open, in mongrel publications like this, but there must be some trick! The editors are listed, the place of publication is listed. It must be to mislead us! The real conspirators are elsewhere, don't you think, underground, supremely sophisticated, funded by China and Cuba and. . . . These people are sick," he said, tossing the newspaper down. "At the very least, Yvonne," he said irritably, "you should have a secretary handle this. Andrew's methods were perfectly—"

"I told you it doesn't bother me," Yvonne said. "I don't need a secretary. I don't want a secretary. I can handle this—I don't answer most of it, I don't even turn it over to the police—I simply look at it and keep it around for a while and then throw it out. I can handle it, I can handle anything. And as I told you, it doesn't upset me; it doesn't upset me in the least."

"Yes, you're very fortunate," Charles said slowly.

The sofas, couches, chairs, cushions, pillows, and carpets have been cleaned. There is a slight chemical smell; there is a persistent dampness to the air. Everything is sharper, each fabric bright, aggressively clean, not quite the color Yvonne believed it to be. The green velvet love seat is a peculiar electric lime green now, bewilderingly

bright when the sun catches it. The carpet throbs with strength; its
once subtle colors now undulate beneath Yvonne's feet. Everything
looks renewed, invigorated, harshly clean and dramatic. The effect is
a powerful one, Yvonne thinks, and perhaps it is worth the cost.

However, there are smudges on the newly painted walls from the
cleaners' hands. There are deep scuff and scratch marks on the hardwood floors, especially in the entryway between the living room and
dining room. The smallest bathroom, the guest bathroom, has been
cruelly used—men's fingerprints everywhere, the small scatter rugs
dirty, the toilet seat itself dirty. The fabrics gleam with a cruel, hard,
bright health, but the walls look nearly as gray as they did previously.

The widow thinks: His things are being desecrated.

She thinks, walking from room to room: I can't stop what is happening.

She signs the check and Fritz Sanderson takes it from her.

"I'll put this into a neutral account," he says, "and make sure the
Pickard family gets it. *From an anonymous donor?*"

"An anonymous donor," the widow says tonelessly.

Time passes, the mail slackens again, drops to no more than five or
six items a day except for Mondays, when a package arrives from the
offices of *Discourses*. She continues to open it, to study it, then to
push the contents aside into small piles. She is unmoved. She reads
some of the letters more than once—the insulting letters, the obscene letters, the letters that accuse Andrew of ugly crimes or
Yvonne of crimes, even of her husband's murder—she reads them,
pauses over them, as if waiting to feel some emotion.

Nothing. She is unmoved.

30

She is on the veranda of the old farmhouse on Fremont Road. He
is working in the garden, which is a mess of weeds and briars and
rosebushes gone wild. *Yvonne? Yvonne, where are you?* She stands
on the veranda, not hiding, not shrinking back against the side of the
house; yet he cannot see her. His fair silvery-blond hair gleams in the
pale sunshine, his smile is visible, appealing. *Yvonne?*

He has been working too hard. It is too difficult, the effort of

bringing together so many years' work. He cannot always read his
own handwriting. Some of the pages are yellowed, wrinkled, torn.
The ideas are not adequately developed—they are scribbles—jottings
—agile astonishing leaps of logic—not translatable into prose. He is
digging in the garden now, giving his mind a rest, wearing a pair of
gardening gloves he found in the workshed, galoshes over his shoes.
He looks strong, robust, but it might be a trick of the light. He is
tired, he is too tired to sleep at night. *Yvonne?* he calls petulantly.
He has been working too hard for months, for years. For a lifetime.
There are lines of bitterness radiating out from his eyes and mouth.
Yvonne? You won't leave me? Yvonne?

In the background is the sound of the river, the gushing rapids.
The river is shallow at this point, the rapids are splashing, churning,
foaming white. But the river is some distance away. The river is hidden. It breaks over rocks, splashes and flies into the air, turns to
foam, to spray, its roar is never constant but always increasing, thunderous, a heavy throbbing in the head.

He throws down the hoe. He approaches her, squinting. Is he
blind? Is he pretending to be blind? He limps, he must be unusually
tired, she knows she must hurry to him—she must run to him, her
arms outstretched. Otherwise it may be too late.

But he is smaller than she remembers. . . . Smaller, and yet
cocky, self-assured. He wears old clothes that are too large for him.
The knees of his overalls are filthy. Yet he is smiling, squinting in
her direction, he has sighted her, has sensed her. *Yvonne?* She will go
to him, there is no question about that. She does not care so much
for—for whatever it is that holds her back; she does not care so much
for her own self, Yvonne Radek, Yvonne the tall, gawky, sullen,
coarse-haired creature, Yvonne the ugly one, Yvonne with the long
narrow hands and feet. In the part of her hair they claimed to see
lice. Lice! And set up a shriek, the bitches. The scrubbing with a
wire brush, the stench and shock of kerosene, afterward the humiliation, the jeers! No, she does not care so much for Yvonne. In fact,
she rather despises Yvonne.

And so she will go to him. *Yvonne?* he is calling.

But he has shrunk, and his face is so fleshy-pink! She sees that it is
an artificial face. *Ah,* she thinks, *they did fix it, inside the coffin.
But not well enough.* A face of liverish pink, putty and paint and
darkened eyebrows, the mouth moist and rosy as if wet with life,
fixed in that demanding smile. Behind him is the vegetation she
hated—the summer before his death it went out of control and she

hated it—hated it. The farm had no memories for her. It was his family, his life. She hated it. Now he limps toward her, he has thrown the hoe down carelessly, his arms are extended and he calls for her, pleading, begging, a whine of fear in his voice.

She steps into view. She will not hide from him.

But my God! His face!

He did not want to die, he did not want his handsome face so cruelly smashed. He limps toward her and she hesitates only a moment and then steps off the veranda and hurries toward him, to help him, to catch him before he falls. . . .

Yvonne? he cries, not seeing her. *Yvonne, are you here?*

31

When the doorbell rang she was reading the preface to the second edition of *The Critique of Pure Reason* in Andrew's old broken-backed Modern Library edition, with its close-packed type and narrow margins and thin paper; she was reading with complete absorption—must have been sitting here for a very long time, in a kind of trance—and taking notes on the countless tiny comments Andrew had made in the book. Nearly every page was annotated. There were some pages, throughout the *Critique*, that were so marked up as to be unreadable; but Yvonne intended to read them.

The doorbell rang again and she went to answer it, indifferently, not pausing to wonder what she looked like—it was eleven in the morning and she was not yet really dressed—and it was only the manager of the apartment building, whose name she continually forgot; it crossed her mind that perhaps she should not have opened the door so readily without inquiring about who had rung. It was not impossible that someone could slip by the doorman or bribe one of the building maintenance men to let him in. . . .

"Yes," she said, interrupting, "I did receive Mr. Wheaton's letter and it was very kind of him and skillfully written, but I don't intend to move out—that's why I didn't reply to the letter."

"We have only been thinking of—"

"Do you have a petition? Do you have signatures?" Yvonne said mildly. "If the other tenants are worried about living here, if they think they're in danger of some kind—you can break their leases for *them,* you can let them move into other buildings of Mr. Wheaton's."

"Mrs. Petrie, I wonder if I could come in for a moment?"

"I haven't any time for you," Yvonne said. "I'm working."

"The offer of— Mr. Wheaton had only in mind— You see, it's a matter of—of the other tenants, yes—a sizable number of them, in fact—as you know, some of the apartments are rented by women who live alone, quite elderly women—widows—and they're very concerned, and their children are very concerned—for instance Gabriel Hendon's mother lives just two floors below and—"

"Who is Gabriel Hendon?" Yvonne said. "I don't know Gabriel Hendon."

"Of course you know Gabriel Hendon!" the man said miserably. "—and so—we thought that possibly—Mr. Wheaton could very easily arrange and help to move you and pay all expenses, and he does own what he personally considers to be a far more *interesting* building than this where you might rent or buy a condominium at your leisure and where—"

"I don't know Gabriel Hendon," Yvonne said. "Andrew never mentioned him. He didn't associate with speculators and he certainly would not move out of this building until he was ready to move."

"Mrs. Petrie, you put us in a very, very awkward position," the man said. "There *is* a petition, yes, and we were terribly upset when it was presented to us—we tried to reason with them, we tried to point out that the Tower is totally impregnable—we have more security guards, I believe, than we actually need—as well as TV surveillance at all the possible points of entry and in the elevators—and Mr. Ryan at the door knows absolutely everyone who lives here and would not let even a close relative come upstairs without buzzing first. We told them, we tried to explain—"

"But it isn't my problem," Yvonne said. "I don't know why you're telling me this. Since I have a three-year lease, and since I don't intend to move, why are you telling me these things and taking up so much time? —Your other tenants have the problem, not me."

"It's my problem," he said hurriedly. She looked at him for the first time. Astonishing!—a gentle, aging man no more than five feet two or three, rimless glasses, a very wrinkled throat, staring at her with such terror. Yvonne looked at him. He was speaking again, his lips were actually trembling. For a moment she felt pity—she felt quite moved.

"—two of the ladies were down talking to me this morning so very

very upset and I tried so hard to reason with them but what can I do or say?—one of them is almost totally deaf, Mrs. Petrie, but she claims to have heard coming from your apartment all sorts of strange noises and voices and that sort of thing—she's so very very certain about it and since she is one of our oldest tenants and has been with us since the first week the Tower opened—and since as I said there are others—not all of them elderly, either—we only thought that perhaps that possibly—if you would be so kind as to consider the situation—and they say you have many visitors?—though Mr. Ryan claims you do *not* and he should know—they swear you have many male visitors and that something is definitely going on—a party or a meeting or something—and though I have tried to explain to them that—"

"Who are these people?" Yvonne said. "I want to see the petition."

"I— They have requested that we keep the signatures confidential until such time—unless—"

"I want to know who's been telling lies about me," Yvonne said. "I want to know who's been saying slanderous things about me."

"Mr. Petrie himself would have been sympathetic with these poor frightened women, I think," the man said hesitantly. "He was *such* a gentleman . . . with ladies of that type . . . so kind and considerate and thoughtful. So very nice to *me* also, but I won't go into that. It seems to me that in memory of him, in a sense, you might—"

"Who are those people? Who began the petition?"

"—and Mr. Ryan *did* say that he believed there have been odd people in the vicinity—across in the park sometimes, as if they are watching the Tower—and occasionally men walk by who don't seem to have much purpose in this neighborhood. Mr. Ryan says he can recognize two of them by now, even when he sees them in another part of the city."

Yvonne stood silent. Then she said quickly: "That's ridiculous. I don't believe that. He's told me that too and I don't believe it—"

"I would feel so much more comfortable if I could come in," the man said, lowering his voice, "or maybe you would consent to come downstairs to my office? If you—after you—I mean, of course, after you were—perhaps on your way out of the building—"

She still pitied him, she did not want to look at him. These weak, frightened people! Andrew's housekeeper had been the same way, a Slavic woman of indeterminate age, no longer young, and Yvonne had found it painful even to talk with her about casual things— impossible to give the woman instructions about the apartment. Her heart turned, she felt not only pity but a flash of shame, guilt, revulsion for herself and for such people, who stared at her, at the outside of *her*, with such trepidation! And it was shameful, too, she knew very well how disgusting it was, that she should manipulate and employ and appear to be superior to them.

"I wish you could help me, Mrs. Petrie," he pleaded, "I wish there were some way that everyone could be satisfied and things return back to normal and—"

Yvonne stepped back, away from him. She was tired of this conversation suddenly. She was tired. What did she care for him, for his terror? Why had she cared so much about the housekeeper, when the woman had clearly despised *her*? She was tired of wasting her time with such people, she wanted only to return to Andrew's study, to his desk, to the only valuable part of her life.

"*Everyone satisfied! Things return to normal!*" she said, mimicking him. "Things will *never* return to normal—go tell them that. Things will never, *never* return to normal," she said slowly.

32

Andrew's battered old copy of the *Critique*, lying there in the narrow space Yvonne has left herself to work in—on all sides, in the pigeonholes of the desk and sticking out of the shelves above and to the side are papers, papers, parts of his manuscript—some of them already edited, some temporarily set aside, others not yet even investigated—and she returns to it eagerly and sees the dark spots on the carpet that was cleaned so recently and, puzzled, sees the dark smears on the chair seat—even so, the open book draws her to it, she leans over it, both hands on the desk so that she can lean far forward, dizzy, intrigued, wondering if—as Andrew claimed had often been the case with him in his youth—the next words she reads may change her life—

But the letters blur, Andrew's underscorings are distracting, she finds herself looking instead at the seat of the chair— Ah, it is blood: *only blood.* For a moment she feels nothing, the lower part of her body is numb, and then it begins, as if from a distance, the slight dull ache of cramps, only that, nothing more. Earlier, in the bathtub, she had imagined some faint curling streams of blood—but very faint —had imagined she'd seen them in the bath water—but her mind drifted onto other things, she took no more notice, she forgot. It is only her blood, only that, the most trivial and negligible sort of blood; though she has not had anything like a full, normal period since sometime in June, this still means very little to her—she could not have been pregnant, after all—she cares very little about these things. Remote, trivial, a harassing ache in her loins—she cares very little, she has forgotten even to be concerned.

33

"Nothing will be the same again. Nothing will be normal again."
"I don't know what you mean," Yvonne said uneasily.
"It can't—it can't return to what it was. You know what I mean."
"I don't exactly. . . ."
"It isn't just that I have no one to talk to, it isn't just that he's dead. It's you too: now it's you too. You know what I mean."
"Please, I really. . . ."
"You *know* what I mean," Eliot said.

She read that the will of the sovereign must be carried out, whoever the sovereign is. It can make no difference who it is. Why would it make a difference, what difference could it make?—there are no differences above or below. Her eyes ached, she remembered the poor, frightened man in the dream—his glazed-over eyes—the artificial heartiness of his face. Whenever she stirred she felt how steadily the blood flowed, a fine feathery-thin stream; the rest of the time she forgot. She did not think of it. She read that even genius has a place in the cruel, tyrannical order of the sovereign: to celebrate, to praise.

"You know what I mean," Eliot said over the telephone.
After a while he stopped calling.

She went to the Elmer F. Clay Foundation banquet in December, to accept an award being given posthumously to her husband. *For Outstanding Lifelong Citizenship in the United States of America.* She wore a dark velvet dress, several strands of pearls, porous fresh-pink paint on her mouth. Her manner was subdued. During the long dinner she tried to let her mind drift, back to the apartment or at least out of the hotel banquet room; but she kept hearing the conversations around her and because she was alone, without Andrew, she suddenly felt the danger of an exterior world crammed to bursting with people she could not tolerate.

If he were with her, they would glance at each other from time to time, accidentally, unconsciously. They would happen to look up at the same moment; they would face each other across the length of a table, suddenly amused, wanting to laugh aloud.

But she was alone, even when people talked to her she was alone, her numbed lips responding, her manner brightly dark for the occasion, a pretense of warmth, something harmlessly womanlike, womanly, not quite human. *The Elmer F. Clay Twenty-Fifth Annual Banquet. A Non-Profit Non-Political Forum for the Study and Preservation of the Ideals of the American Republic. "Give Me Liberty Or Give Me Death!" Twenty-Fifth Annual Award: In Honor of Former Senator Andrew D. Petrie, Outstanding Citizen. With Remarks By.* . . . "This is a century of conspiracies," a man said. "Everything has become invisible," another man said. "Once these people were visible but now they're invisible—they've wised up, they've gone into hiding." "They've crossed the border into Canada." "By the time these poisons have their visible effect," a man said softly, "it's too late. Mr. Petrie wasn't the first and he won't be the last. We are *all* slated for. . . ." "What puzzles me is how everything has become invisible," a man said, addressing Yvonne. "Just like that! Invisible! Overnight—*invisible!*"

Talk drifted to the current Secretary of State. A movement was being started to arrest him for treason; but it would be difficult, very difficult. Everyone was intimidated by the power structure, the big East-West coalition of certain politicians and certain labor-union officials. Blatant acts of treason were being committed each day, lauded in the public press. But a movement was being started, funds were being raised. . . . The organization's headquarters, Yvonne was told, were in Baltimore. Would she like to lend her support?

"There is almost a different species involved here, a different species of human being," a man said slowly. He sipped at his water glass. He had not touched his wine. ". . . Like a murderer, that's what it is. A murderer. If a murderer makes the claim that he won't do it again, why should we honor him? Treason is like that and there are traitors everywhere, you can almost smell it . . . can almost smell them. There's no forgiveness for the betrayal of your country. I can see the forgiveness of sin, when the guilty party repents, but I can't see forgiveness for the betrayal of your country because that . . . that

is the unforgivable sin. Those people are guilty because they are
criminals and they feel the guilt and behave in a guilty fashion because their primary allegiance, if you gave them a lie detector test, is
not to our country but to a foreign power . . . it could be any foreign power at all. They don't care. They just don't care."

"They don't care about anything," a man in a dark blue suit said.
"It's the times. You breathe it in, in the air."

An attractive blond man in his late thirties made the presentation
speech. He was evidently a professor of history at a local institution.
He glanced at Yvonne and then out at his audience, back to Yvonne
again, and back to his audience, dramatically. He was a superb
speaker. His technique of pausing to stare at individuals, looking
keenly from row to row, face to face, was oddly effective. One could
not escape him. His praise of Andrew Petrie continued for fifteen,
twenty, twenty-five dramatic minutes. *Reflective thought—analysis
in depth of all contingencies—distinguished record of contribution—awareness of personal and cultural linkage—decadence of
art, scientific endeavor, the so-called humanities—ecopolitical issues
—finest stylist in the history of American conservative thought—
heroic—martyr—fearless illumination of the darkness that surrounds
us—defense of individual in an era of collectivist mania—liberal-
socialist ideologies not native to North America but imported from
—and above all—*

"Our time will come," the blond man said, shaking Yvonne's
hand, "our time will come—disaster may permit us to return to our
true values!"

Yvonne looked at the people, mainly men, who were looking at
her. It was a curious moment: she was in perfect control, she was
smiling the sort of small, sad smile the occasion demanded, yet none
of it was real. She half-believed she would wake and find herself at
Andrew's desk. The banquet room was overheated and smoky, but
even these discomforts did not make the occasion convincing.

Where was her husband? Where—? She glanced from table to
table, from face to face. She was still smiling. So many men, so many
faces!—but all strangers. It occurred to her that the world was composed of strangers. They stared at her, they did not know her, did
not love her or value her.

"I want to thank you for—for—"

A man rose suddenly from a seat almost directly in front of her.
He took several steps forward, shouting, and before Yvonne could
even step back he dashed a glass of warm water at her—it splashed

into her face, onto her shoulders and chest. She was astonished. She watched as two men grappled with him, subdued him, dragged him into the aisle. The water had gone directly into her face!—he had done it so quickly, no one had been able to stop him—

Afterward, the president of the organization and the speaker and a number of other men apologized profusely. They assured her that individual was a very disturbed, unhappy gentleman who in no way represented the views of the Foundation, and whose prejudice against Mr. Petrie was based upon a failure to comprehend Mr. Petrie's stand regarding the possibility of the reinstatement of capital punishment in New York—an old issue, an old, old issue, fought over bitterly in the past and by no means settled even now—

The man had called her a whore. She was certain of that. He had jumped up from his seat, a man with no identity, no face she could recall, he had jumped up and shouted at her, had called her a whore, had dashed water into her face—all so quickly, no one had known what was happening. She had not known. She still did not know. —So quickly! It had happened so quickly!

The medallion from the Foundation was very heavy. It was nearly a foot in diameter, coinlike, with an elderly man's profile on it, in copper. *Elmer F. Clay. Andrew D. Petrie.* Yvonne put it in a closet, beneath some linens. It was heavy: lifting it, she felt the warm seepage of blood in her loins, again.

But she was not in pain. She felt pleasantly numb.

34

When Andrew's younger brother Stephen was introduced to Yvonne, he shook hands rather stiffly with her—he stared almost as if he believed he knew her, had recognized her. But she did not know him; they had never met before.

Andrew let his hand fall on Stephen's shoulder fondly. He was two or three inches shorter than Stephen but he appeared taller, more powerful; in the awkward silence that immediately followed the introduction, he guided them skillfully, smiling, patting his brother's shoulder as if they were friends. His manner was genial, even sunny. "All of my family are rather unusual, rather *uniquely* individual," he said, still patting Stephen's shoulder, still presenting him to Yvonne. "But Stephen is my favorite; Stephen and I, in a sense, have yet to meet."

It was his quick, clipped, daylight manner—his surface charm, so adroit in society, so really indefinable when Yvonne tried to analyze it afterward. Andrew could talk directly to individuals and yet retain that elusive, intimidating air of being distant, as if he were onstage, protected from his audience by distance and elevation and powerful glaring lights that both illuminated him and blinded him to his viewers. —Yet in the next moment he might change, might become suddenly personal, even intimate. His expression shifted subtly; the gaze narrowed, became intense; the hand on the shoulder gripped.

"But we won't *meet*, will we," he said to Stephen, "in front of my bride . . . ? The last thing poor Yvonne wants is to become embroiled in family disputes."

Stephen did not smile. He drew away from Andrew.

"Why do you think I came here just to fight," he said in a warm, mild voice, not looking at either Andrew or Yvonne, blushing, very self-conscious. ". . . I came to talk with you."

"Yes," Andrew sighed, smiling, "and I can guess about what."

They talked for several hours. From time to time Yvonne could hear her husband's voice raised—and then silence; and then both voices again, indistinguishable. It alarmed and excited her when Andrew was angry; in a way it pleased her. He was so rarely angry, always aloof and in control and subtly amused by his opponents—and then, the effect of his passion, his genuine emotion! Her senses were stirred by his emotions as they would never have been by those of a lesser man.

Midsummer. July. An unmarked day. Opalescent sky, great slabs of dusty cloud, like concrete. A forty-mile-an-hour wind from the mountains that morning. But near noon the sun appears, the wind dies down, the clouds are broken. No storm, not even the threat of a storm; now there is sunshine, a sudden transformation of the mountains and the sky. Yvonne, restless, troubled by something she is working on, climbs the stairs to the attic and then the several steps into the cupola at the very top of the old house.

It is smaller than she expects. No more than ten by fifteen feet. Used for storage, jammed with old books and magazines and several large trunks, everything damp, ill-smelling, dirty. There are bird-droppings everywhere. Dust. Cobwebs. A solitary wasp flies toward her; when she waves it aside, it flies away mechanically, leaves the cupola by a broken window. She looks out—sparrows are chattering a few yards away, on the rotted shingles of the main roof.

She shades her eyes, looks out. From this height she can see the highway that leads to Fremont and to Gloversville; she can even see the small, unpaved road that follows the river fork. The river itself is intermittently visible, obscured by foliage, mainly willow trees growing tight along its banks. She stares at the mountains, not recognizing them. Which one is Mt. Invemere? She cannot remember. She is not very interested.

They are at the farm for a week, alone. Yvonne has never been here before. She is still a bride—offers herself, still, in the guise of a bride—asking questions, curious to know, to learn, to adapt. Her adaptation to this marriage has proven far less difficult than she had anticipated.

She is disappointed, however, with the condition of the farm. The house, built in the late eighteenth century, has been badly neglected: the roof leaks, there is an odor of rot and mildew everywhere, the plumbing is antiquated—has not been improved, Andrew said, since the thirties. But he likes it here, he likes the solitude here, the privacy. No neighbors, no telephone. Less than a hundred miles from Albany, but totally isolated, inaccessible to intrusion. He can think here, he says. He can breathe here. Yvonne is his bride of eight months and she is surprised by, a little disappointed in, his excitement about this place. There are memories here that exclude her, a past that excludes her; here he keeps to himself even more than he does at the apartment.

She is disappointed in the farm, having expected something more impressive. The house is large enough, enormous, with a wide fieldstone front and steep roofs, because of the heavy snows, and many rooms—most of them closed off, so she and Andrew are living in four rooms downstairs. It has little about it that is decorative or ornamental, like other houses of that period: no pillars, no columns, no wood trim. Very functional, plain. More a farmhouse than a country mansion. It is bordered by a stone wall, the front and side yards were used not long ago as cow pastures, and its clayey quarter-mile lane to the highway is bordered by shortleaf pine never trimmed, but allowed to grow free. From Fremont Road the house is hardly visible.

When she first saw it she said *How beautiful,* but the expression was not really meant to be sincere, nor did Andrew accept it; he merely said that she should wait till they got closer. In its way it was beautiful, with so many windows—countless windows—and the flag-stone front and the cupola, peeling white, archaic and fragile and otherworldly, a little comic. The cupola was almost entirely windows and seemed to float above the pines and oaks as if it were not at-tached to the broad, squat house. Wings had been added crudely to either end of the house, ordinary brick later painted white. The main barn had a solid stone foundation; there were two smaller barns, a stable, a springhouse, even a smokehouse. Thousands of acres of land, most of it wooded. *Beautiful*, she thought, with an in-explicable resentment.

"This would be a very valuable property," Yvonne said. "A house built in 1749. . . . Why have you people let it go like this?"

"There isn't any *people*, there's just me," Andrew said. "I'm in charge here. Nobody else cares about it—they've more or less forgot-ten it. They have other things to care about, as you know."

He spoke as if amused, but brusquely, as he always did when she inquired about something insignificant. Or perhaps he did not be-lieve it was any of her concern. "I like it this way," Andrew said. "I won't fix it up until it starts to cave in."

"Yes," Yvonne said.

"It's a place to take sanctuary in, if you know what I mean; there's no sense of time here, all the times are jumbled, the nineteen-seven-ties and the seventeen-seventies, adulthood, childhood—my father used to come out here occasionally, used to bring us out for little vacations— I don't mind things being dilapidated, I like the way the barn roof is falling in and the ivy is taking over, and the moss; I like the squirrels in the upstairs rooms and the owls and the insects and the damage from the storms, and the *irrelevance* of the place. It's like nature: it's here, it exists in its own dimension, and essentially there is something pointless about it, so no one will fight over it."

"Yes, I see," Yvonne said.

Yes, I see, she mimics her voice. She stands in the cupola, leaning out one of the broken windows, restless, ironic, yet rather subdued. Is she in disguise, is it a masquerade? Or is it, on the contrary, working out far more remarkably than either of them had hoped? Not love, not that kind of love; both are tired of *that* kind of love; both are faintly contemptuous of it and never speak of it and never think of it, in fact. *How beautiful. Yes, I see*. The bride, a young woman in khaki trousers and a black blouse, stands at the broken window, squinting into the sun. About the beauty of the trees and the mountains and the stark blue sky there is nothing to say. Words are inadequate, therefore she will not speak of it and consequently will not think of it and, vaguely, she resents *it* for imposing such muteness upon her; she is very verbal, quick-minded, aware of herself as a performer.

If she is a performer, however, she is not necessarily insincere. Sincerity too demands a performance, a face.

"How beautiful," she says aloud, testing the words. "Beautiful. *Beautiful.*"

Most of the mountains are dark with timber. Mt. Invemere and Royal Mountain and another, to the west, have peaks that extend slightly beyond the timberline; but even these are small mountains, hardly more than hills, compared to the Rockies. She does not think of the Rockies, does not remember them clearly. If she has a visual memory of them it is probably based on a photograph; she has no real, emotional memory of them at all. Blank. Null. Dead. Here the mountains are small but comely. She must interpret them as pictures, as background. They surround the farm on three sides, at a distance. Everything is comely, a picture, a backdrop for their work, his work, and as he said—it is irrelevant, it is essentially pointless. The beauty of nature, the muteness of nature: pointless. Foxes and porcupine and raccoons and muskrats and rabbits and deer and pheasants and partridges and hawks and jays and sapsuckers and smaller birds of all kinds . . . ashes and beeches and pines and elms and oaks . . . marvelous, mindless; yet invisible, in a sense, when the human intellect leaps into play and demands its own kind, its own kind in combat.

She sees a movement in the lane. She shades her eyes—sees nothing—waits—then sees the figure of a man, approaching the house from the highway. She had not seen him a moment earlier. It is a shock to see him, so suddenly, as if he has come out of nowhere. . . .

But she should not be surprised; Andrew had told her his younger brother might be coming to visit, from West Virginia.

35

The Manitou was a spirit that used to live in the mountains, in the wildest parts of the mountains. It could take the form of a bear, a panther, or a deer, in order to lead the Indian to his death. This spirit had no other reason for its existence, evidently, except to wreak evil upon men. . . . The Indian might come to his senses at the very edge of a precipice, or as he was about to slip into the water and drown . . . then he would realize that the creature he'd been chasing wasn't a living animal, but a spirit. At the last moment the Manitou turned to him and shrieked in triumph, because it could never resist identifying itself, it wanted that peculiar kind of triumph. . . . Some hunters returned to tell about the Manitou, but most of them never returned, of course. They died. They were found dead in the mountains.

Andrew at someone's house, at someone's dinner table. Telling an anecdote. She cannot remember the setting now—cannot remember who was with them. But a woman did ask, brightly, whether the Manitou was still in the mountains?—whether it was still dangerous there?

Absolutely not, Andrew said. *The Indians are gone from the mountains and with the Indians are gone their devils; we live here now.*

36

She was talking about the fiasco of the previous day—the Republicans in the Senate having overestimated their voting strength on a certain controversial issue, and the majority leader, whom she had always thought a fool, forced to reverse his course in public—to the scornful delight of the opposition; she was talking animatedly, grinning her wide insouciant affected grin, unaware of the shoppers who were forced to go around her and Yvonne. They were on the street floor of Kildare's, not far from the front entrance, in the busiest part of the store; but Pamela talked and talked, oblivious of the irritated stares she was drawing, not noticing Yvonne's discomfort. It was more than discomfort, however: it was close to alarm.

How Pamela had changed! How sick she looked, despite the skillfully applied makeup, the brave wide smile!

Yvonne was so startled at the sight of her, so dismayed and bewildered, that she found it difficult to follow Pamela's words. What was she saying, what was the point she hoped to make, why did she keep taking Yvonne's gloved hand, tugging gently at her. . . ? Mink hat, mink coat, fashionably at midcalf, and youthful suede boots to the knee; her dyed hair flounced out from under the fur hat, ends turned up perfectly, as always; the wide lower lip, the artfully thin upper lip, carefully outlined in a dusky pink tone; the eyes sparkling desperately, as if this were a dinner party or a flirtation, inside their complex structure of black paint, silver-blue eye shadow, and wrinkles caked with makeup. She had aged incredibly since Yvonne had seen her last, at Andrew's funeral.

How was Yvonne? How was the magazine, *Discourses?* How did Yvonne like the weather so far?—already so much snow! How was Hugh? Had Yvonne seen Hugh recently? How was Doris? Pamela had not seen Doris for some time. And Stephen? Did she ever hear from him? Or of him? Did she remember that dinner party early last spring at the Greasons', when they'd all had such a good time? Had she seen Adrienne or Leon recently? What was she doing with herself?—someone said she was editing Andrew's paper—letters?—had gone to an international conference to present one of Andrew's speeches—?

Yvonne managed to draw her off to the side, out of the center aisle. She had always avoided Pamela Bausch—had instinctively feared her—admired her, in a way, for her relentless brassy manner, which disguised an exceptional shrewdness; but she had avoided her, knowing that Pamela was a personal enemy. Greeting Andrew once, the woman had thrown her arms around him, had playfully kissed him, giggling that he was her favorite cousin—pressing herself against him in a bizarre way, as if parodying a seductive embrace— squinching up her face, rolling her eyes—then stepping back to hold him at arm's length, as if to prevent him from crushing her against him. Such forced, feverish gaiety, such a girlish reliance upon her charm . . . and the pretense of being drunker than she was. Yvonne had been angry, though she had not shown it. Andrew liked Pamela, always made excuses for her, alluding vaguely to her numerous difficult marriages and disastrous love affairs; it was clear that he liked her very much. And she was clownish, amusing: after embracing Andrew that time, she had jumped back and then, a moment later, held out his wallet to him—a new trick she'd learned, she told them all, snorting with laughter herself. They were astonished, they applauded her, they seemed unable to resist the woman's manic high spirits.

Pamela was looking searchingly at Yvonne. She paused in midsentence, seemed about to say something, then returned to her subject— chattering about the family, about the vacation in the Caribbean she and Charles hoped to take in another two weeks—all the while holding Yvonne's wrist. Yvonne wondered if she had been drinking.

"I suppose people talk about me too," Pamela said, "I suppose they can't resist talking about us all . . . it's our fate, isn't it . . . and nothing changes, nothing seems to be happening . . . what will we do, Yvonne, if they aren't caught? They must be caught! They must be punished! Andrew was your husband and I was only a cousin of his, a second cousin, we weren't close in the same way, but . . . but we were very, very good friends . . . I valued him so highly though maybe I didn't always show it . . . I'm such a scatterbrain, I always have been. May I ask you something very personal, Yvonne?—or would you take offense?"

"What is it?" Yvonne said uneasily.

But something in Yvonne's expression discouraged Pamela; she grinned, patted her stiff hair nervously, changed the subject. "I wish we had been closer, Yvonne, before it happened . . . I could have comforted you, I'm sure I would have been useful . . . you must have needed someone and there was no one, was there, no one you trusted . . . and I don't blame you. I don't blame you. It has been such a strain on you, it shows in your face, it always shows in the face . . . of course you're still a beautiful woman, a very beautiful . . . beautiful woman. And you're still relatively young. We never did talk, did we? I kept wanting to have you to the house for lunch, just the two of us; but I'm always so busy, and you were always so busy, and Andrew might have disapproved . . . since he didn't always approve, you know, of my life. Marvelous advice he gave me, marvelous! . . . in terms of investments, I mean . . . before I met Charles . . . and then, after I met Charles, I believe it was Andrew who encouraged me to marry him . . . as a kind of investment, you might say," she laughed. Her eyes were bright, merry. Yet there was a queer leaden cast to her face, her skin tone; whenever she was silent, whenever she allowed her smile to sag, she looked suddenly spiritless. "I wanted to ask you, Yvonne, if. . . . It's so strange, it's terrifying, but. . . . I was wondering. . . ."

She stared at Yvonne, utterly blank.

Yvonne shivered.

"Yes. . . ?"

After a moment she shook her head mutely. Then she laughed, went on to speak of the necessity of exercise, of a change of scene regularly, less hectic a social life, and a diet high in protein. "My health isn't as good as it might appear to be," she said evenly, "and

it's mainly because of poor eating and sleeping habits I acquired as a
teen-ager. We lived in Washington part of the time, you know . . .
or maybe you don't know. I doubt that Andrew wasted much breath
talking about *me* to you. Yes, my father worked in Washington, had
a very demanding but thankless job . . . I wish I had had the leisure
to have grown up here in Albany, with the others . . . it might have
done me a great deal of good, a steadying influence, you know . . .
because Washington is frantic, incredible. I loved it, don't let me
mislead you! I loved it. I still would, if Charles allowed me more
freedom, but . . . but things there are changed . . . always new people, new people . . . and the others, well of course the others grow
older or change in different ways . . . or die. Growing up in that city
was very exciting, Yvonne, but I think I lost my childhood or
girlhood along the way, I *know* I lost something along the way," she
laughed. "I'm supposed to be indestructible, people tell me. Men.
They can sense something about me, like dogs sniffing. . . . Is it the
same way with you? You and men? Or don't you. . . ? By now I'm
sure I would be remarried, Yvonne, I simply couldn't have endured! . . . and living in that apartment, *that* apartment,
alone! . . . always thinking of him, always being reminded. . . . I'm
sure I would have remarried by now, practically anyone," Pamela
said, trying to make a joke of it. "Even that . . . that lackey, that
what's-his-name, the editor of *Discourses* . . . or is he already married? Someone was saying. . . . But. . . . There are always rumors, I
don't credit them with much reality . . . especially after *my* history
. . . the outlandish lies told about *me*. If you've heard any of them,
Yvonne, I hope you disregarded them. I would like us to become better acquainted, I wouldn't want anything to stand in the way of . . .
of a friendship. . . . People have told cruel lies about both of us, you
know; but what can you do? They all lie, they all gossip! It would
have been even worse, you know, if Andrew had been in office. That
was the wisest move he ever made, retiring from politics . . . he was
too good for those bastards, wasn't he? . . . I don't care what anyone says. He was too good, too honest. It was almost neurotic, that
man's honesty! . . . but wonderful, wonderful. There are no other
men like him. Willa Fergus wasn't good enough for him, she simply
wasn't intelligent enough and he needed someone to talk to, didn't
he, that was the main thing in his life, he needed someone who
would understand . . . and he was so brilliant, so intellectual, I always gave up, couldn't follow him, agreed with anything he said.
The thing about Andrew was . . . the mysterious thing was . . . he

cared so much," she said, her eyes glistening, "he *cared* so much about the world, that was why he was so angry all the time and couldn't relax and the trouble with his stomach, well that was obvious, I mean it was obvious he was in pain at times . . . he cared too much, he had too much invested in the world, I knew about the ulcers and was so very, very sorry for him and for you both . . . the ulcers, the operations. . . ."

Yvonne wanted to interrupt. What was this! The woman was drunk or drugged, talking like this! Passersby were glancing at them, at both of them. Yvonne had the idea that they were recognized.

"Other men don't give a damn about the world," Pamela whispered. "They want to make money, that's it. They don't give a damn —they don't know the world is there—my father had an important position in Washington but he didn't know anything, he didn't *know* there was a public or a world or . . . or whatever I mean. You have to care about the world to get so angry, don't you."

"Yes," Yvonne said. "But Pamela, really—"

"Don't leave! Don't tell me you have to leave!" Pamela protested. "I've been meaning to call you for months! . . . and when I saw Hugh recently, I made up my mind . . . I was definitely going to call you . . . but . . . at the last minute I always hesitated . . . I always. . . . Because I had the idea you didn't care for me, you know; you disliked me. . . ?"

"Of course not," Yvonne said, embarrassed.

"I can sense even the most subtle of feelings," Pamela said wistfully. "And I thought . . . I always thought. . . ."

"Of course not," Yvonne said. "That's ridiculous."

". . . in a way we're close, close as sisters. . . . Do you have a sister?"

Pamela radiated an odor that was spicy, tawny, tangy . . . not quite clean; her breath smelled of something liquorish and fruity. Yvonne laughed nervously, looking away. Kildare's was a wintry festival, a wonderland of synthetic glittering frost and icicles that turned, twinkling, and clouds of angels'-hair and baurite; above the lavish cosmetics section a gigantic whitely clad Santa Claus plunged with his reindeer and heavily-laden sleigh, stardust glittering in his silky white beard and in his bushy white eyebrows and even in his protruding staring eyes—the reindeers' eyes were jewels, light bulbs, their antlers were sprayed with frost, their hides stark white, a smooth satiny down: an Arctic paradise, this well-heated store. . . . Yvonne hardly knew where she was. She hardly knew what season it was, what might be expected of her. Christmas bulbs twinkled and gleamed from every corner of the ceiling, as if making signals to her; the reindeers' eyes glowed and darkened, and glowed again; and darkened; overhead the synthetic snowdrifts like whipped cream floated without weight, the giant Santa Claus presided, plump and sleekly white, grinning, the whip forever suspended above the beasts' backs, never the release of its angry snap, never the release of its pain . . . only the shoppers, milling in the aisles, most of them dressed like Pamela Bausch, seemed to Yvonne recognizable if not entirely convincing. A fragment of an epic passed close behind her, and then away; she overheard *If a heart could break that was what happened to that poor man . . . no one could have foreseen . . . he hesitated for years and then sold the property for a million . . . in Boca Raton I mean . . . and the new owners sold it for twice that a year later, I'm not exaggerating, now he's lost all will to live and we're hoping this Christmas, with the grandchildren. . . .*

"You don't hate me, Yvonne?" Pamela was whispering.

"What a thing to say," Yvonne murmured. ". . . ridiculous."

"She isn't drunk and she isn't sick and she isn't having a breakdown," Yvonne said carefully, since Pamela's husband Charles had sounded so annoyed, "but I think you might want to come get her. . . . Yes? Good."

Pamela was sprawled on the long leather sofa by the fireplace, her coat on the floor beside her, the hat stuck impishly atop one of Andrew's antique clocks. She had already finished her drink. Her face was puffy, lined, yet her eyes were curiously bright—as if she were a mischievous little girl, temporarily resting.

"Is he coming to get me? Why did you call him? . . . That bastard, that pathetic . . . how dare he make judgments on . . . has no right to amass an opinion on any of us, let alone . . . let alone his superior like Andrew. Can I have another drink? Or are you puritanical, like Andrew, and will you frown at me. . . ?"

She wore a dress of apricot jersey, long-sleeved, with a fringe of dark mink at the cuffs, a heavy chain of a necklace around her thin neck, gold and onyx and pearls; her hair was still perfectly set, though she had snatched the fur hat off as soon as she got inside the apartment. Her body was slender, eelish. Yvonne approached her but did not sit down; she remained standing, as if mesmerized.

"Poor Willa was so offended by me, my mere existence seemed to pain her," Pamela murmured, "but had *she* had the best of him, would *she* have even noticed. . . ? I mean it's so obvious! . . . the poor soul. But you are not Willa, not quite! Not quite. You are so very, very different, dear, I think I know exactly how poor crazed Hugh feels . . . he's infatuated, Yvonne, did you know? . . . but penniless, I have it on the best authority . . . which is *not* him. Penniless. A genius, they say, but . . . but there are so many geniuses now . . . in Andrew's day, when he graduated from Harvard Law, there weren't as many geniuses and he rose to the top immediately as one might expect . . . but now, today, already it's a different world and perhaps Andrew is better out of it, how could his rage have kept pace with. . . . I loved him for that, didn't you, for his fine healthy boy's rage. . . ?"

Pamela patted the cushion beside her, but Yvonne remained standing. It was 5:20 by her watch and she calculated it would take only ten minutes for Charles to get here if he came directly.

"Yes, you certainly are different from Willa," Pamela said with an air of melancholy cheer, ". . . different from all of us. It was astounding, Andrew discovering you . . . or you discovering Andrew . . . however it happened. And the stories you two contrived! Shameless. Hilarious. *I* knew who you were because Tommy K, who did surveillance for my second husband and who befriended me for certain reasons, before and during the divorce, Tommy K gave me a full detailed report, but I loved it . . . I loved it all . . . and the first time I saw Andrew I nudged him in the ribs and asked how his copper heiress was and he colored to the roots of his hair—is that how it's put?—can you blush in that way?—and we had a good laugh together because we were always very close, as close as sister and brother though in fact we were only second cousins . . . we had many a good laugh together in our lifetimes. But now. . . . You won't sit here? You won't get me a drink? It's as Hugh feared, you are a puritan like Andrew, a warrior-princess, a barbarian, eh? . . . and disapproving. . . ? But I haven't anyone else, you are the only person who . . . even your antagonism, Yvonne, would be. . . ."

"Would you like a glass of water?" Yvonne said abruptly. ". . . Would you like to use the bathroom, to wash your face. . . ?"

"My face isn't dirty, Yvonne," Pamela said evenly. "And I wouldn't dare mar or rearrange it this far from home. . . . Death? It doesn't bother me in the least. I like to talk about it, in fact. I like to be utterly frank . . . uninhibited. That's health, isn't it, the open expression of . . . refusal to be intimidated by . . . I could envy Hugh his murderous caricatures, they're so quaintly diseased and obscene! . . . ah, but artistic genius is beyond me, I don't claim to. . . . And Stephen, do you know Stephen? . . . a pity, he's so interesting . . . though I don't know him myself, now that we're adults I find I scarcely know anyone . . . we've all gone into disguise. He was such an intense child, fascinating . . . too young for me . . . too young for me to really notice. You don't know him? At such a time in your life the consolation of . . . a man with such fervent religious beliefs . . . *knowledge* . . . no matter that people made fun of him, *I* never made fun of him . . . a man like that would be. . . . I'm not divorcing Charles, did you hear? We've reached an agreement. Cammie and me, I mean. It's been dragging on so long I scarcely remember which one I'm supposed to be in love with and which one is the . . . which one must be taken seriously, in terms of his attorney; do you know Cammie? You've seen him . . . yes, you have! . . . you've looked him eye to eye, Yvonne . . . about a year ago at the Van Hornes and I was there in a red velvet halter dress and sandals and I introduced you and Andrew to . . . yes, very blond, platinum hair combed flat on his head . . . broad jaw, slightly Slavic look to the cheekbones . . . looks thirty-five but is older than I am. . . . As I said, death doesn't bother me in the least. I wanted to invite you to lunch, Yvonne, so we could talk openly and frankly, but I was afraid . . . I am afraid . . . sometimes you look so fierce and disapproving and while I take it all lightly and can't really be hurt, still, I feel uneasy in . . . in your presence. But I wanted so badly, Yvonne, to talk to you about . . . about. . . ."

Yvonne hesitated. Swift, intense, came a feeling of pity; a sensation powerfully physical, like nausea, spreading in her. She stared at Pamela, at the woman's ludicrous black eyelashes and her glossy, exaggerated lips, not knowing whether to turn away in irritation or come closer.

". . . about your life since it happened, about *how* you are living, Yvonne, *how* it is possible that . . . that you have lived this long. . . ."

"I don't want to talk about such things," Yvonne said weakly.

"But Yvonne! What else is there, what *else* is there?" Pamela asked, genuinely astonished. "Life—death. Life and death. When I was younger I thought there were other things . . . I mean, just a year or so ago . . . I was much younger then . . . and had been young all my life, you know, *very* young . . . and deluded . . . and . . . and reasonably happy, I suppose. But deluded, deluded. And now. . . . Now it's different, isn't it, now we *know* so much more, you and I. But you are closer, that's undeniable! You are closer to him! You know infinitely more than I do. . . . No matter how young I look, Yvonne, I'm feeling my age now, and in a way it's a relief; I put in three solid decades of it, and it's a strain, no matter what they say, it *is* a strain . . . being a beautiful desirable woman and always having to get the most of it, going out when you'd rather lie in bed with the flu, getting fitted for new clothes when you'd rather gorge yourself and gain fifty pounds and close up shop, the hell with it. Those indentations at the top of the thighs are the first real sign, and the breasts sort of sallow and flabby, and lines in the throat they say *cannot* be dealt with . . . but the real sign, in my opinion, is when these things don't register except to make you feel relieved. . . . Thank God! you whisper and kiss yourself in the mirror, congratulating yourself on having come through. . . . But you are indifferent to that sort of thing, aren't you, Yvonne? You truly don't care! You're immune, you're invulnerable . . . impregnable . . . which is why we're all frightened of you and hope you won't somehow turn against us . . . or won't, somehow, be revealed as unworthy of Andrew Petrie? . . ."

"What did you want to ask me?" Yvonne said.

"About his death, about his . . . were there . . . his dying words? . . . no? . . . it's as you told the police, he was already dead? . . . already dead. Yes. I suppose so. And . . . won't you sit beside me, Yvonne?"

She came to the sofa. Pamela coiled into an upright position; Yvonne sat beside her uneasily.

"And . . . And do you dream about him, Yvonne? Do you still make contact with him in any way? Don't look embarrassed, I'm just a silly woman who craves. . . . You don't dream about him? You *do*? I do too, Yvonne, but the dreams are . . . are not . . . the dreams are not very pleasant."

"My dreams are not very pleasant," Yvonne whispered.

"He comes to you? He speaks to you? What does he want?—don't be embarrassed, I . . . I don't want to embarrass you. . . . Suddenly I feel so dizzy, I feel intoxicated," she murmured, taking Yvonne's hands and rubbing them, "both of us are so cold! . . . our fingernails are turning blue, just look! We're so cold, so icy . . . *he* has us, don't you think? . . . *he* has us. There's no warmth in the world, even the sun is turning cold, it's pale and faint, and so much snow already and the winter hardly begun . . . your hands are even colder than mine, Yvonne! . . . what lovely rings . . . such lovely, lovely

rings . . . but you should do something about your nails, dear, you
should have a professional manicurist look after them . . . it isn't
enough just to keep them clean and filed and . . . don't draw away,
please! Oh dear, please! I am always offending you without realizing
it and . . . and I am only hurting myself . . . I feel such pain, pains
. . . pains in my heart and in my head and . . . when people draw
away from me like that, women or men or children, when living people stare at me like that and draw away . . . and . . . I feel such sorrow," she said, beginning to cry, "and there's comfort only in . . .
only in *him,* in knowing that his claim on me takes priority, and why
should I trouble myself about the others . . . why should I continue
to make the effort to . . . year after year, morning after morning,
why make the effort of. . . . Do you see? Do you know?"

    She began to cry. Like a child, she moved into Yvonne's arms—
seemed to insinuate herself into Yvonne's arms—suddenly helpless,
quivering. She was a child, a child!—a mere child. Yvonne's mind
darkened for an instant, she had not enough awareness to resist, to
draw away; and then it was too late, she was actually holding Pamela
and comforting her as the woman sobbed without control, saying
"Yes. Yes. I know, I understand. Yes. I'm the one who . . . I am the
one who understands. I am the one, yes." She was still holding
Pamela when the doorbell rang at six.

37

*Clarity is close to godliness; and when you achieve clarity, you can
dispense with godliness.*

She remembered that, the following morning. It was in the room
with her. The words were his, uttered in his voice. She woke early, before dawn, and though the scene of the previous evening returned to
her with frightening, repulsive force, she countered it at once by saying, "I am not the one, I am not the one who understands, not *that,*
I am not the one . . ."

He had instructed her to avoid Pamela—had not liked to see the
two of them together, even in public.

"I'm not the one," Yvonne said aloud. "I don't understand what
you mean and I don't care to know what you mean and I don't . . .
I am not . . . I am not the one."

She threw herself into the outside world. That was the place of clarity, the place of daylight. There he had wanted, in his way, to reign: not by the simple, brute, childish means of direct power, but by knowledge, by ideas, by the intellectual and ideological control of the structures of power. The world was there, it could not be denied, it seemed so open to her, so desirous of her—both as Andrew's widow and as a person of her own—pushing in upon her when she would allow it, ready to spread itself at her feet. The mail, the invitations, the telephone calls, the requests. . . . She did not think of Pamela, she did not think of her own degrading performance, moved to such morbid and inconsequential and unproductive self-pity. . . .

"I must avoid certain members of the Petrie family," she thought.

Since the conference in San Francisco she had received a number of invitations to participate in similar events. How flattering these invitations were, and how she gloated over them . . . over Andrew's posthumous power . . . the revenge he would enjoy, *Andrew Petrie* presented in another form to these people, many of whom had professed to scorn him in life! . . . and they were mistaken, very much mistaken, if they imagined his widow would dilute his teachings. These foundations and institutes and forums and councils, what were they but intellectual façades for the betrayal of the nation, as he had said repeatedly; what were they but. . . . She leafed through their glossy brochures. She read and reread their letters of invitation, to determine which had been written specifically to her and which were merely form letters typed up and sent out across the country to ostensibly prominent people . . . prominent names. Only one of them, *The Gladys and Randolph Frazer Foundation for the Arts, Sciences, and the Humanities*, had ever invited Andrew himself to participate in a conference. The others were new, new conquests of a sort, and Yvonne considered them with growing excitement, wondering which would be more politic to accept, and which to reject . . . wondering if Andrew had often rejected such offers without telling her, without considering it important enough to tell her . . . or whether, in fact, he had wished to be invited and had been disappointed that they had excluded him.

The Futures Institute. The North American Affairs Council, of Chicago. The Life Studies Forum. The Joseph Crocker Institute. The Samuel P. Barclay Memorial Foundation. The Clarkston Center for the Studies of Democratic Nations. The Moncton Council of World Affairs. The Maisie and Edgar Hollingsworth III Memorial

*Foundation for the Exploration and Promulgation of Ideas: With
Fully Subsidized Scholar-Centers in Washington, D.C., Geneva,
Switzerland, and Acapulco, Mexico. The Seventeenth Annual Con-
ference of the Baxter Fellowes International Congress. The Founda-
tion for the. . . . The American Association to Advance Human
Communications and . . . The Julian P. Morgan Council of. . . .
The Seattle Center for the. . . . The Commission for . . .*

Yvonne spent a morning studying these. She sat at the dining-room
table with the brochures and membership lists and programs and
"brief histories" and letters of invitation spread out before her. It
was a clear, harsh day. Sometime in December. Her thirty-second
birthday had come and gone without her noticing. One hundred
seventy-one days had passed since his death.

—And she answered the twenty-five questions sent to her by a
young man at Kings College, Cambridge. He was preparing a study
with the title *American Conservative Thought from Pre-Revolu-
tionary Times to the Present.* It took her some time, but afterward
she felt as if her head were cleared. She felt as if an obscure but intense pressure had been removed. —Then she typed up what was to
have been Chapter Three of Andrew's book, which she had con-
densed into a thirty-five-page essay; she chose the title "Traditional
Limits to Freedom of Speech" among several titles Andrew had been
working with; Eliot Stacey had wanted this for the April issue of *Discourses.* When he telephoned her now he spoke only of impersonal
matters, and she spoke only of impersonal matters. They were polite
with each other, as they always had been. "By spring the murderers
will have been arrested," Eliot said impulsively. "I have a feeling. I
just have a feeling." Yvonne did not question him, did not care to
talk about it. She listened politely but did not comment. —She spent
hours rereading articles Andrew had published, in *Discourses* and in
other magazines; she spent hours sorting outlines, notes, abortive essays; there were occasional letters mixed in with his papers—as a rule
Andrew had destroyed the personal letters he received: it was his
policy—and she put these in a file she had started. It pleased her to
accomplish so much. She felt as if her head were cleared for that
day. —She attended to the serious letters. She answered some letters
that had been sent to Andrew back in June. Each day she answered
three letters in the morning, three letters in the afternoon, and three
in the evening. Otherwise there would be too many! . . . otherwise
her head would get clotted. As it was, there were times when her vi-

sion swayed, grew cloudy, foggy . . . but when this happened she simply stopped what she was doing, put it aside, and did something else. She read books as Andrew had read them, two or three at a time. It was marvelous, to read Andrew's books, to follow the passages his mind had taken . . . his marginalia, his puckish comments. She did this when the other work was too difficult or when she could not think how to open a letter, or how to conclude it. She did this always in the evenings, before going to bed. It helped to clear her mind, it helped to. . . . There was wisdom, clarity, sanity . . . the possibility of. . . . *Is there no free will?!* Andrew at the age of twenty or twenty-one had scribbled this in his copy of Spinoza's *Ethic.* Philosophy 240 at Harvard. *Is there no free will?!* Andrew did not believe it. Yvonne guessed that Andrew, young Andrew, did not believe such a lie. Throughout the Spinoza there were impertinent high-spirited questions and comments and several places where entire propositions were crossed out, in evident impatience. *In the mind there is no absolute or free will, but the mind is determined to this or that volition by a cause, which is also determined by another cause, and this again by another, and so ad infinitum.* . . . Really! Really! Was that possible, she thought scornfully, who could allow it to be possible!—Andrew was right to reject it, to cross it out. She would have crossed it out also. —She sent photostated copies of several of Andrew's previously published articles to a young man in Palo Alto who was doing his doctoral dissertation on Andrew; she sent copies of articles to a publisher in Boston, who was editing an anthology; she sent "The Failure of Post-War Ethics," "Beyond Mediocrity: The Present Crisis in Public Education," "Genocide in the 'Third World'," and "Three Decades of American Liberalism: 'Beyond Good and Evil'?" to an admirer of Andrew's who taught at a small college in Michigan. These small accomplishments gave her a sense of satisfaction. They had boundaries, were like propositions that might be X'd out, dealt with, terminated. *Clarity.* . . . *Clarity was being served.* . . . —She read Tocqueville and Marx side by side, and added to them Jonathan Swift, taken from the bookshelf beside her that reached to the ceiling; she leafed through an old first edition of a book by Charles Sanders Peirce, whom Andrew had said was related distantly to the Petries, and she discovered, underlined heavily in the preface, remarks of Peirce's that Andrew had taken as his own, had said repeatedly: Peirce had had ambitious plans for philosophy and had wanted, even in his old age, to do a thorough study of the "belief which men *betray*, and not that which they *parade*"

. . . . that was Andrew, Andrew's voice! . . . yet nothing else of
Peirce's was Andrew's, as far as Yvonne could judge; she could not
read more than a few pages of Peirce before losing interest, opening
another book, balancing it on the pile of papers before her and reading, reading quickly, hopefully. Just so had her husband read, with a
certain expectant, childlike urgency for which she had loved him.
—And there was Andrew's copy of *The Leviathan* and his copy of
The Republic, printed in the same series, in the same print; read together, did they not emit the same sounds, were they not the expressions of a single mind? . . . and it intrigued her to juxtapose with
them the letters of Thomas Jefferson, which she scanned, wondering
if the rhythm beneath the surface rhythm of the prose was that same
rhythm. . . . Hume's *Political Discourses*, for which Andrew's journal had been named; and the *Critique of Pure Reason* again, and
again Spinoza, opened at random. Duets, choruses. Combined
voices. Powerful contrasts—contradictions—affirmations. *The Prince*
and Tom Paine and *Fellow citizens, we cannot escape history.* . . .
Sometimes her mind clouded, sometimes the voices jarred and refused to admit their secrets, their secret clarity; she saw a solitary
woman walking through a wet pasture, through a scrawny ash woods,
she saw but did not pity the mute, uncomprehending terror; she did
not pity anyone and she certainly did not pity herself. . . . Not
pitying herself, wasn't she relieved of the burden of pitying others?

   She pushed the books aside. She reached for another. Always, there
were books: near at hand the chorus of voices. Words. Salvation. She
was never alone. There was Andrew's voice hidden everywhere
around her in the desk drawers and in the pigeonholes and in the
cardboard boxes and in the filing cabinet and on the shelves and in
the solid leather-bound back issues of the magazine, a multitude of
voices, yet one man's voice, single, singular, and there were, mingled
with his, the voices of other men—all men—all speaking with that
extraordinary blinding clarity she knew by now she worshiped. The
intellect and its precise measurements, its setting-up of empires,
word by word by word, which nothing could demolish—except other
word-empires, perhaps; she knew by now this was her worship, her
fate.

   A cheap paperback edition, the pages loosened and yellowed, the
margins filled with Andrew's faded commentary: she had reached for
it when her mind clouded, reaching for it instinctively, at random.
The danger in happiness: now everything I touch turns out to be

wonderful. Now I love any fate that comes along. Who feels like being my fate?

38

Shortly after five one dark wind-blown Friday afternoon in December, Yvonne met Hugh Petrie in the lobby of the Andora Hotel, which was a few blocks from her apartment building. There were poinsettia plants in this lobby as there were poinsettia plants in the lobby of her own building. Christmas carols were being piped in and a group of seven or eight children, herded across the lobby by several adults, were chanting in a singsong way, joking among themselves, emphasizing the wrong syllables in the familiar words—O *little* town *of* Bethle*HEM*—so that Yvonne had the uncanny feeling, for an instant, that she was in a foreign country, overhearing foreign speech.

Hugh seemed startled by the sight of her, as if he had forgotten what she looked like. He shook hands awkwardly. He released her hand almost at once. Stiff, formal, yet clownishly eager, he began murmuring in his polite, unconvincingly gallant way. *Ah, how are you!—how good to see you!—what a pleasure after so—*

She saw that he was unnaturally pale. And thin, almost emaciated —but probably no thinner than he had been at their last meeting. He was absurdly well-dressed, but the parts of his outfit did not match. A russet tweed suit with suede trim, which fitted him well and looked expensive; a cheap necktie of eye-boggling zebra stripes, made of a synthetic material, the sort of tie Yvonne remembered having seen in the window of a novelty shop in downtown Albany the other day, priced at three ninety-eight; stylish black shoes with pointed toes, splashed from the street; a white handkerchief in his pocket, too white, pulled too far out. Yvonne wanted to tuck it back down. His hair was wind-blown and frizzy, soft-looking, as if he had just shampooed it. His nose was hawkishly prominent, longer and sharper than she remembered. He was smiling, chattering, obviously very nervous.

In the cocktail lounge he directed the hostess to seat them in one of the corner booths, but these were booths for four or six people; the hostess led them elsewhere. *Do you see!—what it's always like!—* in a way this seemed to please him, as if it were a perverse victory. He went on to complain about the train ride from New York to Albany, the condition of the train, the condition of his fellow passengers, the insolence of a ticket taker who had misunderstood one of Hugh's jokes; and about the filthy weather, which had driven him from his home town as much as anything else, though of course New York City wasn't much better—was in some ways even worse. "What was the winter like in your home town, Yvonne?" he asked. "Snow?—wind?—sub-zero temperatures?"

Yvonne said something noncommittal.

"Cold—cold—cold," Hugh muttered, rubbing his bony hands together. "Do you know I can't remember any summer this year?—I realize we must have had one—*must* have—I know I suffered as usual —my apartment isn't air-conditioned, it's really shockingly dismal and overpriced—and yet I can't exactly remember—I can't remember a typical summer day, can you? Only the day I came to visit you: that *was* this summer, wasn't it? That *was* you, wasn't it?—and me?"

But this was joking, mere joking. Smiling and smiling and smiling. No need for her to reply, really; only a minimal acknowledgment seemed necessary. The man was all elbows, knees, feet. And that slightly clownish grin.

"Time seems to have played some tricks on me in this phase of my life," he said. "In one sense it's stopped: stuck. In another sense it's flashing by. Or perhaps this is a symptom of my age . . . I must acknowledge, you know, the fact that I am in the second half of my life."

His smile shifted, was suddenly fearful. He did not look at her.

After their last meeting Yvonne had analyzed her feelings, unable to account for the effect Hugh had had upon her. A certain disdain, almost revulsion . . . at the same time an odd euphoric giddiness, like hysteria. . . . her nerves tight and jangling for hours afterward, her pulse beat heightened. . . . Yvonne in the presence of an enemy, sensing and recognizing an enemy. Yet she liked him. She liked him. There was precedent of a sort because Andrew had said, once, that he did not mind his brother—in a way he liked him—so long as they were not together for too long a period. She liked him but was wary, cautious, could not relax in his presence. That beaklike nose, those small clever eyes! . . . and the insinuating whine of his voice! Afterward she had tried to analyze her feelings but could not understand them. Hugh had aroused in her uncharacteristic emotions, which were, in a sense, peripheral to her being, irrelevant; to have been frightened of . . . intimidated by . . . trembling in the presence of. . . . She had even thought, for an instant, that he *knew*. He was the one, he *knew*.

But his manner had thrown her off. It had temporarily thrown her off. His jocular conversation, his harmless little jokes and ironies . . . he was one of the enemy, yes, but not an enemy to take seriously. Then the gifts, the flowers and the drawings and the fey, silly surprises, and the occasional telephone calls, which were like stage monologues: he was not an enemy to take seriously.

"Has time played any strange tricks on you, Yvonne?" he asked.

"No," she said.

"You live it straight out, eh?—no convolutions?"

"I'm very busy—"

"Yes, I've heard! I've heard. Busy, very busy—always busy—*busy*—just like your husband—work—work—work—hour following hour—cold cold cold—the kind of people I've always admired, adored, from a distance—yes, I've heard about how industrious you've been. Not even a vacation!—not even a month off, let's say, for a collapse. But should you ever desire a collapse, and want absolute privacy, I could take you in—protect you from the gossip-hounds— That isn't likely, I suppose; you're a paragon of health and strength and virtue. Is it true, really—you live life *straight out* . . . ? Strictly chronological?"

"Of course," Yvonne said evasively. "How do you live . . . ?"

"My God," he laughed. "Must you ask?"

She thought: He's real, he's living. He's like myself. He's real, a human being, a man.

She had gone to intercept him. She had been watching him, now she went to him. She wanted to know: What did they quarrel about, why had her husband gotten so angry?—when it was not Andrew's practice, it was not in his nature, to get angry.

"Must you ask?" Stephen said.

She looked at him directly, now that they were alone. They were not performing for anyone. No one watched, no one overheard. "Of *course* I must ask," she said angrily.

There were darkly glowing orange lights in the cocktail lounge. In this light Hugh was revealed to her as someone quite different from the person she had assumed him to be. His face was lean with desire, his smile lumpy, bemused, twisted with melancholy. *A human being, a man!*—she saw him in that instant and felt such sickness, such an opening, a raw unfathomable opening—something ripped from her through which her soul might fall—

The powder room too was decorated for the holidays. Three poinsettia plants done up in crinkly green paper with bright green bows. Yvonne studied one of the plants, made out the tiny yellow flowers at its core. Near-microscopic, they were. The leaves were a bright, dramatic, unreal red, tapering to green; they were not flowers, not petals, but leaves. Spiky, dramatic, deceptive. But beautiful. The tiny flowers, the genuine poinsettia flowers, were hidden. They too were beautiful, but they were hidden.

"Don't drop no ashes in there, miss—oh, okay, I thought you had a cigarette or something—"

Yvonne went into the other room, ran the cold water faucet. The black attendant was humming to herself in the powder room; Yvonne turned the water on harder.

She dampened one of the linen hand towels. She touched her eyes with it. One eye, then the other. One eye, then the other. A gentle ceremony. A gentle refreshing ceremony to restore vision.

Working hard lately. Working hard. Perhaps she was working too hard.

The alternative—?

She wondered if she had made a mistake, agreeing to meet Hugh. She could not recall exactly having agreed to meet him; that is, she could not recall the moment, the change of heart. *Yvonne? Yes? Please?* And her acquiescence. Then it was written in her little notebook, just below the notation about Dr. Jamison—she was to have seen him at three-thirty that day. But she had crossed out the appointment. She had telephoned, had canceled. She really did not care to be examined and to be interrogated, however kindly, about her physical condition. It did not interest her in any fundamental sense; it was not permanent but always changing. The cramps in the pit of her stomach, the sudden sensation of cold, utter cold. . . . The bleeding had started again according to some erratic rhythm. It had gone on, last time, for seven or eight days. Then, the other night, it had started again, accompanied by unusually severe cramps, which Yvonne did not recognize as a problem belonging to her. She supposed she might accommodate it, however, as she accommodated so much. But it was not her own problem, nothing of *hers*, it was peripheral to her being and insignificant and embarrassing.

"You okay, miss?"

The black woman stuck her head in. She was fairly old—with a zesty quizzical expression—rather insolent. Yvonne thought of that black woman at the school, the principal, whose name she had forgotten.

"Of course. Thanks."

When she left, two extremely tall, beautiful young women were coming in, faces glowing with color, hair to their waists so thick it must have been supplemented with hairpieces. Their dresses were cut low to reveal large, bulging breasts; their bare shoulders gave off a powerful perfumy odor. And what remarkable eyes, like the eyes of beasts in paintings! Yvonne looked away, offended by them. She knew they were call girls, they were probably here with men from the legislature, she did not approve of them . . . still, it pleased her, it touched a secret, cloudy part of her, it pleased her cynically that such women had power over men, any men; it was reassuring.

Nothing else matters, Yvonne. You understand. You are the only person who understands. The truth that must be expressed, must be given its form . . . its perfect form. . . . The truth that cannot be withheld. . . . Our activity, our human activity; our only distinctly human activity. You understand? Of course you understand, you alone . . . the mind of man supreme in the universe, no sympathy for mere matter . . . the purposelessness of nature, what a distraction! But the truth I want to present to the world, Yvonne, keeps breaking into bits. . . . I was drawn outside this morning, for some reason my interest was absorbed by a tree on the riverbank that I had played in as a boy. An immense willow tree, incredible! . . . not far from the cabin . . . I examined it, I was amazed at its size and complexity . . . eight main trunks and they divide into twelve or thirteen smaller trunks, each large and sturdy enough to be, to have been, separate trees. It was colossal . . . astonishing . . . mysterious. One tree, or many? Many trees competing for moisture, or a single tree, nourished by a single source? It was beautiful, a monster. Fascinating. . . . I wasted an hour or more staring at it, contemplating it . . . and when I returned to my work I kept thinking about it, had the most ridiculous urge to go out and look at it again, count the trunks again, study the leaves. What an eerie thing. . . . I could almost have the thing cut down, it was such an exasperating experience. Yvonne, beauty is preposterous; it has no point. It exults in itself, wasting our time, wasting our lives! . . . it can draw us away from our commitments to the world and to one another so easily, be-

*cause you only know it at the moment you experience it: afterward
you lose faith, you forget. So you keep being drawn back to the
source of beauty again and again . . . again and again . . . again . . .
it makes you insatiable, it wastes your best energies, the time you
owe to. . . .*

Hugh was at the bar when she returned. Getting a second drink.
By the meager look of him, his slightly hunched shoulders, she knew
he was not her husband; and his hair was frizzy; and his profile steep.
But when he returned to her he slid into the booth with one arm
around the back, a casual gesture meant to suggest proprietorship.
*Such a striking woman . . . always a surprise to . . . and so kind of
you, to agree to. . . .* He watched as she sipped at her drink. Was
anything wrong? Didn't she care for it?

"Andrew drank more in his late teens than he did later as an
adult," Hugh said. "Drinking is adolescent, I suppose. . . . You
don't drink much, I've noticed, which gives you a certain advantage
over others . . . though at the same time, the world must remain awfully jagged to you, all edges and sharp corners. —Is the drink all
right?"

"It's fine," Yvonne said.

"Yes, the world must be awfully blunt to you," he said slowly.
"Most of the time."

That grotesque necktie!—the white stripes were glowing faintly.
She wanted to pull the lapels of his jacket together to hide the tie.
She wanted to tuck the handkerchief down. She wanted to steady his
nervous hands, which were constantly in motion—his fingers drawing
invisible shapes in the damp spots on the table, or tracing imaginary
words in the air, or plucking unconsciously at his own chin. She
wanted to take his angular face between her hands, wanted to steady
him, calm him.

"I like the world as it is," Yvonne said after a pause.

Hugh snickered.

"What do you mean by that?" Yvonne asked sharply.

"*I like the world as it is.* —What a lie! You insult me, Yvonne, by
lying to me constantly."

"*You* lie. You lie constantly."

"I may lie in my life, but not in my art," he said at once.

"Your art!" Yvonne said. "I looked through that book you sent—
those books you sent. Art, is it?—Andrew would have—"

"Not would have, *did. Did.*"

They were silent. Both were quite excited. Yvonne found she had finished her drink; the ice cubes knocked pleasantly against her front teeth. Hugh called for the cocktail waitress and ordered two more drinks in his brisk, fussy, public manner.

"I realize you dislike me, Yvonne," he said, bowing his head, "but I assume it's partly because of *his* influence. He hated me, was insanely jealous . . . certain childhood affairs . . . and my mother's preference for me . . . matters I won't go into. Though you dislike me, however, I don't dislike *you*. I feel a certain compassion for you. Perhaps you've noticed?"

Yvonne said nothing. She was watching his forefinger trace shapes on the table top. Was he spelling something out?—a word, a name?

". . . grown increasingly concerned about you, about your personal safety . . . and your health. Rumor has it . . . but of course you must live your own . . . on the other hand, as your brother-in-law I . . . sometimes I wake from sleep and . . . not typical, not typical . . . a nightmare of astounding clarity and terror in which someone is trying to communicate with me . . . reaching out to *me*. I feel your presence, and I feel *his*. Sometimes the dream is overwhelming . . . I don't think I will survive . . . have the unshakable certainty . . . somehow knowing . . . that is, *knowing*. . . ."

Yvonne watched the man's fingers. He gave himself away. She wanted to reach out, wanted simply to lay her hand on top of his. And then. . . .

From the high window she watched him approach the house. His figure had appeared at the rise in the gravel drive, then disappeared a moment later behind the scruffy, overgrown pines. Then it appeared again. She squinted into the sunshine, her hand upraised, the instant of her alarm passing. She knew who it was. They expected him. He had planned on borrowing a car from one of the priests or brothers at Brandywine; but he must have hitch-hiked instead. He appeared in the lane, on foot. He was not carrying a suitcase. There was something in his right hand—it looked as if he were carrying something— a flower, a spray of blossoms? He walked easily, not hurrying. She could see he was looking around, looking carefully around. As a child he too had come out here—of course; he too belonged here. He was her husband's brother, therefore closer to this place than she was. She resented him, she did not really want to meet him. Her husband's family intimidated her. They could not get hold of her, though; could not gain power over her. She kept clear of them, wisely. Now Andrew's younger brother was coming to visit and Andrew had said he wanted only one thing: To get money from Andrew for whatever he was involved in at the present time, whatever school or halfway house or work farm or clinic or brotherhood or "family." He wanted money; he even wanted this land, these several thousand acres. He had given his own money away and had nothing to show for it and now, in his adulthood, in his perverted maturity, he wanted to beg money from others. *He isn't quite human,* Andrew said of him uneasily. *He has no shame.*

"Cheap ecstasies don't interest me," Hugh was saying. His voice was less abrasive now. "I know they don't interest you either. Which is why we keep working, always working. We wouldn't betray our destinies. They said you would disappear but you haven't disappeared and you don't intend to—you are *married,* aren't you? I'm frightened by you but I respect you. There are the blessed and the cursed, Yvonne, and it's no good saying there is no original sin, there is an original something, an original distinction between . . . between those who dwell in darkness and those who dwell in light. Do you know what I mean? You do? . . . Though he's dead, Andrew dwells in light. He's a child of light. I am a child of darkness, I can't help my fate, nothing cheap or easy or entertaining or pleasant or wholesome or trivially *human* interests me. . . . Are you sleepy, dear? Or would you like another drink?"

In another booth the two girls were shrieking with laughter. They were with two well-dressed men, one of whom resembled an acquaintance of Andrew's. Yvonne was not certain. She did not care. She was not annoyed by their noisy gaiety. She was not certain if the man was someone she knew or a stranger and she was not certain what Hugh wanted, but there was something sleepily comforting about the atmosphere now, rather warm, close, pleasantly close. Hugh's voice had become hypnotic. It was not really Hugh's voice. It was a voice he had appropriated and was using, skillfully. "Women like *that* don't interest me in the slightest," Hugh whispered. "They're contemptible . . . just pigs. . . . They didn't interest your husband either, did they; he had the most exquisite good taste, I halfway envied him at times . . . of course there may have been things in his life I wasn't aware of, as there are things in my life no one knows about, not even intimate friends. . . ."

She went out to talk with him. He was leaving; he was simply going to walk away.

When he spoke to her, answering her quietly, she realized she had no existence for him: he looked at her, his dark eyes moved upon her, shying away from her own, but she was not really there for him. He was thinking of something else. His complexion was bright, high-colored now because of the quarrel. His eyes were bright, moist, very dark. Like Andrew he had a high forehead; but his hair was thicker than Andrew's and fell forward carelessly, making him appear younger than his age and giving him a peculiar air of self-possession. He answered in monosyllables. He did not acknowledge her now, in her complexity; he refused to be charmed.

At the funeral he had wept. He had hid his face and wept. She thought hatefully: *Now—! Now you're feeling something!*

He was watching her closely, strangely.

". . . not even intimate friends. . . ."

She wanted to reply but could not. Her eyelids were heavy, her lips felt heavy, swollen. The drink had overwhelmed her; she had not eaten since breakfast; it had been a mistake to come here . . . where a man's forefinger was making slow, tight circles and figures in the damp spots on the table top.

". . . things in one's life, in all our lives, even *we* don't quite comprehend . . ." he was saying softly. Head bowed, now leaning close to her, as if they were conspirators or lovers. An air of both gravity and excitement. Very watchful. ". . . Yvonne? . . . you are very lonely, are you? . . . and stubborn, and blind? . . . you won't let me protect you? . . . you could come live with me, incognito; there would be no fuss, no obligation . . . I wouldn't even touch your money, I wouldn't *touch* it . . . his money . . . any of it. You believe me, don't you? . . . you and I understand each other, I'm confident of that, we are both outsiders in a sense . . . not *Petries*, not accepted by. . . . If you were to die, Yvonne, your inheritance would certainly not go to anyone in *your* family, certainly there are provisions to prohibit that, and they say you have no family . . . no one. So it would revert back to the Petries anyway and . . . and nothing would be gained by. . . . The problem is that neither you nor I cares for money and so we find it difficult to believe that others do, that they *truly* do, as characters in movies and nineteenth-century novels do, obsessed by . . . determined by . . . considerations you and I and Stephen and anyone of intelligence and sensitivity find preposterous, degrading, silly . . . uncivilized. If you came under my protection . . . if you were to marry me. . . . Yvonne? Are you listening? . . . If you were to marry me you would be absolutely protected: there would be no way on earth that Harvey could get hold of . . . not even Doris, that gluttonous witch . . . no one, no one! . . . since Andrew was the Crown Prince and his grandfather loved him best and trusted him with infinite powers . . . since he was the Prince and the others of us mere court jesters and unredeemed frogs . . . Calibans of the air. . . . do you see? . . . always astonishing . . . discovery . . . one's own soul . . . fairy tales are exactly analogous to life as it is lived in the family. . . . Let me order us more drinks, Yvonne. No? . . . You'd like to leave? . . . but why, it's hardly night, why, why? . . . is someone waiting for you . . . ? But you do look awfully tired, dear, maybe it would be a good idea to. . . . And then we could talk more freely. . . ."

He was a good man and he died horribly.
We all die horribly, Yvonne.

39

She woke two days later, early Monday morning. The door to the darkened room was ajar and she could see out into the corridor and hear the lowered voices of women; and she could smell the medicinal odor, the unmistakable odor of a hospital.

Her mind seemed to turn over, to raise itself and turn over—exposed now to light, to sanity. She did not panic, she was too exhausted. Her mind raised itself, shook off the hallucinations and the visions and her own complicacy in them; she did not know what had happened but she was at once reassured by the room, the corridor, the sounds of other people, the smells and the feel of the stiff clean linen. . . . She rang for a nurse. She knew how to ring for a nurse: two years ago her husband had had emergency surgery for a stomach condition, she had practically lived with him in his private room, she believed she must be in the same hospital now, though she could not, at the moment, remember its name.

She thought: *They won't kill me. They are not going to kill me.*

40

She was screaming. Her eyeballs rolled in her head. Her body
thrashed from side to side so he could not get hold of her, she felt
his hands on her shoulders, on her neck, she was screaming and at
the same time detached from the struggle, watching or recalling it,
paralyzed, her consciousness reduced to no more than a tiny pinprick
—and she could not will it to expand, to raise itself, to force itself
back into her muscles, her flesh.

Her eyeballs rolled back in their sockets, her chest heaved with the
brutal effort of drawing breath; she could hear that ragged crazy
breath. How hideous, how sickening! . . . someone ran his hands
over her, far away at the surface of her body, muttering, pleading,
begging . . . whimpering . . . she struggled again, her body thrashed,
went wild, she had no control over it or over the ugly screaming or
the precarious pinpoint of light in her brain that was herself and that
he called to, *Yvonne! Yvonne! dear sweet Jesus, what*— He called to
her but her soul was paralyzed, was about to die away. His voice was
distant. An exclamation of disgust . . . pain . . . fury . . . and again
the pleading, the whimpering. . . . *I didn't mean—didn't know—I
am innocent*—

The voice went away, the hands and the breathing and the awkward insubstantial weight of his body, the struggle with him ceased,
yet still she could not wake, could not force herself out into her body,
still she heard her own hideous panting. The room had gone mad:
the walls and the ceiling and the mirrors and the lamp beside the
bed, the play of shadows and the stench of her own blood and someone's disembodied shriek of disgust and rage. *How horrible! How
filthy! I hate you! I hate you all!* But she could not seize upon these
words, she could not make them stay still so that, straining horribly,
she might draw herself out of the madness by concentrating on what
was not mad—she could not get hold of the moment, she was pulled
back, drawn back down, always down, into a swirling of shrieks,
flashes of light, sensations, grunts, pain that burst into stars, and that
terrible muscular struggle for breath—

She wanted to cry for help but could not speak. She could not
speak, could not speak, there were no words, no way to express them,
she shouted and mouthed Help, help me but there was no sound,

nothing, all was dull, blank, dead, echoless, she was running some-where in the mud and aware of herself screaming and aware of the futility of it—but her consciousness, her awareness of herself, was shrunken, reduced to a tiny area of light, she could not control it, could not force it to expand and take control again of her muscles, her flesh, her being. The walls of the room had turned to water. There was a terrible hissing noise everywhere. He had stopped shout-ing at her, had stopped grappling with her; she still felt the clumsy weight of his body but he was gone, there was no one, they might come for her now and she could not defend herself against them. A jumble of faces appeared but did not stay still long enough for her to see them. She felt, she did not see, her eyeballs rolled crazily, and something had happened to the inside of her mouth, and now she was arching her back as if to get free—to force herself free of—even if the effort broke her backbone, destroyed her—she threw herself from a great height and her bare arm smashed against the lamp, the telephone—

The carpet shimmered with them. It had come alive. At first there were patches, like patches of snow or crumpled newspaper, or shad-owy patches of debris; the carpet was a field, the inside of a ditch, there were small broken corpses, there were wet holes into which things were kicked, the carpet awakened and began to quiver and patches of it sprang into life, churning, seething, tiny white grubs—she screamed again but there was no sound—she screamed, screamed, but there was no sound. *Andrew,* she screamed—but it was a word, it could not force itself into being, *Stephen, Hugh*—no sound, no ut-terance— There was nothing but the hissing of the carpet and the wet, cold field, the grasses and the wind and the noise of the river. She did not scream *Mother!—Father!*—because there was no one there, even in her terror she knew there was no one there, the fields and ditches had sprung to life from them, and now could not be stopped: a galaxy of tiny secret writhing seething bits, deathly white, ferociously alive, utterly silent.

41

On December 29 she was released from the hospital. The detox-icating treatment had taken only four days; they kept her longer, for other purposes. They ran blood tests, metabolism tests, gave her

X rays, checked her for tumors and brain lesions, gave her an elec-
trocardiogram, even checked her teeth.

You are neither well nor ill, they told her.

Because she was Andrew's wife, no report was sent to the police.
She supposed that everyone knew, however. Albany was a small city.
When the first of the family called he listened for several minutes
and then interrupted to say: "I told you not to get involved with
him! I told you to avoid him! You said he was harmless and I *told*—"
But she was not going to bring charges against him, and she did not
care about the gossip, so what did it matter? It did not matter.

"No, you can't bring charges against him," she was told. "Even if
you wanted to—you really couldn't."

"It was my own fault," Yvonne said.

"You couldn't prove—"

"I couldn't prove anything."

"As it is, no one knows anything specific. You entered the hospital
for tests, for a checkup. . . ."

"I entered the hospital for tests, for a checkup," Yvonne said.

"We've talked to him and he denies everything, claims he wasn't
even in Albany, but I had the office check the hotels and he was
registered at the Washington. It's possible he didn't know what he
was doing or didn't know how strong the dosage was. . . . He's been
in trouble before, he's been in peculiar situations before, even in
London, and the family bailed him out. Once a young boy was involved . . . drugged . . . hidden away in Hugh's apartment. . . .
The best advice I can give you is to avoid him."

"I will," Yvonne said.

She returned to the apartment and returned to her work and made
arrangements for the hardwood floors to be sanded and polished
sometime in January, though it was quite likely she would be leaving
the apartment after all. The ambulance, the emergency crew, the
stomach pump . . . the furor and scandal . . . the shame of
confronting the other tenants in the foyer and in the elevators. . . .
"I wasn't insane and I wasn't dangerous and I don't take drugs, I
have never taken drugs," she told the owner of the building, "and I
drink very little . . . but I see your point of view and I should probably move out." They had diagnosed a powerful hallucinogenic drug
after all. It was on the medical report. It could not be denied.

"I should probably move out, yes," Yvonne said. "I should go
somewhere where I will be safe."

She knew she had had hallucinations. For the first time in her life, she had had hallucinations—what must be called a psychotic experience. She knew she had gone through a hellish period, hour after hour of it. But she did not care to remember anything specific. She did not care to explore that experience. It would be neither wise nor productive, and it would certainly be humiliating.

42

She returned to her work. She returned to a schedule of meetings, luncheons, receptions, parties, spaced economically throughout the week. She felt rested after the hospital; she believed herself to be in fairly good physical condition after all. She renewed her membership in a downtown club so she could use its swimming pool—she forced herself to go out at seven in the morning each weekday morning, knowing it was necessary, it would help her with her work, it was something Andrew would have approved of. At first she could swim only a few lengths of the pool, then as the days passed she worked it up to twelve, to eighteen, to twenty-five. She did not much care for the water, or for the vigorous effort required of her, but she was pleased, in a way, by the assertion of her will: the increasing number of lengths, the fact that she forced herself to go out on these frigid winter mornings.

She returned to her work; her anxiety that something might have happened to Andrew's papers was unfounded. If Hugh had gone into that room he hadn't disturbed anything. . . . The work was absorbing, challenging; it was always *there*; yet a subtle change had taken place in her, which she could not quite comprehend. It must have had something to do with the hallucinations, the terrible visions and . . . must have had something to do with . . . but she could not remember, could not comprehend. Now she cried more easily. She cried when there was no reason to cry. When she was informed of the fact that the FBI and Philadelphia police had arrested some members of a group charged with the kidnaping and murder of the young son of a Long Beach industrialist, and that it was highly possible that these people had also been involved in the assassination of her husband, she hung up wordlessly and began to cry. She did not know why afterward: she felt no relief, no sorrow, no anger, no emotion at all.

She learned from Eliot Stacey's wife that he had had an automobile accident on the New York State Thruway. He was in critical condition, had a concussion, a ruptured spleen. The wife told Yvonne this news in a tiny hateful girl's voice, and then asked Yvonne not to visit him at the hospital. "I want you to know what all this has done to him," the girl said, "but I don't want you anywhere around."

"He isn't dead," Yvonne said. "He almost died but he isn't. . . ."

"I want you to *know*," the girl said. "You and him, always you and him, *him*, always *him*—and after his death it was you—always you, talking about you—so miserable—it wasn't like Eliot to drink but he had been drinking when the accident took place—it *wasn't* his fault, the accident—I want you to know these things, to know how faithful he was, Andrew Petrie's good little puppy dog, but I don't want you anywhere around him and I don't want—"

"Yes," Yvonne said. "All right."

"He was lovesick for both of you and couldn't see how ridiculous it was—your horrible pompous husband!—getting people in trouble, like Eliot—getting the editors sued—your horrible nasty mean insane husband!—the two of you bossing Eliot around, bossing everyone around—and now—and now I *forbid* you to—"

"Yes," Yvonne said. "I understand."

The girl began to cry but Yvonne was unmoved. She hung up. She was on her way out somewhere, to the library. In the car she turned on the radio and heard about a child allegedly thrown from the tenth floor of a housing project in the Bronx, thrown out by his mother, and for a while she was unmoved by that too but finally, driving in midday traffic, she broke down and cried. There was no point to it, and very little emotion.

43

She ripped open the envelope though she knew whose handwriting was on it and she had been destroying his letters without reading them for some weeks now; she ripped open the envelope and a news clipping fell out—

HUGH PETRIE, PRIZE-WINNING CARICATURIST, DEAD BY HIS OWN HAND, IN MANHATTAN INTIMATES BLAME UNREQUITED LOVE

It was a joke, a fake headline, a fake page of the *New York Times.*
And his scrawl on the envelope—the baby, the murderous fool! She
remembered him pawing at her and she remembered his excited disgust and the whimpering and the terror and—and, afterward, the
hell of her own wastes and blood and madness, the sick, ungovernable madness she had had to endure for so many hours—

"*Unrequited love,*" she said aloud, in contempt.

44

"But there is nothing in writing," Fritz Sanderson said. "You have
nothing in writing, nothing specific . . . ?"

"That man is the executor of Andrew's estate but it applies only to
financial matters," Yvonne said. ". . . property, investments. . . . It
doesn't apply to his work. . . . He would have wanted me to. . . .
We worked together, the two of us worked together, I helped him
. . . I helped him in certain ways . . . I checked references for him, I
. . . sometimes I typed . . . I helped him proofread galleys and I
. . . I. . . . Everyone knows this," Yvonne said wildly. "They know
this at the magazine and they know this in the family, *everyone*
knows this, why are they doing this to me . . . ? Those people you
named are not . . . they are not experts . . . how could anyone be an
expert on Andrew . . . he didn't even care for that . . . that charlatan, that opportunist . . . he was contemptuous of. . . . He would
have preferred Eliot Stacey, at least! You know that very well! And
nothing matters except what Andrew would have wanted, it only
matters that his work be presented . . . that nothing gets lost. . . ."

"Dr. Reynolds has a letter Andrew sent him, evidently," Fritz said.
His tone was carefully neutral. ". . . some time ago, before he was
even divorced from Willa . . . Reynolds was president of the Elmer
Clay organization, and he'd done a favor for one of Andrew's associates by writing up a quite detailed review of a book . . . and they
claim he's an expert, he obviously is an expert, he's a professor at
Fordham, isn't he? It's a very delicate situation, Mrs. Petrie, because
obviously you don't want to antagonize. . . ."

"*Roderick Petrie!*" Yvonne said. She threw the document back
across the desk. "What does that man care about my husband's literary estate—that's ridiculous and I'm insulted they should think—it's
Harvey, I know very well it's Harvey behind this—"

"Well, I don't know that it necessarily is Harvey," Fritz said.

He was sympathetic, but really neutral. She had understood, from the way his receptionist greeted her, so very warmly, so intently, that they were going to betray her here. She had understood, by the half-lies her attorney was offering her, and by the open, direct, frank way he was speaking to her, that he had already betrayed her; he had made a deal with the family's attorney.

". . . and it's only an injunction, it's only an appeal to get the papers in a safe place, in a neutral place . . . until the time when . . . when other matters are settled. You don't have anything in writing, then, that names you specifically as the executor of . . . ?"

Yvonne pressed her hands against her face. It was happening, *it* was happening, something had opened in her and she was in danger . . . she was betrayed and helpless to stop the betrayal, she was going to surrender him to the rest of them, was going to deny him. . . . She sat for a while without speaking. Sanderson was embarrassed; she could hear him shifting his weight behind his desk; she dreaded him calling for his secretary as someone else had done, long ago . . . she could not remember who . . . another man, upset by her and fearful of her and disliking her. . . . She had been crying that morning, effortlessly, changing her clothes in the steam-heated locker room at the club, alone, hurrying, she had begun to cry for no reason and had not tried to stop, being alone, shivering even in the heat of that airless antiquated place, but the weeping had not cleansed her: had had no effect at all. It came and it went. It came, lasted five or ten minutes, and was over. Now, seated on the edge of a chair in someone's office, her hands against her hot, frightened face, she was not going to cry; she was in control; her mind skittered backward, away from the present moment, it tried to reconstruct, tried to fit together the pieces of . . . as if she were Andrew, as if she might appeal to him . . . *Why, why?* . . .

She failed. She was lost, utterly bewildered.

". . . the events of the past few weeks alone," Sanderson was saying sympathetically, ". . . that business about Andrew's brother . . . that alone . . . not to mention the schedule you've set yourself. . . . Why don't you go home, Yvonne, and we'll talk about this tomorrow? You can think it over and. . . ."

"I thought Harvey liked me," Yvonne said. "I thought there was a . . . a feeling. . . . He didn't like Andrew but sometimes he seemed to like me, we got along, I could respect him as . . . as a politician . . . he's much more clever and . . . and manipulative. . . . And he has said certain things to me, I don't think he was joking, he was . . . he seemed attracted to me," she said dully. ". . . I thought he liked me, I thought the Petries liked me, more or less . . . they had swung around to liking me as a person. . . ."

Sanderson laughed uneasily.

"But none of this has to do with persons," he said. "It's circumstances."

"Circumstances. . . ?" Yvonne asked blankly.

"Strictly speaking," the man said in his neutral, balanced voice, "there are no persons involved in this at all. There are only circumstances."

45

The Puritans were capable of extraordinary acts of courage, she read in Andrew's notes, *because they were so certain of themselves, of their own conscience. They were fanatics, murderers, and such energy is required to get things into motion . . . cross an immense body of water, create a "new" world . . . even kill a king and an archbishop, if necessary. Assassination is not murder, it must be distinguished from ordinary murder. . . . Their only problem was that they were deluded, as we know: they thought it was God directing them, but in fact it was history.*

She leafed through other notes, older, yellowed notes. She emptied one of the side drawers, which was stuffed with papers and note-cards and even a few letters, dating back to the early sixties. His voice, these fragments, these bits . . . she felt him brush near her, she felt his presence close about her . . . she knew no one could piece these bits together except her, she knew how he needed her, what terror he felt that she should betray him. . . .

In a cold northeast wind she was crossing the plaza by the Schumacher Building when the solution came to her: it came to her in Andrew's voice.

The Schumacher Building was no more than a year or two old. Made of black-toned glass and precast concrete and simulated marble, it was thirty-five stories high, with an observation deck and a tower that from a distance looked like a church spire. Its novelty as a structure was an entirely open ground floor—it rested upon four immense steel and marble pillars and other, smaller columns; one had to take an elevator even to the first floor. Yvonne saw that something had gone wrong, an area was roped off, there was broken glass and people were skirting it. . . . A tremendous wind tunnel, winds like small tornadoes rushed through the building, made it vibrate, shudder . . . something had gone wrong, the building was a failure, an experiment that could not withstand the winter winds. . . . It represented only itself, an architect's and an organization's monument to themselves, their brainless audacity, it was like the entire ninety-eight-acre Mall Andrew had so bitterly opposed. . . . She saw with an inescapable touch of satisfaction that an area was permanently roped off and tourists and office workers and others were skirting it, bent against the wind, their faces wisely closed against it.

She thought suddenly: I must move against them.

She thought: His enemies—even the family are enemies. I must move, I must not allow myself to be broken.

46

"I don't believe those people are guilty and I don't think anyone believes they are," Yvonne told Harvey. ". . . I don't *feel* they are guilty. Even if they had his name on a list. . . . The case will never hold up in court, I've read about it in detail, I've even talked with someone in the Civil Liberties Union in New York. . . . Yes, I'm serious. I might even go to visit them if I can in Philadelphia. Why not? What? . . . I certainly would. I don't believe they're guilty, there is no case at all against them, the FBI is harassing them. . . . I would just go to the newspaper, I would tell them what I think . . . that it's a political trick, it's a way of distracting . . . because the real murderers are. . . ."

". . . really insane, Yvonne," he was saying angrily. ". . . if you. . . ."

"It's true! It's true! . . . And even if it isn't true, it's possible, and anyone with any intelligence would see that it's more possible than . . . it's more likely, it's more . . . the public would prefer it. . . ."

"You're hysterical, Yvonne. I think I should hang up, to protect you against yourself."

". . . it's more plausible . . . it may or may not be true . . . Andrew himself wouldn't know, he couldn't have guessed at the viciousness in his own associates and in his family. . . . Since his death I've come across. . . ."

"The sentiment was for his son," Harvey said reluctantly. "The boy wanted to be named executor and he was putting pressure on us, he went to Roderick's office and presented his case, it has nothing to do, Yvonne, with you or with me, it isn't political, I really know nothing about it . . . you're entirely mistaken."

"His son? His son?"

". . . entirely mistaken, I'm surprised and disappointed and. . . . We'd better meet about this; when can we meet?"

". . . his son, that boy Michael?"

"An interesting child. Precocious. I'm not at liberty to say what the pressures were he put upon us, I don't know that much about it myself, I'm not in the inner circle, really. . . . I think we should meet, Yvonne. I think we should have a talk."

Yvonne was standing by the window. It was snowing and she could barely see Jefferson Park. Harvey's voice was mixed with the blizzard, suddenly unclear, confusing.

". . . that you should try to blackmail us . . . *me.* . . ."

She said nothing. She tried to picture Harvey and could not remember him. The broad frame, the tolerant, rather ironic expression . . . a habitual impatience. . . . That was Andrew, she was seeing Andrew in her mind's eye.

"*I* am innocent," Harvey said. "I'm innocent of even suspecting what you suspect. Andrew's enemies are my enemies and I want to get them too, but not every one of them is as guilty as the others . . . do you see? . . . and it's a question of gradations of guilt, complicity. . . . Not whoever actually pulled the trigger or even hired the gunman . . . or gunmen . . . though we will get them eventually . . . they certainly won't escape . . . but the interim must be handled cautiously, some very unfortunate and irreparable errors might be made, and lives might be endangered. I can't talk over the phone, Yvonne; I'll be up to see you as soon as possible."

"I don't want to see you," Yvonne said.

"I'm not going to blackmail *you,*" Harvey said. "I have nothing against you."

"You tried to blackmail me once. . . ."

"I did not: I simply informed you of the existence of. . . ."

"I knew about him, I had told Andrew before we were married, I kept no secrets from him. . . ."

"I didn't know that! . . . and in the meantime it seemed to me you might be vulnerable. You still might be vulnerable, if that party is still living, is still around. . . ."

"Of course he's still living," Yvonne said. "I think he's still living."

"If he were dead, we would know it," Harvey said.

". . . he was never a threat, he simply wanted to borrow some money from me," Yvonne said. ". . . nothing political at all . . . he read about me, about my marriage, he came to Albany and looked me up and was very direct and open . . . and there was nothing he could prove, there was no evidence . . . it didn't matter in the slightest to Andrew because he knew how he had canceled out everyone who came before him, he *knew* I didn't care for any other men. . . . He obliterated everyone else, he. . . . Everyone knew. . . ."

"Yes, I'm very jealous," Harvey said. "But I want to hear more."

"I don't want to see you," Yvonne said.

She watched the snowstorm. With one part of her mind she spoke easily, effortlessly, to the man at the other end of the line. He was in Washington. There was no image for him—only a dull fleshy blur. He might have been anyone at all. She might be saying anything to him; any arrangement of words.

". . . always difficult to talk about complex things . . . over the telephone," Harvey was saying.

"I had no lovers. I had no real lovers," Yvonne said. "I never . . . I didn't believe in . . . couldn't take them seriously. . . . I was only a girl, I had no feeling for them . . . Andrew understood . . . we understood each other . . . now you are dragging this up, you're trying to confuse me by. . . ."

"You brought it up yourself. You spoke of blackmail."

"Blackmail. . . ."

"*You* spoke of blackmail."

"It doesn't matter to me, what people think of me," she said quickly. "I know how they lie about me and how your precious family lies about me and it doesn't matter, not to *me*, the only thing that matters is Andrew's work. . . ."

"Andrew's dead, his work is dead," Harvey said. ". . . I could never read him anyway, even his speeches never made sense, it was just the feel of them . . . the rhythm, wasn't it? . . . but now that he's dead, that is dead too, and we'll continue this conversation, Yvonne, as soon as I can. . . ."

"I don't want to see you," Yvonne said shrilly.

47

Fritz Sanderson telephoned the next day. He told her that everything was fine; there had been a misunderstanding; the family had thought, erroneously, that the widow had been unfairly burdened . . . unfairly coerced into working with Andrew's papers . . . that she was breaking down under the strain and the responsibility and, according to a friend, would have been relieved and grateful if the task had been taken up by other people.

". . . a misunderstanding, evidently," he said. He sounded pleased. "The rumor can be traced back to Pamela Bausch, they say, and since the poor woman is so unstable herself. . . . Since she's been so despondent and unpredictable herself. . . ."

"Thank you," Yvonne said.

". . . confidential, of course, I wouldn't want her to know you were told . . . now that everything's cleared up and. . . ."

"Yes, thank you very much," Yvonne said.

48

He had been in San Diego and he flew back to join her in Albany, a day early. She kept his return secret; they would have felt obliged to attend a family dinner that weekend otherwise.

The conference had gone well, he told her. Remarkably well. His ideas about the income tax—the abolishment of it as it now stood— and his ideas about social welfare and civil liberties had been respectfully received though not understood, and of course not taken seriously—but he wanted to leave early, something had gone out of the conference for him, he had had a disturbing dream and wondered if he might tell it to her?—though it was not in their habit to tell each other their dreams. He wondered if they might have a drink, if he could talk about his dream, which was so disturbing and so very real, more real to him than the conference itself—?

. . . *a city half submerged in the sea . . . the waves tepid and flattened. . . . hardly more than ripples. An empty city, a deserted city . . . some of the buildings vaguely familiar, like the skyline from the apartment here or from certain angles in New York. . . . But not recognizable, ultimately. A city submerged in the sea without any defenses or protestations . . . any evidence of life. I was wading along a street and I found a small animal in the water, but it was an infant, it turned into an infant . . . at first I thought it was drowned but it came to life and I was very excited and frightened because the water was thigh-high now and the waves were getting rougher, there was the danger of drowning . . . I didn't want the baby to slip out of my hands and be swept away. . . . I can't convey to you, Yvonne, the feeling of this dream! . . . so much more real, so much more compelling, than San Diego and the people at the conference and myself, even, in that context! . . . so painfully real. I was entrusted with the infant and it was my responsibility to take it somewhere . . . I had to wade along one of the streets . . . the waves were getting higher, rougher . . . my legs were almost knocked out from under me . . . the city was entirely deserted but I knew that people had lived there just recently, now I was the only living person, it was my responsibility to keep the baby from drowning and it was a terrible responsibility . . . I was frightened . . . I was talking to the baby, singing to it, trying to comfort it . . . the waves were sweeping toward me . . . I knew that in another minute I would be knocked over, I would fall into the water, the baby would be swept away. . . .*

After he told her the dream they sat for a while in silence. Andrew, rather emotional during the recitation, was now uneasy, embarrassed; he went to get himself another drink.

Yvonne could think of nothing to say. She too was embarrassed.

They glanced at each other. His eyes were sea-green, sea-gray. He was a remarkably attractive man, his manner always courtly, with a pleasing, subtle irony that showed in his mouth, in his habitual smile. At this time they had been married two years and Yvonne had never seen him poorly groomed; she had heard him speak, occasionally, with anger and contempt and passion, but she had never heard him speak like this, in so hesitant a manner. There was something meager and shameful about him—something that unnerved her. She could think of nothing to say. Her mind went blank. Where were the words one might employ, where were the phrases one might contrive? . . . she could not speak to him, a stranger thigh-high in the waters of a dream, clutching a dream-infant . . . she could not recognize this person, could not speak to him across such a distance.

After a while Yvonne said, "Was the conference interesting . . . ?"

49

He sent her an inexpensive rosary, shiny black beads that looked like roaches, a crucifix of lightweight metal, probably tin, stamped out nearly flat. It had been sent from New York, it must have been another of Hugh's jokes; she had opened it without thinking, absent-minded. It must have been another of his jokes. Enclosed was a typed note. She read it swiftly, with a dreading eagerness, thinking it was only another of Hugh's jokes and not to be taken seriously.

Death, the true goal of our existence, the best friend of mankind. . . . The image of it does not frighten me, but soothes and calms me. For me everything is cold; as cold as ice.

50

She ran along the muddy lane. This was not her world: she did not belong here. Other people owned it, his family owned it, very subtly they hated her and would someday expel her, but now she was the one who was running along the muddy lane, her arms at her sides like an older woman, panting, calling his name in so faint a voice that of course he could not hear.

The door to the cabin was ajar. It was a real cabin, made of logs. Yet it was a playhouse, a playhouse for adults. No one used it now but Andrew, who had retreated to this playhouse, was hiding from her and from the others, sitting every day at a makeshift desk, alone, absorbed, indifferent to everything but his work. The world hung loosely to the side, connected by fibers, by sinews that might break; it did not matter, it was not very real, its gravity was not to be taken seriously.

Andrew? she called.

The door was ajar. She pushed it open. There was the small table, there the aluminum lamp, the portable typewriter, the piles of papers—there was the uncomfortable hard-back chair he used— Andrew? Andrew?

He was standing against the opposite wall, crouched slightly, his arms folded. He was standing in a narrow shadowed recess, between two sets of bunk beds.

Andrew?

His face rigid, his lips drawn back from his teeth in a strange ironic grin. . . .

Andrew, what will happen? Andrew? She was terrified now, seeing him, knowing he would refuse to speak to her. At times he refused to speak to her. Andrew, what will happen? What has happened?

He grinned at her. There was something puckish, sardonic, zestful in his grin. *Why do you people torment me?* he said.

51

Harvey took her to lunch in a place with Corinthian columns and wine-dark velvet drapes and statues of partly clad men with swords, stark white. The carpet was thick and not very clean. The waiters were black men in beautifully decorated white-and-blue uniforms; their voices were exquisitely modulated, velvet-soft. Yvonne, not feeling herself that day, had difficulty understanding their waiter. Her head felt stuffed, her eyes watery. Chemicals from the pool had gotten into her nose, her eyes, into her bloodstream.

Harvey's red-blond hair had been styled recently; one lock fell across his left temple. He was older, thicker, more stubborn than she recalled. He broke his hard-crusted roll and buttered it in two or three brusque, competent swipes, all the while talking to her about the misunderstanding, the matter of Andrew's literary estate, his own baffled innocence, Yvonne's bravery and selflessness and audacity. She asked him to repeat what he had said. ". . . your audacity," he said.

His gaze, set in that large-boned, amiable face, was always clear: it told her nothing.

". . . suicidal tendencies," he said.

He hoped to be Governor of the state in another six years. It was quite possible, wasn't it? . . . everyone believed it was quite possible.

"As well me as anyone," he said, almost gloomily.

"Where will you get the money," Yvonne asked.

He seemed not to hear her. He broke another roll and tiny bits of crust flew onto the tablecloth and into his lap.

". . . important thing, that he did not die in vain . . . his ideas
. . . basic Americanism . . . resurrected, so to speak, in me. As well
me as another. In life we didn't get along. I mean—in his lifetime we
didn't get along. There was something about him, as you know, that
made it difficult to love him—but now that isn't necessary, now we're
relieved of that challenge. I'm not a politician either, Yvonne. None
of us are. I am really a political theorist, an idealist. Politics! There is
no such thing. We are all idealists. Andrew was a messiah with
brains and though I don't pretend to be on his level, I too am an intellectual; I too can play the idea-game. . . . Do you think of me as
a politician? You're wrong. You're all wrong. Rockefeller appropriated the state to make it safe for democracy and education and
building programs and highways, he was an idealist, the 'little FBI'
we have here is for the good of the people, and before your time,
dear, the Governor of this state created his image as prosecutor and
judge and executioner, he was relentless, merciless, he found graft
and corruption and racketeering everywhere—even in the chicken
business," Harvey said fondly, smiling, "even in—in baked goods!
Seek and ye shall find. Seek and ye shall be found out. Andrew too
wanted to be relentless and merciless, but they didn't let him. They
cut him off in his prime. Before his prime. He wouldn't necessarily
have been defeated for a second term when he was a senator—he
stepped down because he was confused about his idealism, about
being a messiah, he *thought* that idealism meant something it
doesn't mean; and now, as you know, he's dead."

Yvonne could not follow him. He spoke freely, smiling, and yet
there was an odd vacant neutrality to him; he sat there in his
cushioned high-backed chair, a handsomely dressed man of middle
age, distinguishable from the others in the club mainly by his broad,
tolerant manner, his extraordinary self-assurance, and that sweetly-
mocking smile. Since Andrew's death he had begun to imitate him in
small ways. He used his hands more gracefully. Yvonne could see
that his nails had been manicured, polished with clear polish. He
gave off an odor of shaving lotion and expensive soap.

"I may reemphasize the liberalism inherent in the Petrie mental-
ity," Harvey said. ". . . It was a Petrie, after all, a spinster lady, who
helped organize the Society for the Prevention of Cruelty to Children, back in the eighteen-eighties; and it was one of *our* people who
got a bill through to ban child labor. I'm neither for nor against
these things. There's much to be said on both sides—on all sides.
However, I may reemphasize latent dreams and ideals. I may do

that. I take very seriously the words of wisdom passed on to us by one of our distinguished Southern statesmen: *Fascism can return, provided it calls itself anti-fascism.* Huey Long said that. I never met Huey Long. He too was an idealist, he too was assassinated. —Where will I get the money? Did you ask where will I get the money?"

He spread his fingers wide. His fingernails gleamed.

"Where do any of us ever get any money?" he said.

Yvonne shook her head slowly. Her eyes filled with tears. In this pleasantly crowded place with the high, ornate ceilings and the immaculate white tablecloths and the weighty, old-fashioned silverware, she could not feel her husband's presence; she could not summon his voice, which would have been raised in immediate witty opposition to this voice, overpowering it, quietly, skillfully.

". . . *fascism!*" Yvonne whispered. "That's obscene."

"Anti-fascism, I said. Anyway the names have all been changed, the terminology is completely different; each decade is a new clean slate; there are no history books now, only weekly news-magazines. As for money, Yvonne, my wife's family has money. Your husband's family has money. *You* have money—or will. Won't you? Even if the court resents you it won't find completely against you, since it doesn't particularly like the rest of us either—it's a Democrats' brewery-and-construction setup. Yes, you'll have money. Even you don't know how much. We'll continue to be friends, we'll become closer friends, and you can do your share in helping me—Irene won't suspect anything, she's a remarkably unimaginative woman."

"But there's nothing to suspect," Yvonne said irritably. "You've always acted as if there were something between us . . . you smile at me, you leer, you allude to things I don't understand, the very first time we met you squeezed my hand and. . . ."

"I may have been a little high," Harvey said. He seemed offended. ". . . may have been carried away by your beauty, by the scent you give off. . . ."

"There's nothing to suspect and there won't be any sharing," Yvonne said. "I intend to use his money as he would have wanted it used—there's going to be a scholar incentive program in his name, and I hope to set up a better arrangement for the magazine, and—"

"Your problem, Yvonne, is that you continually mistake yourself for someone of value," Harvey said. "Of course this is a problem most human beings have . . . like my constituency . . . like the women in our family. It is only your circumstance that gives you value, Yvonne, and the quality of your circumstance can change. In which case you might need a friend: and at the moment you haven't a friend. *He* has a few friends still, and as his wife you're still involved, but that won't last. When I spoke of your role in sharing my future I meant that you would have an emotional and supportive part . . . maybe even ideological . . . though money would not contaminate our relationship."

"Andrew didn't approve of you," Yvonne said tonelessly. She had been hurt by his remark about value and circumstance. She had not really heard the rest of his statement. "He didn't think you were serious . . . he didn't think you were really a leader. . . ."

"*He* was a leader," Harvey said, "wasn't he? A supreme leader. No followers—only a few demented disciples—and at the end no one at all. Yes, *he* was a leader, he did beautifully." He had finished his lunch and was fussing now with his napkin. There was an air of tension between them; Harvey's small tight smile flicked on and off. "There's a possibility, of course, that I won't have a future. That should please you and him both."

"What do you mean?"

He shrugged his shoulders. Something shifted in his expression, he looked now sly, secretive.

"What does anyone mean, in speaking of the future?"

"A future in politics or—?"

"A future. A future on this earth, as a man, in my blood and bones and flesh—in my living body. That sort of thing," he said flippantly. "A future in the sense in which Andrew no longer has a future, despite his genius and your devotion. . . . I'm only joking."

"No one has threatened your life, have they?"

"Why would anyone bother to threaten my life," Harvey said. He tossed the napkin down. He stared at her, frankly and rudely.

52

The cabin smells of damp, dust, cobwebs. It is only a single room, with a fireplace on one side and bunk beds on the other. The beds have not been used for some time, probably for years. They seem to be made up with care—boys' bedspreads, navy blue, with designs of battleships and anchors. There are no sheets or blankets beneath the spreads, however, nor are there pillowcases on the yellowed foam-rubber pillows. The fireplace, made of stone, is attractive, but the

chimney is clogged and has not been used for years. There is a single
rug on the uneven floor, a large braided oval rug, quite dirty. The
floorboards do not fit properly, the four small windows do not give
much light, yet he prefers to work here; he prefers it to any other
place.

He brought his own desk lamp and a small transistor radio so he
could listen to the news occasionally, and his portable typewriter
with its badly worn ribbon, and a small clock in its leather traveling
case, though he has a wristwatch; he props the clock up on the mantel where he can see it whenever he glances around. Time, time! . . .
he likes to hear it clicking and whining and whirring, so that its terrible passage will not be too surprising. He brought a dictaphone too
but he never uses it. And the papers: the mammoth collection of
papers. Sharpened pencils, ballpoint pens in several colors of ink,
fast-drying marker pens, an eraser, a pencil sharpener, a yellow note-
pad and a stack of typewriter paper and a newly published dictionary, still in its glossy black jacket. Outside is the river, shallow and
noisy, inside is a small quiet kingdom where the clock ticks
peacefully and everything is being brought into order, brought into
completion and perfection.

53

Hugh was in a small private hospital in Greenwich Village, not far
from Washington Square. But when Yvonne got to the brownstone
building she could not force herself to enter. She stood at the top of
the steps and could not enter. After a while someone hurried up
the steps, whistling, started inside, paused, held the door open for
her. "Going in?" he said. Yvonne stared white-faced at the man: but
he was no one she knew. He was not one of the family. He was no
one she knew.

"No thank you," she said.

Her lips were dry. It was still winter: mid-February. Very little had
changed.

*Ethics, Eugenics, and Democracy: The Twelfth Annual Forum
of the Braley T. Yaeger Institute for the Analysis of Humanistic
Values in the Contemporary World.* She leafed hurriedly through
the glossy brochure, which was one hundred and fifty pages long.
Photographs of prominent politicians, thinkers, a few artists—several

full-page photographs of the Yaeger Institute's grounds in Virginia—detailed schedules and programs for the four-day conference—even a little map showing the location of the tennis courts and the golf course and the indoor swimming pool. The conference was to be larger than she had anticipated—there were at least twelve seminars in addition to her own, and three evening lectures. Her seminar was called "Tradition and the Future: Our Ongoing Crisis" and there were more people involved than she would have liked: a population biologist from Princeton, a congressman from Oklahoma who was a member of the House Judiciary Committee, the chairman of the board of Anaheim Mutual Insurance Company, Dr. Maynard Wall of the World Medical Council, a woman from the Corporation for National Cable Television and the Performing Arts, and a special assistant to the general counsel of the National League of Cities and U.S. Conference of Mayors.

The conference was scheduled for the first week of April. By then she hoped to have moved to another, smaller apartment, sublet from a friend of Adrienne Greason's who was going to Europe for a year. She hoped to have recovered her health, her sense of well-being; it was even possible that the people involved in the assassination would be definitely found. At the moment, an organization known as the "Prince Kropotkin Study Group" was under suspicion; they had planned but failed the "shame killing" of a black congressman from Yonkers, and it was believed they had been behind a series of bombings in New York. One of the group's members was a light-skinned black man with degrees from Harvard and Oxford, who had given an interview from his hospital bed—he had suffered broken ribs and some damage to his kidneys as a result of resisting arrest—and in the interview, broadcast over national television, he had claimed responsibility for the Petrie killing. Yvonne had watched the tape several times, fascinated by the young man's thick smirking lips and his bushy hair and his clipped, fastidious accent. For some reason, however, she thought he was a liar.

"You can thank me any way you like," Harvey said.

She took the letter out of the envelope. It was addressed to her. *Dearest Yvonne!* Scrawls in Hugh's hand, fifteen or twenty lines of scrawled words, with many X'd out parts, ink blots, and *Love, love, love* at the very bottom of the page.

"Read it," Harvey said. "It isn't obscene. It's touching. Frankly I was moved by it. . . . I didn't think my cousin Hugh was so serious, so thoughtful. . . . Did you? He must have loved you very much."

Yvonne tried to read the letter, but could not. She folded it and
slid it back in the envelope. "He didn't love me," she pleaded. "He
didn't even know me."

"He loved you and that letter is proof," Harvey said flatly. "You
can thank God I retrieved it for you. *Dearest Yvonne! Love love
love!* . . . It's possible word has gotten out unofficially, but I think
you're in the clear and nobody knows and that's the only damaging
thing in his apartment, damaging to us, I mean. Damaging to you.
—The gun was Willa Fergus's, what do you think of that! She claims
he stole it from her."

"Gun . . . ? Willa Fergus . . . ?"

"Wake up, Yvonne, you look as if you're in a trance! . . . you're
turning blue, are you cold? There's no chance the poor bastard will
return to bother you; he's blind and almost entirely paralyzed
and. . . ."

"He didn't love me," Yvonne said in her rapid, light voice. She
had thrust the envelope in her coat pocket, folding it clumsily. "He
didn't know me. We didn't know each other. We didn't . . . we
never . . . we never. . . ."

"You can thank me any way you like," Harvey said.

54

Dearest Yvonne! I must know what you know—was he dead
when you found him or in the throes of death & did he
speak to you, did he SPEAK to you? My God how I want
you & cringe before you & realize I do not deserve you as
others might its true that I *love* you as a normal man loves a
woman but I would be willing to admit that there is something else there is your *secret closeness* to him & your knowledge
of him I crave I am dying to know I cant bear it here without
you & without knowing all that you know how & why he
died & when it must happen again it isn't justice any of us
want Yvonne but our *sanity* I cant live without that & it is
being taken from me & only you can restore it but you have
turned against me & betrayed me like the others & laugh & jeer
at me but still I wld. come to you if you beckoned I am
not afraid of you

                              Love   Love   Love
                                                 Hugh

55

There was an informal but large gathering to celebrate the passage of a certain bill, and one of Andrew's old acquaintances, a state senator from a rural district in Alleghany, slipped his weighty arm around Yvonne's shoulders and held her there for ten minutes while he told a story that concerned himself and his twin brother, who had died several decades ago in France, in the Normandy invasion; the senator had been in a hospital in Hawaii at the time of his twin brother's death but he had felt the death, had felt the explosion that blew off his brother's legs, he had *gone over* to the other side with his brother but had returned and now, he told Yvonne in a coarse, broken voice, "I ask that boy's advice on every move of my life, I mean *every* move, I don't get up in the morning without him there and I don't make a decision, not even a minor decision, without his approval, and I offer up to him my successes—you've got to, you know; you've *got to*. The dead are always near."

"Yes," Yvonne said. "I know."

Mrs. Van Horne, Andrew's great-aunt, her perfect white hair arranged in a thick, elaborate bun, held in her two hands a paperweight of clear crystal with a gigantic yellow butterfly on a leaf embalmed in it, explaining that it was from Peru, a gift of her husband's associates there. She was helping to organize a conference on education to be held at the state university here in the city, in May, and she wanted Yvonne to help her staff the panels and arrange for a luncheon speaker and do a little publicity, a television interview or two, an interview with the magazine *Schools*. "Andrew had already indicated his support," she said; "we are approaching a crisis situation and private foundations must meet such problems head-on, or *they* will take all our freedoms from us, we must govern our own lives and *we* and not the federal government must lead . . . if we must give our money away *we* must give it, *we* must be the donors, and not. . . ."

"Yes," Yvonne said.

"It's so obvious isn't it!" the old woman said.

The Smith-Harrison bill, she was told, would require six to eight months of intense work, contacting sympathetic legislators, courting the unsympathetic, organizing citizens' volunteer committees throughout the state. They would be delighted to have her. She would have to travel, especially to Western New York and the Catskill area where there were sympathetic politicians who were, unfortunately, conservative in an embarrassingly anachronistic way, and she would have to meet with newspaper editors and managers of television and radio stations. She would find it tiring at times and frustrating at times but also exhilarating. There was nothing like it, she was told. She would make many friends, especially with the citizens' committees, whose members would be delighted to meet her and flattered to work with her. There was nothing like it, nothing quite like it. So much to do! So many weeks of activity! And then, when the bill was passed—as it would be passed—what exhilaration, what a sense of accomplishment!

Harvey said: "For Christ's sake why do you let those people use you?"

Yvonne said: "I want to be of use."

Harvey said, disgusted: "There are other ways, there are more pleasurable ways."

She worked, still, on the manuscript. It was not one but several manuscripts—three separate but related books.

She worked, she worked every day from about eight-thirty, when she returned from swimming, to noon. If she had no luncheon engagement, she took only a few minutes for lunch—sometimes ate it at the desk—and returned to work. She had brought a table in from the living room, needing more space for the papers.

At times she felt quite pleased—almost euphoric. She could do anything, nearly. She could accomplish anything. His presence was abstract but always close, comforting. When she read aloud from his papers, she heard his voice behind hers, distinctly. When she stopped, she could hear the echo.

"Individual rights are not to be thwarted by the State. . . . People *are* a great beast and must be governed. . . . An organization of the world's true leaders should be created. . . . Abortion is always and forever immoral and illegal. . . . World government is world tyranny. . . . The beast must not be allowed to continue to breed. . . . The Age of Reason has not yet dawned. . . . The average man is gifted with common sense and knows his enemies on sight. . . . The State is a great hideous machine. . . . The average man is not uneducated, merely stupid. . . . 'Intellectuals' discover the same pseudotruths every twenty or thirty years, and go mad. . . . The working man is slave to the non-working masses. . . . Society will buckle, people will never stand for. . . . The Age of Reason has come and gone. . . . Post-civilization worships Narcissus. . . . Taxation is tyranny. . . . Today's national leaders should be arrested for treason. . . . World government is our only salvation: it is the future itself. . . . The average voter will never stand for, will never condone; society itself will buckle inward, decaying at the top and then collapsing suddenly. . . . Church and State should never have been separated. . . . You tell me every man has a soul to save? I tell you, not one man in a thousand has even a soul to lose. . . . Politics is the highest calling. . . . The ruler is always treasonous. . . . Emotion has no place, superstition no place. . . . Common sense. . . . One-half of one percent of the population: must greet one another, must recognize kinship, must organize. . . . The future is our salvation. . . . The future is a great beast. . . . Individual rights are not to be thwarted by the State. . . . The beast must not be allowed to continue to breed. . . . Politics is the salvation of the contemplative soul; we are fulfilled only in action. . . . Everything not you is the beast. . . . The ruler is humble, the ruler is without ego. . . . Socrates, our first master: *I have nothing to do with the trees of the field, I have only to do with the man of the city.* Hence civilized. Hence redeemed. . . . The individual's rights are sacred. . . . The individual, strictly speaking, does not exist. . . . We are entering a supreme Age of Politics. . . . The politician is extinct. . . . The politician, upon examination, does not exist. . . . The beast is an anachronism but is no less cunning. . . . The beast is sacred. . . . The beast must not be allowed. . . . Who is the savior, who will be broken and humiliated and sacrificed *in saecula saeculorum?* . . . One truth will do for us all; truth cannot be broken down. . . . Everything not you is redeemed. . . . The State is contrary to nature and therefore higher than nature. . . . We all serve the *politeia.* . . . We are humble. . . . We are divine. . . . We are servants of the true religion. . . . Strictly speaking, we do not exist."

56

"I want to be of use," Yvonne said aloud.

The apartment was utterly silent. The clocks had stopped ticking —had not been rewound since her hospitalization.

57

Van Schuyler Boulevard, north of the city, running near to the river. The funeral home of last June: she drove past without flinching. Other mansions, renovated coach houses, brick ruins, razed buildings, a stretch of new single-story homes, and then the nursing home, in an old gabled Victorian house like a fortress. Trees not yet in leaf. Rows of windows, high and narrow, granite walls streaked with damp, reminding her curiously of Hugh's face, the face of his previous self . . .

She drove past the nursing home and intended to circle the block. But on a new, narrow street called Morning Glory Crescent she came to a cul-de-sac; she sat in the car with the motor running, smoking a cigarette. She had not smoked for years, since Pittsburgh. Now she was smoking again, occasionally. She could not remember having begun the habit and often could not remember having lit a cigarette; it was a dull, small surprise to discover a package of cigarettes in her possession.

It was eleven-thirty in the morning of a sharply sunny day in March. Fingers of snow remained, not yet melted, darkly glowing against the browns and greens of the earth. The sky was light, the clouds distant and insubstantial, there was an air of spring—a false air, she knew, but it was dramatic, invigorating. She opened the car window a few inches. She smoked her cigarette.

She conceived of herself as a woman in good health. She had gained back a few pounds, though her collar bone showed through her pale skin and there were odd knobs of bones at her wrists, and her knuckles seemed enlarged, as if belonging to someone else. Her cheeks were less hollow, her eyes less shadowed. She did no more than glance at her reflection, checking to see if she was minimally acceptable—checking to see if she was there—and at times she could confront her image only by slitting her eyes and gazing through her eyelashes, so that the reflection was out of focus. Still, she was in good health now. She could swim between thirty-five and forty lengths of the pool, she slept fairly well, was not quite so drowsy during the day; her appointment book was as filled as she might wish, and her work with Andrew's papers was progressing. It went slowly but it was always, always progressing. She hoped to have one of his unpublished essays ready in a week or two . . . several editors were interested . . . the new editor-in-chief of *Discourses* was a mediocrity whom Andrew had humored for years and whose ascendency to power would have amused and horrified him, so she would decidedly not send the essay there. She was in excellent health mentally as well as physically: her mind worked as well as ever, perhaps better. There were times when she felt she could do nearly anything! . . . anything.

It was ten minutes to twelve. They would be serving lunch at the nursing home. Perhaps she would not visit him after all today. No one had asked her to visit him. No one spoke to her about him. The Petries did not talk with her often now, except about political or financial matters. And she had disappointed Mrs. Van Horne, evidently angered the old woman, by writing a lengthy apology explaining why she had to decline the honor of working with her, after all . . . had meant only to be polite . . . had meant only. . . . Time passed so effortlessly, so cruelly! . . . she had finished one cigarette and lit another and now it was four minutes to twelve and. . . .

She was not guilty. No charges had been brought against her. They were allowing her absolute freedom—it seemed absolute in time as well as in space. She could travel anywhere, she could do anything. They were observing her, but she had absolute freedom. It was not clear whether they were judging her. Hugh had been judged: but she had nothing to do with Hugh.

She was not guilty, except of knowing ahead of time that he would die. But perhaps others had known and were equally guilty. Perhaps he had known, himself . . . ? He gave her no answer, no answer. She could not always hear him. He wanted her to visit the nursing home, wanted her to see his brother or what remained of him; the paralysis was so complete that Hugh had to be kept alive by an iron lung, unable otherwise to breathe, and they said he was blind and deaf and could not speak except in weird unintelligible moans. . . . Andrew wanted her to visit Hugh. She believed he did. But it was not certain. . . . Nor was it certain that he believed her guilty, though others did. In life he had never been influenced by others; if anything, he had recoiled violently against the thinking of others. He did not necessarily believe her guilty. He loved her still, as he had loved her in life and as she had loved him in life: realistically, dispassionately, with a sense of humor and irony, an awareness of certain limitations. . . . He did not believe her guilty, she was convinced of that suddenly. He understood.

She left Morning Glory Crescent and drove out to the cemetery.

58

Not that day, but another. Another prematurely balmy day in March. At the cemetery where she had driven, not exactly knowing where she would drive, having dimly in mind the new library at the state university, there at the cemetery she had seen the concluding minutes of another funeral, another burial a hundred yards or so from Andrew's grave. . . . A dozen mourners, a subdued grouping, the usual dark clothing and dark shadowed eyes and glances of shame and humiliation and impatience and anger, from one man especially, walking to his car ahead of the others, his gaze severe, blue-gray, razorish, his big-boned face rather like Harvey Petrie's . . . as he walked heavily along the graveled path and passed Yvonne he raised his eyes to hers, unsmiling, subtly irritated, rude. She stared at him levelly. She did not look away. He too was a mourner but he detested the role—was hurrying away, had perhaps even quarreled with someone at the graveside. She took his bold masculine assessment of her without flinching, as if she too were capable of assessing herself, detached and unemotional, critical, but determined all the same to fulfill herself as circumstances directed.

"I want to be of use," she whispered.

She was a point in time, was she not? . . . a pinpoint, the mere tip of a needle . . . the point at which certain circumstances touched. At moments this knowledge was exceptionally clear so that her head snapped back with the force of the revelation, and she felt she would faint, would cry out, astonished—but at other times it was not clear and she could not comprehend the revelation or feel that certainty or, in fact, any certainty at all. There was Andrew, there was his work. There was the fact of her widowhood. The circumstances were incontestable; her own existence, so problematic, was not an issue. *I don't much care for individual women any longer,* Harvey Petrie had said coarsely, smiling his mock-genial smile, *but there are certain circumstances that interest me very much. . . .* How Andrew had disliked him! He had disliked the man's values, the man's intelligence, quite apart from disliking him personally; the force of his emotion came to her as she stood by the grave, she could almost feel the revulsion, the small leap of hate.

59

Because she was very busy she was using the answering service once again. One day, checking the calls that had come in, she saw the name L. *Wunsch.* She could not remember this name. *Wunsch?* She knew it was a man, a man's name, but she could not remember the first name. . . . Then it came back to her, that day at the school for handicapped children, her husband's cousin Hannah and the black woman who was principal of the school and one or two other black teachers, and Wunsch, eyeing her so insolently, with such an air of *knowing* her, while the others chatted as people always chat in such situations, lightly brushing against profound issues but drifting away into banalities, always into conversational banalities; she remembered her uneasiness, her distress, could not quite remember why, had it disappointed her that Hannah, a woman her age, a woman with whom, conceivably, hopefully, she might have been friends, was subtly in opposition to her? . . . had possibly even invited Yvonne, the wife of Andrew Petrie, to visit the school in order to display her connection with these people and at the same time to draw away, to define herself as critical, unsympathetic, enlightened? . . . it must have been a terrible, bitter disappointment, since she remembered it after nearly a year had passed.

But *Wunsch,* what had he to do with it? A trivial enemy, an enemy Andrew would have scorned to consider. *Wunsch,* L. *Wunsch.* She had heard the name a while back, again in connection with Hannah . . . they were engaged, maybe? . . . that must have been it.

Hannah had not telephoned her once; but she had not expected her to call. Wunsch was between them. She smiled, thinking

obliquely of him, remembering him blundering into the closet, opening the closet door . . . Wunsch or someone, someone else . . . yes,
she remembered obliquely without real interest. There were circumstances, there were random events. Some were strung together and
others were loose, like beads without a thread, and these did not
matter. At any rate, the contest had been between her and Hannah;
more specifically, between her and Andrew, and Hannah.

She did not return his call. There were several other calls, far more
important, which she had to attend to.

60

Everything ends at the river, everything runs down to the riverbank, to the cabin on the river. The mind, loosed and exuberant and
free, drifts at first toward the river and then, as if sucked by invisible
currents of air, or by the motion of the river itself, begins to speed,
always accelerating, accelerating. At first it drifts and then it begins
to move with more direction, fiercely, helplessly. Everything ends
there, everything yearns for that place and for the ceaseless noise of
the water, part music, part inaudible conversation, part chaotic din.

61

Immediately behind the cabin, on a hillside, is a beech wood.
Behind that and stretching out, fanwise, is a wood of ashes where
old paths are overgrown and walking is difficult. There are innumerable seedlings, shrubs, small trees, wild rose. There are fallen and
decayed tree trunks, there are unaccountable holes, shallow pits, occasionally rusted beer cans or empty soft-drink bottles. There is a
lane leading from the farmhouse to the river, but it is muddy in
springtime, impassable except by foot. Many people have walked on
it though the land is privately owned, though there are No Trespassing signs posted on trees . . . dozens and perhaps hundreds of people
. . . overlapping footprints, a crowd of footprints, a chaos. Fisher-
men from the area. Hunters. Some are probably children. Such a
tide, such a rush of footprints . . . and there are as many, perhaps
even more, leading along the riverbank itself, leading from the open

area surrounding the cabin to a narrow country road a half mile away.

Willow trees grow along the river. Poplars. A jungle-like thicket of anonymous bushes, small trees. There are lilac bushes gone wild, grown too tall, ugly, unpruned for many years. There are unpruned forsythia bushes and here and there more wild rose, climbing rose, with tiny anemic buds and thorns that catch on one's clothing.

That day, the day of his death, she had walked in another direction, restless, bareheaded, her hair swinging loose. She had found a hoe in one of the sheds and had tried to work in the old garden right behind the house, had seen in the flowerbeds rosebushes trapped and stunted by weeds and briars, had wanted with an uncharacteristic vexation to free them, to dig them free, but working with her bare hands was impractical, the briars and weeds hopeless; she hated labor of this sort, hated the quixotic sentimentality of it, and the waste of time, what did it matter that the garden was ruined, that the Petries had abandoned this place because they owned other places, had better things to do, what did it matter, any effort of hers. . . . She was impatient to leave; she hated the country, it bored her, she hated her husband here because he was not himself, his manner was that of another man, an older, distracted man, he was absent from her, always absent, as if in a trance, his thoughts always on what he was writing . . . his thoughts always circling on that work . . . always concentrated on . . .

She threw down the hoe. A tiny blister had begun on her right hand. She threw down the hoe, she whimpered aloud in vexation and impatience and dread. *Something will happen to us,* she thought. It came to her from the outside, impersonal and disembodied. She threw down the hoe, the handle swung over into the choked flowerbed, she left the garden and the vicinity of the house and walked out the front, through the old pasture, rubbing her sore hands together. She walked quickly, as always, not really aware of her surroundings. Her mind raced. It was June: in two weeks it would be summer by the calendar, but here it was still cold, a sluggish chill spring in the mountains. She wore jeans, a soiled sweater, and boots. She was bareheaded. His wife. His widow. *Something will happen,* she thought. And then, defiantly: *Nothing will happen.*

62

Shortly after midday on April 6, in a suite on the top floor of a hotel on Wisconsin Avenue, Washington, D.C., Yvonne submitted to Harvey Petrie's clumsy embrace; not only submitted—wisely, since he seemed frantic and angry and distracted—but embraced him in turn. The room was gold and white, the mirrors on all walls glared prettily, as if through layers of frost, there was the occasional sound of air-hammers from the street twenty floors below but otherwise an intense moody overheated silence, punctuated only by Harvey's mutterings and labored breaths. Yvonne thought: *Nothing will happen.*

The Yaeger Institute was housed in five octagonal buildings of stone, glass, timber, and aged brick, on several hundred acres of rolling countryside a mile or two from Arlington National Cemetery. It was larger and more impressive than the brochure had indicated. There was a library with immense plate-glass windows, floor to ceiling, genuine Oriental rugs, leather chairs for scholars- and thinkers-in-residence, innumerable volumes of books, mainly reference books; there was a small, beautifully decorated auditorium that seated about three hundred people; there were a number of seminar rooms, all with floor-to-ceiling plate-glass windows looking out upon the lovely Virginia countryside. There were fireplaces, hearths, flagstone terraces and walks, there were artificial ponds, one natural stream that flowed through the grounds and was the reason for a small bridge of split logs, and trees and flowering shrubs of many varieties. There were tennis courts, an indoor swimming pool and a small gymnasium, even a golf course (shared with an adjacent country club); there was a banquet room in the Wilson Building with art work by Monet and Picasso and Andrew Wyeth and Mondrian and Diego Rivera and Paul Klee, a dining room that was plate glass on three sides with an enormous fireplace, and raw-looking wooden beams overhead, and giant plants, rubber plants mainly, in buckets of oak and brass. There was a smaller dining area with a brick floor and shaggy fur rugs and low-slung Danish modern furniture, a kind of cocktail area, where members of the Institute or guests like Yvonne could sit and discuss the issues of the day's seminars—peaceful uses of atomic energy, new concepts of genetic control, the philosophy of activism vs. the philosophy of detachment, violence in popular entertainment, man's place in a post-modern age—there were neat, small, surprisingly plain rooms for guests, some with television sets and some without, all with handsome multidrawered desks and swivel chairs and copies of the *New World Dictionary* and the *102 Great Ideas of Western Man*. Yvonne was assigned to a room that looked out upon a small grove of flowering crab trees and the brook.

She wore white linen trousers that flared at the ankle, in the fashion of the day, and a tight-fitting black silk blouse with a drooping bow, and she drew across her mouth several hard, ironic smears of bright red since bright red was once again being worn, and she brushed her hair so it came slightly forward, the sides swinging forward, glossy, black, severe.

When she arrived from the airport one of the college boys who worked at the Institute stood with her luggage for some time, looking at her uneasily before he inquired where her husband was?— should they wait for him or would she like to be shown to their room?

"Show me to the room," Yvonne said.

Harvey had tossed something at her, a small gold pillbox, saying he had found it the other day in his coat pocket in a cloakroom, did she want it?—he had no use for it himself. Later, when he was panting and struggling with her so frantically, gripping both her shoulders as if he felt it necessary to hold her in place, she said, "I don't want the pillbox," but he evidently didn't hear her. He struggled, he grunted, several times he nearly slipped out of her; she tightened her embrace companionably and waited.

In the foyer of the Wilson Building there were gleaming plaques honoring recipients of awards made by the Institute, and rows of framed photographs, and a gigantic wall-sized copper scroll of names and dates. There was Braley T. Yaeger, the founder and first director of the Institute, a cereals manufacturer who had also served as chairman of the board of ANSCO of Chicago and a trustee of the Pennybacher Foundation, and had distinguished himself as an ambassador to the Netherlands during the Eisenhower years; he had been a close though not an intimate friend of President Eisenhower's. He smiled shyly and benignly in a posed photograph of sharp, artistic lights and darks. There were the Reverend Martin Luther King; Madame Ngo Dinh Nhu; Prime Minister Eisaku Sato of Japan; Secretary of State Dean Rusk; Adlai Stevenson in his role of Ambassador; Prime Minister Nehru; President Tito; Willy Brandt; the Shah of Iran; Senator J. William Fulbright; Senator Barry Goldwater; Buckminster Fuller; President Echeverria of Mexico; Prime Minister Golda Meir; William E. Colby, Director of Central Intelligence; John Kenneth Galbraith; Ralph Nader; Sidney Hook; Walt Disney; Senator Charles Percy; the Honorable Henry A. Kissinger; Marshall McLuhan; Robert Heilbroner; Mrs. Clare Boothe Luce; Nikita Khrushchev; King Hussein of Jordan; the Apollo XVI Astronauts; Dr. Billy Graham; John F. Kennedy; Martin Buber; the President of Atlantic Richfield Company of Los Angeles; Robert Frost; a woman on the U.S. Court of Appeals of Ohio; Countess Doenhoff of Germany; the Vice-Chancellor of the University of Nigeria; the Director of the Joseph Crocker Institute; the Governor of Maine; the sculptor Hans Eurich; the Shahbanou of Iran; the publisher of the *Phoenix Record*; Master Goodhall of Kings College, Cambridge; Henry Steele Commager; William Buckley; Leonard Bernstein; Carl Rogers; the Secretary General of the World Population Council of the United Nations; Prime Minister Wilson; Lyndon Johnson; Senator Wayne Morse; Senator Eugene McCarthy; Aaron Copland; Daniel Bell; Asa Dunn of the Council on the Humanities and International Studies; Herman Kahn; Georgia O'Keeffe; Robert Kennedy; Prime Minister Trudeau; Walt Kelly; W. H. Auden; Congressman Frazer A. Powers; King Frederick IX of Denmark; Al Capp; the physicist Egon Stein; Gus Connally of the *Chicago Tribune*; Harald Peckman of the Rockefeller Foundation; Senator Jacob K. Javits; the Executive Director of the Center for Advanced Study in the Princeton University Program on Science, Technology, and Society; Field Marshall the Viscount Montgomery; J. Edgar Hoover; the Director of the National Committee for Cultural Freedoms; the President of the University of California at Berkeley; the Chairman of the Board of Motorola of Illinois; Robert Lowell; James Graham of Gulf and Western; the Chancellor of the University of Indonesia; Senator Hubert H. Humphrey; Vladimir Boer of the Commodities and Trades Division of the Commission for Economic and Social Affairs of the United Nations; Drew Manley of the Union Theological Seminary; James K. Price of the University of Michigan Law School; the editor of *America This Week*; Salvador Dali; Francis Ponge; the Director of the Peace Studies Program of the University of Virginia; the Vice President and General Manager of the Systems Group of IKW; the Director of the Los Alamos Scientific Laboratory; Richard Nixon; Wei Ming of the Asian Studies Program of the University of

Illinois; Snowden Macke of the Coca-Cola Corporation; Nicholas
Wilson of *The Guardian*; Ambassador Inga Thorsson, Undersecre-
tary of State of the Ministry of Foreign Affairs of Stockholm,
Sweden; Alan Watts; Sister Mary Theresa (Warner) of St. Ann's
College of Boston; L. H. Volkemeier of the Task Force on World
Hunger of the Center for Ethics and Society of the Overseas Devel-
opment Council; Lieutenant General Jack Ditsky of the Department
of Defense; the President of the Academy for Fine Arts of the Uni-
versity of Paris; I. F. Stone; Dr. Benjamin Spock; Len Cameron of
the Gestalt and Gurdjieff Institute; Daniel Berrigan, S.J.; Sir Arthur
David Kemp Owen; Nikolai Kozyrev; Duke Ellington; Arthur
Miller; Henri Queuille; Eliot Janeway; Frank Shakespeare of the
United States Information Agency; the Most Reverend Oscar
Knight, Bishop of St. Louis; Stokely Carmichael; Claes Oldenburg;
Thornton Wilder; Sukarno of the Republic of Indonesia; Barry
Commoner; the Director of Foreign Affairs of the American Jewish
Congress; Jan de Hartog; Goodwin Knight; Bernadette Devlin; Pearl
Buck; the Dean of the School of Behavioral Sciences of the Univer-
sity of Pittsburgh; the President of the R. J. Reynolds Industries;
Yakubu Gowon; Grandma Moses; Richard Mellon; Margaret Mead;
Arthur da Costa e Silva; Martha Graham; the Chairman of the
United States Tariff Commission for 1968–1970; Hortense Powder-
maker; John Steinbeck; Walter Reuther; Joan Barclay of the Samuel
P. Barclay Memorial Foundation; Secretary of State John Foster
Dulles; Seyfe Tadesse, President of the Chamber of Deputies of the
Ethiopian Parliament; Lester Cox of the Eisenhower Exchange Fel-
lowships Program; Pastor Charles Worner of the First Presbyterian
Church of Atlanta, Georgia; Governor Ronald Reagan; Chancellor
Konrad Adenauer; Senator Edward Kennedy; the Deputy Director of
the Geophysics Department of Mineral Research and Explorations
Institute of Peru; Senator Andrew Petrie. . . .

Yvonne stared. She awakened as if from a deep trance. Around her
people were chattering—it was the Institute's opening affair, a cocktail party in honor of Nobel Prize Winner Andre Sagendorph—and
for a moment she hardly knew where she was. The foyer, the photographs and the plaques and the gigantic roll of honor: and there,
there, one of the smaller photographs but a photograph nevertheless,
wedged between a swarthy mustached gentleman in what appeared
to be a tuxedo with medals and braid and a handsome photograph of
United States Representative from Michigan John Conyers, Jr., there

was Andrew's face, younger than she recalled, a wry, bemused look to it, his gaze resolutely off to the side, refusing to meet the eye of the viewer.

". . . hadn't known Andrew had ever been there . . . hadn't thought . . ."

Harvey gripped her harder as if to silence her. Droplets of sweat fell onto her; her backbone had begun to ache, as well as her left cheek, which took the full weight of his face. He was enormous, swollen with desperation, panting, gasping, oblivious to her.

. . . Governor George Romney; the Director of the Aquarius to Africa Program of the Boy Scouts of America; Paul Newman; Stanley Kobach of the Sierra Club; the Chairman of the Board of Belmont Park, Inc.; the Curator of the American Museum of Natural History of Manhattan; Yehudi Menuhin; Joseph Wouters of the National Rifle Association; Jacques Barzun; A. L. Klein of Roche Laboratories; Dr. Matilde Frank of the Institute of Society, Ethics, and the Life Sciences of New York; Nelson Rockefeller; the Reverend Tim Porter, S.J., Director of the Division for Justice and Peace of the United States Catholic Conference of Washington, D.C.; the architect Stefan Lewicki of Warsaw; the Director of the Clinical Research Program for Violent Behavior of Stanford University; Norman Cousins; J. M. Goodrich of Allied Chemical; the Mayor of Los Angeles; The Right Reverend Ralph Atwood of the Episcopal Church in the Diocese of Southeast Florida; Merrill Henry of Communications Research of the Xerox Corporation; Brigadier General Austin Rusack of the Pentagon; Supreme Court Justice William O. Douglas; Arnold Toynbee; Congressman Steve Freer of the House Ways and Means Committee; Robert M. Hutchins; Professor E. McNamara of the Harvard Business School; J. McCormick Topping of the Federal Communications Commission; Edward P. Murphy of the U.S. Army Defense Biology Laboratories at Fort Detrick, Md. . . .

Harvey labored over her, his eyes closed, his hands now shut into fists on either side of her head, his body raised slightly from her—and relieved of his weight she felt her mind drift and spin and dart—mixed in with the air hammers and Harvey's strained gasping breath and yet freed of them, soaring away from them—a butterfly—a dragonfly—her mind drifted onto the young man who had been her lover years ago in Pittsburgh—his name forgotten—his green eyes cloudy with passion as he spoke of reform, of revolution, of the New World, his lips continually jerking and tensing—his name Raschke, Raschke—Joseph—Joey—*Should we be less violent than our leaders? Should we subject ourselves to more self-restraint than they do?*— Joey with his spiky disorderly discolored blond beard and his darker shaggy hair and those busy wet lips—a passionate, violent lover—all body—all body as a lover—pinning Yvonne to the sofa-bed in his dreary basement room—a young muscular lover—eyes cloudy and shrewd—his ranting, his arm-thrashing, his anger and his quotations from Marx and Lenin and Mao and Castro—making love to the nineteen-year-old Yvonne with tenderness and patience—bringing her to her own pleasure, finally—and then again and again for the seven or eight months of their relationship—Yvonne lost in him, in what he did to her, infatuated, intoxicated—for a while totally dependent upon him and his whims and passions and plans for the future—for a while totally subordinate to him—Raschke with his raised voice and messy beard and boots and work clothes and his circle of young disciples and his three or four ideas repeated endlessly and his habit of pretending someone might be spying on them and his wet lips and his unwashed body and his swaggering walk on the street and his enthusiasms and his dejections and his boyish plain face and his stubborn lovemaking and his name that was slightly absurd and that she had forgotten over the years— Energetic, bold, always bristling with life, the young man who had been her lover—her lover in Pittsburgh—but who was he, what had his name been—could not remember his name—could not remember why she had been attracted to him—remembered only the sudden cold realization she had had one evening in a cafeteria, listening to him argue with his friends, that he was really not intelligent, not nearly so intelligent as she: In that instant she lost interest in him, lost all feeling for him.

I feel nothing for you, she told him. *It's over.*

Jacob Harley of Columbia Law School was speaking passionately of the need to fully and deeply consider the individual as an individual, never to think in terms of masses or statistics or charts or graphs. He was a handsome, rather stout man in his mid-forties, with glasses and soft coppery hair and a ringing voice; he grew particularly passionate and convincing when he spoke of Congress's need to completely rethink the national budget, to cut back on defense and military spending and put more money, much more money, into *people.*

He was warmly applauded. Milton Gonne of the Economics Department of MIT rose to speak of the folly of overextended welfare and social-action programs, especially in this era of inflation and general economic disaster. He was a surprisingly young man, though balding, beautifully dressed in a cream-colored sports coat and an orange pastel necktie; Yvonne had seen him the day before on one of the tennis courts, in white, leaping and bounding from place to place. The thesis of his fifteen-minute presentation was that the American workingman of all classes of society has become an unwitting economic slave to the unemployed, the chronically poor, the handicapped, the aged, the sick—that is, a substantial number of fellow "citizens" who, though entirely non-self-providing, nevertheless share voting privileges with everyone else. He spoke rapidly, referred to Malthus and Durkheim, and concluded by acknowledging his indebtedness to the late Andrew Petrie for the concept of "economic slavery," and to Professor Raymond Ottiwell of the Economics Department of Harvard for many of his ideas, Ottiwell having been Dr. Gonne's thesis advisor. He too was applauded, at first not so warmly as Dr. Harley had been, but his gracious manner and very likely the presence of Yvonne in the audience stirred people to applause, so that in the end he did as well as Dr. Harley and perhaps even better. The seminar— "Eugenics, Ethics, and Economics in a Fast-Shrinking World"—was being televised by the National Educational Network; it was said, afterward at lunch, to have been one of the most dramatic and successful seminars so far.

The late Andrew Petrie, Yvonne repeated.

Heaving, gasping, pounding himself against her, the man with the damp red face seemed to be saying something, muttering, arguing— but she could not distinguish his words—could not make sense of them. He labored over her, he gripped her tightly and showed his teeth and moaned against the side of her face. He was on a congressional investigating committee these days, had been appointed to take the place of a distinguished southern gentleman who had recently passed away; was involved in a study of the distribution of pharmaceutical and medical supplies in the United States and its territories—a delicate area of investigation—risky—controversial— challenging. He might have thought suddenly of his work, for his desire began to ebb; and then, gritting his teeth again, grunting, he summoned back his strength; he seemed to throw himself upon

Yvonne with ever greater urgency. He murmured something, a word, a name, but Yvonne could not decipher it.

"Mrs. Petrie!"
A stranger came forward to shake her hand. He kept it in his grasp, even gripping her at the elbow with his other hand.
"You don't remember me . . . ?"
It was Dr. Wall of the World Medical Council; the man who had annoyed her in San Francisco, whom she remembered having subtly insulted. But perhaps he had not annoyed her seriously and perhaps she had not really insulted him, because they met now as friends; he was speaking to her animatedly and warmly. Still tanned, though shorter than she remembered, his face possibly more lined . . . it was the same man and yet not the same man.
"I heard the most extraordinary farfetched rumor about you," he said, smiling nervously, "and I almost wanted to . . . wanted to telephone, get in contact immediately. But I was in Ceylon at the time. And it was only a rumor, I was certain of that; the person who told me it didn't really think it could be true. . . ."
Yvonne said nothing. She withdrew her hand from his, she smiled in her ordinary manner, as if what he had said did not upset her.
". . . a rumor that you'd tried to commit suicide, had taken an overdose of. . . ."
"No," Yvonne said.
". . . you were hospitalized over Christmas . . . ?"
"It was just a rumor," Yvonne said. She smiled. She was conscious of herself as a particularly striking woman, in this context especially —most of the participants in the conference were middle-aged, only a few of the attending women or wives were attractive in the usual sense of the word—and she liked it, in a way, that Dr. Wall should seem to be so concerned with her. It was a delusion of his, it was an attempt on his part to manipulate her into thinking he was not an enemy, when of course they were necessarily enemies; he was deluded into actually believing they were not.
"I wasn't hospitalized," Yvonne said. "I wasn't ill."
"You don't *look* ill. . . ."
"Of course I don't look ill," Yvonne laughed. "You don't either."

So many contradictions, so many lies! . . . her cousin-in-law insisting that he loved her while he had made it very clear to her, thoughtfully clear, that he loathed her: long ago, nearly a year ago. His rude vacant stare. His thrill of pleasure, of satisfaction, whenever he thought of her husband's death. So many lies! One could spend a life's energy just in picking through them, sorting the dangerous lies from the merely conventional and from those statements that, failing to be utterly true, turned out to be lies without the liars' knowledge. Her cousin-in-law claimed to be obsessed by her but now, making love to her, she suspected that his mind slid and skittered elsewhere, in a panic, she suspected he was hardly aware of her, had no concern for what she might be feeling or whether she was feeling anything or whether he was hurting her. . . . He claimed to want her, he claimed to want her as a friend as well as a mistress, a woman with whom he could speak and from whom he could get advice, sincere advice, now that everyone flattered him and lied to him and wanted only to manipulate him; yet his body lunged and fell and rose again feebly and his face dripped perspiration onto hers and half-consciously he was groaning *Bitch, bitch* or a word that closely resembled that word. So many deceptions, so many lies . . . misstatements . . . rumors. They said they would be moving to another town but long before summer he was dead: her father dead, mangled, buried, lost. They said she was pretty, then they said she was ugly. They said she must be good and then they said she could think for herself—why was she so stupid, so helpless! They praised her for being smart and then they hated her for being smart and it was only a joke, it had been treated as a joke, when one of them mauled her and pressed himself against her and told her he would strangle her if she screamed. . . . They had always told lies about the Radeks. They lied about everyone but especially about the Radeks. They said her mother was sick and couldn't take care of her, then they said her mother was getting better and would be coming home soon, then they said something had happened—her mother would not be coming home after all—but she could stay with her grandmother. Then they said that wasn't possible and they came for her in a station wagon with chicken-wire protecting the back windows, they came for her and the neighbors watched and whispered as always; they took her away again, but not to the place she knew about. They took her somewhere else so that no one would find her and so that Yvonne would not remember how to get back home. It was useless, useless to listen to them. You could not sort out the malicious lies from the rest. *I don't know any Radeks* that woman had said coldly, but she was lying. Yvonne knew she was lying. Still, she must accept the lie; she must live her life, she *must* live somehow. Andrew had been the only person never to lie: but they had killed him. They said afterward that his murderers would be found but the murderers were still free. He was dead, but the murderers were still free. His enemies were still free. They were everywhere, everywhere, gloating over what had happened.

This man was Andrew's cousin but his face was altered, distorted. She did not really recognize him. He paused, seemed about to break away from her, said something unintelligible: ". . . hurting you? . . . Are you crying?" She wondered if he would blame her for his failure. She wondered if he would close his fingers playfully about her throat.

He regained his strength. He summoned it back. He was wonderfully determined, willful, stubborn; he had told her she would love him eventually, she would learn to love him as she had loved her husband—more than she had loved her husband. He quivered with will, with rage!—she *would* love him, he insisted.

She was excited and nervous and could not remain in one place. It did not matter to her what these people thought—she was independent of them, really indifferent to them—not deceived by their friendliness and their uniformly genial manner. They hated her, they were her enemies, hers and Andrew's, it had been their triumph, his assassination, no matter how they protested: so it could not possibly matter what they thought of her. But she was nervous, anxious, unaccountably excited. She read the many pages of notes she had brought along, she went to the Institute library to look through reference books, taking solace in the simple act of turning pages. It did not matter what they thought: she was apart from them, excluded from their society. She did not want to belong to it. Still her mind drifted back to them, to this place, she could not calm herself by turning pages. . . .

"I want—"

She was warm, her face especially. She was feverish.

"I want— I want—"

His strength ebbed and he summoned it back. It faded, it returned bravely. They were chafed, wet, raw. The air hammer had stopped and now there was a siren down in the street. If she were alone she would probably go to the window to stare curiously down. She would probably stand at the window as she had often stood at the window in the Albany apartment, before they had forced her out. She would gaze at the handsome tall buildings and at the Washington Monument in the near distance; she would rehearse what she would say at the seminar. It was not important but it was very important. It should not have mattered. It mattered very much. *He* would be close beside her, *he* would be listening anxiously. . . . The siren passed. The noise began to fade. It was fairly quiet in this exquisite room once again, except for Harvey's breathing: like any man's breathing, she supposed, in such circumstances. She did not especially dislike him.

"I want to explain—"
Outside were azaleas and lilacs and hyacinth and daffodils . . . jonquils and small coldly perfect crocus . . . and tulips, banks of tulips, red and yellow and white predominating, so beautiful she could not bear to look at them. She stayed inside, stayed in her small cell-like room, leafing through pages of notes or through the dictionary, quickly, distracted by something in the room with her . . . or perhaps it was outside, the narrow meandering stream like a stream in a picture book . . . the flowers and flowering shrubs and the frail blue of the April sky, which seemed too exquisite to be real. Now it was spring again: mechanically spring again. The calendar had swung around, everything had swung around, again and again, repeating itself endlessly, mechanically, without suffering as she did. It was windy: the tulips were being blown almost flat, their leaves shuddered and gave way and eased back into place again, bright green, unhurt. It was windy and then the wind died down and the sun came out and visitors from the North walked about in their shirtsleeves, grinning, childishly pleased. Nothing more was wanted for the moment. Nothing more was necessary. Time swung about, it was three hundred and four days since his death, mechanically and stupidly time had passed, and yet there was nothing mechanical or stupid about the world that so pained her: it was living, alive, fairly beating with its own life, quite oblivious to her own.

"I want to explain— I want to change your way of thinking—"

"It would be tragic for America if drugs were legalized," Harvey had said. He spoke in his flat mocking voice, one corner of his mouth turned up. "I owe it to America to make that as plain as possible. I owe it to my friends, my benefactors. Some of them I have never met and never care to meet, but I get along very well with their attorneys—one of whom, Yvonne, was on the same floor as Andrew when they were freshmen at Harvard. He told me in absolute honesty and without my bringing up the subject—he offered me the information gratuitously, that they didn't know who had killed Andrew: really, *they* didn't know."

It meant nothing to her, it was neither a lie nor a statement of truth; it was merely conversation.

Harvey had squeezed her hand several times. He was nervous as a bridegroom, now that she had consented to meet him in Washington; it was as if she had come to him, homeless, to *him*, and he had to accept her. The apartment would have to be vacated in a few weeks, and the other apartment, belonging to a friend of the Greasons', was not available after all—rather mysteriously, Yvonne thought—so Andrew's furnishings and most of his books would be put into storage in Albany and Yvonne would find somewhere else to live. It did not matter where, she had no desire for luxury, hardly even for comfort; she wanted only privacy; she wanted only the freedom to continue her work. Harvey had not spoken about these matters but she knew that he knew—had probably known, before Adrienne told her, that the other apartment wasn't going to be offered to her after all.

". . . if *they* don't know, then no one knows," Harvey said softly.

Yvonne smiled but said nothing. She did not want to continue this line of talk.

"And those Kropotkin idiots, those liars . . . it would have been too good to be true, an *anarchist* . . . an old-fashioned resurrected *anarchist* as an enemy. . . ."

"Yes," Yvonne said. "It would have been too good to be true."

The seminar room was jammed. Yvonne found she could not look out at the faces—it made her too nervous. There was no reason to be nervous, no reason to be excited, yet her heart seemed to jump erratically and she felt the palms of her hands begin to perspire; those old symptoms of distress, of panic, when there was no reason for them. . . . It annoyed her that the only other woman on the program had canceled out; her substitute was a stocky, beefy, pipe-smoking former presidential aide of several administrations ago, long since discredited in both the liberal and the conservative press, back to his professorship at a New England university: everyone knew what he would say beforehand and no one would be interested. She was the only woman, people would study her as a woman, would be staring idly at her, were already staring idly at her, though the seminar had begun with the clipped, precise, rapid-fire recitation of certain statistics and predictions, read from a prepared paper by the Princeton biologist. He too was a familiar figure. At the lengthy luncheon preceding the seminar—consommé with avocado, lobster mousse too heavily seasoned, to Yvonne's taste, with sherry, and an inedible marmalade soufflé—the man to Yvonne's left had told her contemptuously that this Mathewson, this prophet of doom and irrevocable misery, had had his teeth capped in order to appear more attractive on television, and had brought suit for a million dollars against the paperback reprint house that had done his best-selling book—*Beyond Ethics*—for obscure reasons having to do with advertising and distribution. Still, listening to him now, Yvonne found herself moved by what he was saying. It was impossible not to be moved. According to Dr. Mathewson there would be, despite last-minute technological "miracles," an era of famines and very likely a thermonuclear holocaust in the next decade or two or "possibly sooner." He had done field work in Southeast Asia and India; his description of Calcutta reminded Yvonne of what Andrew had said once, telling her of a fact-finding mission he and other congressmen and government officials had been sent on back in the early sixties—he had been repulsed by the crowds, the filth, the herds of people, though not so distressed as another member of the group, who had vomited uncontrollably in a New Delhi taxicab and once again at an official dinner —had returned home convinced that foreign aid was useless, far more useless than people commonly thought, even as a political strategy it was useless, worthless, a bad joke. *Those people are, strictly speaking, not even people . . . they're not people in our sense of that word.* And now Dr. Mathewson seemed to be saying the same thing, though in different terms. He was a liberal: therefore he used different terms.

Someone rose to challenge him. There was a minute of spirited debate. Other experts claimed—did he know of the most recent—and what about Dr. Roddy's thesis, Dr. Roddy of McGill—

But there was no real disagreement, since the white-haired gentleman in the front row had evidently misunderstood something Dr. Mathewson had said.

Dr. Wall, handsome in a white turtlenecked sweater, tapping his teeth thoughtfully with a pencil, said something about the romance of disaster, sheer catastrophe, the predilection certain people had— the more intellectual, oddly enough, the more susceptible—to want to believe suddenly and irrevocably that all was lost. That the world was lost. Doomed, already dead, gone. Best to turn our vision back inward, onto ourselves . . . far easier, more rewarding. Selfishness given a new name: pragmatism. But, as far as he was concerned, and *he* had just returned from Southeast Asia himself as a member of the World Medical Council Commission, *he* believed that the situation was not really hopeless. There was a difference, after all, between crises and actual catastrophe; and, as a doctor, he believed there was a very real difference between extending aid and medical services to individuals and attempting to extend it to *everyone.* And also—

Others spoke. Yvonne spoke. It came very easily, it was not at all difficult; like conversation. The congressman from Oklahoma, a Republican, said several rather simple-minded things and even asked whether these scholarly professors and self-styled experts were aware that the population crisis was, according to a study he had read, really a political ploy—an "emergency" staged by certain world powers. You had only to ask yourself, he said, who would gain the most by the United States going overboard in any direction, throwing more money down the rat hole, or even, though it wasn't as bad a strategy, *not* throwing money down any rat holes. Yvonne laughed. Others laughed. Out in the audience, sucking on a pipe, was the blond man who had given Yvonne that award some months back—president of the Elmer Clay Foundation—chuckling and nodding and sucking on his pipe. His name was Reynolds. He was sitting beside Alfonso Javaez, who had addressed the conference the evening before, to a packed auditorium, fiery and dramatic, an apostle of utter freedom— in drugs, in experimental life-styles, even in certain therapeutic acts of violence and acts of suicide—and they seemed to be getting along quite well. Yvonne heard herself laugh, though she could not remember why she was laughing.

Liberalism is a mask, Andrew had written somewhere, a phase of personality like any other, a phase of expediency: Adlai Stevenson at the United Nations, for instance, lying beautifully and intelligently about the Bay of Pigs, *on our side for once.* Conservatism is a mask: a phase of personality, a phase of expediency. Yet one must choose, one must determine which attitude was most required by history . . . one *must* jump into the arena.

"To the conservative all life is holy," Yvonne said. "The individual is the highest reality. . . . We must believe that," she said, "or . . . just the opposite."

They heard only the first part of her statement; at once the former presidential aide took it up, animated, deeply moved, shaking his

forefinger at the audience and at the television camera at the back of
the room. He was a Catholic: had been a close friend of the late
Robert Kennedy: had believed at the time of the Supreme Court's
decision on abortion that the United States had begun a horrible
sickening slide into disaster. And it was true. It was true. Every day it
was more true, wasn't it, could anyone deny that the actual affirma-
tion by presumably intelligent and moral men on that level of our judiciary was not the public revelation of a horrible, hideous, cancerous
degeneration of the spirit of America . . . ? That a conference like
this should even be held, that decent, intelligent people should present such insane ideas, wasn't that symptomatic in itself . . . ? Abortion, sterilization, an attempt to distinguish active from passive
euthanasia . . . sickening, unbelievable . . . not surprising that the
United States had lost all pretense of being a world power, *the* power
of the world, that the vision of John F. Kennedy was totally lost in
this morass of. . . . *Eugenics!* What were they talking about except
kinds of murder? Why didn't they give the proper name to what
they were talking about?

Now the discussion shifted violently to "morality." Yvonne felt
the shift of interest, of sympathy; she felt people looking at her. She,
sitting second from the end, in a bitter-green outfit that went very
well with her pale skin and her blue-black hair, she, being a woman
and a widow, would defend morality; they liked it that she was there
to defend it. And so she defended it, more reasonably than the previous speaker. Dr. Mathewson interrupted to restate the thesis of his
book, that the world had gone beyond ethics and ethical considerations, and someone interrupted him, and Yvonne felt the laughter
rise in her but controlled it; no one was laughing now and she would
be noticed. She was in control, fully. She was no longer nervous.
Sweat had run down her sides, the tips of her fingers were numb, and
her head still swam when she looked out at the audience—but really
she was in control because now she understood.

They were talking about traditional Western attitudes toward
progress and man's place in the universe and death and justice; they
were talking about—this from a tall, sportily dressed man at the very
rear, a man famous from his triumphant involvement in the Water-
gate prosecution and obviously a favorite of this conference—about
people, not issues. They were talking about whether scientists should
be autonomous or carefully directed by government officials and by
the voting public—whether there was room for more progress in the
area of genetic control or whether things had already been allowed to

go too far, as in the case of the space program. But one of the Apollo XVI astronauts was at the conference—not present in this room, fortunately, but present at the conference—and someone on the panel seized that issue to speak of the space program and of how, at its termination, so abrupt and wasteful, hundreds and thousands of people had been suddenly unemployed . . . a good example of governmental madness on the highest of levels. Dr. Gonne, wearing the same suit but with a sunny yellow tie, spoke out sharply from where he stood against the rear wall about the lopsided economics of the current administration, the idiot Keynesians still huffing and puffing under new disguises, and this was greeted with laughter though Dr. Gonne was not joking; he looked very angry.

It was then that Yvonne saw a dark-haired man at the rear of the room; she had been looking at him from time to time, without really seeing him. How very much he resembled Stephen Petrie . . . but he was not Stephen, he was someone associated with the *New York Times* . . . or one of the young business executives who kept so quiet at the Institute. She stared at him but could not see him very well across the distance. People were smoking despite the No Smoking signs. Her eyes watered, her head swam, she was fully in control of every facial muscle and every word she spoke, but at the same time she was weary—infinitely weary—and wanted only for this seminar to end—

"I know he's dead now," Yvonne whispered. "I felt it, I knew it . . . the knowledge went through me . . . I understood why we were there and why he had died and why the rest of us would die and why other groups would come along and say what we said . . . it went through me like a flash. . . . One of the wives of the Institute's directors attends all the meetings and seminars, she always sits in the front row, to the side, she does needlework to keep her hands busy, she's a brilliant woman, herself, has degrees from . . . has written several . . . and when I said something she glanced up, she hadn't been listening, she glanced up at the sound of my voice and nodded very slightly, almost imperceptibly, she hadn't heard my words or anyone's words but she had liked the tone of my voice, at that particular moment in that particular hour that tone of voice was required . . . a woman's voice was required . . . and then another tone, another voice . . . another voice must follow. It's a rhythm, a pattern, one speaks and then another and another and still another . . . there are interruptions, there are bursts of laughter, people

sneeze and cough and some leave early and others take their seats
and at a particular moment a door will open, a door will close, someone will make his way in, apologizing for being late, or someone else
will go out by a side exit unobtrusively, or the program itself will be
declared over and everyone will stand and stretch and yawn and mill
around and go across the way for cocktails and then dinner. I understood: I knew. We do these things because we are the people doing
these things because these things are to be done, at this particular
time, and we are the people who are doing them . . . that's how we
know who we are and how we differ from . . . who our enemies are.
Our enemies are everywhere, they steal our words from us . . . steal
them and turn them upside down . . . and we steal their words from
them . . . we steal them back . . . we change them, the words are always the same words but changed, turned upside down, reversed,
they are mirror images of one another and we are mirror images of
one another but Andrew never knew and so he died. He died. He's
dead. I know that he's dead now and lost to me and lost to everyone
. . . he's forgotten . . . he might as well have never existed . . . and
his death does not matter, his murderers do not matter, his enemies
are everywhere but none of them matter . . . they do what they
must do, they say the things they must say, but they mean nothing
by it . . . they are no different from him . . . they are the same person . . . the same words . . . we are all the same person, the same
words, but he didn't know that and so he died: I felt him die, at that
moment. Since his life did not matter why should his death matter . . . ? It's over."

"Life?" Harvey muttered groggily. "Death . . . ?"

—wanted only for it to end, to end. She wanted only for it to end.
For everything to end. Now that she knew, now that she knew why
they were here, why Andrew had died, now that she knew as if from
the inside these strangers with their individual faces, this crowd of
voices . . . now that she knew them . . . how could anyone endure
it, such a carnival? . . . now that she understood, she wanted only
for it to end.

Yet still it continued! . . . in fact it was running overtime. The
words continued, in new voices, in long-familiar voices, a debate, a
word-ecstasy, passionate harangues and miniature speeches and witti-
cisms and ironies and shocking statistics and rejoinders to the statistics and angry questions and angry replies, a successful seminar after
all, varied points of view that, when broadcast across the nation by

the Educational Television Network, would dramatize democracy in action: a successful seminar after all. And she had participated in it. She had helped to make it successful. Others had been more vocal, more passionate, but she had been quietly effective, and had she been more vocal and more passionate she would have struck these sharp-eyed people as hysterical: for what was zealous passion in a man was always hysteria in a woman, as Yvonne was wise enough to know. She did not mind that, she hardly minded that, it was a necessary strategy to leave the arm-waving and the tears and the breaking voices to the opposition, for those who possess the truth must not seem too eager to convince: it is not enough to possess the truth, one must also seem to possess it, or to possess the tricky elusive conviction of possessing it. Andrew had known half of that proposition.

Now he was dead, now she knew; she knew. She was not bitter so much as tired. The nervousness was gone and now she was emptied out, drained, waiting only for this space of time to end. Still they talked, still there were small speeches from the floor . . . she would have to say something once again, she could not sit here mute and unresponsive . . . she would have to say something further if the discussion continued . . . and she loathed hearing her voice now, she loathed the moment, the very moment at which she would begin to speak and out of deference to her someone else would remain quiet for a few seconds . . . still they continued, Dr. Mathewson shrill and bullying now that he had put aside his statistics, Dr. Wall fumbling, disappointing to his supporters . . . but rallying again with a minute-long eulogy to the ethics of the late Dr. Albert Schweitzer . . . *Reverence for life* . . . and again a rejoinder and again a word-ecstasy and again a contradiction . . . only the Oklahoma congressman was mute as Yvonne, clearly bored, glancing surreptitiously at his big old-fashioned wrist watch with its gold stretch-band . . . and now the former presidential advisor was speaking passionately of the Supreme Court decision ordering the desegregation of public schools, speaking of the need for this United States to abide by that decision come what may, to recognize the justice and morality and respect for the individual behind that decision . . . angry, he was, angry to the point of stammering, that certain factions within his own party and many, many factions in the other party should attempt to flout that decision . . . should attempt to argue racist propaganda . . . despicable antihumanistic racist propaganda . . . to the effect that the trauma undergone by certain factions of the society was not worth the progress and the harmony and the justice that would someday

. . . He was greeted with scattered applause and one or two angry outbursts . . . and a voice from the audience that might have been Dr. Reynolds's, jeering, *Trauma! Whose trauma, you old windbag? Yours—or theirs?* and still it continued, it even grew calmer, Yvonne realized she must say at least one more thing because it was her turn . . . long past her turn . . . the session would be ending at any moment and she must do her part to make it even more successful. Now Andrew was dead, now she was not really his widow; now it did not matter who she was; she represented no one, had been wed to no one, had grieved for no one, was utterly free and committed to nothing, now she might say anything at all and it would be heard, would be televised, taped and broadcast across the nation and perhaps even elsewhere . . . now she might say it did not matter that her husband had lived or died or that any of them lived and would die, it did not matter who the assassins were, they had done their part and it was over, and perhaps everyone deserved the same fate . . . perhaps Andrew had deserved it richly, more than most . . . ? Now she was free to say anything and the moderator had been trying to allow her space to speak for several minutes, while others talked, and now there was actually the opportunity: she heard her immediate, graceful response, she heard her cool light rapid sane voice pointing out that they had all strayed far from the original topic of the seminar and now it was too late, really, for them to do much more than adjourn; it was ten minutes past the hour and there was another seminar scheduled for this room and they must be courteous and adjourn, they must have sympathy for the program director who had scheduled these seminars, and since they had strayed so far from their original topic but had covered innumerable others very well—should they not declare the seminar over?

"They applauded for me," she whispered, "they said afterward it was very successful and I had made the most sense . . . a credit to my sex. . . . Each of the panelists was told he had made the most sense . . . separately, enthusiastically . . . congratulated separately . . . applauded, forgotten . . . *Very good, very good!* . . . and then the next panelists and then cocktails and dinner . . . it had gone very well, it had been very successful; it was over."

But still the man despaired, laboring above her, his body quivering with frustration and rage and a boyish determination to succeed. For him it was not over, he could not come to climax, for him it continued horribly, insanely. She had never known anyone so stubborn.

She had never known anyone so robust, so courageous, so manly. Yet it was not enough. It was never enough. His desire ebbed again, she felt him growing smaller, fatally smaller; though he groaned and slobbered and pummeled her he was shrinking rapidly, he slipped out of her and was lost, fatally lost, he could not regain her no matter how he tried . . . and then the weight of his body began to lighten . . . to ease, fade . . . his abdomen, his thighs, his sweat-slick torso; then his breathing, which had been so ugly, so loud, began to lighten, and the weight of the shoulders, the head, the face . . . all began to fade, dissolve, evaporate. The man's anguished whimpering disappeared into the air, merged with the quivering vibrations of the air itself, invisible. His fixed, mad stare was the last part of him to fade. An exhausted, terrified blue washed-out stare: beyond hate, rage, beyond affection, beyond comprehension of any kind.

It hung in the air for a moment. And then his stare too faded, evaporated, was lost.

"Harvey . . . ?"
He was gone.

63

She returned to Albany to discharge her obligations. She believed herself morally bound to discharge certain obligations, one by one.

She walked through the rooms of the apartment without taking off her coat. It was the same place and yet everything was changed. The furniture—the paintings—the old leather-bound books—the view from the balcony—the polished hardwood floors—the bedroom—the study: all were the same, and yet changed, subtly altered. The thermostat had been turned down and it was chilly and there was a smell of dust, of vacancy, of something faintly metallic.

She sat at Andrew's desk and typed a list of instructions for her attorney. Still she had not taken off her coat, she knew herself temporary here, excluded. She had no claim. She was not the man's wife or his widow or a blood relative or a disciple or even a former student. She had loved him, had worshiped him—and he had probably loved her too—but that made no difference.

She had cared for him more than she had cared for any other man; no other man had existed for her, really. But that made no difference, emotion made no difference, had no effect in the larger world—as she had always known. Their true bond had been intellectual, their most powerful union had been through the spirit, through the intensity of their convictions and their words. Now that was over, she knew him irrevocably and rather shamefully silenced, his voice lost— it might never have existed.

The telephone rang when she had been back only half an hour. She ignored it, hunched over the desk, typing out instructions for Mr. Sanderson. Her fingers were cold; she struck the wrong keys, was upset by the look of the page, the words X'd out and the uneven margins. But she had not the energy to begin again. It was late, getting later, she dreaded a knock at the door . . . dreaded seeing one of the family.

I hereby release all claims. . . . I ask that the investigation be terminated. . . . Enough harm has been done. . . .

In this room, seated at the old-fashioned enormous desk, those familiar piles of papers and books all around her, she did miss him; she missed him very much. He would not brush near her now. He would not whisper advice in her own words, gently, cunningly. He was dead. If she looked through his books he would not speak suddenly to her, out of those lovingly annotated pages, he would not draw her into the hypnotic, potent world he had inhabited. . . . She wanted to cry but could not. She wanted to cry bitterly, missing him; missing the illusion of his presence, and her preoccupation with him. It had been an illusion. She had been deceived. But it had been sweet, it had been worth her devotion, her life.

I want to sink back into the obscurity from which I came. . . .

The telephone began ringing again. But she did not answer it. She was in a hurry to leave, in a hurry to get everything concluded, perfected. Perfection: she still desired that, as he had. Completion was denied them, people like themselves, but perfection was always a possibility, a temptation. . . . She would leave everything in perfect order.

Still the telephone rang. There was no reason for her to answer it; in a sense, the apartment was already vacated.

64

She locked the apartment and mailed the key to Fritz Sanderson and drove out of Albany, northwest along the Thruway, past Schenectady and Gloversville, exiting at Fremont. Mt. Invemere appeared to her right. It was a small mountain, pine-covered except at its very peak. She drove slowly, in no hurry. She had no destination. She drove into the lake country, now straight north, through the small town of Fremont, onto the Old Fremont Road, which led to her husband's farm. Still she drove slowly, as if she had no destination, no plan in mind.

The road narrowed. In places it was badly cracked, repaired with tar that had cracked in turn over the winter. On one side of the road was a deep weed-choked ditch. On the other was pastureland, hilly and rocky, posted against trespassers like all of the Petrie property.

It was about six-thirty in the evening when she got to the farm.

There was a chain across the driveway so she left the car at the foot of the drive and walked up to the house.

No Trespassing signs were posted. Still, people had trespassed; their marks were all over. Muddy footprints on the veranda, several windowpanes shattered, bullet holes in the front door. Neighborhood boys must have shot from the road with .22 rifles. Now all was quiet, vacant.

"Is anyone here?" she called.

She had a key. She was not trespassing.

She let herself into the house and wandered through the downstairs rooms. Most of the furniture had been taken out and put into storage; only a few things remained, shrouded in rainproof canvas. The other place, the apartment, had not really been a home; nor was this place a home. They had stayed here for brief periods, probably no more than two months altogether. Now the rooms smelled of damp and cold and were not recognizable. Windows were broken, rocks and clumps of mud lay on the floor. One of the railings on the staircase had been bent out, nearly broken, as if children had been swinging on it.

"Is anyone here?" she called.

She went upstairs. It was very quiet. She intended to climb into the attic and up into the cupola; but she felt suddenly weak and it was getting dark and there was no point to it. There was something she wanted to remember but it eluded her.

Her old curiosity, her old love of exploration—examining closets, drawers, closed-off rooms, bookshelves jammed with old books: it was gone now, now she felt only impatience. She wanted something but did not know what it was. If she had intended to spend the night, she should have brought food and her own blankets. But she did not want to stay here. It was getting very cold, the rooms were drafty, there was a broken windowpane in the bedroom she had formerly used . . . she did not want to stay here.

"I hate this," she whispered. "I hate this place."

But it was silent, the growing darkness took everything equally, every footstep or word. It did not matter what she hated or what she loved.

If she paused, not breathing, imagining she had heard something, she heard only the silence: it was faintly mocking. Of course she was alone. There was nothing, apart from her. There was nothing. She imagined she saw a flash of lights, like the headlights of a car out on the highway; but when she stood at the window, staring, watching closely, of course she saw nothing. No one came out here at night, no one was interested. There was nothing here.

There was nothing. She walked from one room to another, her hands in her coat pockets, forcing herself to breathe easily. There was nothing, no reason to be frightened, never any reason. No one cared. No one was interested. No one observed her: her guilt was utterly inconsequential. Already the small amiable crowds at the Yaeger Institute had fallen into the remote past. She heard voices, she heard laughter, but the words were lost, gone. She heard someone speaking to her, singling her out; she felt someone clutching at her. "Who is it? What do you want?" she said, perplexed. There must be some mistake. She could not help anyone, she could not help anyone with his life, she herself was breathing now hoarsely and shallowly, panic rising in her.

"What do you want . . . ?" she said.

But she was alone. She knew that: she was alone. Alone she had locked the apartment and alone she had driven out to the old farm, the shadow of his death now inconsequential, or at the most no more than a puddle at her feet. It had filled her womb for a while, that dark thick clotted shadow, but she had triumphed over it—had expelled it from her. It had clamped itself inside her, wanting to eat her alive, but she had expelled it and it had run down her legs, streams of dark shadowy blood, helpless, inconsequential. She had triumphed over that. She rarely thought of it now.

If she had brought food and some blankets she could stay here, but she had not planned that far ahead. She was safe here, where no one knew about her. It would be best to stay here. But she had not planned for it . . . she was tired, hadn't slept very well the night before. . . . Something drew her attention: a flash of white outside, in the yard. Her heart beat erratically. Even as she knew it was only a rabbit, could see the rabbit hopping slowly through the matted grass, she was still quite frightened and could not control her alarm.

How slowly, almost lethargically the rabbit moved . . . as if its entire body were abstracted, listening . . . aware of something it could not exactly sense, could not bring into focus and perceive. . . . Yvonne stood at a window, her forehead pressed against the cold pane, her eyes half closed as if she were sleepy. The old garden, the small uninteresting wilderness that was the garden: there, if she chose to look, she would find the hoe. She knew it was there, where she had thrown it, everything lay where it had been discarded, shoved aside, forgotten. These things awaited her. They had not been altered. . . . She had not wished to leave the shelter of the veranda and approach him, though he called for her in that hideous, plaintive voice, cocky, puckish, authoritative, and yet frightened. She had not wished to step into the sunlight and be visible to him and yet she had done it, without hesitation; she had willed herself to perform in that way. And so it had happened, it had happened. A stranger brushed past her, hurrying from a grave, from his fellow mourners. He had noted her widow's propriety; his gaze had fallen upon her scornfully, defiantly. She had not known him. She had not flinched from that odd look of familiarity, however, being too stubborn to flinch from anyone. They judged her! . . . very well, then, they judged her; but she did not acquiesce to their judgment. Her husband's young brother Stephen awaited her, standing beside a stranger's grave, in the presence of a stranger, watching her, holding in one hand gardening shears and in the other a spray of tiny white blossoms. . . . She had hurried from the grave, from the stranger's angry, rather inhuman presence, she had found herself on the graveled walk in a kind of daze, not knowing what was expected of her, wondering why Stephen Petrie stood watching her, seeming to recognize her and yet not recognizing her. She remembered him as gentle, almost timid, self-effacing and at the same time strangely presumptuous, even arrogant. He did not need her, he did not need anyone except as he wished to need them, on the terms with which he required them and none other—he too was rather inhuman. She ran from him to where Andrew awaited her, his arms opened for an embrace, his complexion so bright, putty-pink, unconvincing. He had not wanted to die, not in that cruel way. He had not wanted his handsome face ruined, his gray-green eyes—how lovely they had been to Yvonne!—how striking they had seemed, no matter what other people said!—blasted, ruined—so horribly destroyed. He had not wanted his life to end like that and yet it had happened, was happening still—

Her alarm subsided. Gradually she came back to life, her heartbeat regular again. Something had frightened her but it was gone. It had crept away. She could not remember what it was but it had been inconsequential. . . . And so nothing was to happen? Nothing.

She was alone in the old house. No one knew she was here. In one of the downstairs rooms she and her husband had slept a number of times, like visitors, like guests at a hotel, never really at home; in one of the rooms he and his brother Stephen had quarreled that afternoon, about money; in the old spacious kitchen she had prepared plain, simple meals, not exactly like a wife, more like a girl playing at being a wife, a bride performing the simplest and most demanding of rituals, never fully conscious of what she did. People had driven out to visit them once or twice, though Andrew had not encouraged visits. In the living room they had sat with their drinks and they had talked, laughed, gossiped, they had eaten a light, plain supper, they had lingered over coffee and mints and had driven away again, back to the city. If she listened closely, perhaps she could hear people's voices, laughter . . . ? But no. Nothing. There was to be nothing. A night bird in the distance, nothing more. Another owl in the woods behind the house. But nothing, nothing human. That world had veered away from her now and she felt nothing for it, no passion, no anger, not even any curiosity.

She had not planned to stay. So she must leave, must drive somewhere else.

She had not planned to come here, had not thought about where she was going. If she had thought more carefully. . . . But now she must leave, it was senseless to stay, she was embarrassed, perplexed at her own behavior.

She left by the side door. It was still fairly light; she could see how deserted the place was. The old barnyard, the old barns and the pasture and the garden gone wild. . . . The lane leading back to the cabin: it drew her attention.

Innumerable footprints in the mud. Strangers' tracks.

She walked along the lane, back toward the cabin. She would have lit a cigarette but her cigarettes were back in the car. The air was fresh, exhilarating. She waited for it to awaken her, to cleanse her mind, which seemed clotted and muddy. There was something she wanted to know . . . something she wanted to discover . . . to see for herself. But she could not remember what it was, the knowledge of it eluded her, like a dream-image evaporating in daylight.

She saw someone ahead. A man, two men. They were at the side of the lane, had been walking in the direction of the house, were now stopped, frozen, watching her.

She was startled at the sight of them. But they were only hunters: probably men from the area, trespassing on the Petrie land. They were only hunters.

"Hello," she said. Her voice was level and curt as always.

"Hello," they mumbled.

On a path behind the two men was a third, who was hurrying to join them. At the sight of Yvonne he slowed. Dark hair, a certain tentativeness about him—did she know him?—Stephen? But he had averted his face and she could not see.

They carried rifles in the crooks of their arms. They wore red hunting caps and hunting jackets with game pockets and boots buckled tight below the knee. She looked away. She had only glanced at them, showing no alarm and no interest. They were on her husband's property illegally, trespassing; very well, let them realize what they did, and that she was a witness to it, and that she was coolly indifferent.

". . . Mrs. Petrie?" one of them said. His voice was low and uncertain, as if he were not speaking to her. She pretended not to hear. She walked quickly along the grassy edge of the lane, since the lane itself was muddy. It had been muddy last spring and it was muddy now.

When she reached the cabin she was breathless. A shock: the cabin was partly razed. For a moment she could not think what was wrong. How much time had passed, how many years, when had the shots rung out to awaken her, when had the funeral been held? . . . and the cabin had been boarded up, the property posted against trespassers. It should have been safe. But people had come, evidently, to tear it down piece by piece, wrenching the smaller logs out of place, smashing the windows. They had come for loot, for souvenirs. They could not be stopped.

Now it was spring. Again it was spring. The river swollen and noisy, overflowing its banks . . . ugly, powerful, uncontainable . . . spring had returned without effort and there was mud underfoot as always and nothing had changed, nothing of any consequence had changed. The dead man was still dead. The murderers were still free. A bird was singing overhead but Yvonne could not identify it—did not care to identify it. Nothing changed. Everything changed. In the mountains the snow melted as it must and the smaller streams grew rough and noisy and arrogant, taking their mature shapes, irresistibly swelling, plunging down to lower ground. As Andrew had said so wisely, it was irrelevant; all of nature was irrelevant; its beauty and its power were therefore arrogant, horrible.

Yvonne stood at the edge of the river, on the muddy bank.

"I hate the noise of the river," she said experimentally. "I love the noise of the river. . . ."

Her words were lost, the rapids were no noisy she could not hear her own voice.

A movement in the corner of her eye: one of the men approaching.

She knew they were strangers. Only by the most extraordinary of accidents had they met on the lane. They were strangers but they seemed to know her. *Mrs. Petrie* . . . ?

She staggered away from the cabin, her hands pressed against her face. Nothing was going to happen because it was over, it was concluded. It did not matter. She did not matter. Whatever she had seen was gone now, whatever she had heard was gone, lost, of no consequence whatsoever. She could not be guilty because it was not that important.

Gigantic, a willow tree with innumerable trunks. She stared at it. She would not turn to face them.

The first shot struck her in the shoulder, near her neck.

She fell. She had already fallen. There was another shot and one of them ran to where she lay, bent over her. She could make out the fresh mud splashed over the dry, encrusted mud on his boots. She was dying but she could see that sharply. *That's it*, someone said. *That did it.*

The others ran forward. One of them was carrying an ax. He was big-shouldered, squat. He wore a hunting cap and a plaid wool shirt. She could see him clearly but she could not scream because she was paralyzed: she was already dead. She died, but was still there. *That did it*, one of them said.

The man with the ax stood squarely, his feet apart. He raised the ax, he grimaced, brought it down hard on her wrist—in one stroke it cut through the bone and severed the hand. She could not scream. Everything slipped from her, was mute. She felt the blow as if it were a terrible vibration of the earth itself, or of the water; there was no pain, no sensation, only the terrible weight falling, crashing upon her. He raised the ax again. Again he grunted. He brought it down this time at her shoulder, where the shoulder and the arm joined. The others had turned aside. They were a short distance away, waiting. They were not watching. . . . There must have been a great deal of blood. There must have been some screaming, some protest, before she died. *Hurry*, someone called out faintly. The man with the ax straddled her and struck at the other arm; but his timing was off, the rhythm of the blow was off. He tried again. This time the ax head crashed through the bone. His teeth flashed with the effort, he wiped his forehead with the back of his hand, he balanced himself squarely on the balls of his feet and continued his work.

Part Three **STEPHEN**

1

Stephen sprang forward to help her. She was evidently ill, light-headed. She was going to faint and she groped for him or for someone, her bandaged hand fell against his arm blindly, in a panic—she said something he could not hear—her voice a low, plaintive wail, hardly human.

He sprang forward to help her and she did not fall. She staggered, her head bowed, her heavy-lidded eyes shut. But in a moment she had recovered. She was all right. No one had even noticed, perhaps—the others were clustered around Stephen's brother, Hugh.

She had recovered. The dizziness had come and gone. She was all right now. She drew away from Stephen, saying what sounded to him like *Thank you, there was nothing wrong, I'm all right, thank you, there wasn't any need—*

Out of shyness he said nothing. They were both embarrassed.

—wasn't any need to—

She glanced at him. He recoiled slightly from that bright hard stare of hers, though he knew it well.

—no need to touch me, she said.

I didn't touch you, Stephen said.

She flexed the fingers of her left hand, which were free of the bandage. Evidently he had hurt her hand, had squeezed it involuntarily. She held the hand up against her chest, her chin, in an absurd, rather derisive childish gesture, as if reproaching him. He blushed.

Sorry, he said.

There's nothing to be sorry for, she said. *What is there to be sorry for? —I thanked you, didn't I? And now I'm all right.*

They were leaving Andrew's grave. It was time to leave. The machine had lowered Andrew's coffin and now a bedspread of handsome and utterly lifelike mint green synthetic grass would be laid reverently on it. It was time to leave, they were not meant to linger now, they were not meant to study the grassy spread since it would probably clash with the real grass that bordered it, and they would be troubled.

They left. They walked slowly. Their footsteps on the attractive graveled path seemed unaccountably loud. Ahead Hugh was still sobbing, though more quietly. Arnold Laubach and Doris and Charles Bausch were close beside him, helping him. In the near distance a helicopter hovered, and between each chopping sweep of its propellers their footsteps crashed, crunched, were locked together in a sort of helpless unconscious rhythm that could not be avoided.

The woman was already dead. He had sensed it, beside her in the pew, during the funeral service. But he had thought it was the odor of the church—St. Aidan's deathly sunless damp odor, which he had always hated as a child; he had not known it was Yvonne herself.

Someone else joined them but they were still walking together, still aware of each other, tense, embarrassed, strangely annoyed. He looked at the side of her face quite openly, searchingly. She was already dead. He saw the death in her, in that bright hard glassy defiant stare. Poreless as a statue, the skin bleached white in the last few days and the eyes so dark as to seem almost black, like marbles, and the lips fixed into a small, stiff, slightly derisive smile: the woman smelled of death and yet she was living, walking away from her husband's grave.

All his senses sprang forward, rushed together to a point, flooding him, almost obliterating his vision. *I must save her,* he thought. His brain flooded. There was a terrible tightness, a constriction, in his chest; for an instant he could hardly breathe. . . . *must save you.*

People were talking quietly, gathered at the line of cars, not wanting to be the first to leave. People were talking in her direction and Stephen listened without hearing, watching her, himself silent, alert, his senses stirred almost to the point of pain. *I must save you,* he thought excitedly. As if she were aware of his thoughts she turned toward him. He saw the fine vexed lines on her forehead, raised in irritation, bewilderment, pain; he was struck again by that glassiness in her manner, that slightly mocking yet trancelike, unconscious derision. . . .

The woman was telling him it was too late.

On Sunday he had hiked for over two hours, alone, in the foothills above Brandywine. When he returned to the Center, rather fatigued, he heard the television set turned up high in the common room and he leaned in the archway out of curiosity. A number of people were gathered, watching a news broadcast. They were all standing: that struck him as unusual.

He came into the room quietly. He saw, on the Center's old-model television set, a series of images that were familiar in a ghostly way— an old stone farmhouse, farm buildings, a cabin. He heard the announcer's strident, solemn voice repeating a name, a certain name, and only after several seconds did it dawn upon him that it was his own name: *Petrie.*

One after another they noticed him. They turned to look at him guiltily. Stephen stared at the television set. His hair was windblown and his eyes felt raw, seared. He could not be certain he had heard correctly. *Petrie . . . estate . . . foundation stone 1749 . . . thousands of acres . . . Adirondacks . . . remote . . . Natauga River . . . controversial . . . threats unheeded . . . a career of. . . .* An interview with a sheriff: a newsman with a microphone asking questions about the time of the murder, the circumstances, the possibility of a political assassination. *Roadblocks . . . helicopter and highway patrol . . . New York, Vermont, Massachusetts . . . the Canadian border. . . .*

Stephen stood there, alone. He was not shocked; he was perplexed, off-balance, like a man who has failed to see the point of a joke.

. . . using every available means at our disposal . . . confident that the murderer or murderers will be. . . .

They were watching him. They were embarrassed. Someone came toward him and it was only with effort that Stephen looked at him, at first no one he recognized, then an acquaintance of his, a friend. It was a friend. Stephen wanted to stammer *I have no connection with any of the Petries, there is no longer any connection between us,* he wanted to shout into this stranger's grayish face, *I have no connection with any of you—anyone on earth—*

Where he stood there stood God. Transparency was Stephen's single talent. Where he felt the terror of his brother's death, there God was neutral, mute, in suspension; where he felt the gawkish surprise of a profound and unforgivable insult, there God was indifferent.

Lithe, weightless, infinitely clever: so Stephen trained himself. He was always watchful. Not existing, not wishing to exist, he lived a life of constant surveillance; his host was *Stephen Petrie* and he was forced to dwell within that host, sharing a common bloodstream, common organs, a skeleton, a dim reservoir of memories.

I knew God was going to take one of us, he whispered.

It was the surprise of it, the insult of the television screen. That disturbed him. *That* did not seem necessary. And the way people had looked at him—startled by his presence, then embarrassed, guilty, ill at ease. He realized that the community, his friends, had always known who he was . . . had always known that he was trapped within and defined by . . . had not been totally free, nameless, their brother in Christ and in the Community . . . had not been. . . .

Albert Perle, an ex-seminarian like Stephen himself, told Stephen to fly home; not to risk driving. He was too excited, Albert said. Stephen denied he was excited. He was not excited. The shock was wearing off, it had not been so terrible a shock as the news of his mother's death, which had come to him at school. He was not excited. He was quite calm. Where he stood there stood God: he was the medium, the reed, the glass, God filled him like liquid, quivering with life, sensitive, keen, and yet neutral, without emotion.

I have only to discharge certain obligations, Stephen said quietly.

He borrowed Perle's car, a Volkswagen. It was bright red, with a rusted bumper. Stephen saw it from a distance, a bright red toy making its way four hundred miles to the northeast.

Perle was still talking to him, giving him advice. He had come very close to dedicating his life to being a Scripture scholar in pursuit of truth and so he gave Stephen advice and sympathy. He was a few years older than Stephen; his beard was thin and rather Oriental, revealing patches of a pink, smooth chin and melancholy lips. He wore jeans and a short-sleeved shirt, its first three buttons undone. His hair was gray and blond.

Maybe you shouldn't say you had anticipated it, Stephen. . . .

I knew God would take one of us, Stephen said quietly. He was

ready to leave. He was not anxious, but as long as Perle stood talking
with him he was restrained, held back, not in pace with the red toy-
sized car in his mind's eye, speeding along the road. He wanted to
catch up with that car. His nails were scraping at the side of his
throat, there were small flat welts being raised on his flesh, yet Perle
continued to give him advice.

People will misunderstand, Perle said.

He drove six hundred and fifty miles from Brandywine, West Virginia, to Albany, New York, without once exceeding the speed limit.
He drove out of the humid, nearly stuporous summer of a river valley, across the state border and up toward and around Pittsburgh,
then east on the interstate highway across Pennsylvania, then north
into New York State: out of a full, rich summer into the surprisingly
cool damp of the Adirondacks. The climate changed. There was
light rain. The seasons had stopped here, seemed to have backed up.
Blossoms were beaten down by rain; grass looked pale and blighted.
Still it was beautiful, this part of the world. When he was away from
it he imagined it to be ugly. The farm, the summer place at Fremont:
he would like to see it again. And the cabin. The river. He would
like to see it again, would like to judge. *My former life was beautiful,*
he told himself. *I didn't repudiate it because it was ugly.*

In West Virginia there were yellow and white and deep pink blossoms everywhere. The flowers fell back, were scattered. It was spring
again, early spring, a tentative end of winter. He was not wearing a
jacket or a sweater; he began to shiver convulsively. The mountains
appeared, low at first, heavily wooded. Their peaks were obscured by
mist.

The world is so beautiful, Stephen thought. He was bewildered. It
did not seem right that the world should be so beautiful, that his
gaze should snag in it, his transparency should grow clotted and
dense, Stephen's emotions, Stephen's astonishments, Stephen's inconsequential appraisals. For an instant he envied his brother, now
dead, transported and pure and permanent.

I wonder which one of us killed him, Stephen thought.

He jumped out of the car. The ignition had not been shut off. He
ran toward the house but they were blocking his way. Someone took
a photograph, lunging near him. He hardly blinked. His eyes were
watering at the confirmation of disaster—the patrol cars, the security
guards, the ring of strangers eying him—the police captain who rec-

ognized him and called him by name, in a voice that warned him to
be cautious, to keep still.

Yes, he murmured, *yes all right, fine, I know, I don't believe I'm
in any danger but I'll be.* . . .

A young detective was assigned to Stephen. They shook hands.
Stephen blushed, not knowing what to say. In silence they returned
to Perle's Volkswagen and Stephen turned off the ignition and
reached in for his suitcase, which was made of royal blue canvas and
had a rather wide, cheaply glinting zipper, and handles of bold false
tan leather. He was aware of people observing him. There were two
other photographers now, one of them a long-legged girl in a khaki
trench coat and sunglasses, despite the drizzle. . . . *is it?
Which . . . ? Did you say Stephen, the one who . . . ? A priest . . . ?*
He was not meant to overhear but he could not resist—such was
Stephen's manner, his embarrassing naïveté that was not always his to
control; he could not resist calling over to them that he wasn't a
priest, not even a brother, not a fully ordained member of the
brotherhood but only a lay brother—only a helper, really, a kind of
full-time volunteer. They immediately approached him. They were
delighted. They had many questions and Stephen perceived he had
made a mistake and now it was necessary to be rude, awkwardly
rude, walking up the wide flagstone walk to the old house while they
asked him questions *Have you any idea . . . ? Any suspicions . . . ?
Unofficial, of course.* . . . He was very confused. The house itself
had alarmed him: his parents' old mock Tudor mansion, gabled and
beamed, with leaded windows, innumerable chimneys, aged brick,
stone, slate, a monstrosity out of a cruel fairy tale. Here was the cas-
tle. Here he had begun, now he was returning, would be brought
back to zero . . . reduced again to that frightened miniature adult, a
child with no core to him, awaiting his fulfillment in God and yet not
knowing what he awaited or that he awaited anything. So many
years in this house had been years in a void. Stephen's lips were
quivering. He was going to press the doorbell but the young detective was pressing it for him with a gloved finger, coolly mechanical,
professional. Stephen looked wildly away—past the curious reporters,
past the girl in the sunglasses, so sleek-headed, who rose in her fashionably chunky mannish shoes to take one final picture of him, the
flashbulb going off no more than five feet from his rapt, astonished
face—he looked wildly away, back to the street, to the red car that he
saw, to his embarrassment, was parked crooked. So many years in
this house had been years in a void and why was he returning

now? . . . what had his brother's death to do with Stephen returning to this place? He knew his sister Doris and her husband and family lived here now, had taken the house over, he really knew that his
mother was dead, had been dead for years—for more than a decade
now—and that his father was an elderly dying man in a nursing
home in Palm Springs; he knew; and yet even as the heavy oak door
was being opened he sprang away, muttered something about the
time not being right—muttered something no one could hear—and
astonished everyone by hurrying across the wide, dipping lawn, back
to the street and the car, running with the bright blue suitcase as if
running for his life. Someone called after him. It could not have
been a member of his family, so quickly: he had seen a black woman
at the door, a maid. But perhaps Doris had been close behind her.
Someone called after him, *Stephen? Stephen?* but he did no more
than wave distractedly and toss the suitcase back into the car and
slide in behind the wheel. His face burned. He did such incredibly
gawkish things, he blundered, made a fool of . . . intimidated others
by his . . . *Why are you so arrogant, Stephen?* someone had asked
him once, angrily and bitterly . . . and he had been speechless,
knowing no answer, not wanting to direct the blame toward anyone
but Stephen himself, the least significant aspect of his being.

. . . *will stay somewhere else . . . don't want to intrude . . . be a
burden on. . . . The time isn't quite right for us to meet, I think it
would be better if. . . . I'm sorry, if. . . . Sorry.*

The time when he had arrived unannounced at this house, for his
father's retirement party: sweaty, unwashed, in clothes he had been
wearing for at least a week, back from a visit to Montana, a month-
long stay with friends, his beard grown out to a length of several ragged inches, his face and hands so sunburned as to look painful, raw;
and since the front door was open and the party had sprawled out
through the house to the back patio he had drifted through unannounced, that time carrying a knapsack; he had even introduced
himself to a few mildly surprised guests—noting their hesitation at
shaking hands, their interest in his long, broken, gray-black fingernails—as if preparing himself for the ordeal of confronting once
again certain members of his own family, especially his sister Doris
and his brother Andrew and most of all his father, who had once
shouted at Stephen that the sight of him was disgusting, unbelievable; shaking hands with a few people, *Hello, I'm Stephen, I
don't believe we've met . . . ?* and even sighting, from the back door,

the plump silly-faced woman his sister had allowed herself to become, diamond and sapphire rings flashing on her nervous hands, her
hair tinselly and utterly preposterous, like a warrior's cap . . . and
the fine bold erect figure of his older brother, deep in conversation
with one of their uncles . . . and the woman close beside his brother,
bride-like, watchful, a stranger to Stephen, dressed for the country, in
gray tweed trousers and a white sweater, her bluish-black hair too
long and too straight, her manner puppetlike, stiff, curiously watchful. . . . Stephen did not see his father. He stood at the back, on the
raised terrace, he got in the way of the black servants who were setting up a buffet and who did not recognize him or even recognize in
him any features of the Petrie family or any quality that might
redeem him to them; —*Who the hell this guy? What did he do, just
walk in here from the street? Somebody's going to get in trouble.* . . .
And what had seemed so fine an idea to Stephen was now revealed,
by a profound quivering wisdom that flooded him, that seemed to
rush in upon him from an exterior source, to be mere vanity, egoism,
a sentimental appeal for forgiveness, an insincere plea for his father's
love . . . Stephen the prodigal son . . . Stephen returning to the Petries . . . when of course he was not returning and would never return except physically . . . would never again be one of them.

So he had left. He turned, made his way back through the
crowded house, smiling, smiling, seeing no one he knew and in his
confusion hardly recognizing the house itself except to know that it
was oppressive to him, the trip had been a mistake, the surprise visit
a mistake, and now he made his way back through the mistake and
to the front door and down the walk, joyous with freedom, release,
not even thinking at the time how people were already whispering
about him back there and about how someone would surely mention
it to his father; not thinking that the entire incident merited any
speculation whatsoever as soon as it was over.

Three years ago, his father's retirement from the bench. Three
years since he had returned to what they called *home*.

Afterward he felt wonderfully light and clean and free, almost euphoric with freedom. He knew he had done the right thing. Following Stephen's sentimental instincts he had nearly blundered into the
old intense overheated nexus of the Petries; repudiating Stephen's instincts and allowing himself to be flooded and directed by a higher
power, he had known himself light and clean and wonderfully free, a
soul delivered for a brief time from the pollutants of its circum-

stantial being. *I am never mistaken,* Stephen thought, not for the first time, *when I am with God.*

You're lying, his mother said.
Stephen said nothing.
I hate you when you tell lies, his mother said. *I don't want you near me.* She spoke in a whispery voice, hoarse and alarmed. She stared at him as if he frightened her and he did not dare move so long as she stared at him like that. Everything upset her now: if someone slammed a door downstairs her nerves jumped, her eyes widened like a cat's, all reflex, involuntary. She claimed to have heard Hugh cracking his knuckles one day, in his own room, and went to scold him; and as she scolded him her voice grew more and more shrill until there was no way to break the tension except by slapping him; and then she had burst into tears.
I want to know who you are talking to when I hear you talking, she said.
No one, Stephen said.
She was a well-proportioned woman of moderate height, still quite attractive, though no longer beautiful. Her hair was fashioned into a simple, elegant French knot by a hairdresser who came to the house. Her long, fine hands were never in motion now but were kept clasped together on her lap. . . . *Everything is going so well this summer, everything is as fine as it can be, now Hugh is over his bronchitis and Doris has so many nice friends and Andrew. . . . And your father. . . . Your father's enemies have been. . . . There's only you, Stephen, I worry about you constantly, I can't stand what you're turning into. . . .*
Her eyes filled with tears. Her voice grew huskier.
Where do you hide, who are you talking to, why do you have secrets from me? . . . Like the rest of them. You are like the rest of them. You lie to me and keep yourself from me and. . . . Don't you love me? Now that things are so much calmer here at home and your father is so happy and we are all out of danger. . . . There was a terrible thing that almost happened to your father, Stephen, some men who hate him and are jealous of him wanted to ruin his life . . . but it didn't happen and now things are back to normal and we can be happy again, can't we, and you seem to be lying to me constantly, you have no shame, no remorse. . . .
Stephen said nothing. He watched her, not daring to look away.
Will you tell me who you're talking to? . . . who you think you're

*talking to? Your father knows nothing about it and I wouldn't want
to disturb him by. . . .*

I don't know who I'm talking to, Stephen said. *There's nobody
there.*

Nobody there.

I'm not there either, Stephen said.

She brushed angrily at her eyes. *You're sick*, she muttered. *You're
lying.*

. . . I'm not here either, Stephen said quietly. *I'm not talking to
you from inside . . . from inside me. . . . But I'm not here, I could
be anywhere, I'm just here now because you won't let me go.*

His mother seized both his hands. Suddenly she was crying. *Your
little hands, I remember your little hands . . . your tiny fingers . . .
tiny, tiny fingernails. . . . You were the most beautiful of all the babies and I loved you the most and now you've betrayed me, you're
no better than the rest of them, you have no gratitude . . . and you
lie, you tell such ridiculous lies . . . you have no shame, a boy your
age telling such lies. . . .*

He wanted to draw away but she held him close, kneading his
fingers, begging. Now he could smell her breath. Tears gathered in
the corners of her eyes and were jarred out and ran down her creased
cheeks, and he knew he should be crying also, he knew she expected
it, was demanding it—as she did often with Hugh; but he could not
weep because he was not unhappy. He was very happy. He listened
to his mother's sobbing and half closed his eyes so that he need not
see her face, so close to his own, and by breathing very lightly he
could barely smell her breath. He was very happy. He had another
place, another life. He was not trapped here. She might squeeze his
hands and cry over him, she might suddenly embrace him, she might
push him away angrily and slap his face, she might even—which happened more and more frequently as time passed—turn away from
him with a short impatient disgusted noise, as if she had suddenly
made up her mind, decided against him, and had no more grief to
spare. She might do anything and it did not touch him. He observed
it, he observed both himself and her closely, and yet he was somehow apart, distant, untouched.

I could be anywhere, Stephen thought, *I'm only here with you because you won't let me go. . . .*

God, squeezed into Stephen's six-foot two-inch frame, was not a
graceful experience.

Stephen felt that his limbs were too short, his head too small to bear what he must bear. His eyeballs strained; he feared they might burst. Of course they had never burst. Yet it was a small dim absurd fear of his that he had had since the age of twelve. *No . . . wait . . . don't hurt me. . . .* When this fear came upon him he pressed the palms of his hands against his eyes, hard; he leaned forward; he forgot everything else.

Stephen was praying for his mother and for his dead brother. He began by praying for them. Praying to them. Then gradually the prayer shifted, was no longer verbal, become formless, dark, freely moving, no longer in his control. It was still a prayer but it was wordless. It sank slowly, gradually. It sank and he was drawn after it. He felt himself poised above a dark, fluid space—like a grassy plain at night seen from the highway—like a body of water—a lake rather than a river, since it was silent—and then slowly, effortlessly, with only a prick of fear, he was drawn down into it. He left the surface of his body; he felt himself withdrawing from the touch, the pressure, the subtle tactile awareness of the air. Once there he forgot everything else. In a sense there was nothing to remember—therefore nothing to forget—for the world did not simply disappear: it was revealed to have never existed.

He prayed for his mother to forgive him though he had not wronged her. He prayed for his mother to forgive him for not having loved her enough though he realized that his nature had not allowed him to love her any more than he had . . . or to love anyone else any more than he did; it was his nature, his soul. Yet he always began by praying for forgiveness. And then the prayer sank, the words sank, he might find himself suddenly in the presence of his mother—in the presence of that aspect of God that had been his mother—now mute, silent, begging for forgiveness though he knew she could not forgive him: her nature forbade her such charity. Now he prayed to his dead brother and groped for him, dreading him, yearning for him, a film of chilly perspiration far away at the surface of the body he inhabited, the heartbeat accelerated, something tense and tormented in the muscles, as if he were preparing to meet an enemy—he pressed his hands harder against his eyes and felt the presence brush near him. It brushed near him lightly. But he could not hold it and relinquished it, out of fear. The fear had followed him down. Bodiless, weightless, transparent: nevertheless he remembered fear.

Now he lapsed back into words again. He felt his tense body. The tears on his cheeks, the painful bend of his back—he was leaning forward in an awkward crouching position, shoulders hunched, elbows digging into his knees—the top of his forehead pressed so hard against the back of the pew in front of him that it pained him—and his hair had brushed against someone's back—bodiless he had forgotten himself, had lost himself—but now he returned, startled, distracted, to the confining interior of St. Aidan's.

The Anglican service did not interest him. Rituals did not interest him. At one time the Roman Catholic mass had interested him very much—had fascinated him—but now, grown out of that infatuation, hardly able to recall, even, the young man who had desired nothing so much as to be ordained a priest in order to participate in that rite—in the ostensible evoking of the presence of Christ—he experienced nothing more than a flicker of curiosity, wondering what the priest or the minister or the altar boys might be experiencing. Rituals meant nothing: words meant nothing. It was not necessary to call Christ into one's presence because Christ was already present. It was not necessary to pray God into being, into attending one's soul, because God was already present. Still, it interested Stephen that others might believe in such magic. He was a polite young man, and did not mind that his politeness was sometimes mistaken as timidity; he had learned, had assimilated the knowledge as a child, that one must always respect the magical rites by which others live.

Above the altar was a pallid and conventional and very chaste image of Christ: an English fantasy of an exotic conqueror conquered. Starkly white with starkly black hair. Curls, ringlets. Ribs showing. Feet long and white and beautifully stained with scarlet. The scarlet a mere suggestion. The conqueror safely dead. Stephen did not resent this lie. He stared at it and settled back and clasped his hands together and concentrated on it so that the minister's words would not annoy him, or his brother Hugh's twitches and throat clearing would not annoy him, or his sister-in-law's presence distract him: how intolerable it could become, the world of accident, of material, of flesh in which God is so cleverly hidden He is very nearly invisible! . . . In such a world not even the meek, gloriously pale Christ of the churches, that supreme and idiotic lie, was an insult. Stephen stared at the image until the service was safely concluded.

And then, with the others, he got to his feet and left. With the others he filed out of the church, slowly, solemnly, aware of being watched. He was one of them now, a mourner. He walked with

them, filed along with them, sharing that odd sensation of embarrassment—grief tinged with a sense of awkwardness, clumsiness—
shock stunted by a sense of obscure social shame.

. . . so moving, wasn't it, very moving. . . .
I was afraid he would break down, reading that passage of
Andrew's. . . .
Wasn't it moving . . . ?
No.
It was Hugh who had spoken.
A woman turned away, offended. Harvey's mother in a dove-gray
suit and a feathery gray hat with a veil that slanted across her forehead. Their aunt, always watchful, critical, censorious. She too was a
widow: her gallant son Harvey was escorting her.
. . . did he say? Harvey asked her.
They got into the second limousine and her reply was lost.
A local television station had received a call that morning that
something would happen during the funeral. But nothing had happened. Nothing had yet happened. There were police on motorcy-
cles, police in several handsome squad cars, police on foot. Most
regal of all were the mounted police; their horses were sleek and
beautifully groomed and delightful to watch. For some reason the
crowds did not excite them, yet Stephen had the idea they were well
aware of being watched. Their riders, expressions subdued and yet
proud, showing perfect control, were very clearly aware of being
watched. Stephen noted their excellent posture, their fine uniforms,
the polished wooden handles of their pistols.
. . . in terror of their going berserk . . . spraying us with
machine-gun bullets . . . if we should get trapped in the cross
fire. . . .
Hugh, there isn't any danger of. . . .
He's joking, Stephen said curtly.
I'm joking, Hugh said.

I'm joking, Hugh sighed. He sank into the cushioned seat and
tried to cross his legs, but even in this spacious compartment his legs
were too long. . . . *How lonely, to be the only creature here who is*
conscious of joking . . . that is, of being a joker.
The hearse, the opulent black-curtained black-gleaming hearse, a
vehicle out of a fairy tale. Slow motion. Everything slow, slow. Slow
motion in honor of death. Stephen felt chilled though the day was at

last sunny. The weeks of disappointing weather had been broken; now it was nearly warm enough for mid-June; now their dark clothing and their somber, subdued movements were inappropriate . . . now it was meant to be warm again, but he could feel no genuine warmth. The interior of that church had always depressed him. It had depressed him physically and spiritually. As a child he had been made to admire the bas-relief of a reputed ancestor of his, a profile and a sweep of bald head, a gentleman in high public office who had contributed a great deal to the church . . . along with other such gentlemen . . . he had had certain things pointed out to him in the elegant dark at the rear of the church, and these stony faces had always depressed him. The marble, the stained glass, the vestments, the hushed reverent magic, the glorying in solemnity, in death: he wondered what any of it had to do with him, whether he was guilty of some obscure sin, that his religion must exact atonement from him at such times.

Ah, I'm glad we made it through that neighborhood, Hugh said. *I don't think Andrew has many mourners there. . . . Not many black faces at church either.*

There were black people there, Hannah said. *There were a number of. . . .*

They fell silent. The limousine moved along slowly. Stephen looked out at the street—caught the surprised and then interested glances of strangers—was sorry their procession had to pass this way. Merely injurious, the advertising of death. Exhibition, pomposity, unforgivable expense. And archaic, so that the Thruway was forbidden them and they must drive the long way to the cemetery.

Hugh was beginning to chatter. That was a danger sign. He spoke, thought better of what he was saying, paused, began again, interrupted himself in midsentence, giggled, was abruptly silent, and then, not accustomed to silence, squirmed and tried to cross his legs and began to chatter again. Stephen tried not to hear. He tried not to allow himself to think uncharitable thoughts about his brother. All that was gone, that sort of emotion. He had rejected it years ago. Hatred, dislike, even flickers of disapproval or annoyance. He was not going to be drawn into the net of those old, dismaying emotions. The brothers had always been a temptation for him, each in his own way. And Doris also. Doris had tried to mother him, even before their mother's death. And his father: sitting there at the head of the table, bland, reasonable, always his bland reasonable monologues, displaying an utterly contemptible and even vicious, viciously igno-

rant nature, biased, prejudiced, close-minded, speaking of certain
people . . . naming certain *names* . . . as reverent and worshipful as
Reverend Thayer mumbling about God and death and judgment
and the sorrow that all must bear in a fallen world. . . . But
Stephen did not want to remember. He did not want to remember
his impatience, his shame, his growing disgust. Judge Petrie shaking
someone's hand, benignly, condescendingly, and no matter who it
might be—Stephen's headmaster, for instance, a deceptively respectful, cunning Englishman doing duty in the New World and
brilliantly mocking behind his genial courtesy—the Judge could not
resist dropping a name or two, always a name, a magic name, sometimes the name of a famous man—a politician, a statesman, a
diplomat—sometimes the name of a very rich or very powerful man
who was nevertheless unknown to most people—a financier, an
unofficial advisor of the Governor's or the President's. . . . even, occasionally, a beknighted friend of a friend or a European nobleman.
Stephen had rolled his eyes in frustration and had gnawed at the inside of his lips and. . . . But no: he did not want to think of such
things. His father was ill, he would not live much longer, Stephen
must forgive him. Must forgive. Must avoid the trap of remembering
and reexperiencing certain degrading emotions that were unworthy
of him and of the spirit that dwelled in him. He must. . . . But
Hugh continued to chatter. *Why* did he chatter, *why* couldn't he
control himself? Stephen resisted the impulse to turn sharply to him.
The man was nearly forty years old, after all, no longer a child. Yet
still spoiled, impudent. A child still. Daring someone to chastise him.
He wanted the air conditioner turned off and now he complained of
the stuffiness of the car and now he wanted a window open and now
he wanted it closed and now he was being condescending to Hannah, whom Stephen had always liked, whom everyone liked, and
now he was apologizing to Yvonne in an effusive, unconvincing way,
fairly twitching with excitement.

*. . . today is such a . . . everything is unbelievable, unreal . . . the
situation has been made so . . . you must feel it most of all, Yvonne
. . . so public, such a display . . . common people and outright rabble leering . . . free to say anything they wish or even take photographs. . . . Poor Andrew, how this would have annoyed him! . . .
any public display or . . . though sometimes he rather basked in . . .
but of course it had to be controlled, it had to be his choice. Do you
know, that pompous old clown put the fear of God in me for a few
minutes there . . . like all of us I've been assuming mortality for so*

*long, so comfortably long. Not like you, Stephen, not at all. Not a bit.
Not like Stephen: he's at home with such things. Immortality, I mean.
The soul. That sort of thing. It's hard even to talk about it without.
. . . Do you feel the same way, Yvonne?*

He laughed nervously.

*. . . Yes? No? . . . Well, the old boy had me nearly trembling
. . . of course the last several days have been . . . since the news
came to me Sunday my nerves have been . . . and the police don't
help, do they, with their concern and their thoroughness and . . .
and their ubiquitous presence. It's enough to make anyone feel under
arrest or under surveillance . . . positively guilty . . . criminal. Do
you agree? . . . I was quite moved, yes, by the funeral oration. I've
drifted away from such things, my friends die all the time, of course,
and my casual acquaintances drop dead even more often, but
there's rarely any fuss . . . cremation, usually . . . and "send no
flowers" . . . donations to the Puerto Rican orphans . . . or the
P.E.N. imprisoned writers' fund . . . or a Zionist front . . . that
sort of thing. No fuss. No limousines, no armed guard . . . no ceremony at all. So I'm quite shaken, I must admit. I'm really very sentimental. It's my nature. Sentimentality and sensuousness are linked
. . . and a talent for the visual . . . artistic expression through the
visual. . . . I was moved but I didn't break down as Stephen did. I
wondered if I should have tapped you on the shoulder, Stephen? . . .
you must have made that detective a bit uncomfortable. . . . But of
course you couldn't help it, it was entirely spontaneous, such things
happen at funerals and they must take them in stride. . . . However,
I was brought up short by the old boy's quoting Andrew himself.
That was jarring, wasn't it, that violated the verisimilitude of the occasion, didn't it, hearing Andrew's words in another man's voice at
Andrew's funeral? . . . something wrong with it, something vulgar
and histrionic. The organ music was in good taste, I dreaded something nineteenth century and tearful, that aspect of it wasn't vulgar
at all, but it jarred, it simply jarred for Andrew's words to be pronounced in that quavering voice . . . like God Himself reading a sacred text. Anyway we all know Andrew didn't mean half of what he
said. He was a brilliant stylist, he loved to hear himself talk, and of
course others did too . . . many others . . . but half of what he said
was just repartee . . . not serious . . . not seriously meant . . . don't
you agree? The difficulty, of course, is in knowing which half was serious and which not. His biographers will fall into despair. . . .
Don't you think? A man like Andrew, so unquestionably a genius, an*

aristocrat, a giant towering above the rest of us . . . a man like Andrew has the most to fear from his own followers, his own admirers. He withdrew from politics, didn't he, because he detested the intellectual level of his own supporters? . . . a wise, moral thing for him to do. Leaders must have followers and all followers are impossible. . . . He was ashamed of his disciples, he told me many times. Especially during that capital-punishment debate. And the business about welfare mothers and abortion. Leaders must have followers and all followers are impossible but Andrew's were . . . were rather . . . colorful, shall we say, and utterly lacking in the ability to appreciate his subtlety of argument. Many times he confided in me, admitted that. . . .

Stephen had been gnawing at the inside of his mouth. He turned to his brother, and Hugh, looking at him immediately, began to smile.

. . . we weren't close in recent years, I admit, he said, but at one time we did exchange . . . ask each other's. . . . Am I annoying you, Stephen? What's wrong? You look like a peevish Cupid, your expression is so. . . .

He's nervous, Hannah said quietly. *We're all nervous.*

. . . not nervous, but superstitious, Hugh said. I'm so superstitious that I feel I must keep . . . must keep . . . not joking, of course, since this is a solemn occasion . . . but I feel I must keep the silence at bay or . . . or . . .

Nothing will happen, Hannah said. *We're all just a little jumpy and maybe it would be best if. . . . Dr. Jamison gave Yvonne a sedative, you know, and. . . .*

. . . sentimental and sensuous and superstitious, Hugh said. He spoke in a low, soft voice, still looking at Stephen. Stephen knew he was blushing; he felt his lips pursed tightly together. *. . . a kind of magic, a magic . . . I'm in charge . . . until he is safely buried and the ceremony is completely over and we're all still alive and . . . and reasonably healthy . . . until then I feel the curious need to. . . .*

He spoke softly, softly. Almost pleading. Stephen was struck by a musical whine in his voice, a childlike quality. Beneath his brother's slant gray-blue eyes were lines that bled into one another; yet the eyes, the sockets, were somehow illuminated, as if that part of his face were blanched, leaving the rest of it with the appearance of being healthier than usual. But he was not healthy, his skin was really coarse, sallow, sickly. Stephen pitied him, felt his anger pass hopelessly into pity. He wanted to like his brother and could not.

His brother forbade him. Always, all their lives, Hugh blocked his way, thwarted affection, forbade any kind of sympathy as if it were degrading. Yet now he was pleading, in his peculiar half-mocking way. *Do you understand? Stephen? You, more than anyone else. . . ? The power of magic, of . . . ?*

No, Stephen said. *I don't understand.*

He had not meant to sound so vexed, so heated.

On the far side of the car, staring out the tinted glass, Yvonne sat oblivious to them all. Her profile was impassive, indifferent. Even at the sound of Stephen's voice she did not move. He had the idea she was deaf to them, she was removed entirely, in another dimension altogether. She did not seem especially unhappy. . . . He was grateful that she was not listening to them. It would have been as if Andrew himself could overhear their words.

I don't understand, Stephen said quietly.

This pleased Hugh. He was long-nosed, and his nostrils widened and seemed to darken with a kind of pleasure, knowing he had irritated Stephen. But he had done it in so delicate a way, with so very subtle an art. . . . *You understand perfectly well*, Hugh said, *and are merely being stubborn in refusing me . . . how have I offended you? . . . or anyone? I don't offend, I merely entertain. If I haven't offended Yvonne, how have I offended you?* His voice quivered. Stephen stared at him and could see the tiny kinky hairs in his nostrils. The man was frightened, really frightened. Yet he could not stop himself. His eyebrows were in constant motion, arching ironically and then relaxing, falling; they were quite thin, as if plucked. Stephen wondered with revulsion if they were darkened with pencil. Hugh looked so garishly and pathetically satanic, a jester not equal to his masquerade. . . . *hardly mean to offend . . . impossible . . . it's just the tension of awaiting some messianic androgynous youth . . . a bomb tossed into our midst . . . and the strain of . . . the grief of . . . as I said, I'm not accustomed to . . . the gravity of old-fashioned death. It's a riddle, I'm an outsider. And the family all hate me. Ech! I can smell it on them. There'll be a war council to which I won't be invited . . . maybe there already has been . . . tension, strain . . . natural grief . . . unnatural pomp . . . and the theatricality of it, the self-consciousness, the perversion . . . perversion of . . . being forced to use words that are so shopworn . . . clichés . . . "so shocked" . . . "so devastated" . . . "sorry, grieved. . . ." That sort of thing. The clichés of ordinary life offend me. All the words have been used again and again and . . . senti-*

*mental greeting cards have usurped our grief . . . how can I accept
"deepest sympathy" from people without laughing in their faces?
And how much worse it will be for Yvonne. . . .*

At the mention of her name she turned to them. She and Stephen
glanced at each other. She looked dazed, yet bitter and knowing; she
blinked several times as if she had just awakened from a dream.

You have no right to talk about me, she said.

But surely I have . . . have not . . . have not. . . . Hugh was
stammering in confusion. He seemed really frightened now. . . . *no
intention to offend and no . . . no . . . no awareness of. . . . I
meant only. . . . I wasn't talking about you but talking to you . . .
addressing you. . . . I meant only. . . .*

You have no right to talk about me, she said. Her voice was
neutral, flat, hollow. She licked her lips, as if speaking were difficult.
*. . . He won't let you. Any of you. You don't have the right and it
won't be allowed. . . .*

But Yvonne, Hugh said, *I meant only. . . .*

Stephen could not restrain himself. He grabbed his brother's arm,
he said in a low, rapid voice, *Don't. Please. Stop. . . . Don't do this
to us and to yourself.*

They saw the artificial grass and looked away at the same time.

His enemies will pay for this, Yvonne said.

We will all pay, Stephen said.

It looked as if Hugh were going to collapse. At first Stephen
thought, horrified, that his brother was really having an attack of
laughter—a giggling fit such as he had had as a boy, at the most embarrassing times. His skinny shoulders shook, his eyes popped behind
the thick-lensed glasses, and he had to press his hands against his
mouth to keep it shut. But he was not giggling. There was nothing
mirthful about his look of terror.

But he did not collapse. He was all right. He was led back to the
car, weeping quietly. And Yvonne was all right: she was remarkably
composed.

They walked together without speaking. In the distance there was
smog or vapor hovering about the city's skyline; like a sunset in a romantic landscape painting. Sinister, lovely. Their footsteps were loud
on the graveled walk. And the helicopter was noisy. But Stephen
looked about and saw that the cemetery was a beautiful place,
that there was no shame in Andrew remaining here while they

walked away. Close about his grave were wych-elms, their miniature flowers just opening. There were potted flowers or fresh-cut flowers on nearly every grave; and every grave was neat and clean and its boundaries carefully indicated.

At the limousine he declined to get inside; he told them he would walk back to the city.

The widow was already inside. He did not care to ride back with her, or with any of them. Of course they were annoyed. Doris's face reddened; she could not resist scolding him. Walk back! Walk eight miles back! It was ridiculous, and typical of him . . . an insult to. . . .

He waved her away. He walked away.

Stephen! his sister cried.

But he walked away. He left the cemetery by a side gate and found himself on a hill above the highway. Ah, what freedom suddenly! What joy! . . . He had wanted to save the woman while knowing it was hopeless; it was too late. He had wanted to save her. His impulse, his instinct, was to reach out for her. But really he knew better. He was flooded now with a spacious warming sensation, a sensation of light, an almost physical knowing . . . he must keep away from her. He must never approach her. She was death. She was death, staring at him with those bright glassy mocking eyes, daring him not to recognize her. He did recognize her. He knew very well.

He was suffused with light, now that the funeral was over. His brother was buried and he was alive, he was alone, slipping and sliding down the grassy hill, at last free to breathe deeply, with pleasure. His lungs filled of their own accord, with immense pleasure.

Across the highway a yellow butterfly fluttered over another field, little more than a scrap of color. Stephen crossed the highway, running. He did not look back. He believed the city lay in this direction; he would get there eventually. He was alive, he was life itself. He was in no hurry to get anywhere.

2

God withdrew. God became contemplative. God resisted despair and plunged into good works; God had known beforehand how good works exercise the body and the mind and, once they are begun, plunge onward charged with their own momentum. God stretched his arms and legs but was never restless. He hiked into the foothills above the cramped little town but was never restless. He forgot a great deal. He fasted, he slept deeply, he forgot as much and as often as possible.

He was one of the community's unofficial brothers. But he belonged there; he was incognito in the community and well loved. He could go anywhere, he was allowed anywhere, he was assigned an extra class since he had requested it to keep him active, to keep his mind plunging. He withdrew often, that was a fact. He was silent and contemplative but never in despair. His eyes glowed at times. His complexion was fine, olive-tan, glowing. In a sense he did not withdraw. In a sense he was always standing at attention. He leaned forward on his toes, he was the first to volunteer, he was always offering himself. Perhaps he was too exuberant. He was too healthy. However, he worked at forgetting and it was generally acknowledged that he had succeeded.

They praised God in their diffident, slightly fearful voices. They accepted God's offers. They followed God with their eyes, however, and thought such thoughts as they wished. No one could control them. God was not offended, not even hurt. God was accustomed to it. Life in a human body had accustomed God to a great deal. There had been so many thousands of years of it now; the accumulated wisdom was considerable.

God wandered out above the ramshackle frame dwellings, following the creek toward its source, contemplative, in a way quite content, doing no harm. God did no harm. Yet they followed him; he knew they followed him. He knew they reported him. His former friends watched him and listened to him and scribbled their impressions. Perhaps they were writing memoirs. His students took notes, watching him all the while covertly. There were visitors at the rear of the classroom. If he shifted his weight from one foot to another all glanced up, alert: their eyes darkened with wonder.

God grew heavy, leaden. God's eyelids sagged.

On the contrary, God had never appeared in finer condition: everyone marveled. In the small town of Brandywine the women observed him with more interest than before. They watched him from the unpainted metal chairs in front of the Laundromat, or from the parking lot of the grocery store, contemplative themselves, sometimes frowning. Girls peered at him between their curtains of soft straight swinging hair. They had always observed him but now it was deliberate.

He kept to himself. He worked very hard. He had no appetite; but he slept well. In his sleep he was utterly dissolved—not even God. He sank into nothing. Afterward he could not remember. He must have dreamed but he could not remember. There was no need to consciously forget. He went into nothing, into utter dissolution, God was lost in that dissolution and woke in the morning startled and cleansed and innocent.

They did follow him, however. One day he was squatting by a creek, had been squatting there for some time, not conscious of himself, not even conscious of the creek, and the call *Stephen!* came floating to him. He did not hear at first. *Stephen!* someone called. And then he returned to himself, to his aching thighs and legs, and looked up. He acknowledged *Stephen*. He was willing to acknowledge anyone.

It was late in the afternoon. Climbing toward him across a field of burned-out grass and goldenrod was one of his former friends.

Stephen straightened to his full height. *The police again*, he thought.

His friend was edgy, plucking at his gray-blond beard, approaching Stephen with that familiar strained smile. They were not friends. They were brothers. Both were ex-seminarians but they had not been in the same seminary. Perle was from the Midwest, had gone to school in St. Louis, had entered a Jesuit novitiate there. Stephen had studied in a seminary in Massachusetts.

. . . *the police?* Stephen said.

A telephone call, Perle said.

Is it the police? Is it Albany?

They said . . . they identified themselves. . . . The Bureau of Special Services of the State of. . . .

Yes, Stephen said. *All right.*

He noted the subtle, almost imperceptible satisfaction in his friend's face. Yes, all right, good. Fine. He would not quarrel and would not resist their questions. He cooperated. He offered himself in every way. He never lied; but he had forgotten a great deal. Perhaps that made them suspicious. People were suspicious because it pleased and excited them and kept their blood running.

You don't like it, do you, Stephen said softly, *I mean none of you like . . . are comfortable with. . . .*

They were not friends now. Stephen knew too much, was really too shrewd. He could not prevent himself from seeing the odd quirky frowns of satisfaction. His friends, his brothers? Of course. But they talked about him, they compared notes on him, they slipped away to Fairmont where strangers took them to dinner and asked them idle harmless questions about the murdered man's peculiar younger brother.

. . . *don't be ridiculous,* Perle said, startled.

He looked resentfully at Stephen. Stephen wondered if they would hound him for the rest of his life. *Don't be ridiculous!* the man said.

God had touched Stephen, had slipped into Stephen many years ago. He had been a child. He had not understood. And perhaps the visitations had not been so powerful as the one that changed his life. He had been twelve at the time; God had changed his life. Something had broken in two, had been snipped faultlessly and silently in two, so there was Stephen the boy—Steve, Stevie—whom Stephen the adult could remember only with difficulty as having been himself. He was forever an adult afterward. No one called him anything but Stephen.

Don't be ridiculous, people begged him.

He did not think God had made him ridiculous; he believed his occasional blunders and oversights and excesses of enthusiasm or feeling were natural to him, bound up with his physical being, in his blood and bones and genes, and had nothing to do with his spiritual certainties. Other Petries were ridiculous. Some were physically clumsy, some were socially clumsy, as if acting out of a perverse family pride, refusing to inhibit themselves as ordinary people did. There was an uncle, George Petrie, who cleared his throat violently and was unconscious of how he sounded, though it had been pointed out to him many times. Being told about himself, instructed about himself, was an unconscious experience for the man—he could not absorb it. He refused to absorb it. There was a cousin who had been a year ahead of Stephen at school, far more gauche than Stephen himself, always the butt of jokes, and yet quick-witted, shrewd, like all the Petries. There was another cousin. . . . And Stephen's paternal grandfather. . . . And his brother Hugh. And Andrew also, in a way: in a way he too had been ridiculous. Unlike Stephen, he had never realized.

The family is ridiculous, Stephen thought with satisfaction. *Everyone I know is ridiculous. . . . Human beings themselves are ridiculous.*

They told him over the telephone that a new issue had arisen. They were forced to question him again. He should not come to Albany on his own, however; it would be better for him merely to wait at the Center and a police escort would arrive to fly him up. Stephen asked what the issue was. They told him to wait at the Center. Was he arrested? he wanted to know. They would not keep him more than a few hours, no more than overnight. He could wait at the Center or at the police headquarters in Brandywine. Stephen said he would prefer the headquarters in Brandywine.

Shouldn't the father have died first? Stephen wondered. Even before the mother. That was nature. That was the natural process. Their mother had died too soon, had willed herself to die too soon; so the natural process had been upset. She had fallen down the back stairs of the house on Van Schuyler, drunk, had broken her back and damaged her liver, which was already degenerate, had never recovered from a week's coma. Everyone had grieved, Stephen most of all. He had not known how deeply he had loved her until she was dead; he had felt, in an inexplicable, obscure way, that she was dependent upon him, curiously dependent upon him, though for some time she had been indifferent to them all but particularly cool to him . . . as if he had badly disappointed her. Hugh too had taken the death hard. And their father, despite his numerous infidelities, had been shocked. They knew she would die, they knew she wished spitefully to die, but still they were not prepared and could not really believe what had happened. It was not the loss of her—they had lost her years before—but her absence, her total removal from their lives. She disappeared. She abandoned them. Doris told them that their mother had screamed at her once that *she* would never know what it was like—to lose her beauty—to have married so well and then to lose it; she, Doris, was at least saved that sorrow.

Now Andrew had died, now one of the children had died. The natural order was violated and they were made ridiculous. If the father had died first, perhaps the son's death would not seem so outrageous. Why else were people so alarmed and annoyed? . . . so resentful? *I don't really think of myself as belonging to that particular family,* Stephen explained. *For quite a few years I've been independent of them. . . . As for the antiwar activity and the people I knew then . . . the people with whom I worked during those years . . . there were hundreds of them, literally hundreds, and I have no contact with them or they with me . . . I'm totally dissociated from. . . . The Brandywine Community is nonpolitical except for some money we received under the Rural Extension Act. . . . I am totally nonpolitical now and dissociated from my past and independent of . . .*

He was being led through a series of questions by a portly, courteous man of early middle age, a stranger. It had happened that, the previous afternoon, Royal Canadian Mounted Police had confiscated certain weapons found in the custody of one Joseph Raschke, thirty-five, who had crossed the border at Coburn Gore, Maine, and had been stopped at Customs in St.-Augustin-De-Woburn, Quebec. . . . *I explained to you back in June that I've been out of contact for years . . . I have nothing to do with . . . as soon as the Movement condoned violence I quit, as I explained in June, and I have no political interests at all now.* Stephen spoke in his even, patient voice. *You can't possibly think that . . . there is some connection between my brother's death and Raschke and me. . . .*

He and Joseph Raschke had been jailed together, hadn't they, in Buffalo, New York, picked up with a number of other men and women for blocking the entrance to a U.S. Army induction center . . . ? Stephen's bail had been paid by his family. By Andrew, in fact. And afterward, had he seen Raschke again? Had they participated in similar activities again? No, Stephen said. *You can't possibly think. . . .*

It was just a coincidence. Really, they did not think anything.

None of this has anything to do with me or with Andrew, Stephen said. *I wouldn't recognize Raschke if I saw him. That doesn't look anything like him, that photograph . . . it doesn't look anything like the man I remember.*

Raschke had tried to cross into Canada with five semiautomatic FN rifles wrapped in canvas in the trunk of his 1969 Ford; he refused to explain to police what he was doing, who the rifles were for. The guns were standard issue to NATO troops, the sort that could easily be converted into automatic weapons. As far as Stephen knew, had Raschke been involved in smuggling?—in the Quebec Separatist movement?—where had he gotten his money from, did Stephen know? *I have nothing to do with these people,* Stephen said patiently. *It's a coincidence . . . it's not related . . . Raschke would never kill anyone . . . I hardly knew him except by reputation and he didn't know me at all, I doubt that he even knew my name when we were all herded off together. . . .*

Stephen answered as courteously as possible the questions put to him. At times he knew what they would be before they were asked. Was it God who gave him such knowledge, or the Devil . . . ? But he did not believe in the Devil. He did not believe in his own involvement with a man named Raschke, the various demonstrations and plots and melodramas of nearly a decade ago. It was another life, it was totally forgotten. God had been unpredictable in those years, sometimes rather reckless. A marvel, that God had survived; that God had survived in Stephen, who had been so innocent. The boy beside him had ducked and the club had landed squarely on Stephen's head. It had been raised and brought down again, this time on his right ear. . . . So innocent, that Stephen. But those years were gone. It was difficult to believe that anyone remembered them or that the police kept records of such things. *I must have met hundreds of people in those big demonstrations and rallies . . . the march to Washington . . . it was a time when I believed history might be directed by human intervention . . . I mean immediately, without recourse to God. Without direct and constant appeal to God. I was another person then, I met hundreds and hundreds of . . . None of us would remember the others now. The decade came to an end.*

The murder had taken place in June and now it was the second week of September, nearing autumn; a full season had passed. They asked him a few more questions, giving him more than enough time to reply. They watched him, like Perle. Like the others. *As a Jesuit novice I had a great deal of practice in examining my conscience,* Stephen said seriously. *I worked hard at self-analysis, investigating the state of my soul every morning and every night, and so I feel confident when I say that there isn't the slightest possibility of any connection of any kind . . . there never was, there couldn't have been. . . . I used my own money and I borrowed money from the family, I even borrowed a considerable sum from my brother Andrew . . . to post bail for a friend . . . but I was never guilty of anything other than what I was charged with, I never took part in any violent demonstrations at all, I didn't believe in them . . . I was a coward, also . . . I have always been a coward . . . in a certain sense I have always been a coward. Life is too valuable to be risked. Life is God, God is life. I don't understand why you are suspicious. . . .*

But they were not suspicious, they claimed. Not of him. They merely wanted to ask him questions, that was all. Since Raschke refused to talk. Since they were unable to locate any possible contacts of Raschke's in Canada, or any friends of his in the United States.

I haven't seen the man in years, Stephen said.
Did he know of anyone who might . . . ?
No. No one, Stephen said.

Once he and Andrew had talked at great length, had discussed a certain matter rather heatedly. They had not argued, not quite. Or perhaps they had argued in a way: Andrew probably would have said so. *Andrew* had argued. Stephen had resisted, had not argued. There had been a kind of victory in his resistance, in his warm, loving, and yet rather cruel tenderness, the cruelty of an impersonality of tenderness . . . Christlike, Godly, really inhuman. After the police questioned him this time he left the building and walked into the warm, humid, smoggy air of downtown, in a kind of trance, already forgetting the detectives' insolent questions, thinking instead of his brother's remarks, his own stubborn resistance, the impersonality of his flesh . . . that any weapon might pierce, any hostile consciousness might assault without really touching.

People say I court murder, people say I'm inflammatory, Andrew had laughed harshly, *but in my opinion you are much worse. . . . In you, Stephen, the process seems to be involuntary.*

Stephen had said he didn't understand. He had no idea what Andrew meant.

Yes, you have some idea, Andrew said slowly. *I think you sense the truth of what I'm saying . . . though perhaps you don't understand, you don't rationally understand, you couldn't express it in words. . . . No one can argue with you, no one can take any position in regard to you, because in a sense you don't exist. . . . You say every human being is a miracle, Stephen, and that to me is preposterous . . . the average human being is a cripple, a wreck, a parody . . . but what you mean is that you yourself are a miracle, the center of a miracle, and you invest the world with your transfigured vision; you give birth to the world, you and only you.*

Stephen smiled slowly. Was his brother joking? . . . it was wise, usually, to assume that Andrew was joking. Then one could not be mocked. And, of course, most of the time Andrew was joking.

I don't understand, Stephen said.

You are unconscious of the role you play in people's lives, Andrew said, *so you're unconscious of the degree to which you are responsible for what happens to them and to you.*

That isn't true! Stephen said. *I feel responsible for everything.*

But you feel that responsibility as a Thomist or an Aristotelian would, Andrew said. *Your guilt and what you call "responsibility" are a priori . . . to my mind it's just sentimentality and egotism . . . Christ on the cross once again bleeding all over us and expecting us to mourn, expecting us to be responsible for his assuming that colossal responsibility. But it's an outrage. It's inhuman.*

Stephen had to fight the impulse to walk away from his brother; he wanted suddenly to get free of him, to be free of that careful, relentless, delicately mocking voice. But he managed to say: *. . . You don't know Christ, you don't . . . don't know what you're talking about. . . . It isn't. . . . It wasn't. . . . His life counted, not his death. You have no right to talk like that. It's confusion . . . it's false. . . . No one can be judged by the way he dies or what happens afterward or anything extraneous to the life. . . . God is life, God is living, always living . . . God is living,* he said, his face warm, and for an instant he could not continue; could not even remember what he was saying. *. . . It isn't . . . it isn't what you think. . . . You're deluded. . . . You . . . You have listened to the wrong people. . . . You don't know God. . . . You don't even know Christ. . . .*

Andrew was obviously very embarrassed. He no longer looked at Stephen; he was looking pointedly away.

I'm sorry, Stephen said.

Are you?

. . . but the fact is you don't know Christ . . . you think he was a freak, you think he was divine . . . the only divine being. . . . You think what he experienced is something apart from you. . . . You think. . . . You don't understand. . . . You too are divine, there is no real difference between . . . between . . . between any of us. Christ was a man who became fully human. What he did with his humanity afterward is . . . isn't . . . isn't necessarily that important. . . . I'm sorry.

His voice was that of a guilty child's.

All right, Andrew said.

I'm innocent, Stephen thought at the time. God filled him and directed him. Weightless, he was. Like a reed that might bend this way or that, depending upon the breeze; lithe, willowy, subtle, so that it survived the most violent storms, bent flat against the earth if necessary, having no definable structure, no rigidity of form. *Innocent*, Stephen thought, hearing his own puzzled, hurt voice. He had set himself free from certain people and he had declared himself free of all merely human, entangling alliances; and so it puzzled him to

discover that he sometimes wanted to be listened to, wanted to be es-
teemed and taken seriously and even loved. But that was ridiculous.
That was vanity. If people listened to him and took him seriously,
they would not love him. *Outrage!* they would cry. *Inhuman!* they
would cry, backing away.

But he knew himself fundamentally innocent. After all, he had
surrendered everything except his innocence. He had surrendered the
rest of the world to people like his brother, who turned and turned it
in their hands and could not comprehend it.

He left the municipal building and walked slowly along the
crowded sidewalk. He imagined himself one of thousands out on the
street today. Miracles, all of them; but not distinguishable from one
another. Not really. He blended with them, he fell in step with them
unconsciously. If he were wearing better clothes and hadn't that
mournful look, he would have blended with them perfectly . . .
would have become invisible. He sensed the harmony of the street,
the harmony of the world . . . jarring warring rhythms that were
nevertheless contained in one pulse . . . one gigantic heartbeat . . .
perfected and completed but set back into motion, once more back
into motion, living in time. They were all perfect, all complete; but
they did not yet know it.

The police had released him. They had no further questions for
him at the moment and so he was free to return to the Center. He
was free to go anywhere as long as he kept in touch. . . . A leaf
among leaves, a stream of water passing into a larger body of water,
shifting into invisibility. They knew he was innocent yet they had
watched him covertly, strangely, as Perle had watched him; as nearly
everyone watched him. Waiting for him to tell them a secret, waiting for him to stumble and blunder and reveal himself . . . when
there was nothing for him to reveal, no secret, nothing that was not
evident in his very existence.

The police had watched him with an air of faint incredulity, yet
with an air of dread, too. He had sensed that. He did not understand
it. His mother's sharp-edged voice, that quaver that ran through her
body: a sense of fear, alarm, dread. His father had ignored him ge-
nially. Had not wanted to know him. His brothers, his sister. . . .
His brother's widow. . . .

They wanted him to explain and yet they dreaded his explanation.
They dreaded, in him, something still unformed . . . something still
in the making. *Would you like me to confess?* he might suddenly say

to the police. *I am as responsible as anyone else. I knew he would die.*

But he could not confess to his brother's murder, since he was innocent. It was not going to be his privilege to confess.

3

So you think she will remarry?

It's a question of when. Of how soon.

But she isn't seeing anyone, is she? . . . Of course she isn't seeing anyone. That would be intolerable.

If she has a lover, he's in hiding. They could wait for years.

But does she have a lover?

The woman is very clever, very prudent. The way she seduced Andrew and destroyed his marriage. . . .

That was horrible. That phase of his life was horrible.

How can you people be so certain she has a lover? . . . I'm under the impression she's entirely alone and still in a state of shock . . . she doesn't even realize that Andrew is dead.

They were silent. One of them said quietly: *That's true for all of us, isn't it?*

Stephen sat in their midst, his face heavy with blood and shame. God had slipped from him; he felt himself opaque now, and very mortal. While the others drank he sat with his elbows on the table, staring at the fresh-cut chrysanthemums a few feet away. Back at the old house, back at the old dining-room table. But not in his former place: one of his aunts was sitting there. . . . The flowers were striking, dusty red and yellow. *I belong here*, Stephen thought listlessly. *I'm needed here.*

Doris had wanted him to stay with her. Since Andrew's death she had not been well, she claimed; woke often during the night, her heart racing, her mouth dry. She was terrified of sleep. Arnold did not understand, wasn't capable of understanding, only Stephen could understand. . . . The family was being destroyed. Everything was being destroyed. Father was dying and Hugh had cut himself off from them, had turned out so badly; Stephen must come home for a while, until this crisis was past. *I can't be of any help to you,*

Stephen had said. *To you or anyone.* But she wanted him close, she insisted. And he was too weak to resist.

He did not mean to be spying on his own family. He did not mean to listen to them with such detachment. But his soul had faded, had withered, and he was left at his sister's dinner table, in the old house he had repudiated, listening coldly to their voices. They made plans, they thought aloud, they speculated. Always they spoke of Andrew's widow, always they circled her, round and round. *We're certain she has a lover. We have our reasons for thinking so. . . . No, we don't know who it is; she's too clever to be found out.* The police investigation, Andrew's complicated posthumous affairs, Andrew's very death—these seemed less crucial than the subject of the widow, about whom so little was known.

She'll be a model of grief for a year, Doris was saying tremulously, *and then watch . . . ! I know her kind. Just from looking at her eyes, those sneering eyes of hers. . . . I know her, I know that kind. A year and a half at the most. As soon as the estate is settled she'll marry again. Like that . . . what was her name . . . that awful, awful woman who got Charles's stepbrother to marry her . . . that Cuban or whatever she was, that nightclub singer. . . .*

Is Yvonne still so unfriendly to you and Arnold?

Unfriendly! She positively loathes us. Won't let us near her. I've begged her to give up that apartment . . . it must have hideous memories for her, don't you think? She could live here; we have so much room, so much extra room, an entire suite over the garage, now that Rosalind is at school, and so beautifully decorated. . . . She could live here and work with his papers, edit them or sort them, whatever she's doing, she could work here far more easily than there and I'd be delighted to help her. . . . In fact I think I should be helping her, I think I have a right to help with Andrew's final papers. But she refuses. She won't listen. Isn't that right, Arnold? . . . She loathes us.

I wouldn't say she necessarily loathes us, Doris.

You don't know, you aren't subtle enough to catch her nuances. I only pray that she doesn't disgrace us all. After the horrible thing that happened to Andrew. . . .

Brandywine was lost to Stephen: so he was in Albany, in exile. He touched one of the mums. Gently, very gently. How minute the petals, compact and firm and still living. . . . His spirit had slipped from him, he felt dehydrated, unreal. He knew that his spirit would return. God would return. He did not know when, he never knew.

He sat now with members of his family, trying not to eavesdrop, trying to love them, forgive them. What did it matter, the petty, cruel
things they were saying, what did any of it matter?—they were innocent, they could not help themselves. They were still in shock.

On the bank of the Laurel Creek he had known he would not be
returning to Brandywine. He had known even before Perle came to
tell him about the telephone call. It had been a paradise to him, the
little community, though it was stunted and impoverished and isolated; he had loved it. He had worked very hard there for the last
several years. Miners' children, handicapped children, a special class
of older students that included several parolees. . . . Stephen had
worked with them eagerly, had worked very hard; but in the end it
had not been enough. He did not belong. Since his brother's death
and the ugly publicity surrounding the death, he had known that that
paradise must expel him.

He always knew. Paradise was continually expelling him and he always knew ahead of time; he tried to leave with dignity.

. . . *it might be necessary to get a court order.* . . .

*Yes, we've talked about that. Roddy has talked about that with
George but they're wary of her, they don't want to alarm her—she
could do something impulsive and hysterical as long as the papers
are in her possession. . . . But on the other hand. . . .*

*We've approached the boy, Andrew's son, but so far without any
luck . . . Willa always gets in the way, claims Michael is on the
verge of a breakdown, rants and raves about the psychic damage
Andrew did to him that can't be undone. . . . The usual thing. It
might be true, as far as I know.*

Stephen turned to his uncle, Roderick. The man was high-colored,
totally bald, with surprisingly round hazel eyes and a small, ginger
mustache. His manner was prim, neat, precise, yet at the same time
wide-eyed, almost childlike. He looked far younger than his true age
—which must have been at least sixty—and kept, in circles in which
his elder brother had once reigned, a certain good-humored naïveté,
a semblance of spontaneity. Perhaps it was genuine. Stephen had
never known any of his father's brothers or sisters well. There were
too many Petries, too many older people to be respected; certainly
there must have been, to the older generation, far too many nieces
and nephews to be taken seriously. Of Stephen's generation only
Andrew and Harvey had emerged as really significant, though a girl—
Pamela's older sister Frances—had married the son of the chief stock-
holder of the second wealthiest conglomerate in the world; and one

of George Petrie's boys, Stephen's contemporary almost to the month, had become a quietly famous Washington attorney. Still, Roderick Petrie had always seemed fond of Stephen, had often turned his disingenuous hazel gaze in Stephen's direction. He imagined him simple-minded, perhaps. Like a number of Petrie men of the second or third rank, he seemed to prefer the attention of the uncritical, and so had a reputation as a ladies' man. In fact he was considered very clever, the senior partner of an Albany investment house, and rumor had it—though Stephen discounted most rumors—that only some very extraordinary financial manipulations engineered by Roderick years ago had kept the Governor of the state and Stephen's father and a number of other men from having to face a merciless, opportunistic U.S. Attorney General's investigation. But the story was cloudy, it was really not at all clear. Stephen found it difficult to believe that his uncle, smiling so artlessly and so sadly, would be capable of anything requiring a great deal of mental effort.

. . . *Michael isn't well?* Stephen asked.

Willa claims he has hallucinations, Roderick said, *claims he can't stop talking to his father . . . I mean, talking to his dead father. . . . He sometimes just babbles, she says, and can't understand himself what he means . . . and he's no fool, you know, he's a very, very bright boy! . . . and at other times he's quite rational and just mutters under his breath or whispers or moves his lips. He's always trying to explain something, they think. What was it, Gladys? . . . something to do with. . . .*

Willa told me it's something to do with finances and with Michael's future, his career . . . he intends to be a historian and rewrite certain things . . . or explain them . . . or predict them. Willa and he don't quite know though they've made tapes of some of his conversations. Yes, and he has other subjects too, sometimes he's accusing Andrew and even shouting at him, but Willa says that's just in his sleep . . . they don't think that really takes priority.

Does Andrew reply? Stephen asked.

His question had been an entirely serious one. But it was received in a slightly shocked silence; then everyone laughed. *No, of course he doesn't reply,* Roderick said. *The poor boy isn't raving mad. It's just a temporary problem, like a nervous tic or a cough, they think . . . though it seems more serious to me. . . . When he's in strong physical health, however, they say the problem doesn't bother him because he simply talks to Andrew through whoever he's with, through whoever he happens to be with. He's even well enough to be back at school, they say. At least he enrolled for a course somewhere. But Willa always exaggerates their good fortune, those two . . . they've both become preposterous, you know. But I won't go into details. He might be recovered by now: the family has always had a remarkable capacity for adjusting to disasters, don't you think? . . . It was really very clever of the boy to seize upon the device of addressing Andrew so elliptically, and he's skillful at it, I spoke with him over the phone once or twice and he was even able to refer to his father in the third person . . . "Father," he would say . . . or "Andrew" . . . and there was just the slightest hint of a stammer, but he kept trying and got through without a slip. He said "Good-by, Uncle Roderick," when he hung up. I could hear the strain, but he managed . . . he got through.*

Stephen rolled his eyes suddenly. He felt an impulse to jump up from the table and run out of the room. His heart hammered, he even pressed his hand against it involuntarily.

Stephen . . . ? Doris said at once.

He shook his head wordlessly. For an instant there had been danger, real danger. Ah, to jump up, to fling his chair back against the wall, to run out . . . to run out to the boulevard. . . . Once there he might burst into tears or burst into laughter or simply continue running along the street. It was as if a powerful force had inquired of him whether he might like to be scooped up and flung away, and for an instant he had nearly consented; but now the danger was over, the moment had passed.

That's . . . that news is . . . that seems to me very serious, he said. He spoke easily, though his heart was still hammering. *I mean, it seems very serious. Maybe I should visit Michael, maybe if. . . .*

Doris interrupted. She was so agitated that one of her earrings came loose and she fussed with it, readjusting it as she spoke. *Now Stephen, now you know . . . you know your presence can have . . . sometimes it can have a slightly unfortunate effect on . . . on unstable people. You went to visit them once, just before the divorce, didn't you? . . . and Willa was . . . well, as you must know . . . the visit wasn't a success.*

Willa telephoned me and asked me to come, Stephen said.

She denied telephoning you. . . . Her side of the story was quite different from yours.

Stephen did not reply. He knew they were waiting for him to defend himself; but he was not going to defend himself. He knew they probably believed him and not Willa—they wanted to believe him, not Willa, because they liked the idea of Willa being hysterical, perhaps even a little mad; but he was not going to accuse his sister-in-law of having lied.

Yes, her side of the story was certainly different from yours, one of them said.

Willa had telephoned Stephen late one night, at Brandywine. She had told him she had a bottle of sleeping pills in her hand and she intended to swallow them all unless he came to her at once . . . she was distraught because of Andrew's behavior, she didn't want to live any longer, could not bear the shame and the humiliation of the divorce . . . the knowledge that Andrew had fallen in love with another woman. Stephen had agreed to come. He had agreed at once. . . . But when he got to her apartment she denied having called him. She denied everything. Awaiting him in a champagne-colored negligee, her hair dramatically messed, her manner fierce and triumphant and bitter, she had denied everything except possibly "thinking" of him. She had only "thought" of him. She had "thought" of him to see if perhaps she was capable of making contact with him across the miles. Stephen had a reputation for being psychic, she said, and she too had such powers—though no one took her seriously. So she had called for him, experimentally, with her mind. But now that he was actually there . . . now that he stood before her, Stephen in his living body, Stephen Petrie himself in her Park Avenue apartment, she found she had no interest in him. . . . When he went past her into her bedroom, however, to see if there were sleeping pills by the telephone, she rushed after him and screamed for him to leave; she threatened to call the police. *You have no right! No right to humiliate me! Any of you! I'll expose you one by one—all of you—not just Andrew but all of you*—Stephen had found the bottle of sleeping pills on the bedtable, beside the telephone.

. . . a very nervous, excitable woman . . . too highly strung . . . even before her marriage to Andrew went sour she was too sensitive, Doris was saying sadly. *It's best for us to stay away from her, even if she does sometimes seem appealing. And of course poor little Michael is pathetic. But don't visit them, Stephen, please. Not again.*

. . . if Michael were there also, maybe . . . maybe. . . . If Willa and I weren't alone together. . . . Maybe it would be all right.

No! Please! You don't know the accusations she made against you. I wouldn't embarrass us all by repeating them. It's horrible,

452   THE ASSASSINS

*heartbreaking, how Willa turned against certain members of the
family . . . those of us who loved her, who actually sided with her
from time to time against Andrew. She has got it into her head that
some of us are her personal enemies, out to destroy her. In your case,
Stephen, it might have something to do with the Ferguses' old
hatred of Catholics . . . dating back to the seventeenth century in
England. There's no reasoning with her. Jesuits in particular, Jesuits
more than anyone else, turn her irrational. She says there are historical records in her family . . . all sorts of scandals and outrages involving the Jesuits in England at that time . . . and she won't believe
me when I tell her that you left the seminary, you were never ordained, never took any vows . . . did you? . . . she won't believe any
of us. She says that is part of the plot. The Jesuits' conspiracy. To
convince people they don't even exist, that their membership is
declining. . . .*

*. . . Yes, she hates Stephen most of all. It's uncanny, how she
hates Stephen. And do you know who she likes? . . . she's always inquiring after . . . ?*

Harvey?

Not Harvey: Hugh.

They were silent.

Stephen felt absurdly hurt.

For a moment no one spoke. Then Harvey came from another
room—he had been on the telephone in Arnold's study and asked
what they were talking about, why they had such odd looks on their
faces; and they told him about Willa's affection for Hugh; and he sat
down, smiling, a handsome man in the prime of life, even more ex-
pansive than usual. *The woman enjoys martyrdom,* he said. *She
enjoys being a victim.*

. . . but it was never actually proven that. . . .

*Of course Hugh stole that ring or pin or whatever it was! . . . do
you think he didn't? . . . he'd been trying to borrow money from all
of us, he was pretending to be desperate as usual, and Willa enjoyed
him, his misery, she liked to lead miserable people on and then say
she couldn't help them, Andrew wouldn't let her, and. . . . She did
it even with men, in a romantic sense,* Harvey said bluntly, *she was
deliberately seductive and then conscience-stricken, I've been told,
and I've heard the tale from enough sources . . . very reliable
sources. . . . She could be an icy calculating bitch, as bad as the second wife, and as long as her looks lasted she played that little game
. . . though Andrew knew all about it; frankly, he confided in me*

once himself, and seemed totally defeated. . . . With Hugh, however. . . .

It *was a diamond stickpin,* Irene said suddenly. She had been silent for some time; now she spoke, calling down the length of the table to her husband. Her voice was sweetly piercing, like a sea gull's cry, but subdued, almost melodious. . . . *an old-fashioned diamond stickpin. I remember very clearly.*

. . . with Hugh, Harvey said, nodding in his wife's direction but not quite acknowledging her, *she enjoyed the delicious possibility of his going berserk on his knees before her . . . maybe even murdering her, eh? . . . but I'm only joking, of course! . . . only joking. Hugh is harmless and wouldn't hurt a louse. He wouldn't hurt a louse without being hurt himself, in a psychological sense; he's very sensitive, you know. . . . So Willa's partiality for Hugh doesn't surprise me in the slightest. She liked it that he stole from her and Andrew, she liked it that the poor bastard was suicidal and . . . what was the problem? . . . being blackmailed by an ex-friend. Ah, the women we men marry!* he laughed. He poured himself a glass of brandy and scanned the faces of his audience, his gaze slipping around to everyone, to each place, in an eerily adroit and practiced manner. Yet almost immediately he was speaking again in the same generous, amused voice. It was as if he had seen no one at all. . . . *a bizarre inclination toward the precarious, the forbidden, the wobbling, the dizzy . . . the hopeless . . . the victimized . . . There's a strain in the family that should be investigated by a sociologist like the man who worked up the Jukes, do you remember the Jukes? . . . almost no one does; now they're bleached out and anonymous, they're everywhere. Except for a few of us, a few of us men, the Petries have chosen improbable mates, they've been guided more by romance than reason, and look at the merry chase old Theodore is leading you, Doris! . . . do you think you'll get to him before it's too late and he marries her? I foresee years and years of litigation, trying to break the old boy's will and trying to whittle down Yvonne's haul. . . . Like old times.*

But Harvey had gone too far. Stephen sensed the man's sly satisfaction at having alluded to something not known to everyone at the table. Harvey sipped at his drink and sighed.

Doris's father, Arnold Laubach said stiffly, *is in perfectly good health . . . he's of sound mind and body for a man his age. He is his own agent. You must have . . . there have been . . . some very ugly rumors have come back to me and I . . . they . . . they are ground-less.*

It was late now, nearly eleven o'clock. Yet they remained at the table as if powerless to break away. Stephen was staring at his hands. While Harvey spoke he had tried to detach himself from the man's voice, which he found terrifying; he examined his rather large hands, his bony knuckles, his nicely shaped fingers and irregular fingernails, and hummed under his breath a song he had liked in boyhood, an English folk song from a record of folk songs he had played over and over one year . . . that he had not remembered now for a long time. Harvey answered someone's query and someone else spoke, wrenching the topic back to Yvonne, always back to Yvonne, and Stephen flexed his fingers and hummed so that no one could hear.

> There once was a ship and she sailed upon the sea
> And the name of our ship was the *Golden Vanity*. . . .

What did you say, Stephen? one of them asked.

He looked up. He let his hands fall.

Did you say something, Stephen?

He indicated that he had not. Doris went on to complain about Yvonne, who was always busy; had no time to meet for lunch; and would not listen to their offer of the suite above the garage. Senator Enslin had met the woman at a reception last Christmas and had complimented her on being even prettier than her photographs and she had simply stared at him . . . had stared at him as if she were deaf . . . so that he repeated what he said and everyone was embarrassed except the woman . . . and Andrew was nowhere near . . . and finally when he tried for the third time she interrupted him to say that he looked exactly like his photographs; and that was all she said, just that. *She thinks she can insult anyone. She's horrible.*

She thought she could insult anyone, but that's past tense now. Now the atmosphere has changed.

But she doesn't know it! She won't admit it! . . . Adrienne Greason was shocked at the woman's rudeness to her and Leon, and she's too nice, she's too goodhearted . . .

She's a stupid woman, let's face it.

. . . too goodhearted to see Yvonne for what she is. Even Leon, who has had plenty of experience dealing with criminals, can't seem to. . . .

Can't you get in her confidence, Harvey? one of the women asked.

I! In her confidence! Not at all! he said, raising his hands in dismay. *The respect I owe Andrew's memory, for one thing . . . I hate spies and informers . . . can't bear dishonesty . . . actually feel pity for the poor deluded bitch . . . No, I'm not your boy. Not me.*

Stephen was humming. He raised his hands and flexed the fingers again, watching them. They moved to his face, the fingertips pressed against his cheeks, shifting upward so that his eyes were forced half-closed. There was a ringing in his head. It was his own humming, singing, under his breath. No one noticed. . . . He tried to resist, but he found himself staring at Harvey surreptitiously through his thick dark lashes. *Her lover. Yvonne's lover,* came the thought.

. . . Send the clergy, send the Boy Scout, our little mascot Christ, Harvey said slyly.

Stephen regained his composure. He tried to laugh. Despite the crudeness of Harvey's remark, nearly everyone was laughing. Doris was laughing. Irene. Arnold Laubach, however, sat stiff, isolated. He must have been thinking still of Judge Petrie out in Palm Springs, rumored to be engaged to a twenty-seven-year-old divorcée, a cocktail waitress at the Racquet Club. He looked ashen, meditative.

She would eat Stephen up, one of the men said slyly.

She would not: she certainly would not. That's ridiculous, Irene said. *I think you're cruel to . . . it's cruel to. . . . There are some things that. . . .*

Stephen is staying close to home, Doris said, *he doesn't know quite what to do next and I . . . I really need someone to talk to . . . someone I don't even have to talk to, if you know what I mean. . . . No, we shouldn't joke about any of this. We're drunk. We're saying awful things. . . . I can't remember what we've been saying. . . .*

Stephen and Harvey exchanged a quick, rather embarrassed look. Then Stephen got to his feet, resisting the impulse to jump up. His face was flushed, his heartbeat again fast. He tried to smile as normal people do. But something was flooding in him now, something was rushing back into him, and when he spoke his voice was unnaturally loud, almost exuberant. It was too loud. One of the women winced.

. . . thank you very much and good night. . . .

Not offended with me, Stephen? Harvey said softly.

. . . good night . . . it was very. . . .

The late hour and we've all been drinking and it isn't like any of us . . . it isn't anything we mean to say . . . I don't even know what we've been saying, Doris muttered, *if anyone was listening to us they . . . nobody . . . it would be impossible to know who we were . . .*

*it's all confused and wrong . . . I can't bear it without Stephen here,
he knows that, Stephen, don't you know that? . . . it isn't anything
I can describe but . . . but . . . I need someone close to me that I
don't even have to . . . I need someone who won't. . . . I can't remember what Harvey said but he was only joking as he always is, as
Andrew always was and. . . . Stephen . . . ?*

For some men and women, Stephen began, again too loudly; then
he paused, swallowed, seemed to forget what he was saying; the
flooding sensation was growing stronger, his skull was filling with an
extraordinary light, invisible and insubstantial and yet on the verge
of being painful . . . so he lost track of what he was saying. Then he
remembered. He said, stammering slightly, *For some men and
women . . . the life of celibacy is . . . our natures demand. . . . The
rest of you are ignorant and totally fail to realize that . . . that . . .
that there are human beings among you very different from you. . . .*
The stammer ceased, he spoke now quite readily, quickly, backing
away from the table and addressing them all: *There are men and
women who recognize their limitations . . . they recognize their responsibilities . . . they know they are not like other people and can't
take on the burden of . . . they can't love, they can't marry . . . it
would be evil of them to marry because they can't belong to anyone
. . . to any . . . any one person. . . . It would be using another
human being for them to pretend . . . to go in disguise . . . being
normal, n-normal, what you call normal. . . . the life of celibacy is
our decision . . . celibacy is . . . it isn't . . . it isn't what you think,
it isn't weakness or timidity or impotence . . . it is a sacred duty . . .
respect for other people, who could be hurt. . . . The less human
you are, gravitating toward God or away from God, the more danger
you are to human beings. . . .*

They stared at him in astonishment. It was not Stephen who
spoke, but another. At the same time it was Stephen, Stephen's
voice, even the faint stammer he had outgrown . . . it was a Petrie
speech, in a way: and the sort of exit Andrew had made often, concluding a dinner party, bringing a discussion to an end by simply
stating his case and backing away.

*You are crude, ignorant people and you . . . you fail to . . . you
have always failed to. . . .*

He left without finishing. Suddenly he had to leave the room, had
to leave the house, had to throw the front door open and run out
into the cool moonlit October night. There was a moon, he saw that
at once. He ran down the hill to the street and already he was forget-

ting, nothing seemed of any importance except the pressure in his mind, which was exquisitely painful, exquisitely pleasurable. Still the thought came to him: *Her lover. He is her lover now.* But the idea was preposterous. It was inaccurate. Somehow he knew it was inaccurate. He had got it wrong. But he did not want to get it right, he did not want to think about it at all, already he was away from them and forgetting.

Still certain thoughts came to him, even as he ran from them. He heard one of the women say *Is he . . . ?* and he heard his sister's voice reply *The worst of us all . . . still in shock.* But this was preposterous too. He could not hear their voices. He ran, panting. Slowed to a walk, then ran again to escape such nonsense. Behind him they were still talking of him in their hushed, shocked, slightly thrilled voices, and he knew it was impossible for him to hear; he did not want to hear. . . . *He gave me a murderous look,* Harvey was saying. *That man is dangerous.*

Next morning he telephoned his sister from a pay phone.

. . . am leaving Albany in an hour, he said.

What? Stephen? You frightened us all so. . . .

I'm leaving, I'll write, never mind about my things, nothing is worth much, it's all—all— I'm leaving, he said, *I've got to leave this city today.*

4

Andrew's wife had come up quietly behind him and asked him what they had been quarreling about.

Stephen started, having thought himself alone.

. . . Not what you think, he said.

He had not meant to be rude. The words came out unbidden.

How do you know what I think! the woman said at once, stung. *You don't know what I think.*

The spray of cherry blossoms he had picked was in an old Wedgewood vase, set in the center of the dining-room table. Earlier, the vase had been set on the stone mantel in the living room. She must have moved it while he and Andrew were shut in together for most of the afternoon. She must have assumed he would be staying for dinner; but he would not be staying for dinner.

. . . sorry you upset him, he hasn't been well . . . hasn't been sleeping . . . he needs solitude, needs to be away from quarreling . . . from people who. . . .

Yes, Stephen said curtly. *I know.*

He walked away and she followed him, a few steps behind him; they were in the front drive. Stephen moved without knowing quite what he did. His brother had slapped him, hard: the left side of his face burned and throbbed. Stephen was ashamed, did not want her to see his reddened face, did not want to look at her directly. She was asking again about their conversation. *Please don't leave without telling me,* she said in her quick cool voice, *I have a right to know and I can't ask Andrew . . . he doesn't care to burden me with family problems. Is it about money, is it just that you want him to donate money to your, to the group you belong to in West Virginia? . . . do you want this farm, is that it? . . . he said something about. . . .*

I don't want anything from him, Stephen said over his shoulder.

. . . he said you once borrowed twenty-five thousand dollars . . . bail for one of your friends. . . . And the money was lost, the man left the country. . . .

Stephen rubbed the left side of his face. It did burn: he could feel the heat. He wondered if she would be able to see that he had been struck. *Is it money you want again,* she said, less confidently, *because if. . . . Sometimes. . . . Sometimes Andrew will listen to me if. . . .*

I didn't bring up the past, Stephen said, *I don't intend to bring up the past . . . it's not only insignificant, it's . . . it's gone. All that is gone.*

I don't know what you mean, Yvonne said.

Her voice had sounded faint, baffled. The last word had died away.

Stephen walked without direction and she did not follow. He rubbed his face briskly. By accident he was headed out toward the highway, striding along the grassy lane between the rows of scrubby untrimmed pine. Yvonne remained back near the house and Stephen walked away, rubbing his face and eyes as if trying to wake himself up. When she called after him they were some distance apart. He could not quite hear her. He had nearly forgotten her, had nearly excluded her from his consciousness. He had excluded Andrew as well. But her voice intruded: *Don't leave. . . .* It was too faint for him to hear. He did not acknowledge it. Andrew had ordered him to leave this property but he was not acknowledging his brother's angry voice either. He was simply walking away.

5

God sleeps and man stirs: Stephen's cautious wisdom.

Years might roll by in God's immense sleep, entire lifetimes consumed in agitation, plots and counterplots among human beings, remarkable melodramas, seductive comedies, libraries of intensely argued and convincing logic . . . and then, God's sleep abruptly ended, God awakes and man subsides into silence, hardly time for a shriek before everything collapses. *God stirs and man is broken,* Stephen thought, *and broken and broken. . . .*

Had God come to Stephen as an adult, he too might have shrieked; might have resisted. It was probable that he would have been destroyed. But God had come to Stephen many years before, when Stephen had not known enough to be terrified. So he had not resisted. A sweet-tempered child, rather passive and docile, obedient, content to play by himself for hours at a time: with dark curly hair, a curious abstract cast to his brown eyes, a manner sometimes unnaturally still and then again springy, quick, restless, like a small animal. He was the baby of the family and theoretically everyone loved him. In fact, apart from his mother's occasional sorties against him, apart from the overheated emotional charges she made—and which, even as a very small child, Stephen seemed to want to resist, rather shrewdly—everyone let him alone. He was a child who could be trusted, as it appeared his brother, Hugh, was not; so they let him alone. Asked by a friend what sort of childhood he had had in that family, in that ornate, pretentious house, always with so many relatives and visitors and intrigues, Stephen had replied warmly: *I was free. I was always free.* The ineffable joy of freedom imprinted itself upon him for life. . . . In the foyer of the Petrie home there was a handsome, wide, winding staircase, and beneath the first landing there was an alcove, a nook that might have been specially constructed for children. It had been fitted out with a pewlike bench, of carved mahogany with faded wine-colored velvet cushions, and a miniature wall lamp, and a small bookcase that must have held about seventy-five books, all of them old. When Stephen sat in the alcove he was shielded from the foyer, from the front door, and only at a slant could anyone see him from the living room or the hallway that led back to the kitchen and the servants' stairway. He spent innumerable hours there even before he could read, looking through the books, turning page after page of encyclopedias printed in the 1890's or of old romances of the post-Revolutionary War era like *Rosalie Du Pont: or Treason Close to Home* . . . intensely curious, fascinated, mystified by the sheer bulk of knowledge that evidently awaited him and would be accessible in time. Stacked inside the bench, whose seat lifted, were even older books—rain-warped, yellowed, falling to pieces. Stephen turned their pages, Stephen was attentive to their mysterious hieroglyphics, reverent before their occasional illustrations and frontispieces. It was treasure, though stored away so carelessly. He knew it was treasure. All he required was the key, the secret code, and these revelations would speak to him: the secret message of a tattered dog-eared almanac of 1790, the secret message of the brown-tinted illustration at the front of *Oliver Twist*, the messages of shepherds and sheep and men and women with halos circling their heads and infinitely detailed maps of New Amsterdam and The Colonies and New France and the Indian Nations. . . . He loved the huge leather-bound King James Bible and the poorly sewn quartos of illustrated sermons, some of them by men whose last names were *Petrie*; he loved the illustrated spy narratives, the pictures of Indians leading white men through the brush, scenes of intense but arrested drama. One opened a page and had immediate access, as if by magic, to an instant in another's life; one turned pages until there was a conclusion, THE END in tall dignified letters, a sense of obscure but powerful accomplishment. Stephen loved his hours of solitude, his isolation, he loved the freedom to daydream or listen to the sounds of the enormous house or to study, with a curiously heightened sense of the importance of what he did, any book, any page in any book, any illustration or map, *anything at all*.

They said Stephen was hidden away for hours when he was away for only a few minutes. Time was crushed flat; he was snatched free of it, shaken a little as if to wake him more fully, and then he plunged into whatever he was examining, thinking of nothing else, aware of nothing else. His mind drifted loose. He was utterly content, immobile. In the midst of staring at one of the illustrations that always attracted him—a girl with long wavy hair, arms outstretched, leaning forward into a mirror that dissolved in order to allow her entry—he might find himself suddenly and unaccountably in another part of the house, suspended weightless in his own room,

observing the placid look of the room when it was empty, or he
might discover himself in the old coachhouse, in the semidarkness,
breathing in the pleasant chill odor of metal, hearing a conversation
he could not quite interpret—handymen, strangers?—or he might
be at the farm or at the seashore or only a few yards away, aware of
himself in the alcove, his feet propped up on one of the shelves opposite the bench. He was always placid, immobile, perfectly content.
His heartbeat was imperceptible. He was not aware of blinking or
swallowing or thinking—he did not think at all. He was lifted loose
of his body, he was set down somewhere else, in absolute silence:
with no emotion whatsoever. He felt no terror, no surprise, no giddiness. Everything was intensely vivid, as if illuminated especially for
his observation, brought to a stop, arrested, somehow permanent
even as it moved, flowed, altered in a sequence he knew to be extraordinary. It was extraordinary because it took place, in the way in
which it took place. He was present, bodiless. He too was extraordinary, as a witness; he floated in the air, but he could not move of
his own will, he simply appeared and disappeared with the rapidity
of light.

In a crumbling book with the title *The Settling of North America*
there was a large map that stretched across two pages near the front
of the book, and this map—*New France and the Indian Nations*—
fascinated Stephen nearly as much as the drawing of the girl and the
mirror. Through this, into this, somehow by means of this yellowed,
ripped map, he found himself transported. . . . He lost track of
time, he lost himself, awoke elsewhere, was made to see as if by an
unspoken command a certain flashing, darting, near-instantaneous vision: a red cardinal in one of the big trees behind the house, merely
the flashing of its wings, the flashing of color itself. Or he found himself for a moment at school, in his seat, staring at the blackboard and
what his teacher had written there. Or his father bending over him,
perhaps bending over his crib, years before, contemplating him, expressionless as if judging, but judging without partiality, without bias.
There could be no help from that father: so Stephen guessed. So he
knew. No help from *that* father. Stephen knew without knowing
that he knew. And in the next second the vision would have disappeared, flicked away, as if it were of no real consequence.

Freedom, Stephen thought. As an adult he could think. As an
adult he could think back upon his childhood, which no longer
baffled him. *That was my freedom. The beginning.*

But there was something about the old map in itself that fascinated him. It resembled maps in his geography textbooks and yet it was different, subtly and exotically different. There was no *United States*. This was a section of the world designated as *New France*. Where the *State of New York* now reigned there was only the notation *Iroquois* and, subordinate to that word, *Senecas, Cayugas, Onondagas, Oneidas, Mohawks*. The Adirondack Mountains were indicated; the Catskills; the St. Lawrence River and Lake Ontario and Lake Erie; Lake Huron, Lake Superior; directions of North South East West; and the Atlantic Ocean. But everything that belonged to a specific moment in history, everything specifically human, expressed in peculiarly enchanting human language, was unrecognizable. So he was fascinated, so he could not resist shaping the exotic words aloud, moving his finger across the map slowly, reverently, in a kind of trance: *Chippewas . . . Ottawas . . . Pottawattomies . . . Eries . . . Wenronronons . . . Petuns . . . Nipissings . . . Algonquins . . . Montagnais . . . Tadoussac. . . .* The world had been a different world. It had been different then. Not very long ago. There were modern cities indicated in parentheses, as if they were ghostly, mere ideas or premonitions: *(Detroit) . . . (New Amsterdam)-(New York) . . . (Toronto) . . . (Ottawa) . . . (Albany)*. Many years ago someone had made a tiny mark in black ink beside *(Albany)*. A child, perhaps. Stephen supposed it had been one of his ancestors. The child had marked the spot upon which he existed at the moment he marked the spot, as if to locate himself, to make a declaration of some kind. Then time stopped: the child leaning over the map, perhaps hesitant to mark it, fearing punishment. Still, he had marked it. *(Albany)x*. Stephen, a bolder child, knowing himself free because he was not being watched and knowing himself unwatched because he was not especially loved, and therefore free, released to a life of exquisite indefinable freedom, got an old-fashioned pen out of his father's study and made the mark firmer.

I am here, Stephen said. . . . *I was here*. Afterward, leafing through the book again and pausing at the map, the thought would come to him: *Someone was here*.

And yet no one was there. Repeatedly, no one was there.

They said he stayed away for hours but Stephen experienced the passage of time differently. It flashed, it became very dazzling, blinding, and then it seemed to shut again, like a book being closed or a light simply switched off. Sometimes they did not miss him when, in fact, he was away for hours. They seemed not to notice him, not to be aware of his absence. At the dinner table, at school, he could feel in an instant that extraordinary swelling, that intensification of perception and of light that played about everything, and even as his father was speaking or as his teacher was writing something on the blackboard, even as one of his brothers was approaching him, or his mother fondling him and whining over him, he seemed to escape, to slip out of himself. One of the pastures at the old farm especially drew him. And he was drawn also to the seashore, to the river, to the view from the window of his room. There was no time for Stephen to get his bearings, no time for him really to recognize his surroundings, to give any name to them. He was there, in an instant. Or perhaps the view came to him, slipped itself between him and the others, for a moment, only a moment. There was no time for him to think *This is what is happening here when I'm not here* or *This is what is happening here when no one is here*; there was no time for him to think at all. It was very clean, razor-sharp and clean. His eyes burned with the need to see what presented itself to be seen. He was always alone, and yet totally enclosed, protected. He went empty, he felt himself turning invisible, yet there was no danger—at times, especially as he grew older, he seemed to know that the danger arose at that delicate instant at which he stopped breathing and gave over to the other side, gave himself over to it, so that the air surrounding him flowed into him, into his lungs, taking over the rhythm of his conscious breathing, and he became aware in a shadowy way of his entire quivering body, very much alive, trembling with life, buoyed up by the air that surrounded it and insinuated itself into its lungs, warmed by its streams of blood, a dense clotty shadowy network of blood. No danger, no harm, so long as he gave himself up to it.

No one addressed him in that place. He was alone. Yet there was the presence of a kind of light, tangible and tactile, a humming radiance, sometimes substantial enough to appear to him as liquid. It was like his body, quivering and humming with a strange energy. It existed of its own, had no boundaries or demarcations; it was like himself, but not encased in flesh. When he was in his body he knew the encasement of flesh, the boundaries of skin. It held him intact, it defined him. He was *Stephen:* where he existed, a creature existed to whom they had given the name *Stephen.* But that was flesh, the maplike boundaries defined by the skin, an envelope of flesh that was extraordinarily delicate; that being, to whom they had given a name, was not really him. He was always elsewhere, he was present and yet absent, he was with the others and careful to imitate them and at the same time always apart from them, secret, invulnerable, in that other place, observing himself from a distance. He was alone and yet never alone. One of his brothers bullied him and yet he was not there to be bullied, he gave way, quickly and shrewdly; he could see the child who was himself, babyish, curly-haired, perhaps infuriating, could see that child through his brother's eyes; neither of them were alone. The radiance enclosed them, buoyed them up, flowed through them. They were the same substance. Being touched, Stephen wondered why he did not melt and flow into the other . . . the powerful throbbing energy that lived in them both, why did it not suddenly burst out of its cocoonlike structures and rush into one being? But the boundaries were powerful also, stubborn and resilient. Not only the boundary of skin but the curious hard glazed-over boundary of the eye, through which people looked at him, stared at him, from an immense distance. This too was safety of a kind. He knew himself distant from them, protected and invulnerable; he knew, sensing their resistance to what he so readily surrendered to, that they would never cross over to harm him . . . they were not aware of *him* at all.

The *Stephen* they recognized was not himself, only a fragment of himself. They could not harm him there. They seemed to be speaking to him through a barrier, a thin pane of glass, which they and not he held between them. They scolded him, they praised him, they declared their love for him or their interest in his schoolwork or their worry about him or their plans for the summer or the weekend or the rest of his life; they said he was intelligent, they said he was slow-witted, they pinched him, caressed him, hugged him, shoved him away; they gave him expensive gifts and they were very, very angry at him when he said the wrong thing—that his mother had wanted to die, for instance, that it was right for her to want to die since her life had gone wrong, and why then should everyone seem so shocked, so sad? He too had been shocked, saddened, stunned as if a loud explosion had taken place near him—but very shortly it passed away, the experience insinuated itself into his life, fitted perfectly and properly into it as it fitted into his mother's life; so it was a mystery that anyone should care to resist such perfection. The *Stephen* some of them loved and some of them disliked and a few of them feared was not the person he knew himself to be, but only a creature who stood where he stood, seen through others' eyes. They saw him with their hard, glazed-over eyes, which distorted him and could not really reach him at all; so they addressed that creature, they loved and hated and bullied and pitied that creature, not knowing it was themselves they dealt with. And always, that barrier was between them: exactly like a pane of glass, almost imperceptible. He saw that people did not want to put aside the pane of glass. He saw that they would have hated him, would have been terrified of him, if he tapped and broke it—even if he tapped it to call their attention to it. They did not want *him*, did not want to flow into him, not even his mother truly wanted him in that way. She had wanted a baby, a pet, a toy; she had wanted someone to weep over because her life had gone wrong, the life-energy in her had gone sour, she smelled of something sour, greenish, sickly, willful. She had wanted to die and so had wanted everyone to die. But she could not get hold of everyone—the family eluded her, the world kept apart and certainly eluded her; Stephen came closest to being sucked into her death, but he too eluded her and in the end it was Stephen she denounced most of all, saying he was not her baby, he was not *her* Stephen, she was sorry he had ever been born. . . .

That too was my freedom, Stephen thought.

The barrier between himself and others: was that perhaps his freedom? Was that the guarantee that he would continue to exist as an apparently separate being, a creature to whom a certain name had been given and of whom various things were expected? He did not know. He did not know if he was content with things as they were, or if he wanted, really, to smash the glass and bring the masquerade to an end. He did not know if this impulse came from that other source or from himself, from the least sane and least intelligent part of himself. He was not one creature, but many creatures struggling for dominance inside the same envelope of flesh. They were almost visible to him in his mind's eye, as tiny minnowlike charges, flashes of ideas, memories, insights . . . in his nighttime dreams they appeared in wild, colorful broken-up images, now this figure, now that, a half-glimpsed landscape, an exaggerated vision of his mother's dying face, the child Stephen himself seen from a distance, laughably miniature and inconsequential. Most of his dreams were insubstantial, like television entertainment, clowns and animals and fools and villains wrestling with one another, soldiers and priests and elephants and black-gowned men and trees and clouds and members of his own family in a frenzied dance, all thrown together in a hodgepodge of fragments as if to dramatize to Stephen the essential absurdity of the exterior world, where these fragments daily did battle. Yet they were himself too, he knew they were always himself. The same energy propelled them, the same throbbing heartbeat connected them, they were given life by the same rhythmic flow of air in and out of their lungs—of course they were himself—not a jumble of pieces making war upon one another, but a single whole. Yet they did not want to acknowledge this. Even the people who claimed to love him would not acknowledge it. His mother said he lied: his brothers and cousins laughed at him: he learned not to even hint at his secret knowledge to his father. The barrier that protected them from him also protected him from them, from their devastation of him, their possible mockery and triumph.

At school he was subdued, always quiet, watchful. He knew from the first how important it was to imitate the others. They were like his most trivial dreams, some of them, the noisiest boys especially, but he knew it was necessary to observe and imitate; he did not want to disappoint the exterior world any more than he could help. Through innumerable mishaps and frustrations and bouts of ridicule and rage he learned to take on the attitude of the other, of whoever addressed him or had authority over him, for as long as that other attitude prevailed. He did not slip out of himself but he went near-transparent, graceful and cunning as a young animal, but always obedient, watching with his respectful studious gaze, offering himself to the other but at the same time inaccessible, hidden. No one could reach him. No one could plunge a hand down into Stephen and seize his heart and yank it up—he seemed to offer the heart, not resisting. *Stephen, you are so sweet!* some said. They praised him and petted him, without noticing him. *Stephen, you're able to learn if you try, aren't you? If you try hard enough, you see . . . ? You're able to learn just like the other children.*

He had no interest in arithmetic, but he must learn arithmetic. His mind skittered away from the numerals, the additions and subtractions and divisions and multiplications of numerals, mere squiggly lines on a page or on a blackboard, signifying nothing; his mind skittered away like a waterbug yearning for freedom, but he drew it back, forced it to learn, to imitate the others. He shifted himself, tried to see the world through the eyes of another person—the teacher who was patient with him after classes, or his brother Andrew, who also tutored him from time to time. When he was himself these things meant nothing. He did not care, really, about numbers. He did not care how much they added up to, how stupefying and vast they could be made to seem, a universe of figures people had learned to control. But when he took on the attitude of someone else it was possible, for brief periods of time, for him to sympathize with the effort, the spirit behind the effort. He learned to imitate certain adults, he learned to imitate the attitude of his older brother. At such times he set himself aside, he quite consciously subordinated himself; but he was not altered in the slightest, not touched.

The pointlessness of school was taken for granted. The others seemed to take it for granted, never acknowledging it; in a way they seemed to enjoy it. Arithmetic, math, the memorization of historical dates, the diagraming of sentences—for the preparatory school the Petrie boys attended was very conservative—and the ability to sit still for long periods of time: all were taken for granted, even enjoyed in a perverse, sniggering way. Then there were sports, team sports. And services in the chapel. The pointlessness of that life could not be acknowledged; Stephen could not acknowledge it or they would turn upon him. Often they did accuse him of being strange, of not paying attention, of being secretive and bad. But they were never cruel to him, as they were to the weaker boys. He got through, he imitated the others in their language and gestures, somehow he managed to get through without being hurt. Occasionally older people professed concern over him, sensing a quirky resistance in him they could not deal with. *Why are you so hard to talk to, Stephen,* they inquired in exasperation, *where is your mind? Why are you always so distant?* Out of earshot they said, *Is it possible he's slow . . . ? Ill . . . ? With a mother like that. . . .* But he always came through with the pack of boys. He did fairly well, never at the top of his class, never a failure. There was really nothing the Petries could accuse him of, though they seemed to know he was not one of them; in him, something had gone wrong.

Always they spoke of their *Stephen.* They seemed to imagine they knew him. They imagined he was a possession of theirs, a child they owned. He answered to his name but did not believe in it. How shallow all that was, that aspect of himself! . . . in his deepest being he was nameless, wordless.

Still, he was afraid to declare his freedom. *Stephen?* they said. And he said *Yes.*

One afternoon he slipped away from the overheated classroom and found himself at home. Miraculously, he was in the alcove beneath the stairs. In an instant he was there, the classroom was gone, forgotten. There were the faded velvet cushions, there the shelves of books; the floor of the foyer had just been waxed and the odor of polish was strong but not unpleasant. From the kitchen a radio . . . an an-

nouncer's strident voice . . . from another part of the house someone's footsteps, rather heavy. A vacuum cleaner's whining overhead.
He was at home, in the old place, suddenly and effortlessly back
home.

Ah, the books! He saw them so vividly. He recognized each of
them. Oversized volumes, volumes whose covers had been lost, titles
that ran sideways so he had to turn his head to read them. . . . He
was back home, he had slipped back, he sat now in that secret place
and was absolutely invisible. His hand reached out gropingly for a
book. He would open it at random, at any page . . . he would see
what it had to say . . . what its message was. But his fingers slipped
through, could not take hold. The books were real; but his fingers
had no substance and could not take hold.

Both his hands groped at the shelf. He saw them dissolve into the
books, the image of his hands fading. His desperate clawing fingers:
they could not seize hold of anything, they faded and dissolved.

I want. . . . Wait. . . .

The air that forced itself into his lungs was sharp and cruel. He was
floating in it, he could not locate the floor, could not get his feet
planted on the floor. Everything swayed, became blindingly bright,
throbbed and pulsated about him though he whispered *Wait,
wait.* . . . He knew it was a mistake to struggle. He knew. Yet panic
seized him, he could not regain his equilibrium. *Wait,* he begged.
Help. Don't. He was twelve years old now. He knew it was a mistake
to struggle. He had never struggled before, had never doubted. As a
child he had accepted everything. He had drifted with it, borne by
the current, in no danger and aware of no danger, always at peace.
Even his excitement had been a kind of peace, a surrender. But now
something had gone wrong and he was struggling. His mind examined itself, his being was flooded with doubt. He tried to resist; he
clawed wildly at the shelf in order to keep in one place. But his
fingers went through the shelf. They had no substance. He had no
substance. Panic flooded through him. He was lost.

The alcove disappeared. The house disappeared. He could no
longer see. The physical world had disappeared in light, in sheer glaring light. *Wait,* he begged. *Help.* Even now he was struggling, like a
drowning person. Even now he resisted. He was lost, gone, extinct.
He felt his soul crushed to nothing. He saw nothing, was nowhere.
There was nothing. The universe was not dark, not black, but nothing: a glare that obliterated all sense. It did not exist and he did not
exist. . . . He darted this way, that way. Never had he been so

terrified. And yet he was nothing: the terror did not exist. *God*, he cried, *where is God? God?* If he could force himself to surrender he would be saved: but the panic drove him now this way, now that way. *God, help me; God, please help me; don't leave me. . . .*

He blundered near someone. Passed through someone. Who was it? Who was here? *Stephen*, a voice whispered. But he could not see. His eyes could not function in this radiance, this emptiness. He was aware, suddenly, of a number of other people—a multitude. Strange vaporous forms, formless, no more than sensations. They were invisible to him. Yet he was aware of their murmuring. *Stephen Stephen Stephen* they said, as if they knew him well. His soul was seized with a terrible clammy fright: they were bodiless. They had lost their bodies. They drifted close about him, murmuring caressing him, calling him by name.

God, he cried, *where is*—

Then he was on a sidewalk. He was on a city sidewalk. He was in the world again, in his body. Traffic. People. Sunlight. He could see; his eyes blinked rapidly. He was alive.

A woman holding a small girl's hand brushed near, no more than glancing at Stephen. He knew he must look frightened. He must look ill. But he had to talk to someone, had to ask where he was— what city this was—was it Albany? A ruddy-faced woman carrying a large leather handbag approached him; she seemed to be looking at him with pity. *Excuse me*, Stephen said, *I'm lost . . . can you help me? . . . I don't feel well*. The woman would have collided with him if he hadn't stepped aside. She did not seem to have been aware of him. *What's wrong?* Stephen said. The woman passed by. . . . Then there were others, women and men both, and they passed by without seeing him. He tried to clutch at a man's arm but his fingers went through the cloth and the flesh and the bone. *Help me*, he screamed, *help! Help!* He ran in one direction and then in another. He crossed a street against traffic. There was someone who looked familiar—an acquaintance of his father's—and Stephen ran up to him and began shouting *Help help, help me*—

Then he was in the front yard of the school. On one of the grassy knolls, beneath an elm tree. He looked about in relief. Now he knew where he was. Now he was safe. Then he was in the classroom again —back in the classroom. He had never left, evidently. He saw himself at his desk, the third from the front in the center row. He had never left! He could have wept with relief. . . . *Stephen*, someone was saying, *look up here. Immediately*. But the boy did not move.

Stephen watched himself from a distance of several yards, astonished at the pale, clammy look of his skin and the moronic glassiness of his eyes. His head drooped forward. His left hand had fallen into his lap and his right hand lay limp, across an opened textbook.

Stephen stared at himself in astonishment. He had never seen himself before. The mirrored self was not the real self. *This* self was Stephen, and yet Stephen was a few yards away, observing, helpless. *Wake up! Wake up!*

The teacher, a man in a tan tweed coat with leather elbow patches, was standing beside Stephen's desk speaking to him in an earnest, slightly irritated voice. He was alarmed but kept his voice low. Stephen darted to his place, circled it, could not discover a way back into himself; the voice was angry, calling *Stephen,* now on all sides he heard the cry *Stephen, Stephen* and he himself was begging *Stephen* but he could not find a way in. He plunged at himself, at the forehead; but he could not penetrate it. The teacher's voice was rising and some of the boys were grinning and some were evidently frightened. But he could not get inside himself, he could not penetrate the skin. He saw the teacher's hand on his shoulder, gripping it, giving him a shake; but it did no good. The head wobbled, the eyes rolled, now the right arm slipped from the desk and fell loose. *Stephen! Wake up!*

Desperate, he darted at the eyes, which looked milky and glazed. But he was rejected; it was like flinging himself at a wall. He slid against the throat, then against the soft, tender flesh where the neck joins the body, but he was repulsed, barred. Then he groped against the chest, helplessly, desperately . . . and then he was inside, by a miracle. He came to his senses. He was back in his body, conscious, again conscious, alive.

It had been a terrible shock to him. And shameful, humiliating. His face burned with the shame of what had happened in front of the others. His teacher was relieved but annoyed; what on earth was wrong with him? Was he sick?

Stephen could not speak for a moment. He had come so far, he had struggled so wildly and desperately . . . and now the boys were laughing at him, again they were laughing at him. His face went red. He stammered that he had a cold and he'd taken several aspirin and maybe . . . maybe the aspirin had made him sleepy. There was nothing wrong with him though. Nothing. Nothing wrong.

After class his teacher said *You frightened us all, Stephen: it*

*looked as if you had died. . . . Are you sure you don't want to go to
the infirmary?*

I'm all right, Stephen said.

*. . . had the horrible sensation you were dead . . . or on the brink
of dying. . . .*

No, Stephen said. *It was nothing. It was a mistake.*

6

Now you must regret it, the woman whispered. . . . *Now that
he's dead you must regret it, your hatred for him. Your feud with
him.*

He was a fine man, Stephen said slowly. *There was no feud between us. I didn't . . . I didn't hate him. I don't think he really
hated me.*

He detested you, she said. *He was ashamed of you. The others
might joke about you . . . your so-called religious visions . . . they
might roll their eyes over your conversion to Catholicism and your
years in that Jesuit seminary out in the woods . . . they might speak
of you fondly as one speaks of an eccentric relative or a retarded
child who isn't too badly retarded . . . but Andrew never joked. He
never thought there was anything amusing about you.*

I don't think he really hated me, Stephen repeated. *He was angry,
he sometimes lost patience with me . . . couldn't understand what I
was trying to explain to him . . . how concerned I was about the
way his life was going, the emptiness of his soul, the bitterness in everything he said or wrote, the hatred of his fellow human beings . . .
the distance between himself and God. . . .*

She began to laugh. She laughed in Andrew's manner, sharply and
with a touch of anger, as if she were degraded by such laughter but
could not resist.

Don't laugh, Stephen begged, *it goes through me like a knife . . .
it tears me to pieces, laughter like yours. . . . I hear it in people who
are trapped in their bodies, like dying people trapped in bodies they
can't recognize are diseased; it's horrible, hideous, to hear laughter
from such people and to be unable to help them. . . .*

He hated you and you hated him, she said. *You envied him. Everyone envied him. Everyone wanted to be him: Andrew. He knew it,
he gloated in it, he was sick with knowing it. . . . You sickened him*

*especially, you with your forgiveness and your love he didn't want
and your advice no one wanted, least of all Andrew: couldn't you feel
it, his hatred for you? You drove him mad, the thought of you drove
him mad. He wanted to be proud of the entire family and one by
one you were disappointing him . . . one by one, like the rest of the
world. . . . He hated you all. He was sickened by you.*

The last time we spoke he was angry with me, Stephen protested,
*but I wouldn't say he was maddened . . . I wouldn't say he hated
me. . . .*

He wanted to love you but you disappointed him, she said. *All of
you. All of us. . . . Sometimes he hated me too when I disappointed
him. He couldn't help himself, that was his way . . . he couldn't be
blamed for it.*

I wanted to help him, Stephen said. *I came to help him. I didn't
intend to make him angry, I didn't indicate that I blamed him. . . .*

*Everyone blamed him. Everyone held him responsible. Everyone
wanted him to die and was relieved when he died; and afterward,
what hypocrisy! What nauseating hypocrisy!*

I came only to help him, Stephen said uncertainly. *Of course I
knew he would be contemptuous of me . . . he always was . . . I
knew it might be a mistake . . . but really he invited me to visit
him: he invited me. I meant only. . . .*

That's ridiculous, the woman said. *I don't believe that. He hated
you. He was fond of you, but he hated you . . . hated what you had
become. Like his father, like his mother, like his sister and his
brother and his first wife and his son and his old friends and associates and supporters. . . . He spoke with contempt of you, especially
of you: that you should give yourself up to a delusion, to God or
Christ or whatever it was, that you should have no shame about it,
should go around openly and crazily. . . . He had nothing to say to
you! It was impossible that he should even want to look at you.*

I don't think I imagined it, Stephen said. *I don't think . . . don't
dare to think . . . that I have imagined everything.*

He believed you were crazy, she whispered. *That was his only consolation, the thought that you must be crazy.*

I must be . . . ?

He woke to sleet being blown against the windowpane.

He woke to the first storm of the winter; the first dark, vicious
morning of his new life in Ogdensburg.

I didn't hate him, he thought. *I have never hated anyone.*

He walked a mile to the institution, hunched over in his long coat, the collar turned up about his face. Snow and sleet whirled about him, stinging his face and bare hands. Behind him, his footprints disappeared. No one had passed this way. No one followed. He wanted oblivion, and behind him the brutal young snowstorm would swallow everything up, so that in a few minutes it would seem that no one had come from the cabin he rented and no one had entered the boys' detention home by the east door and no one had shaken the wet snow from his hair, grateful to be inside.

Good morning Stephen, someone said.

It took him a moment to get hold of his surroundings. He had been alone all weekend, totally alone in the cabin. He had spoken to no one and had not even spoken to himself, had forbidden himself to talk out loud. So it took a moment for him to become adjusted. *Stephen,* he was. *Stephen Petrie.* But they did not know, or gave no hint of knowing, which *Stephen* and which *Petrie* this awkward young man was.

Good morning, he said.

7

A young giant: nearly seven feet tall. Hulking, fat-thighed. Odor of armpits, crotch, soiled clothing. *My name is Kevin.* Surprisingly high, bold voice, like a giant doll come partly to life.

Yes, Stephen said. *Hello Kevin.*

. . . I don't want to put those on. I'm not going to put those on. But the floors are cold and. . . .

Fourteen years old, he was. They said he weighed well over two hundred fifty pounds. Had not weighed him for some months. Had not wanted to upset him—he was easily upset.

. . . your feet must be cold, aren't they cold? Stephen asked.

The boy was panting slightly. Though he was sitting on the edge of his cot, he gave the impression of looking down at Stephen, sighting him along his cheeks. His skin was mealy-pale, as if dusted lightly with flour or chalk. It was mottled, pitted with tiny, nearly microscopic holes. Perhaps they were simply enlarged pores.

My name is Kevin, the boy said slowly. *I been here a long time . . . this is my corner here . . . I don't need to leave it . . . I don't*

*know who you are and I don't need to listen to you. I been here a
long time, I don't know which one of them you are . . . I don't give
a damn which one of them you are.*

He spoke slowly and laboriously, in that stilted, high voice. He
paused, panting mildly. His head was small for his body, and hairless
—the pale, lard-colored skull was covered only by a fine white fuzz.
From a short distance he appeared to have been shaved, but that was
not the case. He was simply hairless, covered with a white fuzz that
reminded Stephen of the thin fur on a dog's stomach. *I been here a
long time,* Kevin said thickly. *You better not touch me.*

*. . . cold air coming up through the floorboards. . . . If you
don't like to wear shoes you could just wear. . . . Are those your
socks . . . ?*

My name is Kevin Kasser, the boy said, staring at Stephen. *I been
here before you came.*

He was one of nine children, Stephen learned. Brought to the Ogdensburg boys' home several years before, having been first hospitalized for minor injuries. His father had evidently beaten him. Had
beaten him and his brothers and sisters. There was no mother: they
believed she had just walked away. The father was in prison now, the
children scattered—the three "normal" ones with an aunt in Watertown. Kevin had attended special classes at Ogdensburg Junior High
School but he had gotten into trouble with the other students and
had been expelled after a fist fight with the shop teacher; at the age
of ten he had been over six feet tall and had weighed about two hundred pounds. *How did the father beat him?* Stephen could not help
but inquire.

A shovel, they thought.

Was he beaten on the head? Stephen asked timidly.

What difference would that make?

There were other tall boys, but they were thin. There were other
odd, disturbing, intimidating boys, but Stephen did not pity them as
he pitied Kevin Kasser.

. . . he was always a little strange? Stephen asked.

*His I.Q. has been measured at 70, then again at 98, then
again at . . . at something much lower, like 55. He isn't strange at
all. When you get to know him.*

He fascinated Stephen. A giant, and yet a child. A child—and yet
a giant!

Considering his huge frame, he was really not ill-proportioned. His head looked small but that was partly because he was bald. Only around his waist was he actually obese; there, he wore three or four lardish layers of fat that rested thickly on one another. His lips were layers of flesh also, which rippled as he sat in silence, evidently thinking. *What are you thinking of?* Stephen wanted to inquire, *are you lonely, are you unhappy, do you miss your brothers and sisters, will you be looking forward to Christmas? . . . to the Christmas party?* There were tiny white granules in the corners of Kevin's mouth. His breath stank: Stephen had to force himself not to draw away.

Most of his dreams still were unimportant. He could not trust them. As a seminarian he had drifted into the habit, presumably a habit others shared, of allowing his nighttime self, his more bodily, instinctive self, to deal with physical preoccupations: so that he, the conscious, intelligent agent, might be freed from them. He did not really know if the others relied upon this self-regulating, therapeutic function—perhaps they did not; perhaps, unlike Stephen, they took themselves seriously enough to be conscience-stricken.

In Ogdensburg he rented a cabin in the country, a winterized shanty with an oil-burning stove and a lavatory. The lavatory was outside, but adjacent to the cabin; of course it was unheated. He settled himself in to living there and working at the boys' home. When he was at the cabin, he did not think of his former life, or even of his present life. He worked from 8:30 A.M. until 6 P.M. He could not have said whether he liked his work—he did not believe it mattered whether one "liked" his activities. He liked them well enough; he always had.

When he was away from the institution, alone in his rented cabin, he did not think of his former life or of his present life, though occasionally he found himself thinking of the future. But it was pointless, it was perhaps harmful, misleading. The future would accommodate itself. The future had always accommodated itself, without the intervention of man.

Have I found my place? Stephen wondered.

He slept wrapped in two blankets, in his underclothes and socks. Snow swarmed against the windowpanes. It was good to be alone at last, good to be exhausted from a day's work, his brain shuddering with fatigue, always on the verge of extinction. It was good, good. His place on earth. God might inhabit the entire void, spread in all directions and never to be tasted—never small enough to be squeezed into a fist—never cajoled into answering Stephen's questions: nevertheless God was present in that bald fuzz-covered child and presented himself to Stephen openly and boldly. *Am I of use, finally?* Stephen wondered. His breath gleamed in the dark as he sank from consciousness. Sometimes he dreamed of *Stephen,* a future self, leading the child along a country lane—into a field where other children played innocently—sometimes he was taller than Kevin, an older brother to him, and Kevin was truly child-sized—his hand meek in Stephen's hand—grateful to be loved. *God is in us, God is everywhere. There is nothing not God,* Stephen's head rang.

There were other dreams, of course. About the woman; about the dead brother; about his former life. But Stephen did not dwell upon them.

I have found my place, he thought in the morning. *I am of use.*

8

Letters came for him occasionally. Some were forwarded from Brandywine and some were sent directly to the Ogdensburg address, though he could not recall having given the address to anyone. He did not shrink from the letters; he carried them to the squat smelly stove and tossed them inside.

Our private lives are temptations, Stephen thought.

Since the age of seventeen he had known that God cared not at all for history, still less for private history.

God flowing into God flowing into God. . . .

They said he was absent for hours, when he sensed himself gone from their presence only for a few seconds; at times he sensed himself not related to time at all. He was in two places at once. There was no strain. . . . But they did not always comprehend his absence: it was a mystery, how little they really knew. He wondered if he should pity them. He wondered if he should try to explain God to them.

For one thing, there was no death. It was questionable whether there was life. Birth seemed to be personal, like death; but one could not take them seriously. They were too solemn to be taken seriously. *Poor Stephen,* they murmured out of earshot, and then *Poor Theodore*—since Stephen's father had been so disappointed in him.

But why *Catholic?* Why *Roman Catholicism?* —The Petries could not comprehend, were personally stung. *Catholicism!* They could not comprehend and Stephen saw no reason to explain. His life was directed so powerfully by God, from the other, deeper, more radiant side of his own personality, that it never occurred to him to seek out reasons; the purity of his actions would have been defiled, in fact, by any attempt on his part to rationalize them. Yet the exterior world begged for excuses, apologies, explanations—no matter what lies— and held it against Stephen that he would not obey.

But why do you want to do this?—to do this to your life? they asked, as if he had any choice. *Why do you do these things to us?*

He had tried to explain, however, years afterward. He had confided in Andrew, rather unwisely as it turned out—though at least his brother's customary disdain was tempered, from that point on, with an air of bemused affection. And he had confided in Yvonne, at a time when they had been strangers; years before she married Andrew. And of course he had shared confidence with others like himself, when they happened to meet. *God-stricken people, God flowing into God flowing into God. . . .*

It was a mistake, my becoming Catholic, Stephen said. *Specifically Catholic. Specifically a priest, a Jesuit. I wanted. . . . I wanted to. . . . It was a mistake but at the time I had no choice. I didn't know. I might have been broken in two otherwise; I might have gone mad. Everything was God, everything was alive, flowing, ceaselessly flowing, like a dam that had burst, I wanted to plunge into it, I wanted to be carried along by it without being smashed. . . . I brought myself to the Church filled to the brim with God, on the brink of overflowing. Of catastrophe.*

You have had experience of God? Yvonne asked.

Stephen ignored the skepticism in her voice.

Not one of the letters was from Yvonne. He could not resist checking the return address to see. But no: never. She would never write to him.

He threw the letters into the stove, even the official-looking ones. *Stephen Petrie:* address unknown. Gradually the letters would stop coming. Gradually he would be released. They would find his brother's murderer someday and after that everything would be forgotten, everything would pass. He had only to wait and have faith.

9

You ridicule other people for the ways in which they want to control the world, Stephen told his dead brother, rather contemptuously. *But you want nothing less than that yourself: your only quarrel with them is words.*

Andrew's lean, sane face had taken on a luminous quality. It looked far more womanly than Stephen remembered.

You have no faith, Stephen sneered.

The dead man lifted both hands in a gesture of startled dismay. Yet there was something mocking about him, even now. Dead, unnaturally silent, he was mimicking Stephen's expectations of his behavior. Dead, he must have learned all that Stephen knew; he could only be pretending surprise.

You want to take away the faith of others! Stephen cried. *I gave up hope and I gave up despair and I gave up my life and even thinking about my life and now you want to take away even my certainty of what I did—*

Andrew watched him. His expression was still mock-serious. They were not in the room Stephen remembered, there was no furniture around them, no windows, no possibility of his glancing out into the garden as he had that day: but even the memory of that day was being taken from him. They were sealed in together. *Your only quarrel with the world is words,* Stephen said, less certainly. *You and your enemies disagree about concepts . . . ideas. . . . You want only to change places with them. . . . You don't know . . . can't know . . . what it is to be utterly dead. . . .*

That day the giant child grabbed hold of another boy in the recreation room. There had been no warning, no raised voices. Suddenly one grabbed the other and the smaller boy twisted free and was caught again, by a finger. Stephen heard the *snap* of the finger as it broke—heard it across the wide crowded room.

He lay wrapped in his blankets, sleepless. *You have no faith,* he said aloud.

10

The stairs were steep and narrow and poorly lit. On the first floor there lived an elderly Polish couple . . . on the second floor a contingent of dark-skinned students, probably Africans . . . on the third floor one day he saw a small child in diapers crawling out into the drafty corridor; a girl in a maternity outfit stood a few yards inside her apartment, smoking a cigarette, staring sightlessly out of the doorway as Stephen passed. On the fourth floor someone played a radio loudly. *Who are you looking for?* a man in a soiled bathrobe asked Stephen, the second time he climbed the stairs. The man's grin was lopsided, he smelled of tobacco and stale dried urine. *You don't live here, do you? Are you new here? Are you in a hurry?*

The door of the room next to Yvonne's was bravely decorated: posters of *art-nouveau* tulips and elongated white-skinned faces. Yvonne's door was plain. Utilitarian green. The three or four times Stephen knocked on it, he could not help shrinking from the sound he himself made. He half hoped no one would be home.

. . . They said you were sick. They told me you lived here. Is there anything I can do?

She blinked at him, not recognizing him. She did not know his name; they had not really been introduced. He knew only her first name—Yvonne—and it was not from Raschke, but from a young woman, that Stephen had heard she was ill.

It's very nice of. . . .

He saw she had been lying in bed. The bedclothes were rumpled and not very clean. There was only the single room, a single window. *. . . very nice of you to come,* she said uncertainly. A tall, rather awkward girl, lean-hipped, her hands and feet long, narrow, pale. She was barefoot. Her hair had not been washed recently. He could smell the sickness about her . . . believed he could see, from where he stood, a dark brown-red stain on one of the bedsheets.

He visited with her no more than ten minutes, the first time. She was alternately groggy and anxious, as if she had taken a drug for the pain and was trying to wake from it, slightly fearful of him, not trusting him. The air in the room was close, but not unpleasant. He had liked it there. The second time he climbed the stairs and knocked at the door no one answered. The third time, a week later, she was in—evidently feeling better—though still very pale, with that air of being both weary and agitated at the same time. She was in her early twenties, Stephen supposed. As they talked she stared at him openly, as if noting every detail about him. At first she did not even sit down, but stood with her back to the window, watching him. . . . *he didn't send you?* she asked.

No, Stephen said, *I'm really on the periphery of that group. I'm just an acquaintance of his. . . . How long have you known him?*

Not very long, she said. *I don't intend to go back to him. It was a mistake, I made a mistake . . . I wasn't the first one, was I, with him. . . . the first to make a mistake. But I'm all right now. The fever or infection or whatever it was is gone. I'm going back to work, I think I'll move out of here. I can't bear this place any longer.*

She had had a miscarriage, Stephen knew. It was quite possible she knew he had been told; but she gave no indication. Her hair was dark, straight, shinier than before. There was something fierce and strained about her. While they talked she stared at him, rapidly blinking her eyes, and from time to time her mouth stretched into an anxious unconscious smile. Stephen was surprised to learn that she had no interest, really, in politics: her indifference to her former lover's plans seemed genuine.

Of course I hope he isn't arrested or hurt, she said, *but if he insists upon taking risks . . . if they all insist upon taking risks. . . . Are you going with them to Buffalo? . . . No, I'm breaking off with them, I have no faith in what they're doing. . . . And I don't want to be near him again. Or any other man.*

She spoke flatly, sincerely.

Stephen asked if she might need help moving; but she dismissed his question. She hadn't another room yet. She didn't know her plans yet. *You're very kind,* she said hesitantly. *You're the only one, and I don't even know you. . . . I didn't love him, it was a mistake. It was a delusion of some kind. Do you believe in love? . . . You don't, no, I'm sure you don't, they said you were an ex-priest. I tried to fall in love but it was a mistake. There is just . . . just . . . just a kind of physical grappling, horribly awkward and embarrassing, it's always been like that but I thought: ah, I must grow up! I must fall in love! . . . So I don't even mind what happened, or how badly people think he treated me; I learned a great deal.*

She spoke so frankly, so disingenuously, that Stephen laughed.

Are you really an ex-priest?

I was never ordained, Stephen said. *I was never even close to being ordained.*

And now what are you doing?

"I do what I am doing"—as the Jesuits would say.

You're not involved with—? I mean very seriously?

Not any longer, Stephen said. *Still, I think I'll stay with them a while. The Movement is disintegrating as it is.*

I didn't care for him very much, she said slowly. *I wanted a friend. Just a friend. A brother, really. . . . I wanted a friend, a brother, someone to talk with, someone to be close to, to trust. No, I didn't want him at all: I didn't want a lover. Not him. . . . Yes, the Movement is disintegrating, everything disintegrates, bleeds away. I cared, I was involved, and then it passed away from me. I don't care now. I'm grateful to have survived. . . . I don't care about anything now,* she said.

Stephen stayed for no more than half an hour. They were silent much of the time, awkward with each other, obscurely embarrassed, as if something had passed between them they could not recall. There was nothing Stephen could do for her, she made clear; she didn't want money, didn't want his help in looking for another room or in moving. Yet at the same time she seemed to be pleading with him. . . . *I didn't want a lover, I wanted only a friend . . . a brother . . . a friend, a brother. . . .* Yet she was dismissing him. Her manner was coolly bright and formal; she wanted him gone. He reminded her of her former lover, perhaps. He reminded her of folly.

If there's anything I can do. . . . he said hopefully.

At this time in my life: no.

He returned again but there was no answer when he knocked. And then he forgot her. He left Pittsburgh, broke with his friends, spent a year and a half traveling . . . wandering, really; in the West and the Northwest, as far as Prince Rupert, British Columbia, where he worked for several months in a logging camp. He forgot her, he forgot that phase of his life, casting it from him as he had learned to do —as one must learn to do. When he met her again they had both changed considerably and there was no link between them, no need for them to acknowledge each other.

Andrew introduced them and they shook hands. They smiled at each other. . . . *But of course we don't know each other,* Stephen wanted to assure her. *There's no reason for us to know each other. . . .*

She was not so thin as he remembered. But still intense, sharp-eyed, rather anxious. By his manner Stephen tried to let her know he remembered nothing, would make no claims, no sentimental acknowledgments. It was a coincidence, but not a significant one. And not that much of a coincidence, really, because Stephen had encountered many people in his short lifetime, many hundreds of people. His brother's wife was only one of those hundreds.

What do you know about her? they asked.

Nothing, Stephen said. *Only what I've told you.*

You're not very close to her?

I wasn't very close to her or Andrew . . . or any of the family.

There was a break between you and your father . . . ? And you weren't close, you weren't in the confidence of your brother Andrew? . . . And you obviously didn't get to know your sister-in-law. So you don't have any information for us.

None. Nothing.

There's nothing you can . . . ?

Nothing.

11

God fluttered outside the window and surrounded the cabin on all sides. The sky was opaque, had been bunched and curdled for days. God broke, fell, drifted downward, fluttered and swirled against the windowpanes, and then, when the light was off, seemed to concentrate in one of the room's corners. God drew everything out of Stephen, darkness and radiance both, and all awareness of motion; finally Stephen was empty even of his desire to sleep and to be obliterated.

Then he could sleep.

God squatted and hopped clumsily about and hunched his shoulders and screwed up his fat floury-pale face. There was a sudden sickening odor in the corridor.

Kevin, Stephen cried, *what are—*

Friends came in a pickup truck to bring Stephen back to their home for dinner. Wherever Stephen went there were friends; they seemed to be waiting for him, for him specifically. He was sweet and unassuming and never argumentative. He never got drunk. He appeared grateful nearly all the time.

One of his new friends in Ogdensburg was a psychiatric social worker in his late thirties named Peter. His wife's name was Molly and she wore her hair braided and coiled about her head. She was attentive to Stephen, curiously reverential. He wondered why. He wondered what they said about him. . . . They did inquire about where he'd been and he told them about Brandywine and about the seminary and how he had never finished college, and they seemed satisfied with that; still, they did not ask if he was related to Andrew Petrie. He thought that odd, their not asking.

. . . *not married?* they inquired. *Up here new people get married fast . . . either that or they leave. The winters are interminable, it's so lonely. . . .*

Lonely? Stephen asked.

He frowned as if perplexed. Lonely? What did that mean? What, exactly, did that mean? He had never been sure.

I'm never lonely, Stephen said. He spoke slowly, almost with regret.

Some of the boys at the Home were teachable: they went to area schools, they attended regular classes or special classes. Some of the boys were not teachable.

Stephen worked in one corner of the recreation room, teaching arithmetic. There were three unteachable boys in his small class—Audie Baker, twelve years old, ostensibly brain-damaged; Jimmy Smith, thirteen years old, squat, rotund, no more than four feet six inches tall, flesh packed in solid so that even his eyes were squeezed out of shape; Kim Ryan, fifteen years old, with an odd milky cast to his gaze and a trailing voice.

Not hopeless, Stephen said.

He was excited about teaching them. He worked with a portable blackboard and colored chalk. The boys sat for several minutes at a time, watching him. *Not hopeless*, Stephen thought excitedly. He wanted Kevin too. He was going to try for Kevin too.

Diagnoses are sometimes wrong, Stephen told his friends at the Home. *I.Q. tests are sometimes misleading. . . . My point is only that no one is hopeless. No one who is alive is hopeless.*

12

DEAR BROTHER: THE FAMILY IS CLOSING RANKS
AGAINST ME. THE WIDOW WILL BEAR FALSE WIT-
NESS AGAINST ME. I FEAR THEY PLAN TO COM-
MIT ME. DISINHERIT ME. DESTROY MY CAREER.
BELIEVE NOTHING OF WHAT THEY TELL YOU OR
THE WIDOW'S LIES IF SHE CONTACTS YOU. THERE
WAS A MISUNDERSTANDING BETWEEN US. SHE IS
MURDEROUS NOW BECAUSE I HAVE KNOWLEDGE
OF HER. CARNAL I MEAN. I DO NOT BEG FOR
YOUR PRAYERS OR YOUR GOOD COUNSEL BUT
ONLY FOR YOUR COMPREHENSION SHOULD THEIR
LIES SPREAD TO YOU. YOU ARE MY ONLY BROTHER.
ANDREW'S ENVY OF ME CONTINUES FROM
BEYOND THE GRAVE. HE WISHES TO DESTROY ME.
NO NEED TO REPLY. HUGH PETRIE.

When Stephen received the telegram, missent to Brandywine several days before, he opened it at once, without thinking. As he began
to read he noticed he was trembling. But why? What did he fear?
He detested such signs of weakness in himself. He could not comprehend them. There was nothing to fear, nothing to anticipate, everything was past, settled, completed; he had only to live out the span
of his life, hadn't he, had only to flow with it, to give way easily,
never to resist . . . ? He had only to have faith.

Jill, a part-time nurse, asked him what was wrong: why was he
standing there with a telegram in his hand? Was it bad news? News
from home?

Stephen folded the telegram carefully and put it in his pocket. He
would read it later, after work. He was in no hurry.

*. . . I do not beg for your prayers or your good counsel but only
for your comprehension . . . you are my only brother . . . Andrew
wishes to . . . No need to reply.*

He did not reply. He folded the telegram again and put it away beneath a loose floorboard.

13

One long winter he studied all seventy-three volumes of *The Jesuit Relations and Allied Documents.* He read with great interest of the Jesuit missionaries who had died as martyrs for the Christian faith, especially the first eight martyrs in North America. They were saints, they had been canonized by the Church after their brutal deaths, their very names came to sound sacred: *Isaac Jogues, Jean de Brébeuf, Gabriel Lalemant, Antoine Daniel, Charles Garnier, Noël Chabanel, René Goupil, Jean Lalande.* Stephen read with an almost feverish excitement of the tortures . . . the hideous and always very complicated rituals of torture to which the Indians subjected the men of God, angered by their stubborn defiance, their refusal to give way to agony. *Jesus, have mercy! Jesus, have mercy on us!* was their only cry. Stephen read, reread, shut his eyes and tried to envision . . . tried to slip into the consciousness of . . . tried to suffer with them, to *know.* He must know, he must yield himself to them. *We are made a spectacle to the world, to angels and men.*

The Iroquois broke bones and tore out fingernails and ran flaming torches about their victims' bodies . . . but their victims did not surrender. They prayed aloud. They addressed the multitudes who stood watching. The Iroquois hacked them with knives, stabbed them with javelins, thrust red-hot irons down their throats, fastened strips of bark, smeared with pitch, about their naked bodies, hung collars of red-hot hatchets around their necks . . . but the martyrs never flinched. They did not even cry aloud except to call upon Jesus. Even when strips of flesh were cut from their legs and arms and devoured before their eyes they did not flinch. Five hours of torture, ten, eleven . . . fifteen hours of torture, a long night of martyrdom: and then eye-gouging, scalping, the eating of hearts and the drinking of blood. Stephen read and reread and had to put the book aside; his brain reeled, he felt ill with dread and excitement.

All the Jesuit martyrs had prayed for martyrdom; they had wanted to die, to die in that horrible way, and had only wondered, occasionally, if they were worthy of it. Stephen identified with the youngest of the Jesuits, Noël Chabanel, because he sometimes expressed a dread of torture and being burned alive and because, in a long spell of depression, he was tempted by God to reject martyrdom

. . . God whispering to him through the medium of the Devil, hinting that his faith was a delusion, his martyrdom pointless, his impending death a folly. Yet he conquered all temptation: he vowed more passionately than before to continue in his mission, though he hated it. He hated every moment of it, hated the Hurons and the wilderness, the vermin, the boredom . . . and yet he vowed ever more passionately to remain in the New World and to fulfill his destiny. *I pray, then, O Lord, that Thou wilt deign to accept me as a permanent servant . . . that Thou wilt render me worthy of so sublime a ministry.* He half yearned for martyrdom, but felt himself not good enough. And in a sense he did fall short, for he was murdered by a solitary Indian, not tortured at any great length. Still, he was canonized, his martyrdom was accepted. Of all the Jesuits he seemed to Stephen the most remarkable, in that he pursued a destiny without regard for his own desire for it; almost, in a sense, he lived out the destiny of another person, an antithetical self.

And he had been intelligent, too. His intelligence had led him in one direction but he had balked, had refused to surrender. And so his willful life was a triumph, even greater than his anticipated death at the hands of the Indians.

We are made a spectacle to the world, to angels and men, Stephen thought.

He had first discovered the *Relations* as a boy, but he had read abridged and edited versions. He read them in full in his sixteenth year, decided at the age of seventeen that he would become a Jesuit, and, some years later, disillusioned with his training, returned to them to see what had originally struck him. And again it was the rather minor figure of Chabanel that drew his sympathy. To hate one's mission and yet to bury oneself in it, willfully, stubbornly, against all temptations and against, even, one's common sense . . . ! What a peculiar triumph, what unnatural courage, what extraordinary grace. The physical tortures were perhaps exaggerated, but had certainly occurred; the dying Jesuits had possibly cried out in agony, no matter what the accounts insisted, but they had died, still, they had died in approximately the way described; the *Relations* were fiction, but at the same time entirely real. . . . They were fictional, no doubt; but real. Authentic. Stephen skimmed through the passages he had once known by heart and saw there not his former self nor even his present self but a timeless, perfect, God-bound self, immune to all change and all temptation.

Like Chabanel, he made another vow. No matter if God withdrew from him—which happened occasionally and unpredictably—he would not withdraw from God. God was perpetual, permanent; "Stephen" was of no more consequence than a fluttering leaf. He could not take "Stephen" seriously, not even when "Stephen" was all he had. He knew "Stephen" would pass away. His alliance must be with God, not "Stephen." Such decisions came to him calmly, as if from a great distance. He was no longer feverish and maidenly, no longer obsessed with the idea of martyrdom. If martyrdom was to be his, very well—it would be his. If not, not. But he did not consider himself unworthy of martyrdom as the Jesuits had; he rather believed, in his heart, that he was as worthy as any of them.

14

As soon as they were alone Andrew surprised him by asking him to sign his name on an index card—*his* name, that was, Andrew's. *Just write my name as if it were yours, as if it were your signature,* Andrew said. Stephen smiled. He smiled as if his brother had said something clever and must be waiting now for Stephen to catch on.

Well—go on, Andrew said, *why are you hesitating?*

Stephen blushed. He took the pen from his brother and signed his brother's name in his own handwriting, as if it were his own.

Andrew Petrie

Andrew studied the card briefly. Then he set it aside. He turned back to Stephen as if nothing unusual had taken place. That was his manner: Stephen remembered it well. Always that imperial, amiable air, never explaining and never apologizing. But of course he would be wonderfully gracious if he were asked to explain. He would not explain voluntarily, he would force others to appeal to him. Stephen felt himself at a disadvantage, too tall, ungainly, somehow in the wrong. His sense of balance was disturbed. He wanted to know why Andrew had asked him to sign Andrew's name but he did not want to ask. They had not seen each other for years but already, already there was a tension between them, the promise of a skirmish, a collision of wills. *Sit down, sit anywhere,* Andrew was saying hospitably, while Stephen stood with his fists clenched, not wanting to give in to curiosity and yet knowing that his stance, his rigidity, were ridiculous.

Sit down. We have a great deal to talk about, I suppose . . . ? Andrew said mildly.

Stephen extracted from his hip pocket a much-folded copy of the March issue of *Discourses*. He tried to smooth it out with his hands, so patiently and fastidiously that Andrew sucked in his breath to show irritation. But Stephen continued for a moment longer, quite deliberately.

I thought you didn't read such worldly things, Andrew said.

You appeared to me in a dream, Stephen said, *carrying something that looked like this . . . though it also appeared to be alive . . . you wanted to talk to me, you seemed quite anxious. . . .*

Andrew jumped to his feet. *What shameless bullshit,* he said. He laughed. . . . *One of these days we'll get you committed, Stephen, my boy. You would benefit from some shock treatments, you even more than Hugh. You're shameless, really,* he laughed.

. . . it looked like a small animal you were carrying, or maybe an infant, Stephen said, *but when you got closer I could see it was just some paper . . . papers. . . . The next morning I drove to Fairmont and got some back copies of* Discourses. *It's true, I usually don't read such things, not even the liberal magazines any longer . . . I've been living a different life, as you know. So I was fascinated to read* Discourses *again, to see how nothing at all has changed with you, nothing at all . . . after what you people did to the Movement in the late sixties, after the total victories you won . . . you're still as frightened as ever, still as paranoid and vicious . . . exactly as if nothing had happened! . . . It was extraordinary, really. I read four issues cover to cover, I was fascinated, mesmerized, I could hear your voice in every line and I began to wonder: do you write the entire magazine, all the articles, or do these people all get to sound like you eventually?*

Yes, and yes, Andrew said.

But he was joking. He smiled fondly at Stephen.

I hadn't remembered you being so concerned with me, with my soul, he said. *It's comforting. It's flattering. . . . Excuse me, though, if I find it difficult to take you seriously . . . ?*

Stephen looked up at him. *I know,* he said.

There had been rumors about Andrew's health but he looked strong: he was even fairly tan. Stephen stared at his brother, un-

smiling. He was struck by the similarity between the living man who
stood before him, hands rakishly on his hips, and the image of
Andrew in his dream. *A brother*, Stephen thought. *My brother*. He
did not know if he felt an irrational love for the man or if his emotion was totally impersonal, like a beacon shining for the moment
upon this particular man. He stared, his eyes filled with tears, until
Andrew turned away in embarrassment.

Would Stephen like something to drink? he inquired. He usually
had tea at about this time in the afternoon. Real coffee was forbidden him now and he hated substitutes, but tea, if it was weak
enough, was all right . . . he hoped it was all right. When he worked
he had an insatiable craving for something to drink, a habit that had
gotten worse in the past few years.

Stephen didn't want anything to drink but he felt he should say
yes.

. . . You'll be staying for dinner of course?

If you want me, Stephen said.

Of course I want you, Andrew said. *I haven't seen you for years.
You've come all this way. . . . What would it look like if. . . . Excuse me a moment, I'll get us some tea, I'll ask Yvonne to make tea
for us.*

He seemed suddenly nervous; he wanted to get out of Stephen's
presence.

An attractive, well-lighted room. It had been a sunroom years ago,
filled with Stephen's grandmother's plants. Now the old furniture
was gone and Andrew had replaced it with handsome rattan sofas
and chairs, starkly white, with gaily colored orange and scarlet and
bright green cushions. Everything smelled fresh, as if it had just been
shipped up from New York City. There were no curtains on the tall,
narrow windows; Andrew had had translucent, off-white shades put
on instead. Stephen went to the window and looked out through the
antique glass that slightly warped his vision. The side pasture was
overgrown but looked familiar. As a boy he had played there. There
were trees he recalled, hardly changed, several giant oaks at the far
edge of the pasture. The day was sunny, warm, ordinary. He had
changed but nothing else had changed. The house, the circumstances of their lives, the deaths, births, everything human had
changed, but nothing important had changed—there, suddenly, was
a flash of red—a bird flying by too quickly for Stephen to identify.
Nothing had changed. His boyhood was here and in the other house,

in town, unchanged. All this would survive him. . . . Yes, he looked
upon it warmly, knowing it would survive them all.

His brother's wife wore a dark blouse that was shot with green and
purple threads. In the sunlight it appeared to be iridescent, like
something glimpsed beneath the surface of the sea. As she moved
the colors changed, shifted subtly. Her black hair too shifted tone. It
was very black, silky-black, with genuine bluish highlights. Like Indians' hair, except it was not so straight and lank. Her eyebrows were
stern, level, rather thick. Her eyes were shining with a peculiar false
levity, like a dog's eyes, though he could see they were beautiful—in
a manner of speaking, they were beautiful. The cords prominent in
her throat, the tension in her jaw and shoulders . . . the way her
voice broke and faltered and then rushed forward again, in imitation
of Andrew's confidence. . . . He wanted to take her hand again, not
to shake it formally but to squeeze it, he wanted to declare his innocence, his good intentions, his inability even to remember clearly the
circumstances of their knowing each other: except for the fact that it
certainly did not matter and that he would never happen to mention
it to Andrew.

Discourses: Essays in Contemporary Culture was now nearly
twenty years old. Andrew had started it as a young man just out of
law school, in imitation of certain English weeklies he had admired.
At first it had been quite scholarly; he had named it in honor of
David Hume's *Political Discourses,* had subtitled it *Independent
Inquiries Concerning Ethical Principles in Our Time.* Most of the
original contributors were university professors in the Boston–New
York area or in England, apart from Andrew himself. Then, as time
passed, as Andrew became more committed to politics, the magazine
changed shape, dropped its footnotes, acquired a handsome glossy
cover, and though it never made a profit—not even in the sixties did
it make a profit, when contributions from right-wing organizations
were generous—it grew to have a respectable circulation. When
Andrew was too busy, acting editors did most of the work, but his
control over the magazine was complete: he owned it, it was his.

Stephen smoothed the March issue on his knees. He leafed
through it. He had studied it carefully, knew certain passages by
heart, and now he leafed through it again while Andrew poured tea
for them and spoke lightly of family matters, with that air of
bemused tolerance he always assumed when speaking of the family.

Stephen was not listening. He knew that his brother—his true brother—had come to him in despair, was appealing to him for help; he knew that the voice in the room with him, like the voice in the magazine itself, was distracting, false. God assuming the dizzying tactics of the Devil. God with a single essence but many warring faces. . . . In this issue there was an article questioning U.S. foreign policy in a year-old African nation, an article exposing the clumsy corruption of a federal commission named to study malnutrition in the United States, an article heavy with statistics that dealt with the history of "semi-socialized capitalism," with examples drawn from contemporary Japan, the Byzantine Empire, and Hitler's Germany. There were less formal essays and reviews; a black-bordered page called *Appraisal of Folly*, with a number of amusing items— *Reverend Scrunt Tyer, known as the "Man of God of the Oppressed Peoples," named by Washington officials to head HPTHT ("Helping People to Help Themselves") was arrested by Baltimore police and arraigned on charges of having misused two million dollars in funds, having conspired to thwart federal investigation of the program's records, and having participated in the corruption of minors. The Reverend Tyer, readers will recall, was singled out by the American Foundation for the Advancement of Minority Peoples for his "selfless service" in 1973 and was feted by none other than Our President Himself.* There were a number of cartoons, a page or two of letters from readers, and a modest number of advertisements. Stephen paged through the magazine until he came to the paragraph that had leaped out to his eye as if Andrew had been shouting at him from it.

Stephen, Andrew said politely, *will you have cream? sugar?*

Stephen did not hear. The paragraph, midway in a lengthy essay by a man unknown to Stephen, touched very lightly upon the possibility of a world-wide "unopen" conspiracy to deal with "quality control of population and culture." For some reason Stephen was struck by this paragraph and read it to Andrew in a strange, halting voice. When he looked up he saw that Andrew was frowning irritably.

So?

Did you write that, is the author's name a pseudonym? Stephen asked. . . . *For some reason I have the feeling that.* . . .

But so what! Andrew said impatiently. *You come here to interrupt my work . . . you stride up the driveway and frighten my wife and myself with your . . . your overheated evangelic tone. . . . What does it matter, what is the point of your visit? Discourses comes out*

*twelve times a year and I'm sure if you, or anyone, chooses to thumb
through it looking for trouble, trouble can be found—our most violent objections, in fact, come from very conservative groups in the
South and the Southwest. In the past year alone. . . .*

But did you write that essay? Stephen asked.

*A gentleman named T. W. Springham wrote it. Accept the evi-
dence of your senses.*

Stephen noticed a small tic in his brother's cheek. He closed the
magazine and held it for a moment, distracted, not knowing what to
say.

Put it down, lay it aside, Andrew said petulantly.

But I. . . I was under the impression that. . . .

Andrew snatched the magazine from him and tossed it onto a
table. *For Christ's sake,* he said, *try to be . . . try to maintain . . . at
least give the appearance of being sane, will you? When you look at
me like that I'm unnerved . . . I feel as if I were in the presence
of. . . .*

But you called me here, Stephen said slowly. *You begged me. It
was you . . . I knew nothing about the magazine, I hadn't seen it for
years, I don't even have time to read the newspaper now and . . .
and . . . I haven't thought of you for months. I didn't come up here
of my own free choice. You must want me, you must have called
me. . . .*

Andrew sipped at his tea. He held the cup in one hand, the saucer
in another, up close to his chin. *How tasteless this is,* he said. *How
horrible.*

Stephen watched him helplessly. He knew it was maddening to
Andrew to be observed at such close quarters; but he could not look
away. The thought came to Stephen again, as if from the outside,
that this frowning man, this handsome graying man in the sports
shirt and the pale green summer trousers, was his brother, was himself: that man set in such rigid opposition to him was actually a form
of himself. And he would die soon: he must die soon. But he did not
know it. He knew nothing, nothing at all. He was like a baby, knowing so little. He had summoned Stephen to him to be told of his
fate, but now he did not want to hear it.

I . . . I only wanted to know if you had written that article. . . .

What does it matter! Andrew said.

*. . . "quality control of population and culture" . . . that phrase
stuck in my mind . . . I was only skimming the magazine but I had
the distinct impression I could hear your voice,* Stephen said.

Ah yes: you're quite mad. We know you're quite mad. Harmless, engaging, mad. . . .

. . . I felt that you might want to talk with me . . . or to talk with someone. Maybe I shouldn't have come.

I have my wife to talk with, Andrew said, *but I'm grateful for your concern. I really am. It's just that I can't take you seriously. . . . No, I did not write that article. A man named Springham wrote it, as the byline says. However, there is nothing in the article I fundamentally disagree with. He's harsh but he's just. He's brilliant. Isn't he? Impeccable logic . . . irresistible. . . . The world's population must be brought under rigorous, intelligent control; he only dares to state openly what everyone else thinks. He's brave, he's reckless. He could make enemies. But I stand by him as I stand by nearly everything that is published in my magazine. And it's none of your business, Stephen, is it? Not at all.*

Stephen acquiesced. He studied his brother silently.

He would die soon: somehow they both knew. But nothing would be said. There was nothing to be said. . . . *I can't know,* Stephen thought miserably, *I can't know such things; I must be mistaken.*

This really is tasteless, Andrew said suddenly. He set his cup down so quickly that the tea spilled. *Tasteless. Horrible.* He grinned at Stephen angrily, as if Stephen were to blame. *Tasteless! Everything tasteless! Horrible! Sickening!*

15

Beneath the blankets the huge body shuddered and wheezed and quivered. The fat arms and legs were outstretched; the feet made enormous mounds. The head, turned to one side on the pillow, seemed to have no focus to it—ear, eye, nose, mouth were murky in the half light, lost in the chalky sameness of skull and pillow.

Stephen hovered over the bed but did not speak.

Don't let him die, he thought.

Someone was making inquiries about him, Stephen was told. It was mid-January now. Peter came to visit, bringing a six-pack of beer. He did not take his jacket off, however, since Stephen's cabin was rather cold. *A friend of ours told Molly,* Peter said. *What do you think it is?*

Making inquiries? Stephen asked dully.

. . . about you, asking questions about you, Peter said.

What questions?

I don't know, Peter said. *I wasn't approached.*

Life in the flesh hurts, Stephen sometimes thought. The revelation surprised him anew each time.

God had no feelings, no sensations, no nerve endings. When God departed from man, pain was a possibility. It was quite a possibility.

But is it supposed to hurt so much? Stephen wondered. *Is it meant to be this bad, or did things go wrong?*

16

When Stephen had been arrested, years before, along with a number of other protestors against the draft, Andrew flew to Buffalo to post bond for him. He had been so angry as to seem almost demented—shouting at Stephen despite the fact that they were not alone.

You idiot! You stupid bastard! And all for nothing! Nothing! You want to be a martyr but you'll see, you'll see whose scheme you're aiding!

Stephen had not been well at that time. Too many people had shouted at him. They had hated him, had wished him dead. A young patrolman had smashed him on the head with a billyclub. Stephen could not believe all that had happened to him and all he had witnessed, and for several months he very much doubted that it had happened; only when his strength was back did he dare acknowledge it.

His famous brother arrived, glowing with anger. In a rented car he drove Stephen to a doctor in Amherst, a friend of a friend; Stephen must have a complete checkup. And then he must come home with Andrew. He must rest, must regain his health and his sanity.

The first law of our era is that nothing influences anything, Andrew said contemptuously. *You'll see, you'll see! One day you'll see!*

Stephen declined his brother's invitation to return to Albany. He accepted money from him, however. He accepted medical care. Over a period of five or six months he regained his strength, as always. When he was broken, obliterated, empty, he simply waited until life returned. It had always returned in the past. God withdrew and then God returned. The flood of God, the flood of God's triumphant return, was always violent, ecstatic. Stephen regained his soul. God eased into God. The memory of the crowds and the Buffalo police and the stinking jail and the blow to his head and the hatred, the maniacal hatred, abated; and God returned in triumph.

Stephen remembered, however, his brother's pitying rage, his exasperation, and the odd incomprehensible things he had said before he had regained his control. *Nothing influences anything! —You'll see, you'll see. You'll learn.*

He worked hard. He worked harder than he had ever worked in his life. And he walked to the Home and back. It was good for him, the mile hike, it cleared his head and made him absurdly grateful, like a child or an animal, for the comforts of warmth. *Hello, good morning,* people said. *How are you,* people said. He worked hard, harder than the other attendants. But he did not call attention to himself, so the others were not resentful. In the seminary, years ago in another lifetime, he had been perhaps too dazzlingly good—too obviously a child of God. The other seminarians had come to detest him. Even his teachers had disliked him in the end. Now he was silent most of the time except with the boys, who liked him, or gave the impression of liking him. They sometimes obeyed him. They sometimes quieted down when he pleaded with them. Even the giant boy, hulking in his cubbyhole of a room, reluctant to come out for meals and showers and recreation periods, seemed to like Stephen. *I won't hurt you,* Stephen said cajolingly. *You can trust me. You can trust me.*

He worked hard and was exhausted at the end of the day. There was no time to think, except perhaps about the boys. Sinking to sleep he concentrated upon Kevin's face, forcing himself to envision it, thinking deliberately *He too is God, he too is God.* That way he was safe. If he dreamed of his dead brother or of his brother's wife or of his living brother, or of Stephen himself, he did not remember in the morning.

17

The elementary arithmetic lessons were a success. Kim Ryan had to be disbarred from them because he gnawed on his knuckles and whimpered and soiled his pants, but two other boys were brought in and even Kevin sat through one ten-minute session without causing trouble. In the staff lunchroom on the second floor talk was of the State Legislature's move against the Governor—who had neatly finessed them in a complicated maneuver that allowed him to appropriate more tax money for one of his pet projects, a Futures Museum adjacent to the Empire State Plaza—which involved cutbacks in the budget for education, health, and welfare; but Stephen did not listen closely. His mind raced with small plans, projects of his own.

They grappled together in a sweaty, impassioned struggle. Stephen could smell the stench of their lust though he was far away from them . . . watching them through half-shut eyes . . . his hands clenched, heart pounding. They grunted, they wheezed with the terrible effort of love. It was a failure, how could it not be a failure, two bodies locked in so comically dismal a struggle . . . ? Guzzling, burrowing, grunting: the larger of the bodies more desperate, thrusting itself against the other, again and again—like this!—like this!—*this!* But the woman, too, strained for union, her labor was perhaps more brutal, her nails clawing helplessly against the man's back: Stephen pitied her. He pitied them both. He watched the struggle from a distance, eyes narrowed so he would not see too clearly. *Life in the flesh hurts,* he thought. *But was it meant to hurt so much?*

It turned out that the giant boy played checkers. He liked to play checkers, he said shyly.

For weeks he had been watching Stephen play with other boys during his free hour from four to five. He was enormous, mute, had a new habit now of screwing his face up when he talked, half his face rising an inch or so, remarkably, the other half frozen as if made of plaster. He picked his nose almost constantly; it must have been a nervous, mechanical gesture. But since the attack of bronchitis he was more subdued. He looked Stephen full in the face occasionally, and smiled.

As another man might keep away from alcohol for weeks and then drink steadily for hours, for days, until he was obliterated, so Stephen kept away from the outside world and then, on a certain day, for no reason he could have named, he traveled as far as was necessary to a large library—at a university or downtown in a fair-sized city—and read newspapers and newsmagazines as quickly as possible, turning their pages, skimming their columns, until his eyes ached. He rarely felt emotion during these sessions; he simply read, read, skimmed columns, turned pages, impersonal and driven as a robot.

He read about the Petrie case: quite deliberately he searched out stories on the case and studied them. But there were not many now. In December and January—very little. Very little. The name *Petrie* caught his eye in a *New York Times* of late January but it was not *Andrew* named; it was *Harvey*. An item of no importance, two inches of print on page seventy-nine. No mention of Andrew at all.

He sat in the library at Watertown for several hours, hardly moving except to turn pages, more and more rapidly. He could not have said what he was searching for. He was not aware of his surroundings, hardly aware of what he read. Columns and columns of newsprint . . . names, names . . . names. Name-labels. Names of places, persons. Dates. Events. Labels that were words, mere words. Word-labels. His fingers were filthy from the newsprint. He had been touching his face unconsciously—his face was probably dirty too. Should go to a washroom, check himself in the mirror. Check his reflection. There, in the mirror, *Stephen* the label of Stephen. A name, a word. . . . The tumult of words was jarring at first and then mesmerizing. Ah, how little mattered! There were papers and magazines before him on the table, pages and pages he had scanned that afternoon, and now—what did it matter? *Petrie* was a word like any other. It was lost in the tumult of words. And it was good, natural, necessary that it be lost. Stephen knew that. He approved.

But was it meant to hurt so much? he wondered.

18

Your existence on earth is part of a political agreement, Andrew told him. *Father and Mother were estranged for years and she was terrified of divorce, terrified he would leave her though she hated*

*him. He was the only man who could really remember her beauty,
she used to say, the only one who could testify that she had been
beautiful at one time—physically beautiful, she meant, not just her
face but her body as well. Father did his best, he managed to be civil
at all times, at least as far as I know . . . but she kept antagonizing
him, testing him, saying insulting things in public . . . she suspected
him of being unfaithful long before he actually was. She had no
shame, like you.*

Stephen stammered that he did not want to hear this.

. . . Her mother was paying the big bills, Andrew continued
blandly, *she was bribing Father, more or less, to stay married. She
helped him in many ways: he told me once, in an unguarded moment, when I was complaining about some Albany crooks, that he
owed his excellent reputation as an honest judge to my grandmother.
When our branch of the Petries needed money, the Paxtons came
through. But Grandmother was primarily bribing Father to stay married. And at a certain desperate point Mother got the idea—from
something she read, I think, a gift book of poems someone gave her
for Christmas—that everything would be right again in her life if she
had another baby. And—*

Stephen jumped up and put his hands over his ears, exactly like a
child.

This is ridiculous! he said. *You're lying!*

*—and of course Father was violently opposed. The poor man was
sane, after all. But eventually Mother and Grandmother forced him
into an agreement; there was even a contract signed, I believe,
though of course I've never seen it. Mother wanted a baby because
the rest of us had disappointed her and a new baby was to be her salvation, her last chance, her lifeline . . . so she could tell the rest of
the world to go to hell, as I remember her saying. Yes, I remember! I
remember. I predate you, Stephen, and I know things you don't
know; I know many, many things you don't know. . . . So there was
a formal contract, with witnesses, and Mother was given one more
pregnancy in exchange for a certain sum of money.*

No, Stephen said, *it's really ridiculous. I don't believe you.*

*So perhaps you shouldn't mistake yourself for Christ, my boy,
whose birth may have been just as prescribed as your own, but at
least wasn't—*

Stephen found himself at the window, his back to Andrew. He
was staring sightlessly out at the pasture. A rail fence, grass, trees,

sky. But he was sightless. He said slowly: *I . . . I never . . . there was never. . . . I don't believe. . . . It isn't possible that. . . .*

Isn't it? Andrew said.

Later he said: *What difference does it make, Stephen? You're here, I'm here. We're all here. We owe each other the courtesy of. . . .*

But by then Stephen had absorbed his brother's hatred.

. . . you will be staying for dinner? . . . you aren't distressed?

By then Stephen had come to terms with Andrew. He did not believe him: but he did not disbelieve. The matter was simply not important.

Of course I'm not distressed, Stephen said calmly. *Of course I'll stay. I'll stay here as long as you need me.*

But you seem a little upset.

I don't think so, Stephen said. No.

You haven't touched your tea. . . . Would you like a drink? A cocktail? I might have one myself if. . . .

I don't think so. No.

19

Hugh appeared before him. He wore an overcoat that was too big for him and drooped well below his knees. His shoulders were rounded, his hair uncombed. He was grinning. Giggling. His body moved in tiny spasmodic jerks, as it had at Andrew's grave, when Stephen had had the impression his brother was weeping.

I have a secret too, he told Stephen. *I'm not alone. I'm not the freak of the family—the freak of the world! I'm not the only one you can read so easily, all of you, I'm not the only transparent person in the world! I'm not! I'm not! !*

They were on a city street but it was deserted. Stephen could not move his head: he saw, however, out of the corner of his eye, a row of cars parked at a curb and what must have been garbage cans. It was winter, both his and his brother's breaths were steamy.

I have a secret too! Hugh gloated. *I have my plans and I know how to execute them!*

He fumbled in his pocket and took out a pistol. He waved it at Stephen. *Do you see! Do you!*

Stephen stared mutely. He could not move, could not draw away. He could not speak. His brother leaned forward but he too did not move; he leaned far forward, almost crouching. He waved the gun at Stephen without aiming it, he waved it freely, rather gaily, as if it were necessary to keep the gun in motion so that it would not take aim.

Long after he woke, Stephen was troubled by the dream. He kept hearing his brother's voice—it was in the cabin with him. As soon as he left for the Home, however, it abated somewhat. The day was clear and frosty, the temperature about zero.

It never took very long for Stephen to walk to the Home. He rather wished he lived farther away. The exercise was good, the freezing air good. He believed he could walk great distances even in this cold—even when the wind was blowing. He could walk great, great distances. Once he was out in the fresh clean air, once he got started, he could do anything.

Good morning, they said, *how are you.*

At noon talk was of the legislature once again. A strawberry-blond girl with horn-rimmed glasses tapped her cigarette into an ashtray and complained bitterly, and Stephen's friend Peter complained bitterly. *Those bastards,* they said. . . . *They don't give a damn about anything,* they said.

Stephen excused himself and left the lunchroom. There were things he wanted to do, certain matters he must check. Did they talk about him afterward?—he did not care.

Did they talk about him? One Sunday he was treated to a big formal Sunday dinner at a friend's. The friend lived on a small farm outside Ogdensburg; he taught at the local college. He was a friend of Stephen's friend Peter, and his wife was a friend of Stephen's friend Molly. There were three other guests—warm, curious, lively, cheerful. They shook hands with Stephen and smiled. They liked him. Everyone liked him—it was not difficult to like him. He was shy, he stammered occasionally, he was obviously grateful for their company—or appeared to be grateful; the women liked him, liked him very much, and worried that he lived alone and perhaps did not eat right. How friendly everyone was!—new friends awaited Stephen everywhere across the continent.

Where are you from, Stephen? they asked.

How do you like it here?—the climate's brutal, eh?

Pete was saying you'd been in the seminary for a while, I wonder if, one of my cousins had a roommate at Penn, quit in his senior year to enter a seminary somewhere, think it was in Indiana, maybe Benedictine?—I wonder if you knew him, his name was something like—

Pete was saying you get along pretty well with the director, how do you manage—all we ever hear is he's a really mean bastard—

Not married? Never been? No plans?

Think you'll stay around for a while?

They talked about him afterward. Of course they liked him: but they talked about him. He did not mind, he was not annoyed. Word got to him that someone had been asking questions of the widow in town who was renting the cabin to him, but he did not telephone her to find out more information. What did it matter? He was innocent. He was innocent of absolutely everything. . . . Footprints in the snow, circling his cabin. A stranger's prints. They did not come near the cabin, however. They kept a respectable distance. A photographer, maybe, Stephen thought. But that did not matter either.

Hugh appeared again. But the vision was blurred and disappointing. Stephen had been trying to get his mind clear, had been sitting with his eyes shut, trying to clear himself out, to dislodge himself from the space in which he now existed, but the image of Hugh interfered: it grinned, giggled, flapped its arms about, ran its hands through its messy hair and even gave the scalp a yank as if it wanted to pull the top of the head off—

No, Stephen shrieked, *no—leave me alone—no, don't!—there must be some mistake, what do you want with me?*

20

The following morning at approximately ten-fifteen, God departed from Stephen with a swift, sickening wrench; he was left staring at the hideously ugly face of a freakish child-giant, whom he loathed with every particle of his being.

No, Stephen thought. *No,* he said aloud.

They asked him what was wrong and he could not explain. He was still nauseated. He had no time to explain, no interest in explaining. What did it matter! . . . The stench of the boys made him nauseated. He would have to get outside as quickly as possible; there was no time to be polite. *No*, Stephen murmured, but it was too late. For one instant he had looked upon the boy—who, at that moment, was picking his nose with a busy, ungraceful forefinger—and had seen him with an astounding clarity. Now he had to escape, he had to escape all of them. *No, it's too late, let me go, leave me alone.* The gigantic mealy-pale face set so oddly flat in that head did not follow him: it retreated, it fell back. Stephen jumped back. He jumped a step or two back. Raw, hideous, astounding—that face, that body— not God, not even human—

He could not explain, hadn't the words. His head reeled. He put on his jacket, pulled a wool cap down low over his forehead, and stepped into his overshoes and did not have time to buckle them. They asked him what was wrong but he had no time to be polite, not now.

Are you ill? they asked. *You look so white—deathly white—*
Ill, yes, Stephen muttered. *Ill.*
Would you like a ride back to—?
I'm ill, Stephen said. *Let me go. . . . I won't be back.*
Stephen—
Stephen's ill! Stephen's finished! he cried.

But the boy was human, there was that qualification. He was human, in his way. Quite human. Surpassingly human. The glimmer of intelligence in his dark shiny eyes—the way the face creased and relaxed and creased again, as if parodying the concentration of others —and that busy, busy forefinger that distended the nose and seemed about to mutilate it—

God has forsaken me, Stephen thought in the cold. *Why has God forsaken me? . . . forsaken all of us?*

21

It was Hugh: crossing the wide windy avenue against traffic.

In a coat too big for him, the sleeves too long, in thin-soled shoes without boots or galoshes, he strode forward oblivious to everything, head bowed against the wind. His fair, fine hair blew. Stephen caught sight of the man who was his brother before he realized he was his brother. Stephen stopped dead on the sidewalk. He gaped.

Hugh . . . ?

But his voice was too faint to be heard over the traffic.

He had been on his way to Hugh's apartment in the Village. This was Hugh's neighborhood, of course, so it should not have seemed remarkable, the sight of Hugh on the street. It was not a miracle, after all. Hardly a coincidence. But since the incident at the Home several days earlier Stephen had not been himself: everything surprised and distressed him and left him oddly weak.

He ran across the avenue as the light changed.

Hugh? Hugh? Hugh?

The eyes dilated, the lips thin, mean, bitter. It was Hugh and yet not Hugh. Stephen stared at him, frightened. He began by trying to explain—stammering nervously—he even took the telegram out of his pocket—apologized for not having replied or come sooner— But Hugh professed not to know what he was talking about. He waved aside the telegram, even slapped lightly at Stephen's arm as if Stephen were a child annoying him. It did not seem to surprise him, their meeting on the street.

Spying on me, eh? Hugh said indifferently. *I no longer care.*

I'm not spying on you, Stephen said. *I thought you wanted to see me. But I want to see you . . . want to talk with you. . . .*

Really! Hugh said.

Hugh had been standing on the sidewalk, gazing over an iron railing into an old cemetery. Stephen had not known such cemeteries were preserved in New York City. A flock of sparrows were picking in the thin dirty snow nearby and when Hugh turned, turned abruptly to walk away, most of them darted into the air.

Don't have time for you, for any of you, Hugh muttered. He did not speak directly to Stephen. . . . *sanctimonious little liar, spying so crudely . . . a vulture drawn by my obituary in the* Times. . . .

What? Obituary? Stephen asked, cupping his ear.

They were heading back toward Sixth Avenue. Hugh charged across the street and Stephen followed. *I wanted to come to New York sooner,* Stephen panted, *but I was . . . I was involved in. . . . Hugh, why are you angry? Has something happened?* Hugh entered a grocery store as if he were alone. He extricated a shopping cart from another shopping cart and pushed it briskly back along one of the aisles, to the rear of the store. At the fresh-produce counter he stopped and examined heads of lettuce carefully. He held a head in each hand, as if weighing them. His lips moved silently. *What did you mean, an obituary in the* Times? Stephen asked.

He stared at his brother's thin, peaked profile and felt that he really feared and disliked this man. He did not know him at all and did not care to know him. It was too late. . . . But in the next instant he recovered, he made a move to help Hugh with the shopping cart, which could not be pushed in a straight line. Its front wheels turned inward.

Very nice, very nice of you, Hugh muttered. *Unfortunately I can't invite you to dine with me. I have another engagement. A previous engagement. A young person of exquisite beauty . . . who would not wish to share my company with anyone else.*

I'm sorry. I had wanted to come sooner. . . .

Sooner? Sooner? Than what, sooner?

He pushed the cart away. He headed for the dairy counter.

I don't understand why you are so angry with me, Stephen said. *We haven't seen each other since Andrew's funeral. . . .*

That ghastly boring day, Hugh muttered. *Don't remind me! . . . Don't follow so close, Stephen, I'm liable to jab you with my elbow.*

. . . had the impression from the telegram. . . .

He stooped for a carton of something, cottage cheese or yogurt. The dairy section was almost depleted; only a few cartons and containers were left, and there was a stale, sickish odor about the refrigeration unit. The carton slipped from his fingers and fell and he retrieved it, grunting, embarrassed. . . . *worried about you . . . thought we could talk for a few minutes. . . .*

Hugh let the carton drop in his basket and turned to Stephen and began to shriek. *Fuck off! Fuck off, you! Fuck, fuck, fuck off!*

Stephen waited for him outside the store.

Not so tall as he remembered, but agitated as always, rather round-shouldered: so Hugh appeared in a few minutes, carrying a bag of groceries. His face was flushed, his cheeks especially reddened. He grinned at Stephen.

Theater, he said softly. *Eh?*

What? Stephen cupped a hand to his ear.

Theater—theater, Hugh said airily. *Everything is theater. The world's a stage—don't you know? And I'm one of the stars.*

Yes, Stephen said. *I wonder if—*

Come back to the apartment if you absolutely must, Hugh said, *but don't expect to stay very long. I can't start this sort of thing at my advanced age—a warm-heartening tête-à-tête with a blood relative —not even when the blood relative is my only living brother. It goes against my sense of propriety, my sense of the grotesque.*

I won't stay long, Stephen said quickly.

Of course you won't! There is only one bed, which will be occupied. But where will you return to, my boy? A monastery? A convent? A churchyard, beneath the stones? Father always said—and said again when I visited him a few weeks ago—

Stephen flinched. *You visited him—?*

Of course. He wanted to see me. He misses me very much. Now that Andrew is dead he feels he has only one son: embarrassing, the love he evidently feels for me. Of course I feel nothing for him. Very nearly nothing. I could hardly have survived my childhood had I actually cared about that man. You were wise, Stephen, to blot us all out. Father and Mother especially. . . . How brave and defiant and melodramatic you were to enter the seminary, to leave home and declare yourself independent and even to disinherit yourself—well done, very well done, a nice bit of theater! But you can hardly grieve now over the fact that Father will never forgive you. He just isn't the type; none of the Petries are.

My father doesn't know me at all, Stephen said. *He never did. He never knew any of us.*

No one knows anyone else; it's an utterly boring platitude, Hugh said. *Father, for instance, has only the vaguest idea of who I am, of what my talent means. He tries, poor dear, but his grasp is limited. Ah, how he prattled of his love for me!—has collected every bit of work I've done, isn't it remarkable? Poor senile drooling dear! Has a clipping service—keeps everything framed and under glass—inconsequential cartoons I had more or less forgotten myself—what a surprise, there, on his living-room wall! . . . Father and I have had our differences, of course, but he is truly making an effort as death draws near. . . .*

Did he speak of me at all? Stephen asked.

Why, you know the old boy is anti-Catholic! It runs in the family, Hugh laughed. *Don't ask such asinine questions.*

You don't approve? he cried gaily. *Too bohemian for you?*

Stephen was distressed at the look of the room. And the odor: it was nearly as bad as certain areas of the Home.

. . . never cared for my work, eh? None of you.

Hugh went into the kitchen to put his groceries away. Stephen did not follow. He did not want to walk through the mess. He stared in silence. His nausea returned.

The main piece of furniture in the room was a workbench, which was piled high with papers, glasses, articles of clothing, towels, linens, crumpled bags, plates, cups, forks, and spoons. Candy wrappers lay underfoot. On the walls were extraordinarily ugly drawings and caricatures—Stephen did not know if they were his brother's or not. He knew little about his brother's art. Atop the mess on the drawing board was a line drawing that seemed to be of a crucifixion. But it was messy, blotted. Stephen stared, fascinated. A crucifixion! . . . A creature with an angel's immense outspread wings, nailed upon a cross that was actually a woman's body upside down. Stephen drew closer. He picked up the sheet of paper. It seemed to him that the angel had his own face. Impossible, of course: yet the face resembled his own, and the dark curly hair was his. The woman's face was unclear but it too seemed familiar.

He let the sheet fall.

. . . little prudes mustn't touch, Hugh said mockingly. He carried a bottle and two glasses. *Such wisdom is not for you.*

What does it mean? Stephen asked, blushing.

Art does not mean, art simply exists, Hugh said. He sat heavily and let his head fall against the back of the chair. *It exists eternally and gloriously and autonomously in its own realm, kicked loose of the bourgeois categories people like you inhabit—beautifully, beautifully free, do you hear? And the artist too is free. Free, free, free,* he said boldly. *Join me in a drink before you leave, eh?*

Thank you, but—

Then leave now! Go! If you won't drink with me after all these years, go at once! Go to hell and good riddance!

He was shouting, but his manner was good-natured. He poured himself a drink. He took a swallow, sighed, squirmed with pleasure.

I know why you're here, you ghoul, he said. *You can smell the stink of my decay—want to close in for the kill, pray for my soul, con me into kneeling in the filth and abandoning myself to God. Right? But it's too late. I'm already with God.*

There were bluish-gray pockets about the man's eyes. But the eyes themselves were bright. They reminded Stephen of Kevin Kasser's eyes. *Here too is God, here squats God,* Stephen thought helplessly. His brother crossed one long lanky leg over the other and began to jiggle his foot. In a way he seemed quite pleased, even excited. He was chattering about how no one ever visited him now, his friends had all abandoned him, had all betrayed him, were spreading rumors about him and no doubt writing their memoirs in order to include sensational anecdotes concerning Hugh Petrie . . . but Stephen must sit down, for Christ's sake, and stop looking so frightened.

. . . *of course they've pumped you full of lies, I suppose . . . the Widow especially . . . so you're afraid of your own brother. And all because they want to discredit me! . . . they hope to have me committed to a mental home, as they did poor Pamela, so they can take over my copyrights, my royalties . . . my bank accounts . . . my prestige. It's all a plot, Stephen, as it was a plot to destroy Andrew because he had gone too far in making certain accusations. . . . Plots, plots! The world is a network of plots and all of them cruel, sinister, subterranean. Innocents like you and me haven't a chance for survival in such a world. . . . Sit down, please! I have begun to find you tolerable and you mustn't press the issue.*

Stephen looked for a place to sit. He located a cane-bottomed chair, overturned behind a large cardboard box—*Ivory Soap*, the box proclaimed—and brought it to within a few yards of his brother. Hugh kicked a pillow toward him languidly; it was bright green, with markings in red yarn to indicate eyes, nose, and grinning mouth. Stephen ignored the pillow. He sat, unbuttoned his coat slowly and self-consciously, but did not take the coat off. Hugh offered him a drink again. . . . *You're still so pure, it's a catastrophe in one so reasonably young and attractive, and still so innocent, they say; what a pity. Mother wanted a baby forever and so she got one: though not precisely the baby she had desired. Well, may she rest in peace,* Hugh said softly. He poured a little more Scotch into his glass and sipped at it. *Sometimes I know very well what Joseph Stalin meant when he said . . . what did he say . . . that the death of his mother killed any warm feelings he had had for anyone, for all of humanity. . . . One must be connected to the world, they say, but how?— how? They don't tell us. . . . They scold and lecture and punish and pass legislation and revoke legislation, they tell us we must marry and then they tell us it might not be necessary after all, they tell us it's only through a woman, then it isn't necessarily, they tell us . . . lecture us . . . insist. . . . The individual is all, the individual is the end of everything . . . and so we are, so indeed we are, we princely ones! . . . but that doesn't quite solve the overwhelming problem of our era: how to get through the long weekends. . . . Well, may she* rest in peace, poor woman. You might have loved her more, you know.

I had no choice, Stephen said.

I didn't either, Hugh said, sighing. I never do.

Hugh was silent for a while and then returned to the subject of plots. He knew there was a plot against his life: and that he could not protect himself against it. How? With what weapons, what strategy? The innocent are always defenseless. . . . They think I know too much, when in fact I know too little, he said. He shrugged his shoulders; his entire frame shrugged. Perhaps there were several plots against him, the most devilish being the plot among his acquaintances and rivals and fellow artists and certain editors to completely demolish his reputation. Stephen would know nothing about it, of course; Stephen knew nothing of New York City. The shifting alliances, the vogues that come and go, the intense rivalry, the denial of true talent . . . rumor, backbiting, vicious anecdotes. Word was out that Hugh Petrie was unreliable. That Hugh Petrie was an alcoholic. Had had a breakdown of some kind. Why, they told him such things in person! . . . Death itself would not upset me nearly so much, Hugh said, as the destruction of my talent. As you can see from the work I'm doing now . . . was hard at work doing, in fact, when you knocked at the door and interrupted my concentration . . . I'm getting better all the time. I am not yet at my peak. That won't come until I'm sixty or more, I have decades and decades, a small lifetime before me! . . . and they are trying to hurry me to the grave, the cruel bastards. Once there, what will I do? Stephen? Even in your ghastly God-universe, in which I don't believe, what would I do?—my talent, my wit, my charm would go for nothing.

You're joking, aren't you, Stephen said slowly. But I. . . .

But what! But! But—? You came to interrogate me about our sister-in-law, eh? And have no interest whatsoever in hearing about my plight. . . . Yvonne is a clever sluttish creature, now fully in alliance with the family against me; they've convinced her that the investigation should go no farther than it has—do you know that arrests are imminent?—they've found someone to confess—yes indeed!—they've convinced her to join with them, to close ranks, to look to the future and ride the swillish tide of public opinion as far as it will take them . . . him, that is . . . Harvey is headed for the governorship and beyond that who knows? . . . as they used to gloat about Andrew. Yvonne is one of them now. She crossed over. And she wishes me

*dead, because of a . . . well, a certain indiscreet session . . . the two
of us fairly drunk . . . and. . . .*

Stephen found himself on his feet, unconsciously. He was very
nervous.

*What? Sit down. Relax. . . . Yes, the two of us got quite drunk
and she invited me back to . . . up to . . . poor old A's apartment
. . . bedroom . . . bed, actually, to be frank . . . and afterward had
regrets, the morning after and subsequent mornings after . . . yes, indeed, unfortunately . . . for me . . . her regrets assumed flood proportions and she tried to take her own life, they say, an overdose of
sleeping pills. You didn't know? Doris didn't tell you, eh? The dear
thing tells me everything! . . . Yes, Yvonne tried to kill herself out
of spite, pure and simple. She left a suicide note blaming me for . . .
blaming me for . . . for what we did together, certain acts of abandon and experimentation . . . not what one would expect from a
cold bitch like her. Most surprising, actually. . . . Stephen?*

You are joking, Stephen said slowly. It was difficult for him to
speak; he had the irrational idea that his tongue might come loose
and begin to rattle helplessly against the roof of his mouth. And
then Hugh would laugh. . . . *You are joking or lying, aren't you? Always, forever, joking or lying . . . your entire life. . . .*

*What are you mumbling, dear boy? . . . As long as you're up,
would you toss me that box of Kleenex? My nose is running, I can't
seem to shake a filthy cold I picked up back in December . . . an ear
infection and headaches. . . . Thanks.* Stephen watched as Hugh
poked his small finger, covered with the tissue, up into his nostril.
He poked and pried and distended his long, rather patrician nose.

Joking or lying or telling the truth, Stephen murmured, *it's all one
to you. . . .*

Hugh ignored him and returned again to the subject of plots. His
head rested on the back of the chair and from time to time he closed
his eyes; he seemed fairly comfortable, not at all frightened, though
he was speaking of the probability of his own death . . . unless he
could outwit his persecutors. Evidently he had been meeting with his
nephew, Michael. Evidently there was something . . . something impending, or possible . . . something about the two of them embark-
ing upon a publishing scheme, taking over a magazine, perhaps . . .
it might even be *Discourses* . . . what delightful revenge that would
be! But the magazine was near bankruptcy and no one wanted to
touch it and the alliance with Michael was something that must be
worked out for the future . . . couldn't be rushed . . . required capi-

tal . . . required Willa's good will. . . . It was necessary for Hugh to
outwit his many enemies, but he must not rush into any alliances or
schemes. Look at Andrew's fate: desperately seeking help from one
side, then from another, until he was abandoned, left to die. *Of
course he was killed by someone he knew,* Hugh said, affecting an air
of indifference. *Andrew kept a gun with him at the farm, had one in
the cabin with him, and would certainly have shot down anyone who
approached him . . . anyone suspicious. No one has ever made that
statement in public and yet it's perfectly obvious. Of course he had a
gun! I know. I'm sure. And it was stolen along with those other
things simply to mislead us. A network of plots, Stephen, crisscross-
ing one another, threaded backward and forward in time. . . . Hideous, intolerable.*

Hugh's face was frail, vulnerable, his eyes brimming with tears.
Stephen, staring at him, was reminded of Hugh's behavior at their
mother's funeral—the quiet, choked, helpless weeping, almost like
retching. *Hideous, intolerable . . . life itself a maze, a network . . .
plots composed by other people . . . sinister creatures who wish
us harm . . . who devise for us the most outrageous, merciless
scenarios. . . . Unless we get there first, of course. Unless we get
there first!*

. . . get there first?

Hugh blinked rapidly at him. He managed a faint, fond smile.
You're simply too innocent to understand me, he said.

You give the impression of being innocent, he was saying, *in order
to be forgiven the need to understand. But it's done unconsciously.
You don't know what you're doing. . . . Most people are like that;
most people live their lives unconsciously.*

But you are different, Stephen said.

*Yes. Frankly, yes. I am quite different. After all, someone must
take on the burden of being awake . . . constantly awake . . . always
conscious, always responsible. So that the rest of the world's population can drift along in its eternal sleep. So that people like you,
Stephen, can dream virtuous dreams in which heroism is possible, in
which everything works out for the glory of God . . . as in those Biblical stories written by lunatics and hermits and cranks, while the
real business of governing the world falls to responsible men. . . .*

You consider yourself one of the responsible men, Stephen said
quietly.

What do you consider yourself? Andrew said at once.

Andrew smiled at him. It would not have been possible, that day, to guess Andrew's age. He wore pale green trousers and a white, finely knit sports shirt; the shirt was unbuttoned at the throat and Stephen could see a few hairs that were starkly white, wirelike in texture.

. . . you consider yourself responsible . . . and men like your pseudonymous prophet, Stephen said. *You and your "Springhams" . . . your lunatics and hermits and. . . .*

Who could buy and sell the rest of you, Andrew said, *who could buy the land out from under your little community of saints and evict you in six months. . . . Or, if we liked, could give you all the land up here . . . the farm, the farmland, half of Natauga County. If we liked. This wonderful old house, for example. If we liked.*

And . . . ?

And what?

But you don't . . . ?

Andrew shrugged indifferently. There was a small, nearly imperceptible tic in his left cheek that he tried to anticipate by smiling suddenly. His smile came and went, flashed, departed, and came back again with no connection to the rest of him. Stephen watched, fascinated. Intimidated. Perhaps his brother was not going to die: Perhaps he was simply going to go mad.

Don't . . . ? Andrew said softly.

You don't want to do that for me, Stephen said. *Do you?*

I don't know, Andrew said. *I suppose not.*

It needn't be all the land, it needn't be thousands of acres, just the house and a few acres, some farmland we could cultivate. . . .

In exchange for what?

What do you mean? I haven't anything you want.

Yes, Andrew said, *you have something I want.*

What?

Life. Your life. . . . You are alive, aren't you?

Stephen could not comprehend the joke. He knew it was meant to be amusing, mocking; but he could not understand.

I said—you're alive, aren't you? Stupid, childish, bungling, unconscious—and alive. I want that. I want to know that.

. . . were saying about Yvonne attempting suicide . . . ?

Yes, I thought you'd pick up on that, Hugh giggled. *Yes. I was waiting for you to inquire. . . . You won't join me in this tiny meal, then? I must admit there isn't quite enough for both of us. A sip of*

Scotch, a spoonful of yogurt: surprisingly tolerable. The Scotch aids in the stomach's chore of metabolizing the yogurt. The yogurt is packed with vitamin-bearing bacteria that flood into the bloodstream and aid in the circulation of the alcohol . . . so that, in no time at all, one's color returns and one is anxious to return to work. . . . Yes, Yvonne is our subject, our worthy subject. You want to know . . . what?

Is it true she tried to kill herself, Stephen said irritably, *or was that one of your jokes? It's very serious, you shouldn't joke. . . .*

You know very little about the art of "caricatura," Hugh said, *if you think joking isn't serious. It is always serious—deadly serious. My master, James Gillray, for instance, always held that everyone gets his deserts . . . everyone gets what he deserves. All the objects of his ferocity eventually died. He made them into dogs and pigs and he drew their corpses for them to contemplate and he gouged out their eyes and hacked off their noses and ears . . . as Nature would do, with less art; he chopped their arms and legs off, even, but in jest. He was a superb draftsman but, as one might suppose, he was denied recognition as a serious artist . . . just as they are denying me. But I won't commit suicide as poor Gillray did. I refuse to give my enemies that satisfaction.*

Stephen listened to his brother's high-pitched, rapid chatter with increasing restlessness. He wanted to run out—wanted to escape. It was difficult to look upon Hugh and see, in him, a brother; without the medium of God to link them, the invisible connective tissue Stephen had always sensed in the past, it was very difficult indeed. He knew he was related by blood to this man and that he was related by spirit to this man and yet, each time Hugh snickered or cast him a mocking glance. . . .

Of course you won't commit suicide! Stephen said. *Why do you talk like that? . . . And what about Yvonne, what were you saying about . . . ?*

Hugh stared at him. He paused, the spoon halfway to his mouth. *Yvonne? Were we talking about Yvonne?*

You said. . . .

No, I believe you said. YOU.

Just a few minutes ago you said. . . .

No, no. You. You, my boy. You brought up the subject of our dear sister-in-law, not me. You're panting with curiosity and lust, not me. Quite frankly . . . quite frankly, I don't believe I care to approach that fierce young woman a second time. Yes, he said, sighing, raising the spoon to his mouth and then licking it clean while Stephen watched him in exasperation, *it was you and only you.*

Hugh, only a few minutes ago you said something about . . . she had tried to commit suicide, you said. I heard you.

Like boyhood, this is! Hugh laughed. *A boyhood quarrel. I said, you said, no, I said, no you said . . . no, NO, I said. But really it was you. It was you, you, you.*

Hugh. . . .

Why, your cheeks are red and your eyes are glowing, you're like an advertisement, Hugh said in surprise. *There really are such creatures in our species. . . . I thought you were all posed and faked. I thought you were plaster. . . . The strangest thing, Stephen, I've discovered a mannequin uptown . . . in Saks's window . . . exactly like Yvonne she is, even more frightful . . . beautiful . . . with her synthetic glittering black hair and her two-inch black eyelashes, like paintbrushes . . . ah, so lovely! . . . so harsh to the soul and one's skin. If it wasn't dark I'd take you up to look. Love at first sight! . . . Even though it's dark, I believe the show windows are lit. Shall we go up, Stephen? A quick cab ride . . . no trouble. . . .*

What are you talking about? Stephen cried.

. . . haven't checked in for a few days, but last time I saw the dear thing she was surrounded by daisies and golf clubs and mats of bright green grass like the sort draped over poor A's coffin as we trudged away. She's all in white . . . dazzling . . . white sleeveless sweater-blouse and white white glaring white blinding white trousers that flare so cutely at the ankle . . . she's swinging a golf club but her composure is as always, porcelain-smooth, impregnable . . . and her lips are pursed, her lips are closed. . . . Shall we go up and say hello?

Please, Stephen said, *don't torture me. Don't do this.*

Why, what do you mean? Hugh asked. He looked at Stephen quite innocently. *. . . I don't know what you mean.*

Don't pretend to be . . . pretend to. . . . Don't behave like a. . . .

I don't know what you mean, Hugh said softly.

It struck Stephen that his brother spoke the truth.

They hated each other. They would not touch each other. But there was the instinct to touch—the yearning to come nearer, nearer. Stephen hated his own weakness, hated the fact that his eyes were brimming with tears; and that Andrew could see. Andrew could see. He grinned.

He saw, he grinned defiantly. The tic was quite perceptible.

Andrew hated the fact that Stephen hovered above him, trembling with emotion, his eyes filling with tears. How crude he was, how embarrassing. . . . He embarrassed everyone. He embarrassed the family, he embarrassed even strangers. His love, his pity, his tears were not wanted. They were loathsome. Andrew knew that Stephen knew how he was despised, and he knew that Stephen's knowledge deepened Stephen's pity, not for himself, but for those who despised him; and this angered Andrew all the more.

Crazy, you're crazy, my only consolation is to know that you're crazy . . . have been since childhood . . . and that nothing you say applies to the world in which I live. . . .

You, Stephen whispered. *You're the one. You.*

I'm . . . ? What?

You're the one who is crazy, Stephen said.

Andrew stood and, without hesitation, as deftly and casually as if he had been planning it, slapped Stephen hard across the face.

. . . bastard!

Stephen's head jerked to the side. But he did not step back, did not lose his balance. For an instant he considered turning the other cheek: how that would madden his brother, that sly Christian gesture! But he knew he would only be struck again. And he knew the second blow might not be a slap.

The one thing that is always true about me, Andrew said ironically, *my minimal virtue, in fact . . . is my sanity.*

Stephen's head reeled. Even now his instinct was, perversely, to submit to his brother's physical violence; for some reason he did not understand, he would have liked to be assured of Andrew's enmity—would not have minded another symbolic blow. They were not enemies but brothers; Andrew, however, imagined himself to be an enemy. And that was important. But it would have been wrong of Stephen, it would have been a violation of his own sanctity, if he goaded his brother into striking him again.

Get out of here, Andrew said.

If you insist, Hugh said sleepily, *if you must know. . . . She reduced me to a quivering shrieking brainless protoplasm . . . a monstrosity that begged for mercy and at the same time burrowed ever more deeply, more blackly, into the monstrousness. . . . She made a jelly of me, of my spine and brain case and knee caps; I slobber even now to recall it. . . . But afterward she regretted unmasking herself. Perhaps it was simply that I am one of the family and might tell tales. She cavorts as she wishes, you know, with men she picks up on the street. Everyone knows that.*

. . . *everyone?*

Doris told me. Everyone in Albany knows. *Private investigators are hardly justified, when the woman behaves so freely, so defiantly. . . . She's a filthy slut, really; a whore. And so it's incredible that the family should take her word against mine, should actually elevate her to my level. . . . Incredible, incredible! And you too: I suppose you believe her rather than me? You look like a young knight, slightly demented, ready to charge off and protect your lady. It's charming, really, though rather frightening. . . .*

Why should I take her word against yours? Stephen said. What does she accuse you of . . . ?

Hugh sipped his drink reflectively. He belched. . . . *a female plot, a typically female plot . . . outraged virtue and all that . . . virginity . . . not that she was a virgin, of course . . . but she maintains that air of . . . something cold and fierce and ruthless . . . amazonian. . . . But bloody! Ah yes: bloody. So I discovered to my chagrin. My horror. One simply can't believe . . . can't, can't . . . can't believe the loathsomeness of. . . . The smell is almost negligible compared to the . . . the metaphysical hideousness of . . . of. . . . Of them.*

Them?

Women. A woman.

I don't know what you're talking about, Stephen said. You've been drinking. . . . What does Yvonne accuse you of? What happened?

Ask the family. Ask Doris. They are ganging up against me . . . want to use this issue to humiliate me and manipulate me. . . .

What happened?

. . . *blackmail me, like everyone else . . . every slutty little bitch. . . .*

Stephen touched his brother's shoulder. What happened? he said.

Don't stand so close, Hugh cried. He pushed Stephen away. . . . *Nothing happened. Nothing at all. I exaggerated our love-play to tease you . . . I was innocent then and am innocent now. She accused me of, of . . . of . . . But Andrew was there also. In the apartment. In the bedroom. He was there watching, he deliberately enticed me there in order to. . . . But I discovered the plot and fled.*

Fled. And nothing happened to her. Now will you move away, will you button your coat and leave? Now. Nothing happened to her, as Andrew knows very well, since he presided over it all; but she was unconscious and claims to have been raped and . . . and claims I fed her pills with the intention of . . . well, I hardly know! . . . of killing her, perhaps. I hardly know what she has told them. A hysterical woman will say anything.

Hugh's right hand moved and jerked and pulsated as if he were drawing; as if he clutched an invisible pen or pencil that moved of its own accord, jabbing at an invisible paper. As soon as he set the glass down, this spasmodic movement began. He did not seem aware of it.

. . . will say anything, he muttered.

But you didn't harm her.

I wish I had! I wanted to. I wanted to fuck her, I wanted to strangle her, I don't know what I wanted . . . all at once, everything at once, everything! I don't know. I didn't know then and I don't know now. Maybe I love her and I wanted to . . . I wanted to do what people do in such circumstances, normal people, people who are not loathed and mocked . . . wanted simply to make love to her; and my life would have been changed. She would have fallen in love with me then. And I would have been normal like the rest of you . . . like everyone . . . would have taken my place as . . . as. . . . I don't know. Maybe I just wanted to get revenge. I suspected that Andrew would be watching. . . .

What do you mean, watching? You know that isn't possible, Stephen said. *You know he's. . . .*

Hugh belched again. *Dead? Yes. Sure.*

Then what do you mean?

. . . watching us, surrounding us. Listening. Spying. Laughing up his sleeve as in the old days. . . . She told him everything, every tiny detail, somebody's father's yacht or sailboat, one of the bunkbeds, and she told him everything, shameless, drunk on wine and giggling and flush-faced, but I loved her anyway and forgave her . . . Pamela, I mean . . . you didn't know her . . . were too young. . . . I vowed I would kill him that day. When I realized. That he had instigated her. That she had told him everything and that they laughed about me together afterward. . . . I forgave her, but not him. Not him. Never.

Stephen could not follow most of this. He said: *Vowed to kill him? Do you mean Andrew?*

Of course I mean Andrew, Hugh said thickly. He was quite groggy now and his hand, no longer restrained, was twitching and jerking from side to side. He might have been drawing tiny circles or heads. . . . *But I never had the courage to do it.*

You never had the courage to do it, Stephen said.

Never. That was my personal failing. My art . . . my career . . . that's another dimension entirely. Another dimension . . . entirely.

You wanted to kill Andrew, Stephen said quietly, *but you never had the courage. So you didn't kill him. It wasn't you.*

Hugh muttered something unintelligible.

It's tasteless, isn't it, Andrew said suddenly. *No wonder you don't want any. I made it too weak. . . . Tasteless. Horrible. But I'm not supposed to drink it strong any more. Tannic acid and caffeine as well. . . .*

What's wrong with you, Stephen asked, without thinking. *Is it your stomach, your nerves . . . ?*

My stomach. My nerves. Yes. My heart as well, Andrew said ironically, *not to mention my gall bladder . . . which may have to be removed, but may not; we are waiting to see. It's a minor point, really. Not like the liver or the heart or the brain. But don't look so absurdly sad, Stephen, I'm not going to collapse at your feet! . . . I'm in reasonably good health. I had an ulcerous condition a while back, was even operated on . . . but kept it quiet, didn't even tell the family. Only Yvonne knew. Shortly after our wedding . . . my poor bride . . . but the operation was a success and I'm fully recovered . . . as you can see. Really. No need for you to look so doggish and solemn.*

I'm sorry to hear. . . .

No, no. It's all right. I wish I hadn't mentioned it. I find myself saying things to you I wouldn't ordinarily say. . . . But you seem to be in radiant health. I could almost be envious. You've never been ill, have you? . . . seriously ill? . . . With your health, your body, and my mind. . . . But Yvonne is remarkably healthy too. She's in superb condition. Likes to walk long distances, likes to swim . . . we have a membership at the city club, you know, and she goes by herself to the pool . . . she's so strong, so remarkably . . . remarkably young and strong and reliable.

Yes, Stephen said.

. . . a superb woman.

Yes.

Without her my life would be very difficult. Without her I'm not sure that . . . that. . . . Would you like a drink, Stephen? Anything at all? She's a beautiful woman, isn't she. Beautiful. Beauty is a minimal requirement in a woman; but there must be more.

Yes, Stephen said.

Of course there must be more, the voice said emphatically; as if it were being challenged. *There must be more, always more.*

Stephen nodded faintly, not wishing to agree or disagree. He was sitting somewhere, ramrod straight as someone had encouraged him to sit or forced him to sit in another lifetime. He was sitting in a handsome fresh-smelling white chair with gay green and orange cushions; he was in the presence of his brother, his famous, doomed brother. He showed no sign of uneasiness. He was confronting Andrew Petrie, who despised him, who was a hole, a hollowness, a vacuum into which he, Stephen, might suddenly plunge and be lost —might suddenly be wrenched from the fixed state of his own being, which was complete, which was with God. He was confronting a brother, an enemy; he was confronting another human being. . . . He sat as relaxed as possible, pretending to study the checkerboard. His were the red plastic checkers; the boy's were the black. Must pretend to take the game seriously. Must pretend to worry. Must not pretend, however, to be stupid . . . for the boy would sense it, the boy would be quick to sense it, and Stephen would be guilty of not accepting him as a human being. *Stephen,* he was. *Stephen,* he knew himself. That too was a mystery into which he might be drawn at any time, if God chose to draw him in. But he could not anticipate it. He must live his life, fulfill his obligations, go where he was needed . . . perform as he was required to perform. Must not allow the boy to win the game too easily; must be very careful not to provoke his rage. *You did that on purpose! You let me win on purpose!* the giant boy had accused him once in a throaty whisper. . . . *I hate you.*

Beauty is a minimal requirement for me, Andrew was saying. *In a woman. There are so many, many women, Stephen . . . so many! Washington, New York, London . . . everywhere. After Willa disappointed me I went into a kind of frenzy . . . became involved with so many women, one after another, sometimes two or three at the same time . . . I used them, we used one another, I loved that freedom for a while, I went a little crazy with it . . . but only for a while. I didn't love any of the women but I loved my own freedom, I loved what was possible . . . the different structures of power, the different relationships in which power could be expressed. You don't understand, I know; you've never tasted power and you don't know. It's like tasting blood. . . . It's like tasting blood must be for an animal, that first taste. I think it must be like that. I'm sure it must be. . . . But where power is so easily achieved it isn't valued; it soon becomes boring. So I moved on from one woman to another to another . . . and then I gave up, something seemed to die in me, I was only in my late thirties but I felt aged, I had always felt older than my chronological age but now I felt very, very old, as old as Father. At about the time I flew to Buffalo to bail you out, Stephen—do you remember?—I was at my lowest point. You probably weren't aware of the fact that I was sick . . . I hid it from everyone. My career had gone well enough but then I lost interest in it: I wasn't forced out, I wasn't even disgusted by certain things I came to know, and I certainly wasn't afraid of being defeated in another election. I would not have been defeated. I simply lost interest. It went dead for me, quite rapidly, in a matter of days . . . three or four days of a particularly stormy week, a very exciting week, the President threatening to veto certain proposals unless . . . and certain deals being made and unmade furiously . . . all very exciting, I loved it, I loved it for years, but then it seemed to go dead for me in a few days . . . slipped from me as if my soul were slipping from me, through my fingers, through my pores . . . and after that I felt nothing for that sort of politics. I made up my mind that I must have power but I must be able to control the structures in which that power is exercised . . . otherwise one's energies are gulped down by other people, always by other people, by the world, by history itself . . . otherwise everything is lost. So I retreated for a while and made up my mind that I would create a great work . . . a political treatise . . . a philosophical treatise that would change our way of thinking, our way of . . . would change our lives . . . if it is possible to change lives . . . in this epoch of human civilization. . . . If it is even desirable. . . . I still kept in the public eye, of course. I intend to keep in the public eye forever. I no longer love the excitement, the brutality . . . the acclaim . . . the hatred . . . but I seem to need it, a part of me seems to yearn for it, though I would rather retreat to this farm and write and write and write until my work was finished; I have obligations still to the magazine, to my friends, to people who believe in me; do you know, Stephen, that there are people who believe passionately in me? Even now, years after I've retired from that sort of thing. They want me to return, they write the most pathetic letters . . . send me the most ex-*

traordinary gifts. . . . When I give a lecture or a speech they are there and the mere sight of me drives them into a frenzy . . . they interrupt my speeches with bursts of applause, I have to beg them to stop . . . have to beg them, beg them, to allow me to continue. . . . Even those who threaten my life seem, in a way, to be addicted to me. They too love me—in their way. They need me. Can't do without me. The last speech I gave, in Boston, I think . . . no, in Ohio . . . I was totally convincing, I was interrupted many times by applause . . . I seemed to feel how my self had spread out to the farthest reaches of the auditorium . . . my presence expanded, enormous . . . and then oddly drawn out of me by the people, as they cheered and applauded, so that it split from me . . . as it always had, as I remembered from other times it did, but this time it didn't return. . . . Or perhaps it had never returned after the first time and I could not remember; the rewards of a public life, Stephen, are many, but the most valuable reward is obliteration . . . extinction . . . you are so totally, totally exhausted that you don't remember what you've said or done a few days later . . . even a few hours later. You can't remember. You hear a tape of your own speech and it's a stranger's speech, a stranger's voice. You hear the applause that punctuates the speech and you feel . . . jealousy. Envy. Spite. A rival! That stranger is a rival! . . . But no, no, it's you. It's always you. The rewards of a public life are many, Stephen, including fame and power and the attention of serious, intelligent people, the attention of attractive people . . . the attention of many, many people around the world; but the most valuable reward is that lovely lovely exhaustion . . . when even the voices in your head, which are tiny mimics of your own voice, are stopped. So I retreat and then I emerge and then I retreat again, and prepare to emerge and astonish and draw the applause I deserve . . . not simply from the rabble, either, but from you all. You can't resist. You can't. Superior natures recognize one another. One may as well admit it. . . . My true interests are philosophical, however. Intellectual. I want to alter the course of intellectual history more than I want to influence the next election or see my enemies denounced and hounded from public office . . . much more than I want to see my friends rewarded. . . . I'm not sure my friends deserve much more than they already have. They're anxious about my support and they should be. You're wise, Stephen, to have no friends . . . no one who knows you, no one who sleeps with you and may overhear you grinding your teeth or whimpering or practicing a speech . . . no one who even

knows you. You're wise, but I couldn't live as you do. Poverty, chas-
tity, that pose of constant humility . . . those big brown doggy
eyes. . . . No, I couldn't live for an hour like that. I couldn't inhabit
you for an hour, a minute. I'd go mad. I'd slash my throat. I don't
want God to envelop me—I want God to keep away—I don't believe
in God but I believe in being overcome by what you call God—I'm
terrified of it, I want no part of it or of you. For me the world is
spinning freely and beautifully and I cling to it for my life . . . I want
it never to stop.

I don't think it will.

No, I don't think it will. But it did once. Once it did. For me. To
me. It wasn't the world but a wheel . . . a wheel in my mind's eye
. . . spinning freely and beautifully, so beautifully I wanted to weep
to see it. I was hypnotized by it. I was enchanted. I wanted it never,
never to stop because if it stopped I would die, I would be sucked
into the hollow of it, I wanted to see the spokes and the rim move,
move faster and faster, I wanted only the blur of motion, I didn't
want it to stop but it stopped . . . it slowed, it stopped. And then I
knew what would happen to me. I knew what must be done. I knew,
I knew; but I hadn't the courage. Someone had to do it but no one
would, except me . . . no one knew about it except me . . . and I
made plans, I made fantastic plans, of acting without being discov-
ered . . . of acting in such a way, so cunning a way, that I would
never be discovered and my immense contribution to American po-
litical and philosophical thought would not be discredited. But I
hadn't the courage. . . . I flew to Buffalo to rescue you and it did
me good. And then I met Yvonne, afterward. And then the wheel
was in motion, I kept so busy that one day I realized it was in mo-
tion again, I was in love again, passionately and overwhelmingly in
love, in love, in love again with . . . with whatever I had been in
love with before; its attractions had not died. They will not die. I
have my work, I have my public, I have my plans for the next century
. . . when perhaps my ideas will be put into practice . . . if not in
this wretched country, perhaps in another; who can tell? . . . I have
my work, my life's work, my complete commitment to posterity, my
willingness to sacrifice a little of the present in return for future as-
surance of . . . of . . . of triumph.

Then there is Yvonne. There is always Yvonne now. She alone of
all the women seemed worthy of me. Seemed to understand me.
She's even more intelligent, more shrewd than she appears to be . . .
there's a certain coyness about her in social situations that is mislead-

ing. She inclines, as I do, to be rather intolerant of fools . . . but she won't show it, as I'm afraid I sometimes do. Of the two of us she's possibly the more subtle, the more deceptive. Our marriage is a perfect partnership. We really are equals. Without any training in law she seems to see life from the point of view of a lawyer . . . knows how we must always assume opposition, must declare only what we wish to be recorded, must be very, very careful of improper alliances. Her only limitation is that she finds it difficult to follow an abstract philosophical argument when it deals with conflicting points of view that are expressed in approximately the same language; that's a curious blindness in her, which comes out when she does research for me, or copyedits something I've written. But apart from that she's marvelous, completely reliable . . . like no other woman I've known. She's superior, isn't she? Superior. The voice grew shrill, ever more shrill. *Superior, isn't she? Aren't we? Superior? Superior? Superior?*

Hugh had reached drunkenly for the green pillow and now cradled it against his chest. Through half-shut eyes he looked at Stephen and muttered something about having another appointment that evening . . . a date . . . a very important date. Hadn't they been together long enough, hadn't Stephen drained him of his energy and interrupted his work and. . . . And upset him, too, forcing him to recall episodes he would rather have forgotten . . . accusing him of . . . spying on him and blaming him and accusing him. . . . *Get out of here,* he muttered. *Out. Out. Out of my life.*

I'm afraid to leave you, Stephen said. *You don't seem. . . . You seem so unhappy. . . .*

"Seem"! You punk! You crude little punk! If you weren't my brother I'd hold you at gunpoint and go through your pockets . . . see what you've lifted from the apartment when my back was turned . . . or maybe you've picked my pocket, eh? . . . lifted my wallet? His eyes rolled. He was holding the green pillow tight in an embrace, his chin resting on it; Stephen saw that the pillow was meant to be a head. It had stitching to indicate facial features and two floppy ears sewn on. It was bright green, with red markings; it was a very bright green. . . . *but you're Stephen, you don't steal, you probably didn't take anything. However, I want you out.*

Stephen buttoned his coat. He was exhausted. . . . *gun? Do you have a gun?*

Yes I have a gun! Everyone has a gun! Yes yes yes! Hugh cried. He tried to get up, slipped back, fell heavily into the chair; but in the next instant pushed himself up again. Though he was pale with exhaustion, his face waxen, he managed to stumble toward Stephen, waving the green pillow menacingly. *Out, I said! Out of my studio and out of my life! Out before I brain you!*

Andrew too ordered him out. He slapped his face, then ordered him out. *I alone am sane*, Andrew said coldly. *It's not a burden I would have chosen, especially in this dying epoch.*

Yes, Stephen murmured. Yes. All right. I will leave.

I didn't call you here. Under no circumstances are you to repeat that asinine story of . . . that grotesque business of a dream or a vision or a hallucination . . . whatever it was. Under no circumstances. And don't speak to Yvonne unless it's necessary. Leave without saying good-by if you can. I didn't call you here, didn't invite you here, Andrew said quickly, *and . . . and . . . whatever I told you today, whatever slipped out, is not to be repeated. Do you hear? Not to be repeated. . . . Suddenly it stops, Stephen. The wheel. It is spinning freely and beautifully and then it slows, it stops . . . it comes to a dead stop. You don't understand. You can't. You haven't tasted the glory of its spinning; you simply don't know. You never will. The wheel is spinning and perhaps it will never stop again for me. I think it might not. But if it does. . . . If I decide to. . . . You are not to repeat anything I've said, Stephen, and you are not to pity me . . . I really don't think I deserve the pity of a thirty-year-old virgin, a failure at everything he has attempted, a charming but ultimately exasperating fool . . . eh? Really I don't deserve that sort of pity. . . . You don't understand me, Stephen, even though you look solemn and sympathetic and Christlike. You can't understand me. There's nothing you can tell me. There's nothing I want from you. I saved you in Buffalo and I'll probably save you again from your own folly. You don't know the world and I do. You don't know the intoxication of the world as it spins, the beauty of that movement . . . and so you can't know the horror when it stops. You can't know how dead, how desolate, how unbearable everything is, even success, even love, when that wheel stops . . . and how overwhelming our need is to get it started again, spinning again; or how overwhelming our need is to. . . . It's a physical need, Stephen. Self-murder. Murder of one's self. One must die and there is no one to commit the act—no one. No one else. And so one must do it to one's self, because there is no one else. But it won't happen, Stephen. It won't. I vow to you it won't. And even if it did, depend upon me to have constructed*

*such a situation. . . . Well, depend upon me to be inventive. But
don't pity me.*

Out, I said! Out, out! Out of my life!
Though his eyelids dropped and his voice was syrupy-thick and his
legs storklike and shaky, he managed to swoop upon Stephen with
the pillow and beat him about the head and shoulders. *Out, out! No
more of your pity! Out of my studio and out of my building and out
of my life!* As Stephen hurried to the door Hugh threw the pillow
after him—the bodiless bright green head—and it struck Stephen between his shoulders and bounced off. For a pillow, it felt quite hard.
But Stephen was more astonished than hurt. And he did not dare
look back.

22

Thank God, they said. *Thank God it's over.*

For days they talked about the young light-skinned Negro who
had confessed to the murder—the "assassination of Andrew Petrie,"
as it was usually phrased. For days they watched him on television,
they read about him and his organization, they wept, they were relieved, they stayed up late and talked and questioned one another
but came to no conclusions. They were exhausted, drained. They
were very relieved. They were puzzled at the young man's bright, insouciant manner and the presentation he gave of himself: he was
both articulate and flippant, something of a comedian. But very serious, of course. Very serious, like all revolutionaries.
Acting as spokesman for his organization, the young man coolly
claimed not only the murder of Andrew Petrie but the murder of a
black police captain in Manhattan, the murder of a Democratic congressman from Maryland, and the murder, years back, of a New Jersey industrialist and philanthropist. None of these murders had been
"solved." The group claimed a number of recent bombings: one of a
Wall Street brokerage, another of a public-schools administration
building in Brooklyn, another of an A & P store. There were even
theatrical "shame" killings planned and a list of the prospective victims was publicized. But the group was thwarted when attempting to
kidnap from the stage of a Yonkers high school a certain contro-

versial congressman—he had been giving a speech on good citizenship to the assembly—and what the media called "three and a half years of ingenious terrorism" came to an end.

Thank God, they said.

It would have astonished and dismayed Andrew, they said, to learn that his assassin had a B.A. in history from Harvard and had studied at Oxford as a Rhodes scholar . . . and to learn that the young man had not especially hated him; did not seem to have followed his career very closely.

Society must be leveled! the young man piped.

He doesn't seem like a black man, they said. *He has no accent at all.*

They're just animals . . . they're insane.

That list included poor Sam MacCannon . . . maybe the publicity will help his career.

They probably will never be tried for what they did to Andrew, isn't that a shame? Why is the law so strange?

. . . just as well, maybe. Avoid publicity.

Yes, I tend to agree with you.

There didn't seem to be much racial point to it, did there? I just don't understand. . . .

There was no point to it at all. To anything they did.

Norman Lutz said in his column this morning . . . did anyone notice? . . . he quoted Andrew from years back and said. . . . He said. . . .

The dangers of anarchy, wasn't it?

. . . so it's fortunate, in my opinion, that the family will be spared any more publicity. The investigation will probably continue for a while, so they say, but there won't be any trial . . . any open hearings . . . that sort of thing. There shouldn't be too much more publicity.

First-degree murder charges brought against them for that poor man they killed in Maryland . . . and then the bombings, two or three people killed. . . .

One of them was an infant, you know. Eight months old.

Imagine, a young mother and her baby, killed in a stupid, senseless explosion. . . . Those people are insane, they're animals, they should be put to death. . . . What if they're paroled in a few years?

They would be arraigned again and tried again for another murder.

. . . but not for Andrew's?
No. Not for many years. . . .

They talked about Hugh, sometimes even in Hugh's presence. But not at any great length. There seemed very little to talk about.

I keep thinking he'll just wake up someday and laugh at us all, he was always so good-humored . . . joked and teased so. . . . Isn't it a pity?
. . . He's conscious right now. He's awake.
His eyelids are quivering.
Yes, he isn't in a coma now, he's awake. They say he's awake. They have ways of telling . . . a brain scan, isn't it called a brain scan? . . . At certain times he's awake no matter how it appears to us, they say. But he can't hear us.
I wouldn't be too sure of that.
No, I wouldn't be too sure of that; he was always so sharp, so clever. . . . And you sometimes hear about people in comas or anesthetized who pick up every word. . . .
His heart was so strong, they say. So very strong. It just keeps going and going and. . . .
There's no possibility he will recover?
Of course there's always . . . I think there's always the possibility of . . . of . . . some kind of recovery, partial recovery maybe. . . . Isn't there?
He did come out of the coma. He did survive that.
But they said something about brain damage. . . .
His eyelids are fluttering. The poor creature, I halfway think he can hear us . . . can sense us. . . . Hugh? Hugh? Can you hear me? Hugh . . . ?
Isn't it a pity!

They talked about Stephen, sometimes in his presence but most of the time when they believed he was out of earshot.

. . . taking this so hard, isn't he, just not himself any longer. . . .
. . . hasn't been himself for years. . . .
. . . can't you get him to see a doctor? . . . seems so quiet, depressed, just not like Stephen at all. . . .
He blames himself for Hugh but that's ridiculous.
Of course that's ridiculous.
. . . any plans?

. . . wants to leave, has been talking about a mission some-where. . . .

A mission?

Religious community in the Southwest, I think they're called the Clarentians. . . . Catholic priests and brothers.

Would they take Stephen? After so much?

. . . really should make an appointment for him with a doctor. He isn't himself at all.

But he's stubborn.

Yes. That's always been part of his illness.

They talked about Yvonne, whom they never saw now. They low-ered their voices and talked about Yvonne. She was being evicted from her apartment building, they said; they talked about that and about where she might move. They talked about her odd habits, her odd personality, her refusal to listen to counsel. They talked about threats she had made against Harvey and against the family. They talked about the danger she was in, which she seemed to ignore. . . .

When do you think her lover will appear? they asked.

23

Raschke's hair was cut short; he no longer wore a beard; it was ob-vious that he did not recognize Stephen. Nor would Stephen have recognized him.

They bought me two new teeth to replace them, he laughed. *And I had some kind of itchy scabby thing on my scalp . . . starting on my face too . . . they gave me some shots and some ointment, cleared it up in a few weeks.*

What plans do you have, then?

He laughed nervously and his shoulders moved inside his thin can-vas jacket. From time to time he shot Stephen a curious, un-comprehending glance; he licked his lips and made an effort to speak as clearly as possible, as if he believed their conversation were being recorded.

Plans. . . . Plans. . . . I have certain plans, I have definite. . . . I have definite plans. . . . Now that I can't cross the border . . . can't get together with my friends. . . . Well, I will have to rethink my position. For one thing I'm a very, very lucky man. It could have gone the other way . . . they could have been very angry at me for not cooperating. They had me in their power, after all. They could have done anything. They did do a number of things . . . certain things. . . . But they could have done a lot more. I expected the worst. . . . So, Stephen, you're related to Andrew Petrie, are you? . . . his brother? That's very interesting. He laughed again, as if baffled. *That's very . . .*

But you don't remember me, Stephen said. *Or her.*

Of course I remember her; I remember her. I remember someone. But I didn't keep track of her . . . have lost track of so many friends . . . and so I . . . I. . . . Yvonne: I remember the name. And her. She walked out on me, she was too young, she was politically unformed . . . and too emotional, I seemed to remember she was too emotional for my taste.

We were all a lot younger then, Stephen said.

Raschke expelled his breath harshly. But it was meant to be a sigh; his lean face sagged. *Yes. That's so. But. . . . Nevertheless. . . . I am contemplating certain . . . I have definite plans . . . they're watching me, I suppose, probably have been watching me for years . . . nevertheless . . . I have definite plans that involve purely legal activities . . . advisory, cautionary . . . staying two jumps ahead of the Government, if possible. They scared me with this Petrie business, I must admit; all the talk about capital punishment being reinstated. . . . I don't mind dying in a legitimate cause, in fact I more or less expected to be dead by now, but . . . this sort of arbitrary, whimsical . . . this sort of . . .*

He made a gesture with both hands as if pulling a net. Stephen understood at once.

. . . it's a very American thing, Stephen said.

Yes, this sort of arbitrary, whimsical death . . . death by accident, almost . . . It's very American and very frightening. So I'm not sure. I'm not sure about the future. My friends are scattered; they're out of the country, or they've changed, they've betrayed their ideals . . . and some of them, of course, are dead. You worked with me, you say, in Pittsburgh?

. . . do you need money? Because if. . . .

No thank you. No. That's all right, Raschke said rather coolly. *I'm all right.*

Because if . . .

No. Not at all. But thank you, Stephen.

Whatever I am doing must be sanctioned, Stephen thought. It must be sanctioned because I am doing it.

Thoughts blew into his face. One blew into his eye and the eye bled. Tears would wash it away, however, without any effort on Stephen's part; he must only have faith.

You let us all win on purpose, he addressed God.

But God had withdrawn. Was coy. Stephen, bereft, muttered to himself as if to punish God. He was empty, cleansed, weightless, shadowless, totally without sin and without hope. He was ready for God once again but God eluded him. Just before Joseph Raschke rose to leave, at the moment when Joseph Raschke—a scared, hollow-cheeked man who looked ten years older than he was—took a soiled tissue out of his jacket pocket and dabbed at his eyes, for an instant moved by something he must have remembered, Stephen believed that God would return to him; stricken with despair, pierced by a sensation of pity for this stranger, he was empty, ready, ready for God as he had not been for months. But nothing happened. Nothing. *I am empty and I am ready. Please—* But nothing happened.

Raschke left. Walked away. Stephen watched his retreating back and had not the strength to wish the man well. Raschke was doomed anyway.

The secret was out: everyone was doomed.

The secret was out. It was no secret. Everyone knew it, had known it all along. Andrew had known, Hugh had known, Stephen had known without exactly knowing he knew—one of God's tricks of grace—one of those features that distinguish God's servants from the rest of the servants.

Ah Stephen, one of them murmured uneasily.

Yes, he said, *all right.*

. . . rather late, isn't it, for a . . . Are you going for a walk?

That's all right, Stephen said. *Fine.*

. . . might be dangerous if. . . . There are gangs of. . . .

All right, Stephen said.

Around the paralyzed creature they gathered, usually on Sunday afternoons. They spoke over the contraption. It could not hear—so they were told—but they were told it could sense their presence and it appreciated visits. Its eyelids fluttered; there were occasional twitches in the face; occasionally, it looked as if it were swallowing.

Blind and deaf, they were told. However, they sometimes believed this was not the case. He had been so lively, so good-natured in life . . . so clever, always such a . . . always joking. . . . It was possible, wasn't it, that he really knew what was going on? It wasn't impossible.

Stephen studied his brother's ruined face and did not think he had much in common with that face. He hadn't much in common with anyone or anything.

Artificial lung. Iron lung. Miracle. Stephen knew there was no choice any longer—you accepted the miracle and that was that. You opened your lungs and it flooded you. That was that. Simple. Useless to brood upon it or philosophize or mourn or make jokes. The street was crowded with miracles, the nursing home was crowded with miracles, that was that. The miracle is the most irresistible form of necessity.

Hugh? he whispered. *I'm sorry.*

The eyelids were not fluttering. The face was still. Hairless, mottled, scarred, the reddened scalp was so still as to resemble something inanimate, like plastic.

Sorry sorry sorry.

. . . *in the end one is left with . . . one can only be . . . can only. . . . In the end one is only accountable for. . . . Can't be blamed. . . . One must make the attempt to live, after all, and . . . and . . . and one must, in the end, only. . . . One is only committed to. . . . One is only conditioned by. . . . Must make the attempt to live: in the end. First premise. None other. Useless all analysis . . . all reflection . . . all emotion . . . regrets . . . sorrow. Useless all that is not sanctioned.*

A passer-by gave him a lewd triumphant smile, as if mocking Stephen's look of distraction.

What did you imagine you could do for these people? . . . what, in fact, have you ever done for anyone? . . . even for yourself?

He wanted to tell her about Raschke. He wanted to tell her about Hugh: that no one blamed her, no one spoke ill of her. He wanted to see her just once more.

Michael is engaged! . . . did you hear? . . . haven't heard from Willa in five years and I picked up the phone and it was. . . . Such a surprise, who would have expected. . . . Twenty-three years old,

*the girl is . . . I.Q. of a genius and not very easy to talk with . . .
four feet nine or ten inches tall . . . Willa met her just once: says
the girl is taking Michael over . . . babies him and bullies him . . .
interrupts him. Getting her Ph.D. in economics at Columbia. Poor
Willa doesn't know whether to be happy that Michael is evidently
more normal now . . . the voices have stopped . . . or whether to be
upset. The girl's family lives in the Bronx. Who would have expected it! Hardly more than a child and engaged to be married to a
genius. . . .*

Stephen read newspapers one day. One morning and one afternoon of a day in late March. He read, read, read. His eyes hurt from
the newsprint. His fingers were filthy. There was a young man who
had confessed to the crime and who was willing to be guilty of it. He
gave interviews, he advertised himself and his organization. The organization was a "study group" but it had performed certain terrorist
acts. *Among the group's victims are. . . . They are alleged to
have. . . . Police are continuing investigation. . . .* Stephen turned
pages, flipped through sections of the newspaper. He did not bother
to read the story, where it was continued. Why should he read such
lies? It frightened him, that he was always reading lies and always
ready to believe them.

He had thought himself empty, but perhaps that was not really
the case—perhaps, at bottom, he retained some measure of hope.
Andrew . . . ?

A pile of newspapers lay on the table before him. Exhausting,
these hours. Futile. The effort of reading, searching the columns, the
task of trying to absorb so many facts . . . trying to concentrate
upon so many details that shifted meaning with every passing moment. . . . Everything was entangled, entwined: lies with the convincing appearance of the truth, truths indistinguishable from lies.
Stephen liked to think of himself as perpetually ready for God. He
liked to think of himself as living beyond both hope and despair, no
longer expecting anything. But perhaps that was not true. He did
want to know where truth ended and lies began; he wanted desperately to *know*. . . . At the same time he realized he was not going to
know. He was never going to know.

Andrew, he said, *why did you do this to us?*
The dead man ignored him. Snubbed him. He brushed close to

Stephen and then moved away; it might have been an accident, his
having come so close.

Andrew . . . ?

24

I don't care to hear about it, the voice said uneasily. *I . . . I . . . I
don't think it has anything to do with. . . .*

*. . . but he didn't even know who I was. And he didn't remember
you very clearly,* Stephen said. *We talked for an hour or so and discovered we had nothing to say to each other.*

I hardly remember him, Yvonne said. *It was so long ago.*

But aren't you curious? They suspected him for a while of. . . .

Why should I be curious? With my life what it is now?

Stephen stood with the telephone receiver pressed tightly against
his ear. It pleased him that his voice should sound so calm. In his
mind's eye her image glimmered, pale and tense and urgent. . . .
What is your life now? he heard himself ask.

*. . . too difficult to explain. I'm going to Washington for a few
days. . . . To Virginia. . . .*

She fell silent, as if unable to imagine further.

Yvonne? Stephen said. *Are you . . . is it. . . . Do you think things
will be. . . .*

Yes? What?

. . . tolerable?

I don't know what you mean, she said.

You know what I mean.

I don't.

He shut his eyes and for an instant held her image there: the face
pale, the eyes dark, exaggerated, doomed.

*I mean—is your life going to be tolerable as his widow? Don't you
think it might be better to—*

No.

*. . . Would you like me to drive you to Washington? I'm going to
be leaving Albany in a few days. I could rent a car. I was going by
bus but if you'd like a ride, if you'd like me to drive you, I would be
happy to. . . .*

You're leaving? Why? Where are you going?

My first stop is the home of some friends in Chicago, people I haven't seen for a while . . . very nice people from a few years back. I have friends all over. Did you know? All over the country. I'll stay with them awhile . . . a few days . . . and then, after that, I'm not exactly sure where I will be going. But I'll find out. When it's time for me to know I'll know.

So you're leaving again. . . .

But before I leave. . . .

They were both silent.

. . . but why are you leaving? she asked.

It's time.

It's time! . . . Andrew always spoke of you with such affectionate contempt, did you know? she said rather sharply. *He said you were an anachronism; he said you were medieval. His enemies, he told me, made more sense. There's no place for you now in this world. . . . I think he was right.*

Stephen did not reply. He waited, as if expecting her to apologize; when she said nothing he said, *But do you want me to drive you to Washington? I could rent a car and. . . .*

I couldn't take the time. I'm flying down. But thank you; you're very kind. You've always been very kind.

Don't you think we should meet, Yvonne, and talk?

Why? Why should we meet and talk? I don't see any reason for it . . . I don't see what would be gained. I advise you to accept the solution they came up with, that black man's confession . . . accept it and go your own way, forget about Andrew. Forget about me.

. . . for just a few hours?

You were kind to me years ago, Stephen . . . very kind . . . but I didn't take advantage of you, of what you offered. Now it's too late. My life is too complicated. There are people I must meet and arrangements I must make and letters I must write . . . and this conference is extremely important, Andrew must be represented as powerfully as possible, as clearly and intelligently as possible. . . . It's a very important event in the history of . . . in the history of Andrew's relationship with American intellectual thought. . . . I don't have time, Stephen.

Yes. All right, Stephen said. *I'm sorry.*

25

Sorry.
Sorry!
Upon a cloud great as the sun you once stood and cried in your loud blasting voice to all the fowls that fly in the midst of heaven that it was time, now it was time, after so many centuries it was time, and now they might come and gather themselves unto the supper of the great God; upon a cloud you once stood, fierce-eyed, merciless, crying: "Come and gather yourselves! That you may eat the flesh of kings, and the flesh of captains, and the flesh of mighty men, and the flesh of horses, and of them that sit on them, and the flesh of all men, both free and bond, both small and great." And the creatures gathered themselves in readiness. And they did feast. For as it happened once, so it will happen again. So it has already happened and will continue to happen. Again. I am the way, the tooth, the might. The beast arose and inside its membrane vast as the sun it was many beasts; but I slew them. The kings of the earth gathered but no membrane contained them and they were not one and yet I slew them. The beast was taken, and with him the false prophet that wrought miracles before him, and both were cast alive into a lake of fire that burns even till this day, and the remnant were slain with the sword of him that reigned, which sword proceeded out of his mouth: and all the fowls were filled with their flesh. So it was in the beginning, is now, and ever shall be. The fowls that fly in the midst of heaven gathered together and did feast until they were filled with flesh and could no longer fly. Look! There they are! They eat and eat and eat until, stupefied, they flop about thrashing their wings, by the thousands and the millions they succumb, you can hear their plaintive chirping and peeping even now. Even now. Listen! Sorry, are you, running wild amidst the sufferers, you who dared descend from your cloud? "Come and gather yourselves!" you cried. And the earth is rocking and seething—feel it?—and now the Devil whom you cast down a thousand years ago into that bottomless hole is stirring, from all the excitement up here, and you run ever more wildly crying: "Come and gather yourselves! Come!" Out of the mouth of the Devil are springing goblins, tiny perfect specimens, *Tat tvam asi* they are peeping, none among them that is not peeping *Tat tvam asi*, and

you cringe with your hands over your ears and your eyes shut tight crying *Sorry, sorry* as if any human word can satisfy me. I am the why, the tithe, the lite. I am the loot. The night. The teeth shining upon the waters. The only begetter of the drops of dew and the Leviathan. And you. I am your wail, your pruta, your kickshawses. Hurry. Don't wait. Be first. The next stop is Cleveland. It's midnight. We're behind schedule. It's noon. It's late. It's light. It's night. It's time. The ship is trembling. Move over. God is in a rush. First come, first served. First in, first out. What are these stains? Whose? Wipe your nose. Are you ready? Do you have your ticket stub? There once was a ship and she sailed. She sails. I am the way West. I am the exit. I am the light that shines in darkness. Sure. Where else is light needed? Darkness. Don't doubt. Don't fear. You can ask for a refund. Money back. Certainly. Guarantee. Don't you believe me? Have faith. Faith! More to come. Always more. Newest and sharpest models. Fantastic prices. Slashed. Cut to ribbons. Once-in-a-lifetime. Savings. I'm everywhere democratic as maggots you'll pay for this Stephen your pretty face will pay for this the boys are going to gang up on you and make you pay with your blood and I am sending from all corners of the earth ferocious waters to batter you and matter you the conduits are flooding even now from all corners of the earth the fowls that fly amidst heaven peeping *Tat tvam asi* are flocking in a vast company: listen! The voice of the wilewind will not help you, the joys crying in the wilderness will not, are not, the mites creeping upon the face of the waters are not, none are, you aren't, no one is: listen! You can't know! Once-in-a-lifetime. Cut to ribbons. Slashed. Refund. Have faith. Don't doubt. Don't

Cleveland!

Stephen woke suddenly to a stranger's voice, hoarsely amplified. Woke curled in his seat. Aching. Legs, backbone. Head. Brain. For some seconds unable to move, paralyzed, his brain aching with the new knowledge that, from now on, even God must be repudiated.

26

In the late afternoon of April 4, Stephen arrived at his friends' home in Chicago. The city was unfamiliar to him. His friends lived in a three-story frame house in a block of similar houses, each with

the same number of windows facing the street, the same meager
front stoops, and the same narrow sidewalks. He was pleased to see,
however, that his friends' house had been recently painted; and it
had new aluminum shutters, hunter green.

Stephen! . . . didn't recognize. . . .

A chain-lock. Two chain-locks, in fact. And a man his own age,
unshaven, greeting him in surprise.

. . . didn't expect you until tomorrow.

Across the country, scattered, were friends of Stephen's who did
not know him. They had never known him very well; but they liked
him and were friends of his. He was a friend of theirs. When he
disappeared they forgot him and when he appeared they remembered him, they welcomed him, they insisted he spend the night with
them or even stay a few days. He explained that he would probably
be leaving quite soon: he was on his way to. . . .

They had other guests, they explained apologetically. And now,
with another child, their extra bedroom was taken. But if he didn't
mind . . . if it wouldn't be too uncomfortable, there was a sofa-bed
he could use. . . .

Thank you, Stephen said. *I can accommodate myself to anything.*